DUGOUT

THE ZOMBIE STEALS HOME

BY SCOTT MORSE

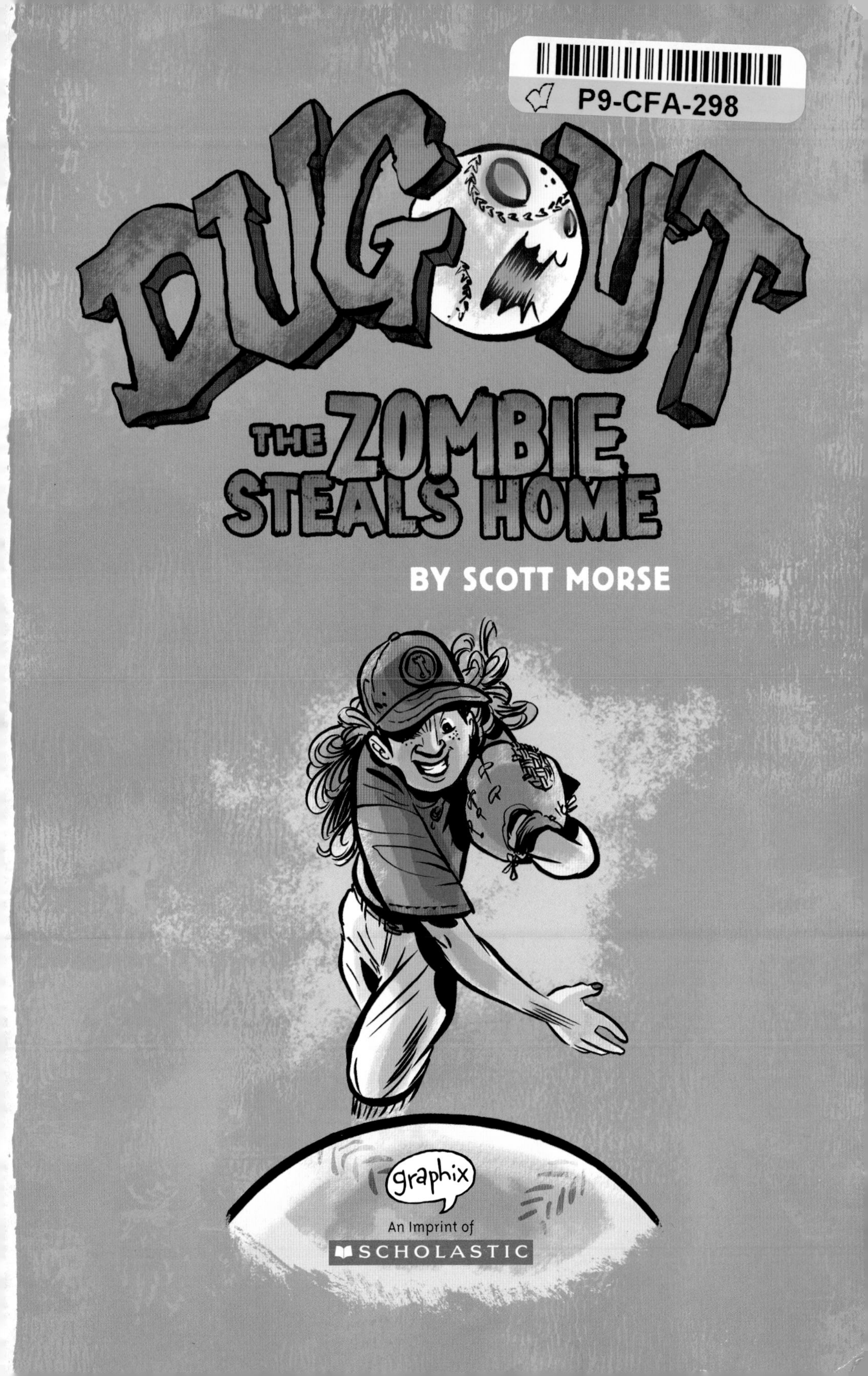

graphix
An Imprint of
SCHOLASTIC

Copyright © 2019 by Scott Morse

All rights reserved. Published by Graphix, an imprint of Scholastic Inc., *Publishers since 1920*. SCHOLASTIC, GRAPHIX, and associated logos are trademarks and/or registered trademarks of Scholastic Inc.

The publisher does not have any control over and does not assume any responsibility for author or third-party websites or their content.

No part of this publication may be reproduced, stored in a retrieval system, or transmitted in any form or by any means, electronic, mechanical, photocopying, recording, or otherwise, without written permission of the publisher. For information regarding permission, write to Scholastic Inc., Attention: Permissions Department, 557 Broadway, New York, NY 10012.

This book is a work of fiction. Names, characters, places, and incidents are either the product of the author's imagination or are used fictitiously, and any resemblance to actual persons, living or dead, business establishments, events, or locales is entirely coincidental.

Library of Congress Control Number: 2018949530

ISBN 978-1-338-18810-3 (hardcover)
ISBN 978-1-338-18809-7 (paperback)

10 9 8 7 6 5 4 3 2 1   19 20 21 22 23

Printed in China   62
First edition, July 2019
Edited by Adam Rau
Book design by Shivana Sookdeo
Color by Guy Major
Creative Director: Phil Falco
Publisher: David Saylor

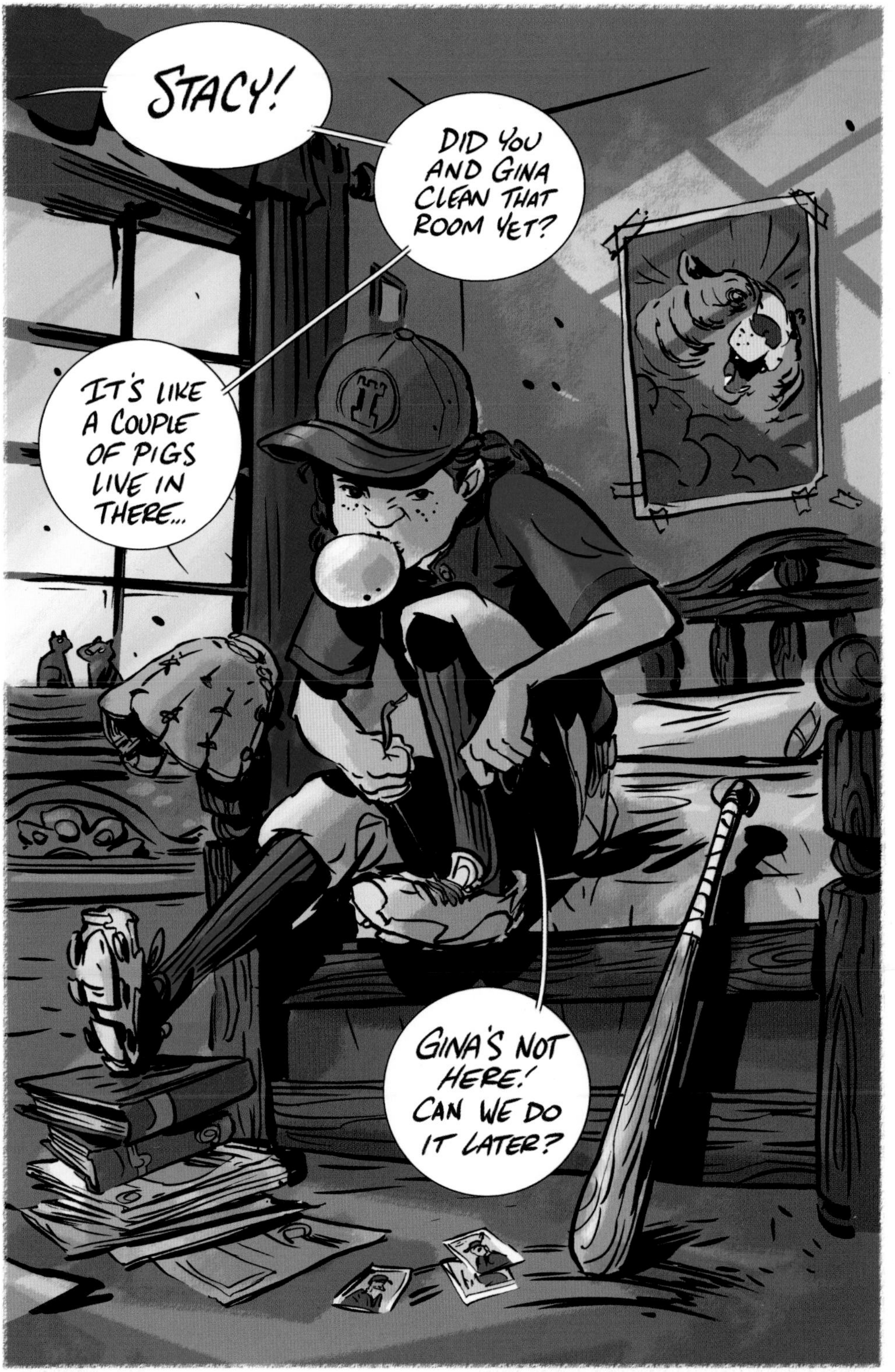
STACY!
DID YOU AND GINA CLEAN THAT ROOM YET?
IT'S LIKE A COUPLE OF PIGS LIVE IN THERE...
GINA'S NOT HERE! CAN WE DO IT LATER?

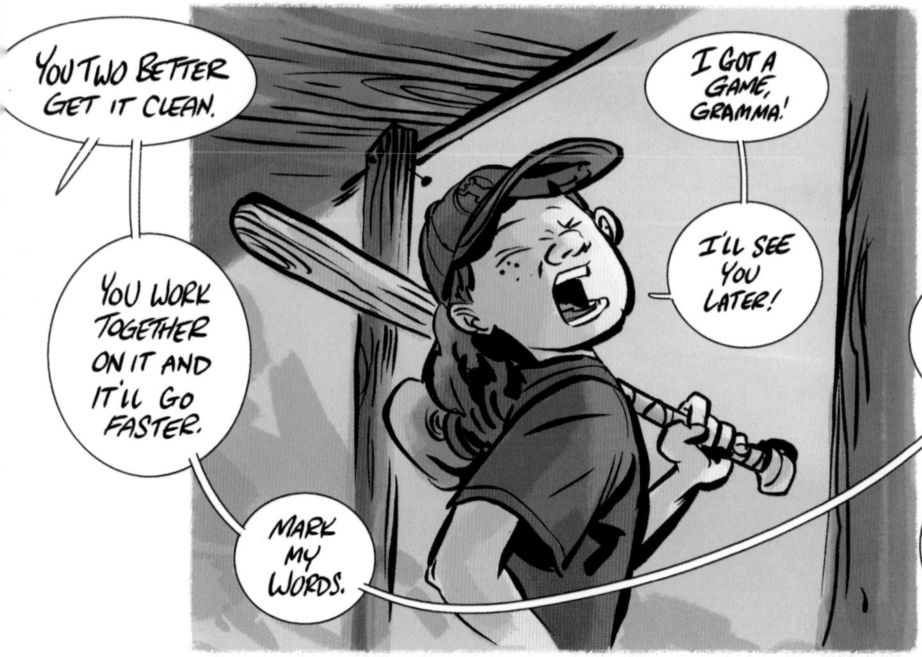

YOU TWO BETTER GET IT CLEAN.
YOU WORK TOGETHER ON IT AND IT'LL GO FASTER.
MARK MY WORDS.
I GOT A GAME, GRAMMA!
I'LL SEE YOU LATER!
GO GET 'EM, KID.
SHOW 'EM HOW IT'S DONE.

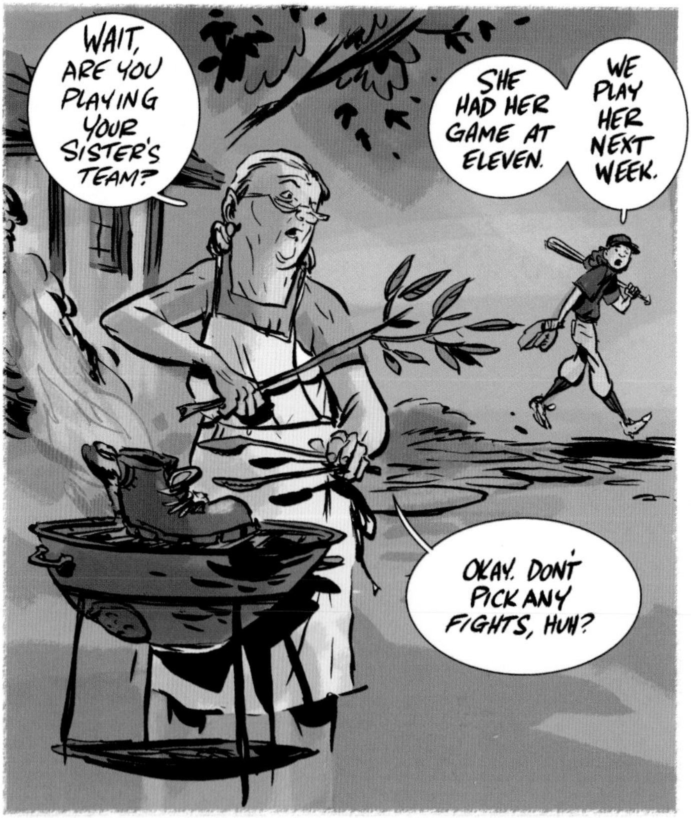

WAIT, ARE YOU PLAYING YOUR SISTER'S TEAM?
SHE HAD HER GAME AT ELEVEN.
WE PLAY HER NEXT WEEK.
OKAY. DON'T PICK ANY FIGHTS, HUH?

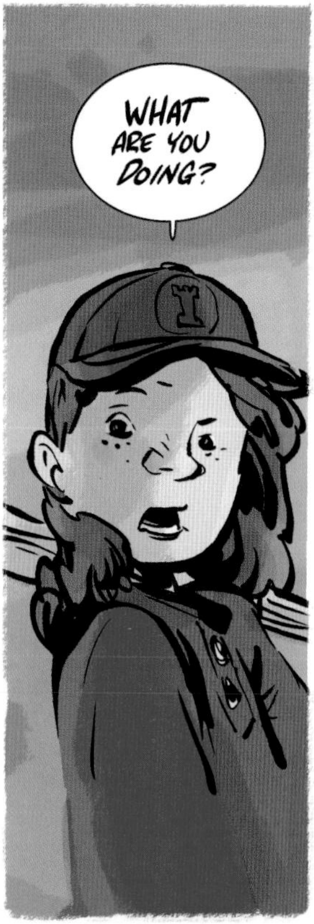

WHAT ARE YOU DOING?

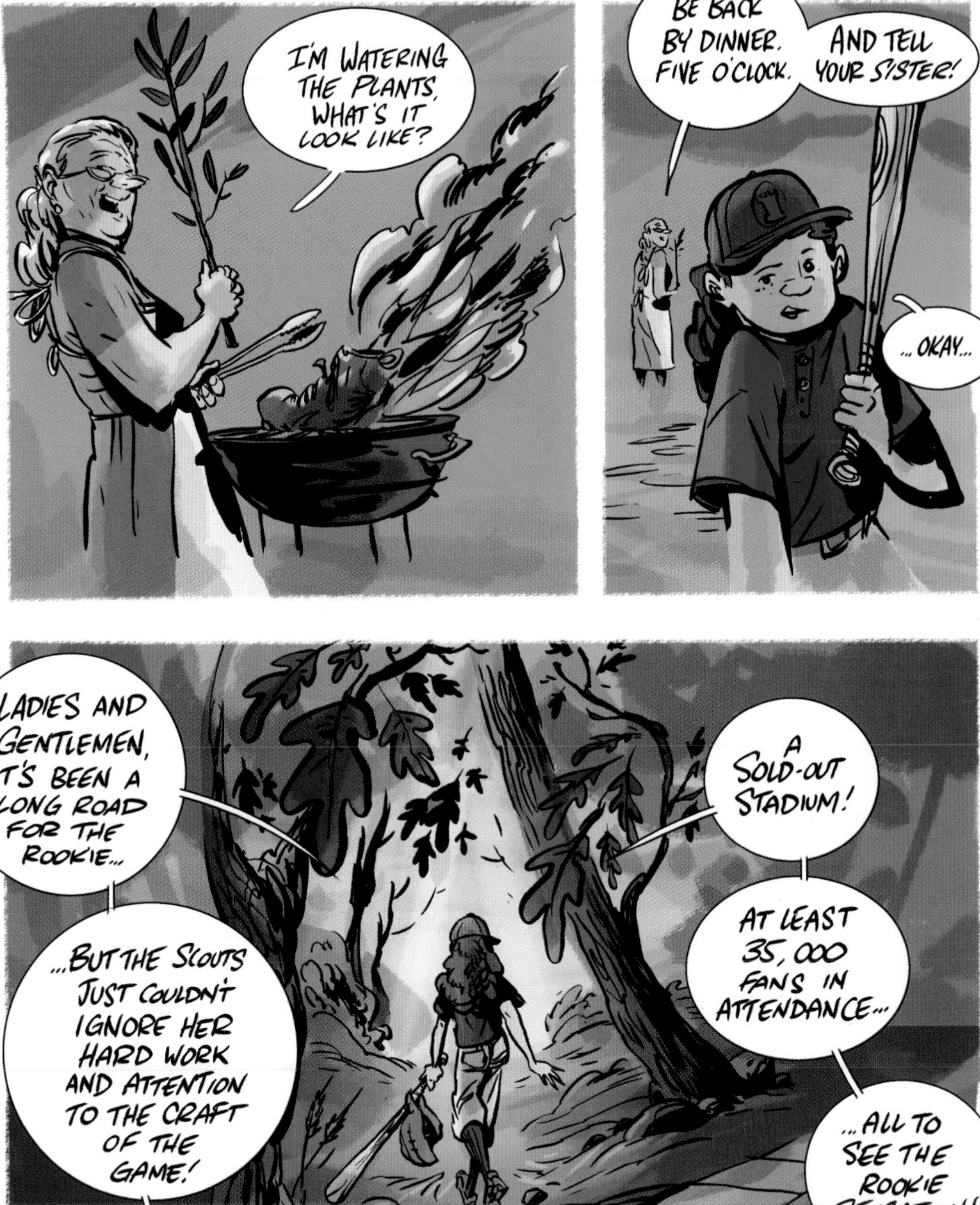
I'M WATERING THE PLANTS, WHAT'S IT LOOK LIKE?
BE BACK BY DINNER. FIVE O'CLOCK.
AND TELL YOUR SISTER!
...OKAY...
LADIES AND GENTLEMEN, IT'S BEEN A LONG ROAD FOR THE ROOKIE...
...BUT THE SCOUTS JUST COULDN'T IGNORE HER HARD WORK AND ATTENTION TO THE CRAFT OF THE GAME!
AND, WOULD'JA LISTEN TO THAT CROWD TODAY?!
A SOLD-OUT STADIUM!
AT LEAST 35,000 FANS IN ATTENDANCE...
...ALL TO SEE THE ROOKIE SENSATION!

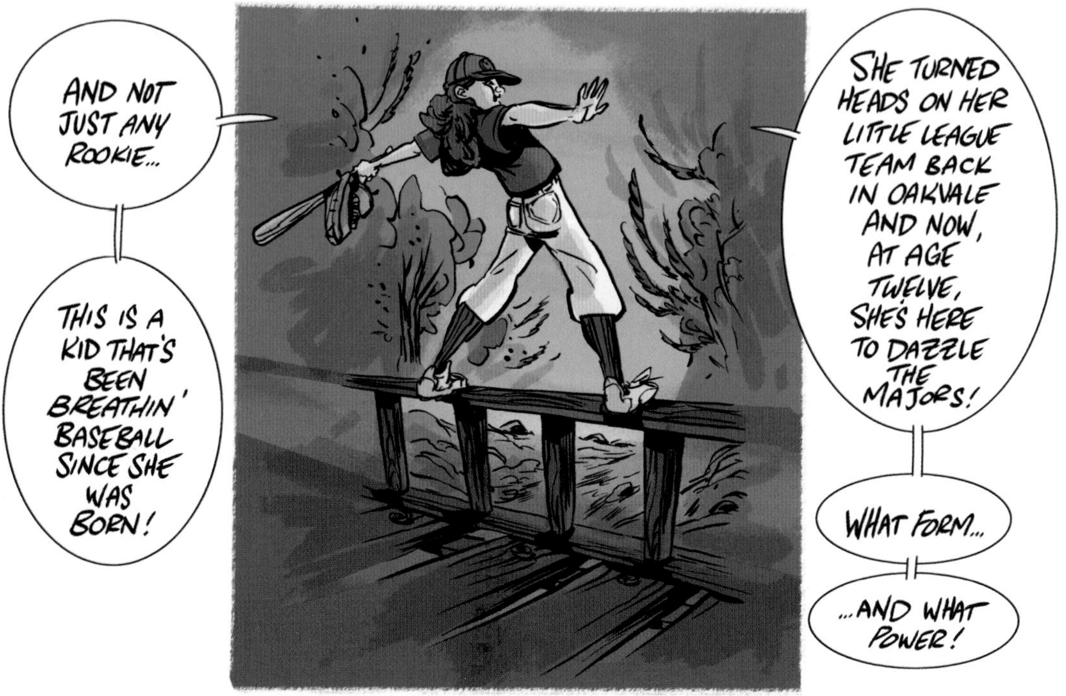
AND NOT JUST ANY ROOKIE...
THIS IS A KID THAT'S BEEN BREATHIN' BASEBALL SINCE SHE WAS BORN!
SHE TURNED HEADS ON HER LITTLE LEAGUE TEAM BACK IN OAKVALE AND NOW, AT AGE TWELVE, SHE'S HERE TO DAZZLE THE MAJORS!
WHAT FORM...
...AND WHAT POWER!

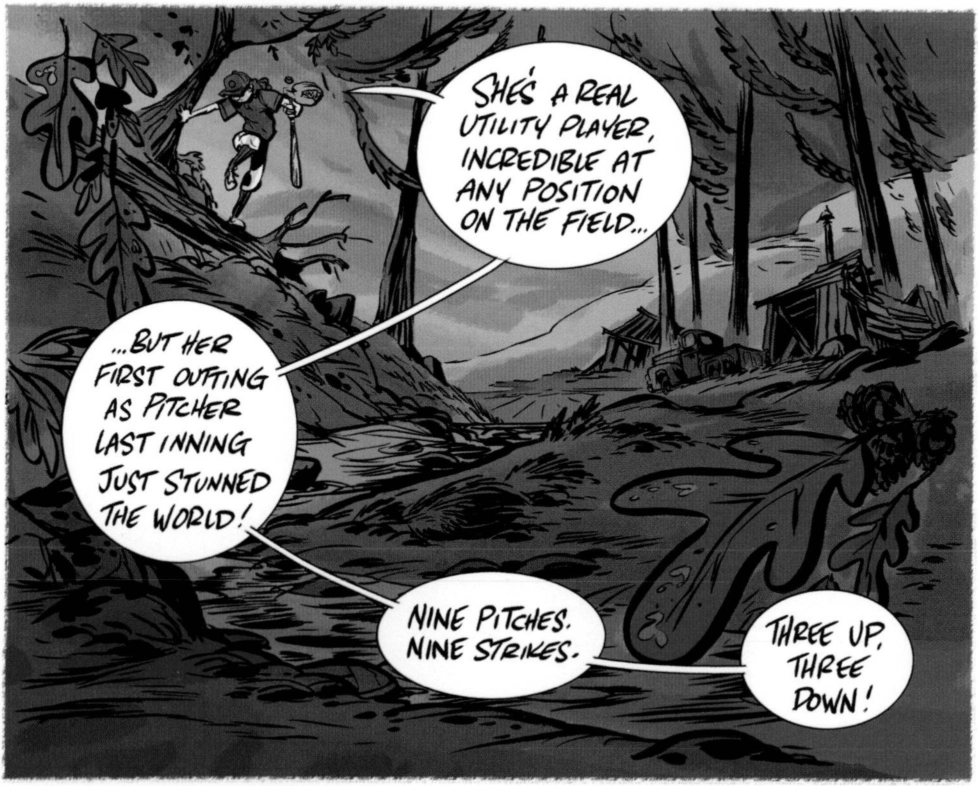
SHE'S A REAL UTILITY PLAYER, INCREDIBLE AT ANY POSITION ON THE FIELD...
...BUT HER FIRST OUTING AS PITCHER LAST INNING JUST STUNNED THE WORLD!
NINE PITCHES. NINE STRIKES.
THREE UP, THREE DOWN!

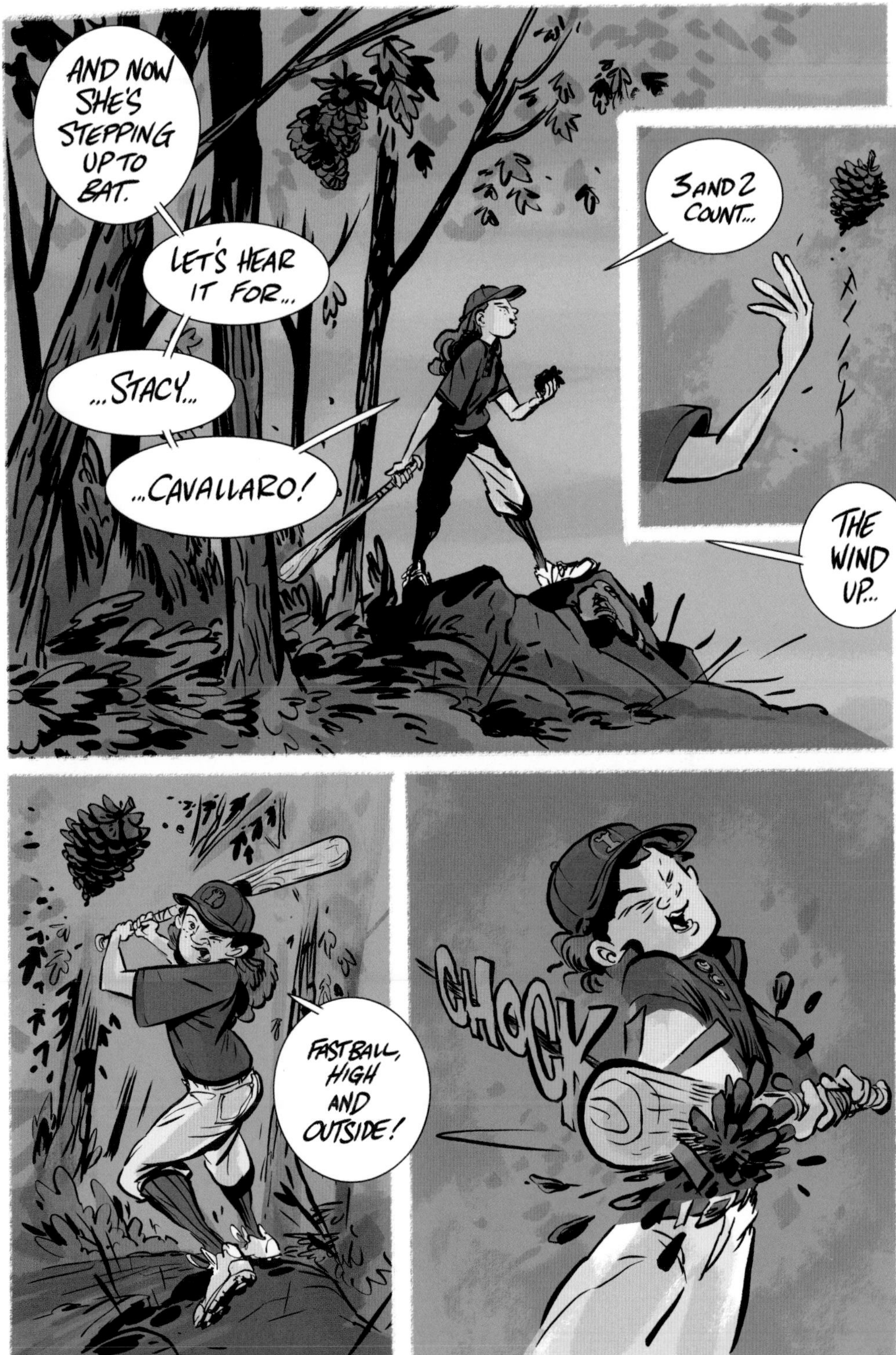
AND NOW SHE'S STEPPING UP TO BAT.
LET'S HEAR IT FOR...
...STACY...
...CAVALLARO!
3 AND 2 COUNT...
FLICK
THE WIND UP...
FASTBALL, HIGH AND OUTSIDE!
CHOCK

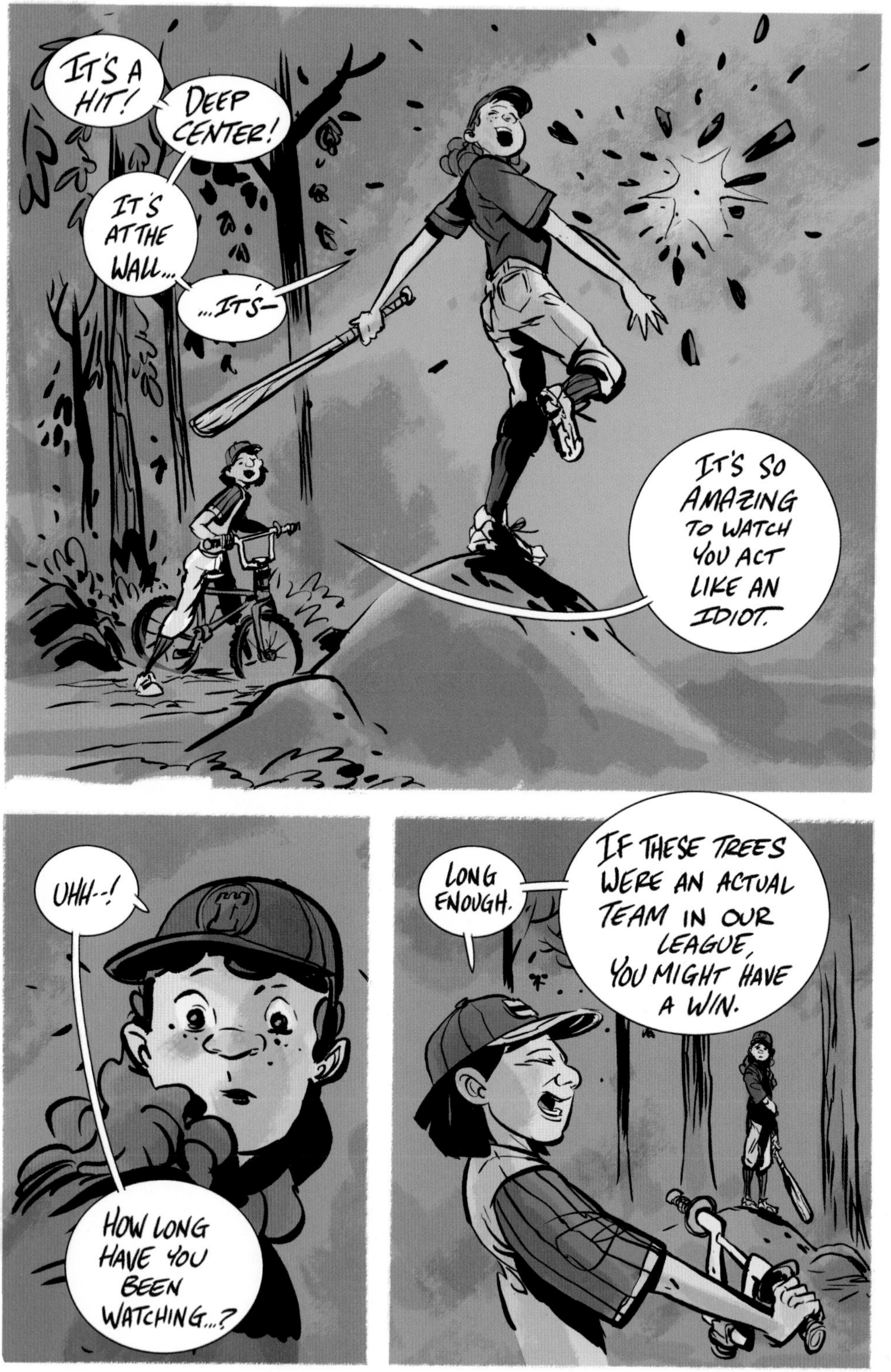
IT'S A HIT!
DEEP CENTER!
IT'S AT THE WALL...
...IT'S—
IT'S SO AMAZING TO WATCH YOU ACT LIKE AN IDIOT.
UHH--!
HOW LONG HAVE YOU BEEN WATCHING...?
LONG ENOUGH.
IF THESE TREES WERE AN ACTUAL TEAM IN OUR LEAGUE, YOU MIGHT HAVE A WIN.

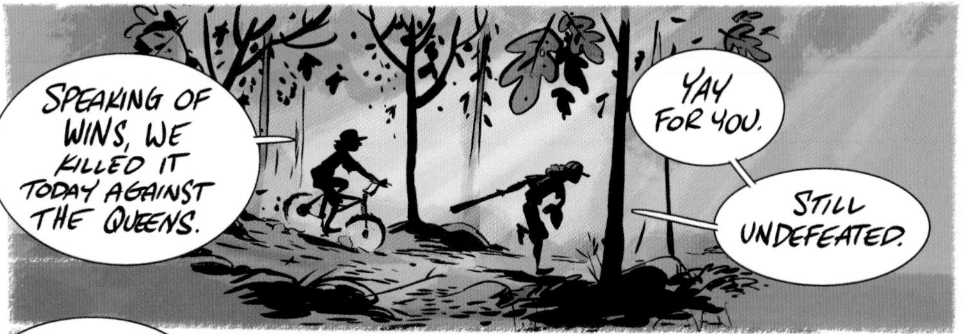
SPEAKING OF WINS, WE KILLED IT TODAY AGAINST THE QUEENS.
YAY FOR YOU.
STILL UNDEFEATED.

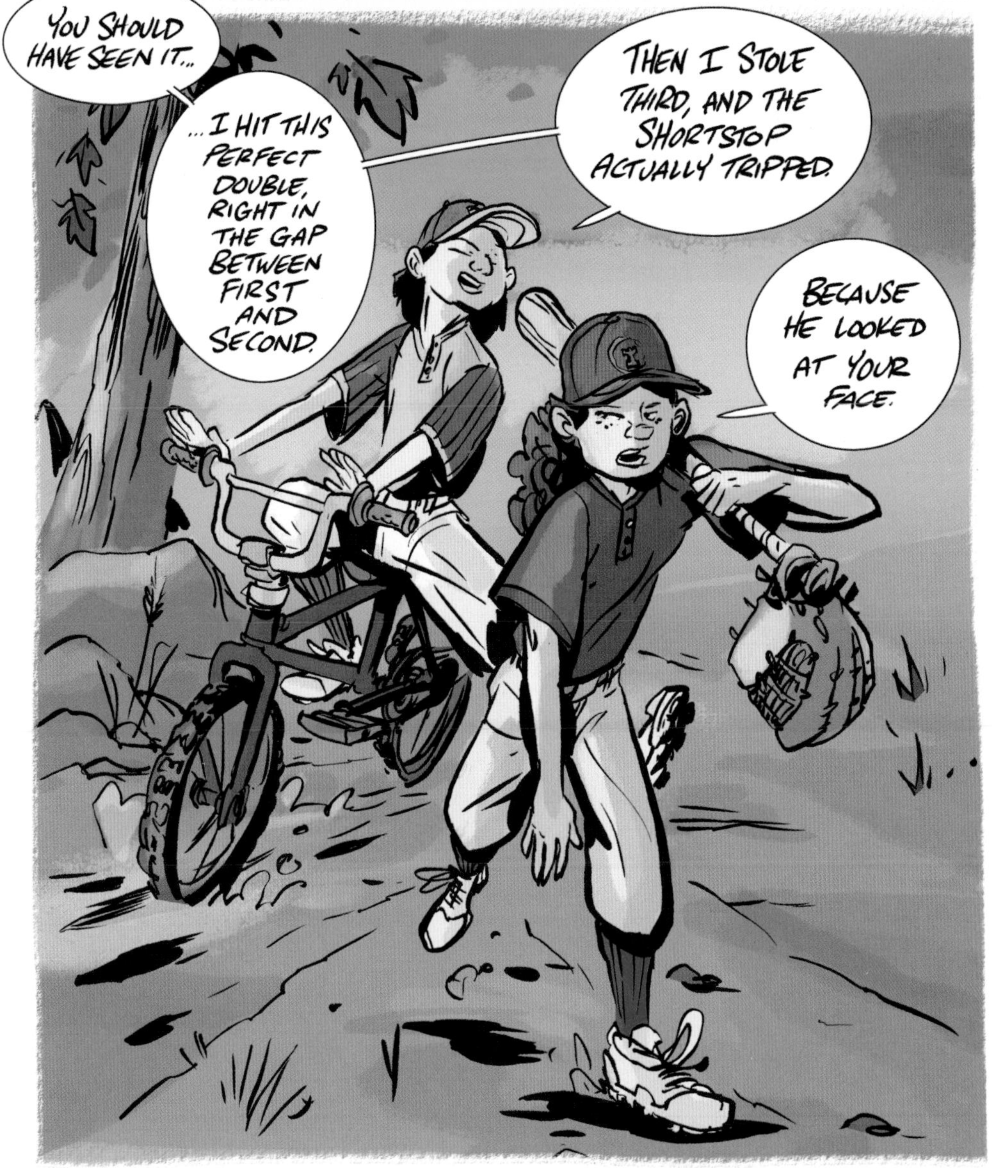
YOU SHOULD HAVE SEEN IT...
...I HIT THIS PERFECT DOUBLE, RIGHT IN THE GAP BETWEEN FIRST AND SECOND.
THEN I STOLE THIRD, AND THE SHORTSTOP ACTUALLY TRIPPED.
BECAUSE HE LOOKED AT YOUR FACE.

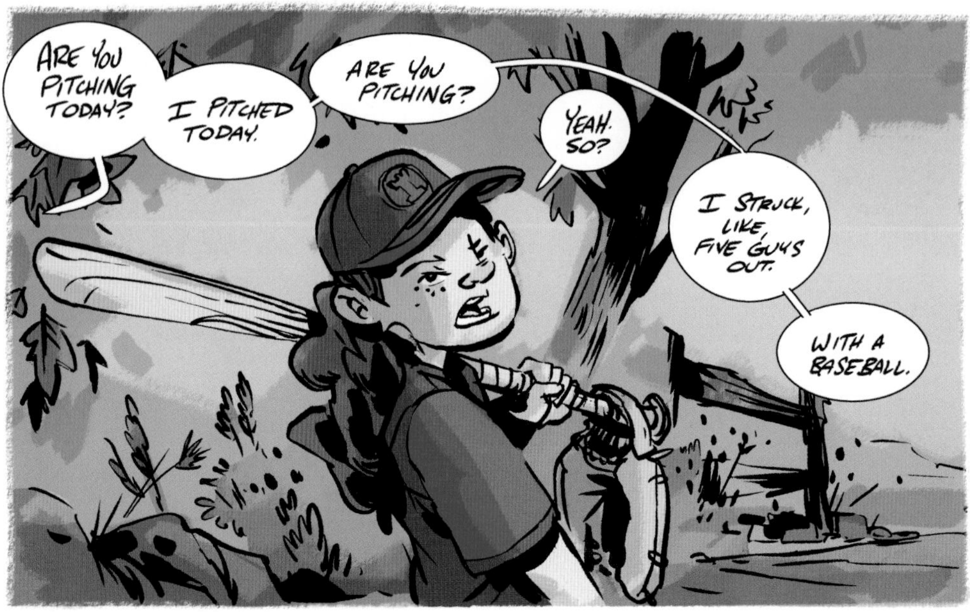
ARE YOU PITCHING TODAY?
I PITCHED TODAY.
ARE YOU PITCHING?
YEAH. SO?
I STRUCK, LIKE, FIVE GUYS OUT.
WITH A BASEBALL.

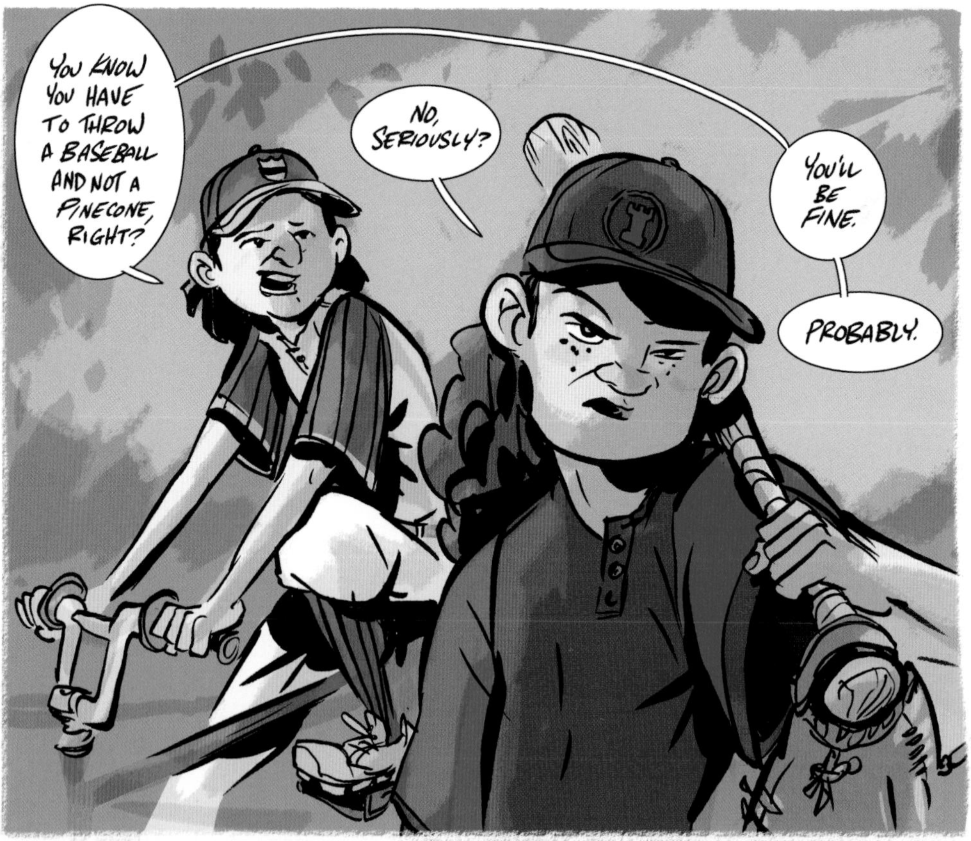
YOU KNOW YOU HAVE TO THROW A BASEBALL AND NOT A PINECONE, RIGHT?
NO, SERIOUSLY?
YOU'LL BE FINE.
PROBABLY.

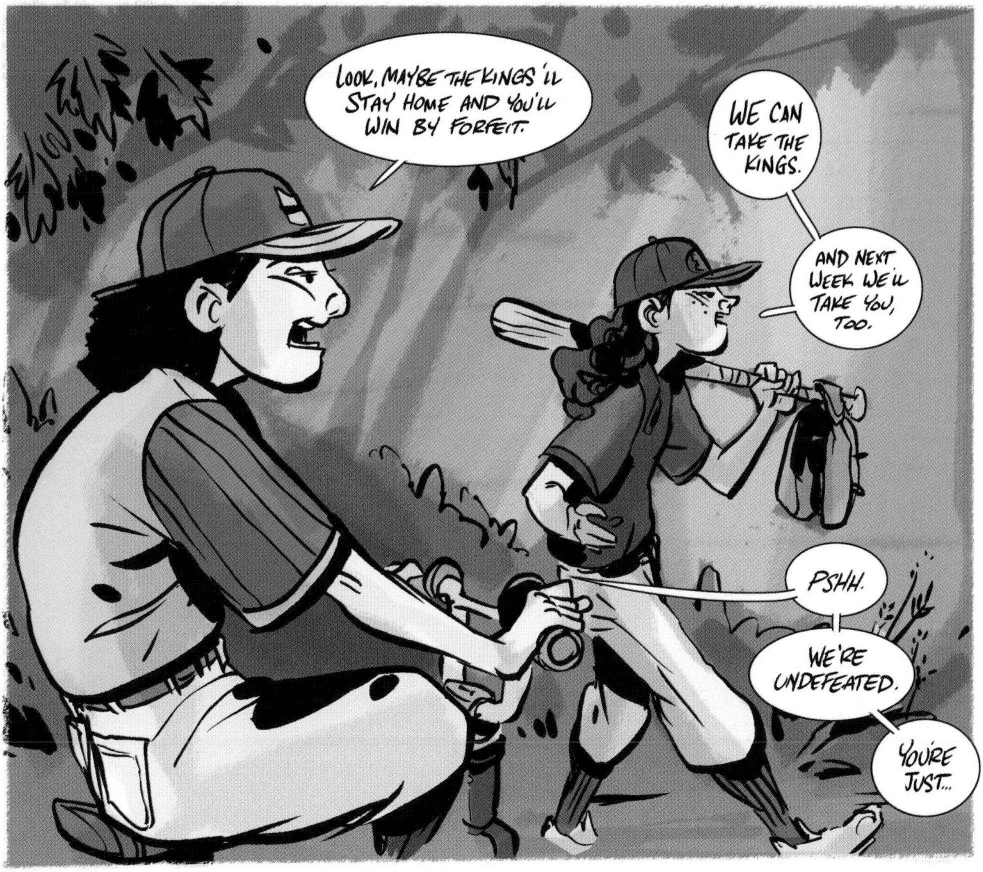
LOOK, MAYBE THE KINGS'LL STAY HOME AND YOU'LL WIN BY FORFEIT.
WE CAN TAKE THE KINGS.
AND NEXT WEEK WE'LL TAKE YOU, TOO.
PSHH.
WE'RE UNDEFEATED.
YOU'RE JUST...

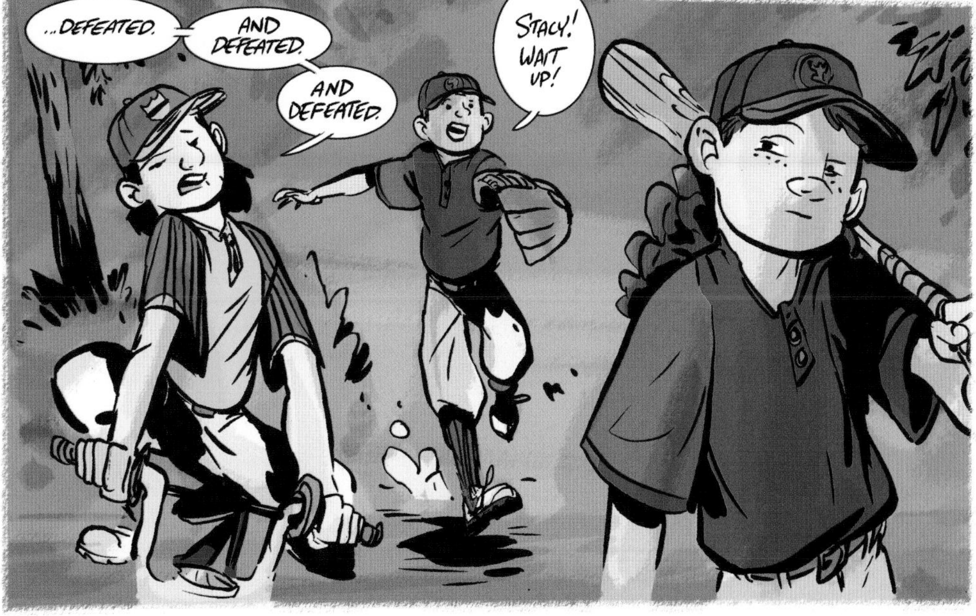
...DEFEATED.
AND DEFEATED.
AND DEFEATED.
STACY! WAIT UP!

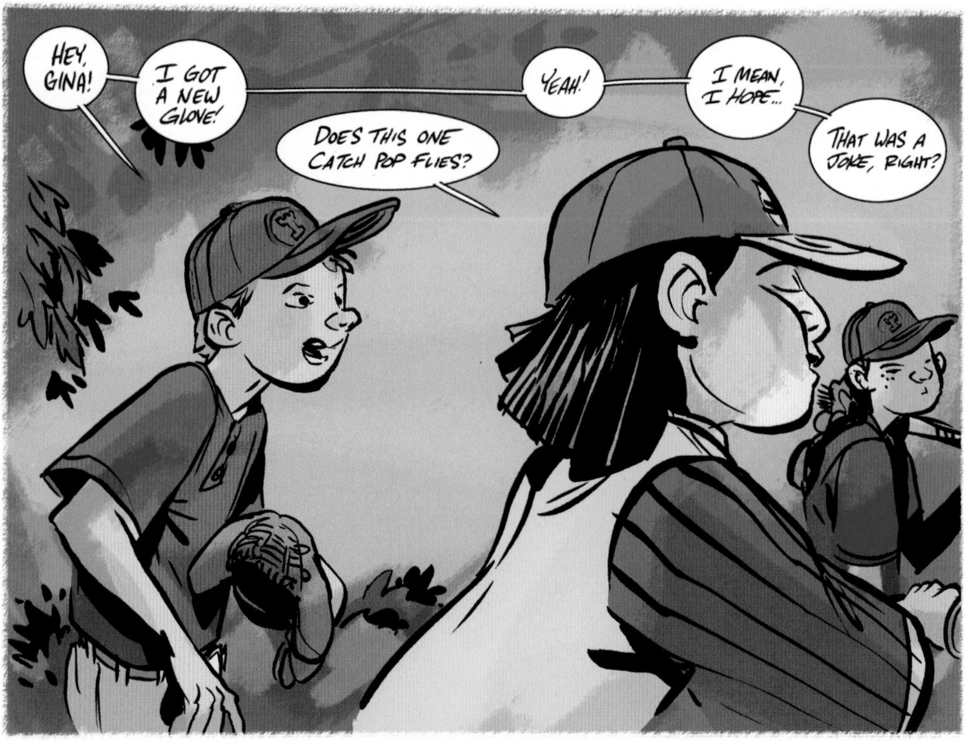
HEY, GINA!
I GOT A NEW GLOVE!
DOES THIS ONE CATCH POP FLIES?
YEAH!
I MEAN, I HOPE...
THAT WAS A JOKE, RIGHT?

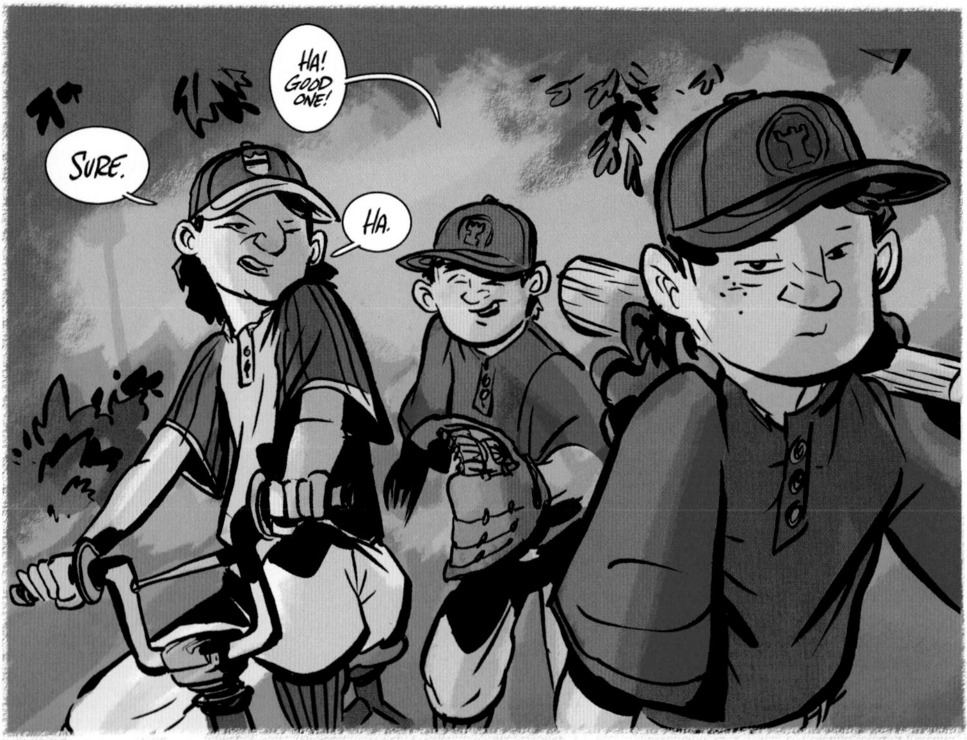
SURE.
HA! GOOD ONE!
HA.

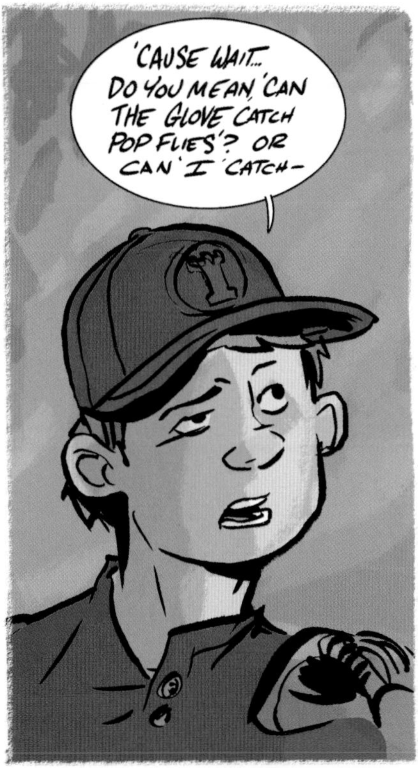
'CAUSE WAIT... DO YOU MEAN 'CAN THE GLOVE CATCH POP FLIES'? OR CAN 'I' CATCH-
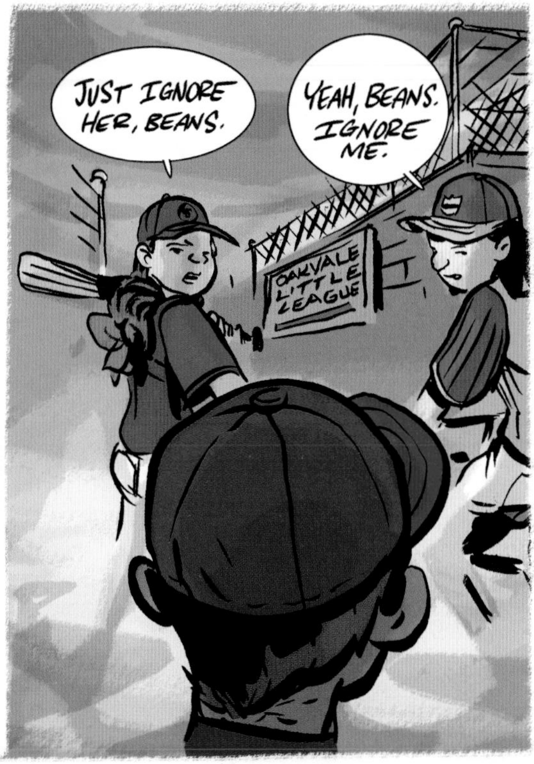
JUST IGNORE HER, BEANS.
YEAH, BEANS. IGNORE ME.
OAKVALE LITTLE LEAGUE
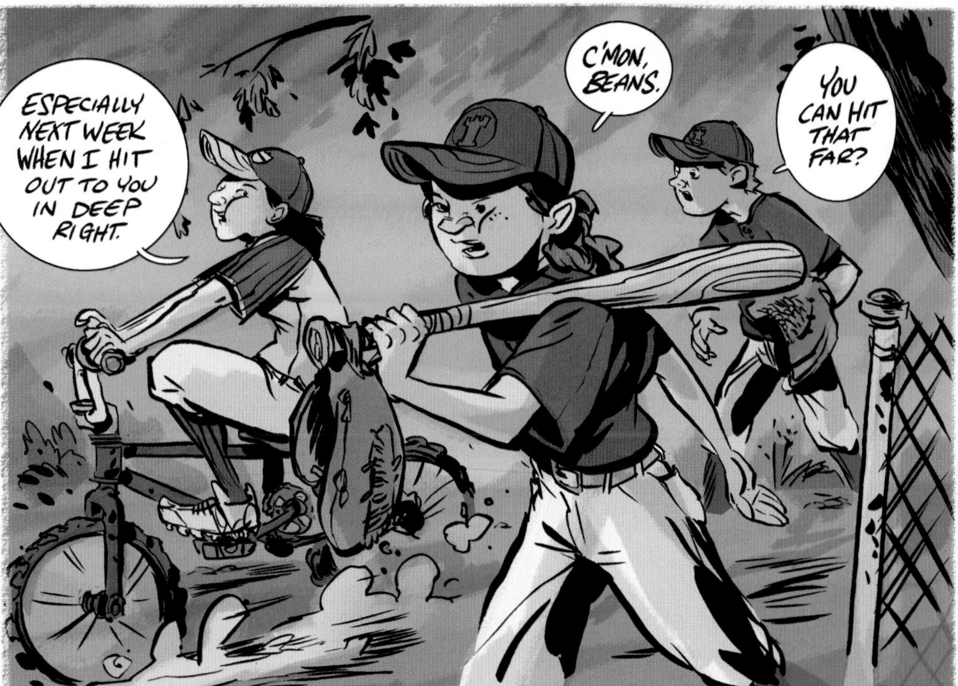
ESPECIALLY NEXT WEEK WHEN I HIT OUT TO YOU IN DEEP RIGHT.
C'MON, BEANS.
YOU CAN HIT THAT FAR?

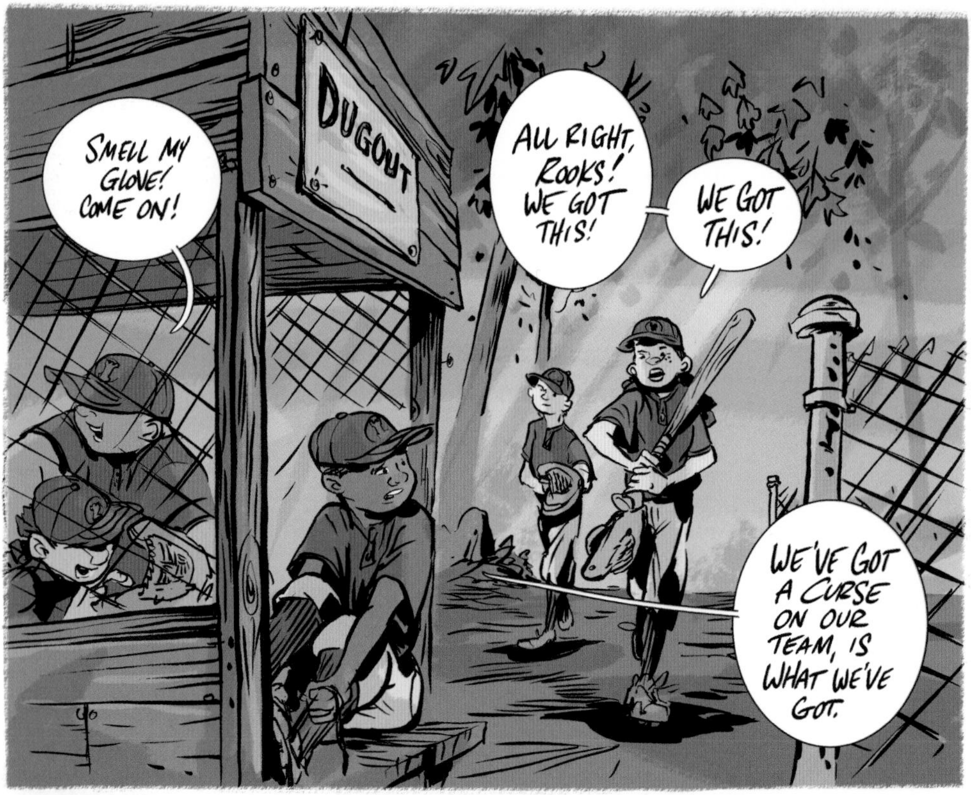
SMELL MY GLOVE! COME ON!
DUGOUT
ALL RIGHT, ROOKS! WE GOT THIS!
WE GOT THIS!
WE'VE GOT A CURSE ON OUR TEAM, IS WHAT WE'VE GOT.

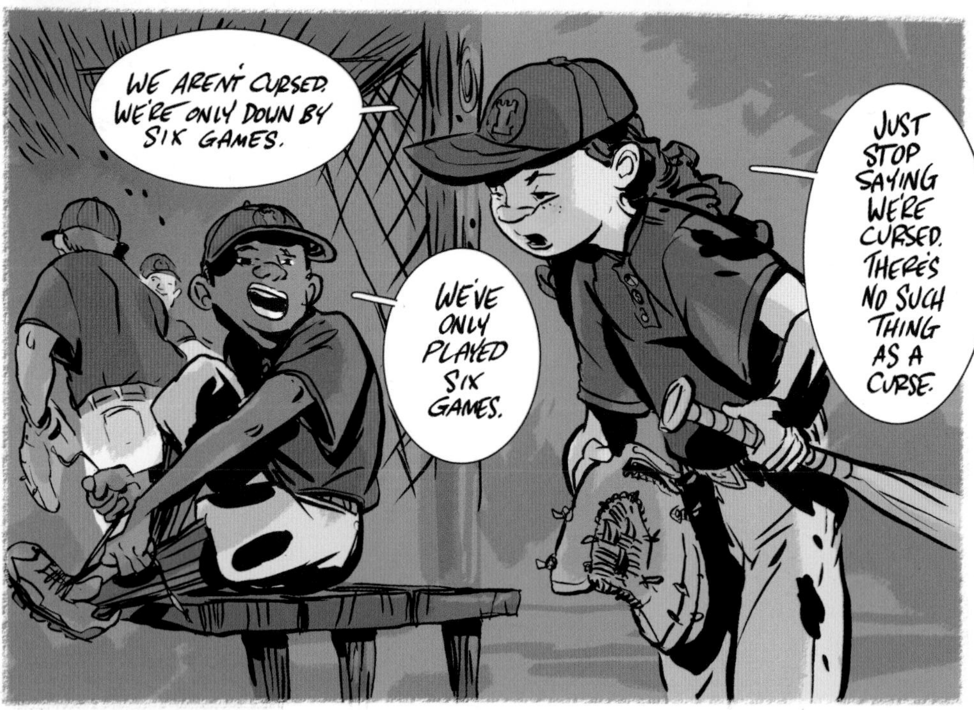
WE AREN'T CURSED. WE'RE ONLY DOWN BY SIX GAMES.
WE'VE ONLY PLAYED SIX GAMES.
JUST STOP SAYING WE'RE CURSED. THERE'S NO SUCH THING AS A CURSE.

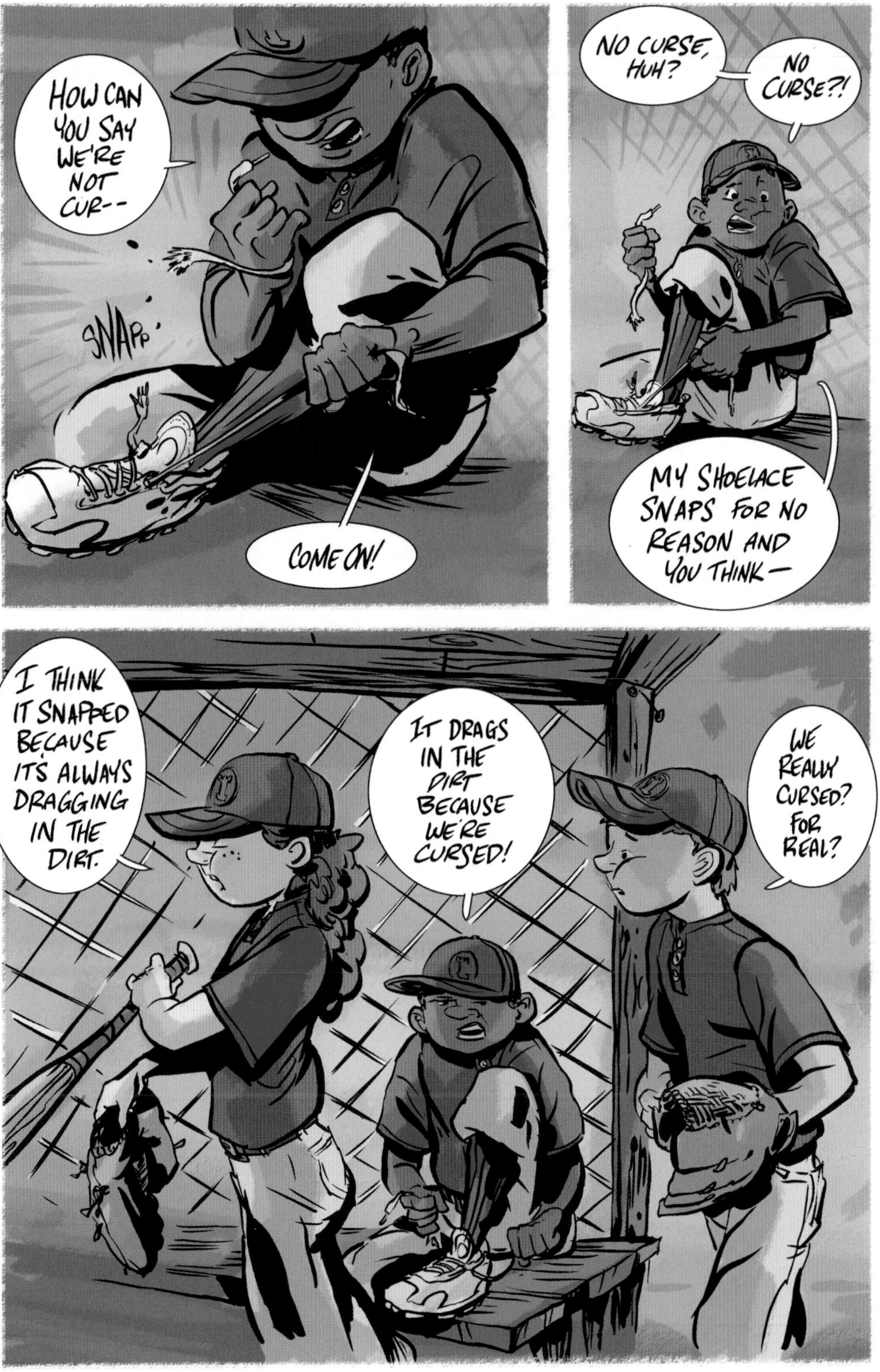
HOW CAN YOU SAY WE'RE NOT CUR--
SNAPP
COME ON!
NO CURSE, HUH?
NO CURSE?!
MY SHOELACE SNAPS FOR NO REASON AND YOU THINK—
I THINK IT SNAPPED BECAUSE IT'S ALWAYS DRAGGING IN THE DIRT.
IT DRAGS IN THE DIRT BECAUSE WE'RE CURSED!
WE REALLY CURSED? FOR REAL?

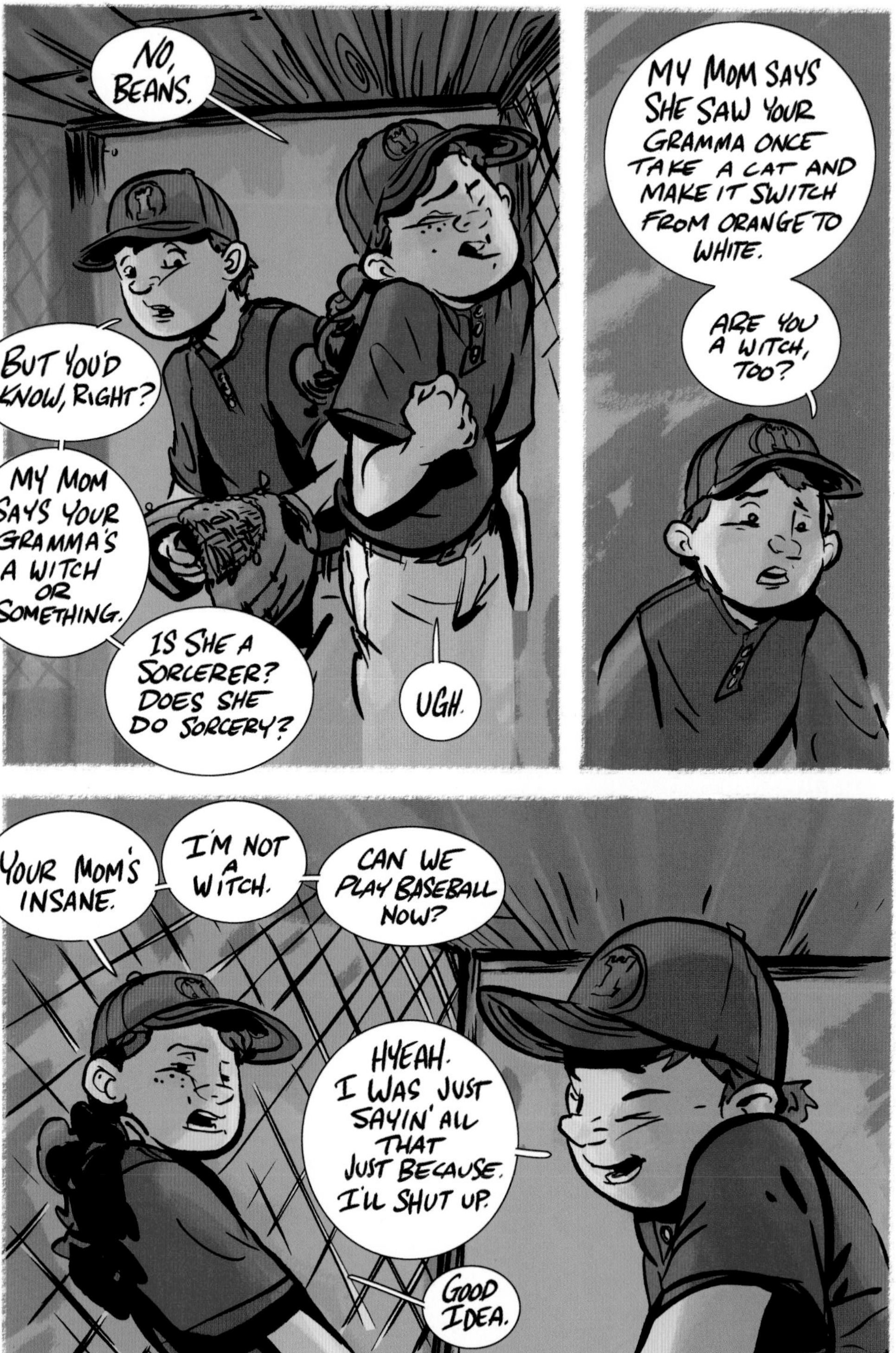
NO, BEANS.
BUT YOU'D KNOW, RIGHT?
MY MOM SAYS YOUR GRAMMA'S A WITCH OR SOMETHING.
IS SHE A SORCERER? DOES SHE DO SORCERY?
UGH.
MY MOM SAYS SHE SAW YOUR GRAMMA ONCE TAKE A CAT AND MAKE IT SWITCH FROM ORANGE TO WHITE.
ARE YOU A WITCH, TOO?
YOUR MOM'S INSANE.
I'M NOT A WITCH.
CAN WE PLAY BASEBALL NOW?
HYEAH. I WAS JUST SAYIN' ALL THAT JUST BECAUSE. I'LL SHUT UP.
GOOD IDEA.

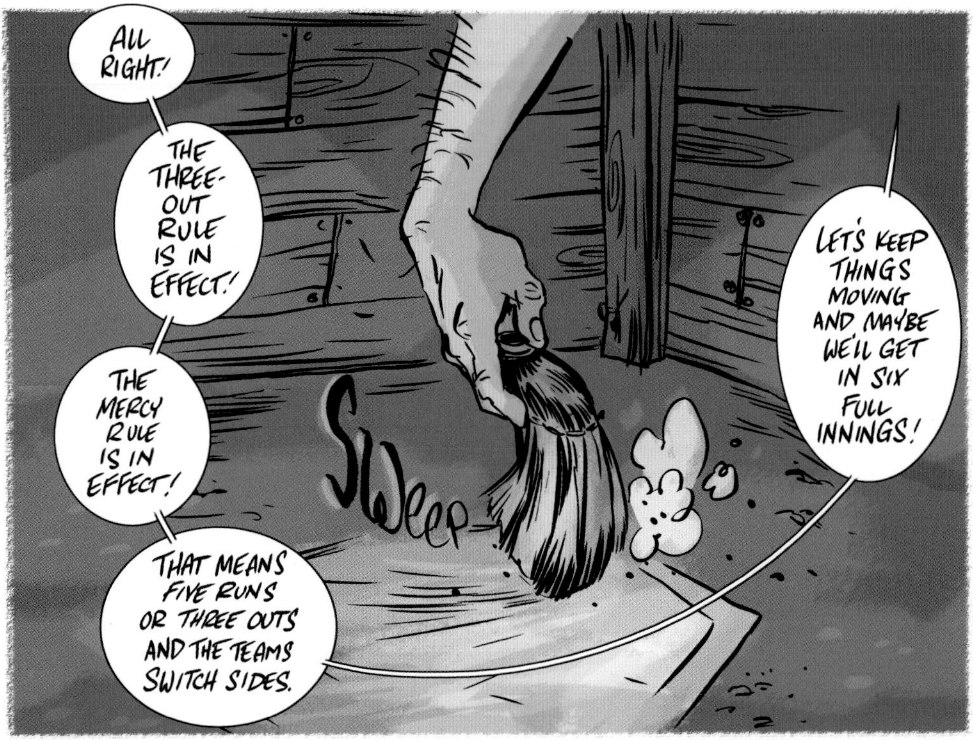
ALL RIGHT!
THE THREE-OUT RULE IS IN EFFECT!
THE MERCY RULE IS IN EFFECT!
THAT MEANS FIVE RUNS OR THREE OUTS AND THE TEAMS SWITCH SIDES.
LET'S KEEP THINGS MOVING AND MAYBE WE'LL GET IN SIX FULL INNINGS!
SWEEP

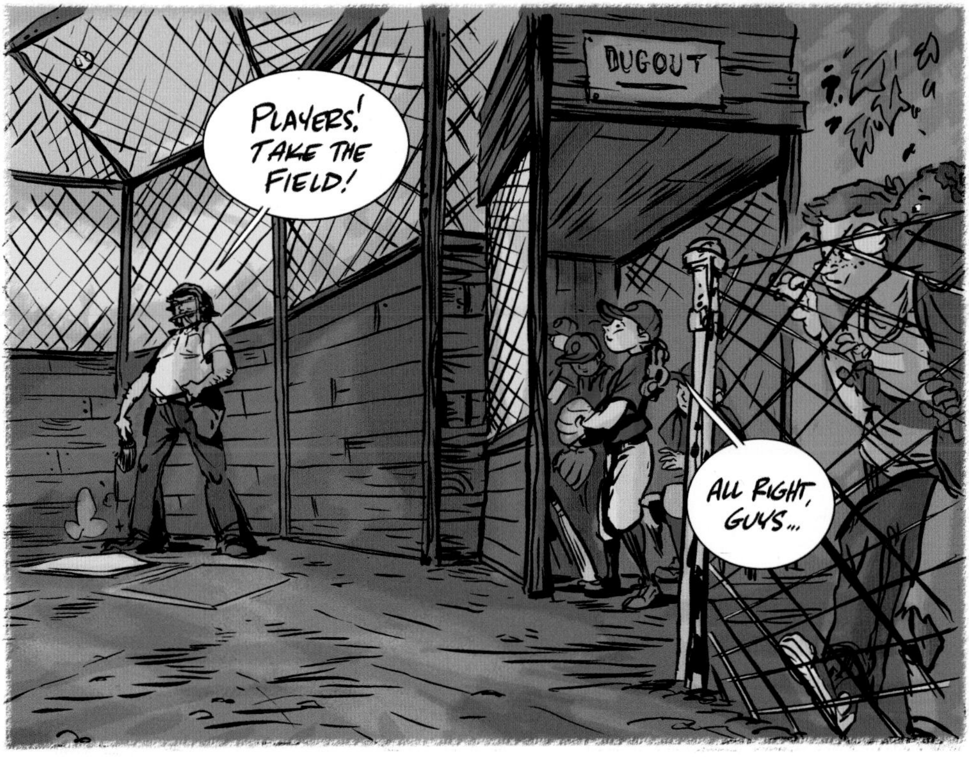
DUGOUT
PLAYERS! TAKE THE FIELD!
ALL RIGHT, GUYS...

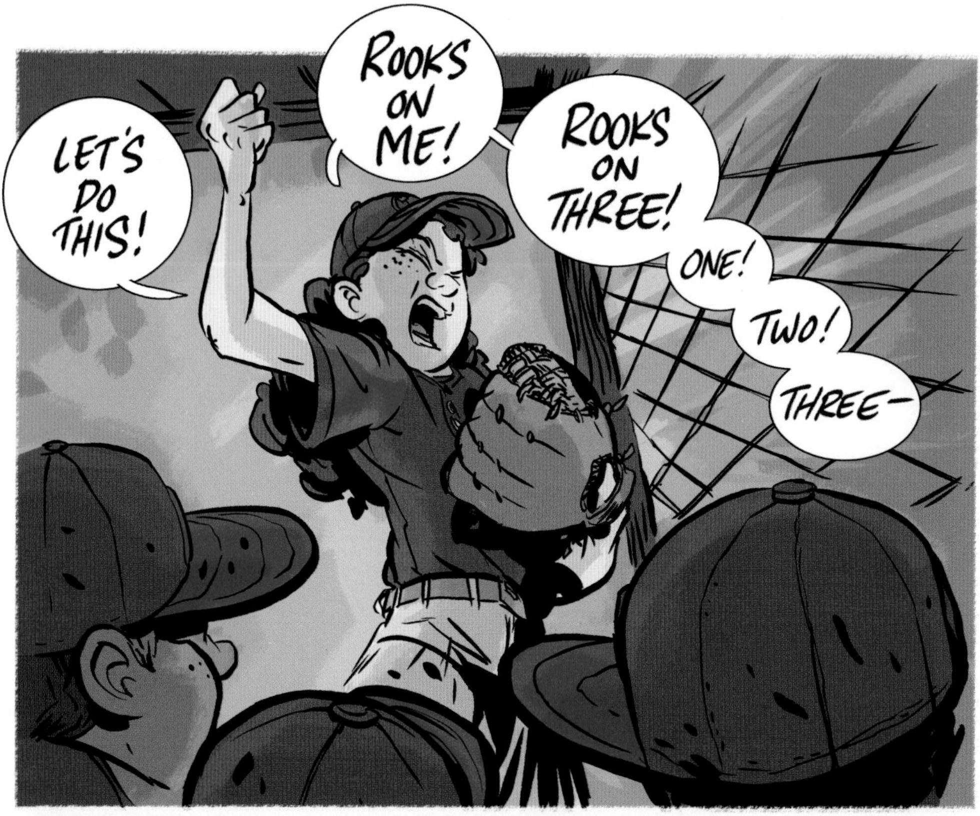
LET'S DO THIS!
ROOKS ON ME!
ROOKS ON THREE!
ONE!
TWO!
THREE-

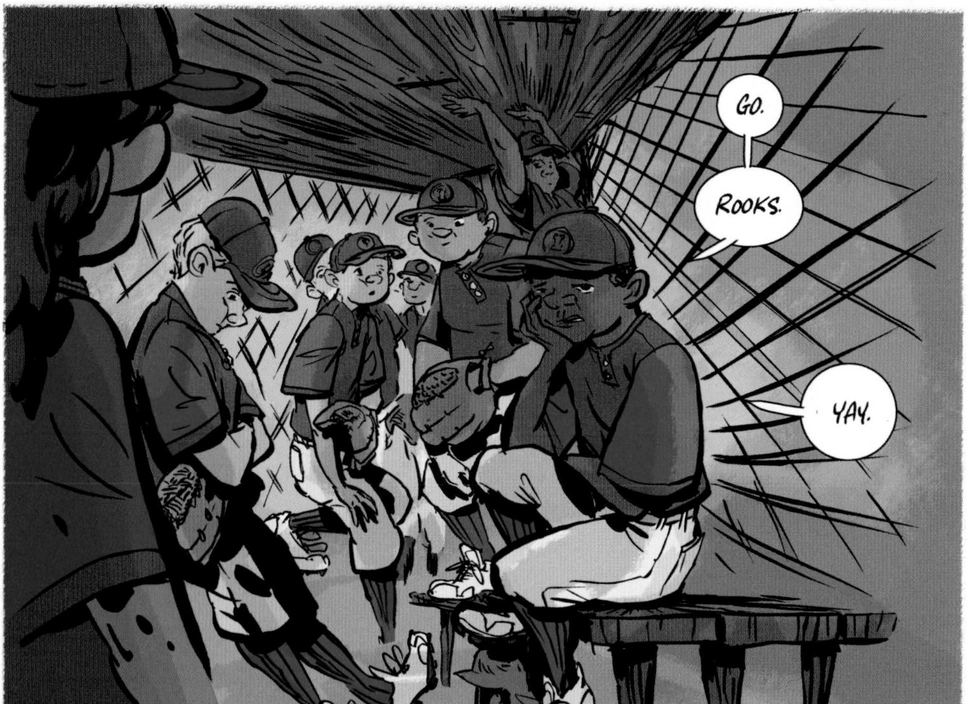
GO.
ROOKS.
YAY.

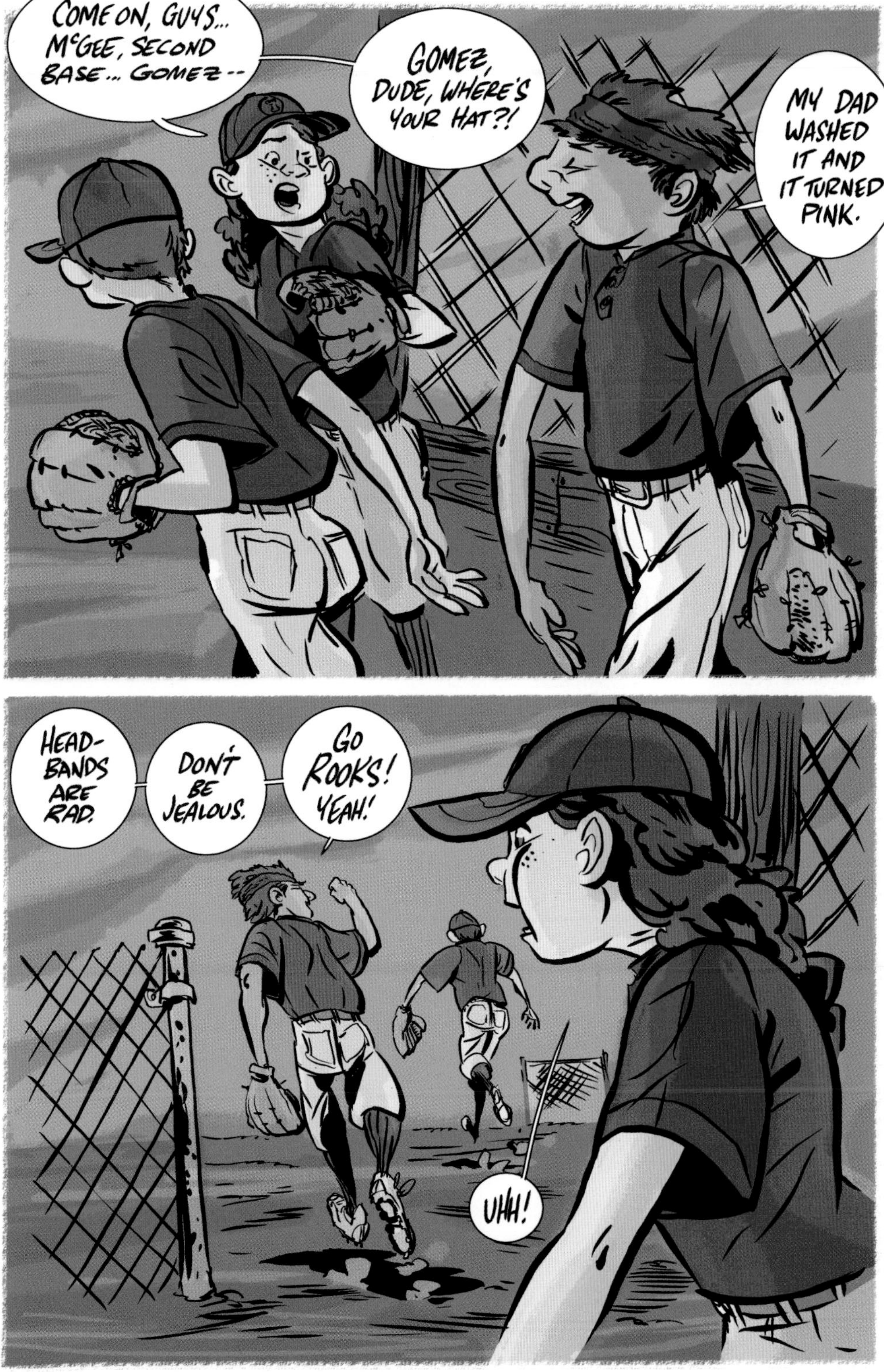
COME ON, GUYS... McGEE, SECOND BASE... GOMEZ--
GOMEZ, DUDE, WHERE'S YOUR HAT?!
MY DAD WASHED IT AND IT TURNED PINK.
HEAD-BANDS ARE RAD.
DON'T BE JEALOUS.
GO ROOKS! YEAH!
UHH!

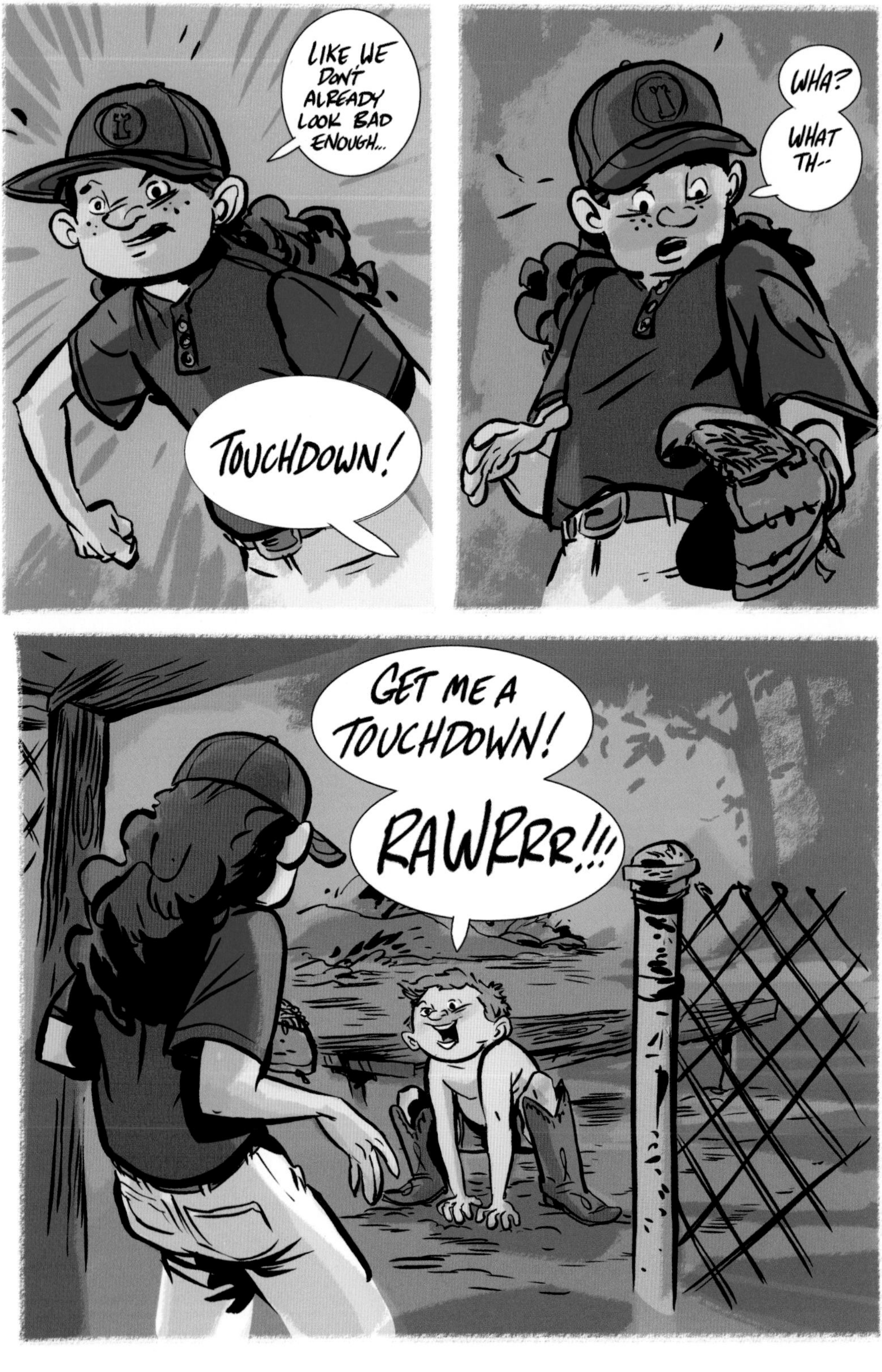
LIKE WE DON'T ALREADY LOOK BAD ENOUGH...
TOUCHDOWN!
WHA?
WHAT TH--
GET ME A TOUCHDOWN!
RAWRrrr!!!

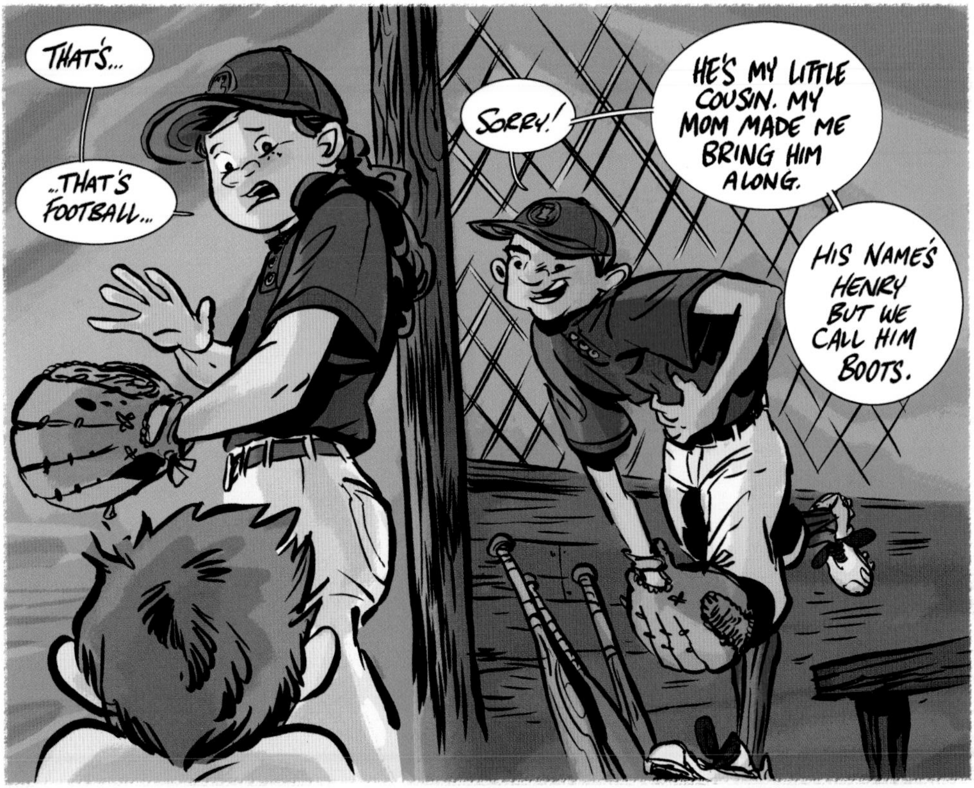
THAT'S...
...THAT'S FOOTBALL...
SORRY!
HE'S MY LITTLE COUSIN. MY MOM MADE ME BRING HIM ALONG.
HIS NAME'S HENRY BUT WE CALL HIM BOOTS.

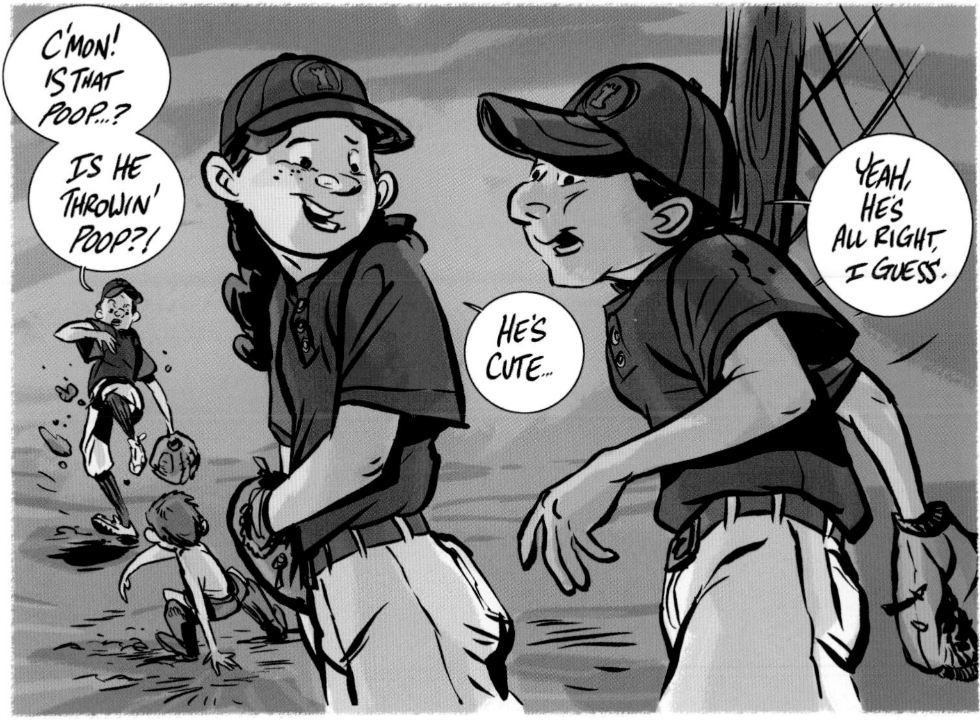
C'MON! IS THAT POOP...?
IS HE THROWIN' POOP?!
HE'S CUTE...
YEAH, HE'S ALL RIGHT, I GUESS.

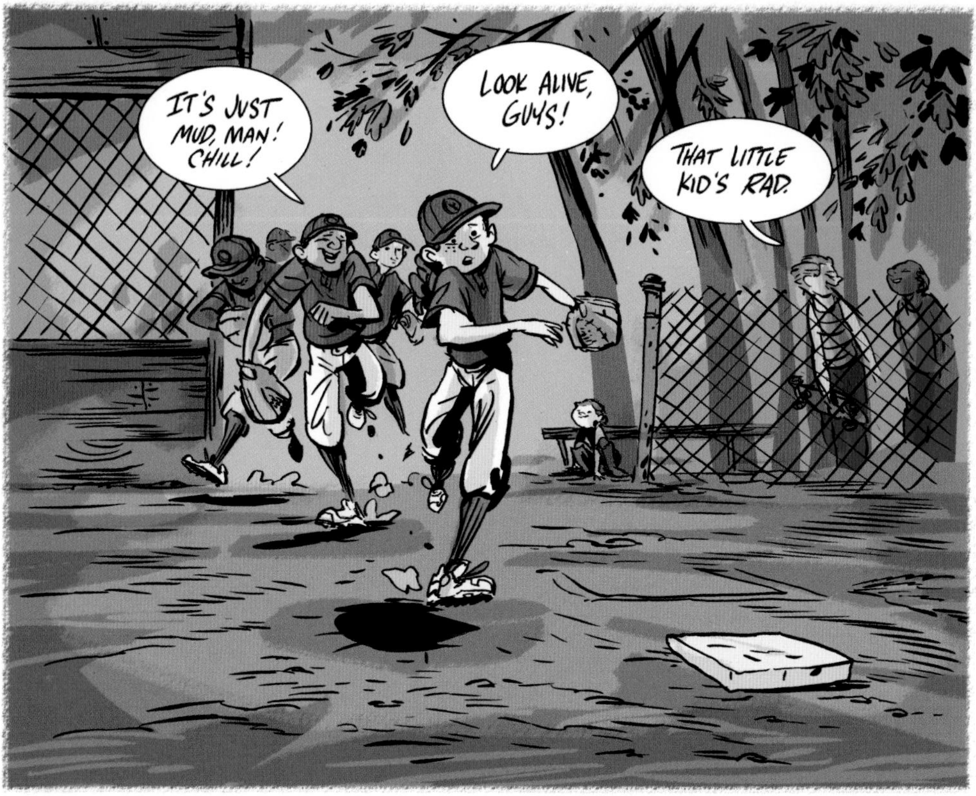
IT'S JUST MUD, MAN! CHILL!
LOOK ALIVE, GUYS!
THAT LITTLE KID'S RAD.

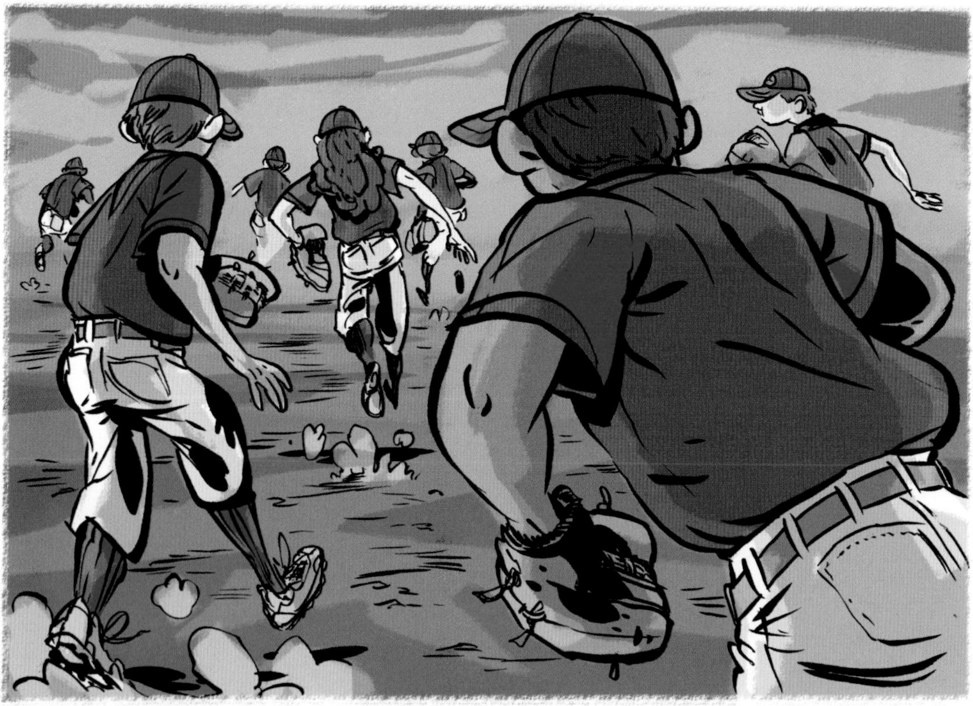

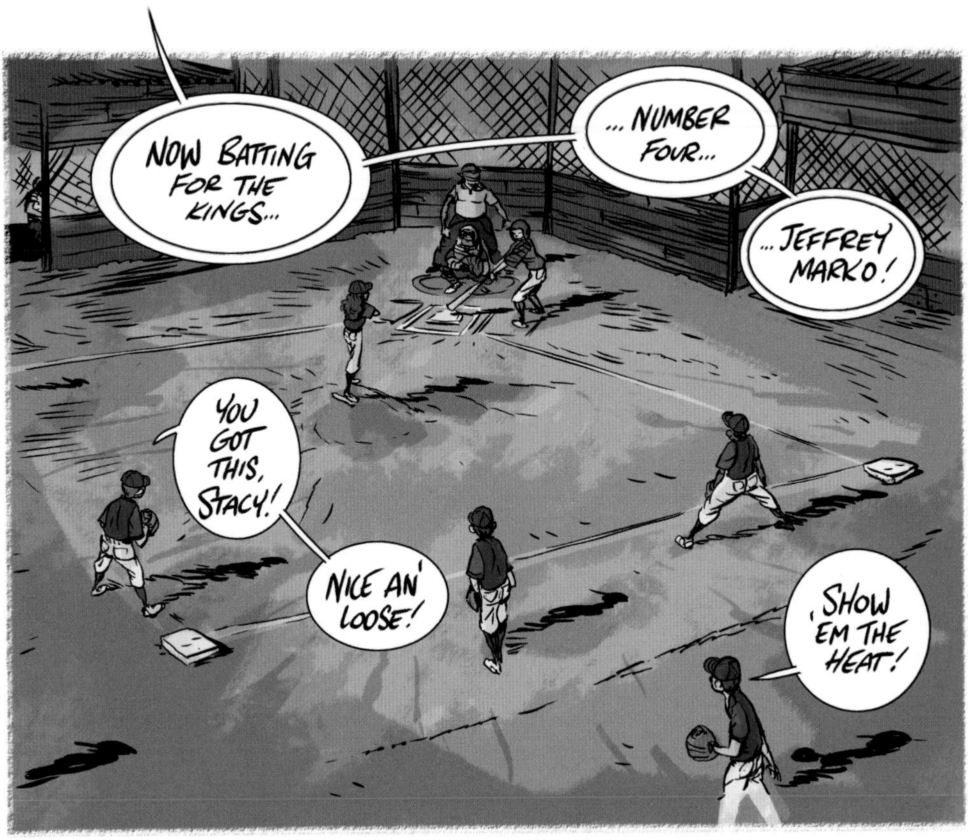
NOW BATTING FOR THE KINGS...
...NUMBER FOUR...
...JEFFREY MARKO!
YOU GOT THIS, STACY!
NICE AN' LOOSE!
SHOW 'EM THE HEAT!

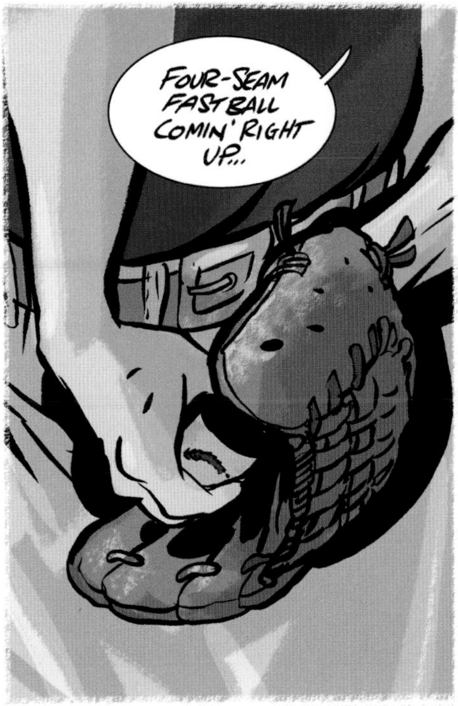
FOUR-SEAM FASTBALL COMIN' RIGHT UP...

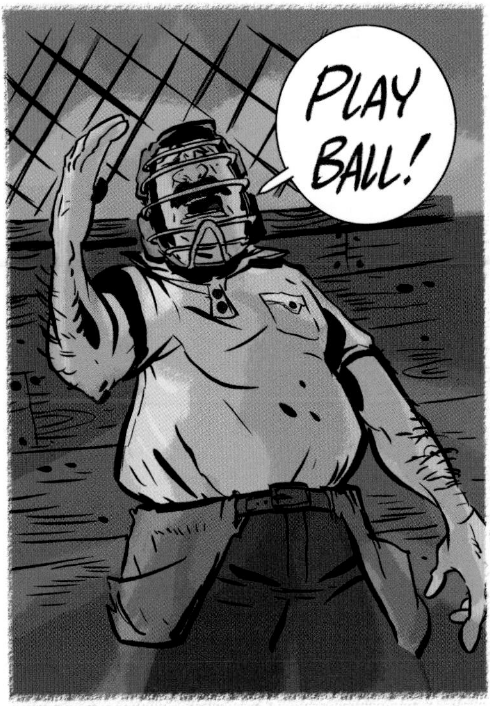
PLAY BALL!

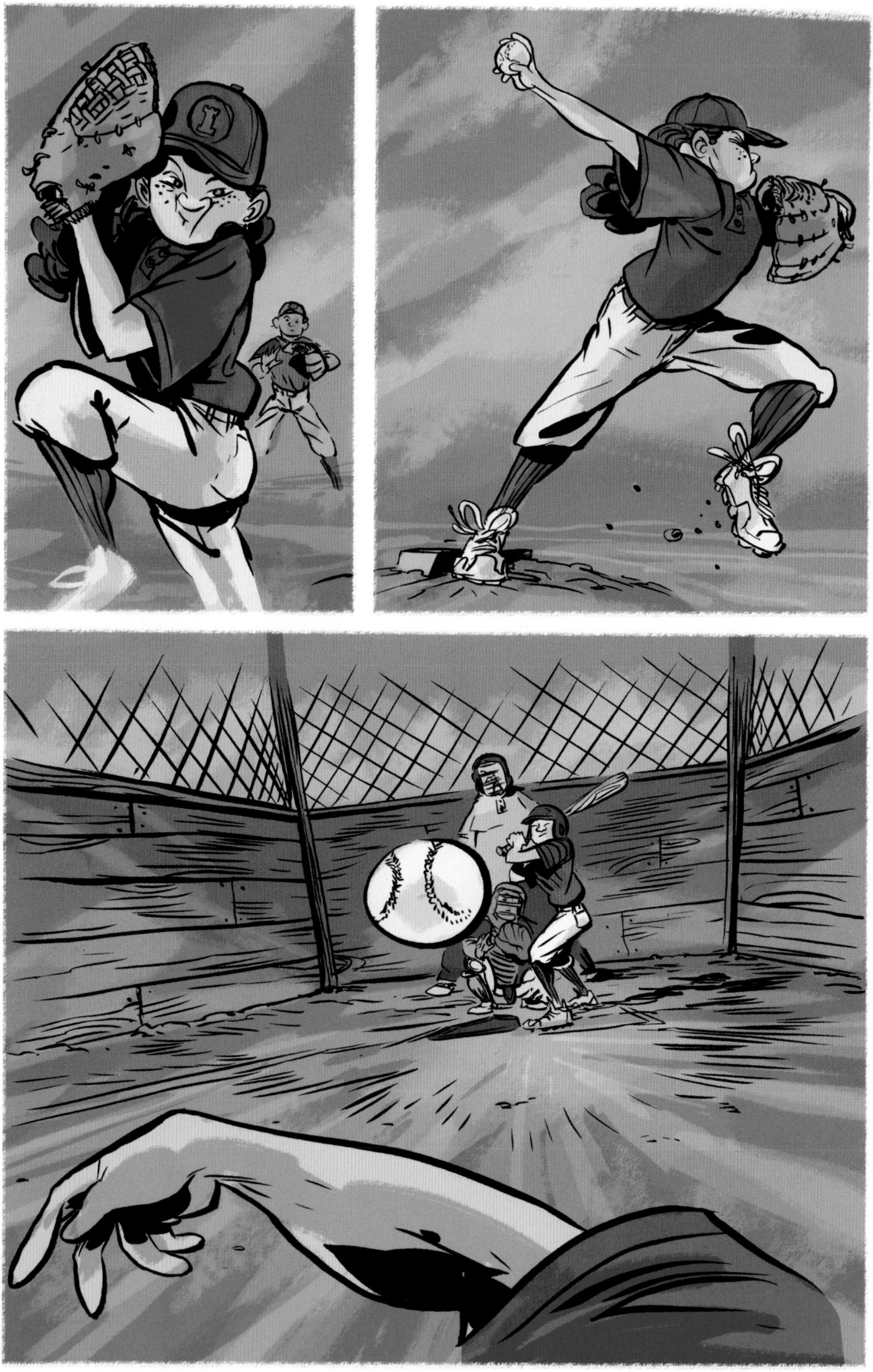

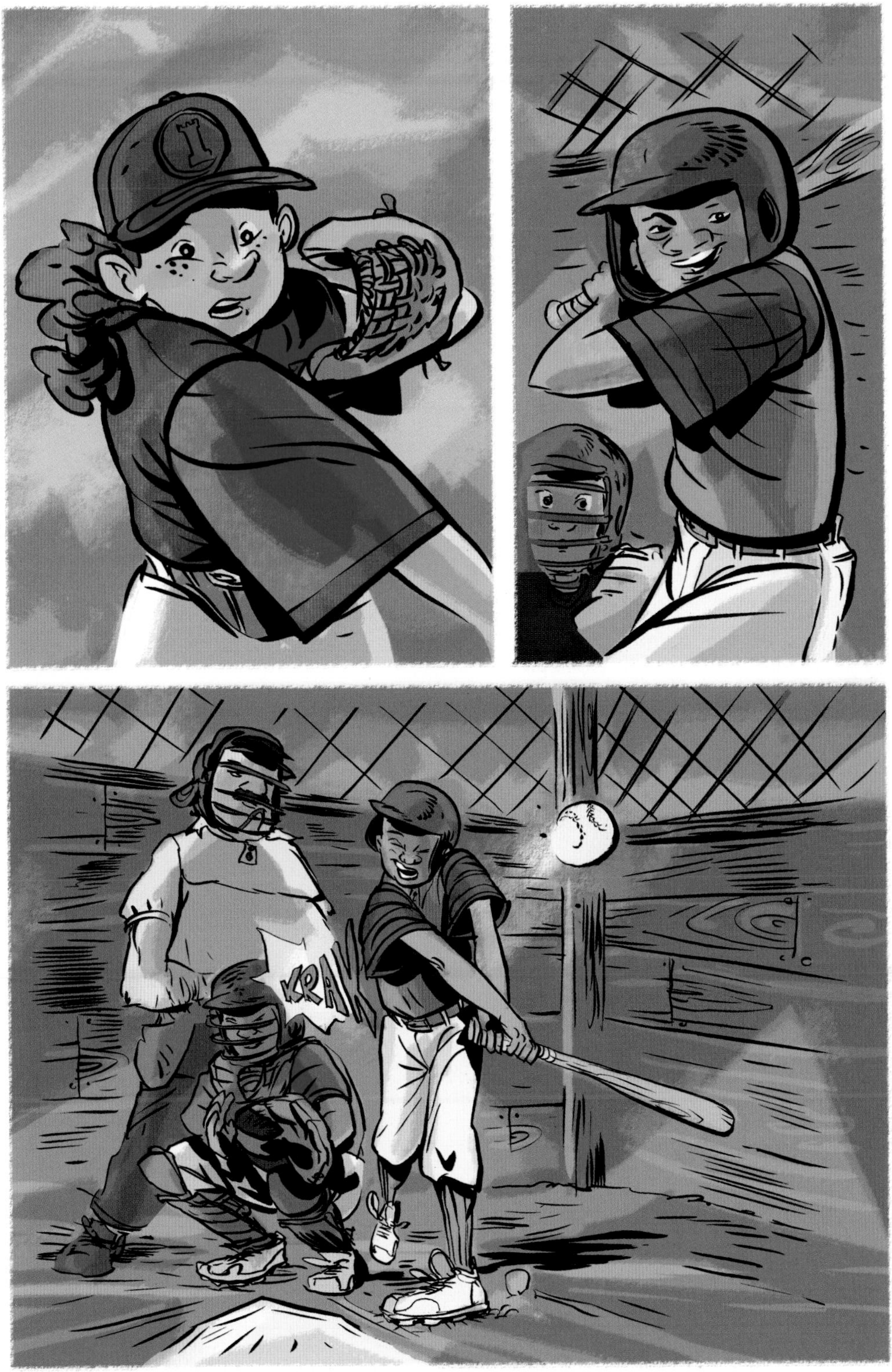
KRA

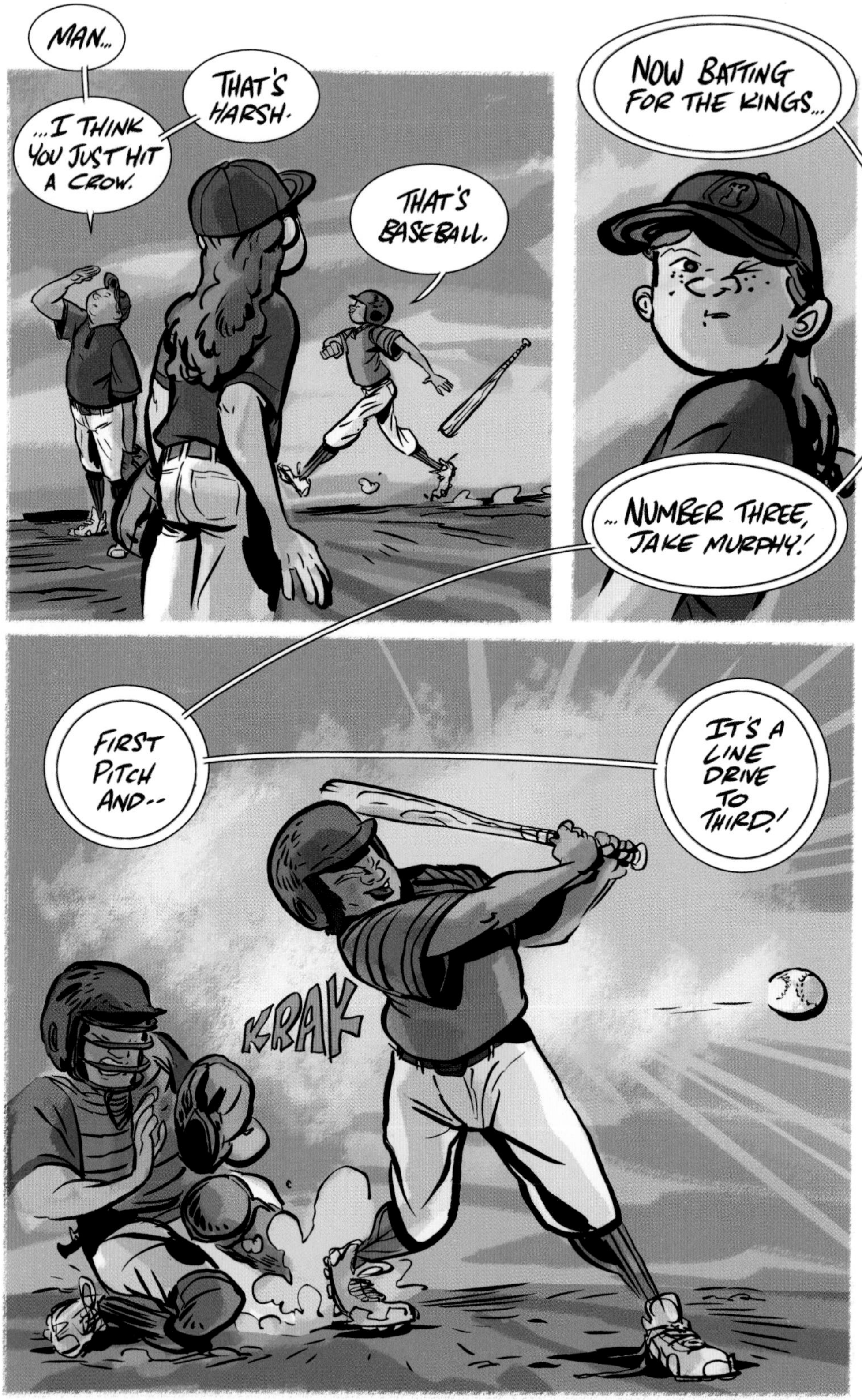
MAN...
...I THINK YOU JUST HIT A CROW.
THAT'S HARSH.
THAT'S BASEBALL.
NOW BATTING FOR THE KINGS...
...NUMBER THREE, JAKE MURPHY!
FIRST PITCH AND--
KRAK
IT'S A LINE DRIVE TO THIRD!

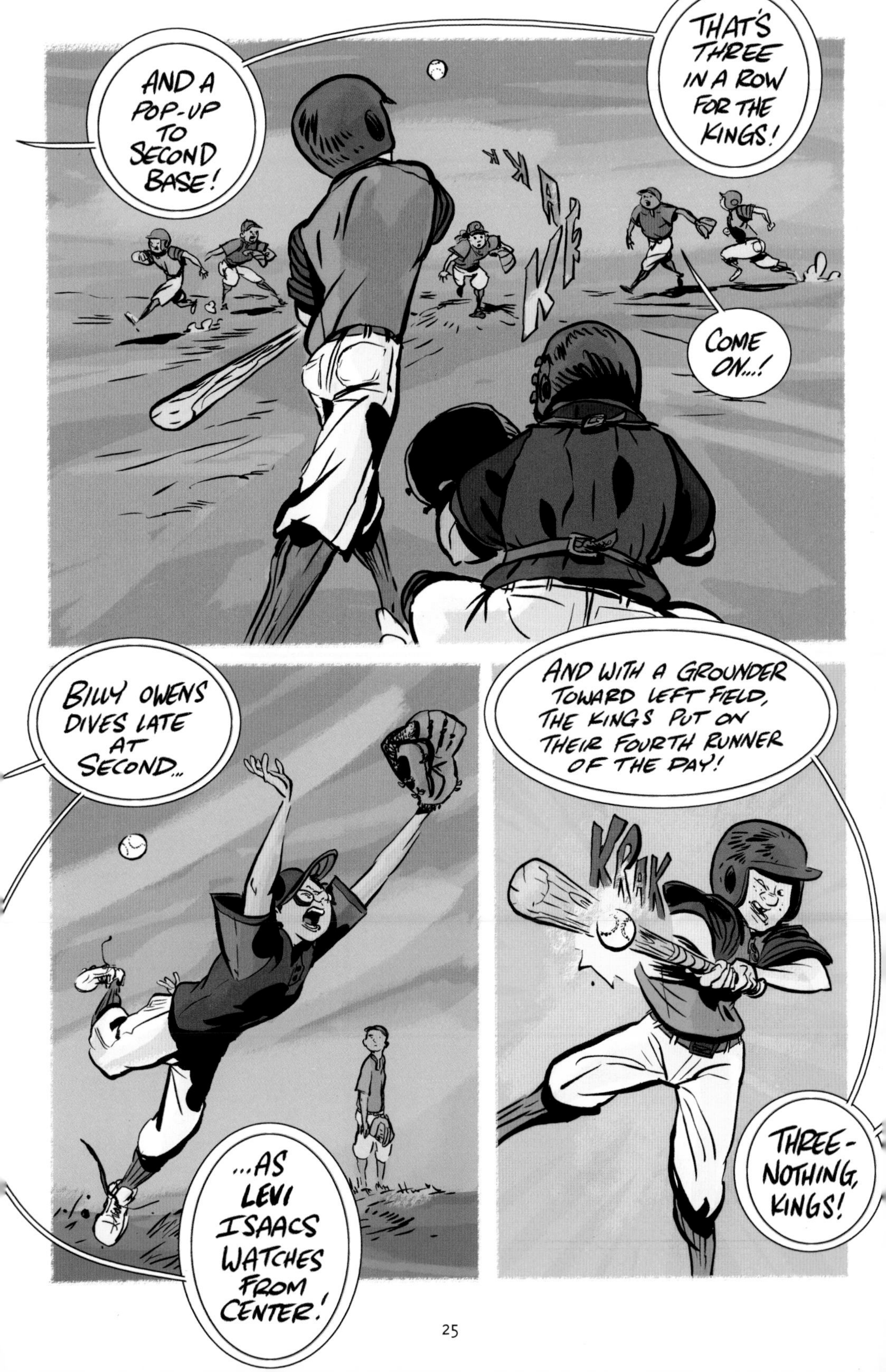
AND A POP-UP TO SECOND BASE!
THAT'S THREE IN A ROW FOR THE KINGS!
KRAKK
COME ON...!
BILLY OWENS DIVES LATE AT SECOND...
...AS LEVI ISAACS WATCHES FROM CENTER!
AND WITH A GROUNDER TOWARD LEFT FIELD, THE KINGS PUT ON THEIR FOURTH RUNNER OF THE DAY!
KRAK
THREE-NOTHING, KINGS!

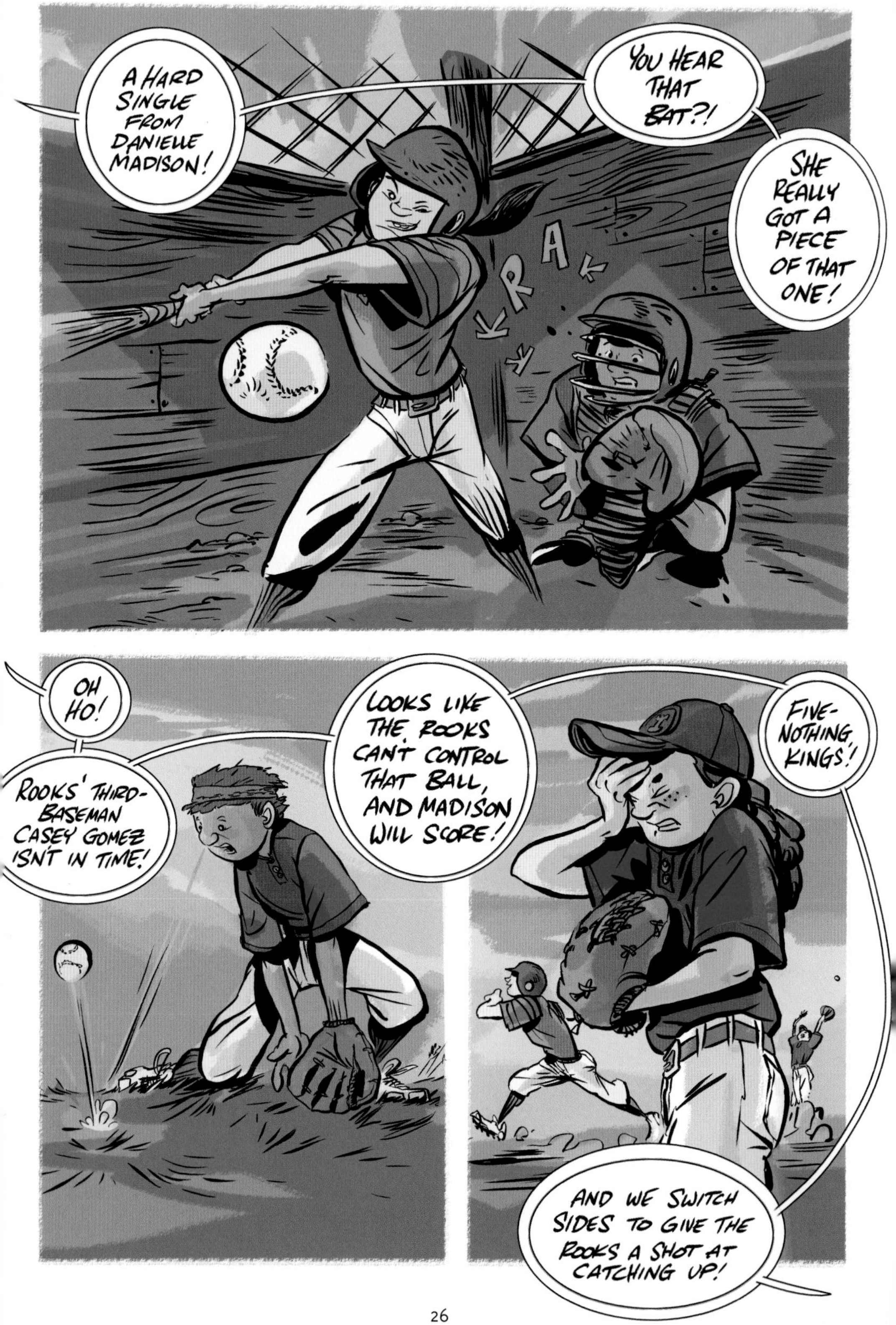
A HARD SINGLE FROM DANIELLE MADISON!
KKRAK
YOU HEAR THAT BAT?!
SHE REALLY GOT A PIECE OF THAT ONE!
OH HO!
ROOKS' THIRD-BASEMAN CASEY GOMEZ ISN'T IN TIME!
LOOKS LIKE THE ROOKS CAN'T CONTROL THAT BALL, AND MADISON WILL SCORE!
FIVE-NOTHING, KINGS!
AND WE SWITCH SIDES TO GIVE THE ROOKS A SHOT AT CATCHING UP!

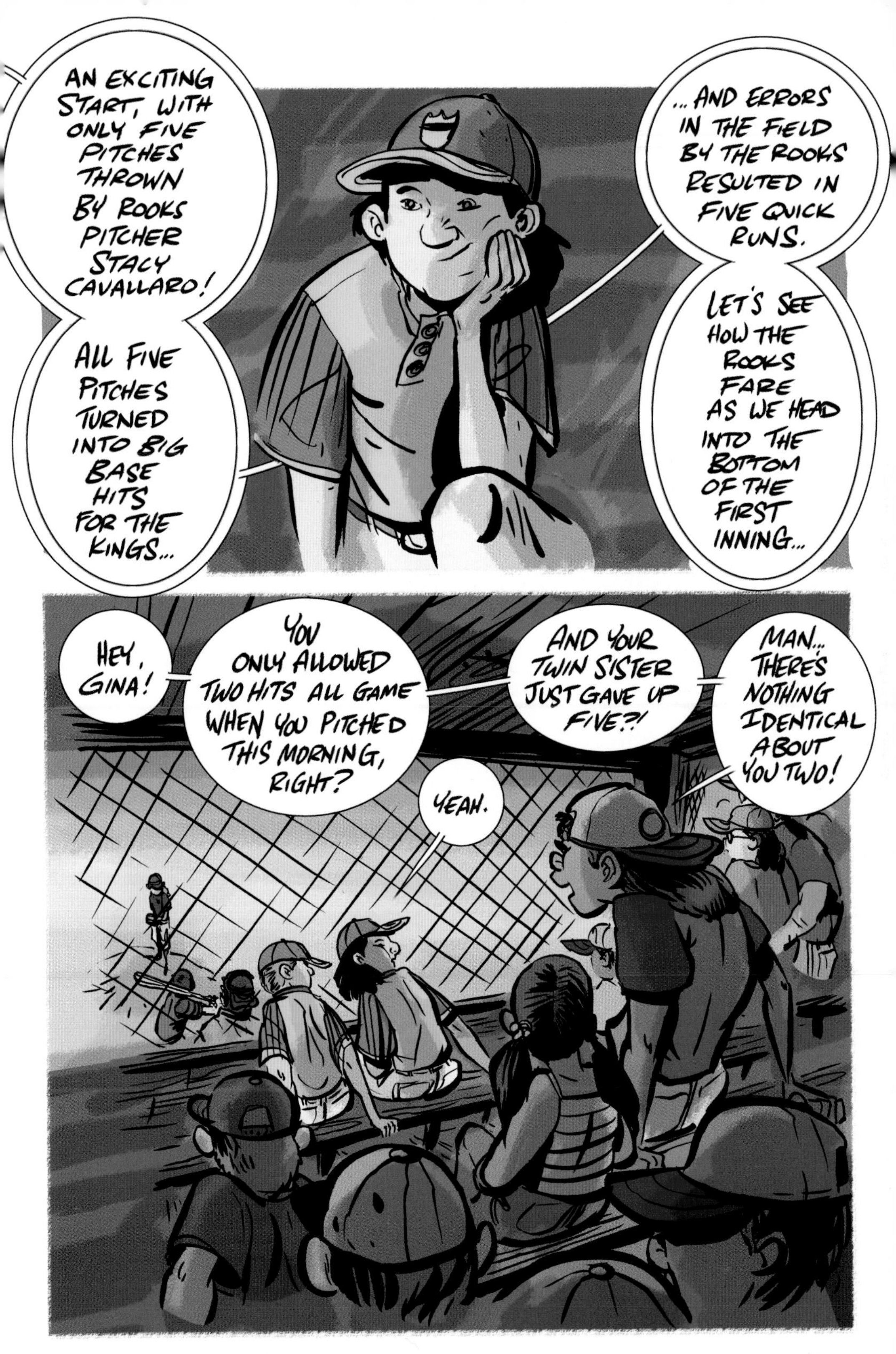
AN EXCITING START, WITH ONLY FIVE PITCHES THROWN BY ROOKS PITCHER STACY CAVALLARO!
ALL FIVE PITCHES TURNED INTO BIG BASE HITS FOR THE KINGS...
...AND ERRORS IN THE FIELD BY THE ROOKS RESULTED IN FIVE QUICK RUNS.
LET'S SEE HOW THE ROOKS FARE AS WE HEAD INTO THE BOTTOM OF THE FIRST INNING...
HEY, GINA!
YOU ONLY ALLOWED TWO HITS ALL GAME WHEN YOU PITCHED THIS MORNING, RIGHT?
YEAH.
AND YOUR TWIN SISTER JUST GAVE UP FIVE?!
MAN... THERE'S NOTHING IDENTICAL ABOUT YOU TWO!

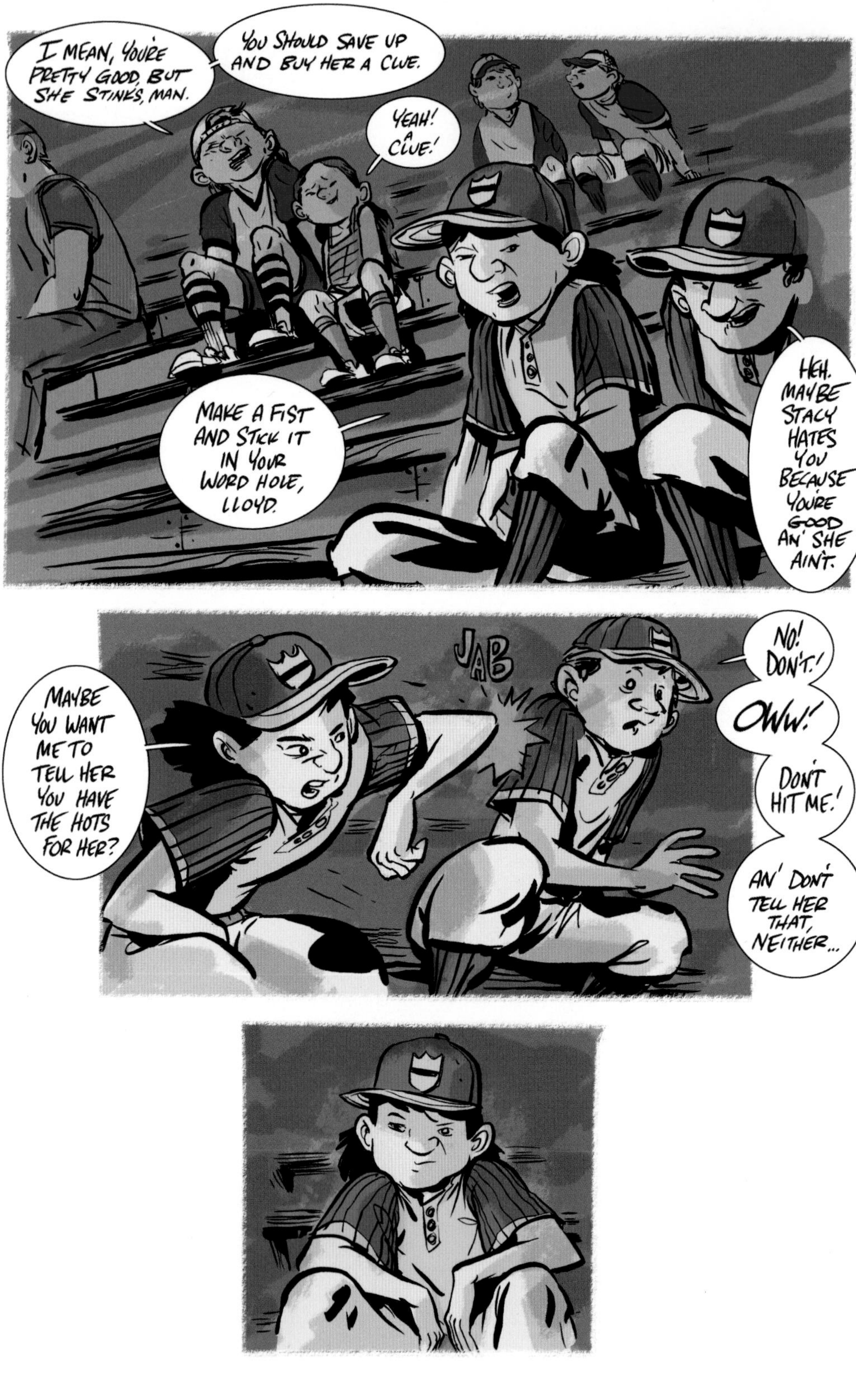
I MEAN, YOU'RE PRETTY GOOD, BUT SHE STINKS, MAN.
YOU SHOULD SAVE UP AND BUY HER A CLUE.
YEAH! A CLUE!
MAKE A FIST AND STICK IT IN YOUR WORD HOLE, LLOYD.
HEH. MAYBE STACY HATES YOU BECAUSE YOU'RE GOOD AN' SHE AIN'T.
MAYBE YOU WANT ME TO TELL HER YOU HAVE THE HOTS FOR HER?
JAB
NO! DON'T!
OWW!
DON'T HIT ME!
AN' DON'T TELL HER THAT, NEITHER...

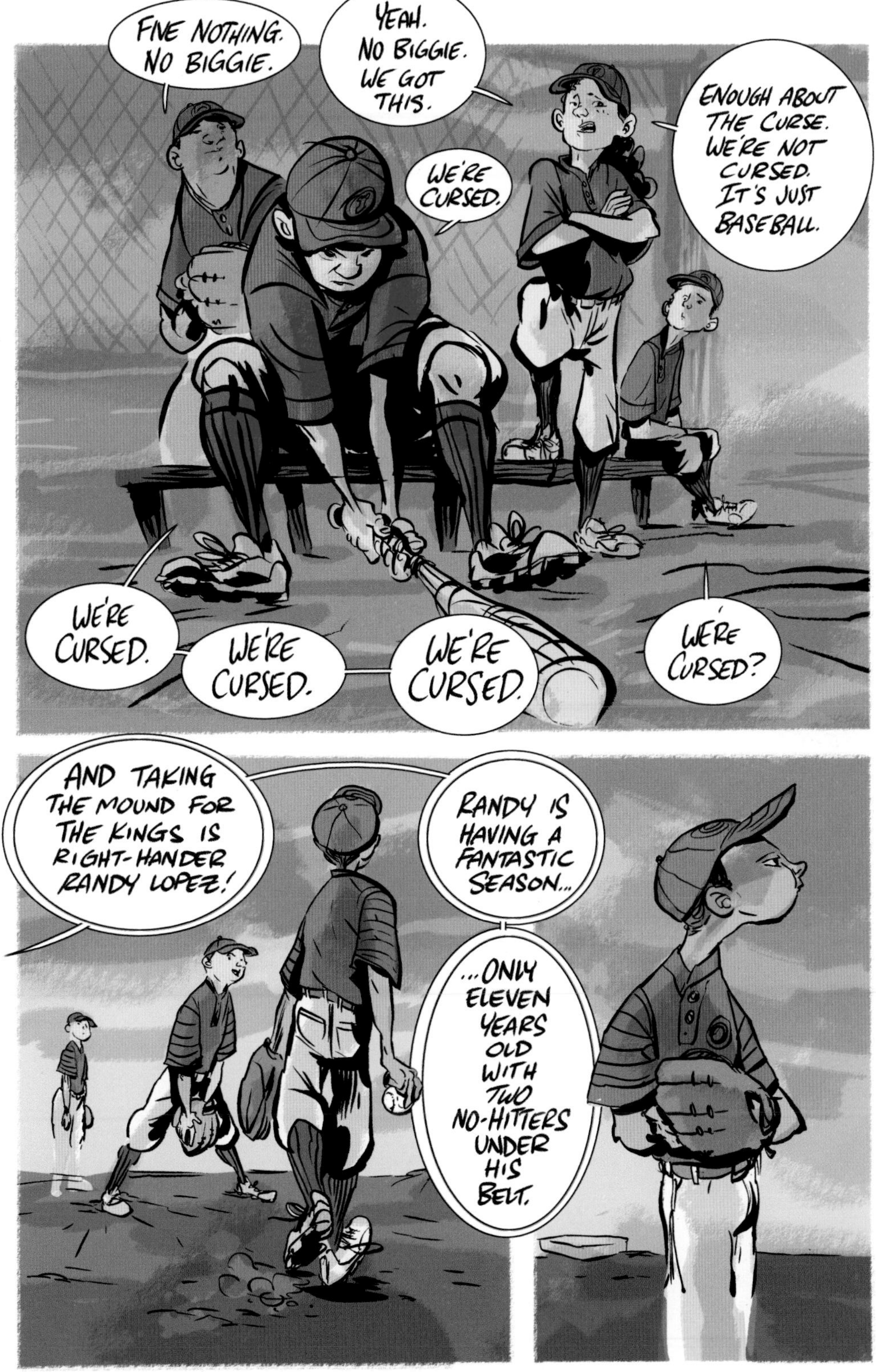
FIVE NOTHING. NO BIGGIE.
YEAH. NO BIGGIE. WE GOT THIS.
WE'RE CURSED.
ENOUGH ABOUT THE CURSE. WE'RE NOT CURSED. IT'S JUST BASEBALL.
WE'RE CURSED.
WE'RE CURSED.
WE'RE CURSED.
WE'RE CURSED?
AND TAKING THE MOUND FOR THE KINGS IS RIGHT-HANDER RANDY LOPEZ!
RANDY IS HAVING A FANTASTIC SEASON...
...ONLY ELEVEN YEARS OLD WITH TWO NO-HITTERS UNDER HIS BELT.

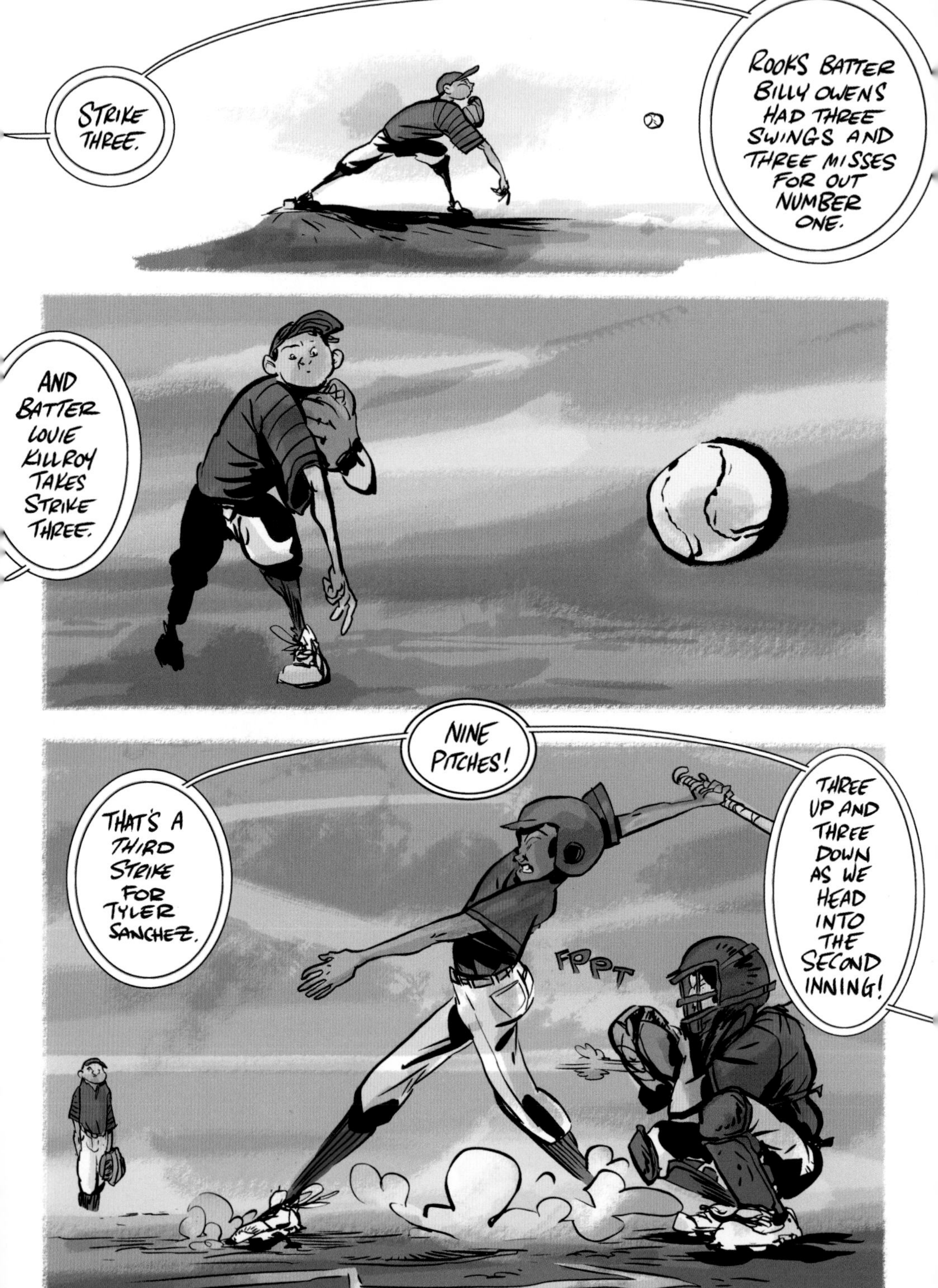
STRIKE THREE.
ROOKS BATTER BILLY OWENS HAD THREE SWINGS AND THREE MISSES FOR OUT NUMBER ONE.
AND BATTER LOUIE KILLROY TAKES STRIKE THREE.
THAT'S A THIRD STRIKE FOR TYLER SANCHEZ.
NINE PITCHES!
THREE UP AND THREE DOWN AS WE HEAD INTO THE SECOND INNING!
FPPT

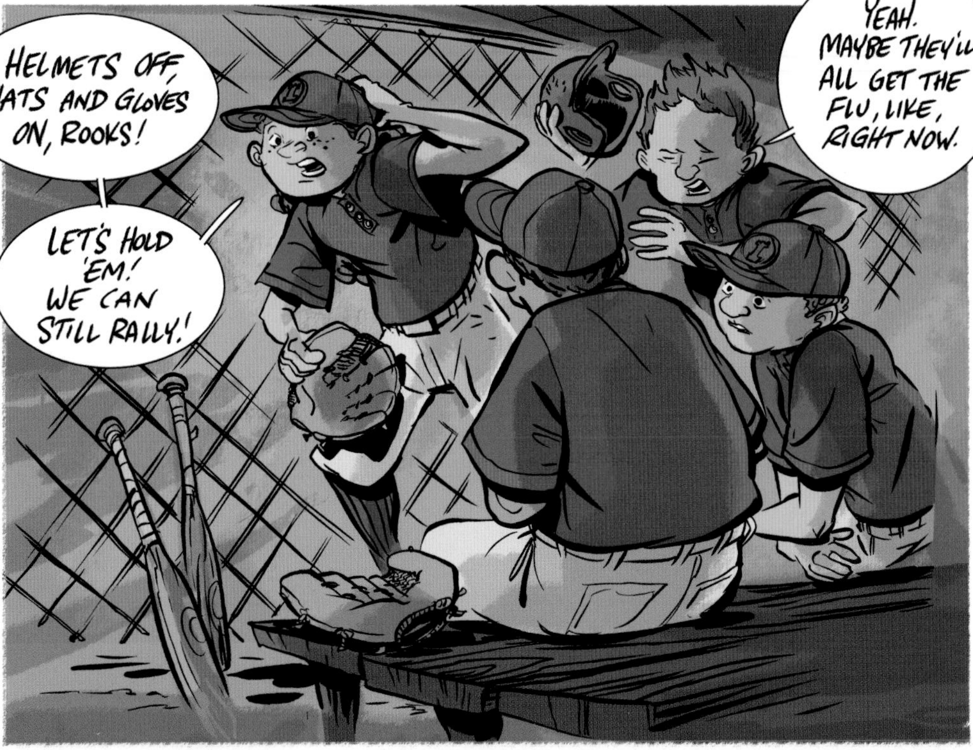
HELMETS OFF, HATS AND GLOVES ON, ROOKS!
LET'S HOLD 'EM! WE CAN STILL RALLY!
YEAH. MAYBE THEY'LL ALL GET THE FLU, LIKE, RIGHT NOW.

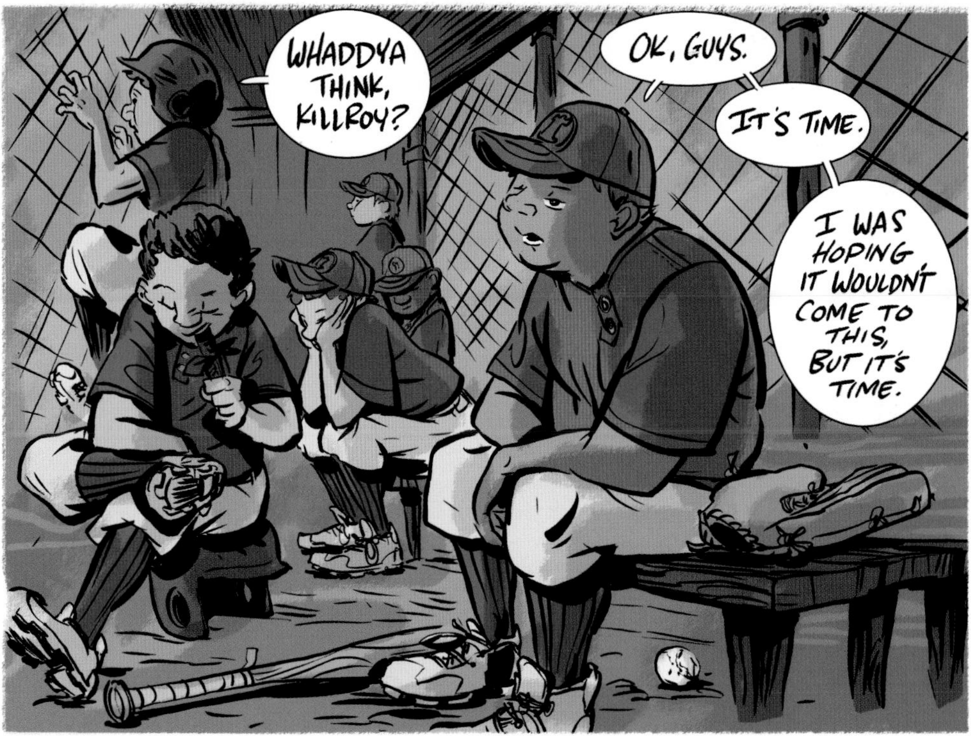
WHADDYA THINK, KILLROY?
OK, GUYS.
IT'S TIME.
I WAS HOPING IT WOULDN'T COME TO THIS, BUT IT'S TIME.

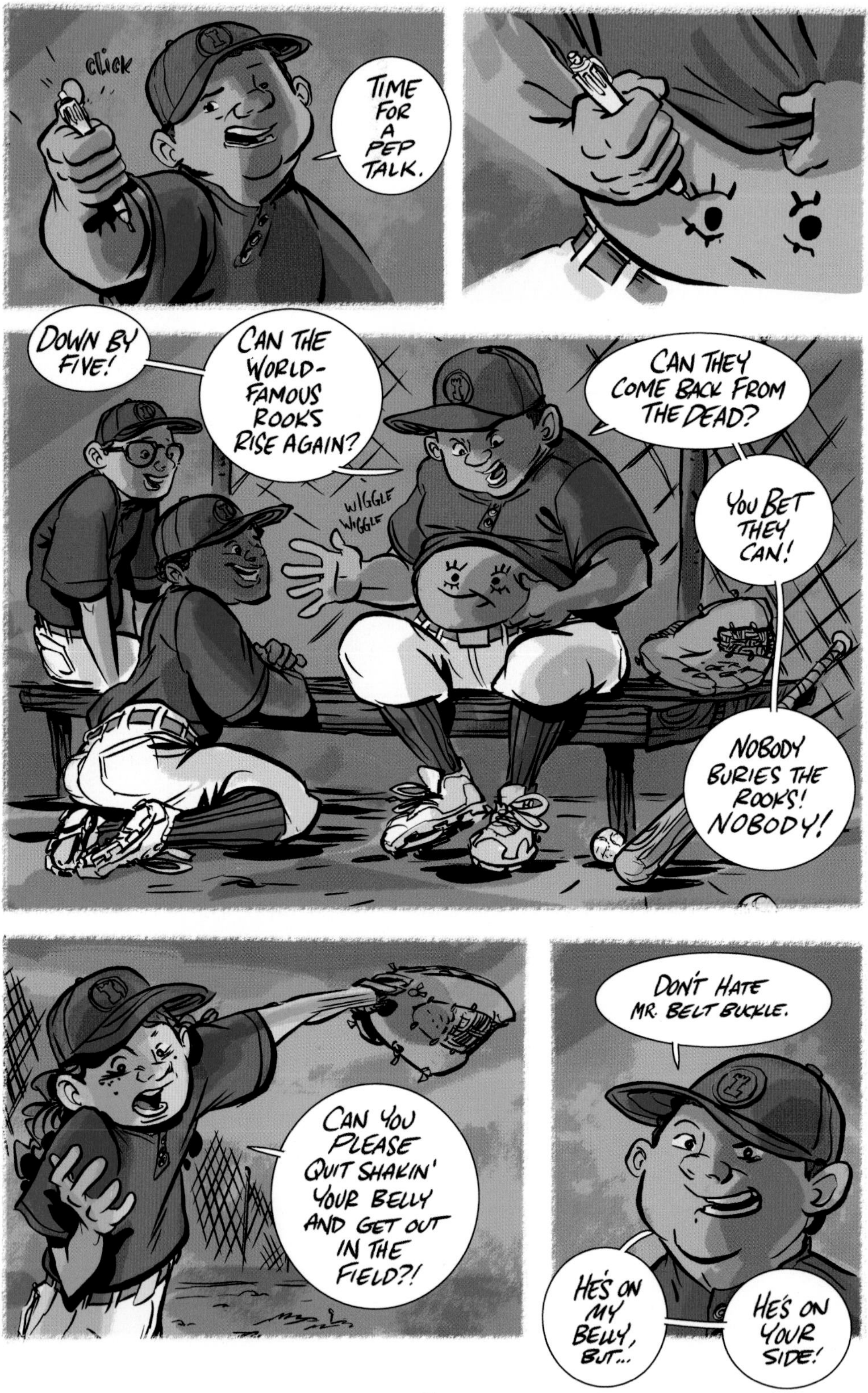
CLICK
TIME FOR A PEP TALK.
DOWN BY FIVE!
CAN THE WORLD-FAMOUS ROOKS RISE AGAIN?
WIGGLE WIGGLE
CAN THEY COME BACK FROM THE DEAD?
YOU BET THEY CAN!
NOBODY BURIES THE ROOKS! NOBODY!
CAN YOU PLEASE QUIT SHAKIN' YOUR BELLY AND GET OUT IN THE FIELD?!
DON'T HATE MR. BELT BUCKLE.
HE'S ON MY BELLY, BUT...
HE'S ON YOUR SIDE!

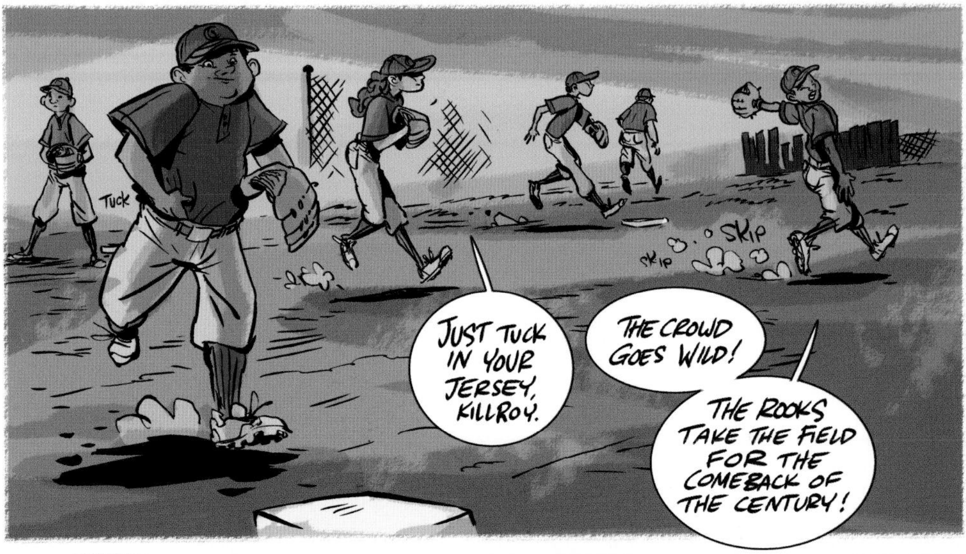
TUCK
SKIP
SKIP
JUST TUCK IN YOUR JERSEY, KILLROY.
THE CROWD GOES WILD!
THE ROOKS TAKE THE FIELD FOR THE COMEBACK OF THE CENTURY!

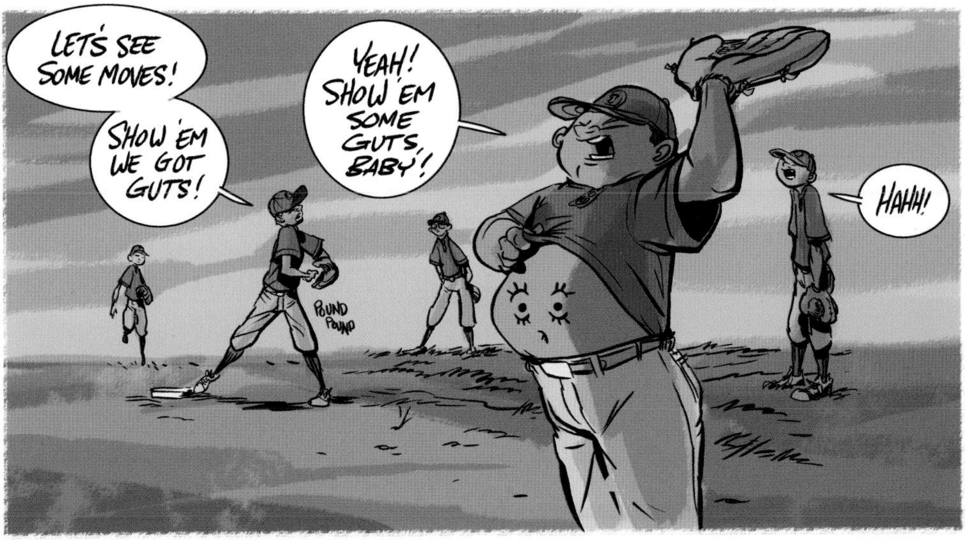
LET'S SEE SOME MOVES!
SHOW 'EM WE GOT GUTS!
POUND POUND
YEAH! SHOW 'EM SOME GUTS, BABY!
HAHH!

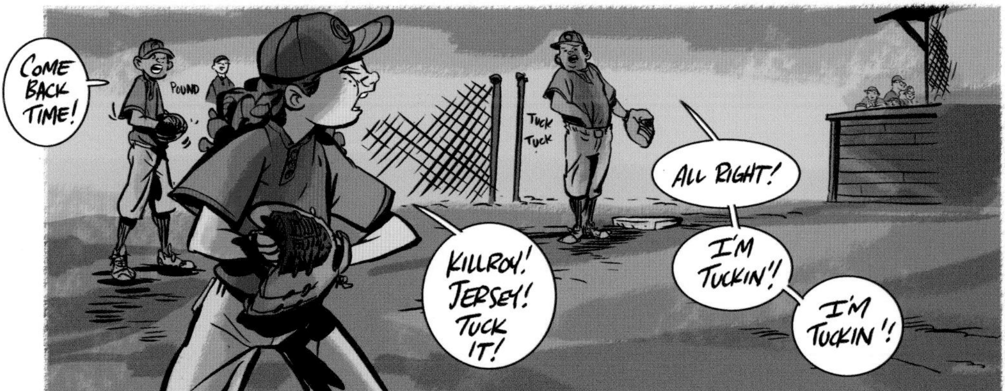
COME BACK TIME!
POUND
TUCK TUCK
KILLROY! JERSEY! TUCK IT!
ALL RIGHT!
I'M TUCKIN'!
I'M TUCKIN'!

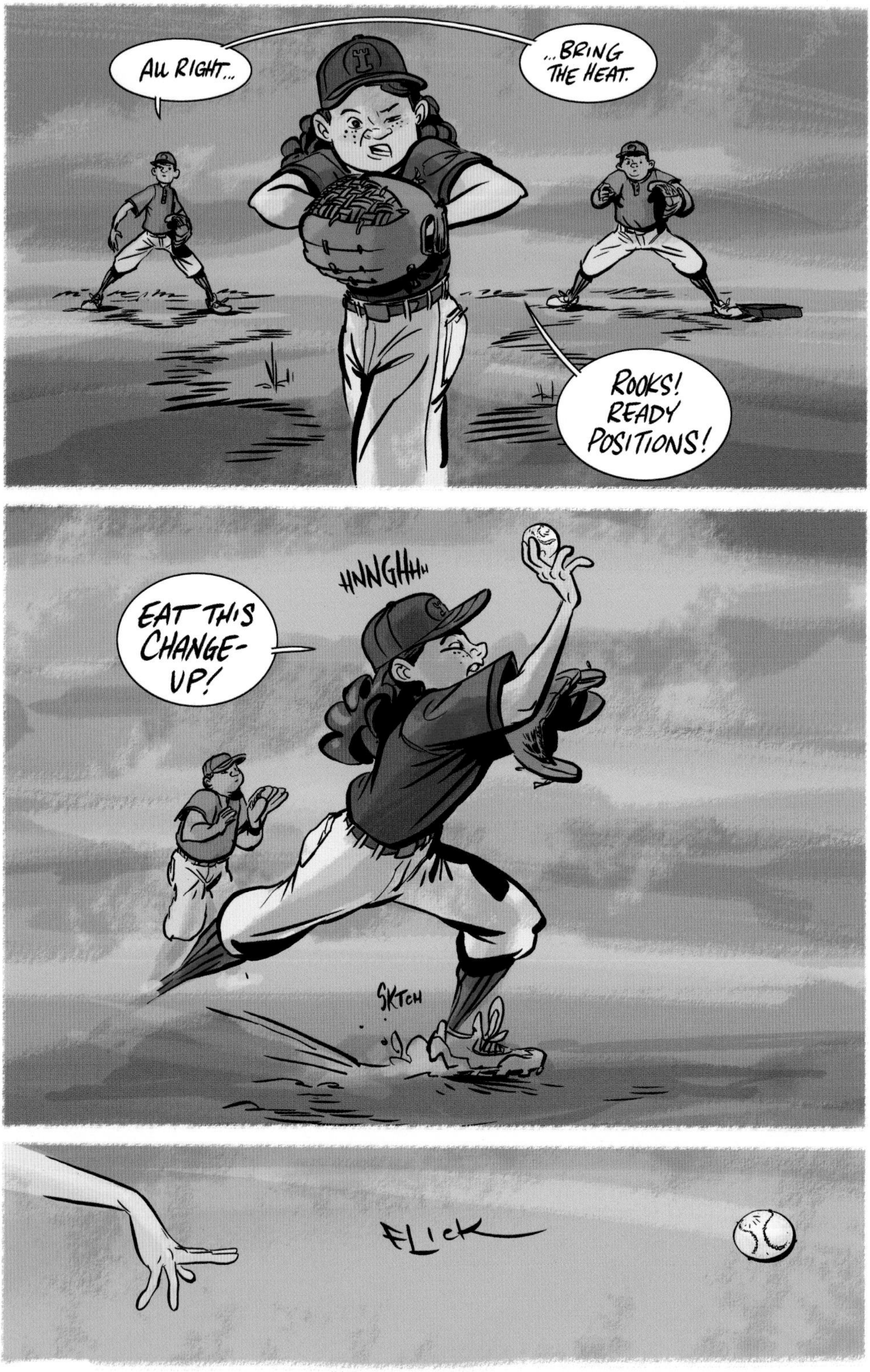
ALL RIGHT...
...BRING THE HEAT.
ROOKS! READY POSITIONS!
HNNGHHH
EAT THIS CHANGE-UP!
SKTCH
FLICK

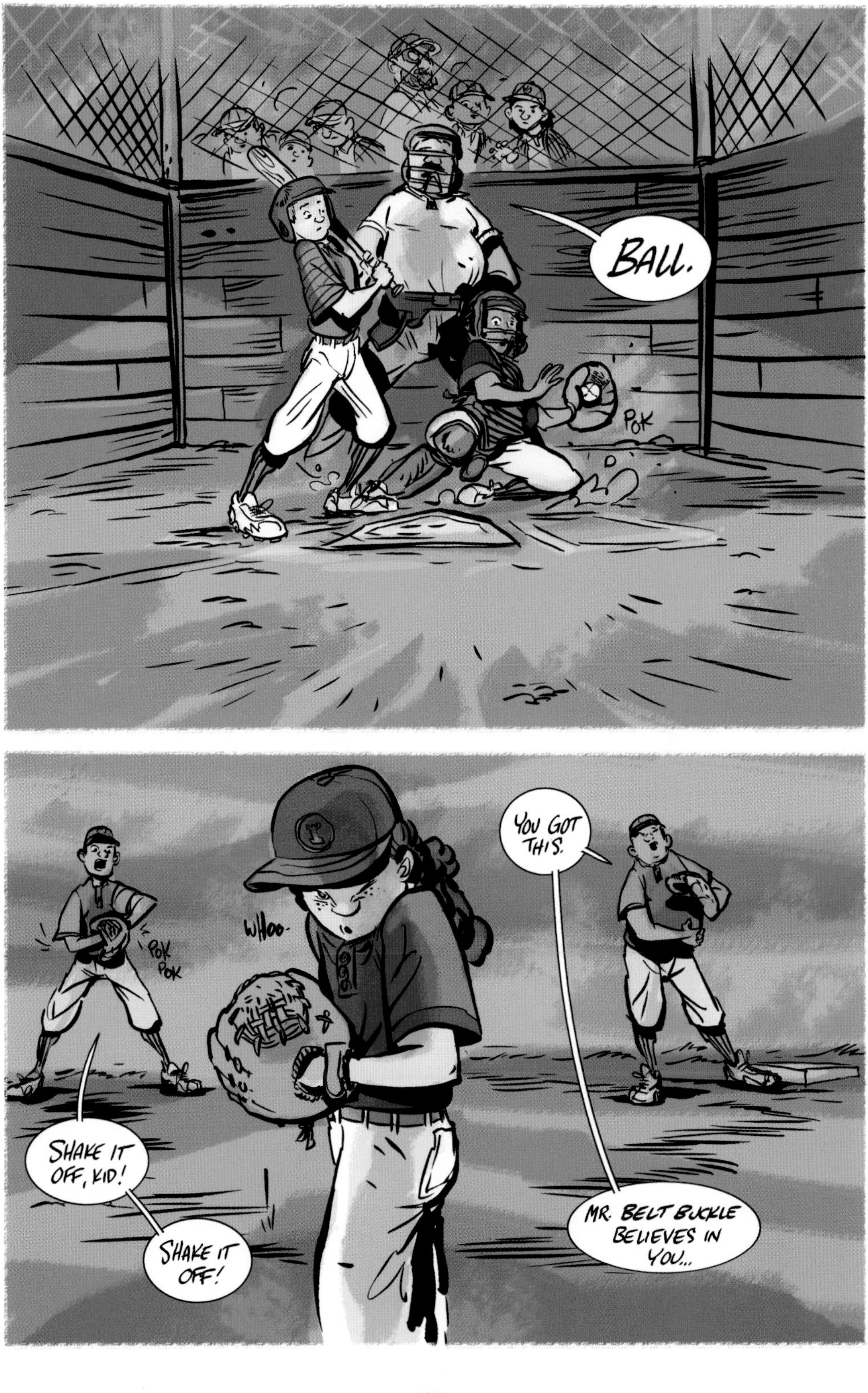
BALL.
POK
WHOO.
POK POK
YOU GOT THIS.
SHAKE IT OFF, KID!
SHAKE IT OFF!
MR. BELT BUCKLE BELIEVES IN YOU...

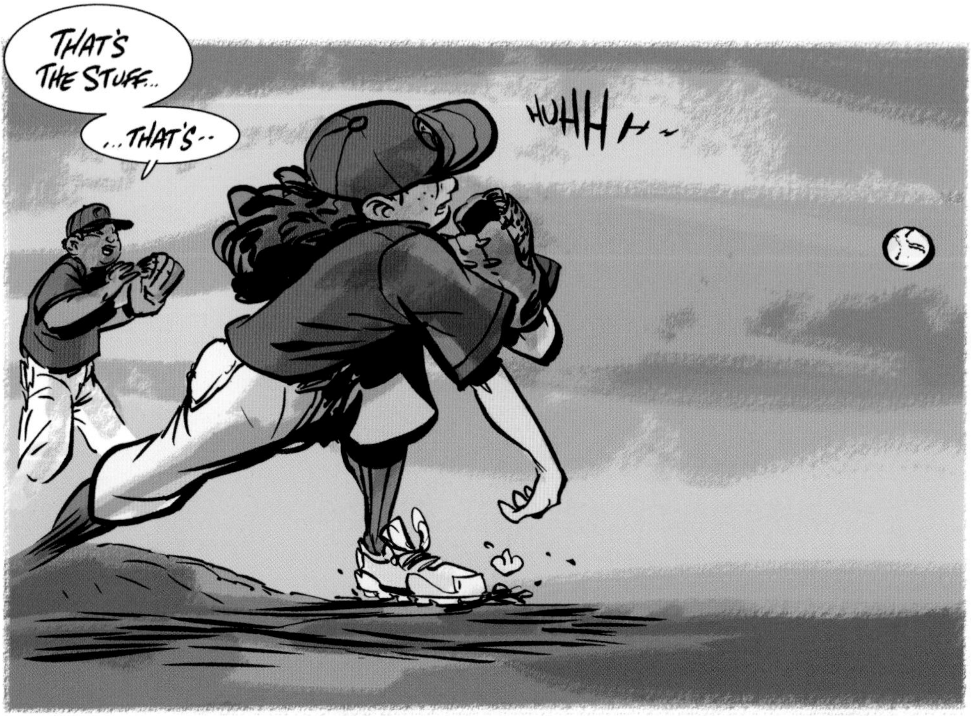
THAT'S THE STUFF...
...THAT'S--
HUHHH--

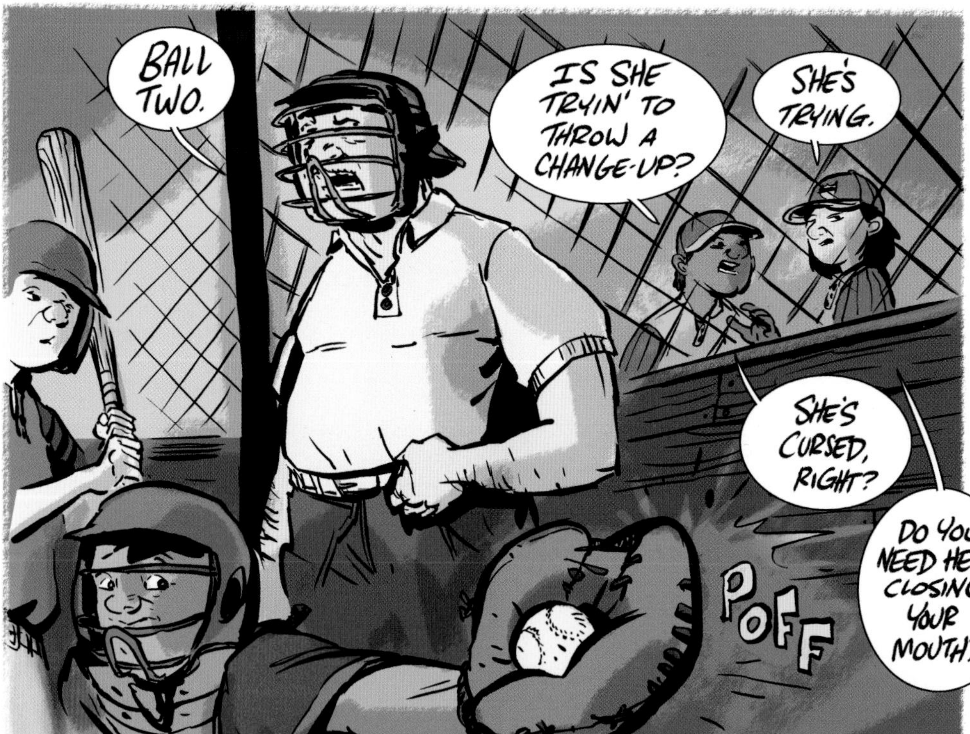
BALL TWO.
IS SHE TRYIN' TO THROW A CHANGE-UP?
SHE'S TRYING.
SHE'S CURSED, RIGHT?
DO YOU NEED HELP CLOSING YOUR MOUTH?
POFF

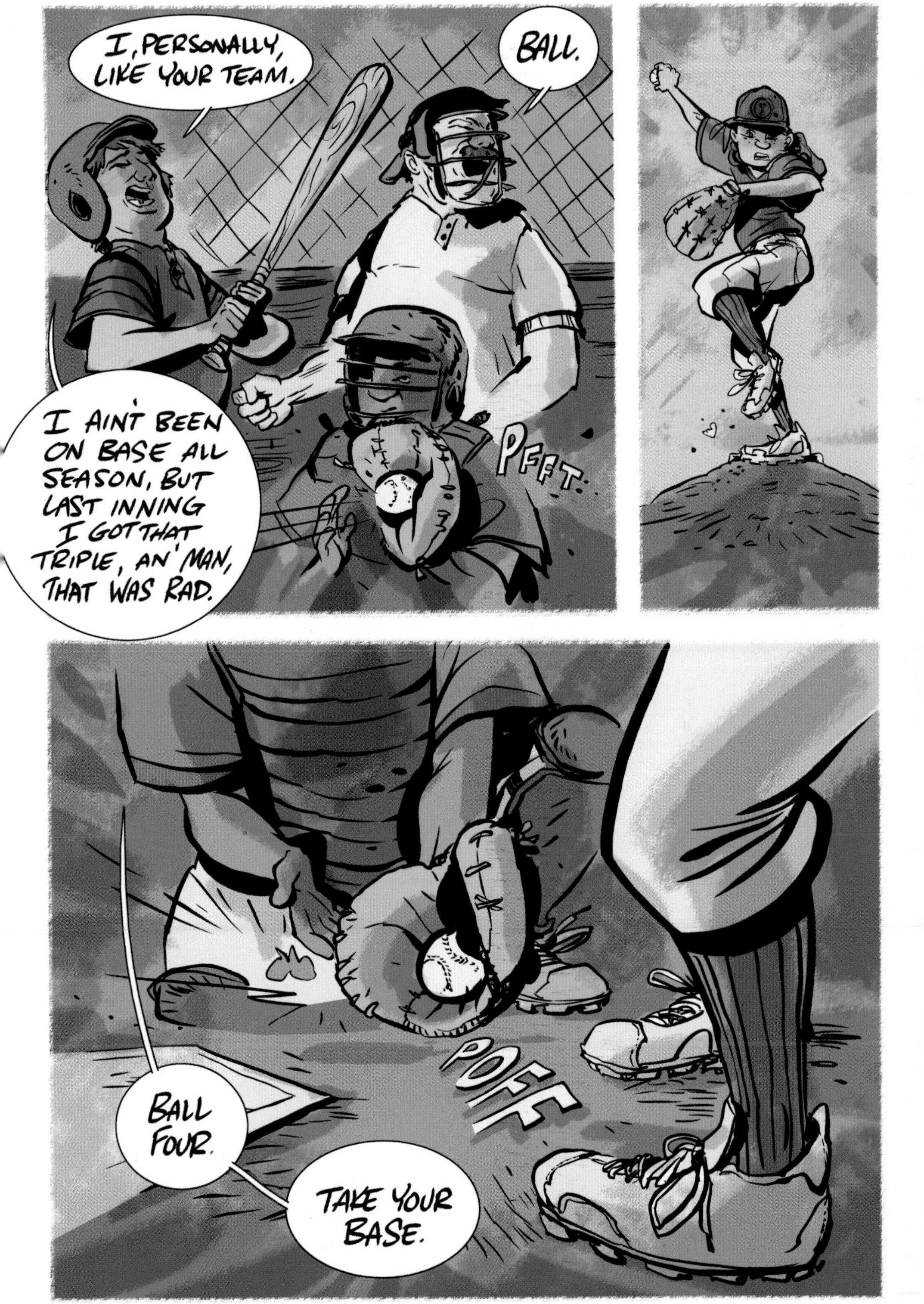
I, PERSONALLY, LIKE YOUR TEAM.
BALL.
I AIN'T BEEN ON BASE ALL SEASON, BUT LAST INNING I GOT THAT TRIPLE, AN' MAN, THAT WAS RAD.
PFFFT.
POFF
BALL FOUR.
TAKE YOUR BASE.

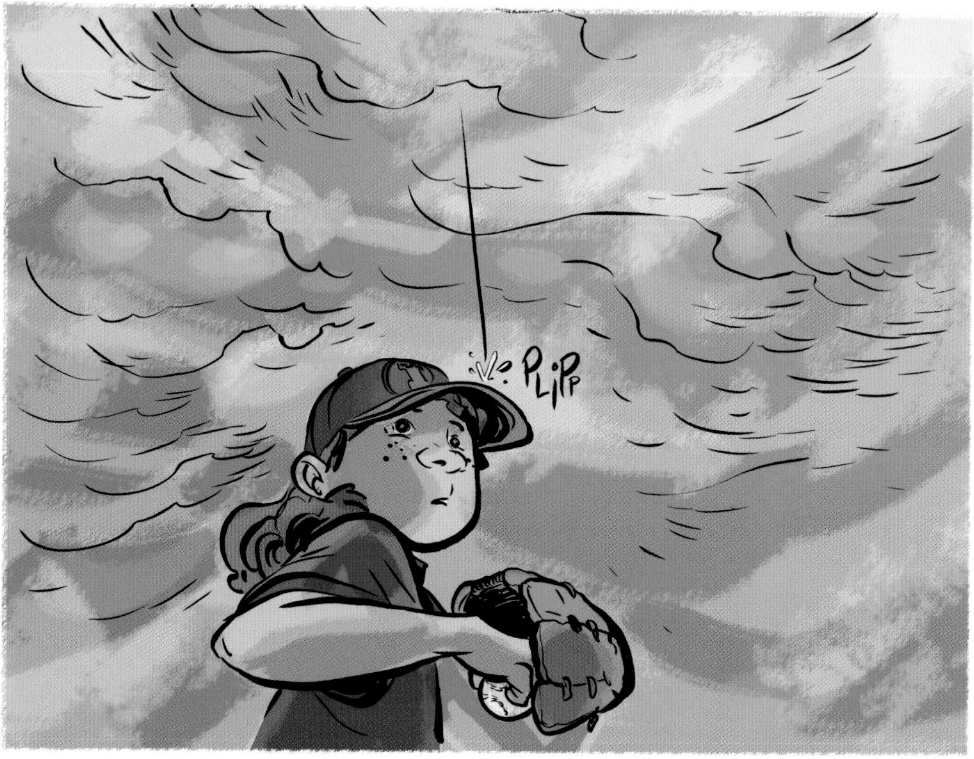
PLIPP

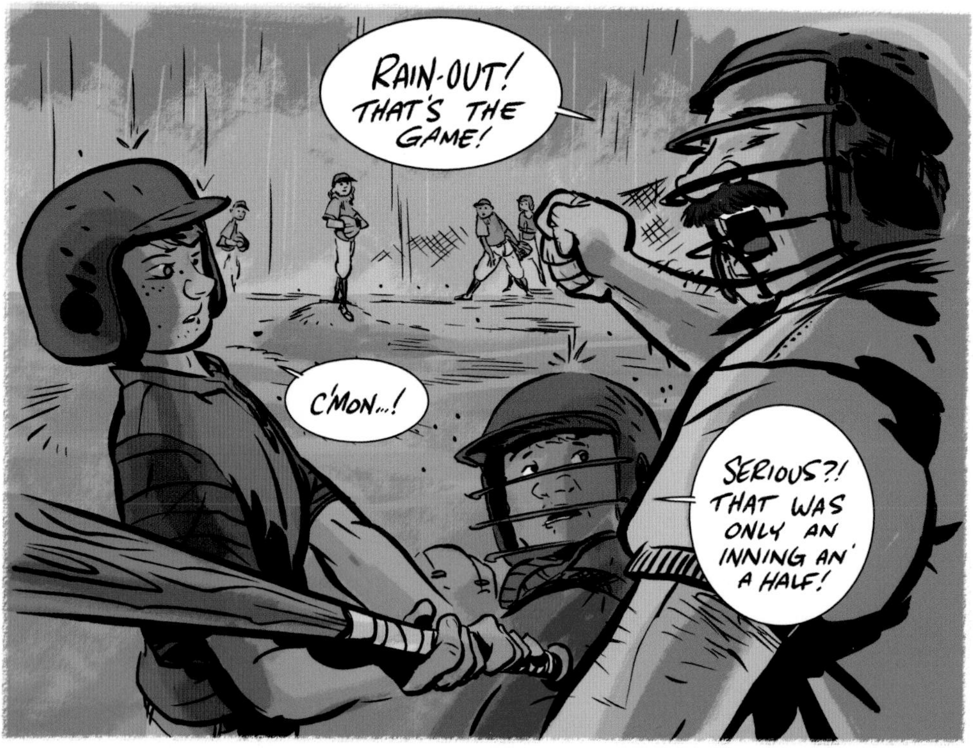
RAIN-OUT! THAT'S THE GAME!
C'MON...!
SERIOUS?! THAT WAS ONLY AN INNING AN' A HALF!

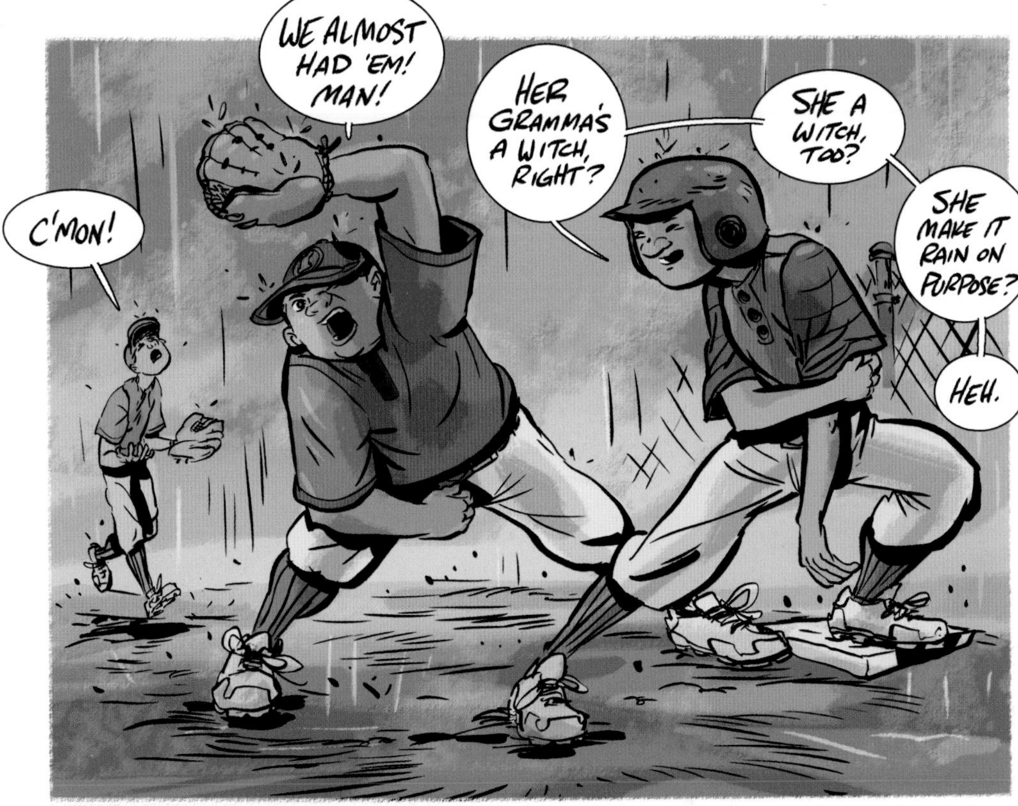
C'MON!
WE ALMOST HAD 'EM! MAN!
HER GRAMMA'S A WITCH, RIGHT?
SHE A WITCH, TOO?
SHE MAKE IT RAIN ON PURPOSE?
HEH.

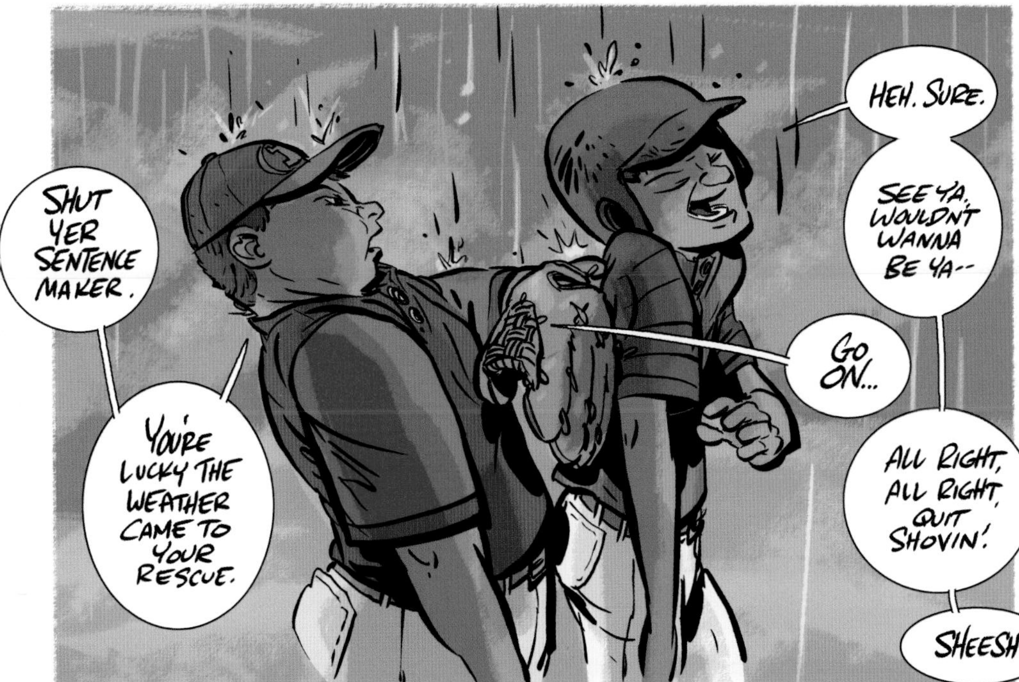
HEH. SURE.
SEE YA. WOULDN'T WANNA BE YA--
SHUT YER SENTENCE MAKER.
GO ON...
YOU'RE LUCKY THE WEATHER CAME TO YOUR RESCUE.
ALL RIGHT, ALL RIGHT, QUIT SHOVIN'.
SHEESH.

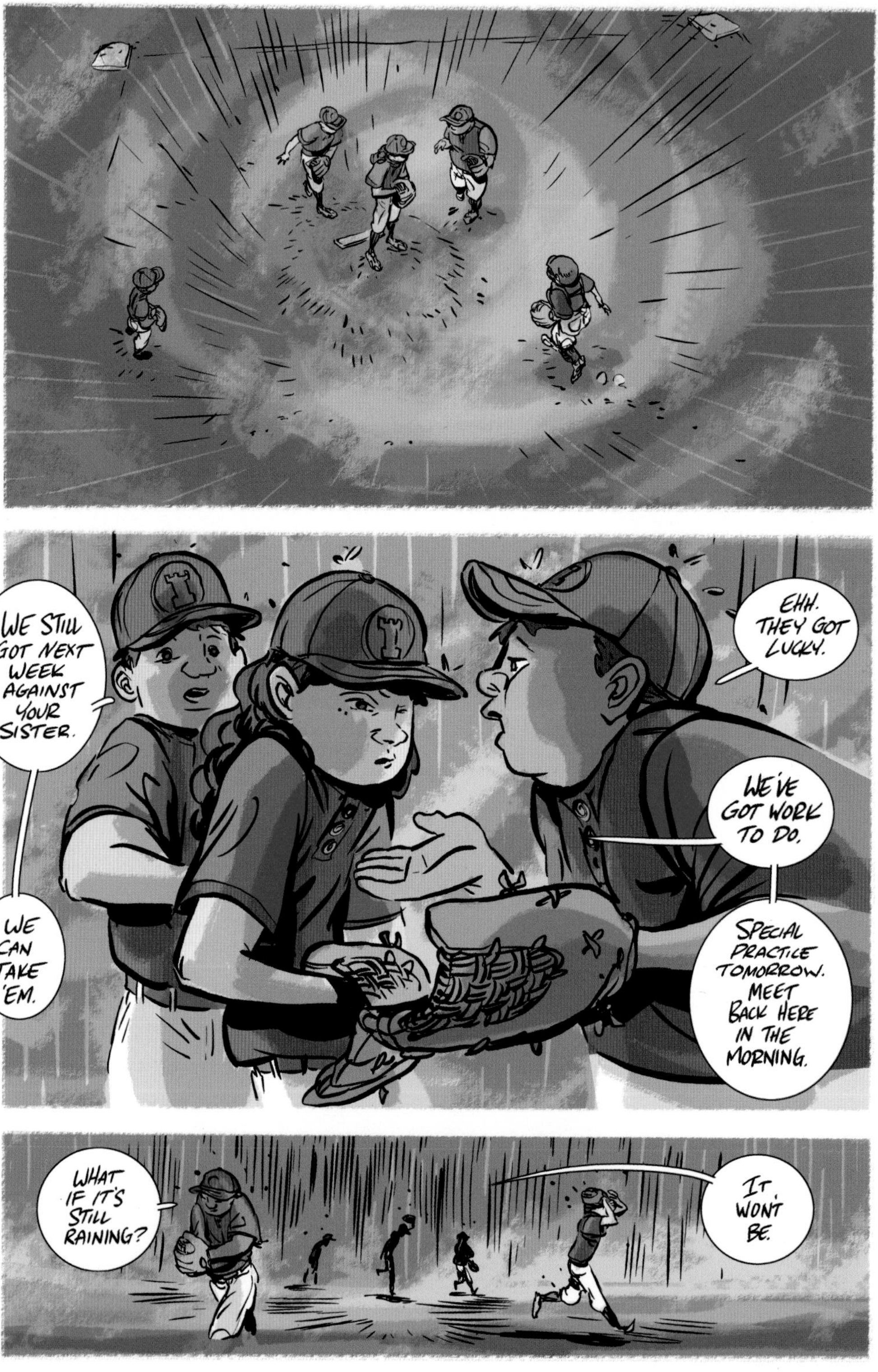
WE STILL GOT NEXT WEEK AGAINST YOUR SISTER.
WE CAN TAKE 'EM.
EHH. THEY GOT LUCKY.
WE'VE GOT WORK TO DO.
SPECIAL PRACTICE TOMORROW. MEET BACK HERE IN THE MORNING.
WHAT IF IT'S STILL RAINING?
IT WON'T BE.

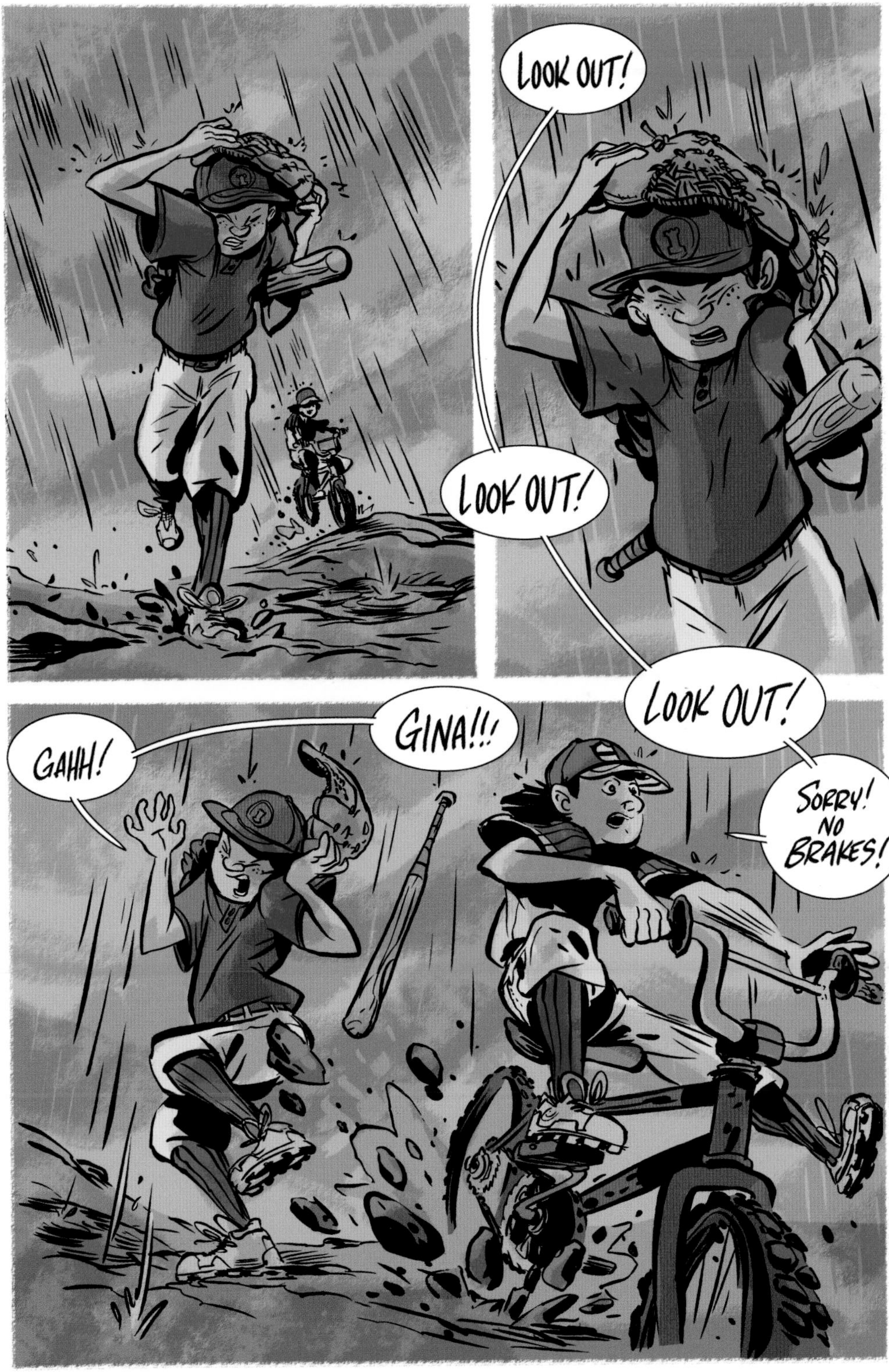
LOOK OUT!
LOOK OUT!
LOOK OUT!
GAHH!
GINA!!!
SORRY! NO BRAKES!

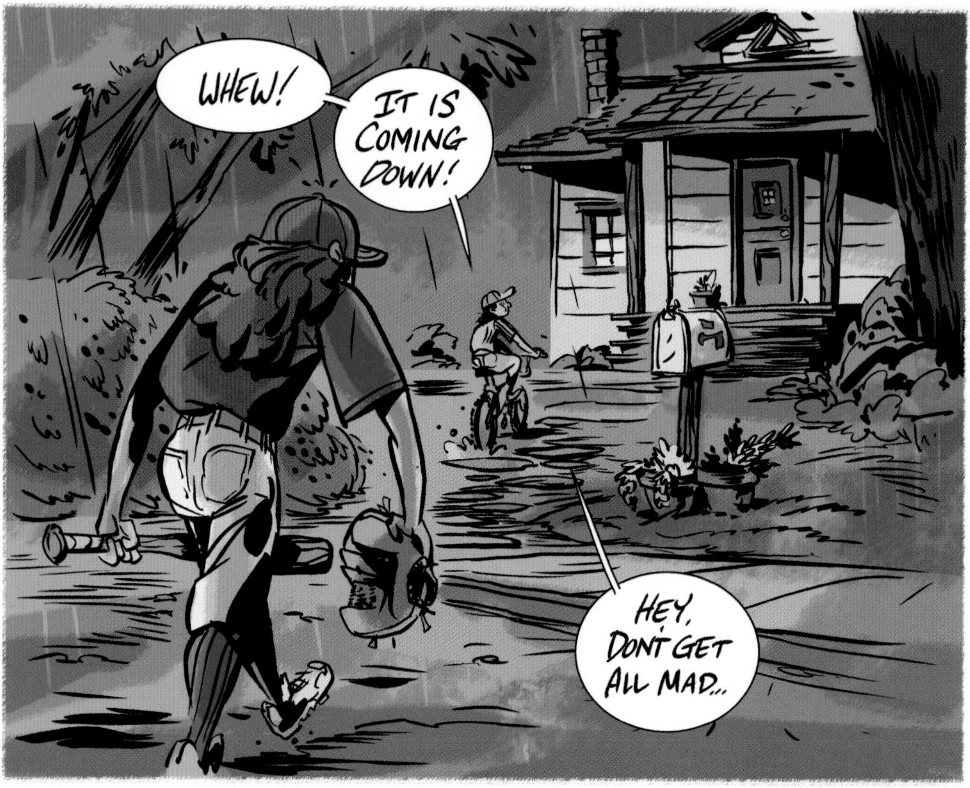
WHEW!
IT IS COMING DOWN!
HEY, DON'T GET ALL MAD...

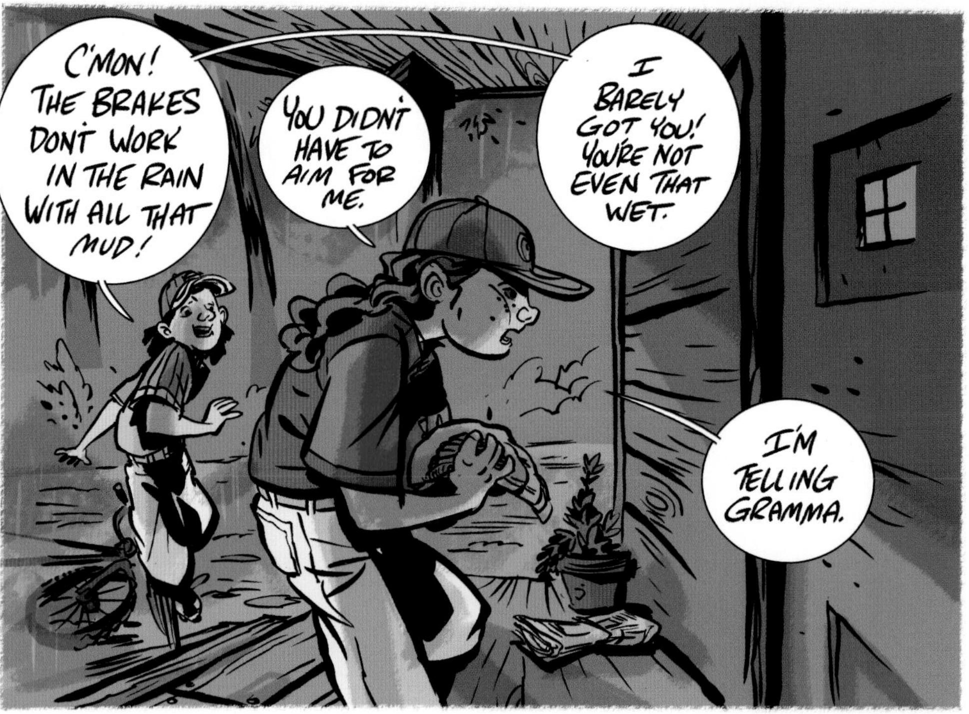
C'MON! THE BRAKES DON'T WORK IN THE RAIN WITH ALL THAT MUD!
YOU DIDN'T HAVE TO AIM FOR ME.
I BARELY GOT YOU! YOU'RE NOT EVEN THAT WET.
I'M TELLING GRAMMA.

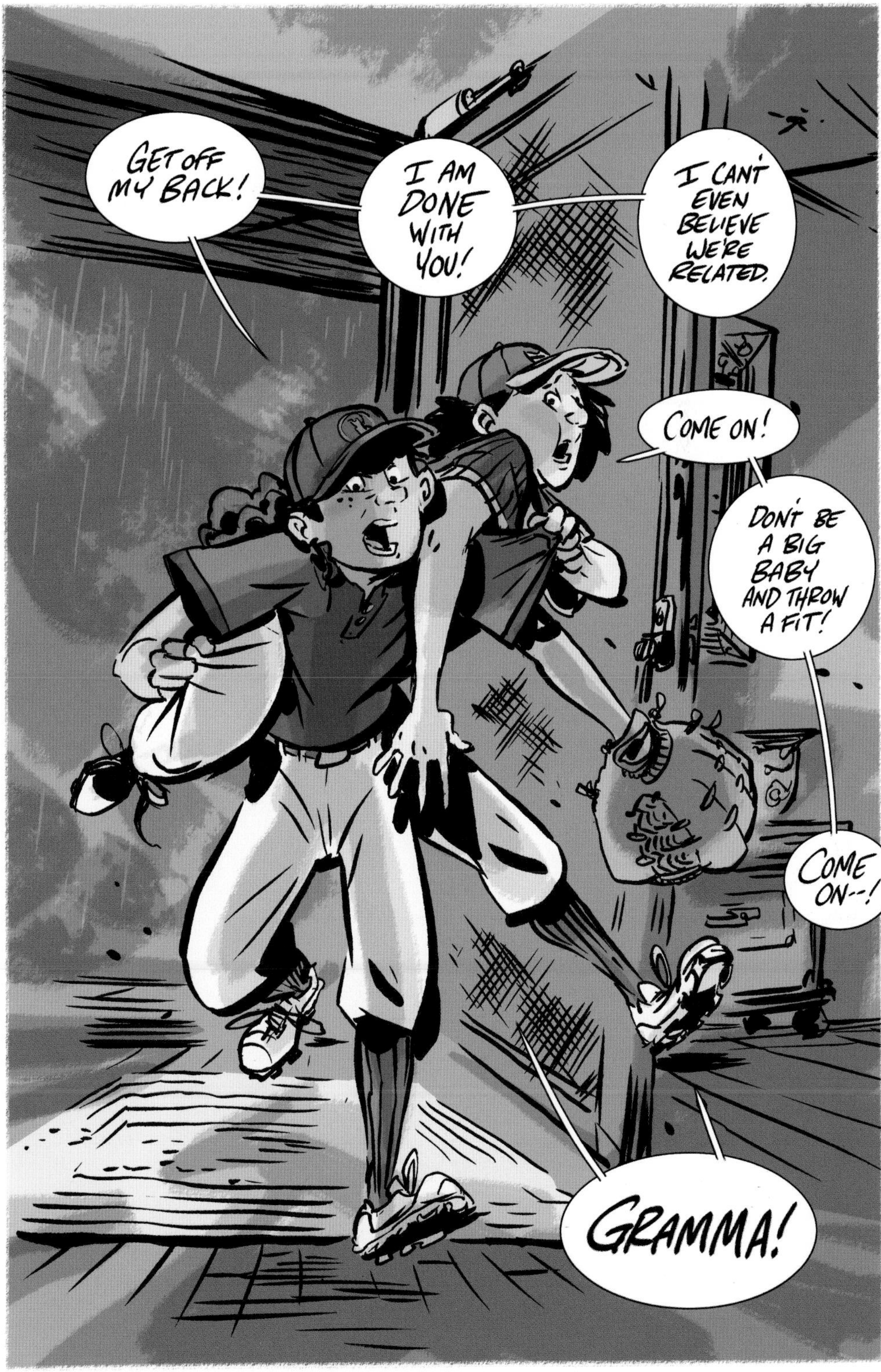
GET OFF MY BACK!
I AM DONE WITH YOU!
I CAN'T EVEN BELIEVE WE'RE RELATED.
COME ON!
DON'T BE A BIG BABY AND THROW A FIT!
COME ON--!
GRAMMA!

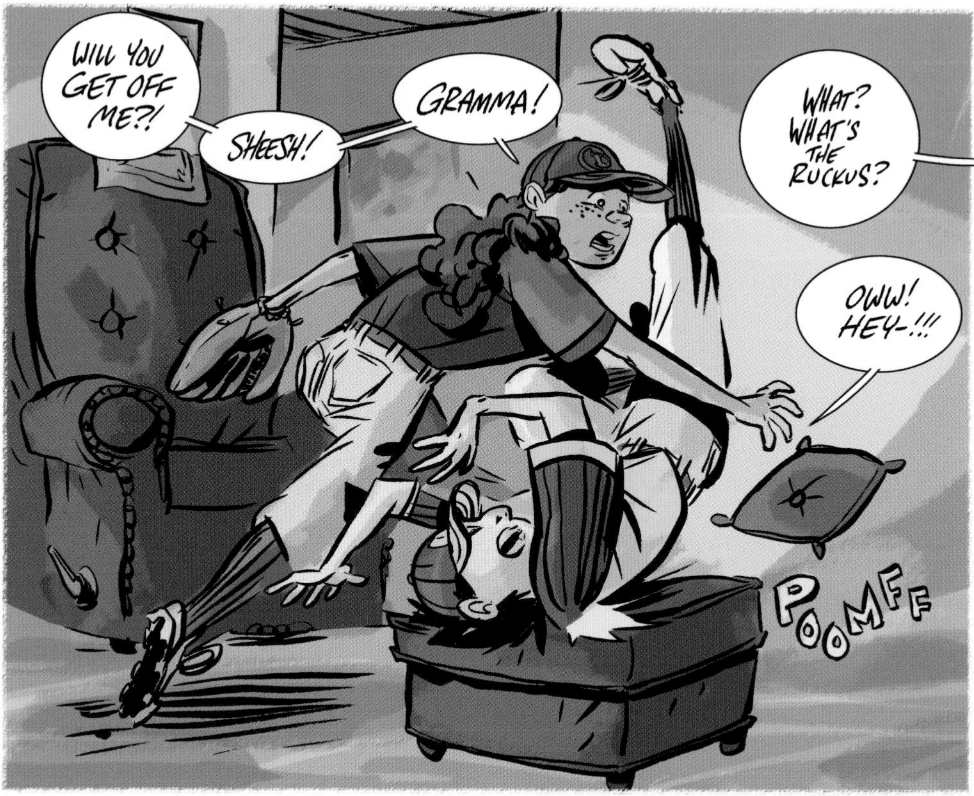
WILL YOU GET OFF ME?!
SHEESH!
GRAMMA!
WHAT? WHAT'S THE RUCKUS?
OWW! HEY-!!!
POOMFF

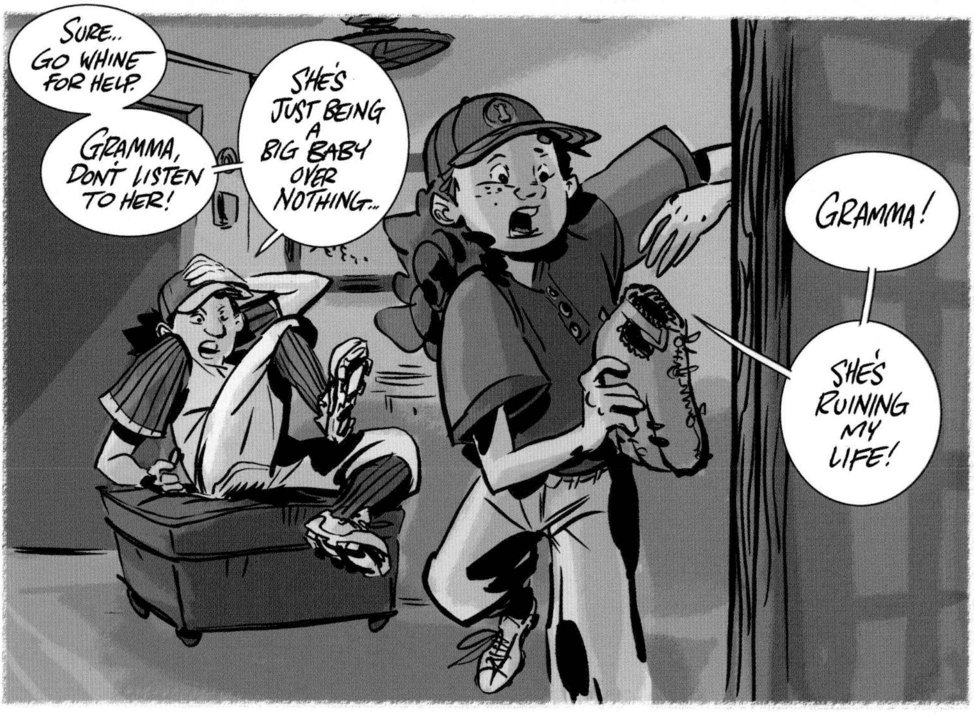
SURE... GO WHINE FOR HELP.
GRAMMA, DON'T LISTEN TO HER!
SHE'S JUST BEING A BIG BABY OVER NOTHING...
GRAMMA!
SHE'S RUINING MY LIFE!

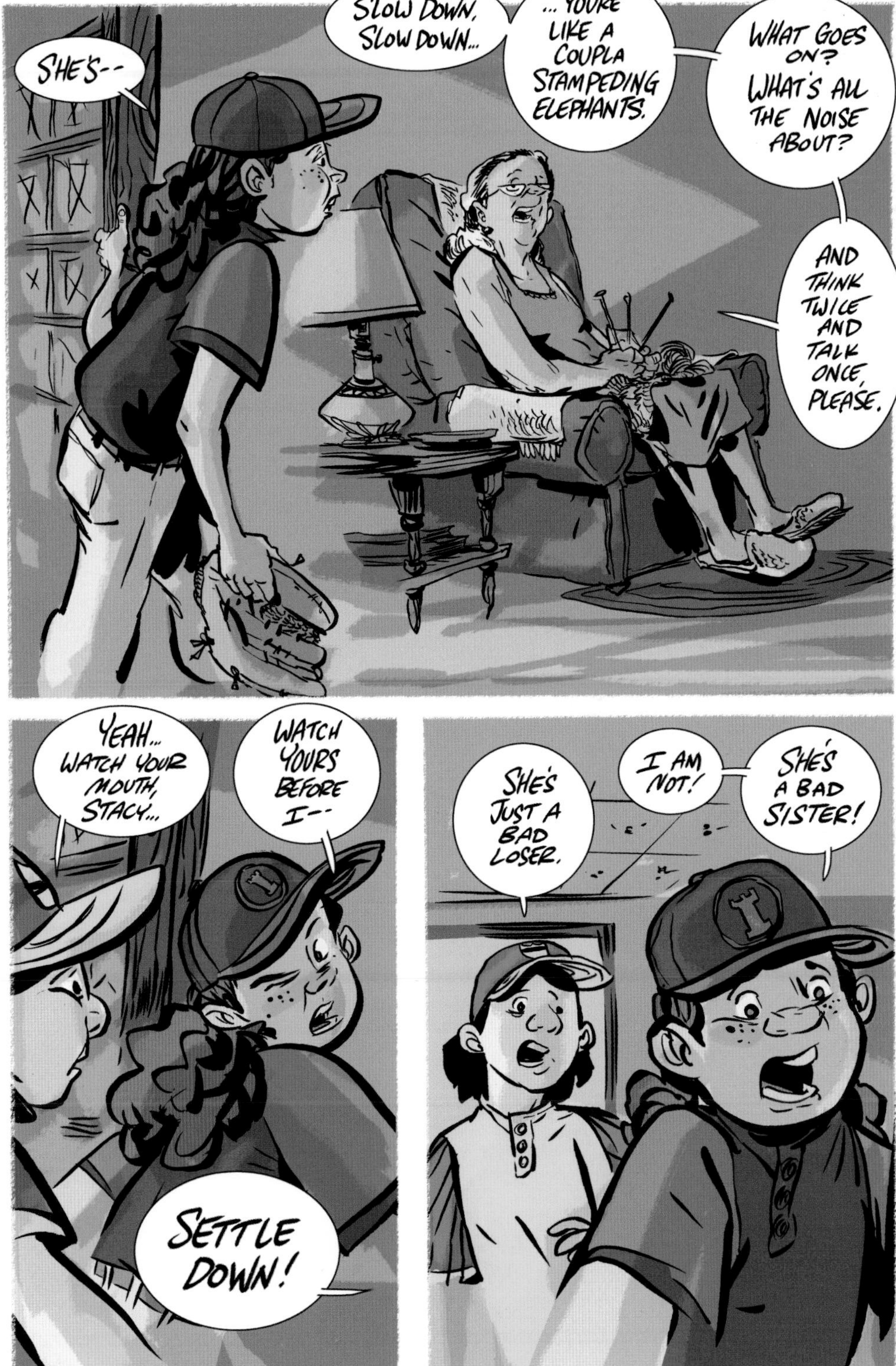
SHE'S--
SLOW DOWN, SLOW DOWN...
... YOU'RE LIKE A COUPLA STAMPEDING ELEPHANTS.
WHAT GOES ON? WHAT'S ALL THE NOISE ABOUT?
AND THINK TWICE AND TALK ONCE, PLEASE.
YEAH... WATCH YOUR MOUTH, STACY...
WATCH YOURS BEFORE I--
SETTLE DOWN!
SHE'S JUST A BAD LOSER.
I AM NOT!
SHE'S A BAD SISTER!

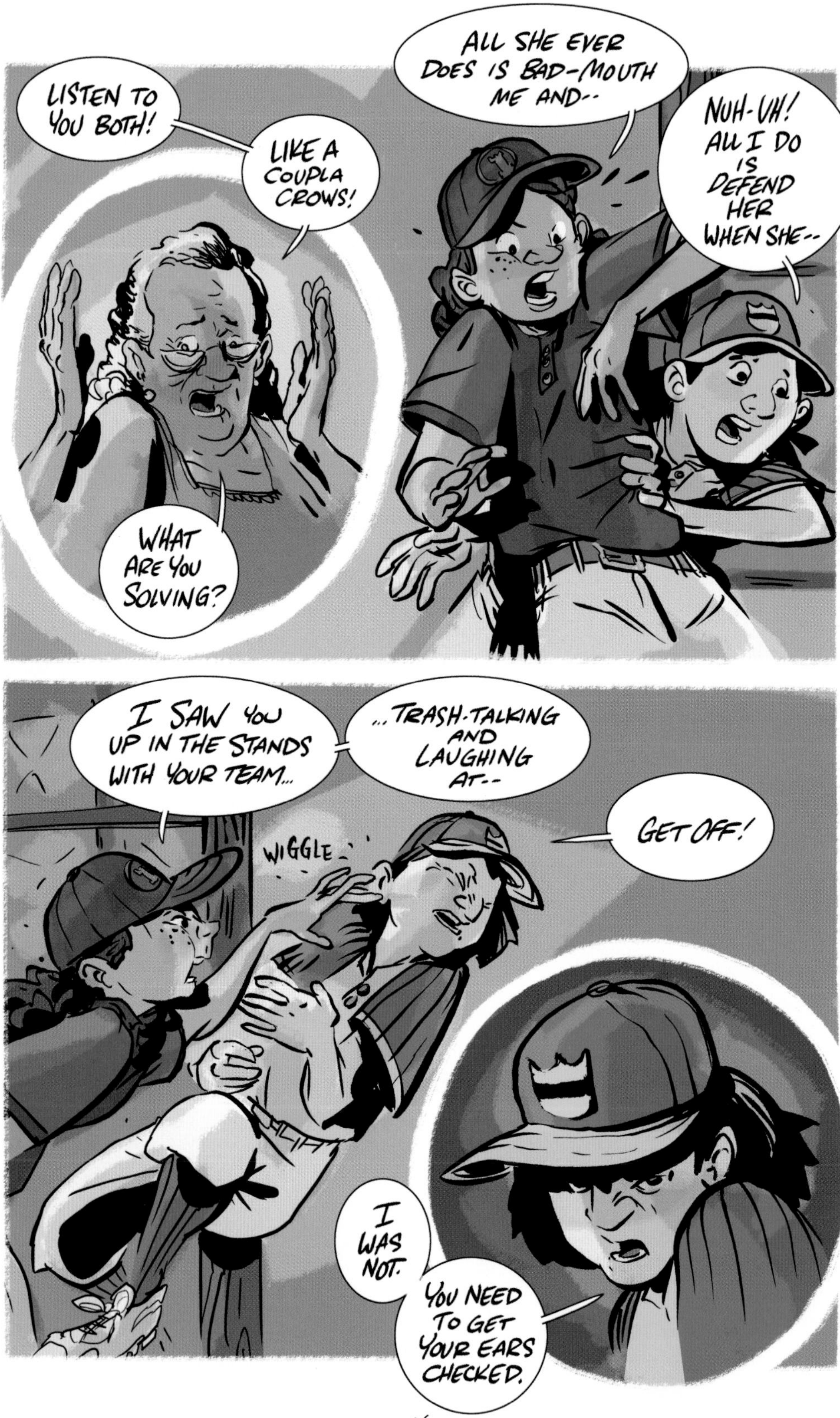
LISTEN TO YOU BOTH!
LIKE A COUPLA CROWS!
WHAT ARE YOU SOLVING?
ALL SHE EVER DOES IS BAD-MOUTH ME AND--
NUH-UH! ALL I DO IS DEFEND HER WHEN SHE--
I SAW YOU UP IN THE STANDS WITH YOUR TEAM...
...TRASH-TALKING AND LAUGHING AT--
WIGGLE
GET OFF!
I WAS NOT.
YOU NEED TO GET YOUR EARS CHECKED.

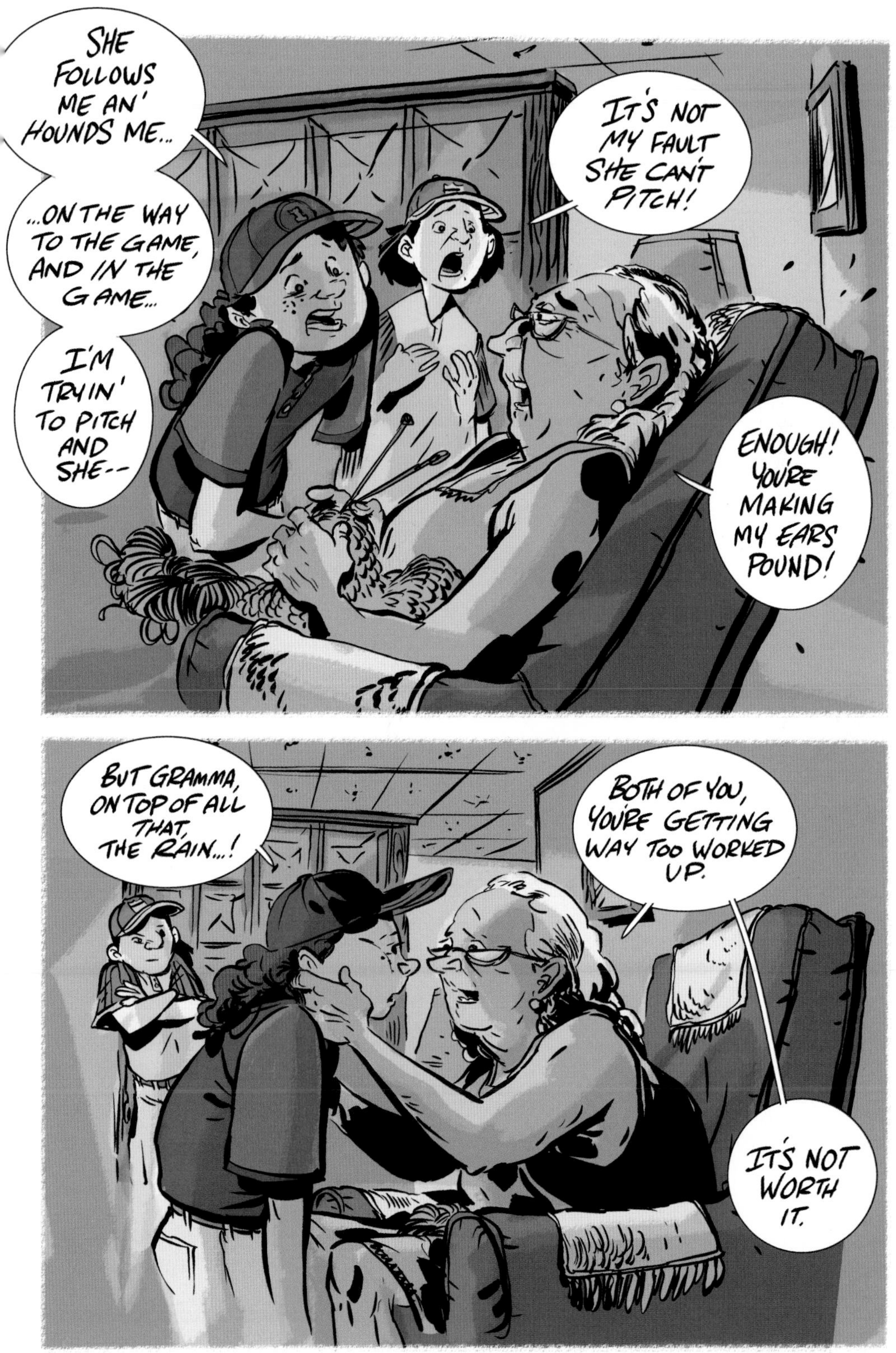
SHE FOLLOWS ME AN' HOUNDS ME...
...ON THE WAY TO THE GAME, AND IN THE GAME...
I'M TRYIN' TO PITCH AND SHE--
IT'S NOT MY FAULT SHE CAN'T PITCH!
ENOUGH! YOU'RE MAKING MY EARS POUND!
BUT GRAMMA, ON TOP OF ALL THAT, THE RAIN...!
BOTH OF YOU, YOU'RE GETTING WAY TOO WORKED UP.
IT'S NOT WORTH IT.

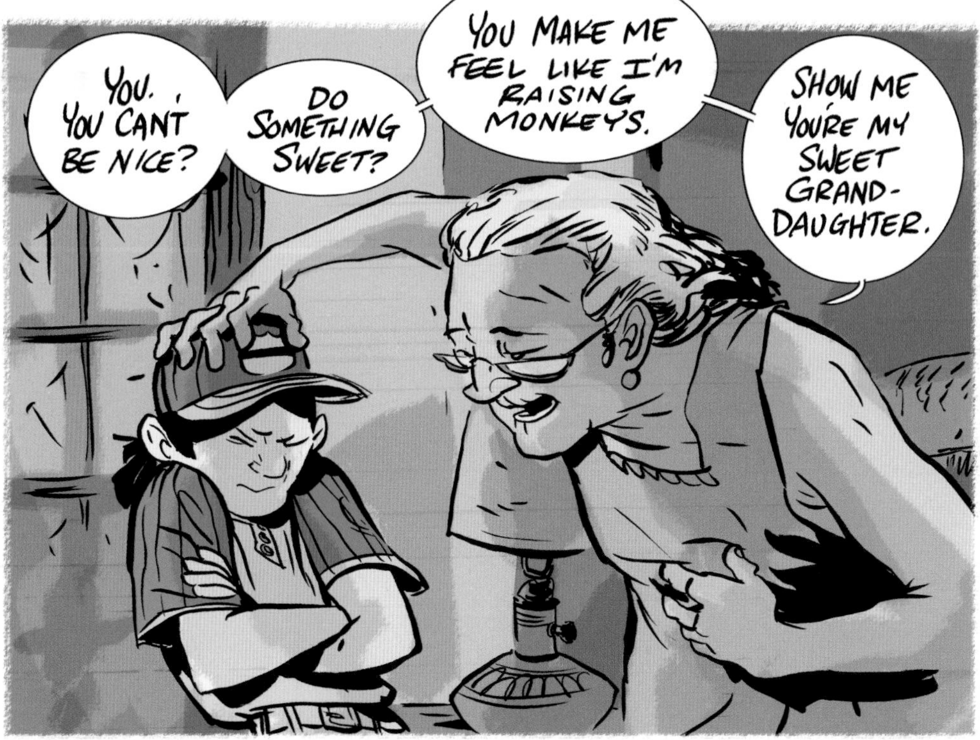
YOU. YOU CAN'T BE NICE?
DO SOMETHING SWEET?
YOU MAKE ME FEEL LIKE I'M RAISING MONKEYS.
SHOW ME YOU'RE MY SWEET GRAND-DAUGHTER.

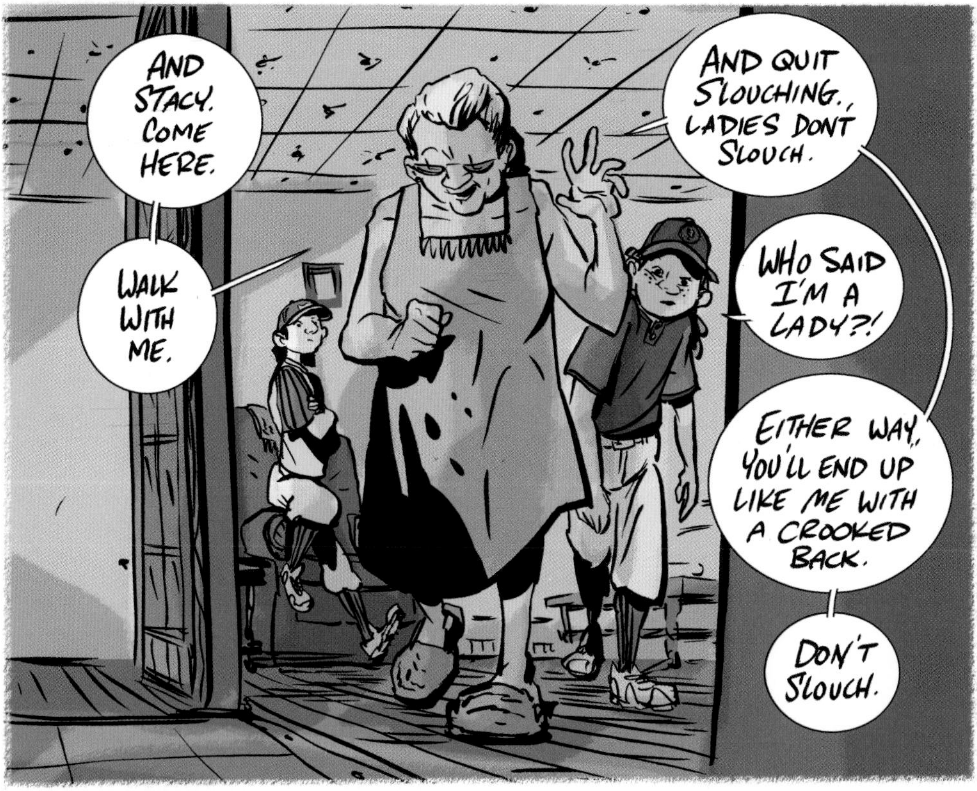
AND STACY. COME HERE.
WALK WITH ME.
AND QUIT SLOUCHING. LADIES DON'T SLOUCH.
WHO SAID I'M A LADY?!
EITHER WAY, YOU'LL END UP LIKE ME WITH A CROOKED BACK.
DON'T SLOUCH.

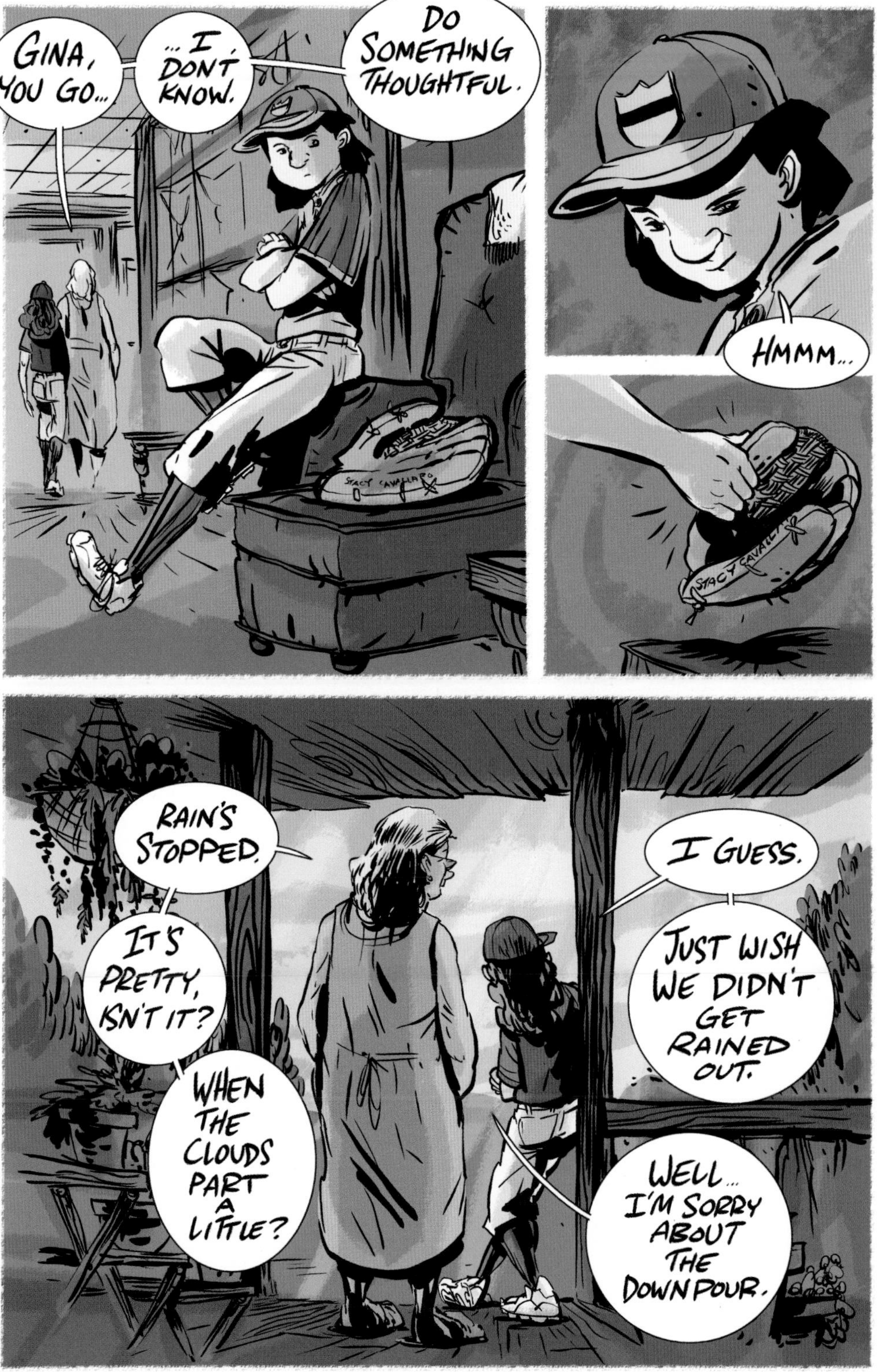
GINA, YOU GO...
...I DON'T KNOW.
DO SOMETHING THOUGHTFUL.
STACY CAVALLARO
HMMM...
STACY CAVALLI
RAIN'S STOPPED.
IT'S PRETTY, ISN'T IT?
WHEN THE CLOUDS PART A LITTLE?
I GUESS.
JUST WISH WE DIDN'T GET RAINED OUT.
WELL... I'M SORRY ABOUT THE DOWNPOUR.

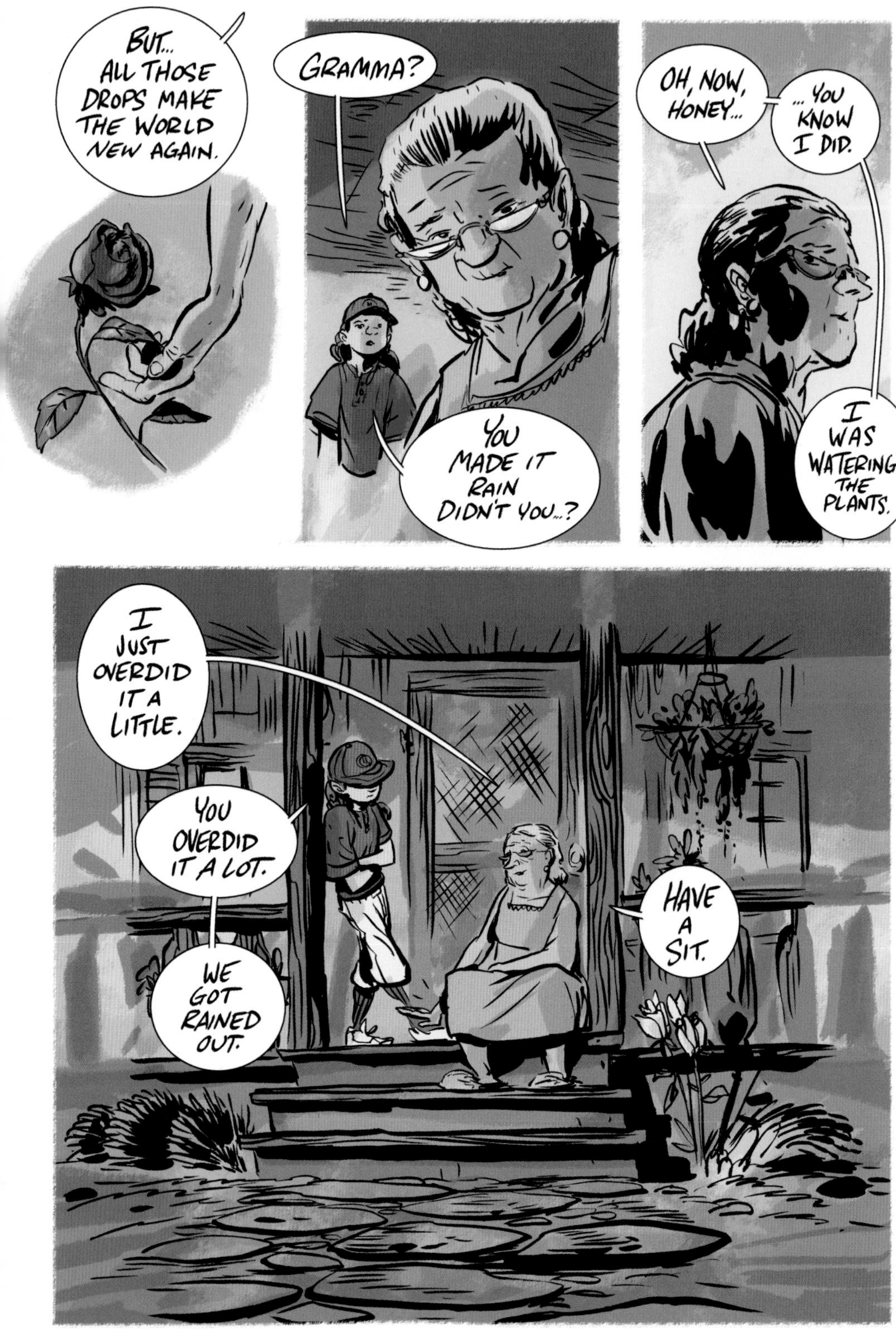
BUT... ALL THOSE DROPS MAKE THE WORLD NEW AGAIN.
GRAMMA?
YOU MADE IT RAIN DIDN'T YOU...?
OH, NOW, HONEY...
...YOU KNOW I DID.
I WAS WATERING THE PLANTS.
I JUST OVERDID IT A LITTLE.
YOU OVERDID IT A LOT.
WE GOT RAINED OUT.
HAVE A SIT.

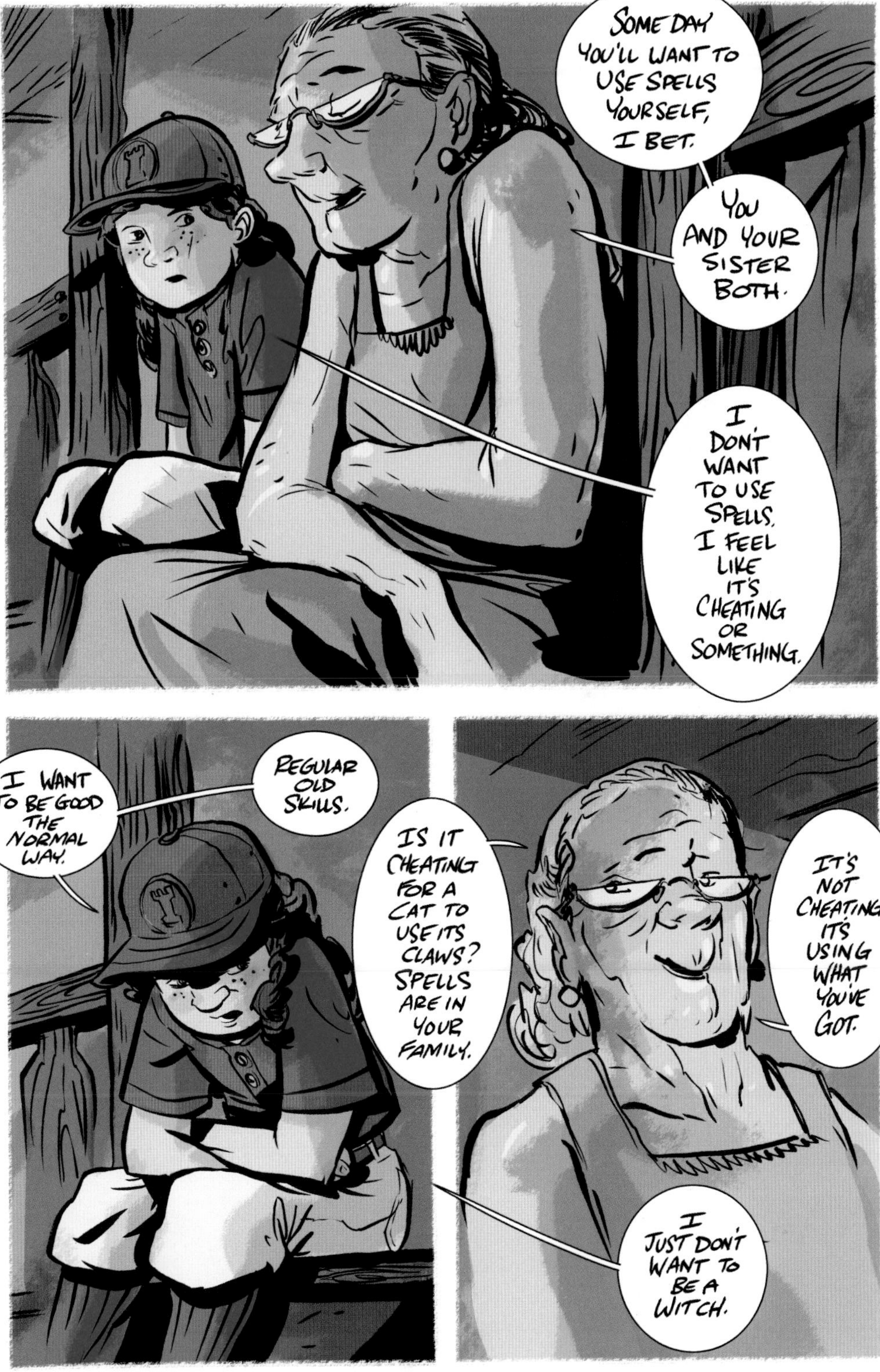
SOME DAY YOU'LL WANT TO USE SPELLS YOURSELF, I BET.
YOU AND YOUR SISTER BOTH.
I DON'T WANT TO USE SPELLS. I FEEL LIKE IT'S CHEATING OR SOMETHING.
I WANT TO BE GOOD THE NORMAL WAY.
REGULAR OLD SKILLS.
IS IT CHEATING FOR A CAT TO USE ITS CLAWS? SPELLS ARE IN YOUR FAMILY.
IT'S NOT CHEATING. IT'S USING WHAT YOU'VE GOT.
I JUST DON'T WANT TO BE A WITCH.

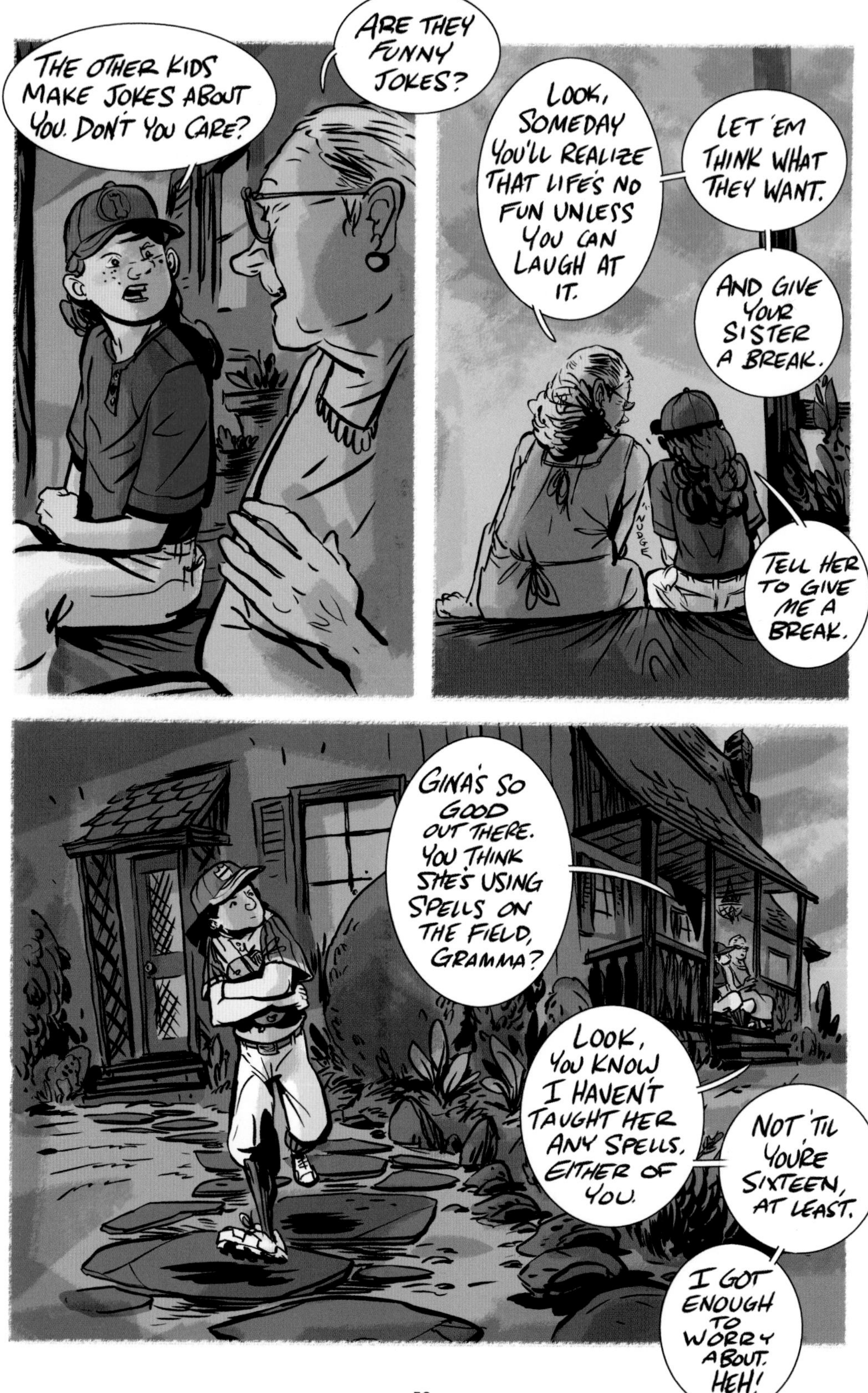
THE OTHER KIDS MAKE JOKES ABOUT YOU. DON'T YOU CARE?
ARE THEY FUNNY JOKES?
LOOK, SOMEDAY YOU'LL REALIZE THAT LIFE'S NO FUN UNLESS YOU CAN LAUGH AT IT.
LET 'EM THINK WHAT THEY WANT.
AND GIVE YOUR SISTER A BREAK.
NUDGE
TELL HER TO GIVE ME A BREAK.
GINA'S SO GOOD OUT THERE. YOU THINK SHE'S USING SPELLS ON THE FIELD, GRAMMA?
LOOK, YOU KNOW I HAVEN'T TAUGHT HER ANY SPELLS. EITHER OF YOU.
NOT 'TIL YOU'RE SIXTEEN, AT LEAST.
I GOT ENOUGH TO WORRY ABOUT. HEH!

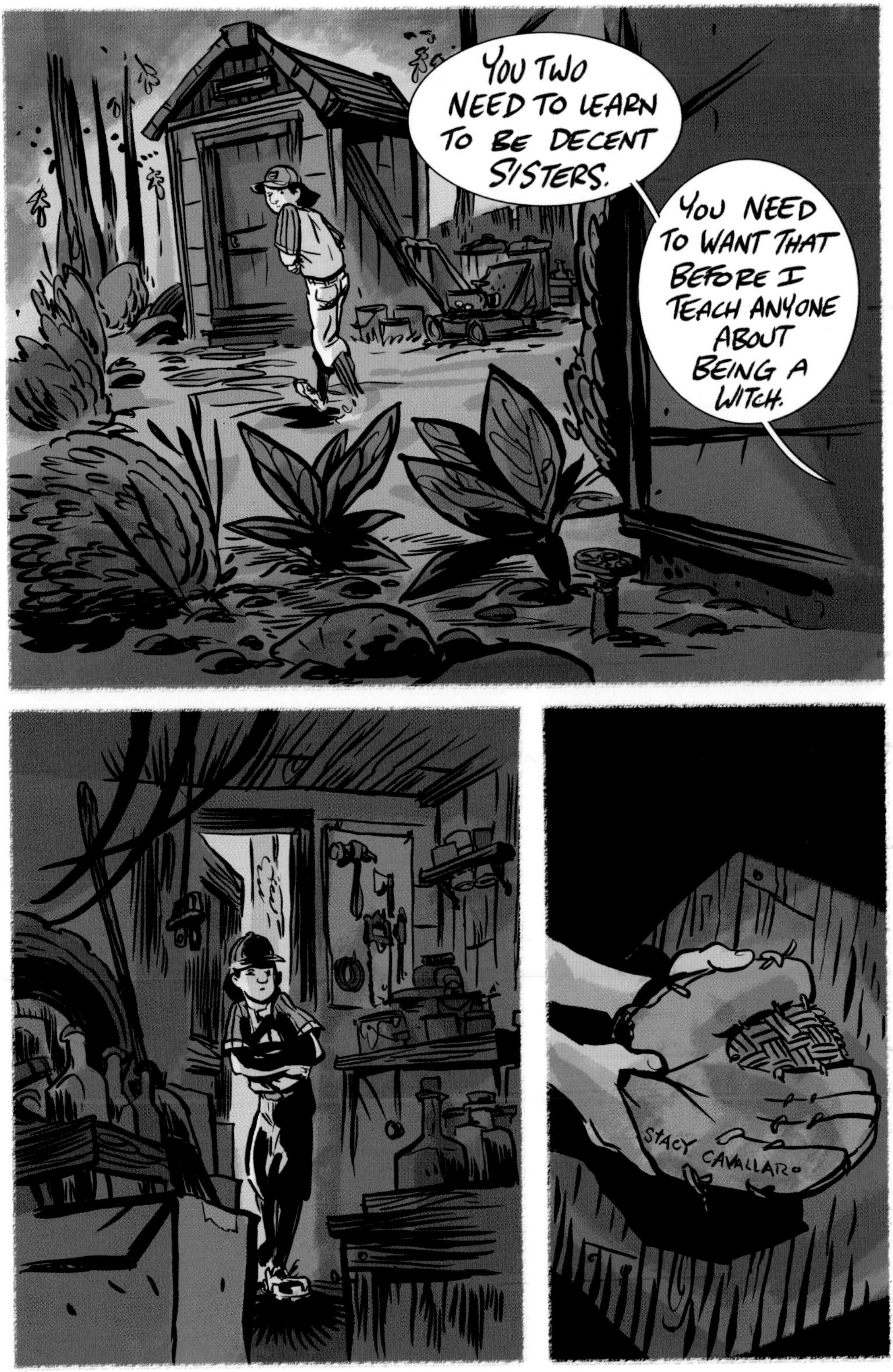
YOU TWO NEED TO LEARN TO BE DECENT SISTERS.
YOU NEED TO WANT THAT BEFORE I TEACH ANYONE ABOUT BEING A WITCH.
STACY CAVALLARO

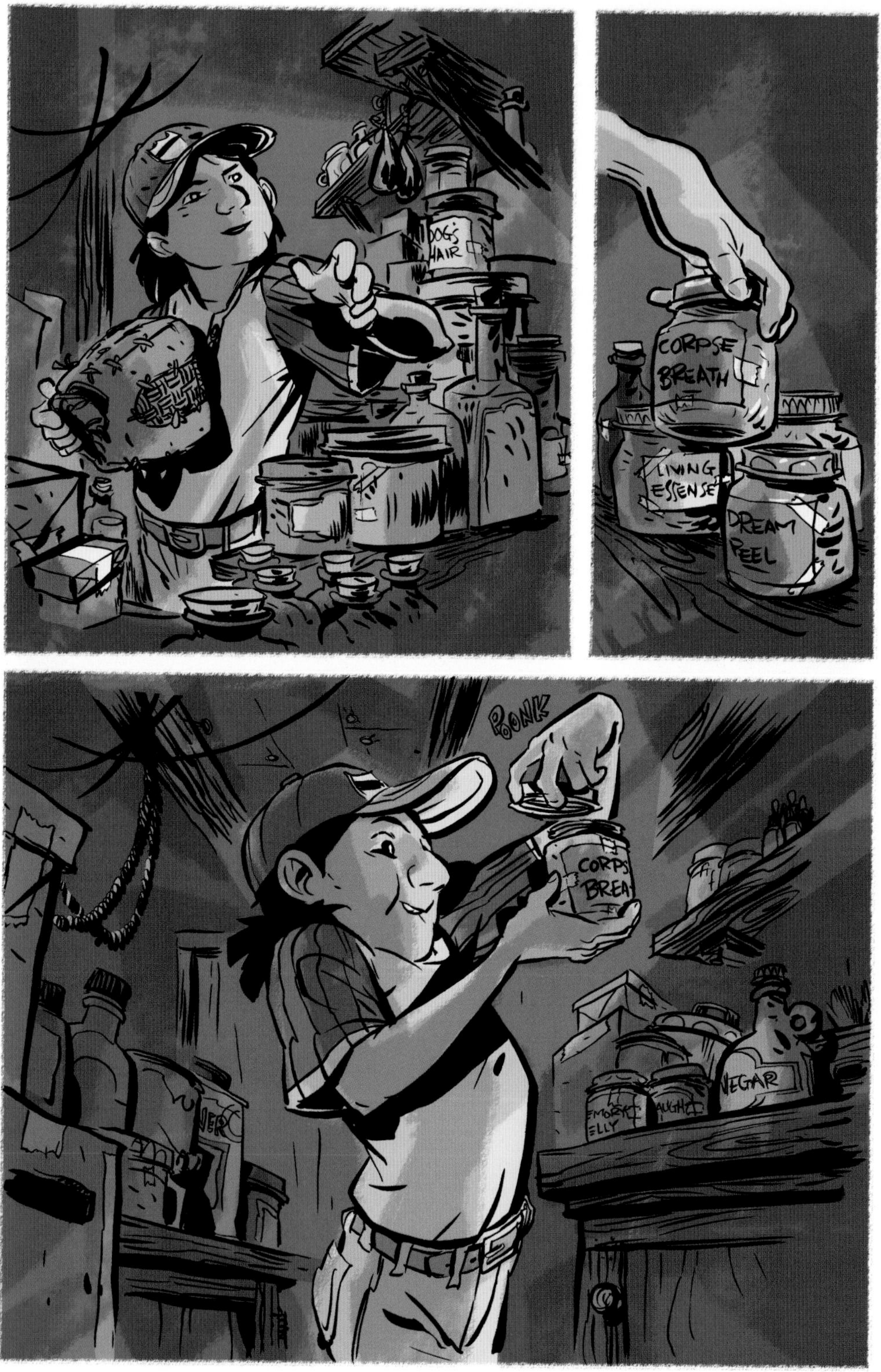
DOG'S HAIR
CORPSE BREATH
LIVING ESSENSE
DREAM PEEL
POONK
CORPS BREA

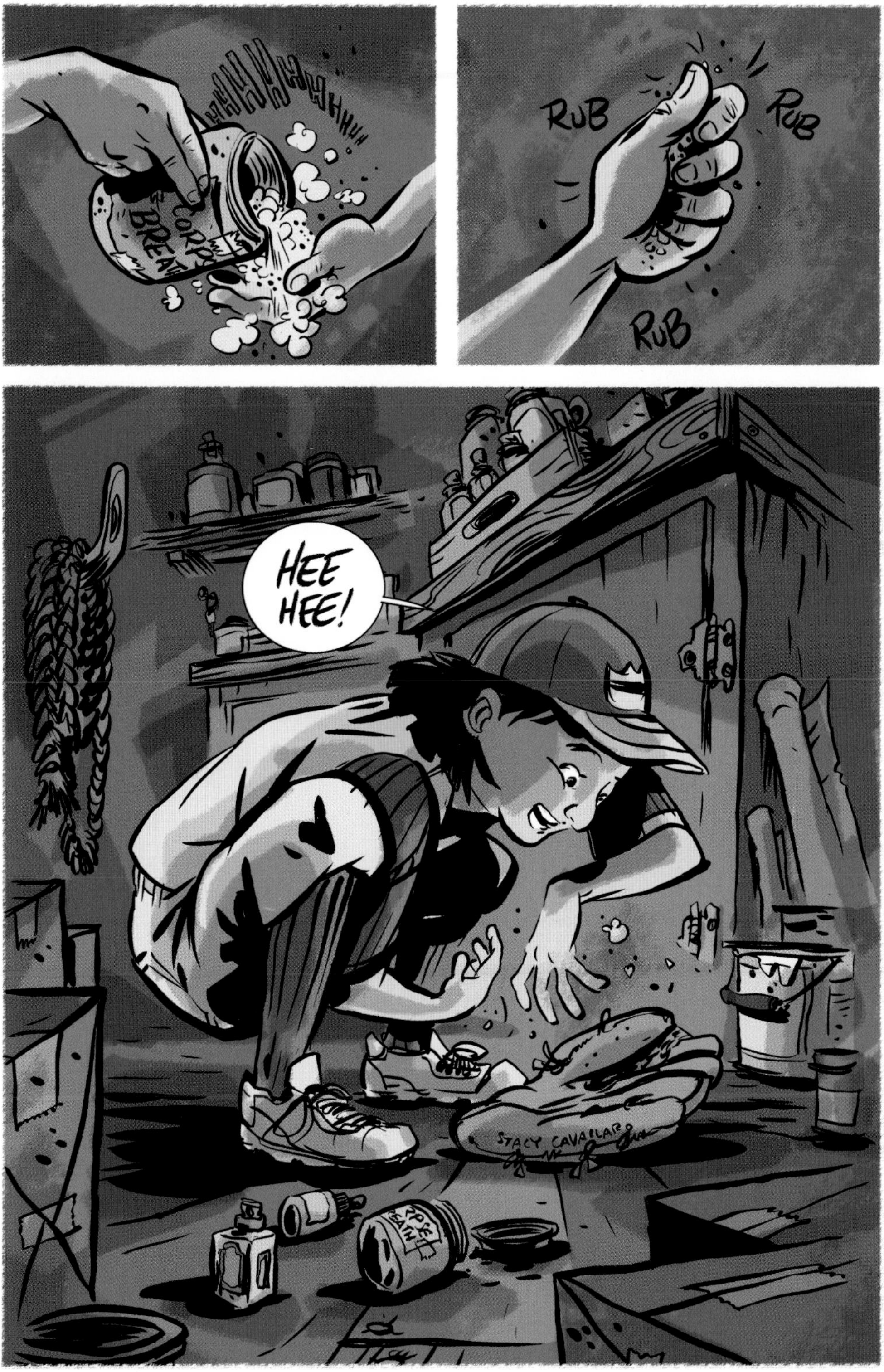
RUB
RUB
RUB
HEE HEE!

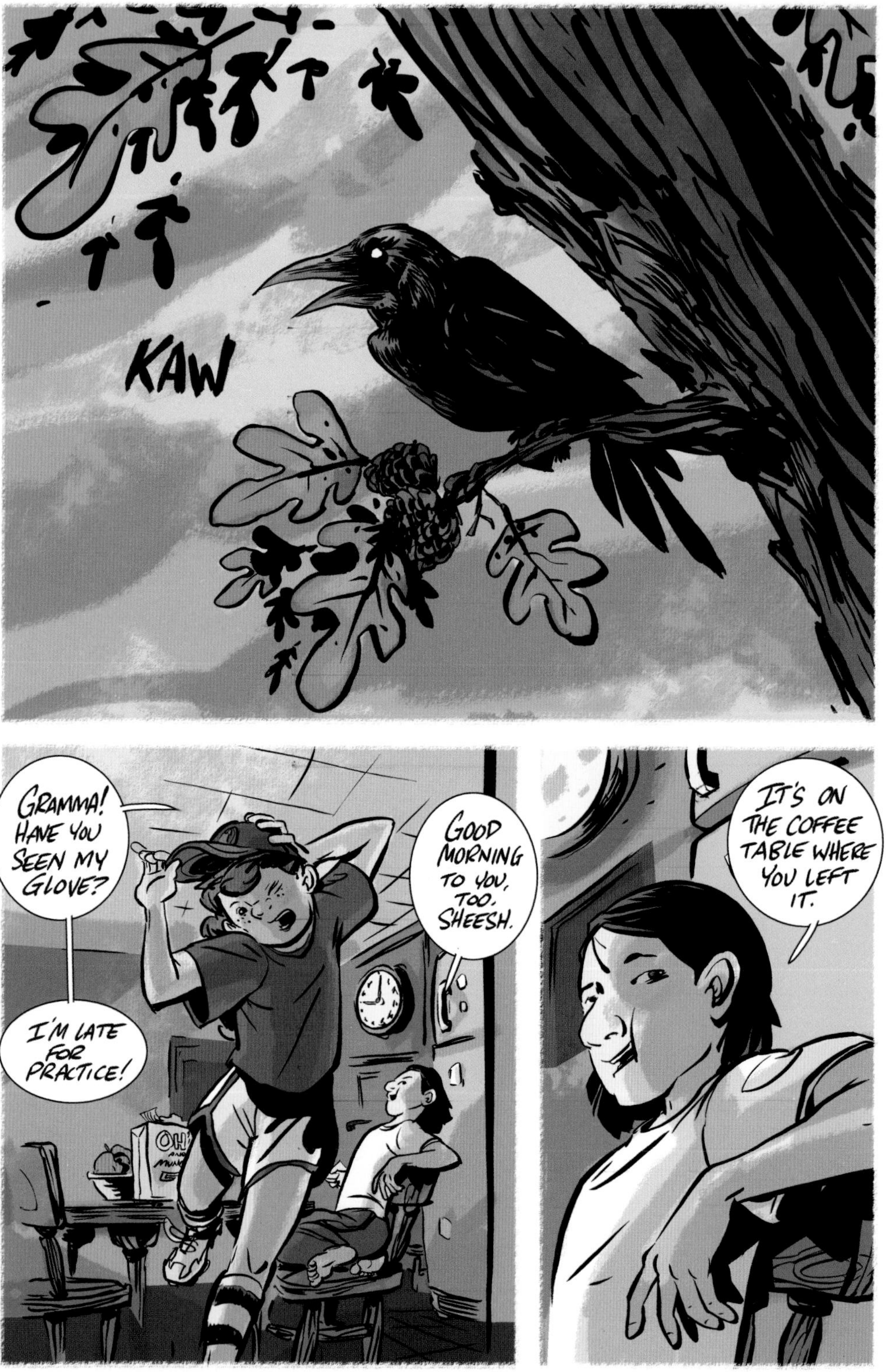
KAW
GRAMMA! HAVE YOU SEEN MY GLOVE?
I'M LATE FOR PRACTICE!
GOOD MORNING TO YOU, TOO. SHEESH.
IT'S ON THE COFFEE TABLE WHERE YOU LEFT IT.

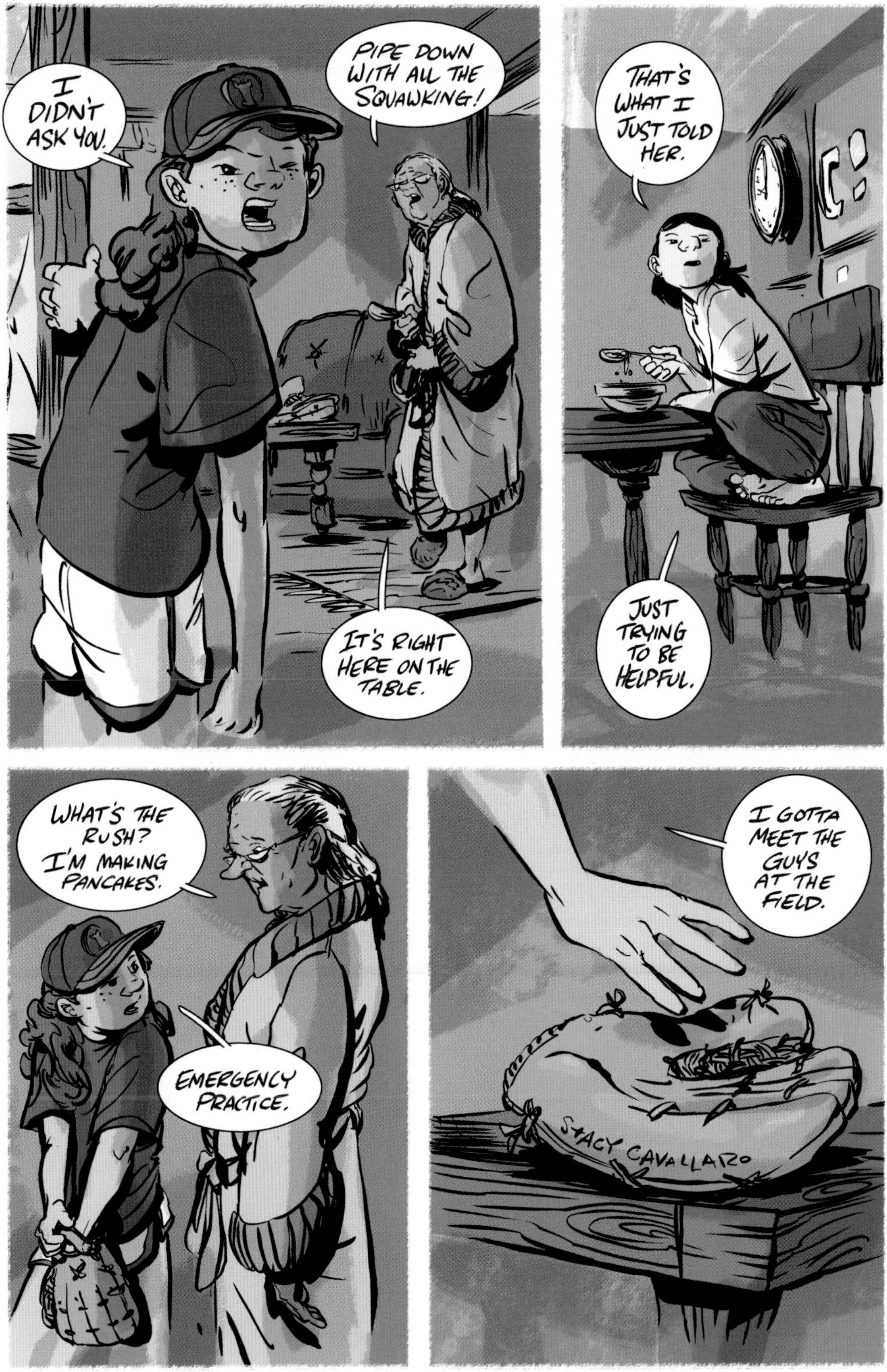
I DIDN'T ASK YOU.
PIPE DOWN WITH ALL THE SQUAWKING!
IT'S RIGHT HERE ON THE TABLE.
THAT'S WHAT I JUST TOLD HER.
JUST TRYING TO BE HELPFUL.
WHAT'S THE RUSH? I'M MAKING PANCAKES.
EMERGENCY PRACTICE.
I GOTTA MEET THE GUYS AT THE FIELD.
STACY CAVALLARO

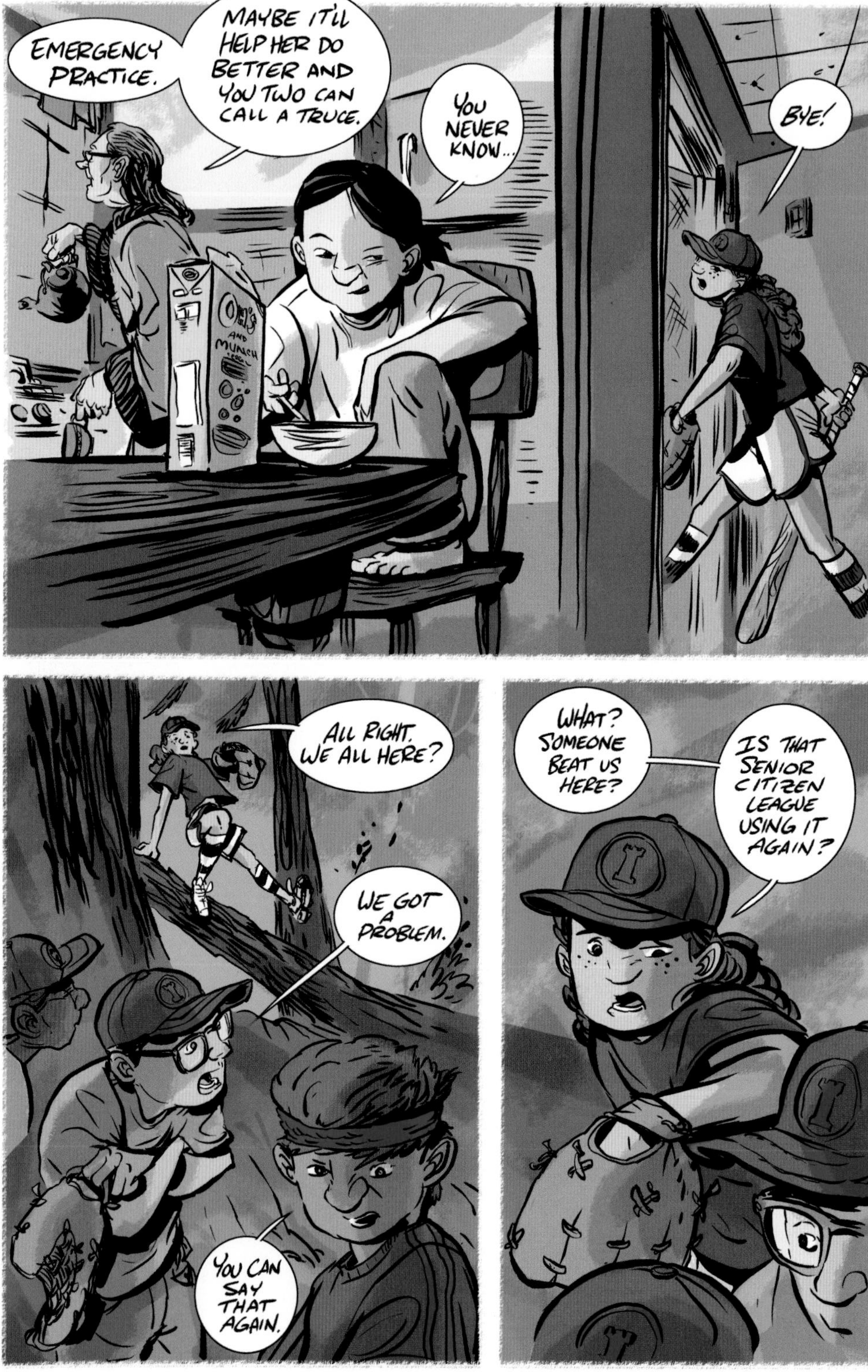
EMERGENCY PRACTICE.
MAYBE IT'LL HELP HER DO BETTER AND YOU TWO CAN CALL A TRUCE.
YOU NEVER KNOW...
OHS AND MUNCH
BYE!
ALL RIGHT. WE ALL HERE?
WE GOT A PROBLEM.
YOU CAN SAY THAT AGAIN.
WHAT? SOMEONE BEAT US HERE?
IS THAT SENIOR CITIZEN LEAGUE USING IT AGAIN?

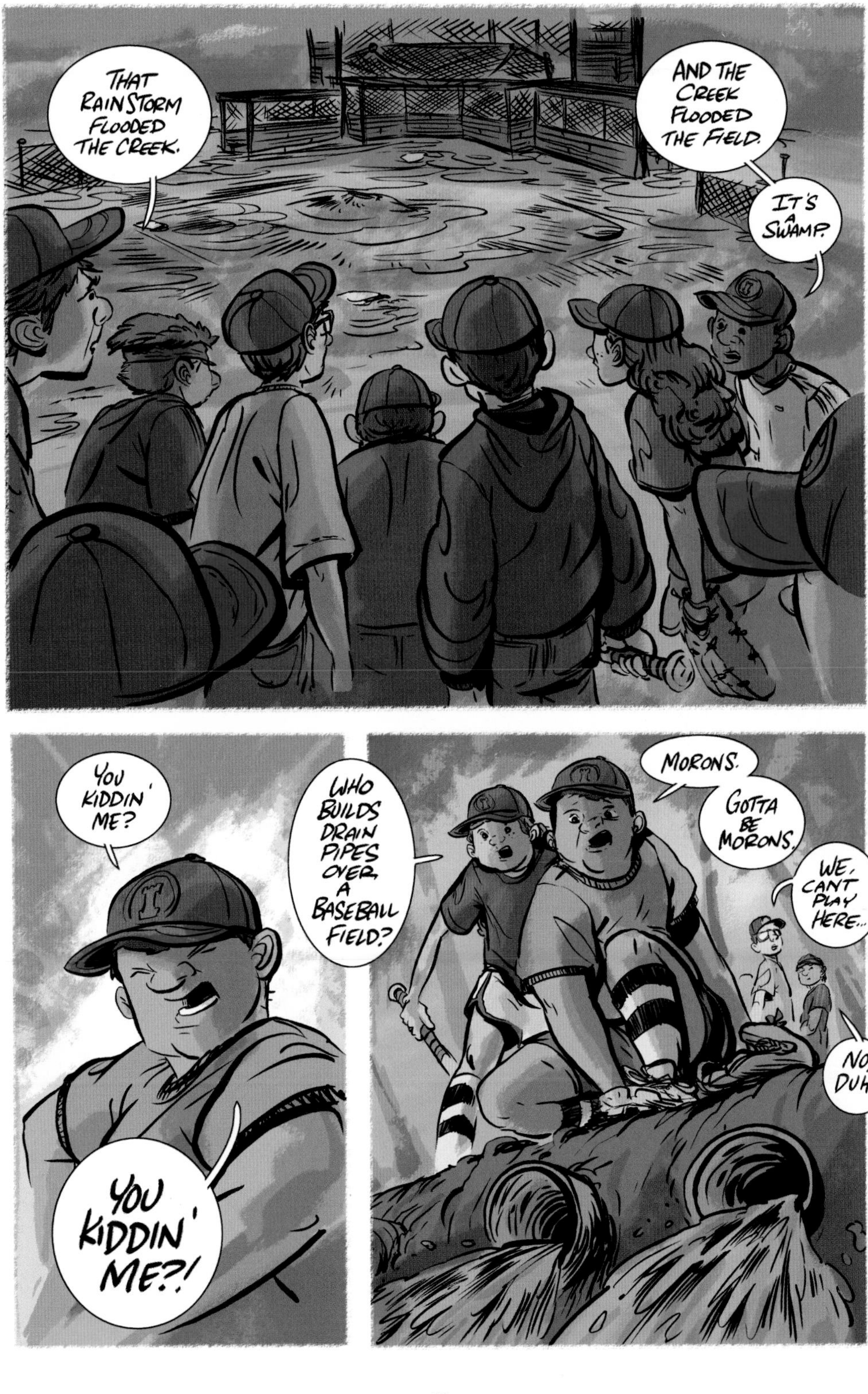
THAT RAINSTORM FLOODED THE CREEK.
AND THE CREEK FLOODED THE FIELD.
IT'S A SWAMP.
YOU KIDDIN' ME?
YOU KIDDIN' ME?!
WHO BUILDS DRAIN PIPES OVER A BASEBALL FIELD?
MORONS.
GOTTA BE MORONS.
WE CANT PLAY HERE...
NO, DUH.

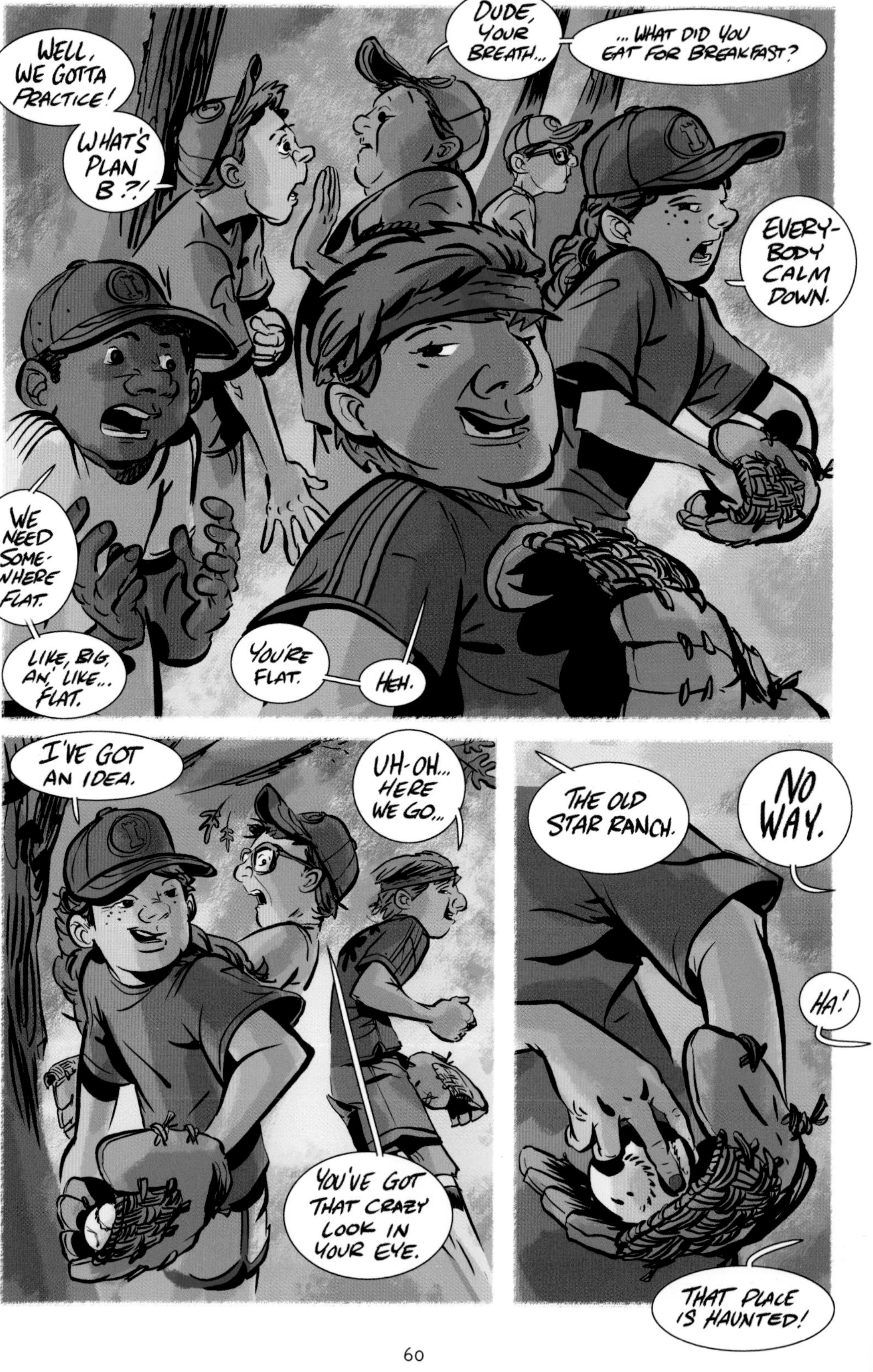
WELL, WE GOTTA PRACTICE!
WHAT'S PLAN B?!
DUDE, YOUR BREATH...
...WHAT DID YOU EAT FOR BREAKFAST?
EVERY-BODY CALM DOWN.
WE NEED SOME-WHERE FLAT.
LIKE, BIG, AN' LIKE... FLAT.
YOU'RE FLAT.
HEH.
I'VE GOT AN IDEA.
UH-OH... HERE WE GO...
YOU'VE GOT THAT CRAZY LOOK IN YOUR EYE.
THE OLD STAR RANCH.
NO WAY.
HA!
THAT PLACE IS HAUNTED!

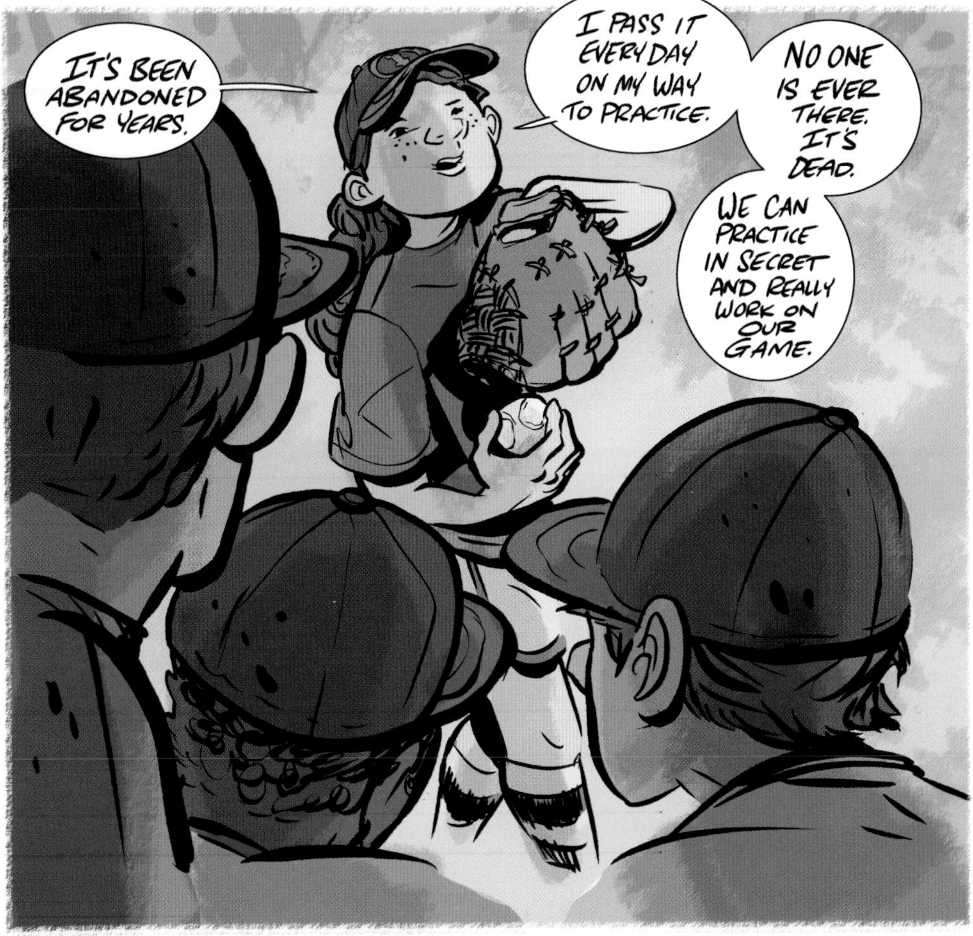
IT'S BEEN ABANDONED FOR YEARS.
I PASS IT EVERY DAY ON MY WAY TO PRACTICE.
NO ONE IS EVER THERE. IT'S DEAD.
WE CAN PRACTICE IN SECRET AND REALLY WORK ON OUR GAME.

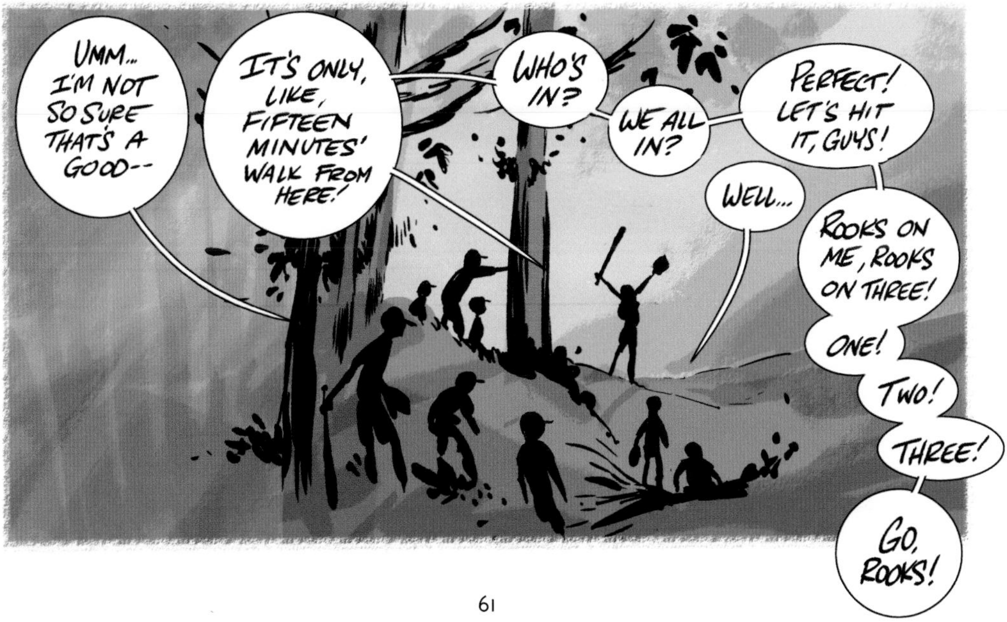
UMM... I'M NOT SO SURE THAT'S A GOOD--
IT'S ONLY, LIKE, FIFTEEN MINUTES' WALK FROM HERE!
WHO'S IN?
WE ALL IN?
PERFECT! LET'S HIT IT, GUYS!
WELL...
ROOKS ON ME, ROOKS ON THREE!
ONE!
TWO!
THREE!
GO, ROOKS!

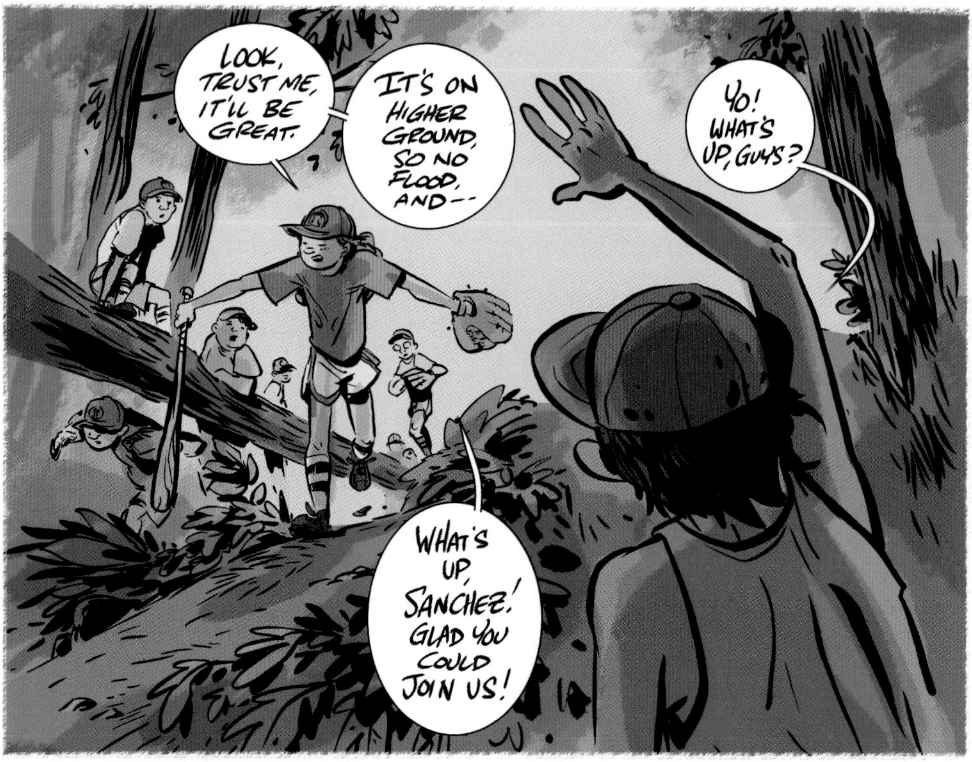
LOOK, TRUST ME, IT'LL BE GREAT.
IT'S ON HIGHER GROUND, SO NO FLOOD, AND--
YO! WHAT'S UP, GUYS?
WHAT'S UP, SANCHEZ! GLAD YOU COULD JOIN US!

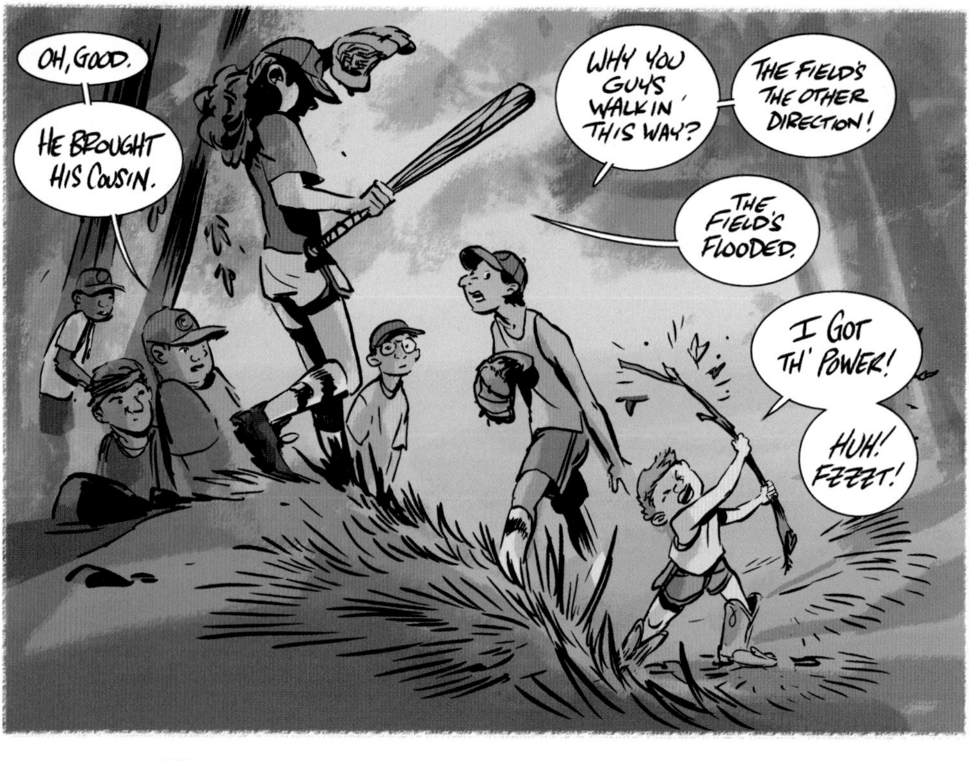
OH, GOOD.
HE BROUGHT HIS COUSIN.
WHY YOU GUYS WALKIN' THIS WAY?
THE FIELD'S THE OTHER DIRECTION!
THE FIELD'S FLOODED.
I GOT TH' POWER!
HUH! FZZZT!

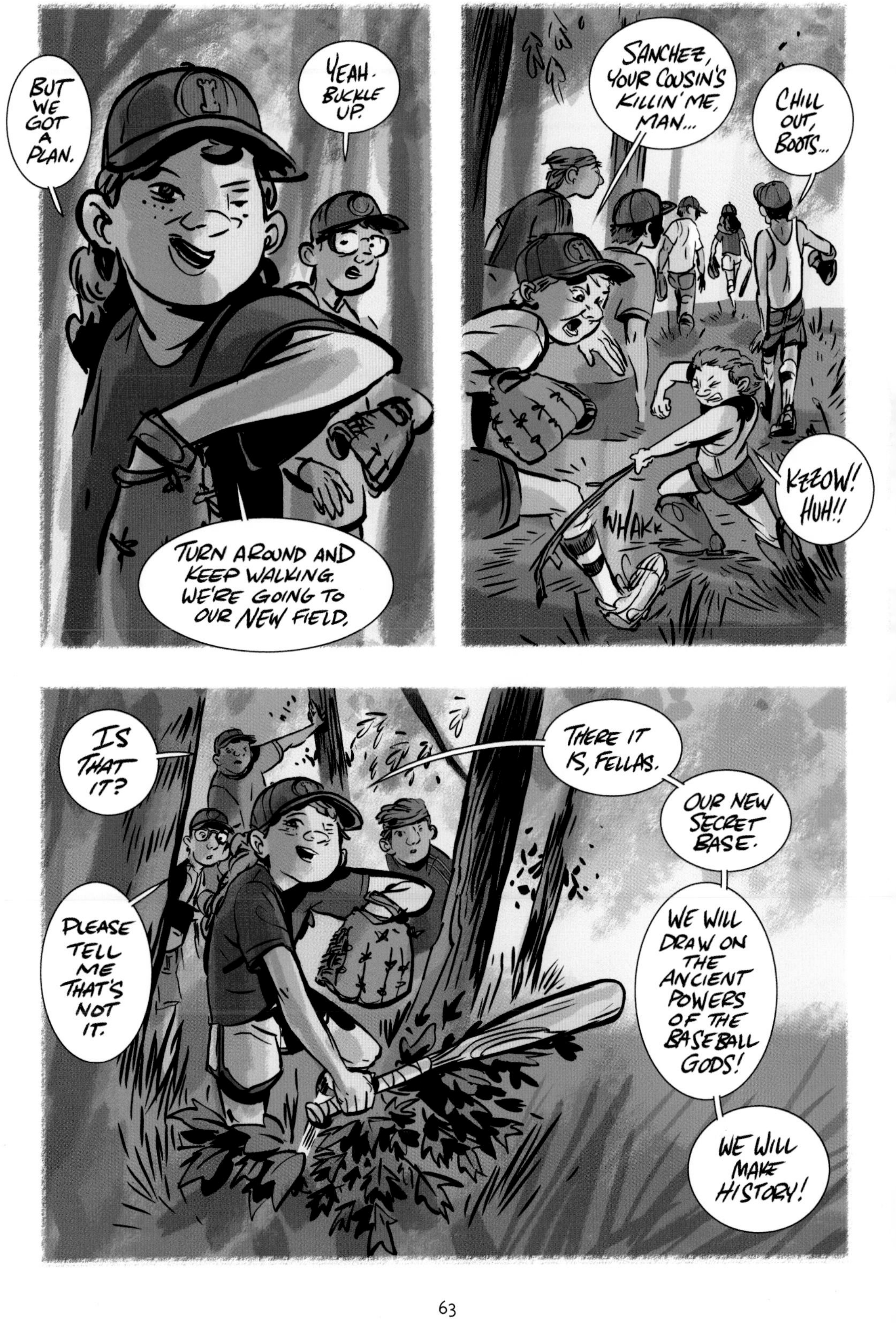

BUT WE GOT A PLAN.
YEAH. BUCKLE UP.
TURN AROUND AND KEEP WALKING. WE'RE GOING TO OUR NEW FIELD.
SANCHEZ, YOUR COUSIN'S KILLIN' ME, MAN...
CHILL OUT, BOOTS...
WHAKK
KZZOW! HUH!!
IS THAT IT?
THERE IT IS, FELLAS.
OUR NEW SECRET BASE.
PLEASE TELL ME THAT'S NOT IT.
WE WILL DRAW ON THE ANCIENT POWERS OF THE BASEBALL GODS!
WE WILL MAKE HISTORY!

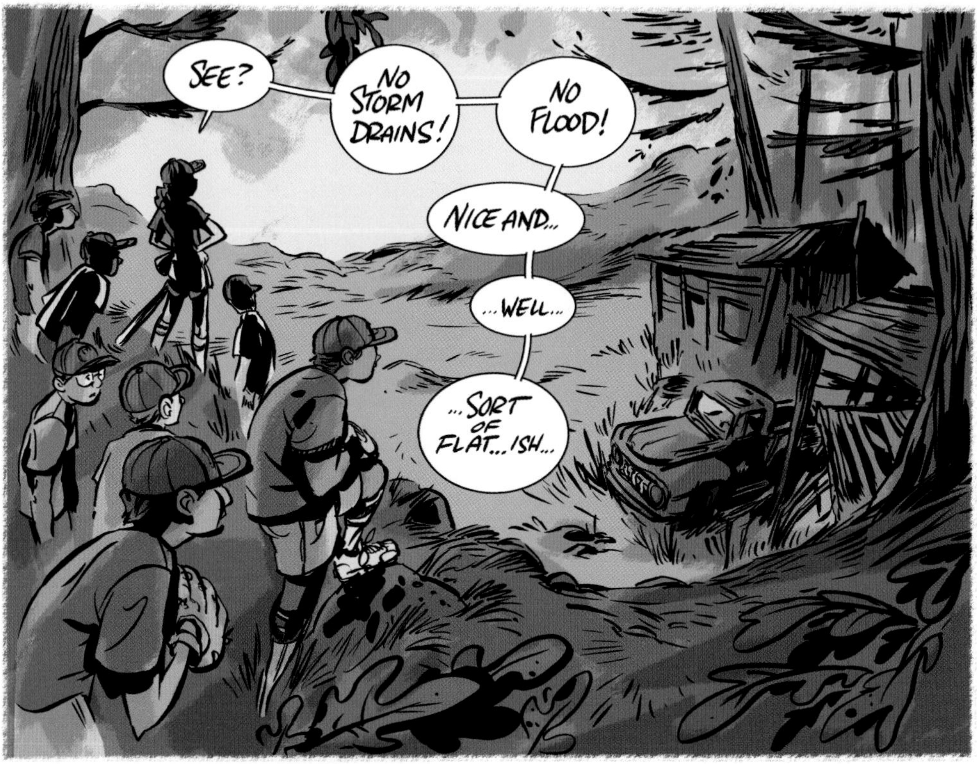
SEE?
NO STORM DRAINS!
NO FLOOD!
NICE AND...
...WELL...
...SORT OF FLAT...ISH...

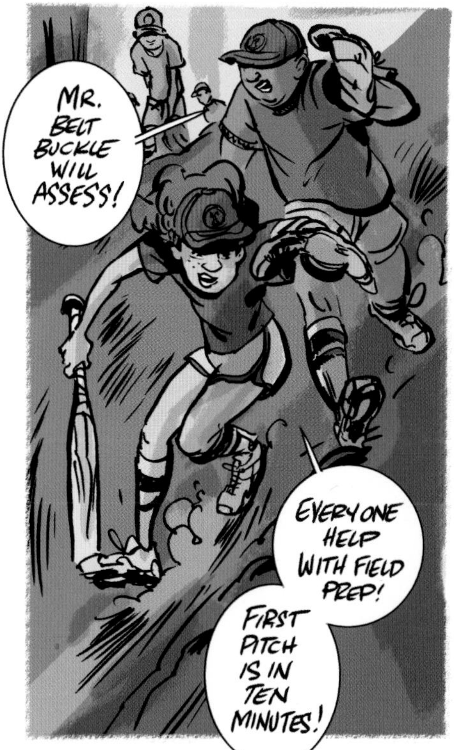
MR. BELT BUCKLE WILL ASSESS!
EVERYONE HELP WITH FIELD PREP!
FIRST PITCH IS IN TEN MINUTES!

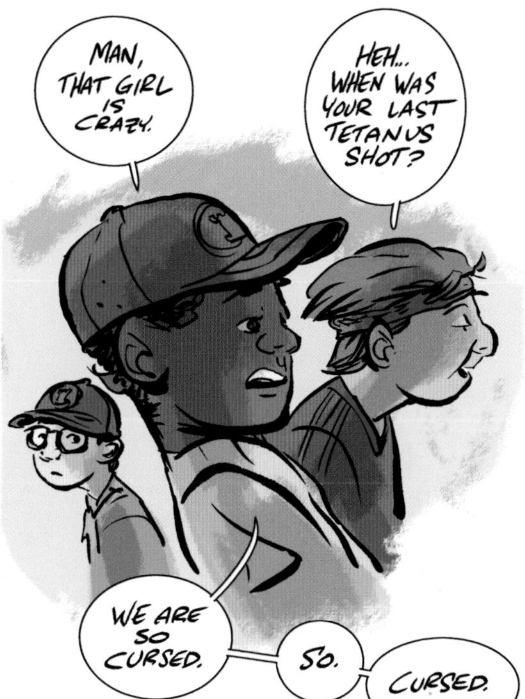
MAN, THAT GIRL IS CRAZY.
HEH.. WHEN WAS YOUR LAST TETANUS SHOT?
WE ARE SO CURSED.
SO.
CURSED.

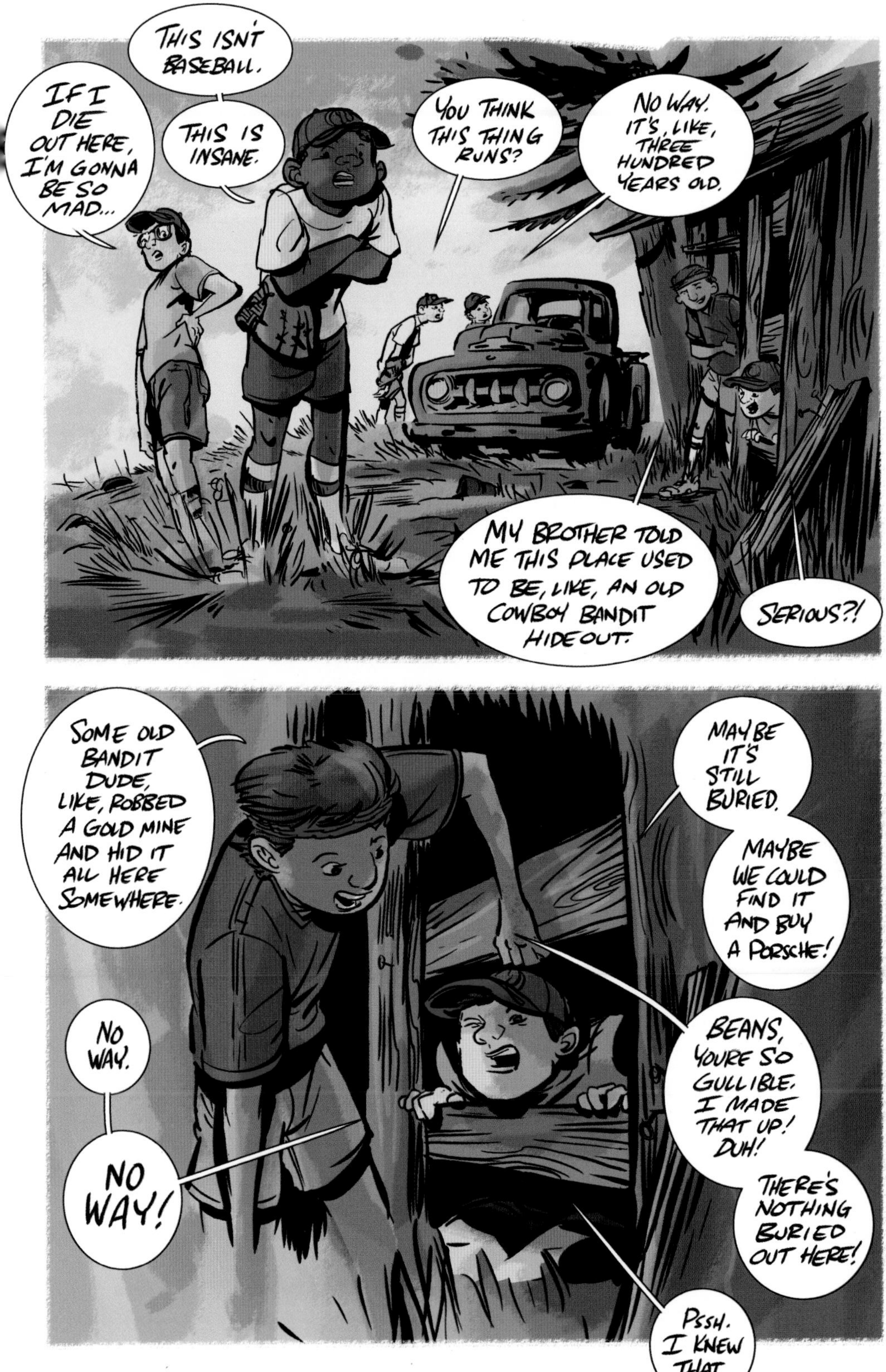
IF I DIE OUT HERE, I'M GONNA BE SO MAD...
THIS ISN'T BASEBALL.
THIS IS INSANE.
YOU THINK THIS THING RUNS?
NO WAY. IT'S, LIKE, THREE HUNDRED YEARS OLD.
MY BROTHER TOLD ME THIS PLACE USED TO BE, LIKE, AN OLD COWBOY BANDIT HIDEOUT.
SERIOUS?!
SOME OLD BANDIT DUDE, LIKE, ROBBED A GOLD MINE AND HID IT ALL HERE SOMEWHERE.
MAYBE IT'S STILL BURIED.
MAYBE WE COULD FIND IT AND BUY A PORSCHE!
NO WAY.
NO WAY!
BEANS, YOURE SO GULLIBLE. I MADE THAT UP! DUH!
THERE'S NOTHING BURIED OUT HERE!
PSSH. I KNEW THAT.

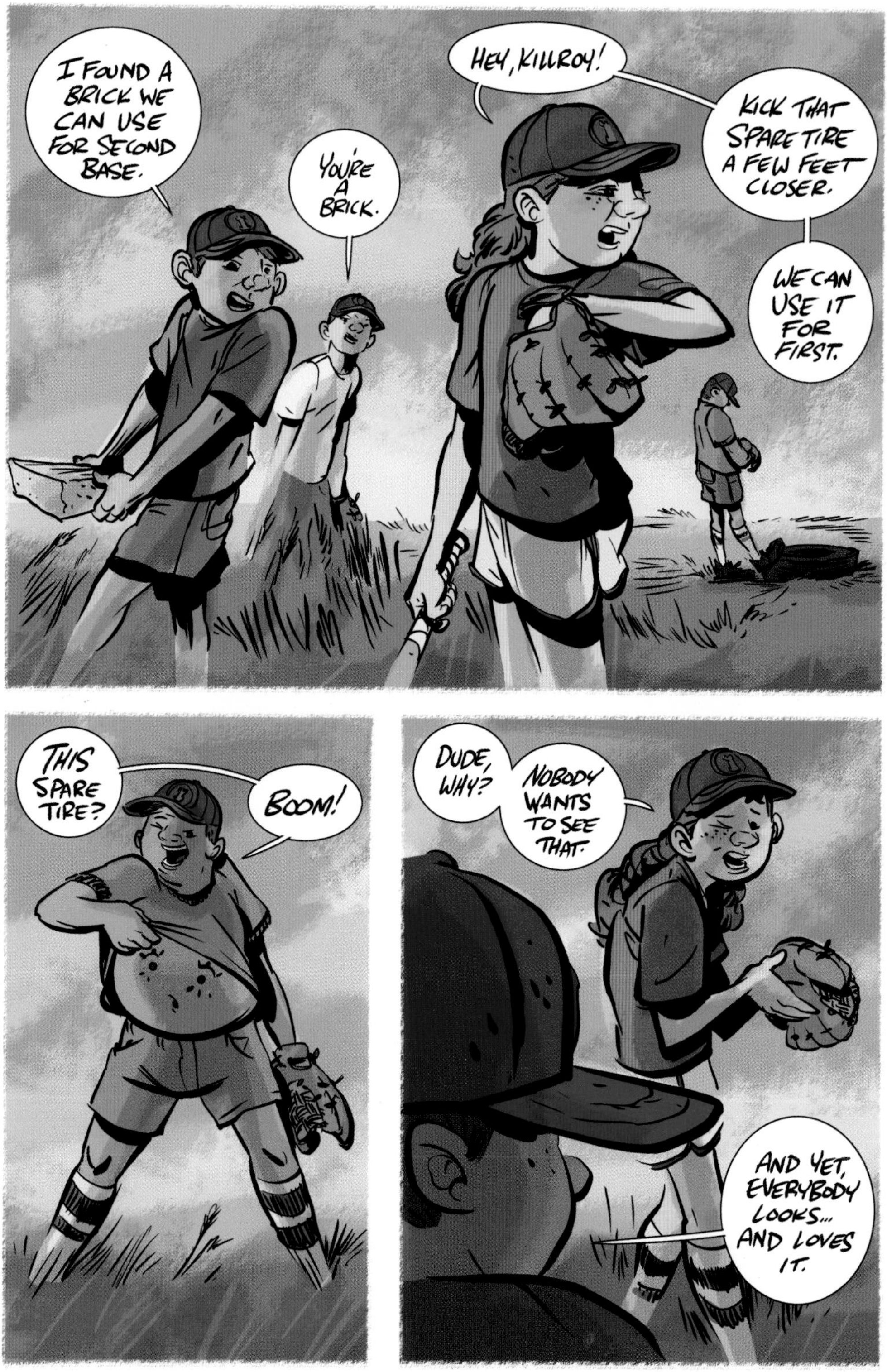
I FOUND A BRICK WE CAN USE FOR SECOND BASE.
YOU'RE A BRICK.
HEY, KILLROY!
KICK THAT SPARE TIRE A FEW FEET CLOSER.
WE CAN USE IT FOR FIRST.
THIS SPARE TIRE?
BOOM!
DUDE, WHY?
NOBODY WANTS TO SEE THAT.
AND YET, EVERYBODY LOOKS... AND LOVES IT.

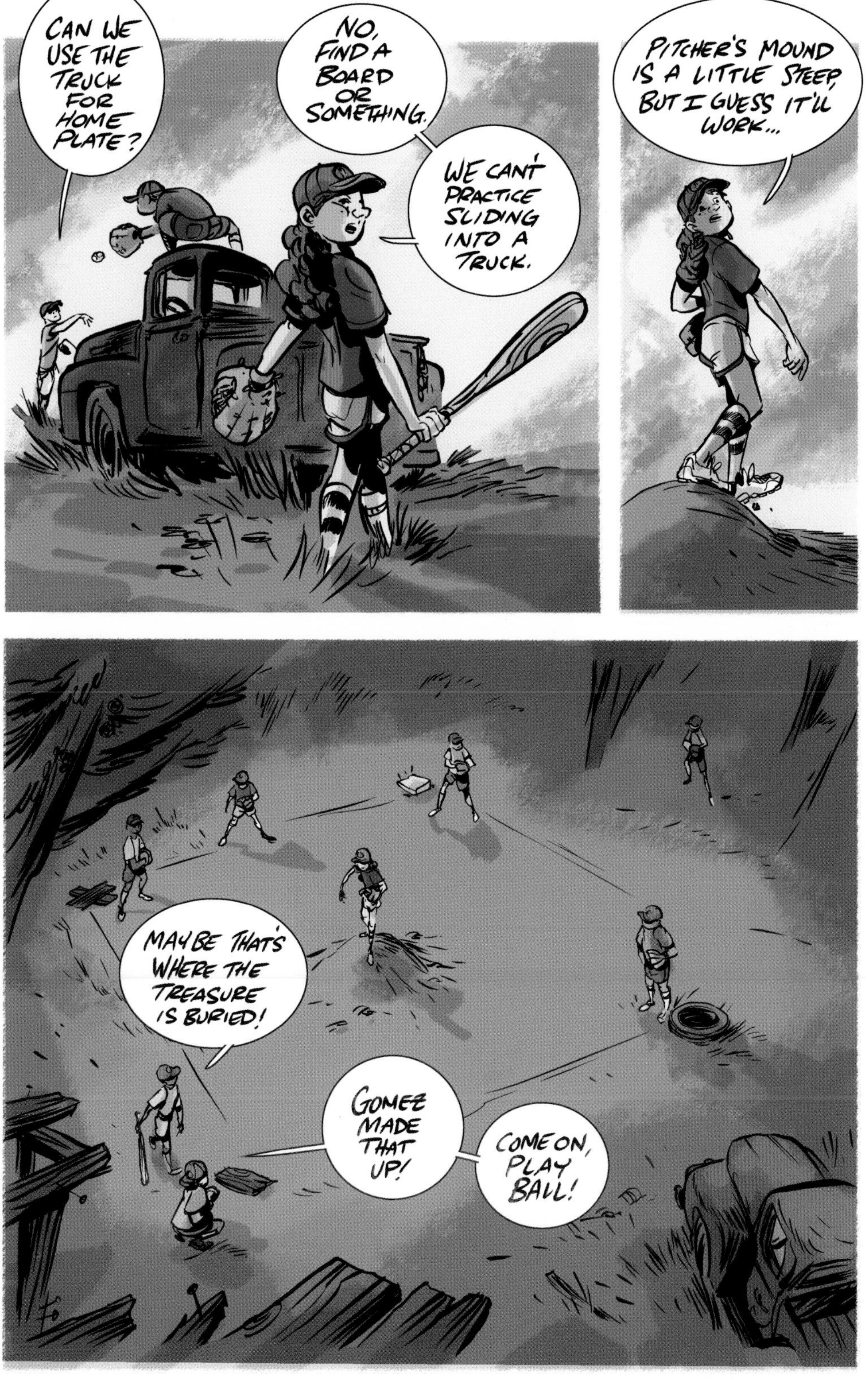
CAN WE USE THE TRUCK FOR HOME PLATE?
NO, FIND A BOARD OR SOMETHING.
WE CAN'T PRACTICE SLIDING INTO A TRUCK.
PITCHER'S MOUND IS A LITTLE STEEP, BUT I GUESS IT'LL WORK...
MAYBE THAT'S WHERE THE TREASURE IS BURIED!
GOMEZ MADE THAT UP!
COME ON, PLAY BALL!

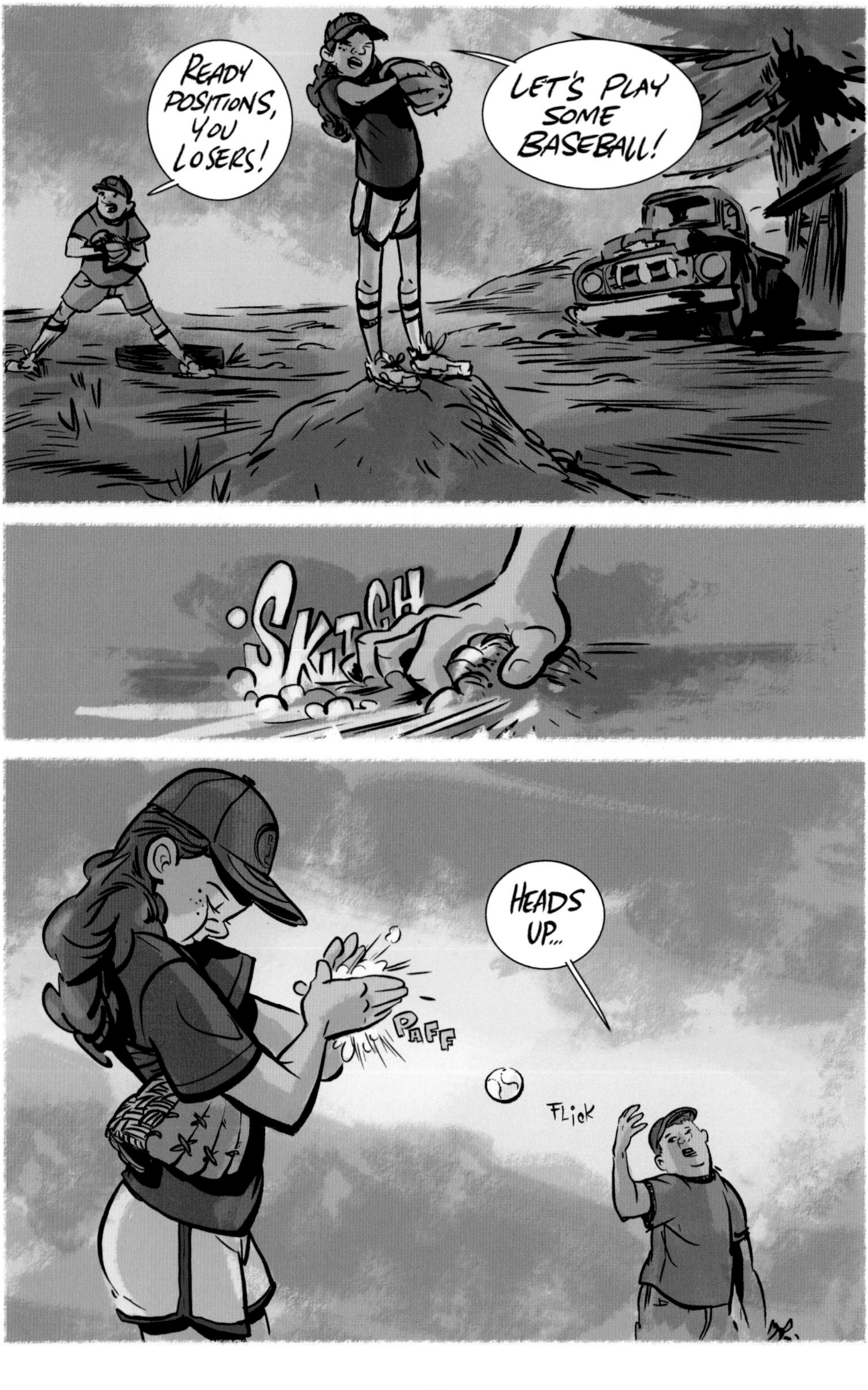
READY POSITIONS, YOU LOSERS!
LET'S PLAY SOME BASEBALL!
SKITCH
HEADS UP...
PAFF
FLICK

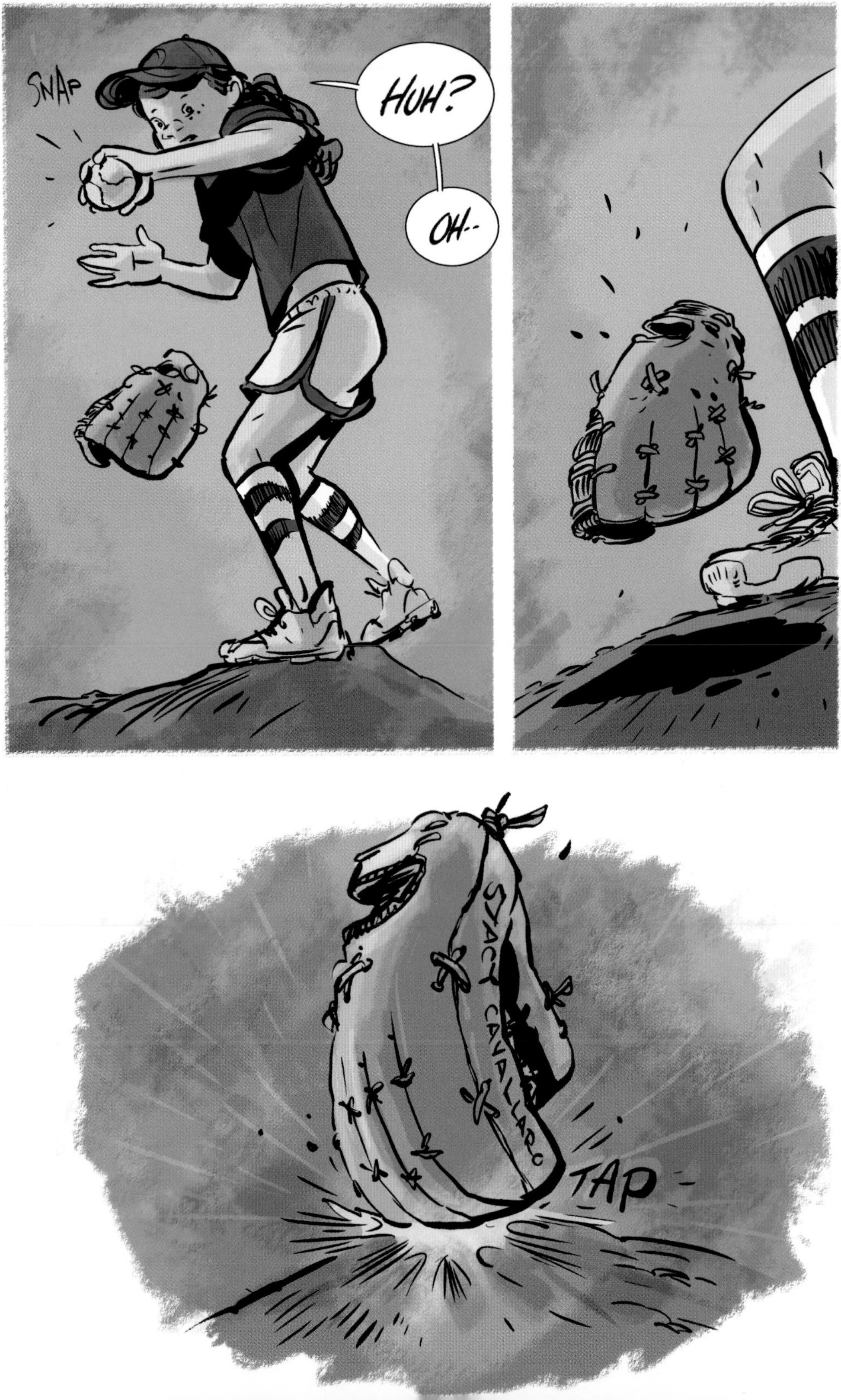
SNAP
HUH?
OH..
STACY CAVALLARO
TAP

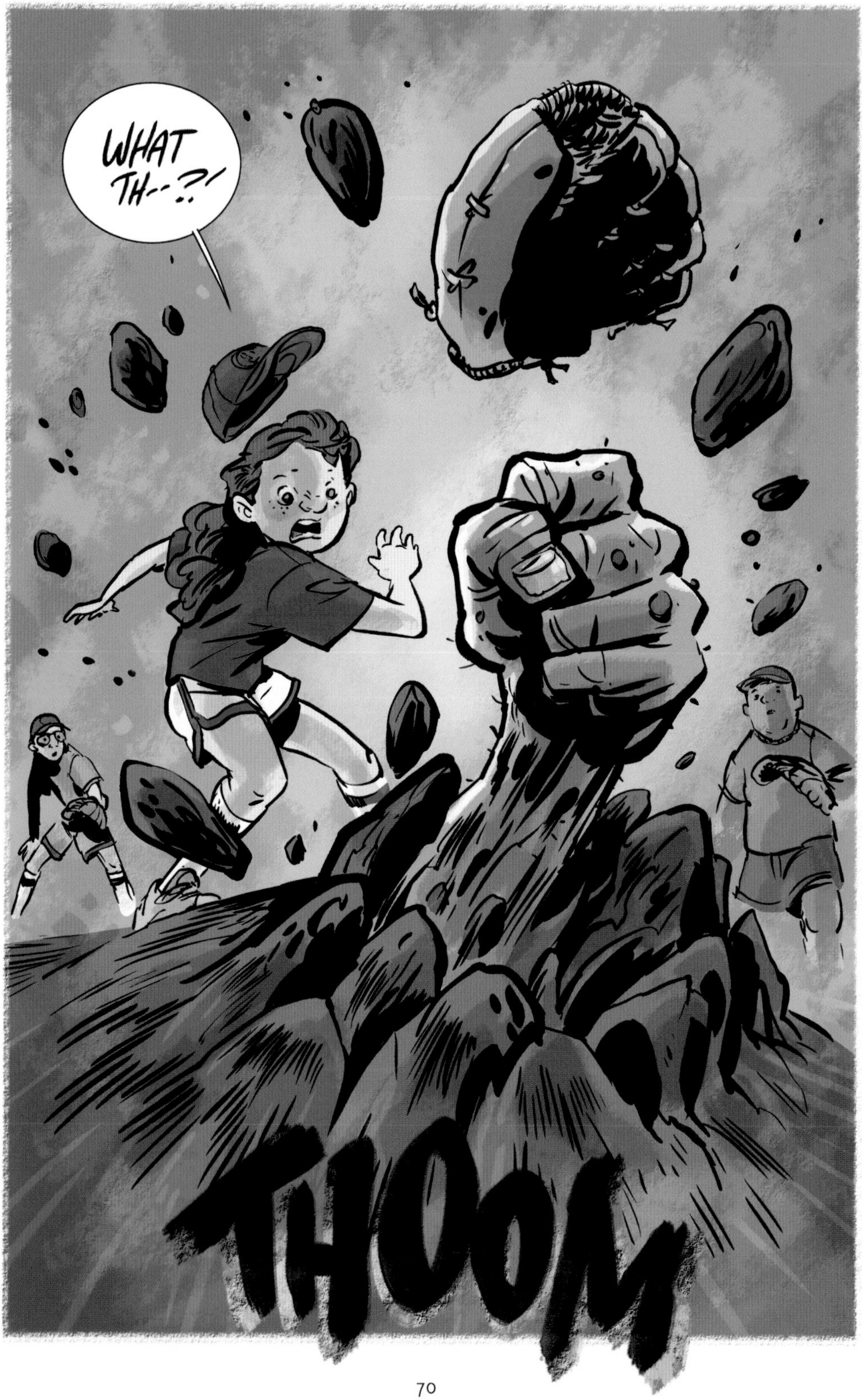
WHAT TH--?!
THOOM

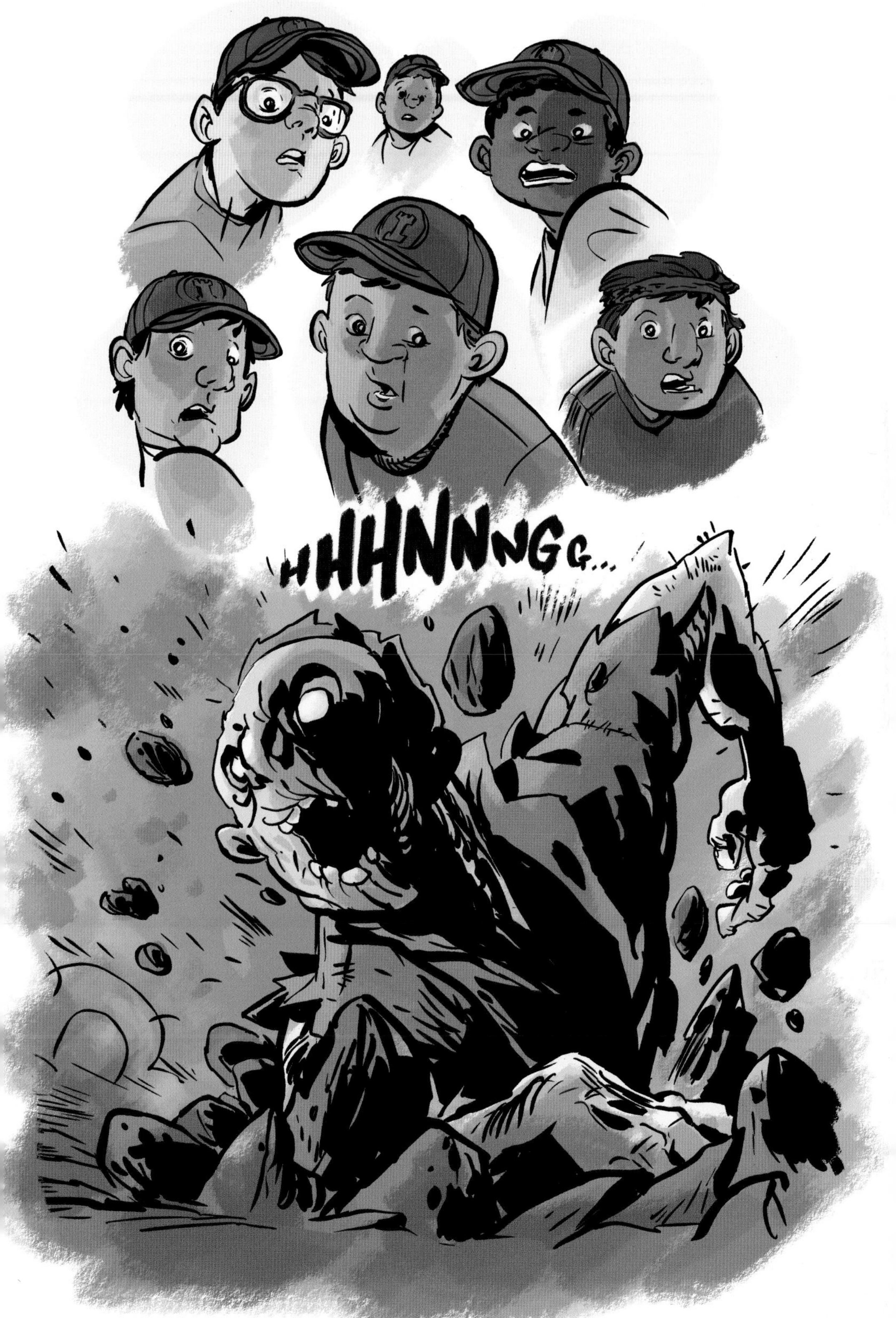
HHHNNNNGG...

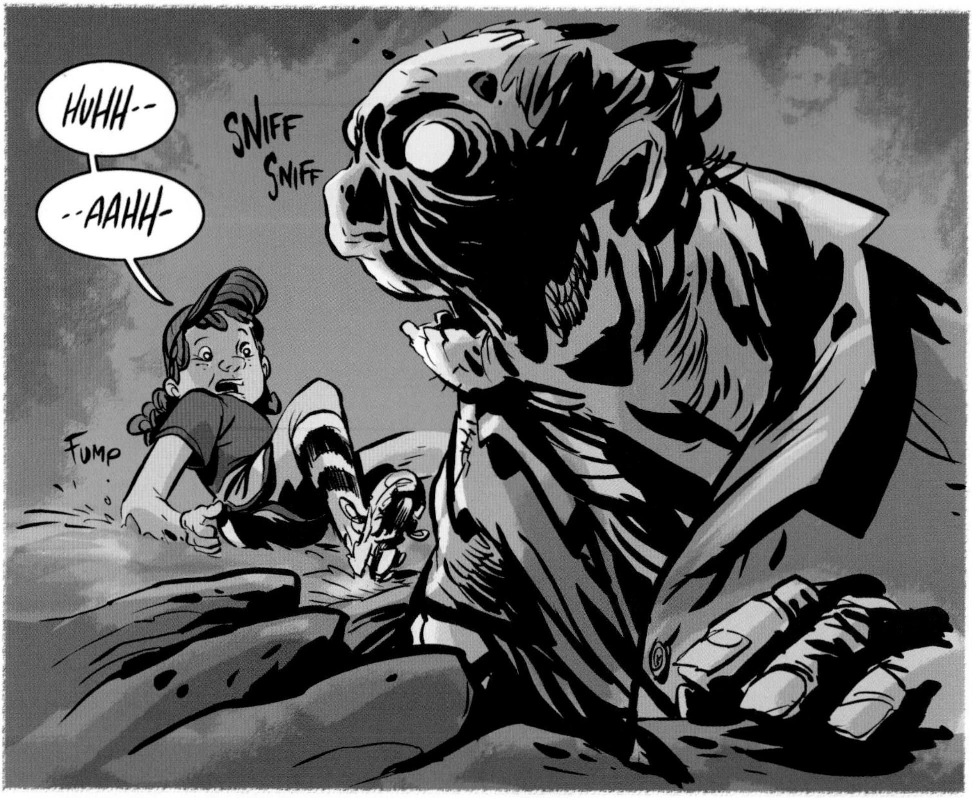
HUHH--
--AAHH-
SNIFF
SNIFF
FUMP

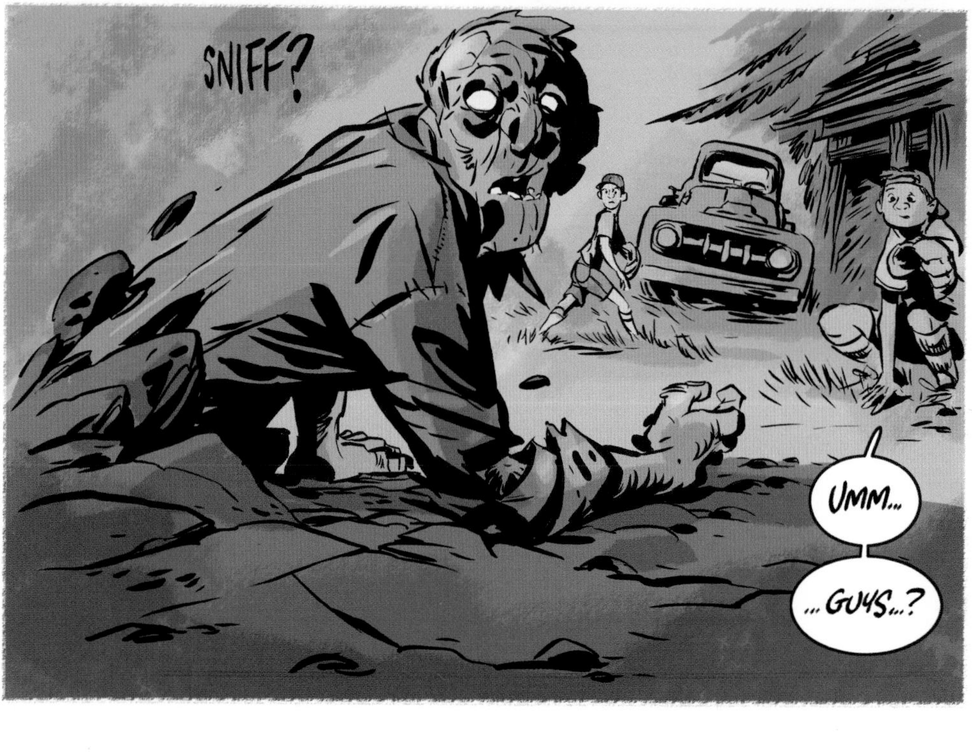
SNIFF?
UMM...
...GUYS...?

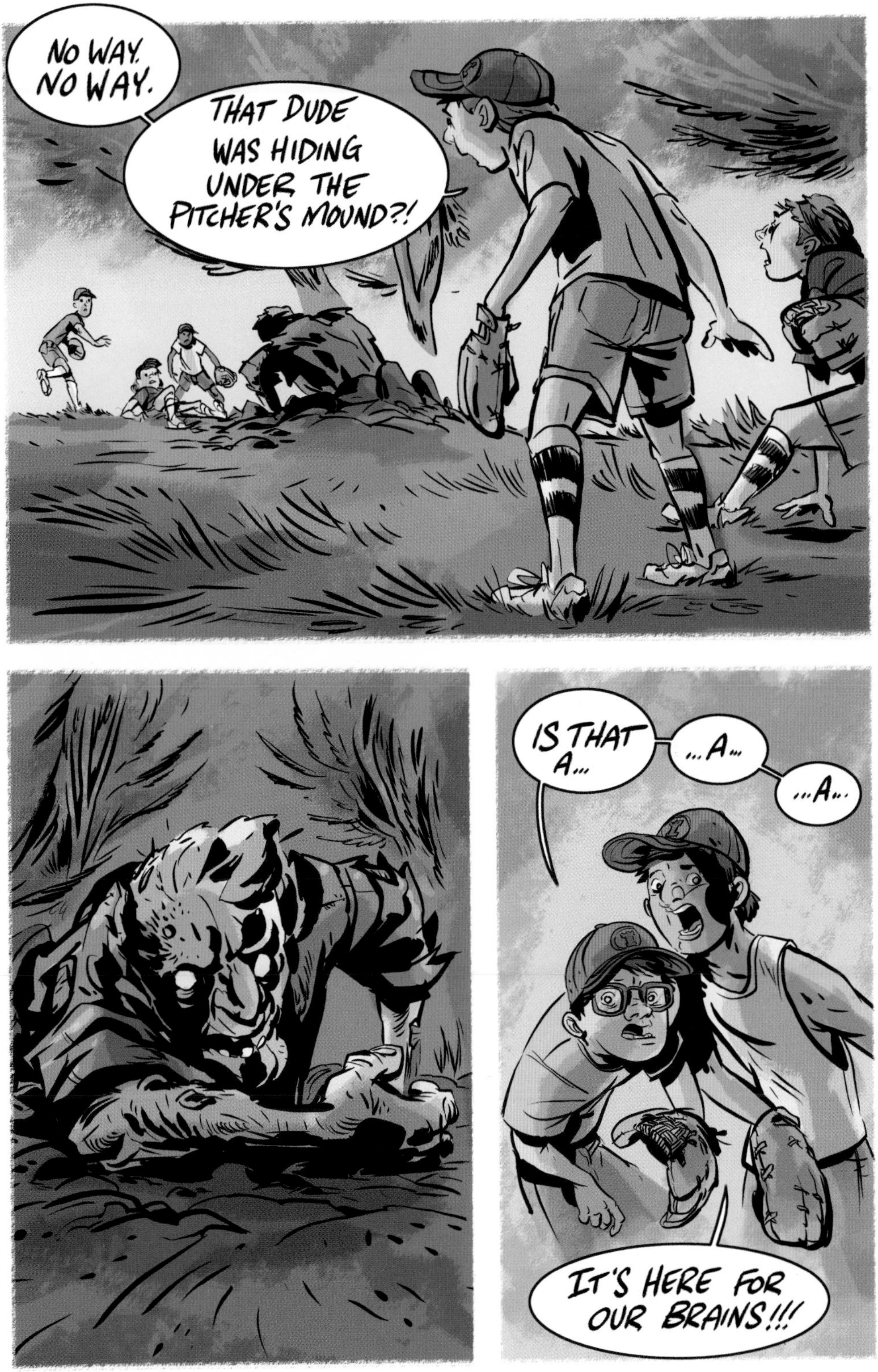
NO WAY. NO WAY.
THAT DUDE WAS HIDING UNDER THE PITCHER'S MOUND?!
IS THAT A...
...A...
...A...
IT'S HERE FOR OUR BRAINS!!!

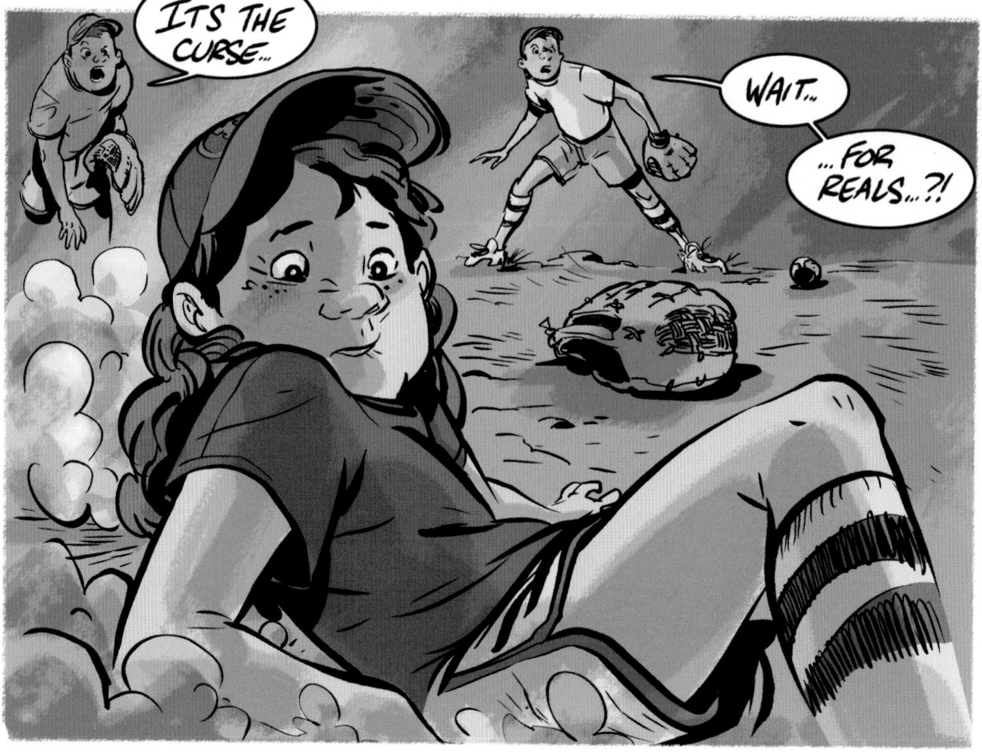
IT'S THE CURSE...
WAIT...
...FOR REALS...?!

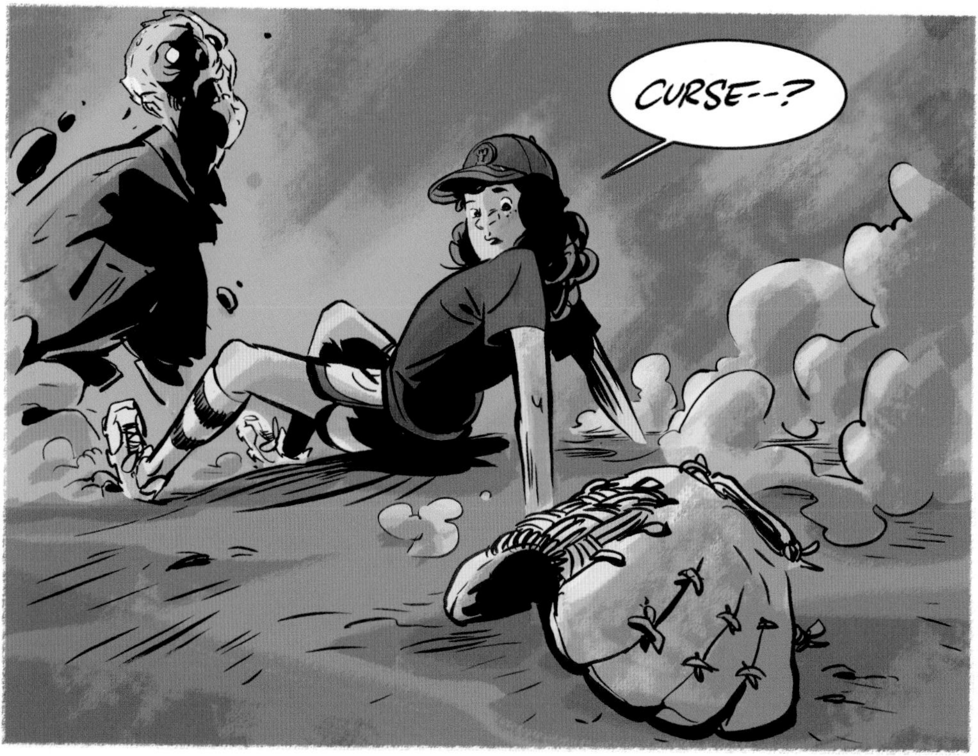
CURSE--?

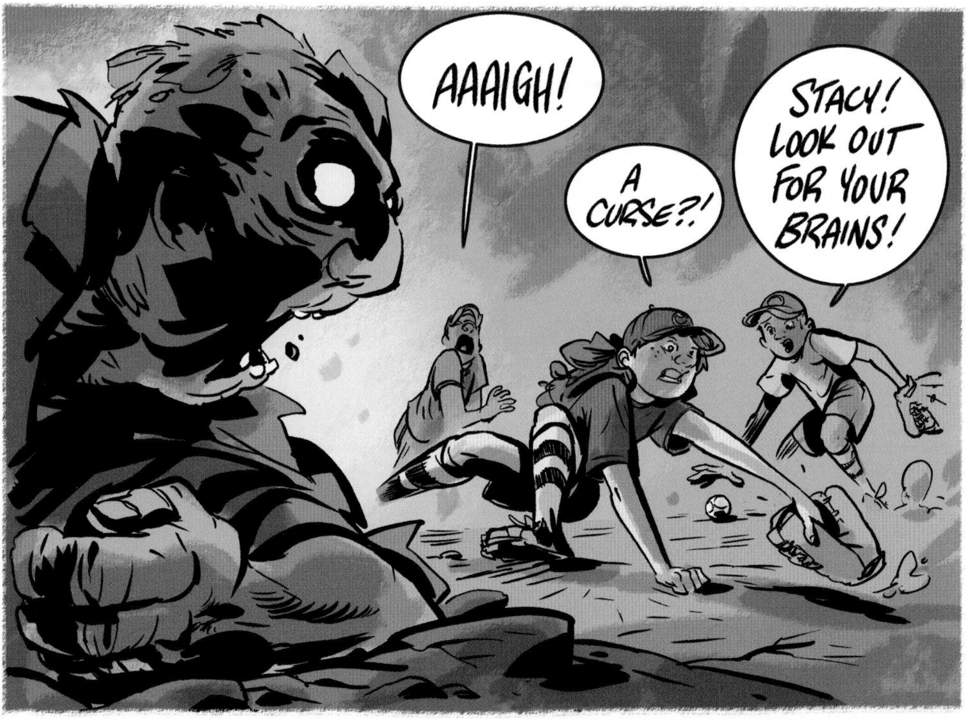
AAAIGH!
A CURSE?!
STACY! LOOK OUT FOR YOUR BRAINS!

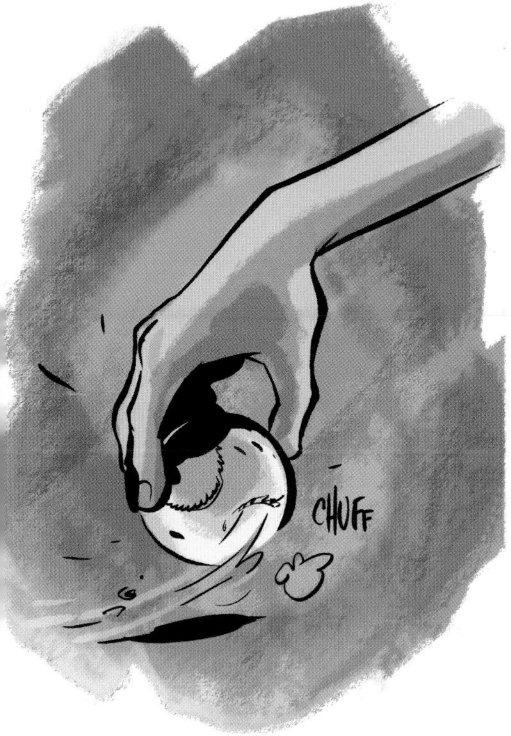
CHUFF

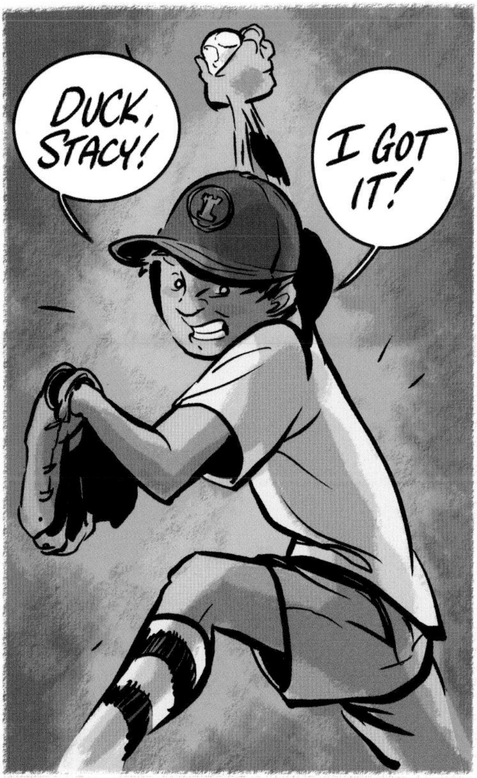
DUCK, STACY!
I GOT IT!

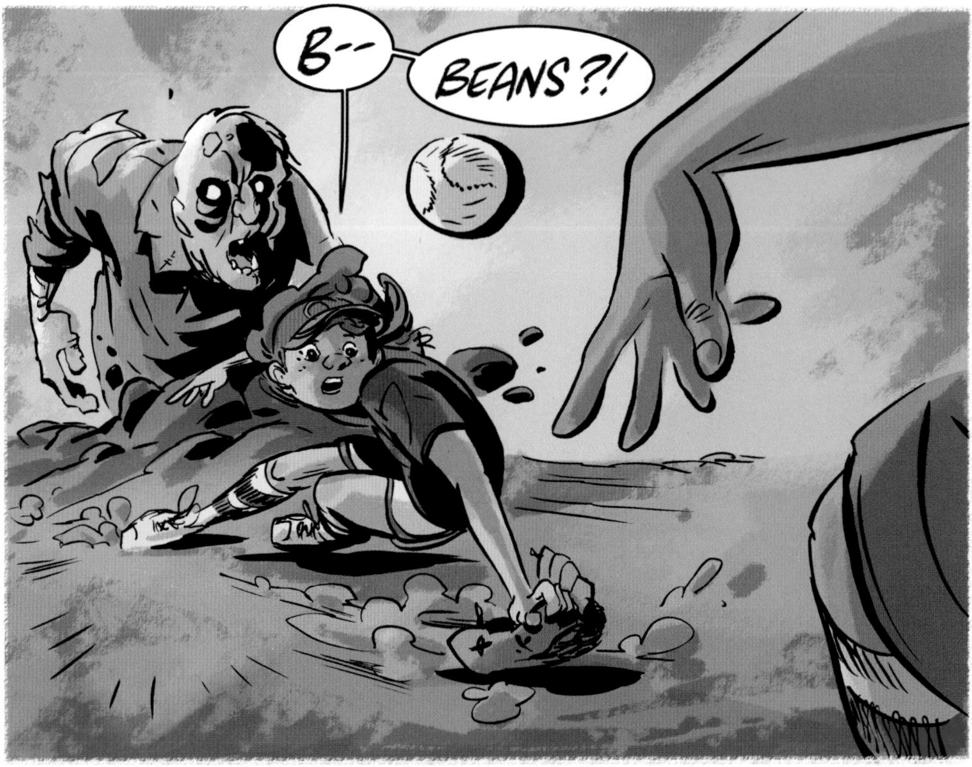
B--
BEANS?!

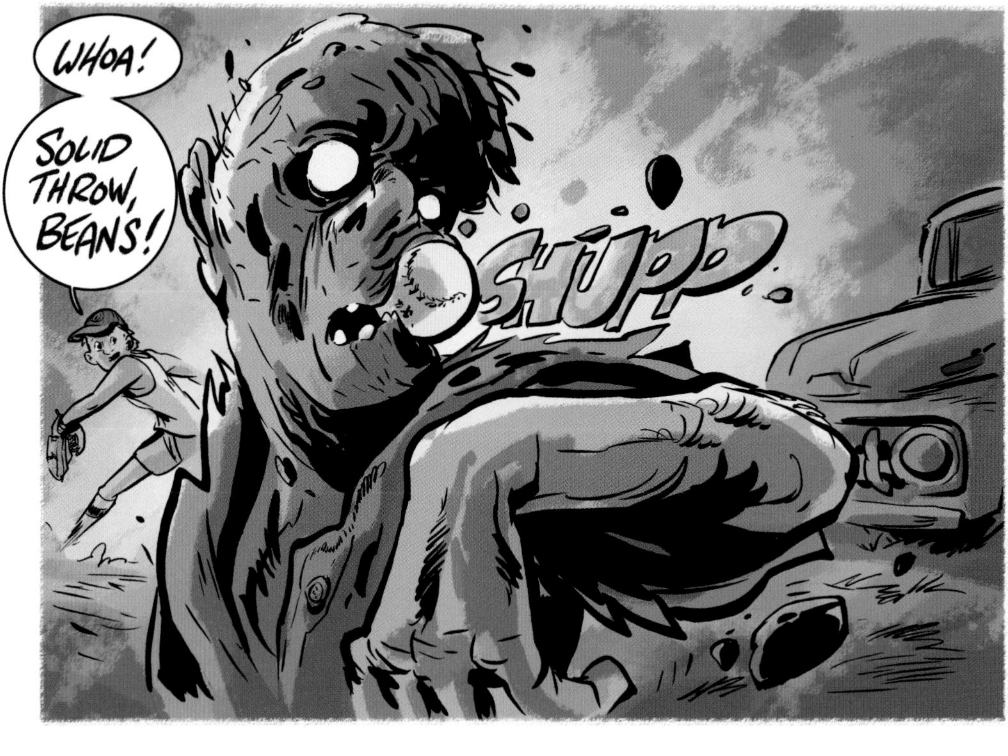
WHOA!
SOLID THROW, BEANS!
SHUPP

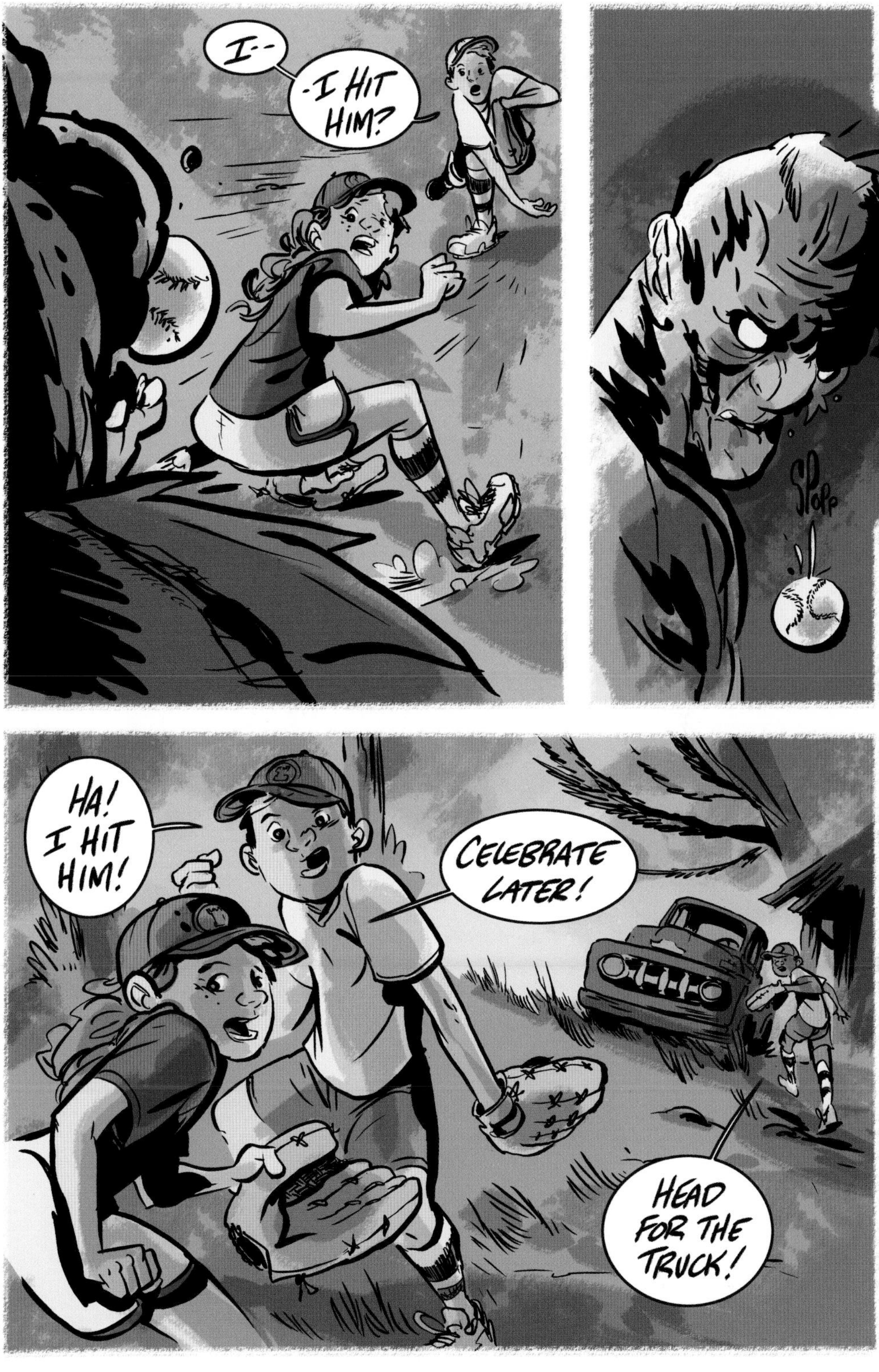
I--
-I HIT HIM?
SPOPP
HA! I HIT HIM!
CELEBRATE LATER!
HEAD FOR THE TRUCK!

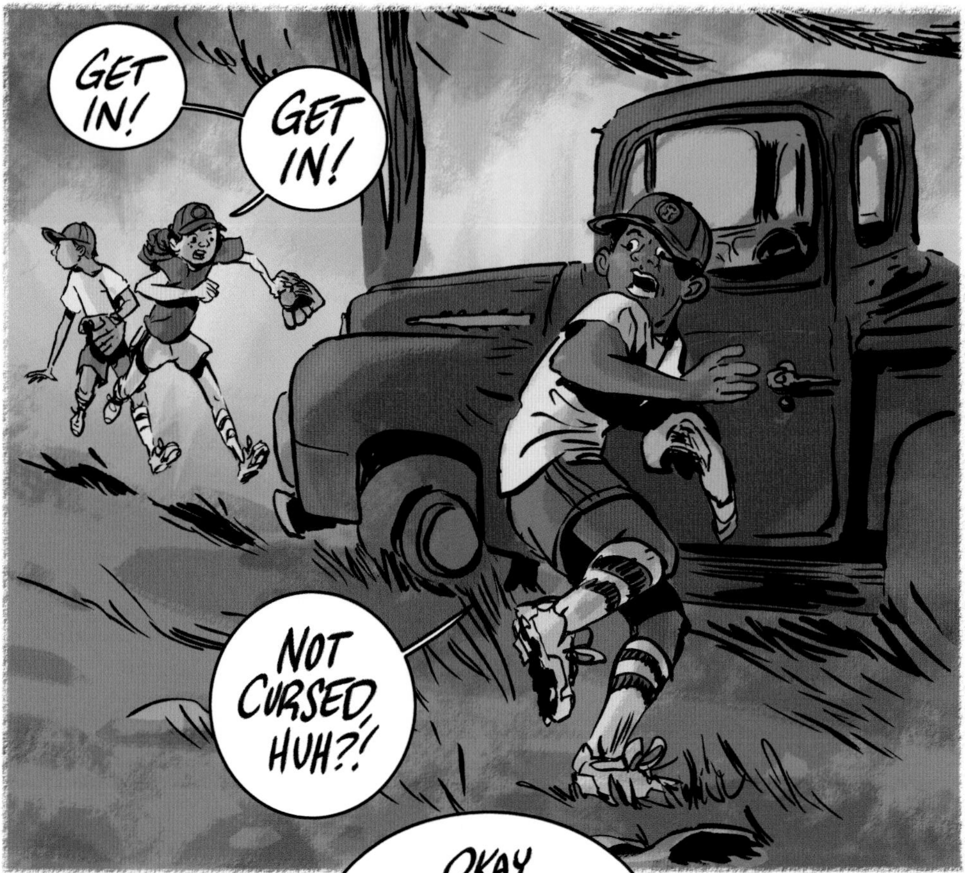
GET IN!
GET IN!
NOT CURSED, HUH?!

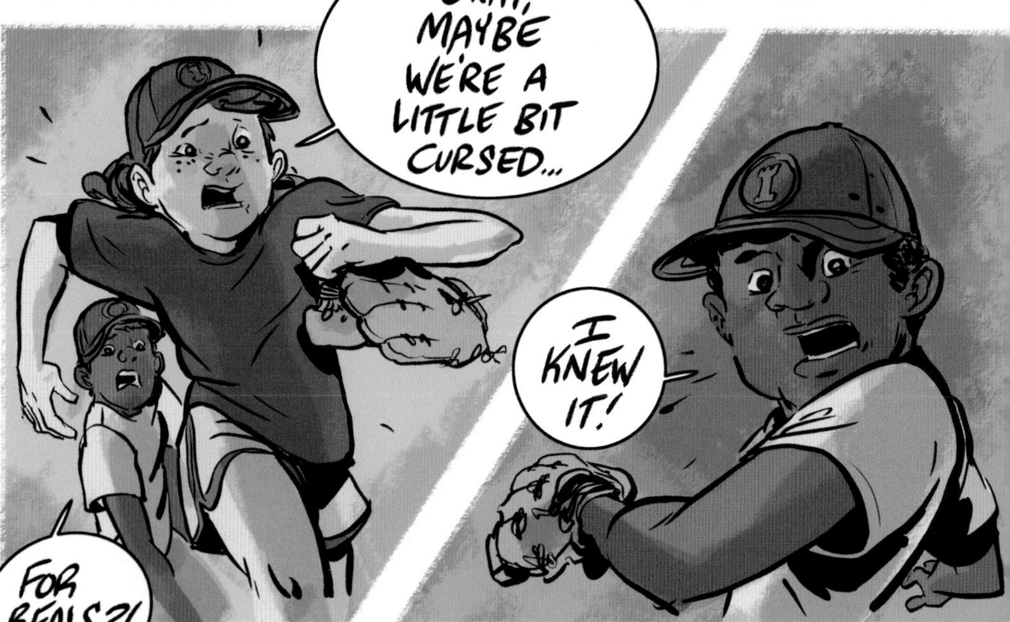
OKAY, MAYBE WE'RE A LITTLE BIT CURSED...
FOR REALS?!
I KNEW IT!

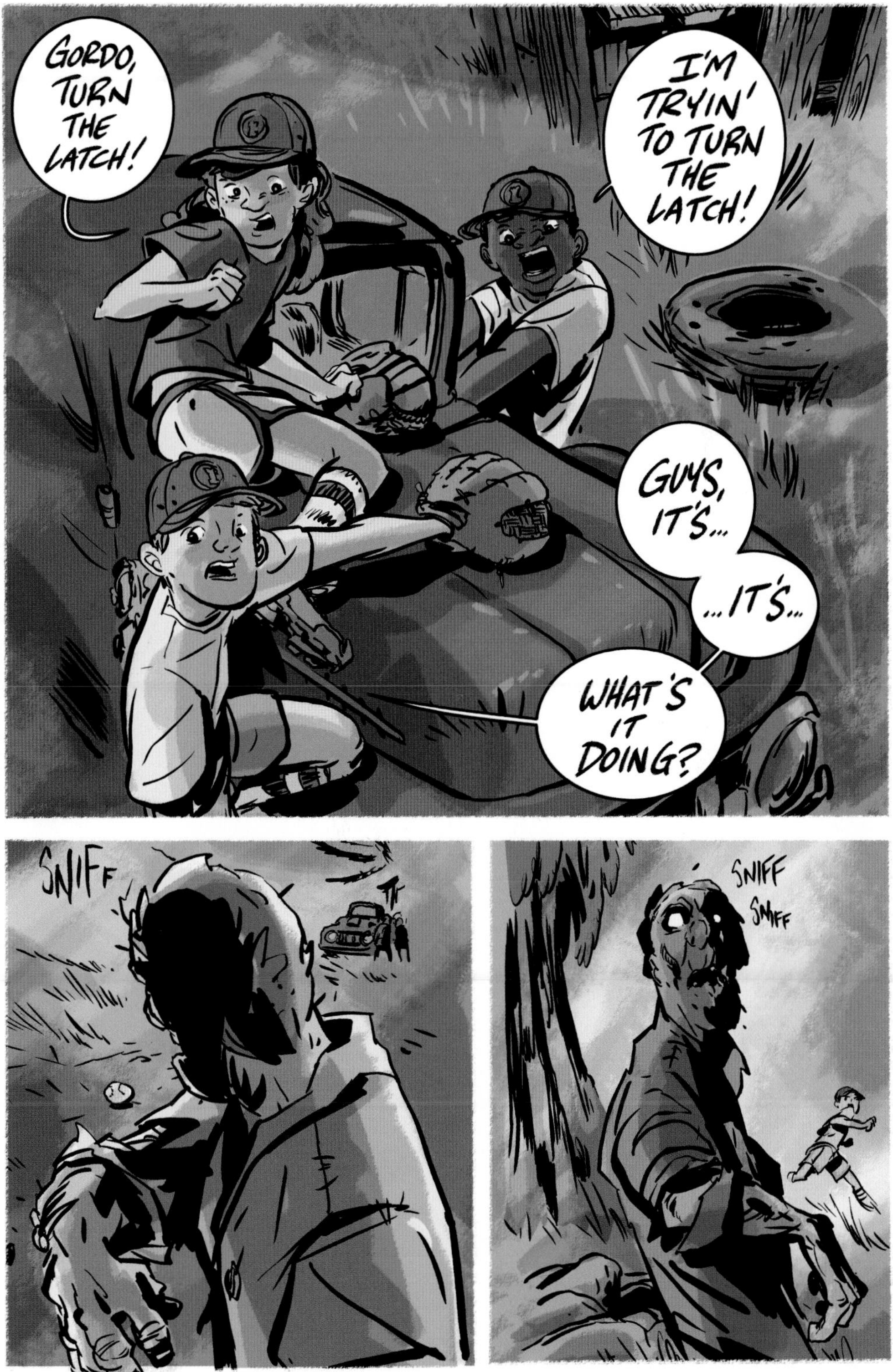
GORDO, TURN THE LATCH!
I'M TRYIN' TO TURN THE LATCH!
GUYS, IT'S...
...IT'S...
WHAT'S IT DOING?
SNIFF
SNIFF
SNIFF

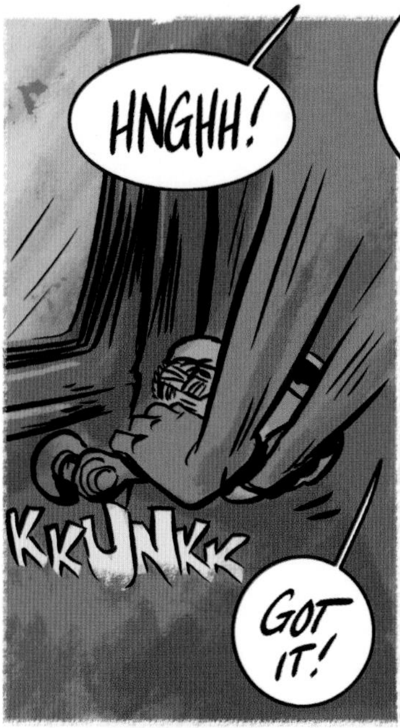
HNGHH!
KKUNKK
GOT IT!
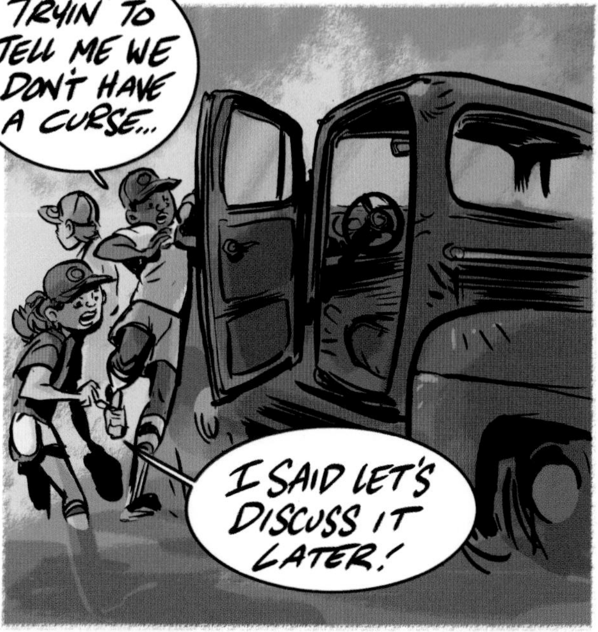
TRYIN' TO TELL ME WE DON'T HAVE A CURSE...
I SAID LET'S DISCUSS IT LATER!
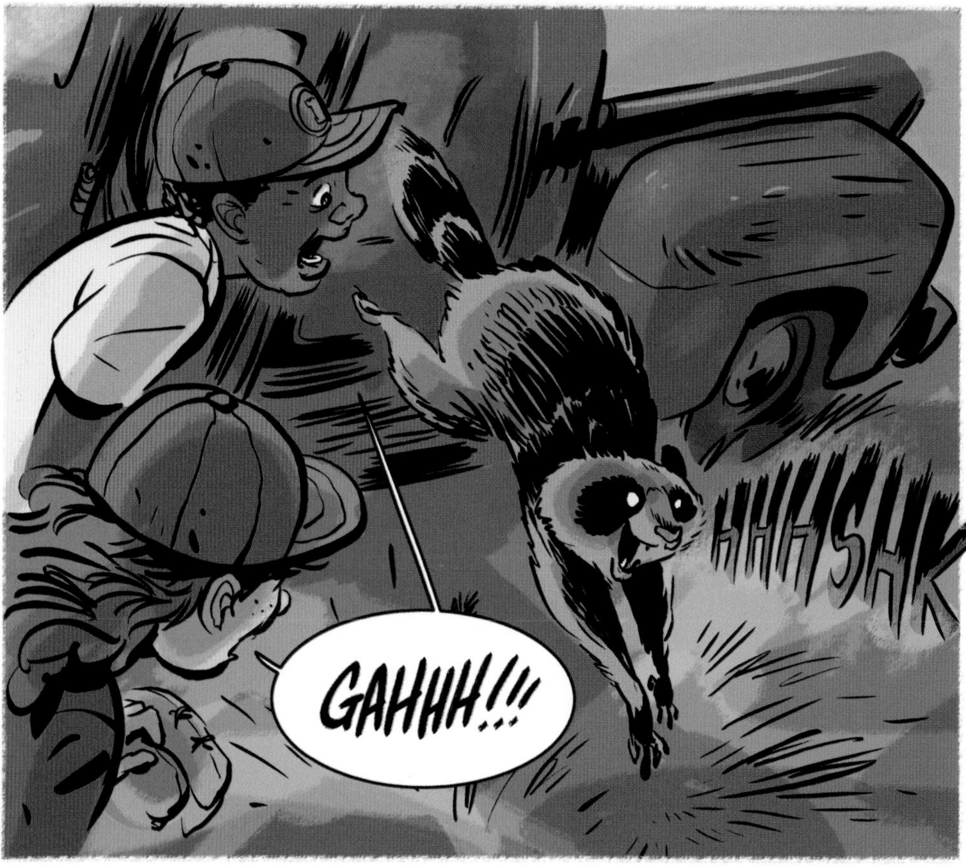
HHHSHK
GAHHH!!!

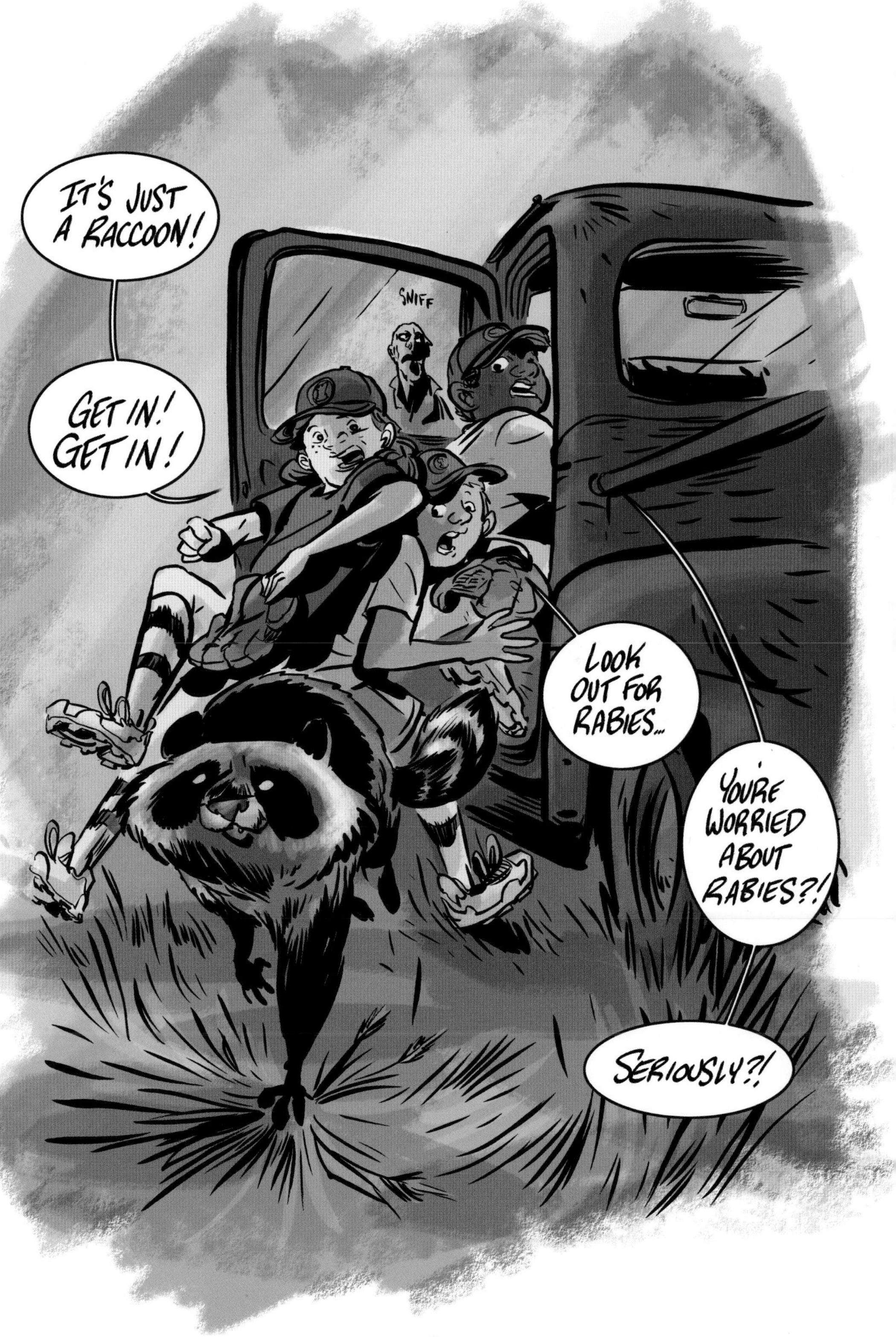
IT'S JUST A RACCOON!
GET IN! GET IN!
SNIFF
LOOK OUT FOR RABIES...
YOU'RE WORRIED ABOUT RABIES?!
SERIOUSLY?!

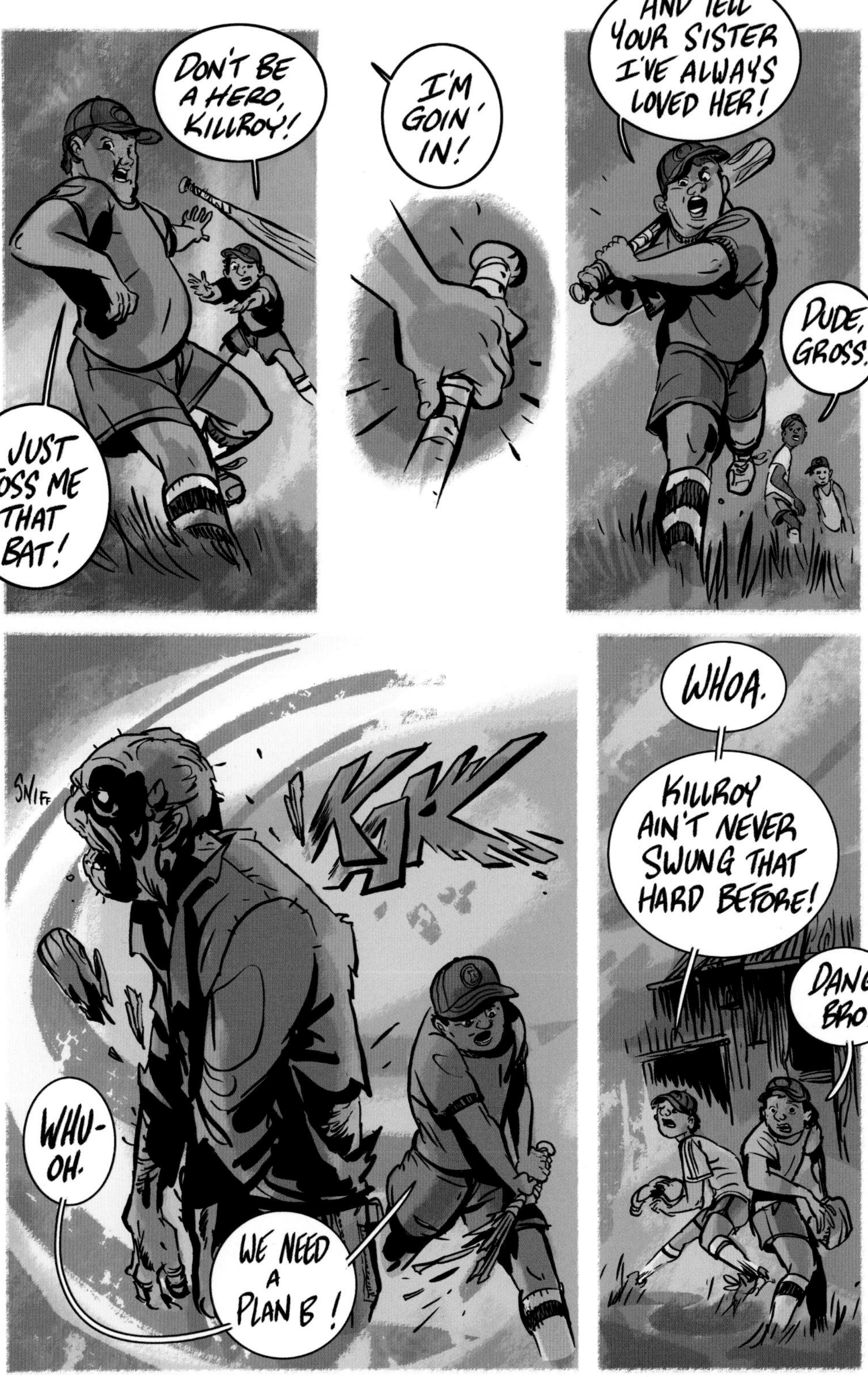
DON'T BE A HERO, KILLROY!
JUST TOSS ME THAT BAT!
I'M GOIN' IN!
AND TELL YOUR SISTER I'VE ALWAYS LOVED HER!
DUDE, GROSS.
SNIFF
KGK
WHU-OH.
WE NEED A PLAN B!
WHOA.
KILLROY AIN'T NEVER SWUNG THAT HARD BEFORE!
DANG, BRO!

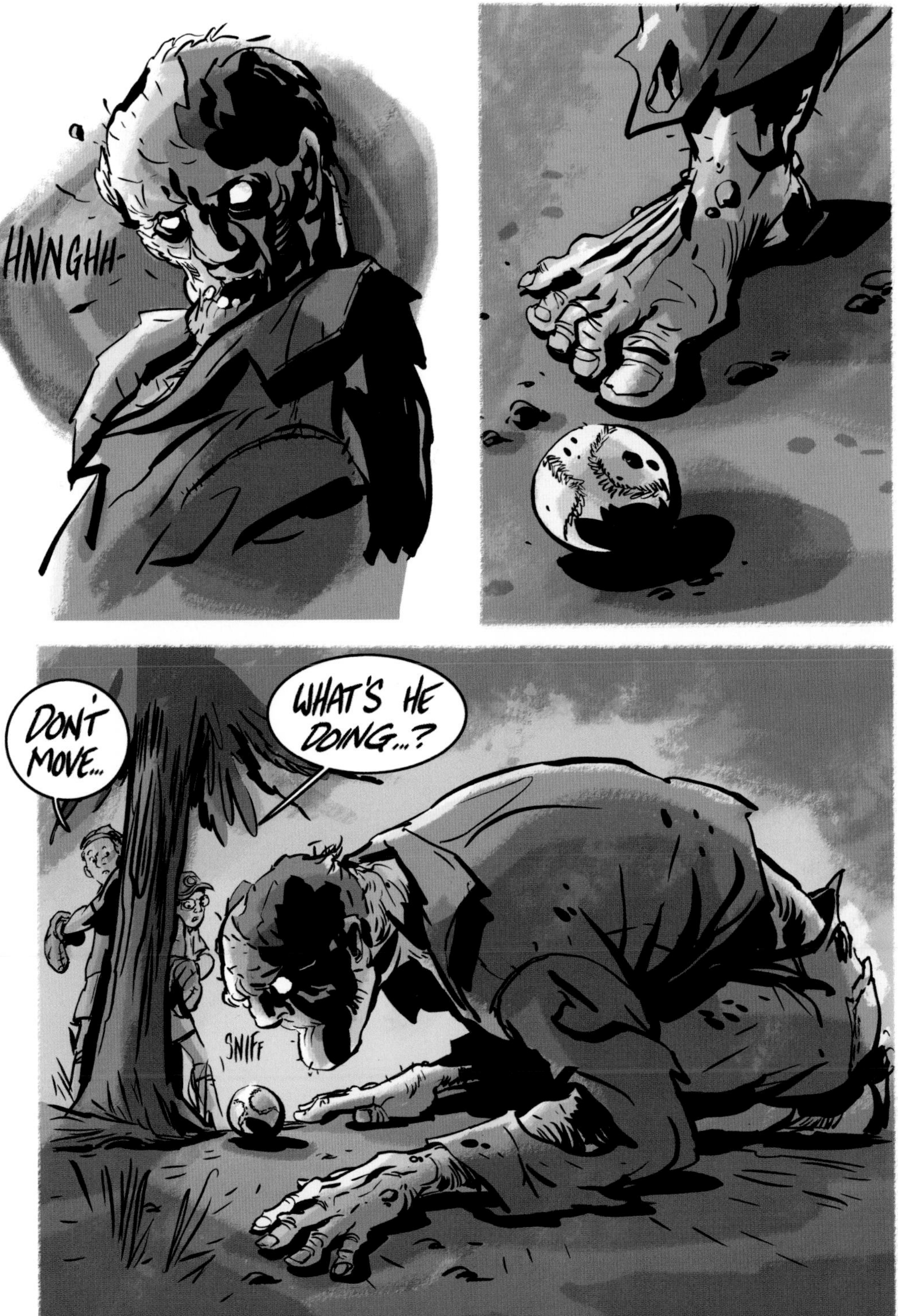
HNNGHH-
DON'T MOVE...
WHAT'S HE DOING...?
SNIFF

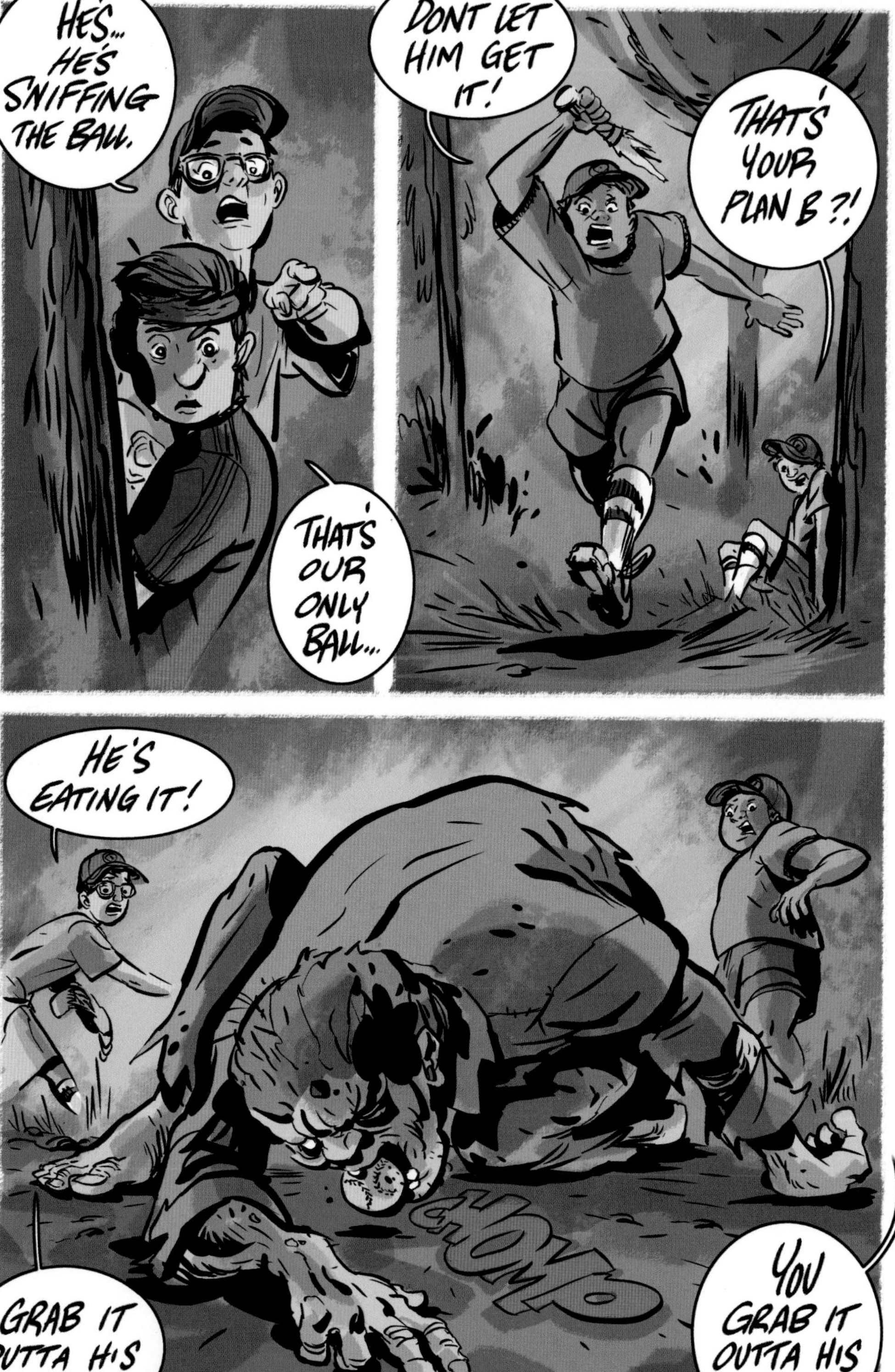
HE'S... HE'S SNIFFING THE BALL.
THAT'S OUR ONLY BALL...
DON'T LET HIM GET IT!
THAT'S YOUR PLAN B?!
HE'S EATING IT!
CHOMP
GRAB IT OUTTA HIS FACE!
YOU GRAB IT OUTTA HIS FACE!

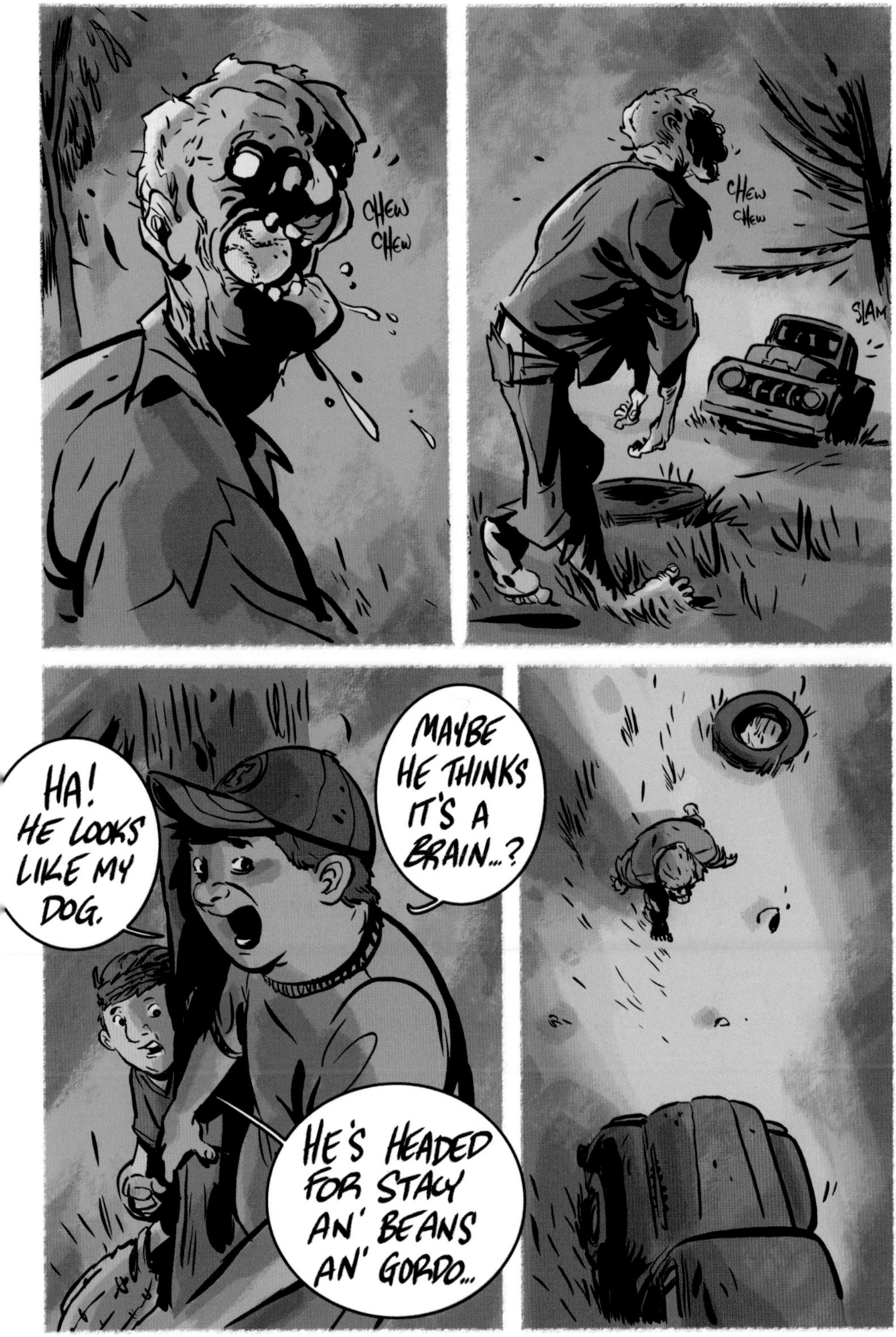
CHEW
CHEW
CHEW
CHEW
SLAM
HA! HE LOOKS LIKE MY DOG.
MAYBE HE THINKS IT'S A BRAIN...?
HE'S HEADED FOR STACY AN' BEANS AN' GORDO...

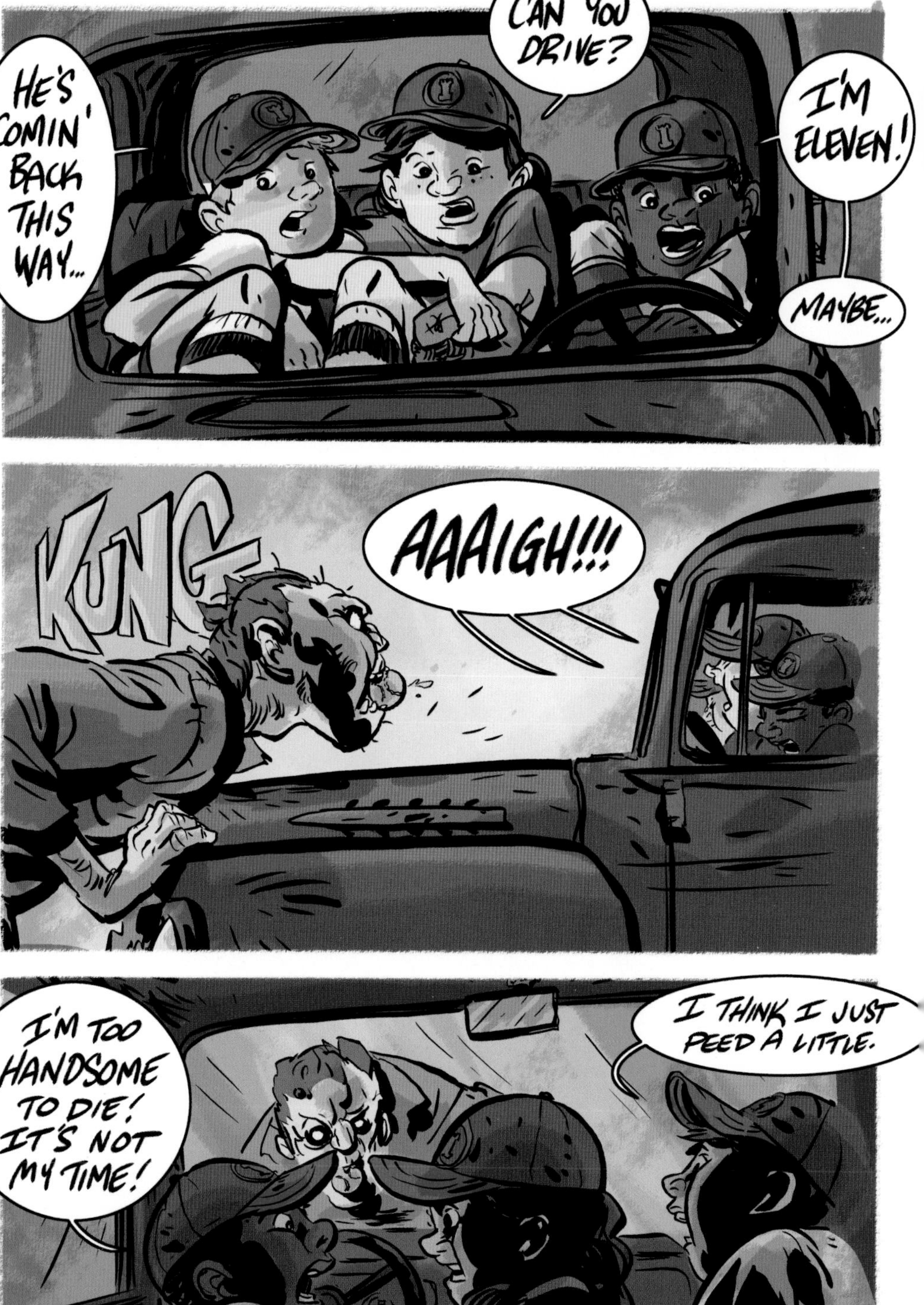
HE'S COMIN' BACK THIS WAY...
CAN YOU DRIVE?
I'M ELEVEN!
MAYBE...
KUNG
AAAIGH!!!
I'M TOO HANDSOME TO DIE! IT'S NOT MY TIME!
I THINK I JUST PEED A LITTLE.

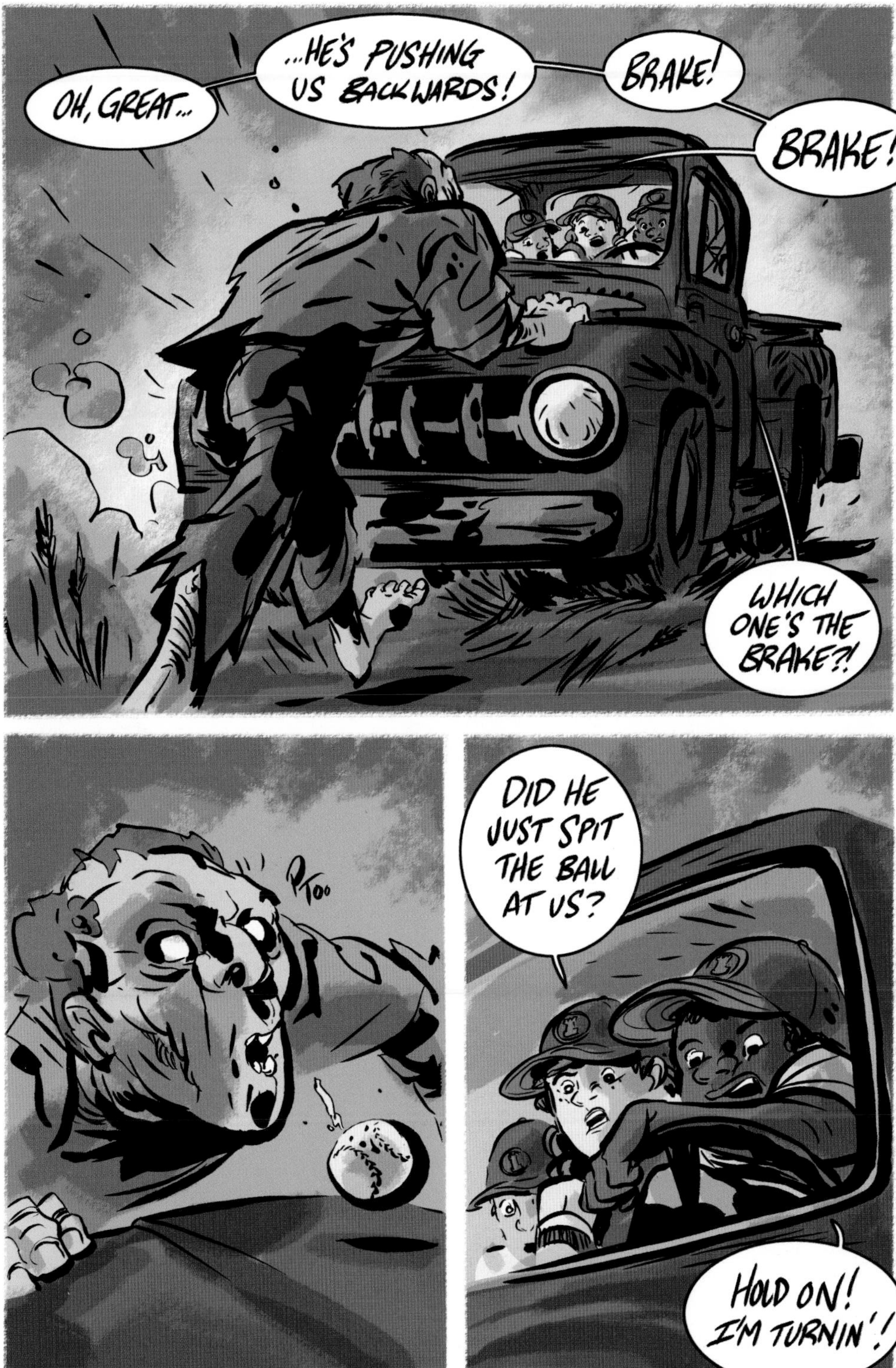
OH, GREAT...
...HE'S PUSHING US BACKWARDS!
BRAKE!
BRAKE!
WHICH ONE'S THE BRAKE?!
PTOO
DID HE JUST SPIT THE BALL AT US?
HOLD ON! I'M TURNIN'!

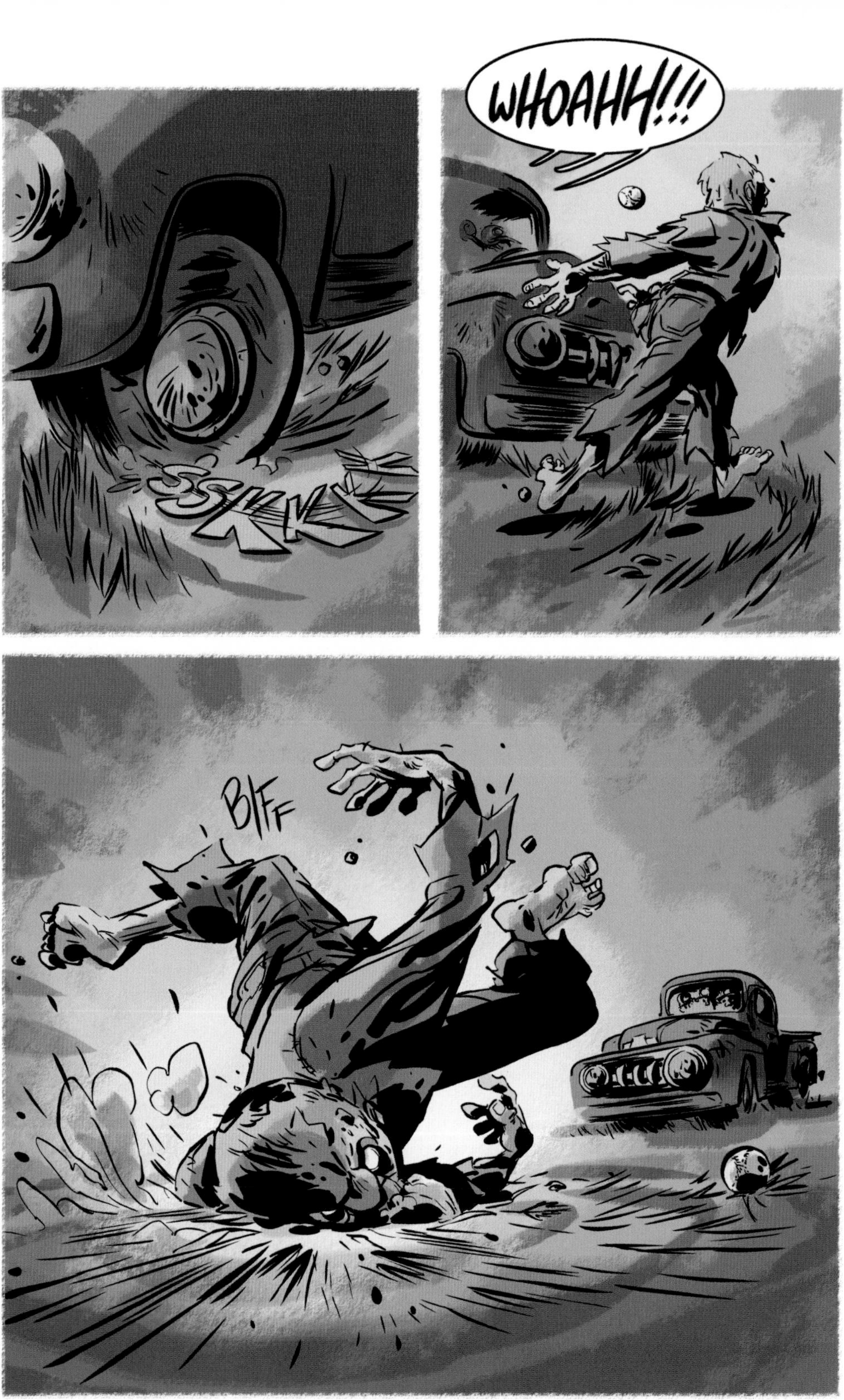
WHOAHH!!!
BIFF

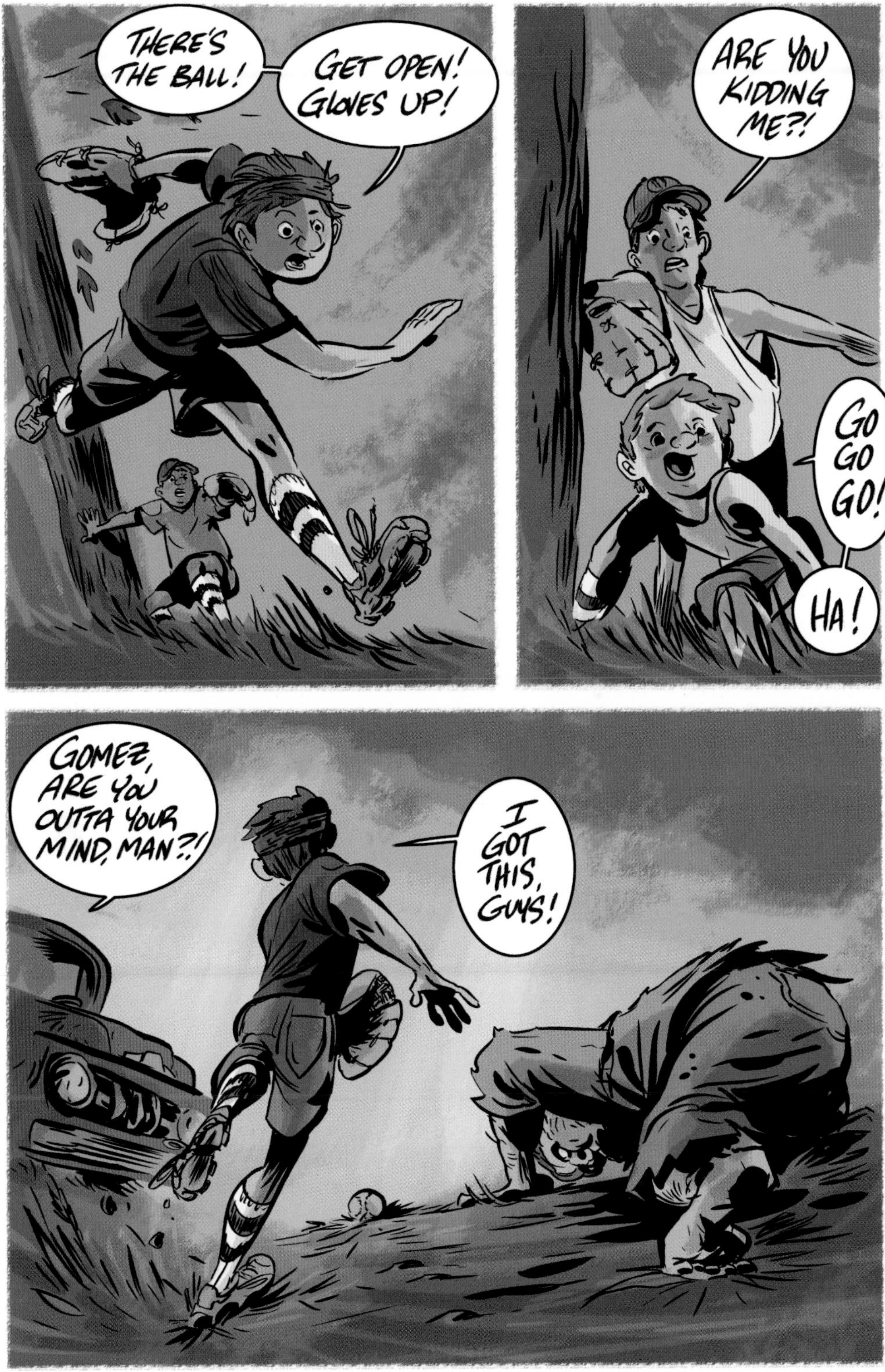
THERE'S THE BALL!
GET OPEN! GLOVES UP!
ARE YOU KIDDING ME?!
GO GO GO!
HA!
GOMEZ, ARE YOU OUTTA YOUR MIND, MAN?!
I GOT THIS, GUYS!

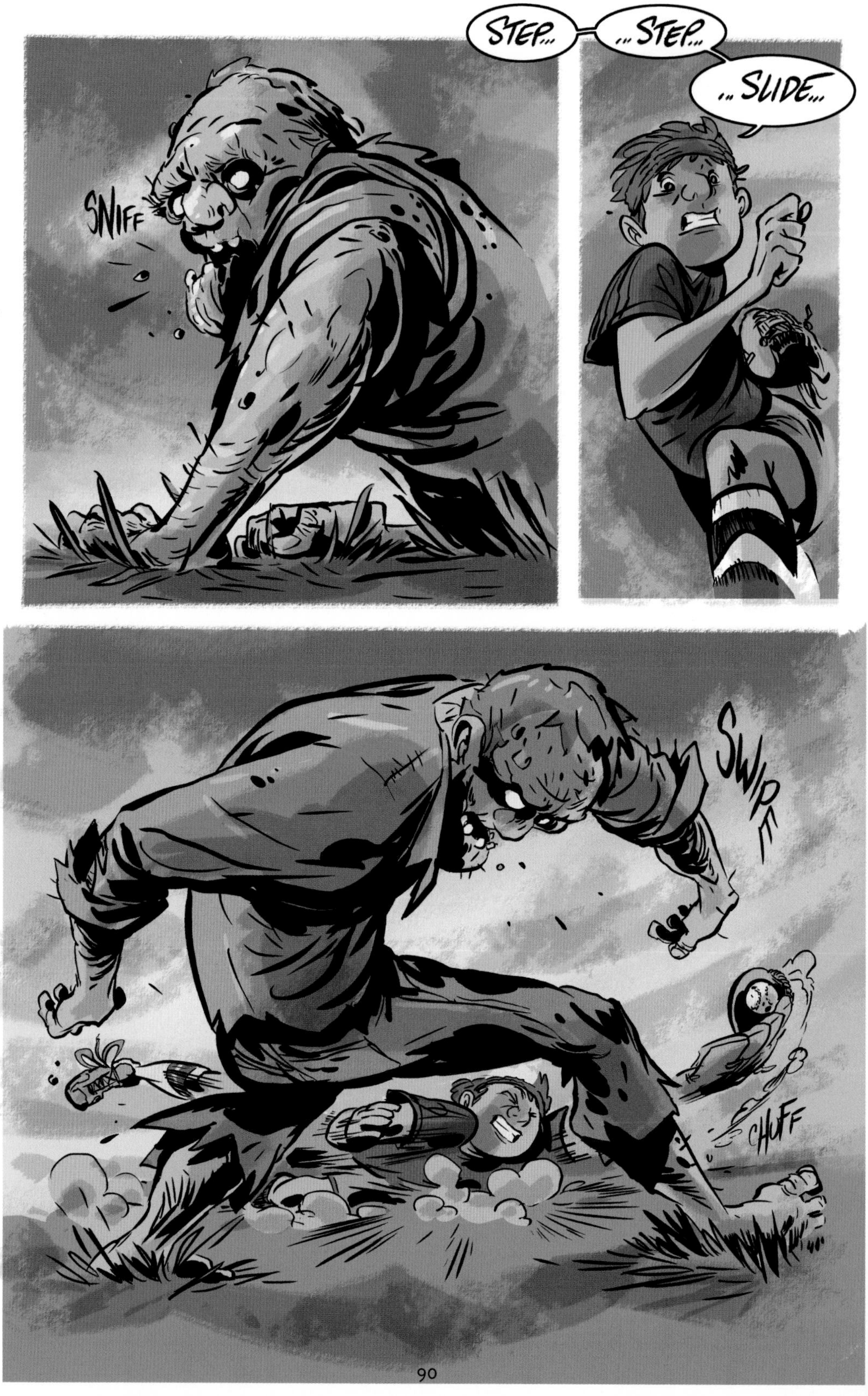
STEP...
...STEP...
...SLIDE...
SNIFF
SWIPE
CHUFF

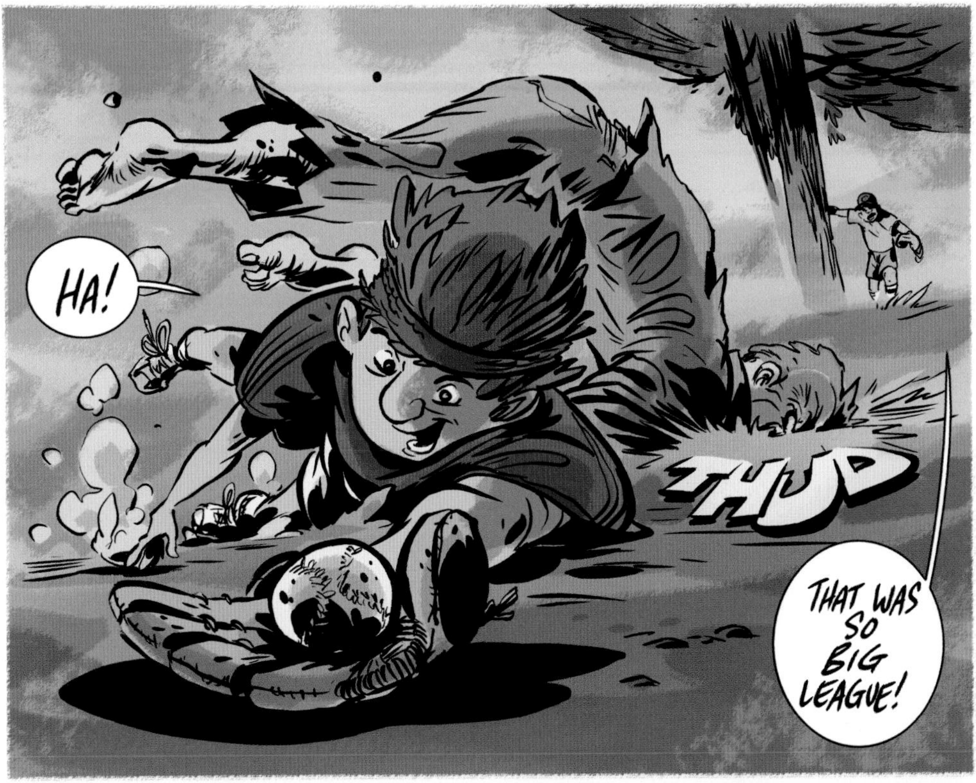
HA!
THUD
THAT WAS SO BIG LEAGUE!

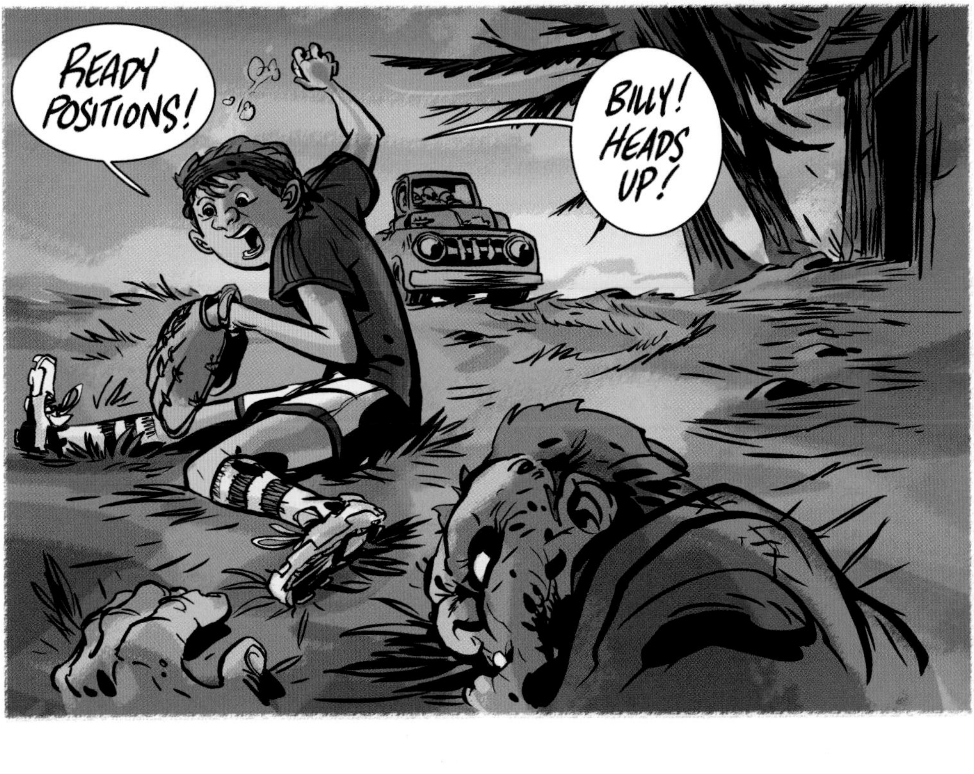
READY POSITIONS!
BILLY! HEADS UP!

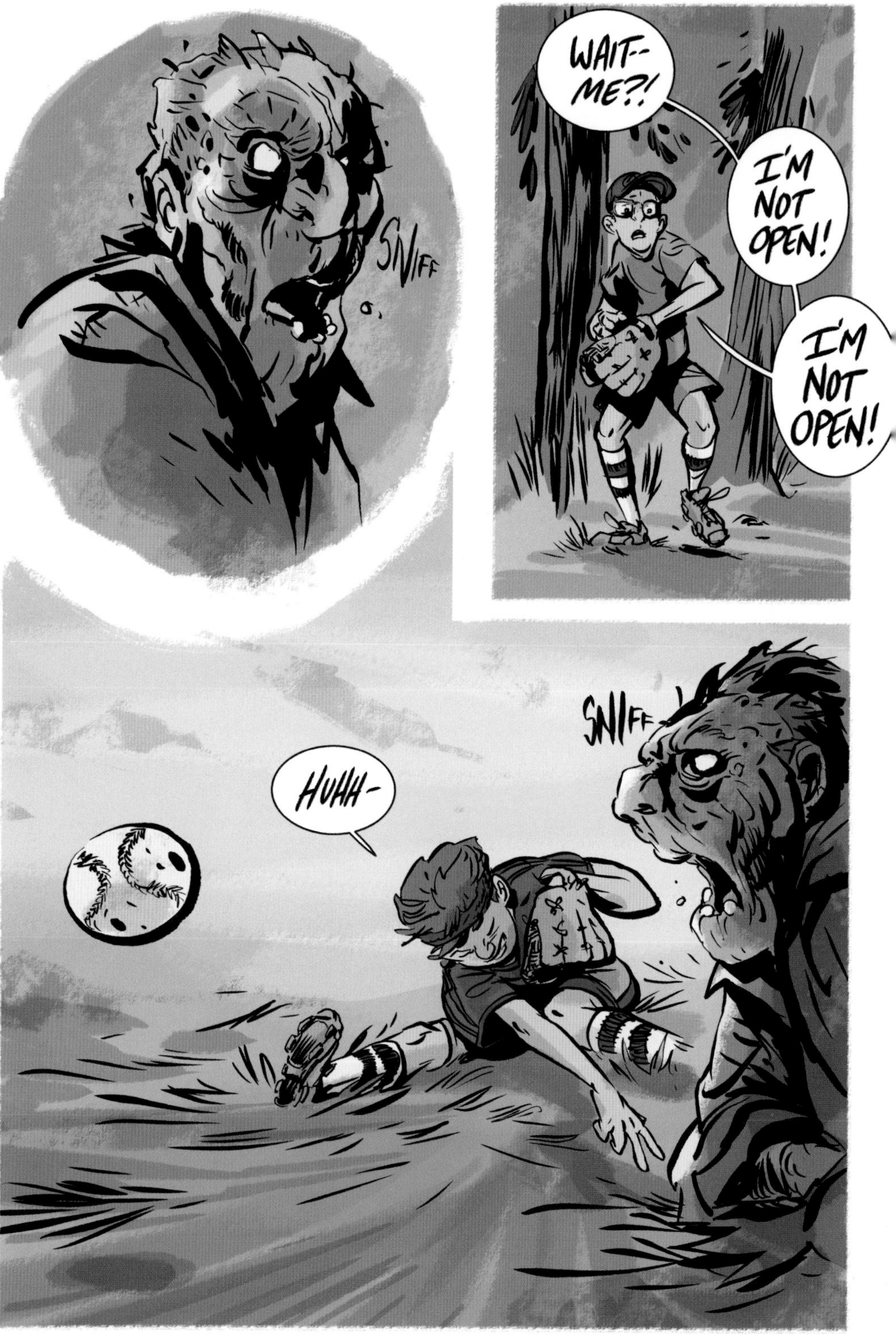
SNIFF
WAIT-- ME?!
I'M NOT OPEN!
I'M NOT OPEN!
SNIFF
HUHH-

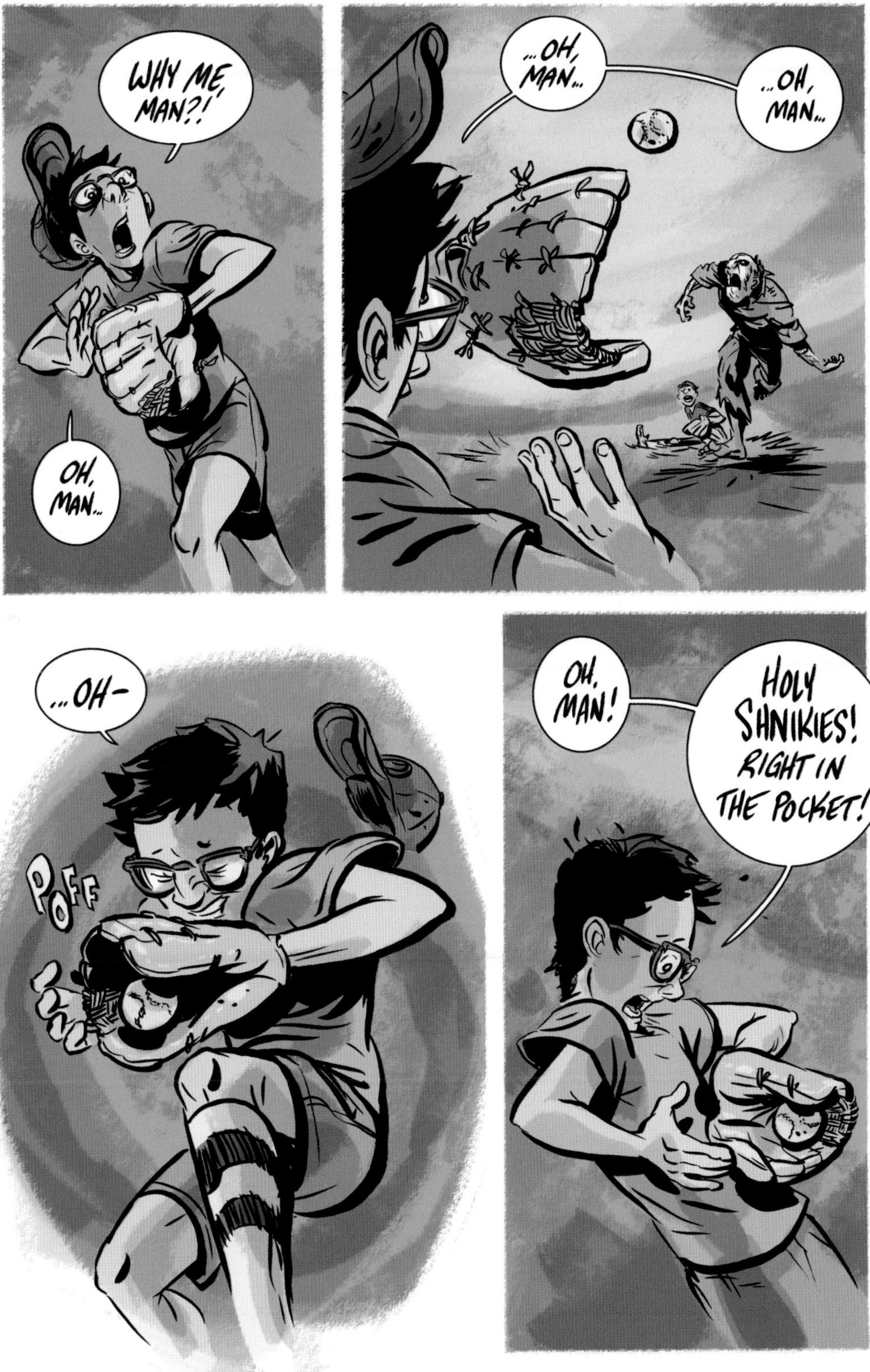
WHY ME, MAN?!
OH, MAN...
...OH, MAN...
...OH, MAN...
...OH-
POFF
OH, MAN!
HOLY SHNIKIES! RIGHT IN THE POCKET!

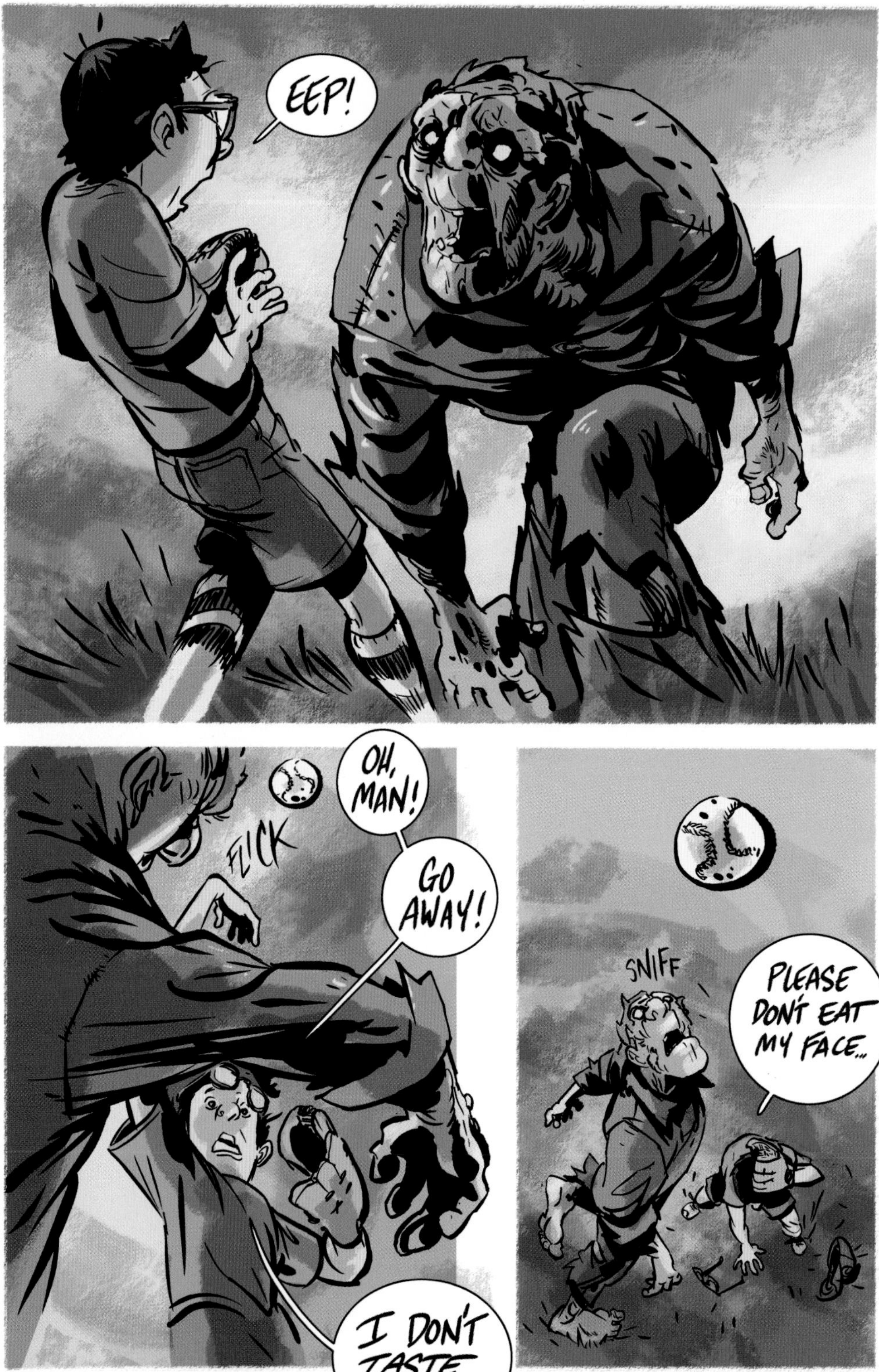
EEP!
FLICK
OH, MAN!
GO AWAY!
I DON'T TASTE GOOD!
SNIFF
PLEASE DON'T EAT MY FACE...

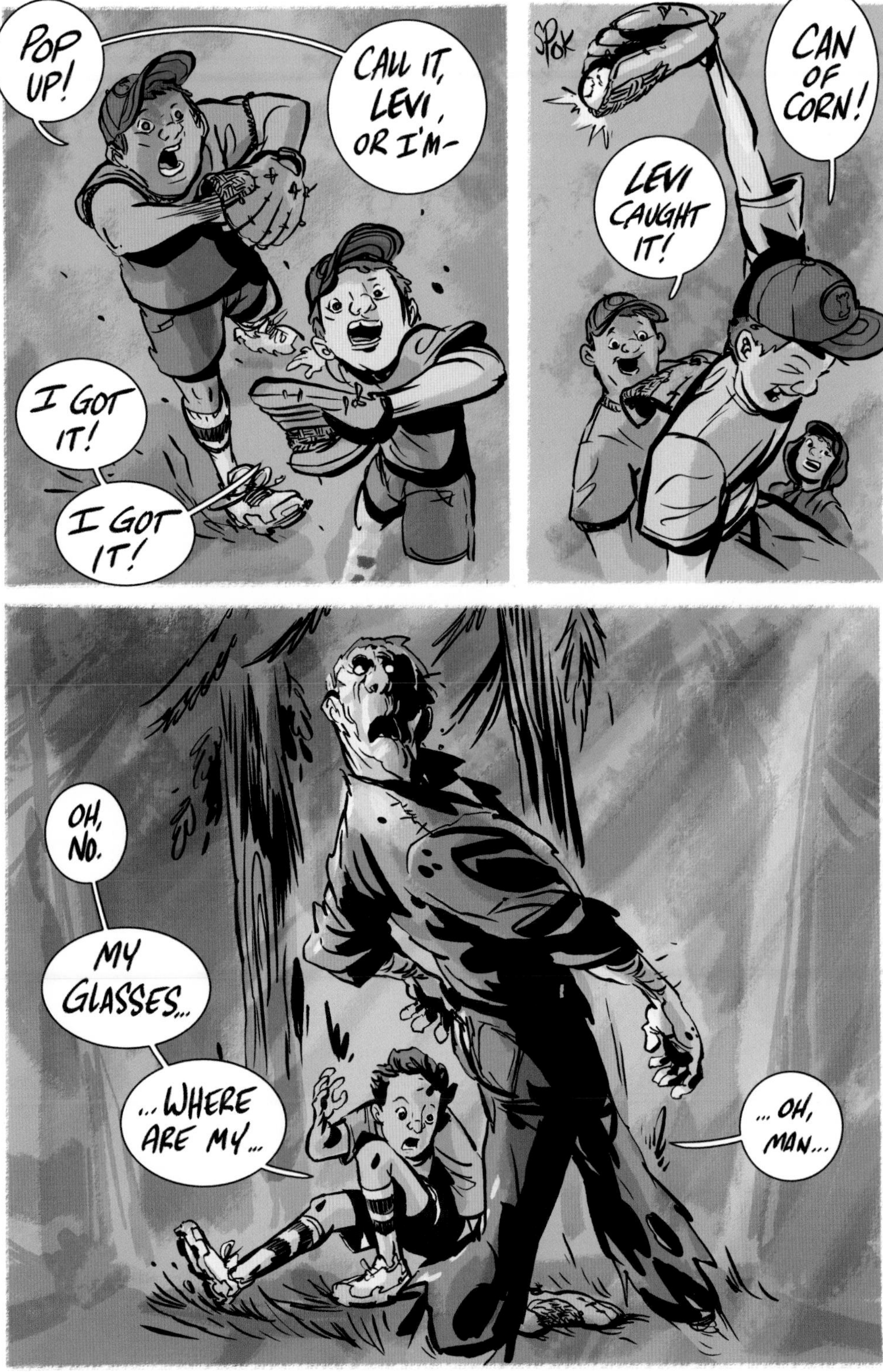
POP UP!
CALL IT, LEVI, OR I'M-
I GOT IT!
I GOT IT!
SPOK
CAN OF CORN!
LEVI CAUGHT IT!
OH, NO.
MY GLASSES...
...WHERE ARE MY...
...OH, MAN...

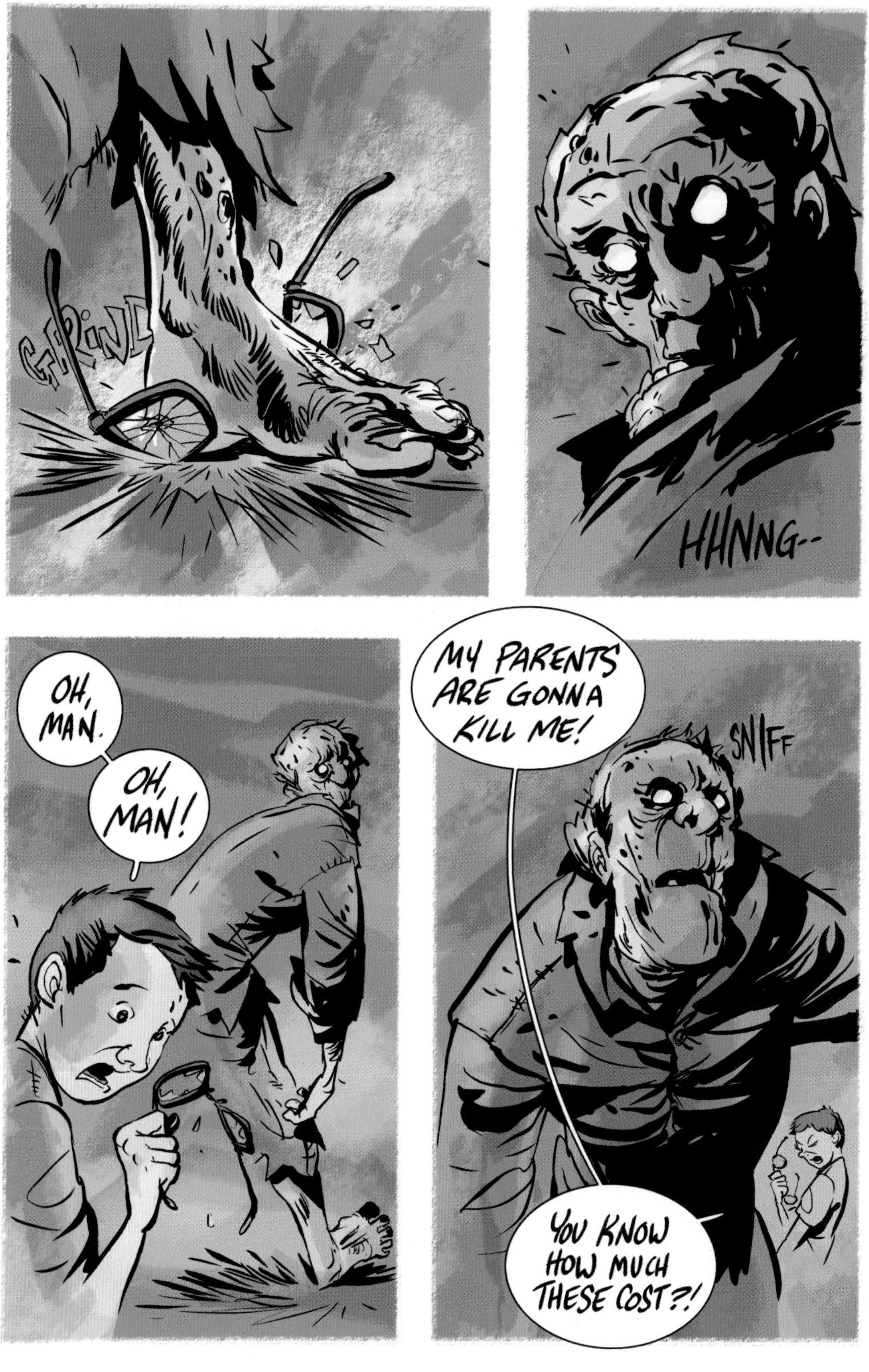
GRIND
HHNNG--
OH, MAN.
OH, MAN!
MY PARENTS ARE GONNA KILL ME!
SNIFF
YOU KNOW HOW MUCH THESE COST?!

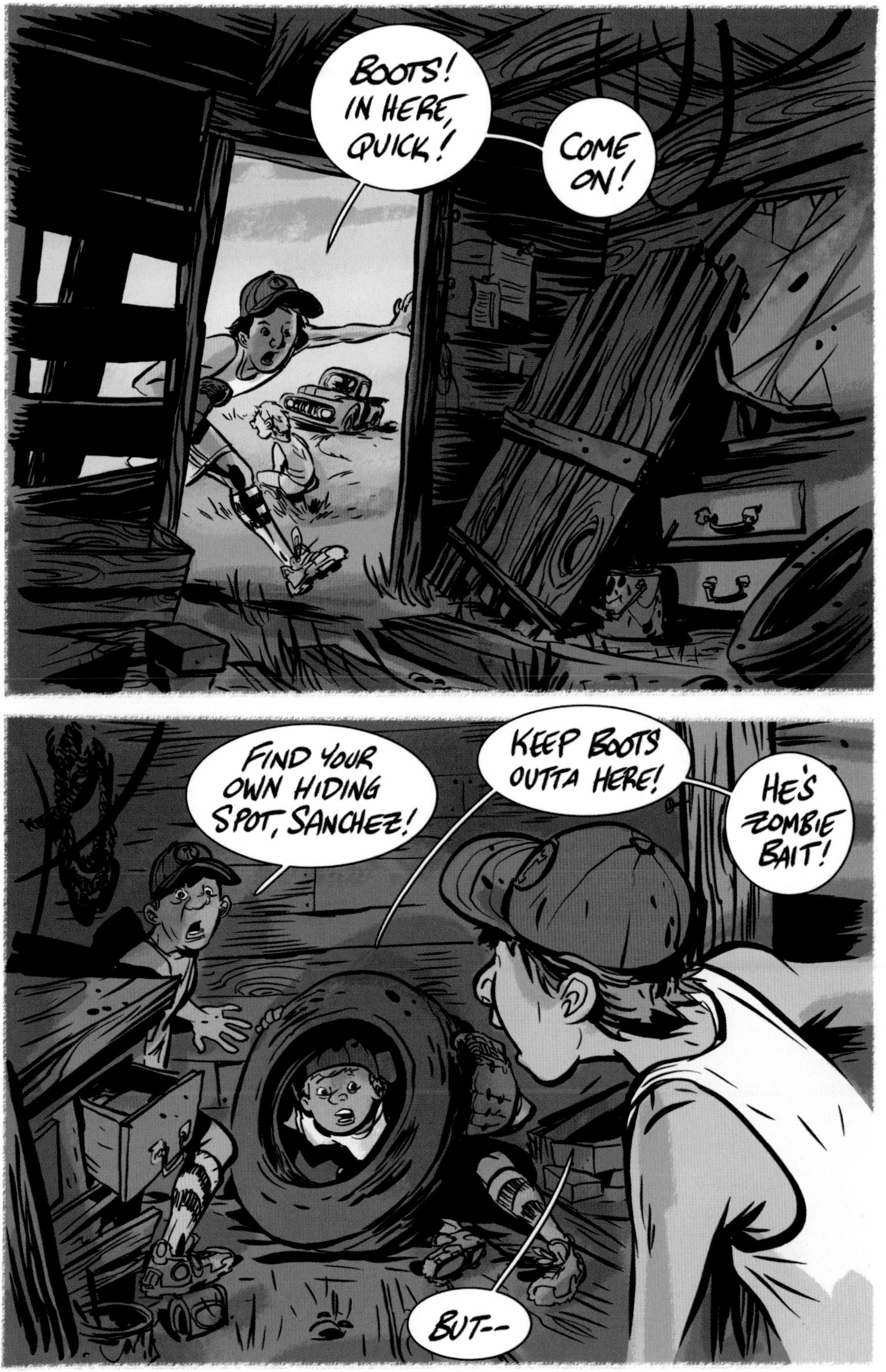
BOOTS! IN HERE, QUICK!
COME ON!
FIND YOUR OWN HIDING SPOT, SANCHEZ!
KEEP BOOTS OUTTA HERE!
HE'S ZOMBIE BAIT!
BUT--

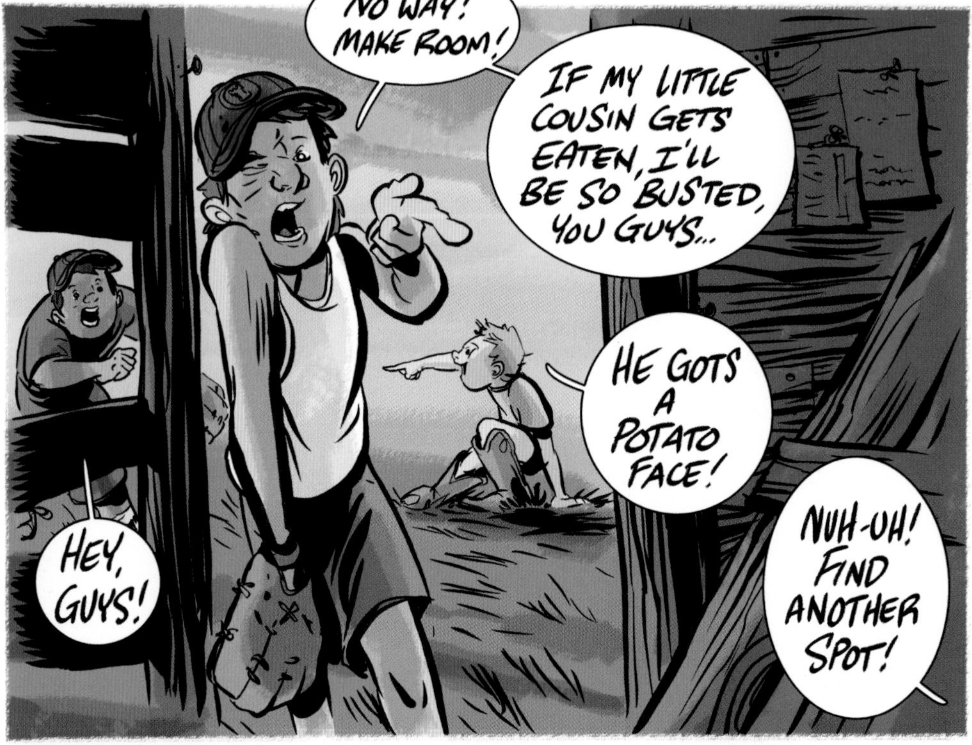
NO WAY! MAKE ROOM!
IF MY LITTLE COUSIN GETS EATEN, I'LL BE SO BUSTED, YOU GUYS...
HE GOTS A POTATO FACE!
HEY, GUYS!
NUH-UH! FIND ANOTHER SPOT!

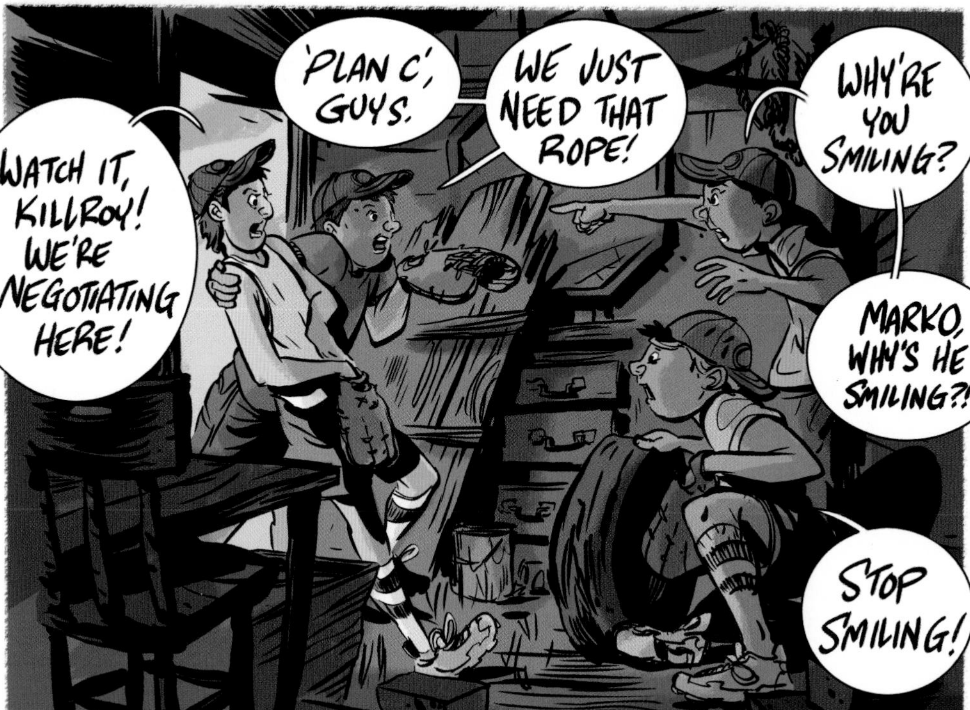
'PLAN C', GUYS.
WE JUST NEED THAT ROPE!
WATCH IT, KILLROY! WE'RE NEGOTIATING HERE!
WHY'RE YOU SMILING?
MARKO, WHY'S HE SMILING?!
STOP SMILING!

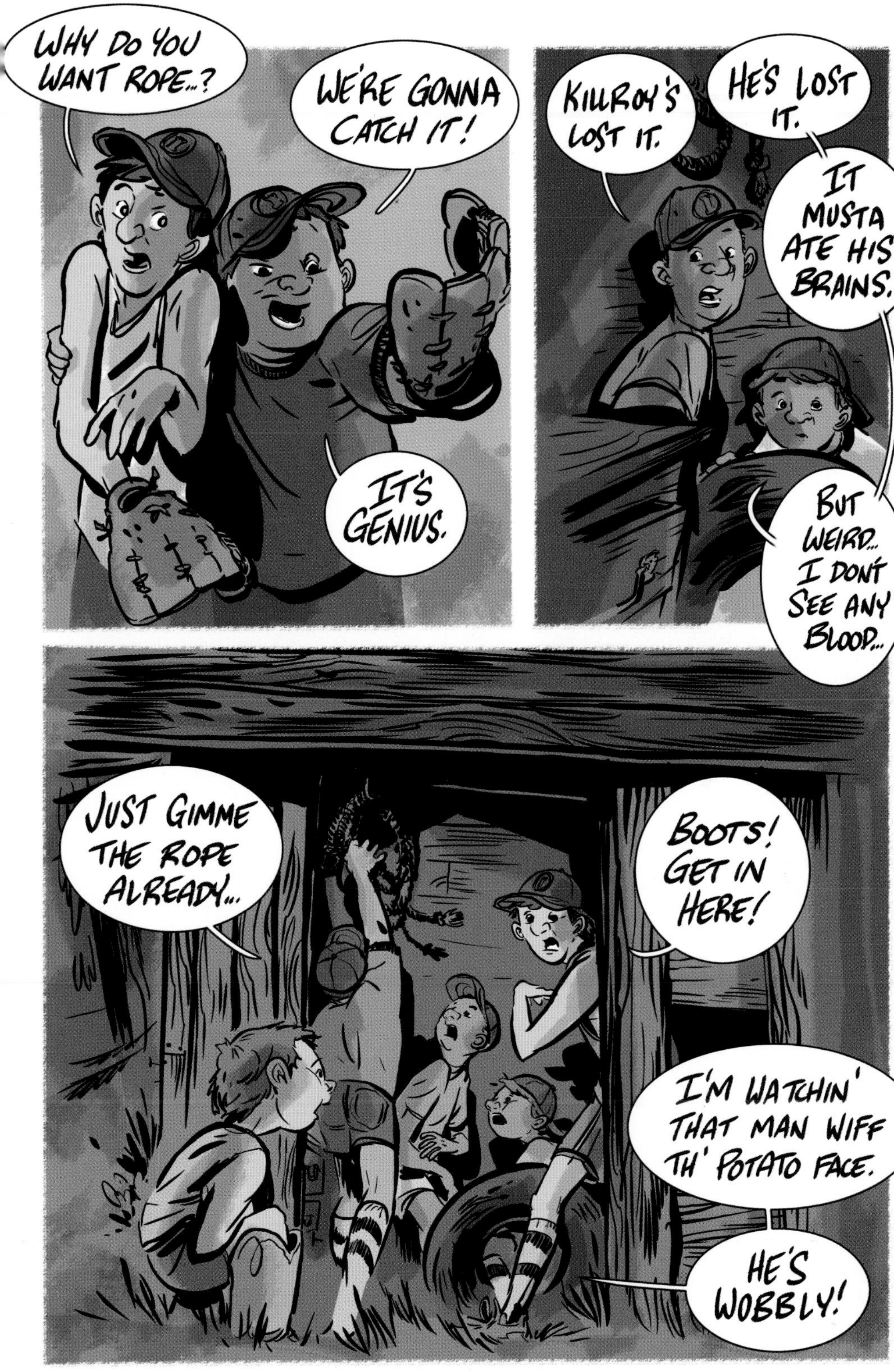
WHY DO YOU WANT ROPE...?
WE'RE GONNA CATCH IT!
IT'S GENIUS.
KILLROY'S LOST IT.
HE'S LOST IT.
IT MUSTA ATE HIS BRAINS.
BUT WEIRD... I DON'T SEE ANY BLOOD...
JUST GIMME THE ROPE ALREADY...
BOOTS! GET IN HERE!
I'M WATCHIN' THAT MAN WIFF TH' POTATO FACE.
HE'S WOBBLY!

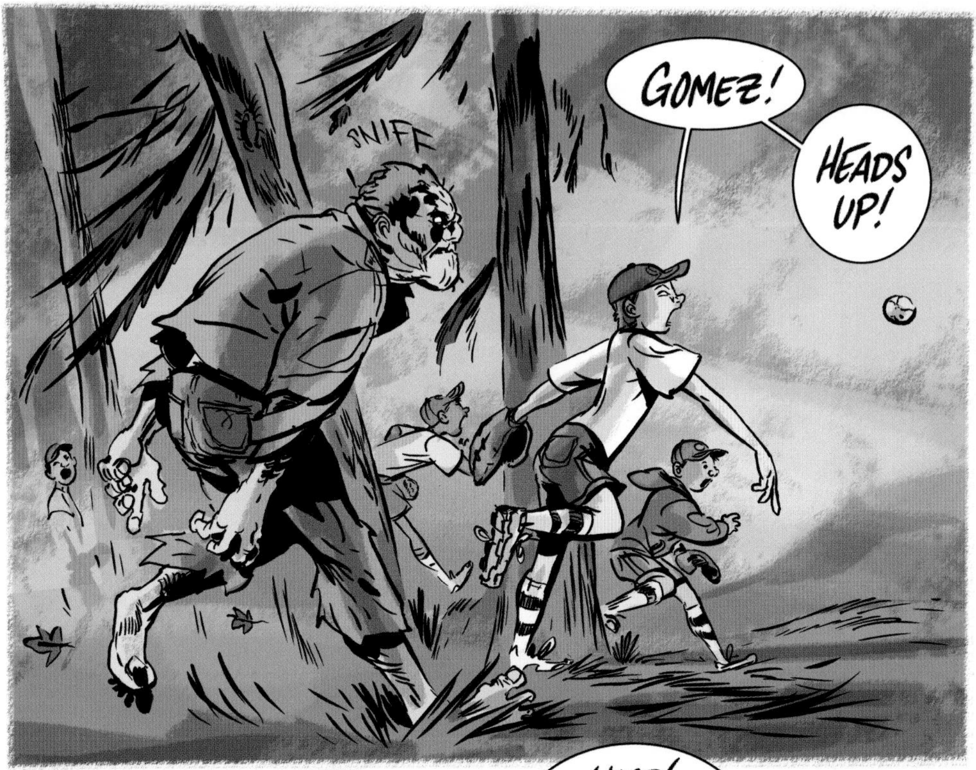
SNIFF
GOMEZ!
HEADS UP!

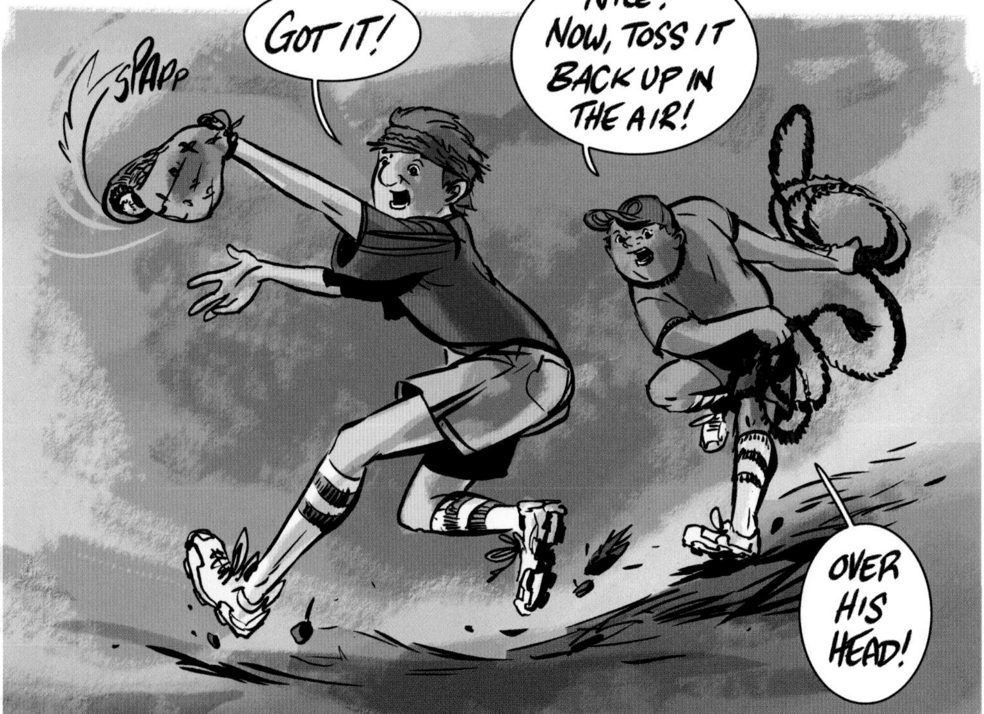
SPAPP
GOT IT!
NICE! NOW, TOSS IT BACK UP IN THE AIR!
OVER HIS HEAD!

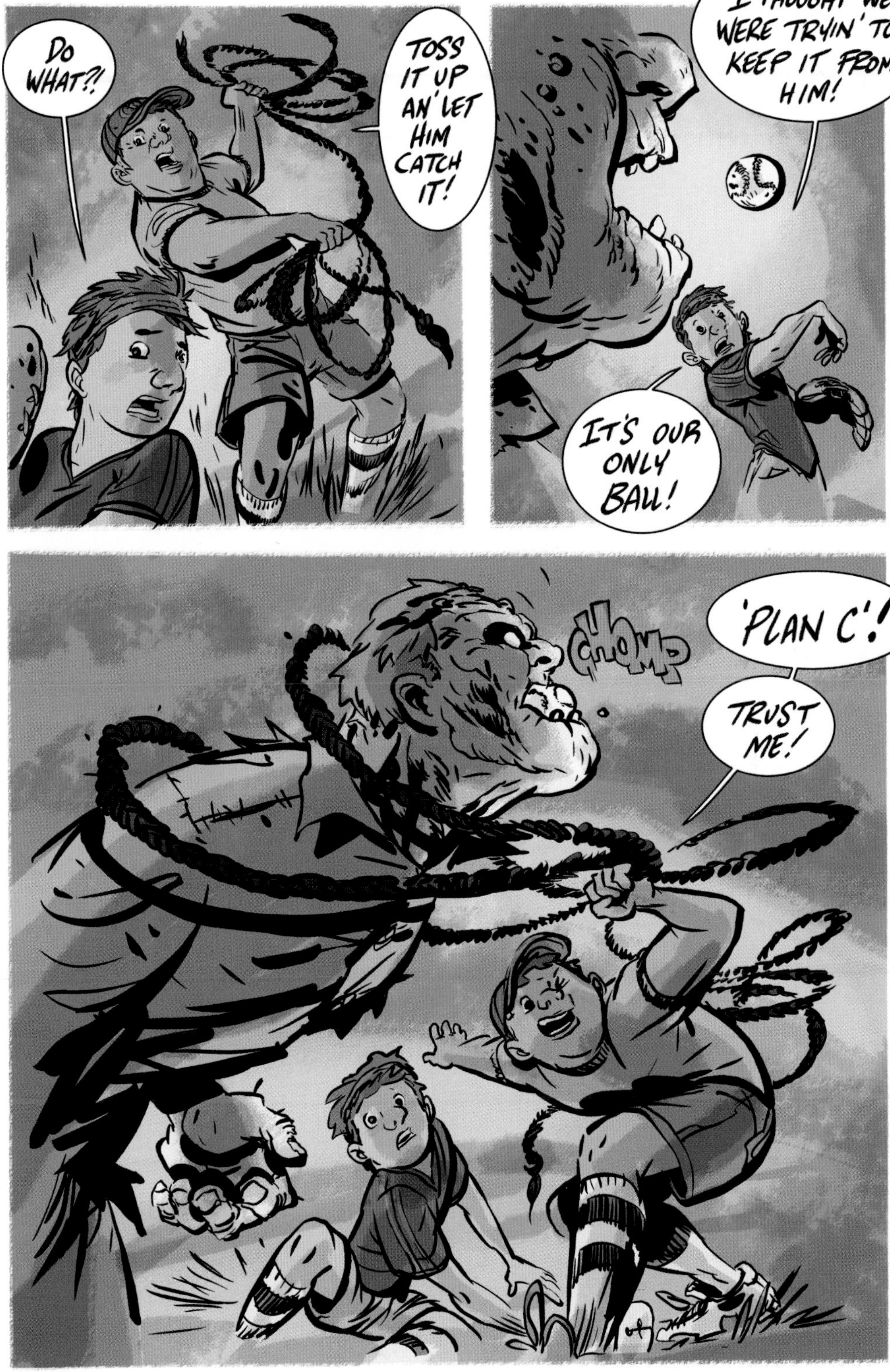
DO WHAT?!
TOSS IT UP AN' LET HIM CATCH IT!
I THOUGHT WE WERE TRYIN' TO KEEP IT FROM HIM!
IT'S OUR ONLY BALL!
CHOMP
'PLAN C'!
TRUST ME!

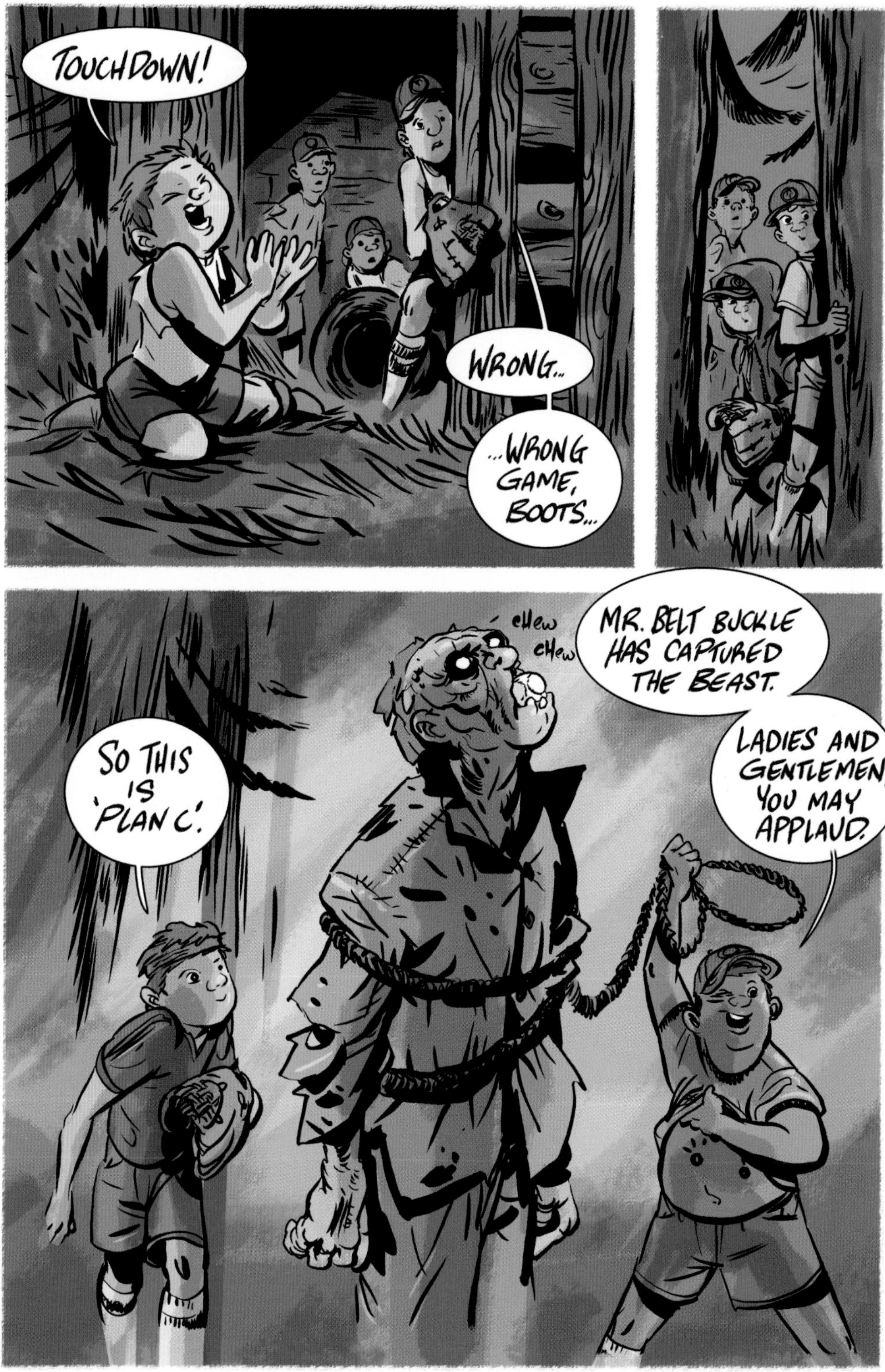
TOUCHDOWN!
WRONG...
...WRONG GAME, BOOTS...
chew chew
MR. BELT BUCKLE HAS CAPTURED THE BEAST.
LADIES AND GENTLEMEN, YOU MAY APPLAUD.
SO THIS IS 'PLAN C'.

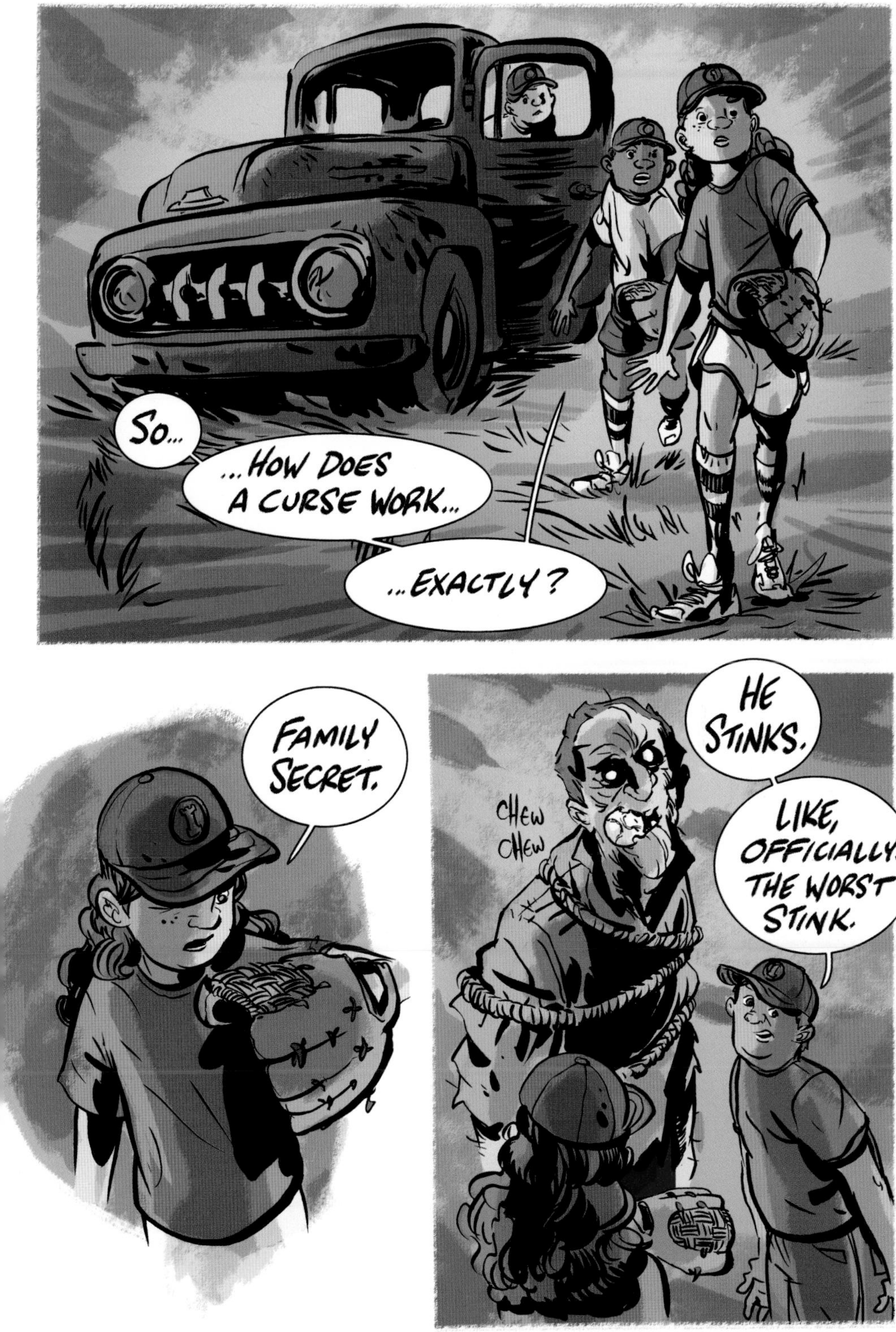
So...
...How does a curse work...
...Exactly?
Family secret.
He stinks.
CHEW CHEW
Like, officially. The worst stink.

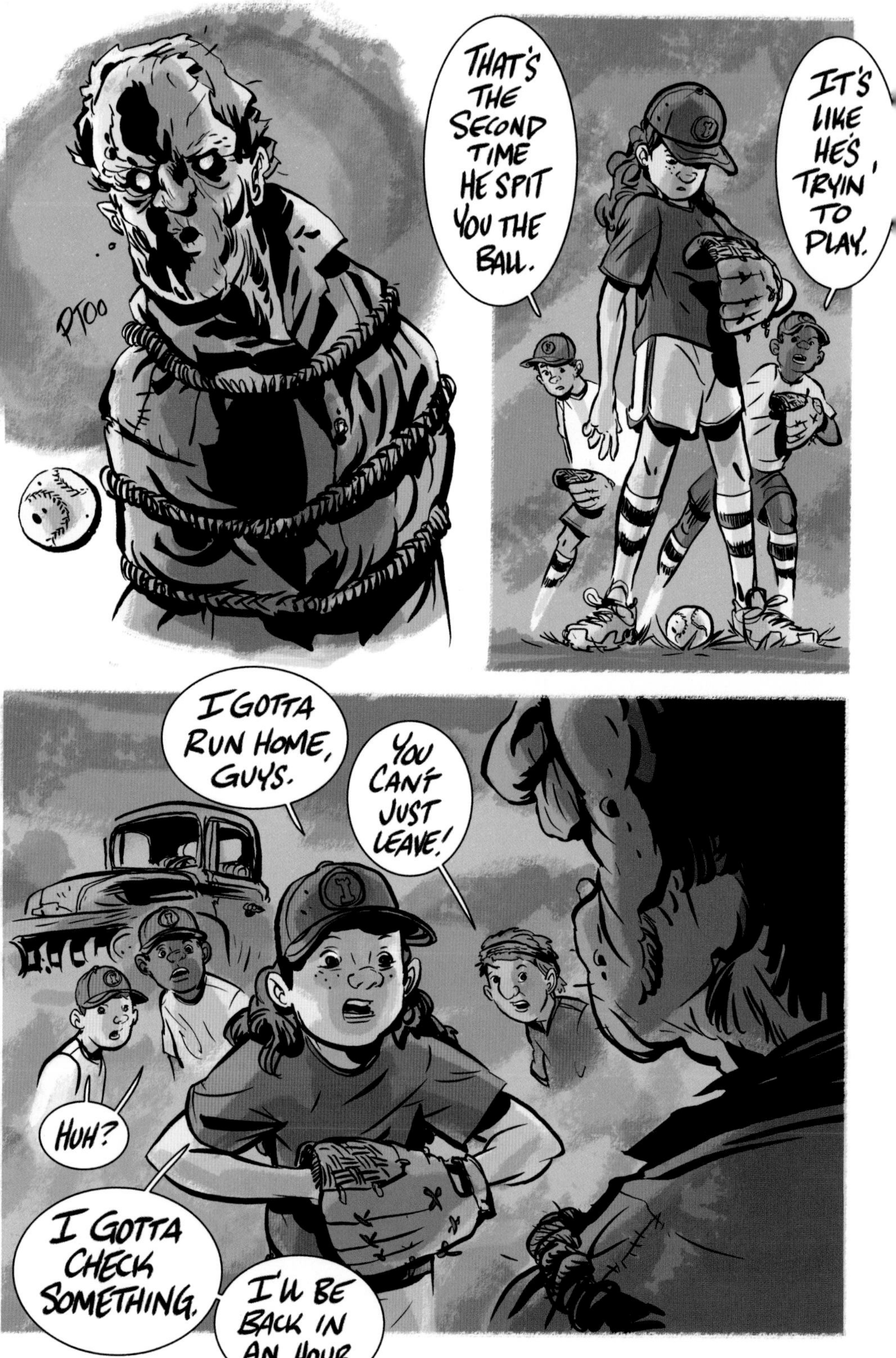
PTOO
THAT'S THE SECOND TIME HE SPIT YOU THE BALL.
IT'S LIKE HE'S TRYIN' TO PLAY.
I GOTTA RUN HOME, GUYS.
YOU CAN'T JUST LEAVE!
HUH?
I GOTTA CHECK SOMETHING.
I'LL BE BACK IN AN HOUR.

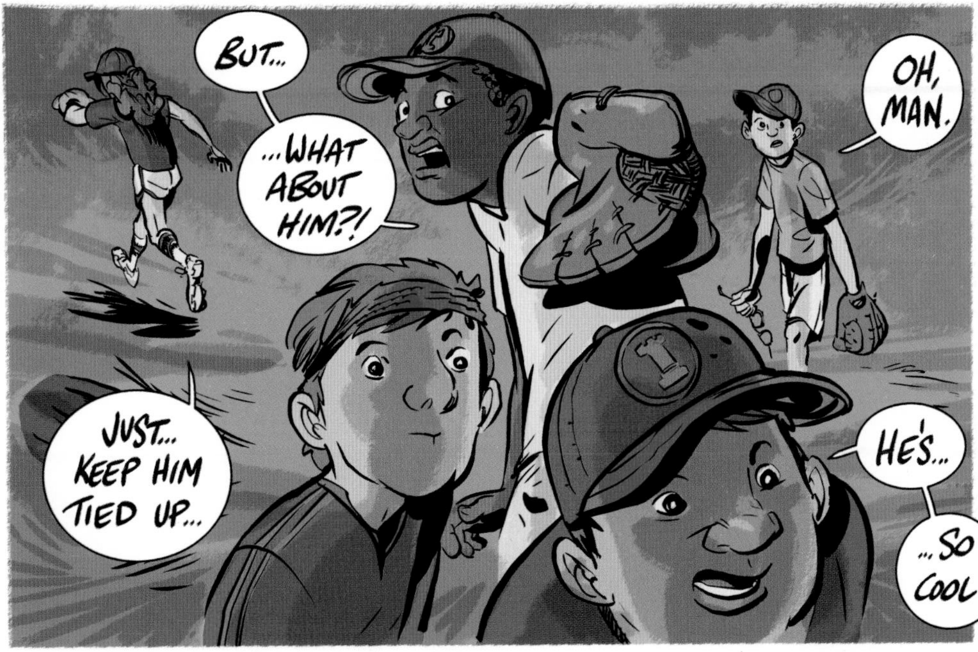
BUT...
...WHAT ABOUT HIM?!
OH, MAN.
JUST... KEEP HIM TIED UP...
HE'S...
...SO COOL.

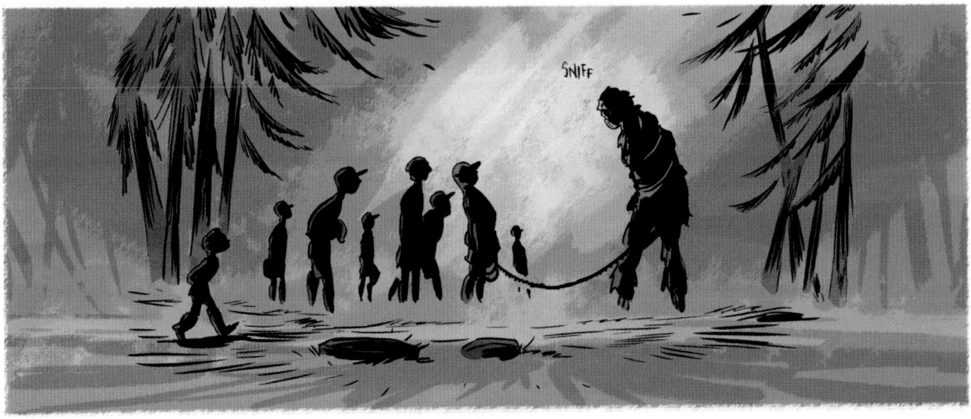
SNIFF

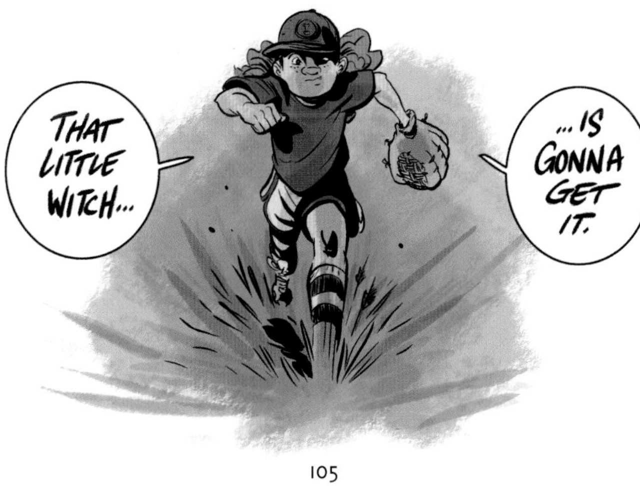
THAT LITTLE WITCH...
...IS GONNA GET IT.

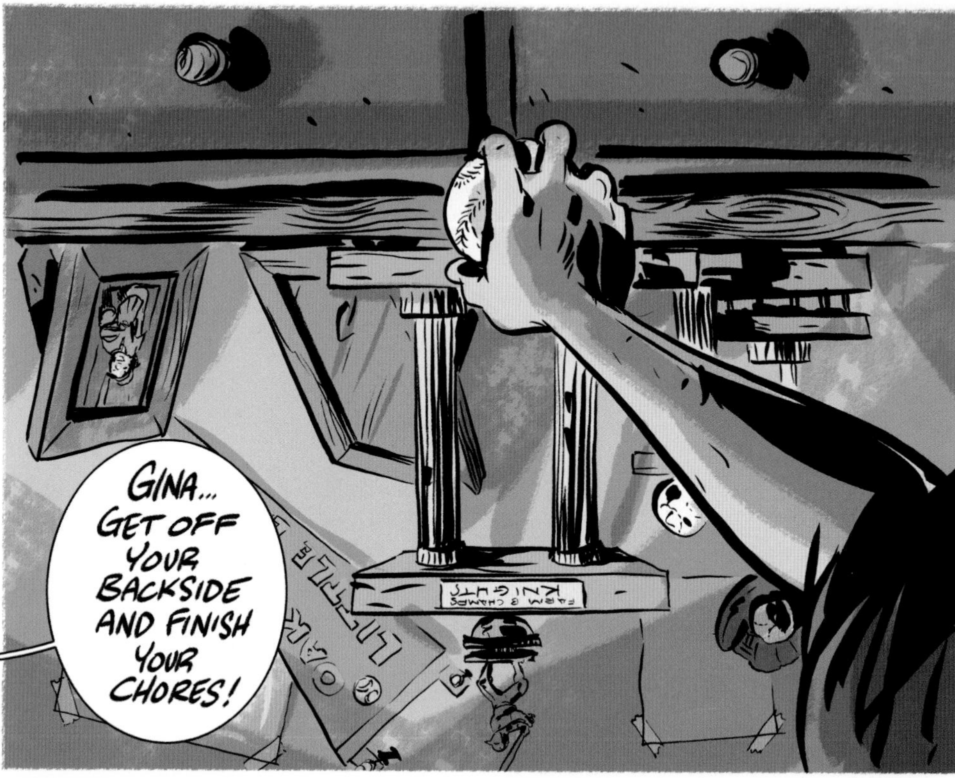
GINA... GET OFF YOUR BACKSIDE AND FINISH YOUR CHORES!

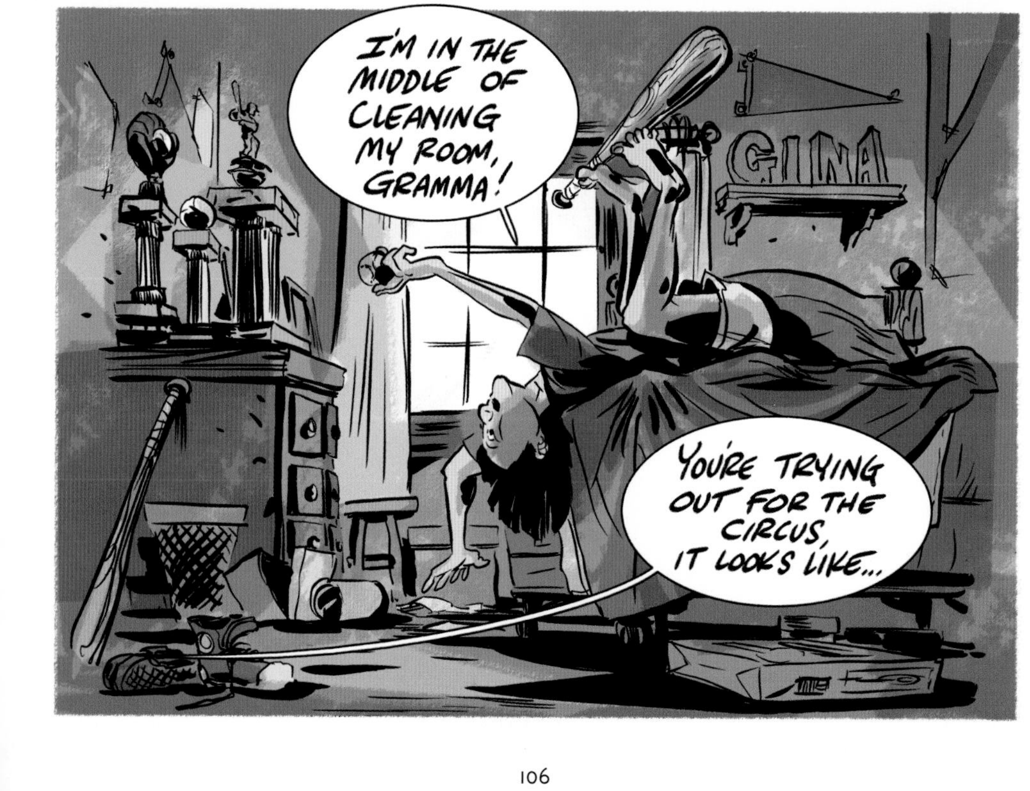
I'M IN THE MIDDLE OF CLEANING MY ROOM, GRAMMA!
GINA
YOU'RE TRYING OUT FOR THE CIRCUS, IT LOOKS LIKE...

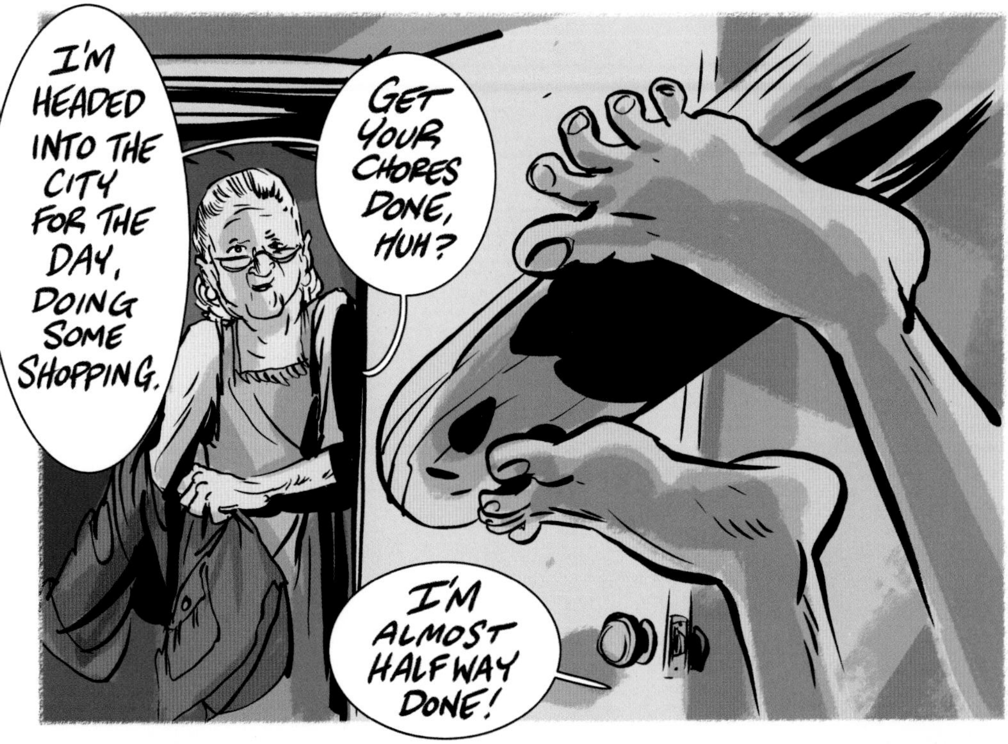
I'M HEADED INTO THE CITY FOR THE DAY, DOING SOME SHOPPING.
GET YOUR CHORES DONE, HUH?
I'M ALMOST HALFWAY DONE!

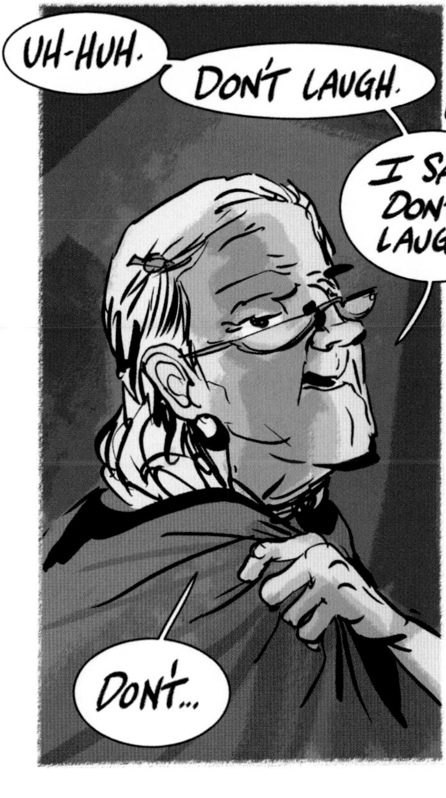
UH-HUH.
DON'T LAUGH.
I SAID DON'T LAUGH...
DON'T...

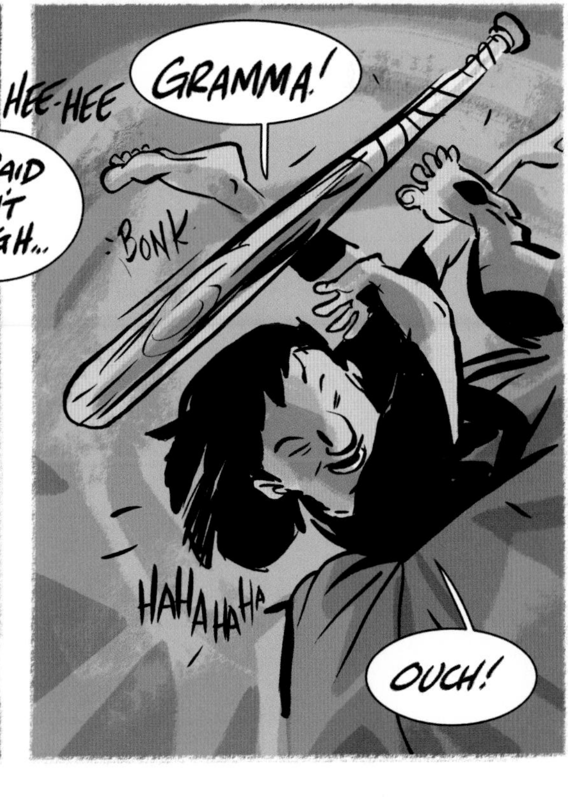
HEE-HEE
GRAMMA!
BONK
HAHAHAHA
OUCH!

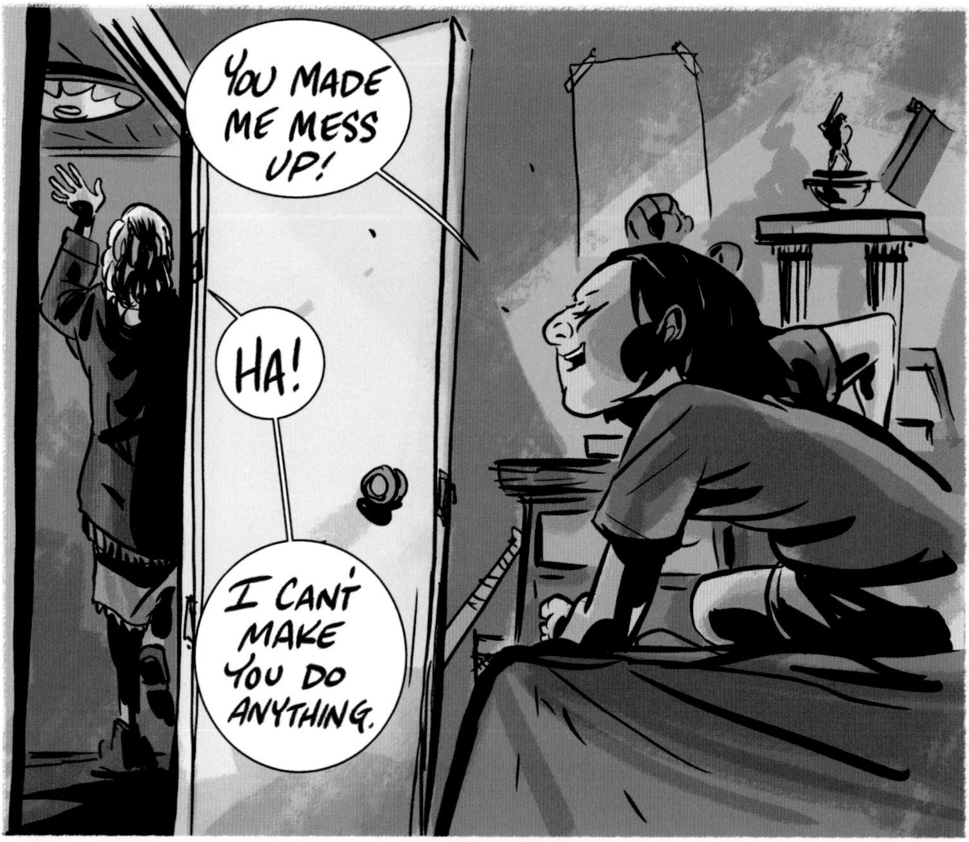
YOU MADE ME MESS UP!
HA!
I CAN'T MAKE YOU DO ANYTHING.

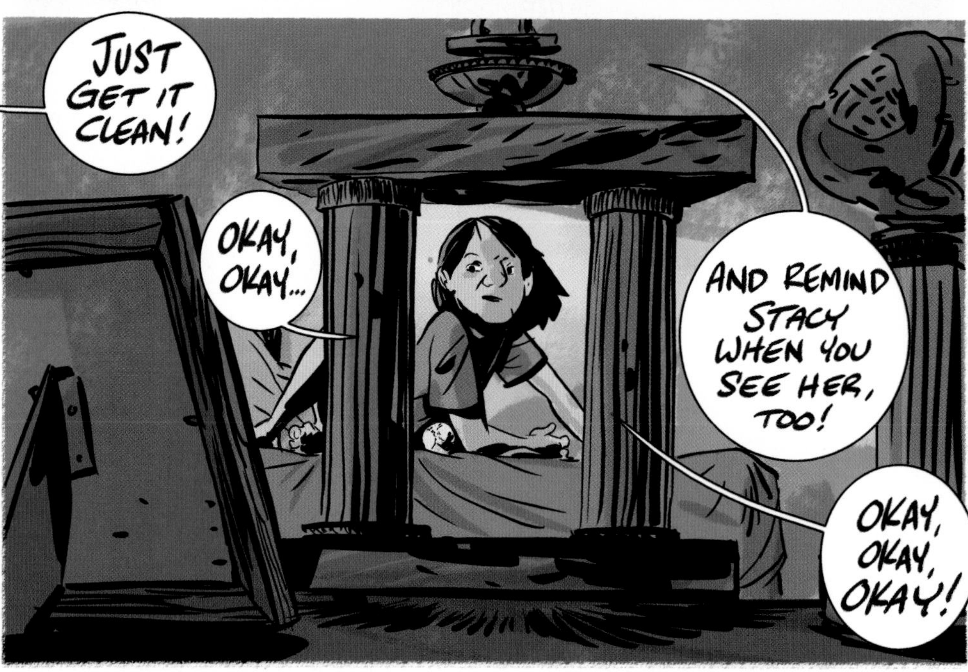
JUST GET IT CLEAN!
OKAY, OKAY...
AND REMIND STACY WHEN YOU SEE HER, TOO!
OKAY, OKAY, OKAY!

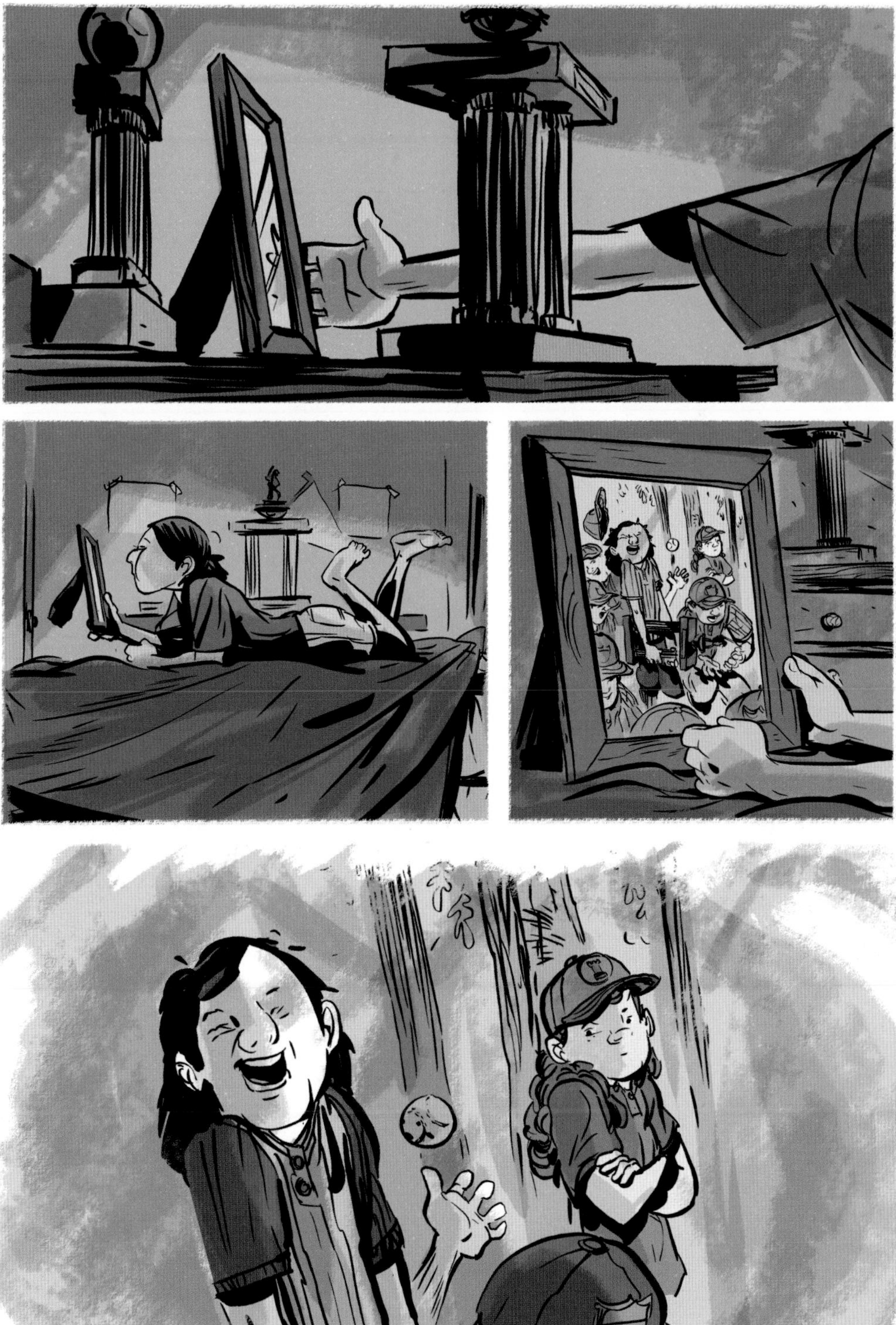

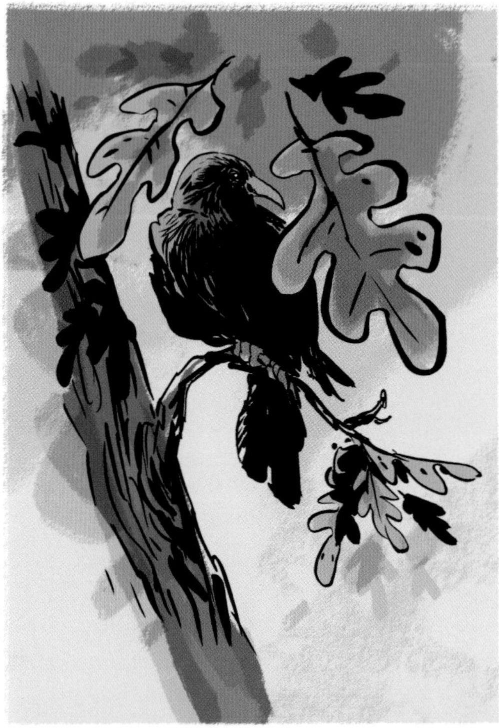

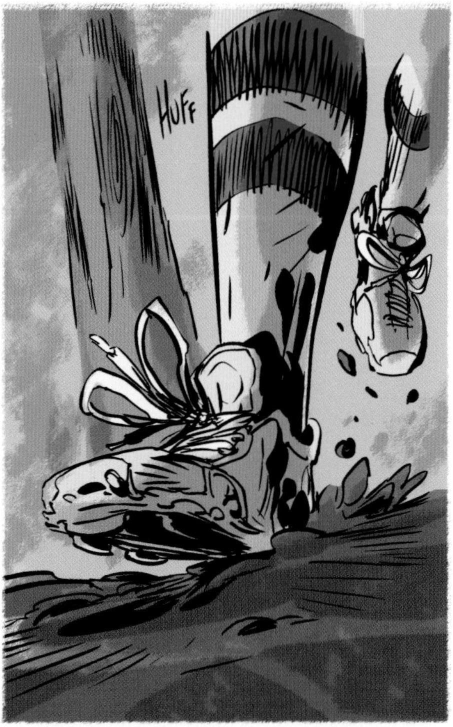
HUFF

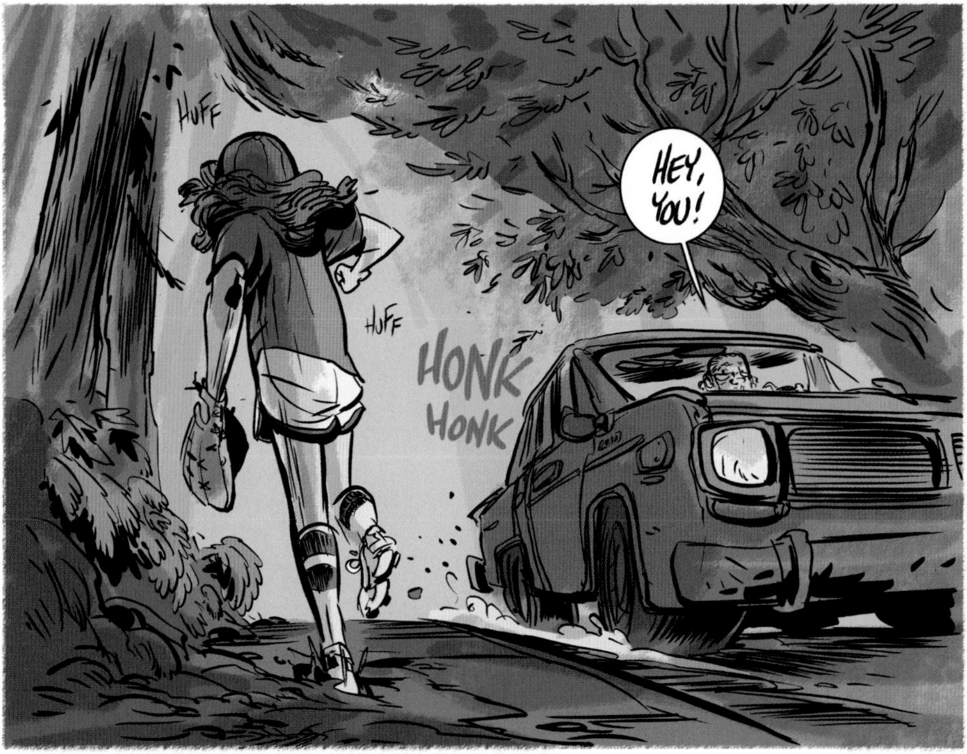
HUFF
HUFF
HONK
HONK
HEY, YOU!

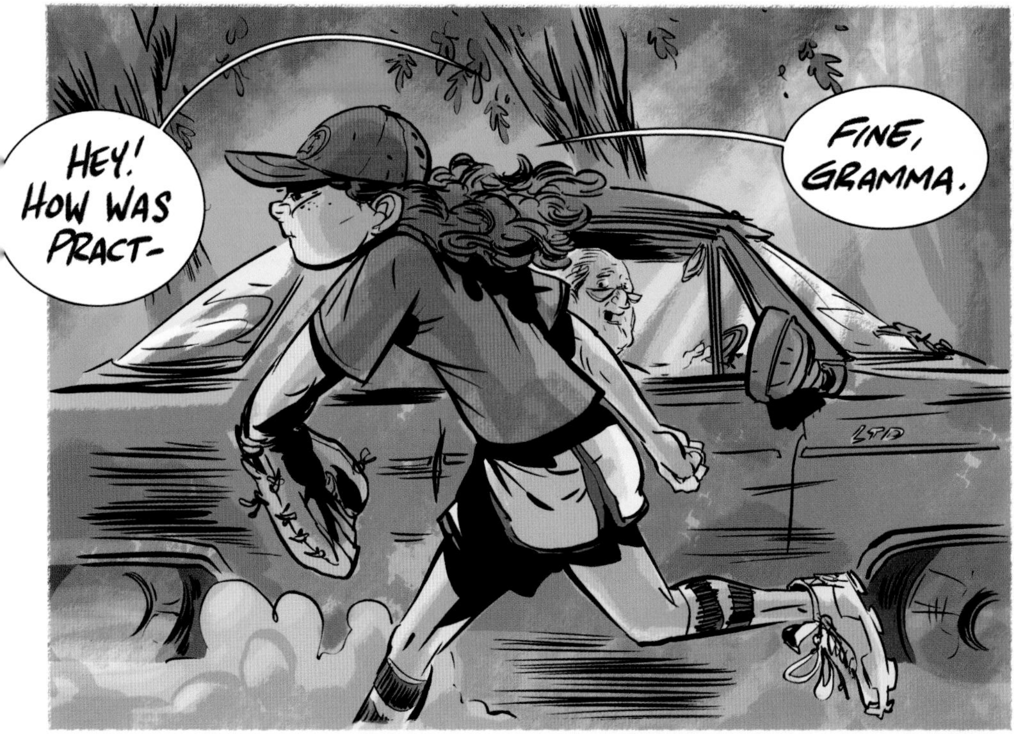
HEY! HOW WAS PRACT-
FINE, GRAMMA.
LTD

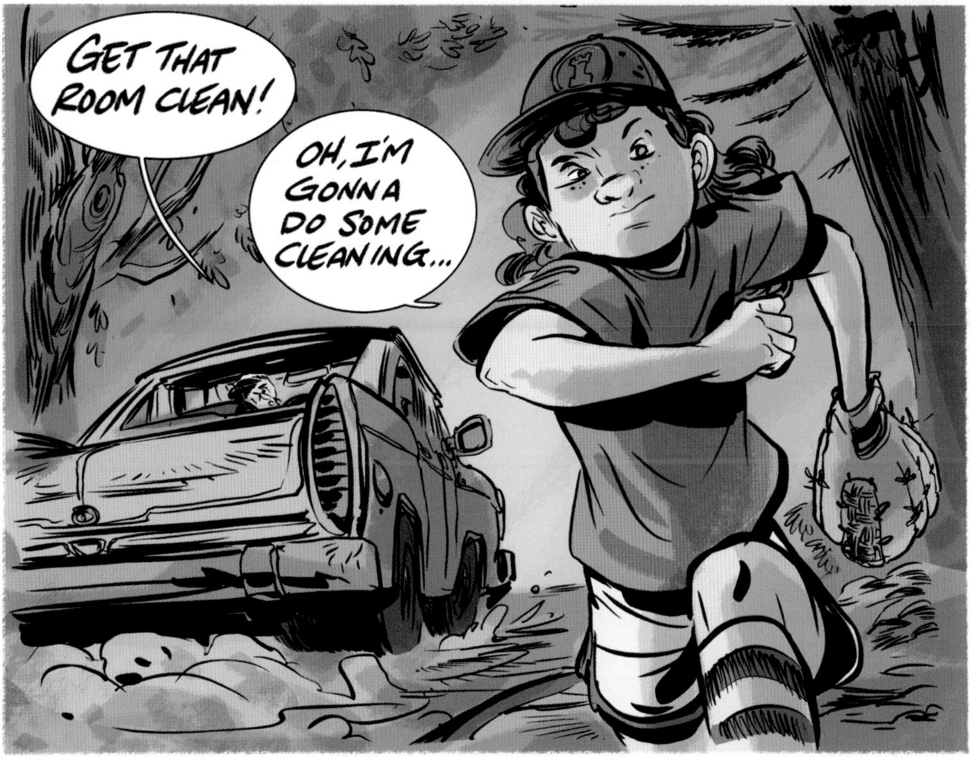
GET THAT ROOM CLEAN!
OH, I'M GONNA DO SOME CLEANING...

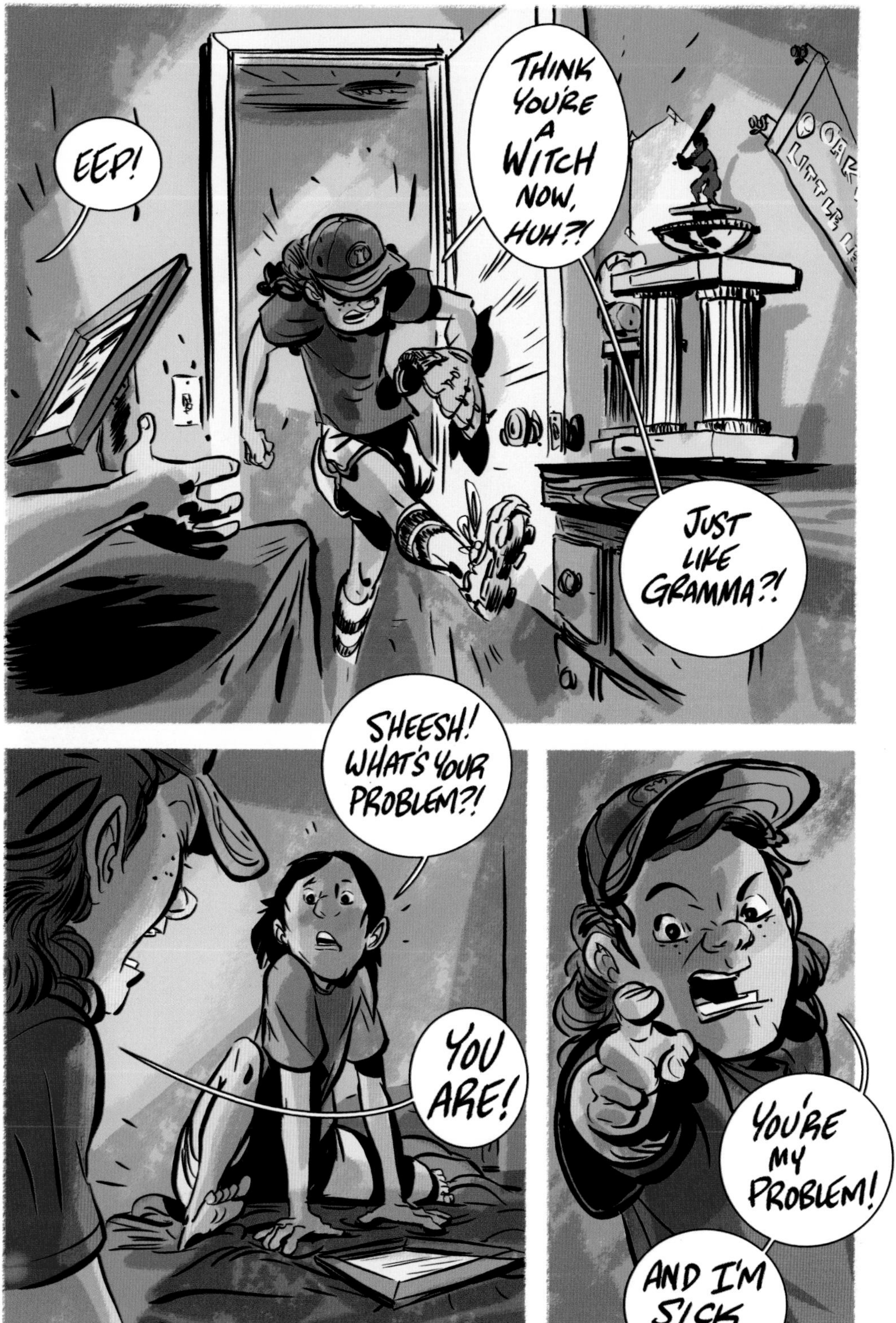
EEP!
THINK YOU'RE A WITCH NOW, HUH?!
JUST LIKE GRAMMA?!
SHEESH! WHAT'S YOUR PROBLEM?!
YOU ARE!
YOU'RE MY PROBLEM!
AND I'M SICK OF IT!

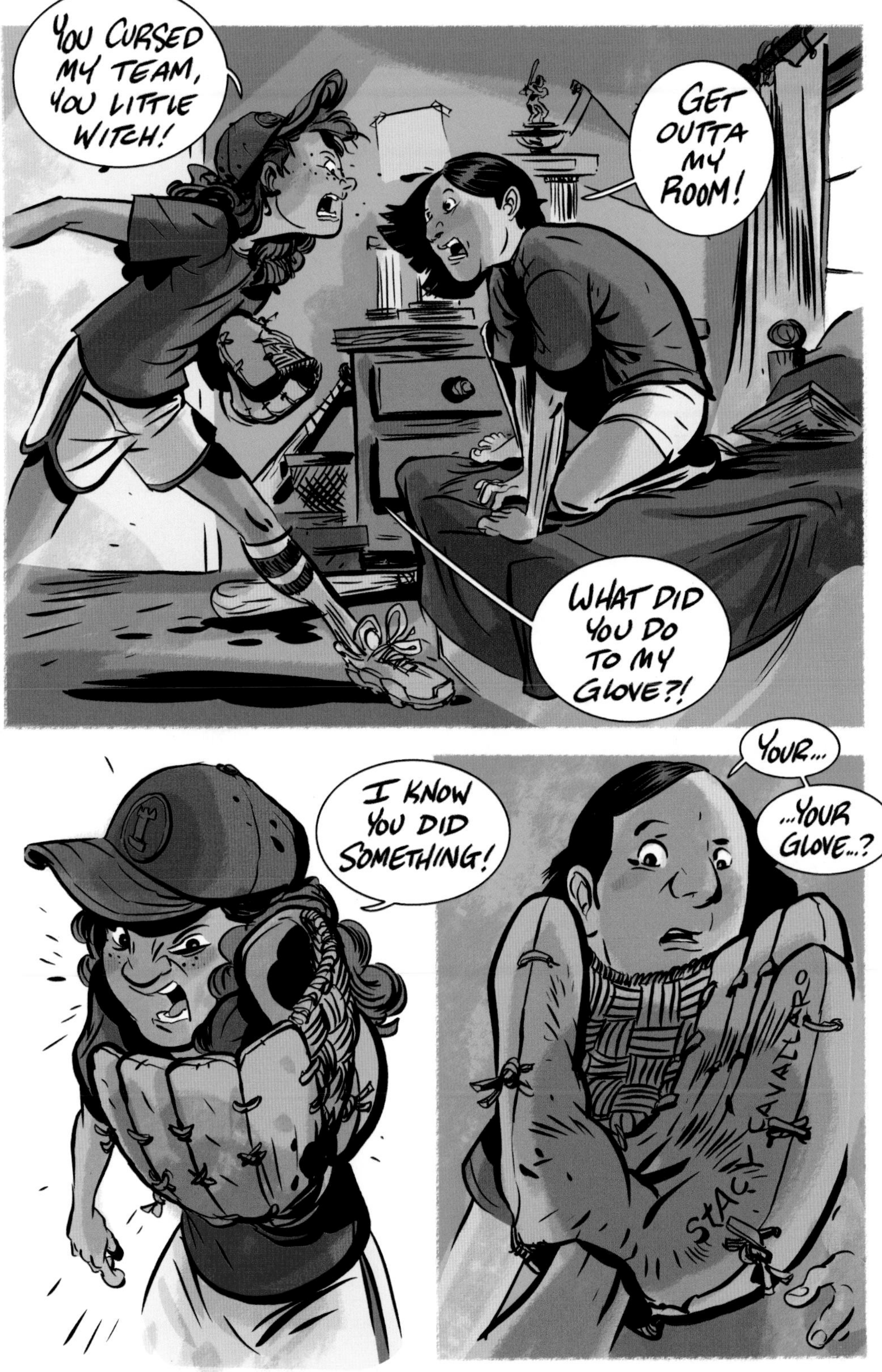
YOU CURSED MY TEAM, YOU LITTLE WITCH!
GET OUTTA MY ROOM!
WHAT DID YOU DO TO MY GLOVE?!
I KNOW YOU DID SOMETHING!
YOUR...
...YOUR GLOVE...?
STACY CAVALLARO

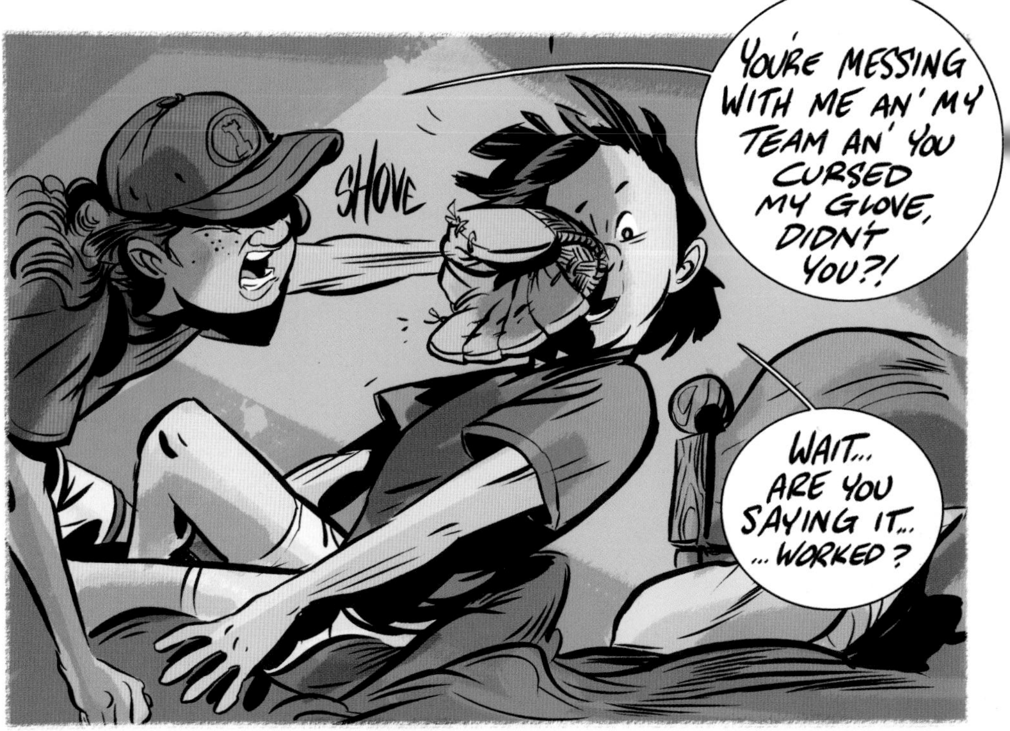

YOU'RE MESSING WITH ME AN' MY TEAM AN' YOU CURSED MY GLOVE, DIDN'T YOU?!
SHOVE
WAIT... ARE YOU SAYING IT... ...WORKED?

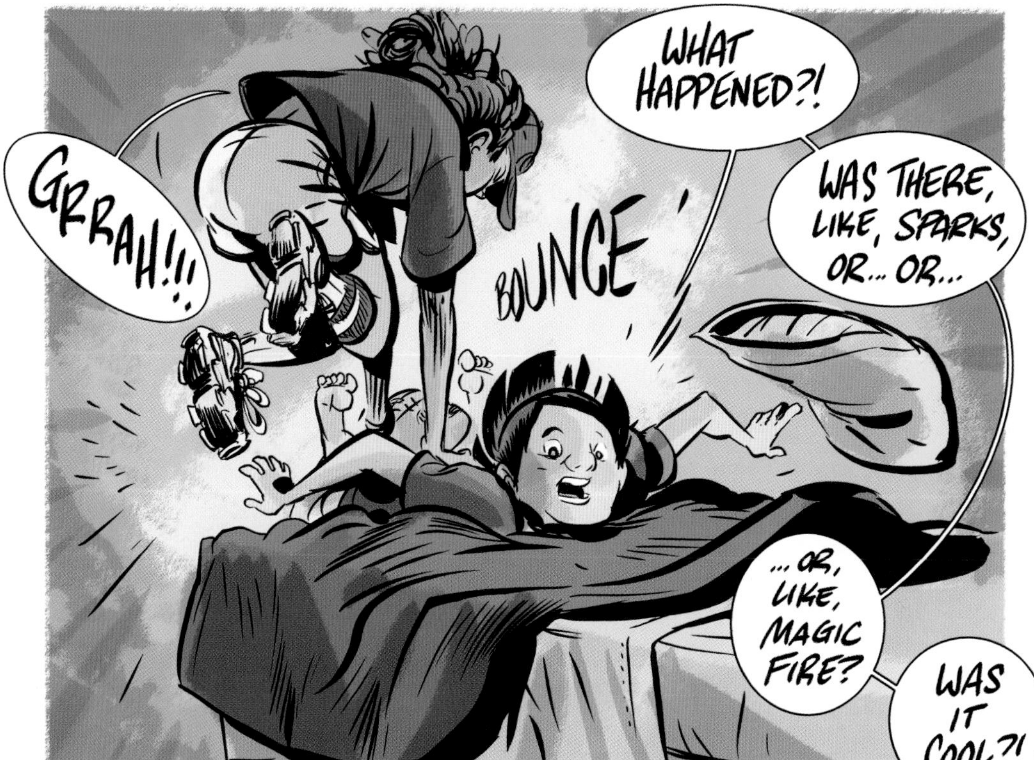

GRRAH!!!
BOUNCE
WHAT HAPPENED?!
WAS THERE, LIKE, SPARKS, OR... OR...
...OR, LIKE, MAGIC FIRE?
WAS IT COOL?!

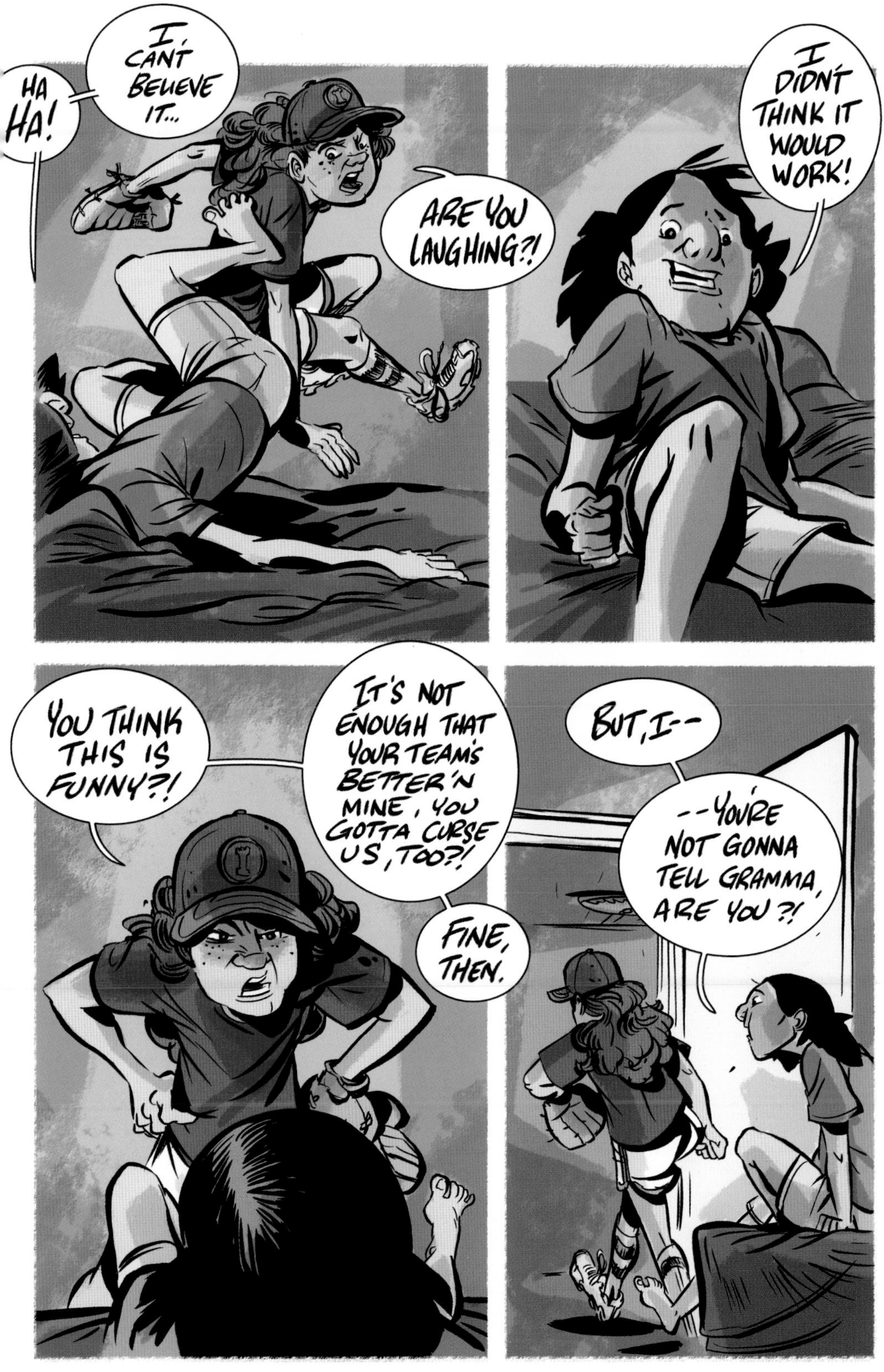
I, CAN'T BELIEVE IT...
HA HA!
ARE YOU LAUGHING?!
I DIDN'T THINK IT WOULD WORK!
YOU THINK THIS IS FUNNY?!
IT'S NOT ENOUGH THAT YOUR TEAM'S BETTER 'N MINE, YOU GOTTA CURSE US, TOO?!
FINE, THEN.
BUT, I--
--YOU'RE NOT GONNA TELL GRAMMA, ARE YOU?!

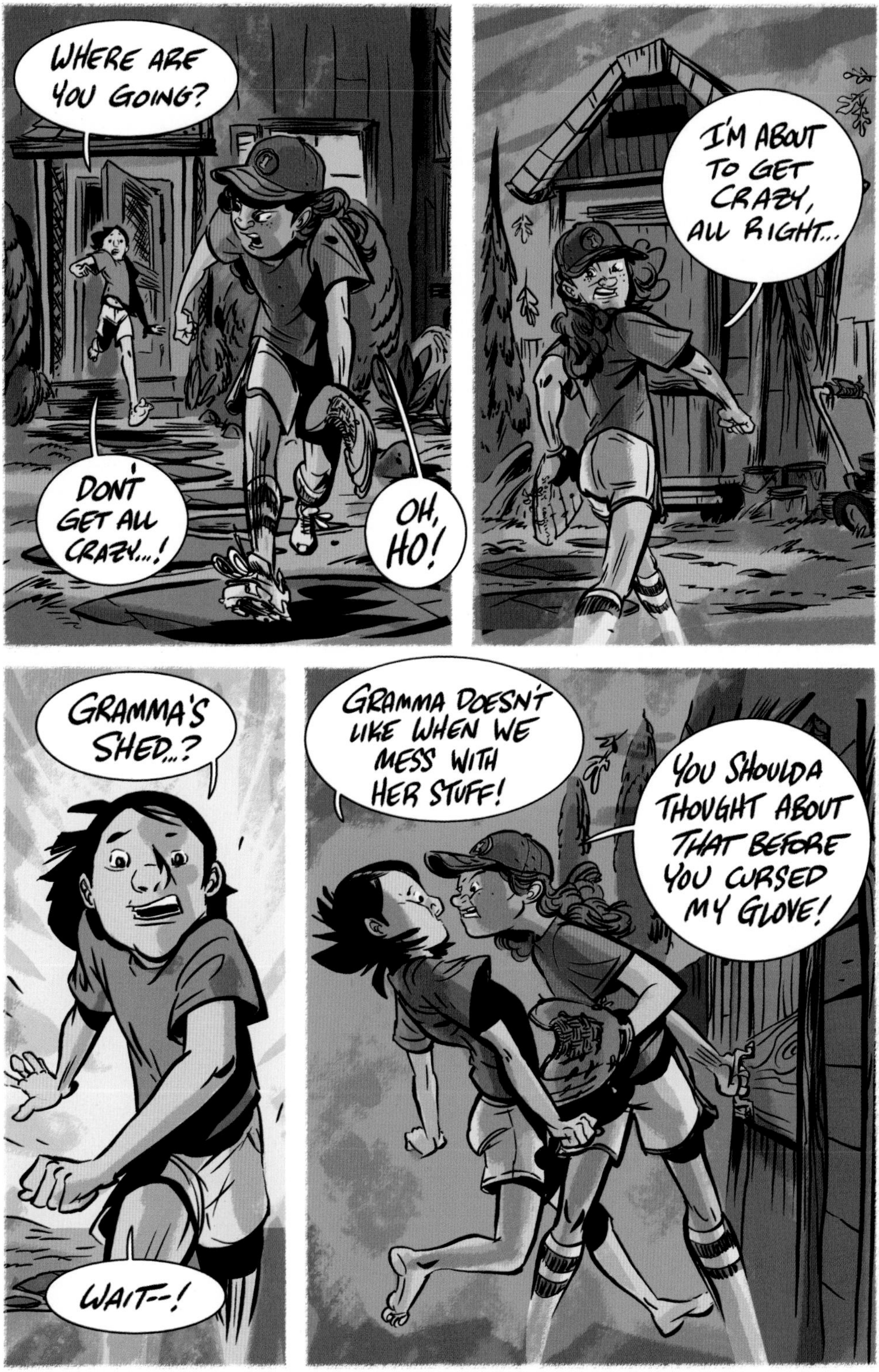
WHERE ARE YOU GOING?
DON'T GET ALL CRAZY...!
OH, HO!
I'M ABOUT TO GET CRAZY, ALL RIGHT...
GRAMMA'S SHED...?
WAIT--!
GRAMMA DOESN'T LIKE WHEN WE MESS WITH HER STUFF!
YOU SHOULDA THOUGHT ABOUT THAT BEFORE YOU CURSED MY GLOVE!

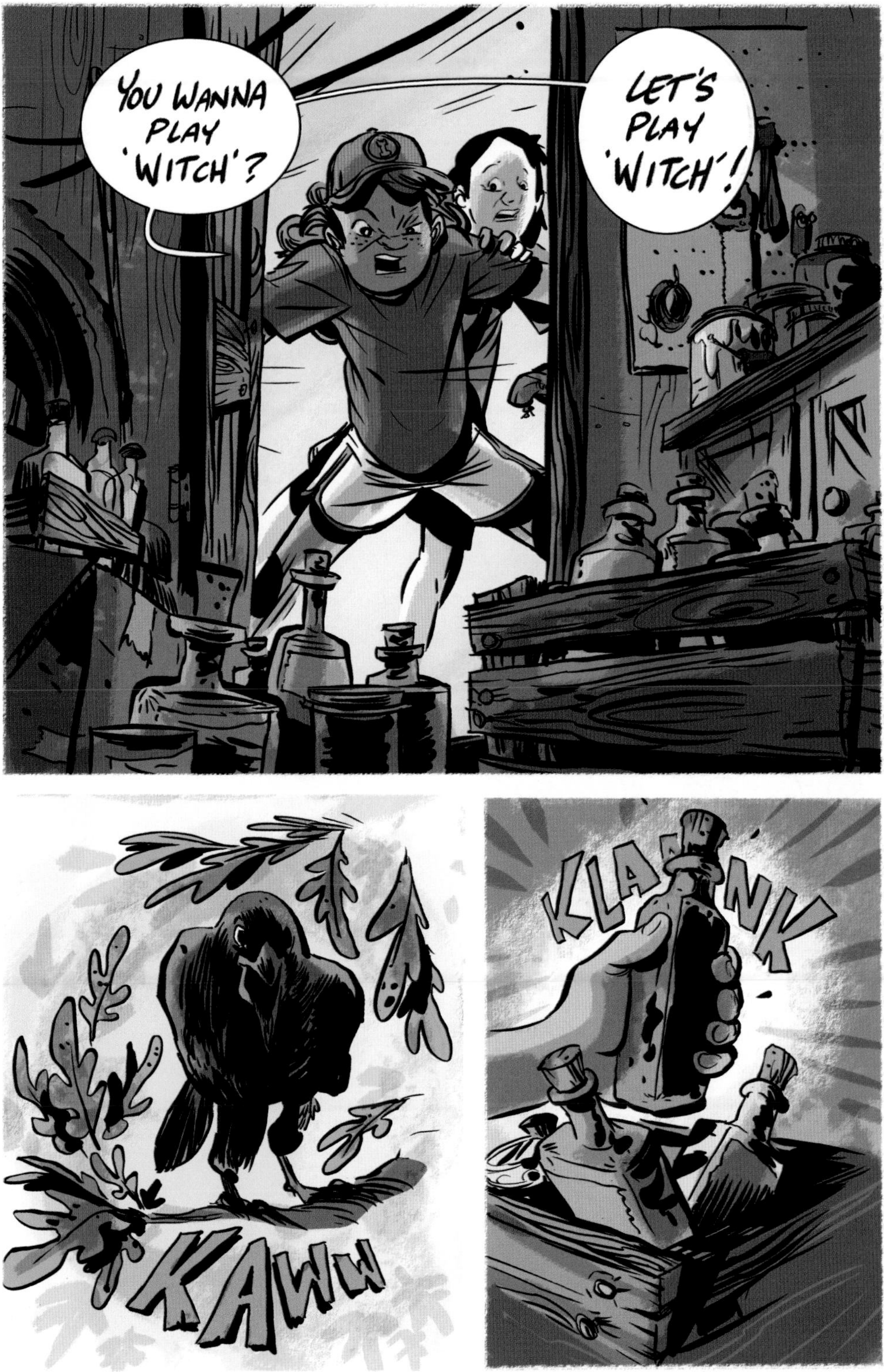
YOU WANNA PLAY 'WITCH'?
LET'S PLAY 'WITCH'!
KAWW
KLA NK

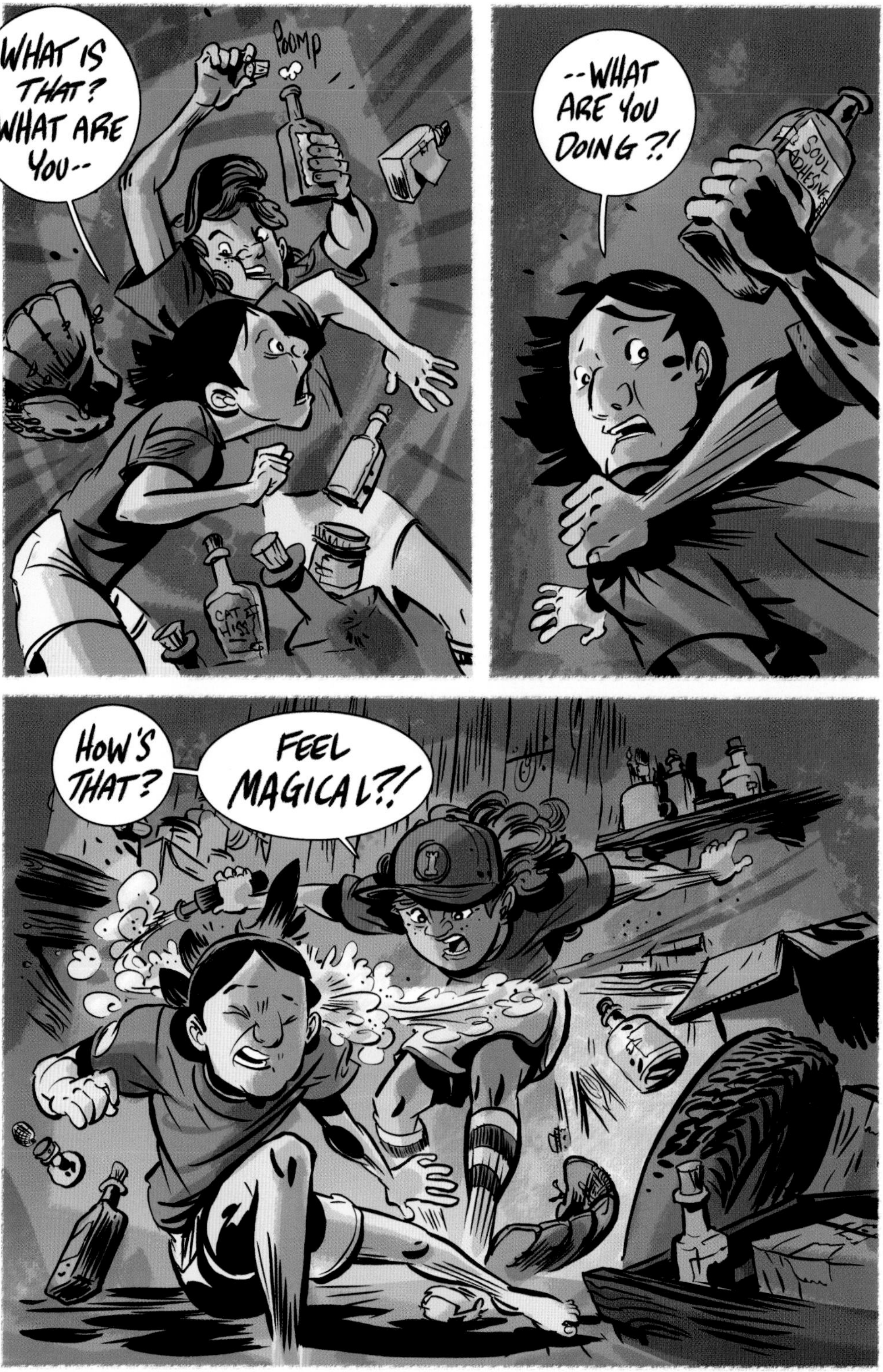
WHAT IS THAT? WHAT ARE YOU--
POOMP
--WHAT ARE YOU DOING?!
SOUL ADHESIVE
HOW'S THAT?
FEEL MAGICAL?!

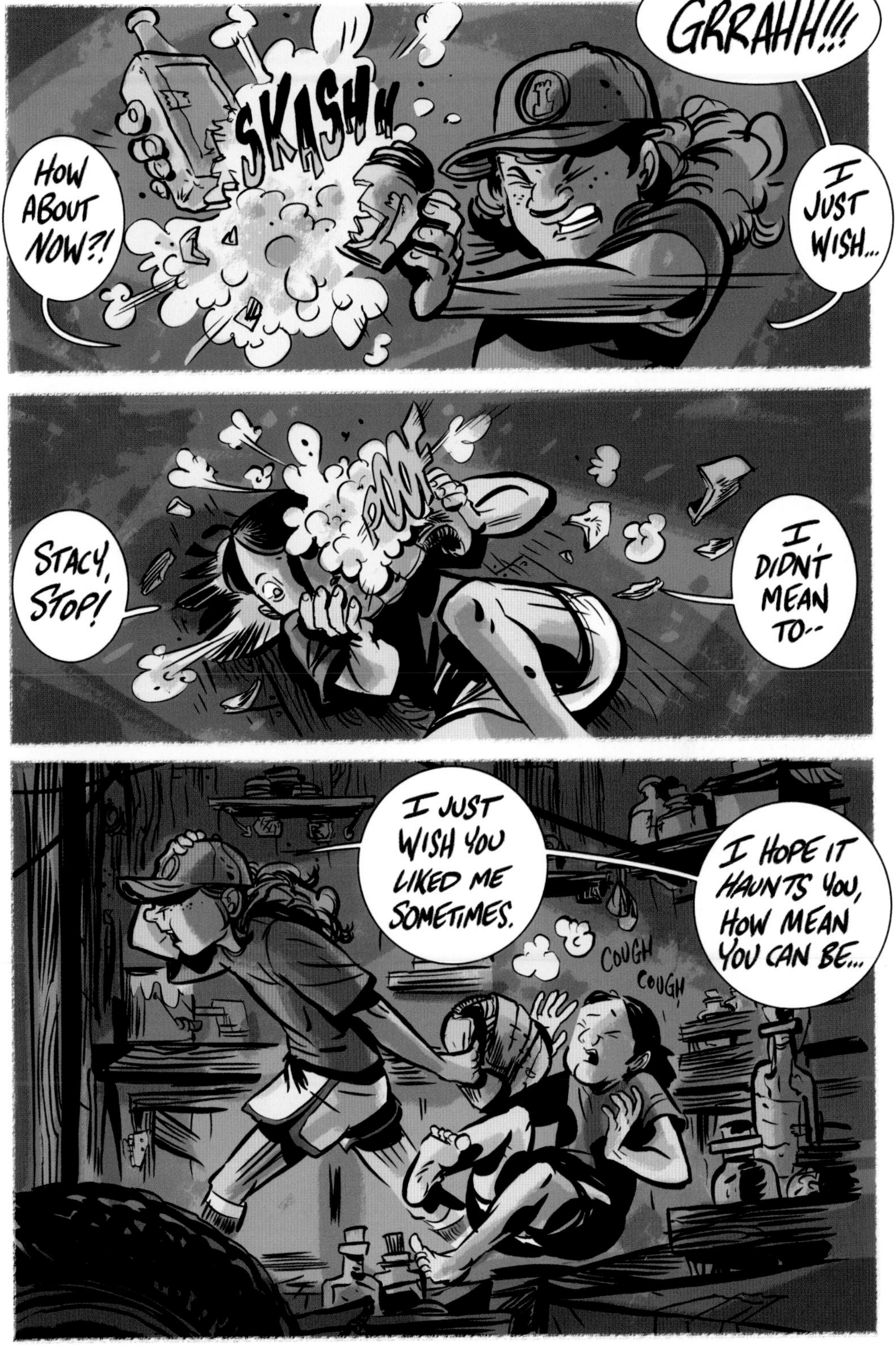
GRRAHH!!!
I JUST WISH...
SKASHH
HOW ABOUT NOW?!
I DIDN'T MEAN TO--
STACY, STOP!
I JUST WISH YOU LIKED ME SOMETIMES.
I HOPE IT HAUNTS YOU, HOW MEAN YOU CAN BE...
COUGH COUGH

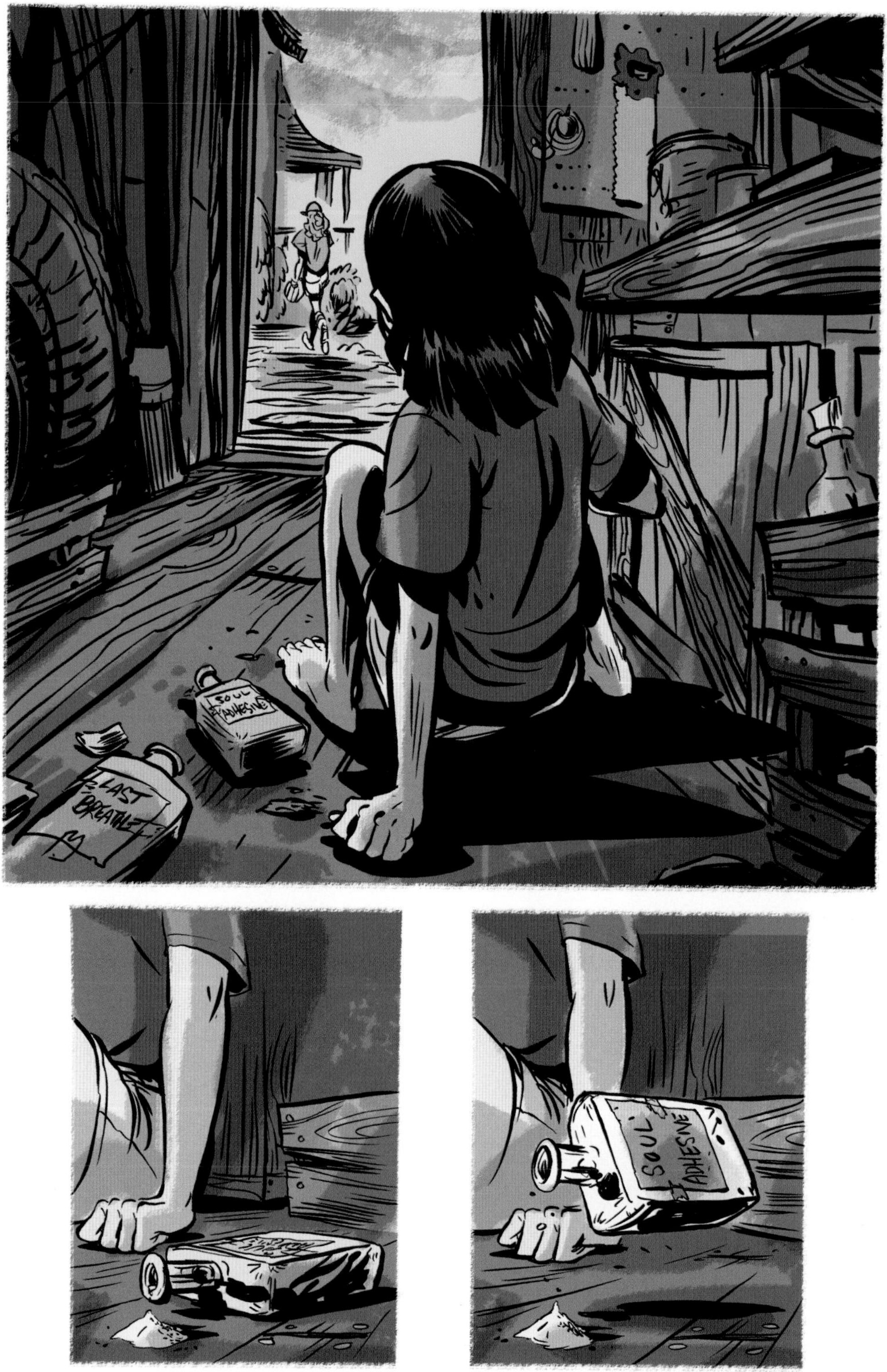
SOUL ADHESIVE
LAST BREATH
SOUL ADHESIVE

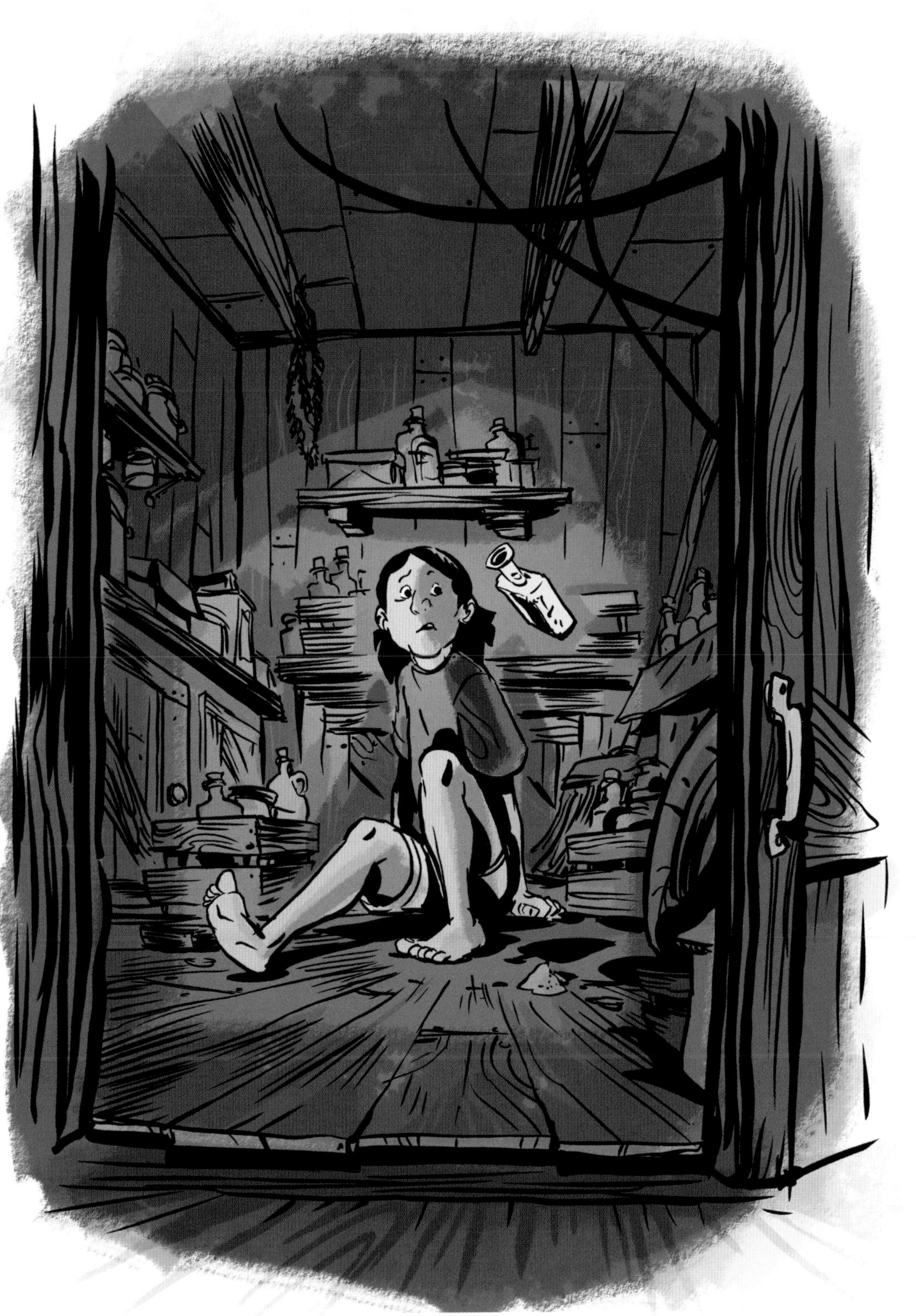

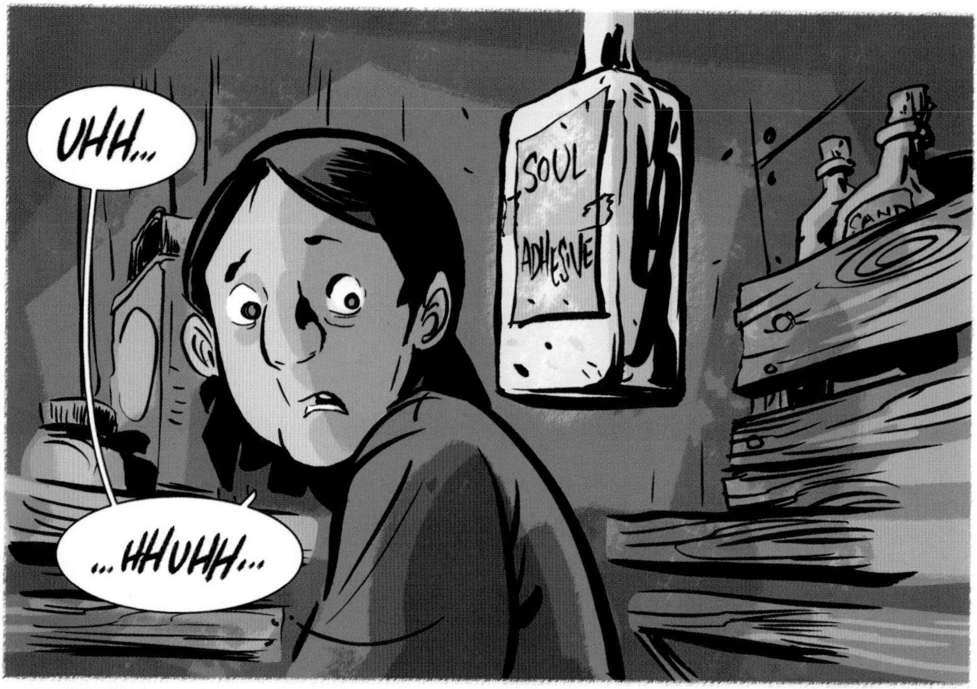
UHH...
...HHUHH...
SOUL ADHESIVE
SAND

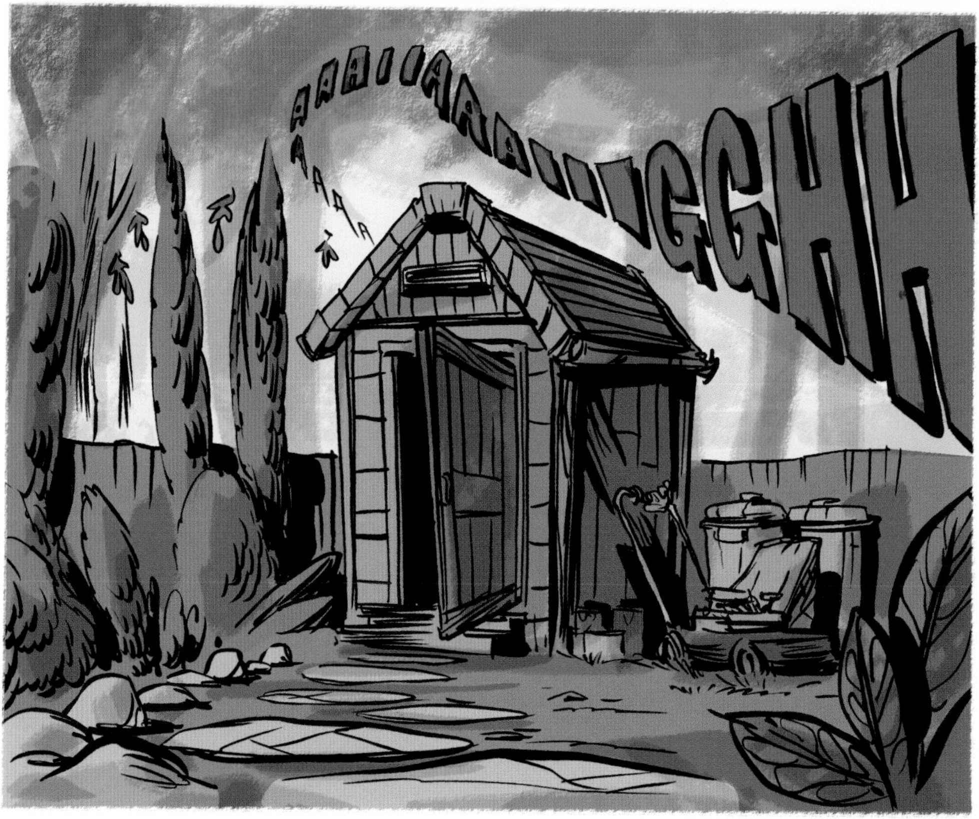
AAAAAIIIAAAAAAAIIIGGHH

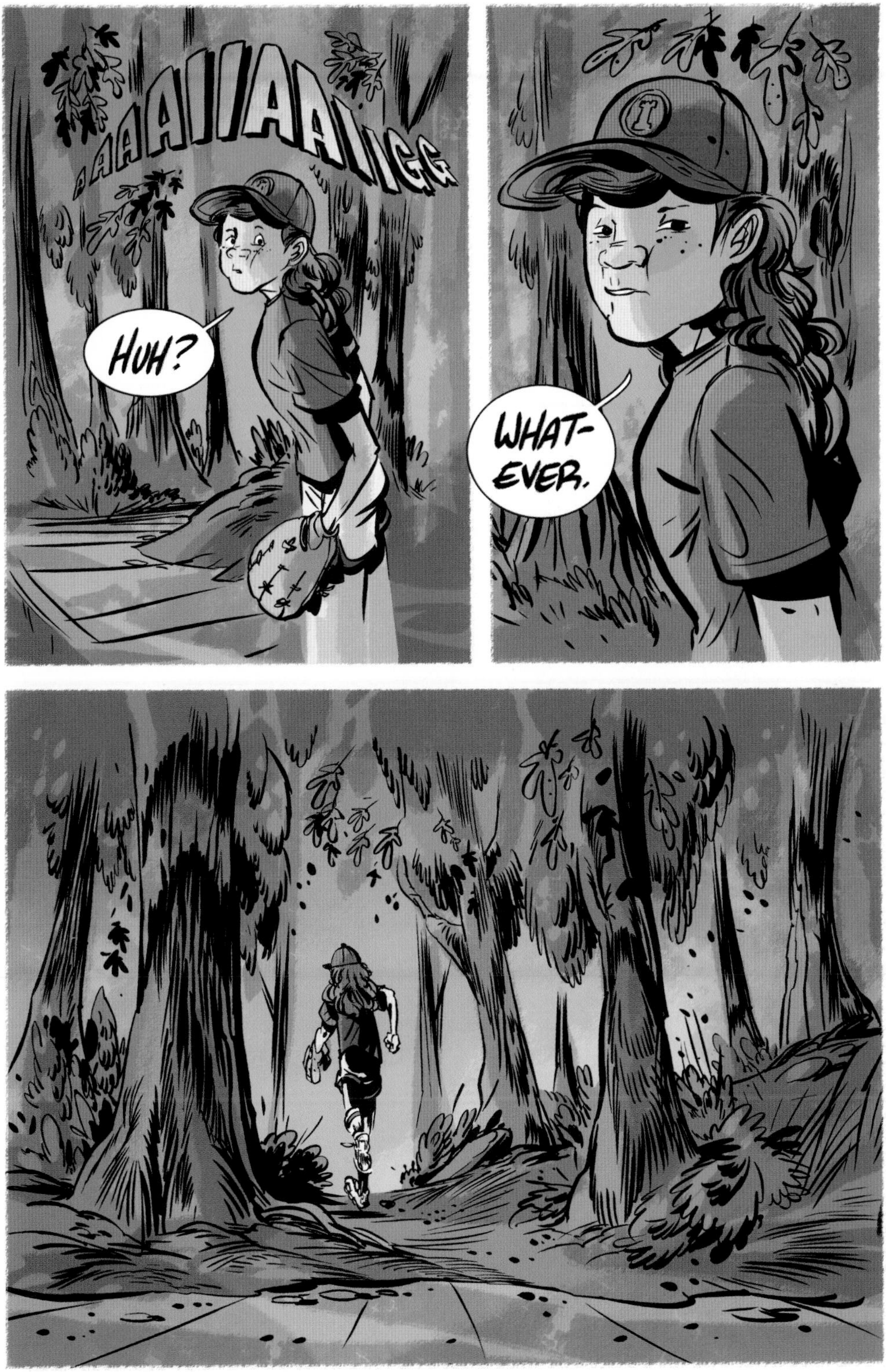
AAAIIAAIIGG
HUH?
WHAT-EVER.

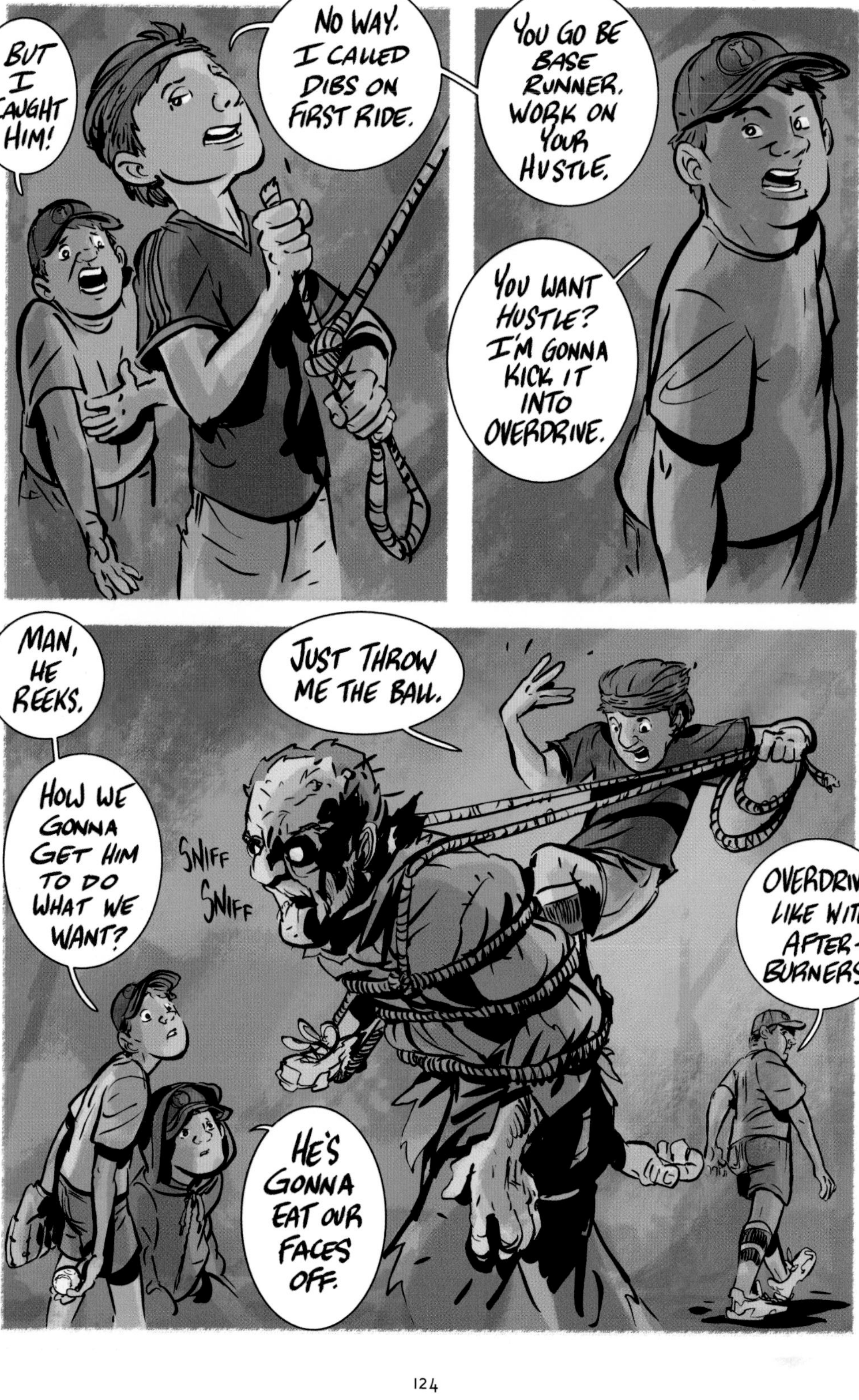
BUT I CAUGHT HIM!
NO WAY. I CALLED DIBS ON FIRST RIDE.
YOU GO BE BASE RUNNER. WORK ON YOUR HUSTLE.
YOU WANT HUSTLE? I'M GONNA KICK IT INTO OVERDRIVE.
MAN, HE REEKS.
HOW WE GONNA GET HIM TO DO WHAT WE WANT?
JUST THROW ME THE BALL.
SNIFF
SNIFF
OVERDRIVE. LIKE WITH AFTER-BURNERS.
HE'S GONNA EAT OUR FACES OFF.

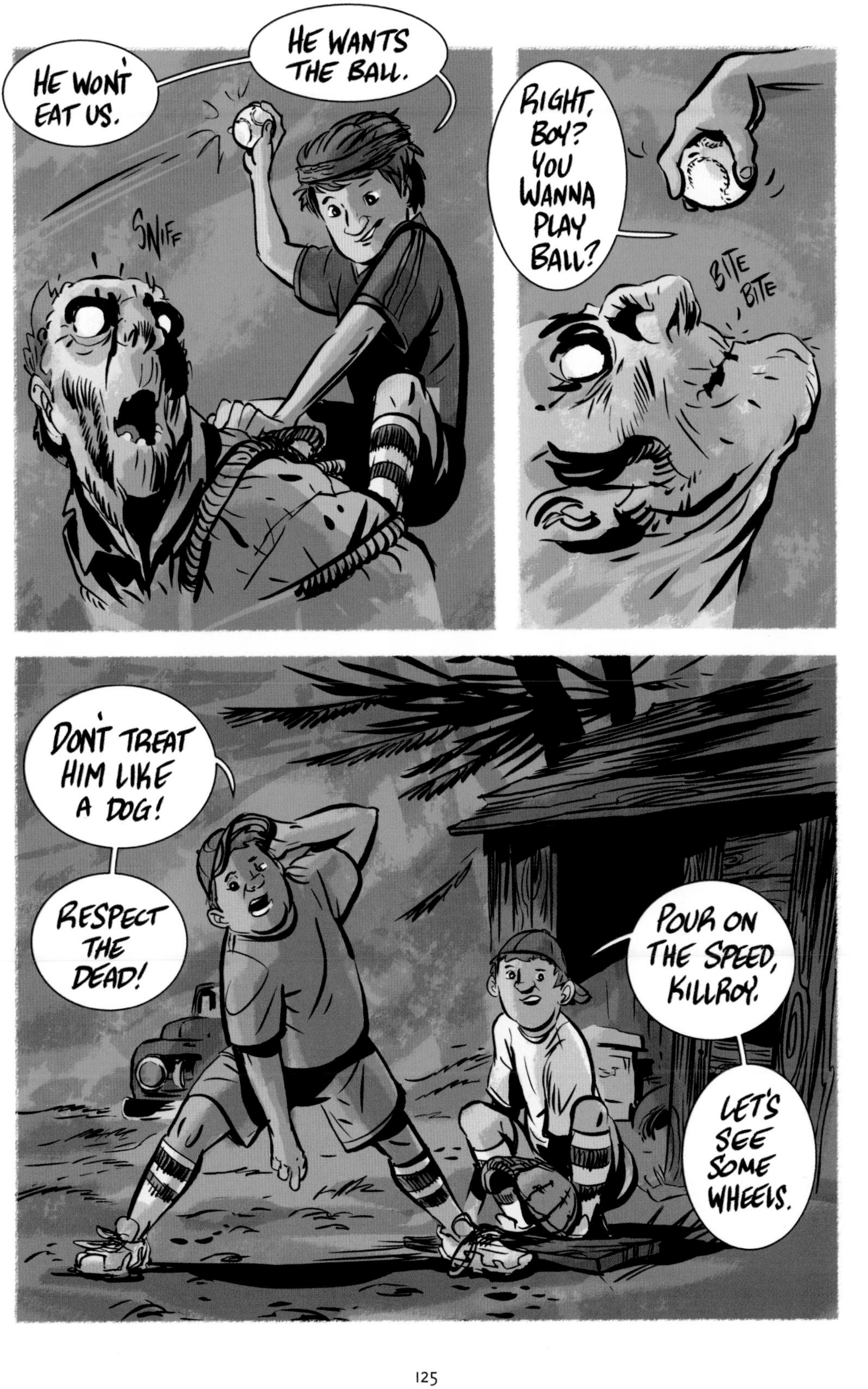
HE WON'T EAT US.
HE WANTS THE BALL.
SNIFF
RIGHT, BOY? YOU WANNA PLAY BALL?
BITE BITE
DON'T TREAT HIM LIKE A DOG!
RESPECT THE DEAD!
POUR ON THE SPEED, KILLROY.
LET'S SEE SOME WHEELS.

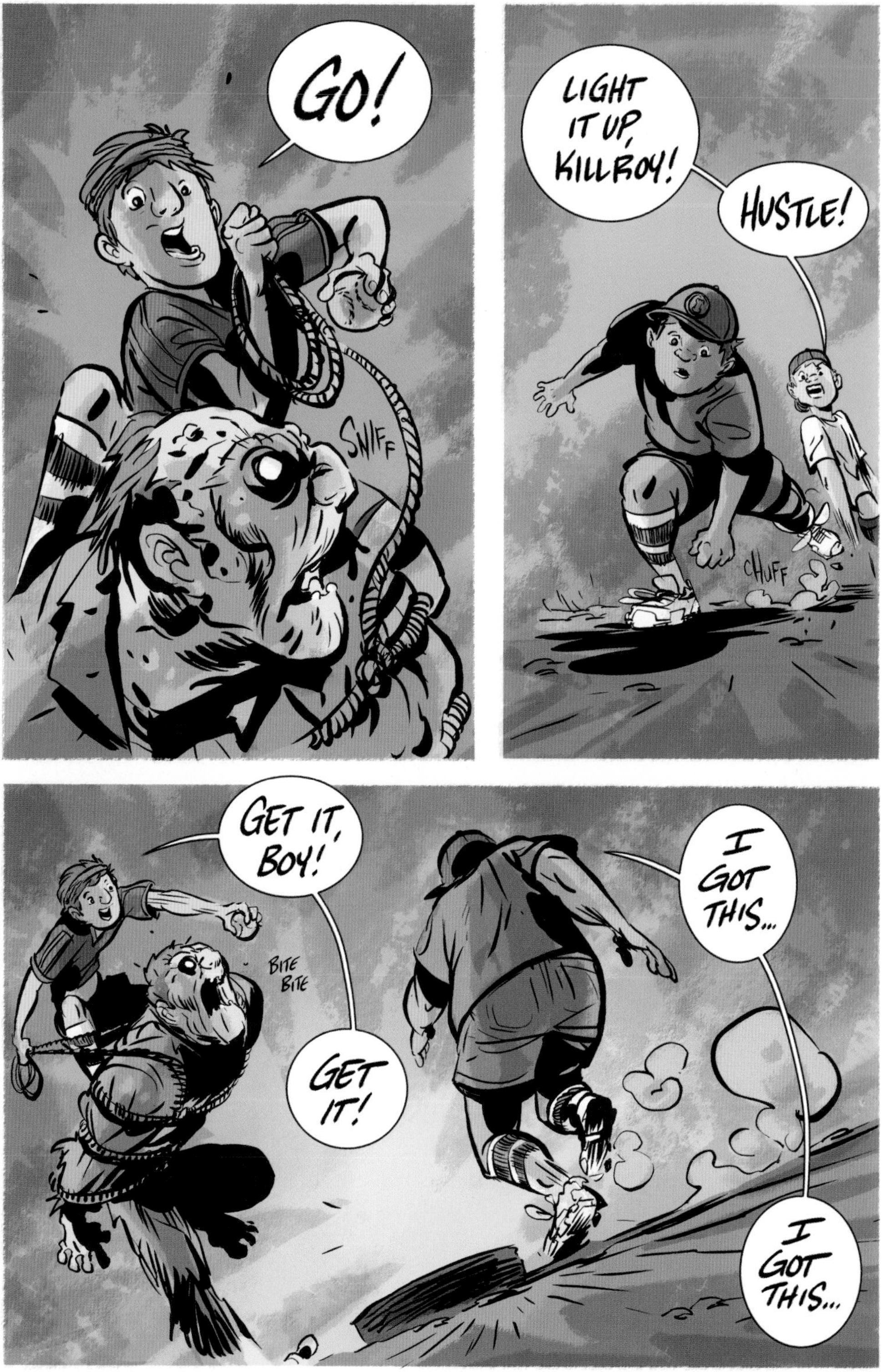
GO!
SNIFF
LIGHT IT UP, KILLBOY!
HUSTLE!
CHUFF
GET IT, BOY!
BITE BITE
GET IT!
I GOT THIS...
I GOT THIS...

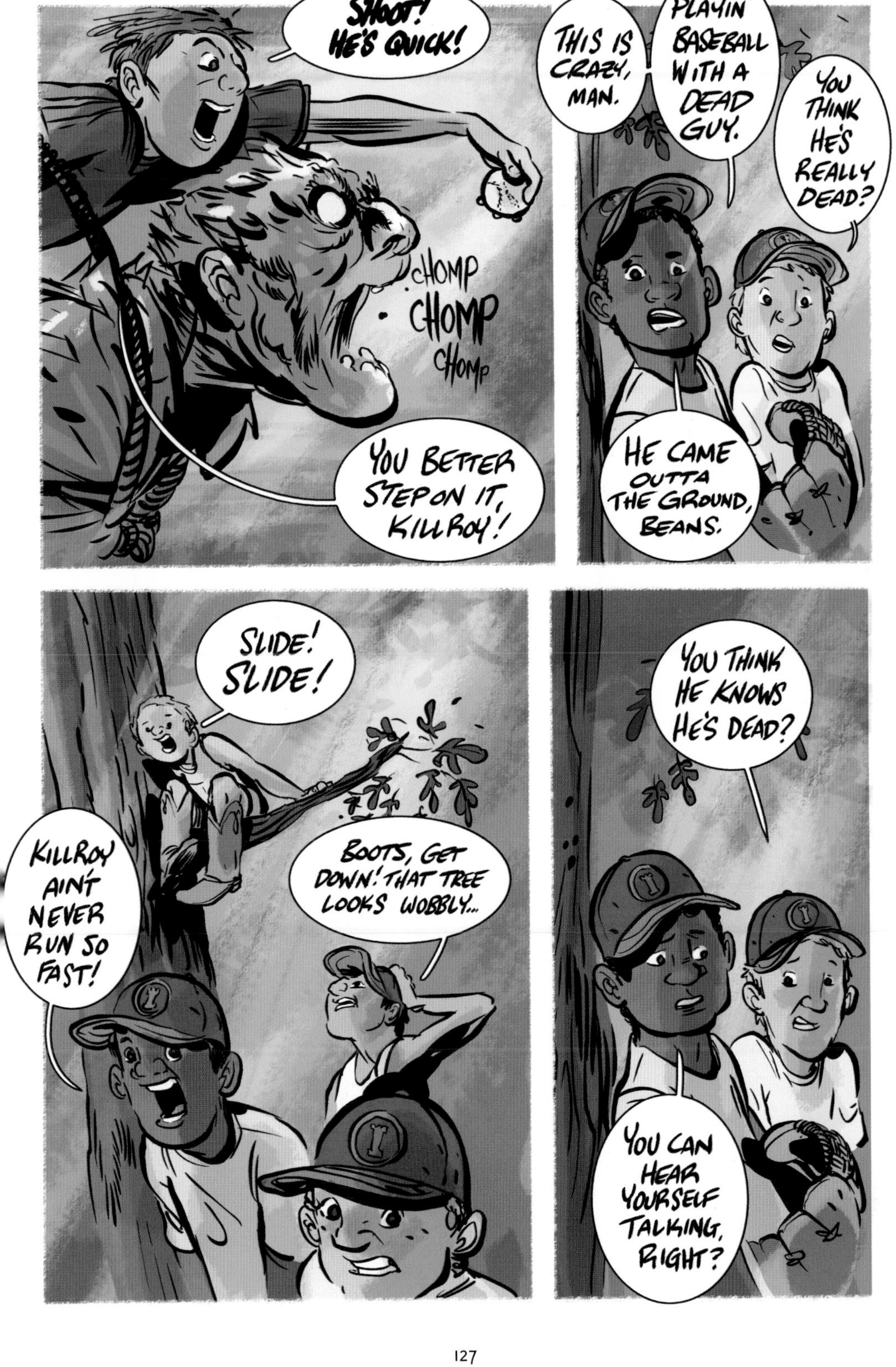
SHOOT! HE'S QUICK!
CHOMP
CHOMP
CHOMP
YOU BETTER STEP ON IT, KILLROY!
THIS IS CRAZY, MAN.
PLAYIN' BASEBALL WITH A DEAD GUY.
YOU THINK HE'S REALLY DEAD?
HE CAME OUTTA THE GROUND, BEANS.
SLIDE! SLIDE!
KILLROY AIN'T NEVER RUN SO FAST!
BOOTS, GET DOWN! THAT TREE LOOKS WOBBLY...
YOU THINK HE KNOWS HE'S DEAD?
YOU CAN HEAR YOURSELF TALKING, RIGHT?

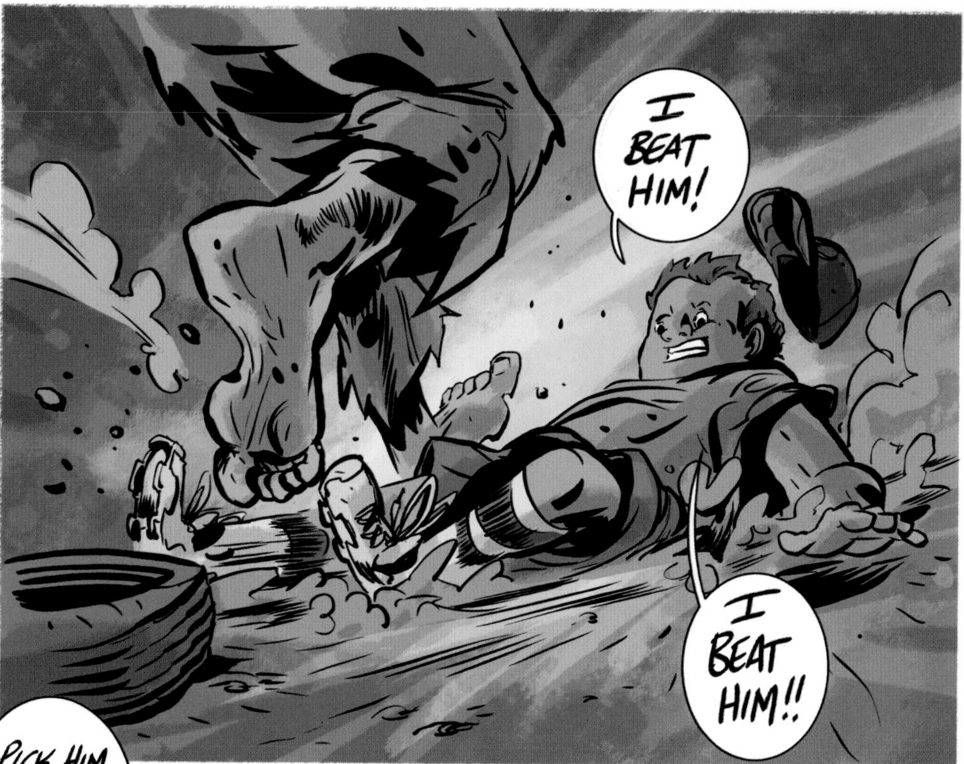
I BEAT HIM!
I BEAT HIM!!

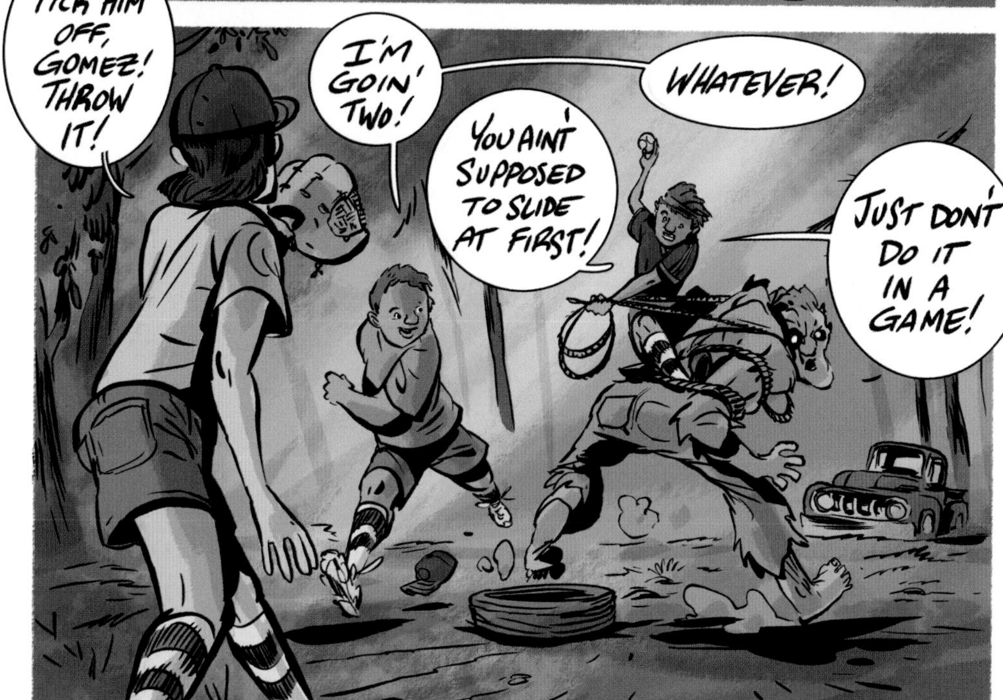
PICK HIM OFF, GOMEZ! THROW IT!
I'M GOIN' TWO!
WHATEVER!
YOU AINT SUPPOSED TO SLIDE AT FIRST!
JUST DON'T DO IT IN A GAME!

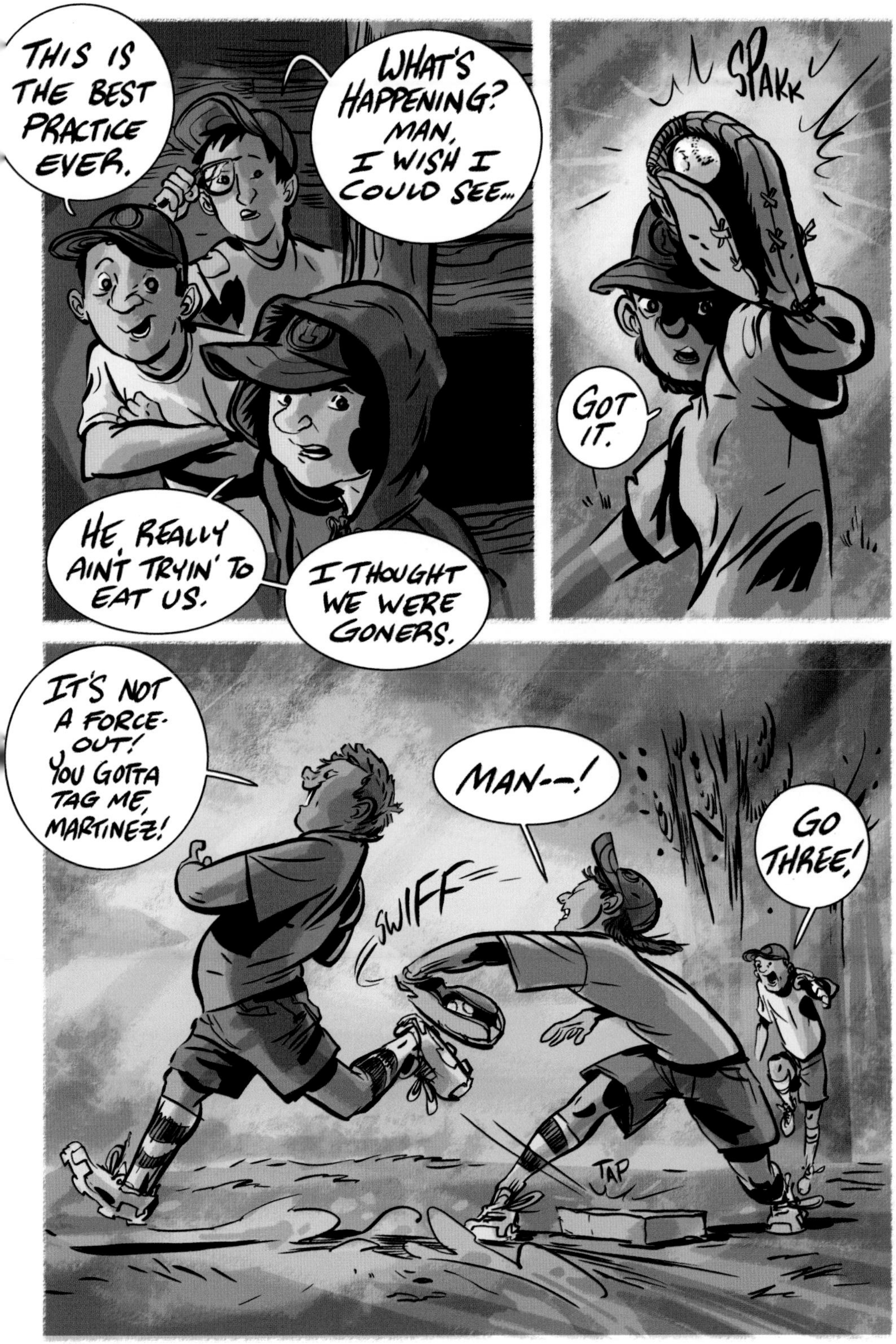
THIS IS THE BEST PRACTICE EVER.
WHAT'S HAPPENING? MAN, I WISH I COULD SEE...
HE REALLY AIN'T TRYIN' TO EAT US.
I THOUGHT WE WERE GONERS.
SPAKK
GOT IT.
IT'S NOT A FORCE-OUT! YOU GOTTA TAG ME, MARTINEZ!
MAN--!
GO THREE!
SWIFF
TAP

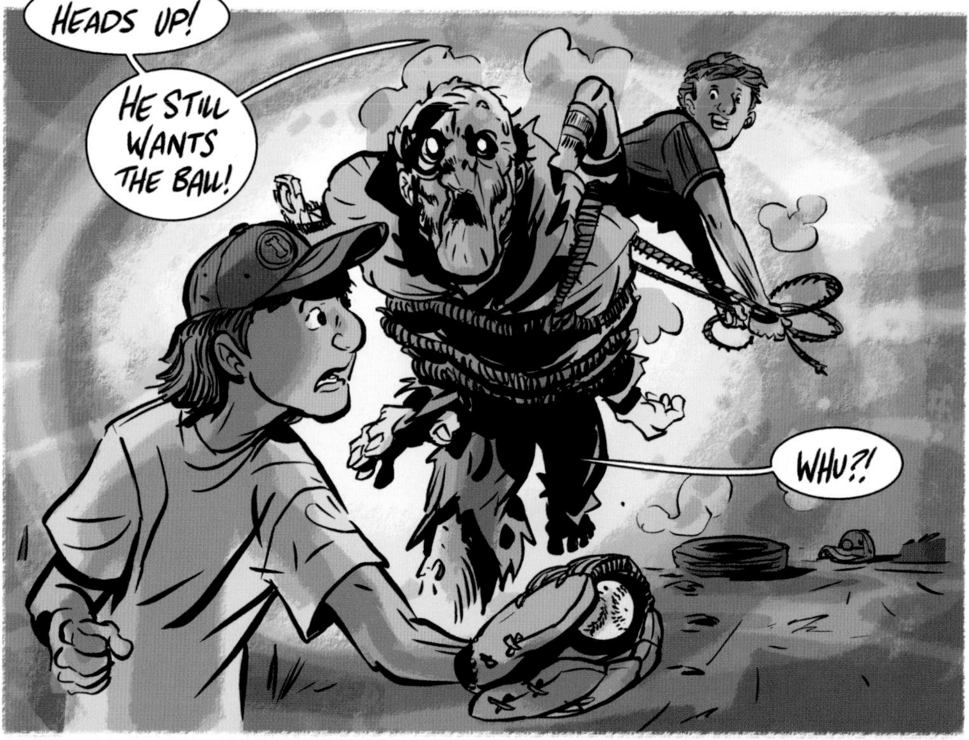
HEADS UP!
HE STILL WANTS THE BALL!
WHU?!

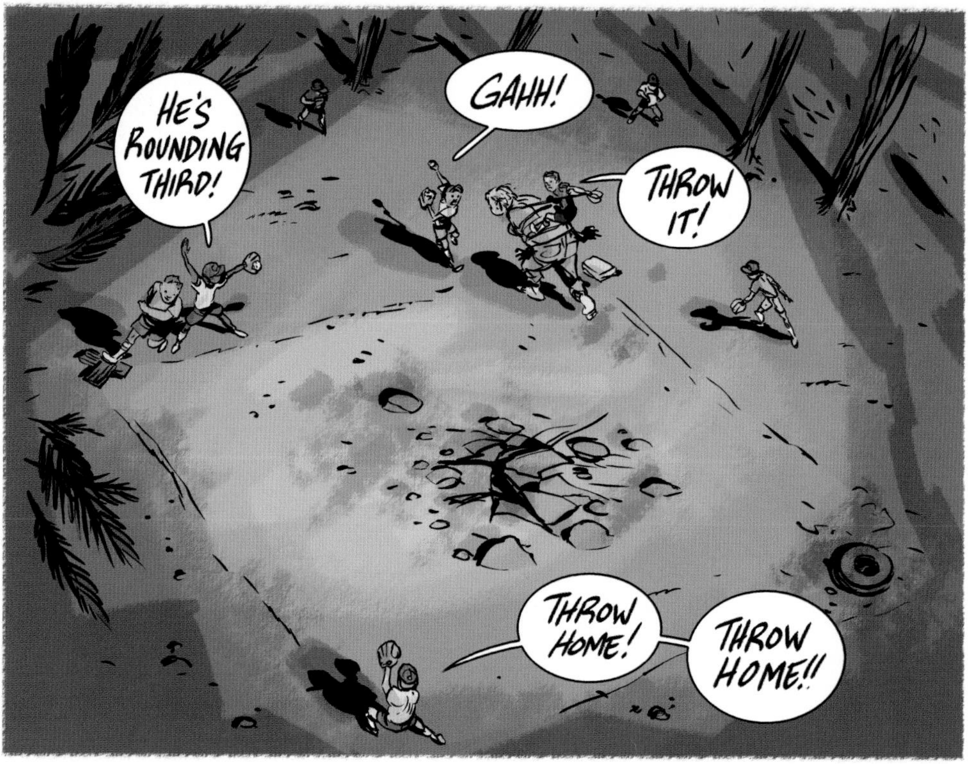
HE'S ROUNDING THIRD!
GAHH!
THROW IT!
THROW HOME!
THROW HOME!!

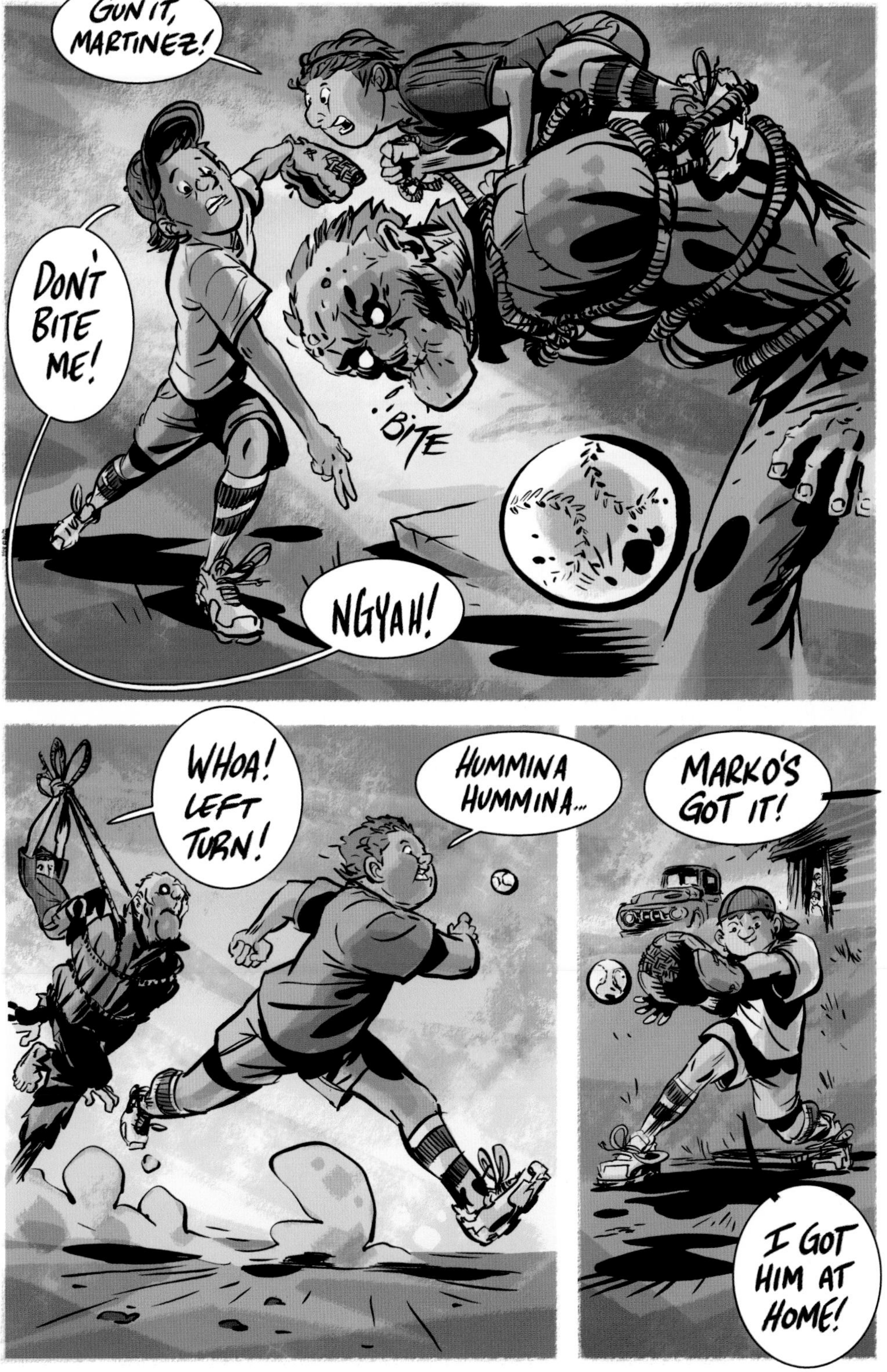
GUN IT, MARTINEZ!
DON'T BITE ME!
BITE
NGYAH!
WHOA! LEFT TURN!
HUMMINA HUMMINA...
MARKO'S GOT IT!
I GOT HIM AT HOME!

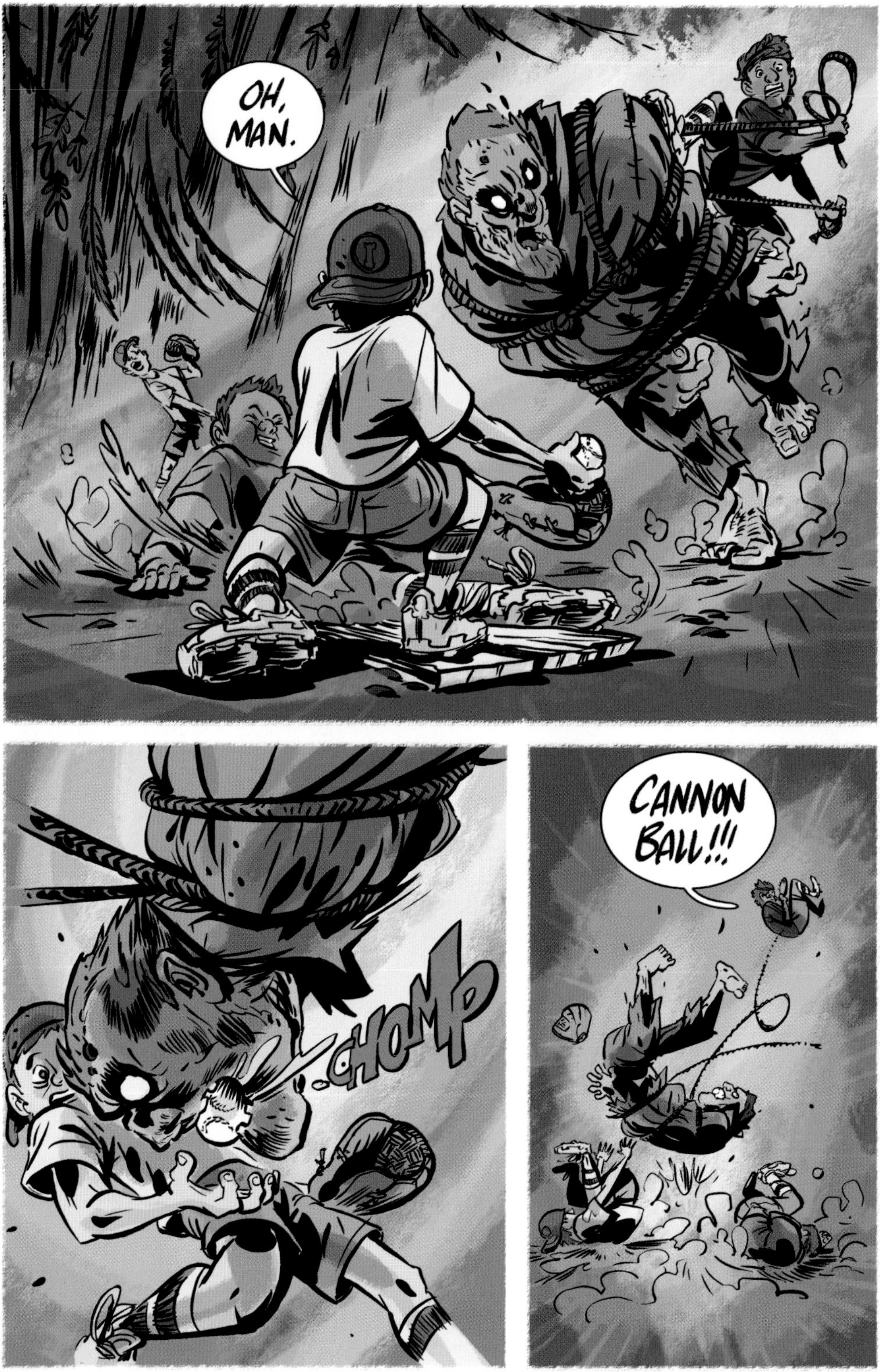
OH, MAN.
CHOMP
CANNON BALL!!!

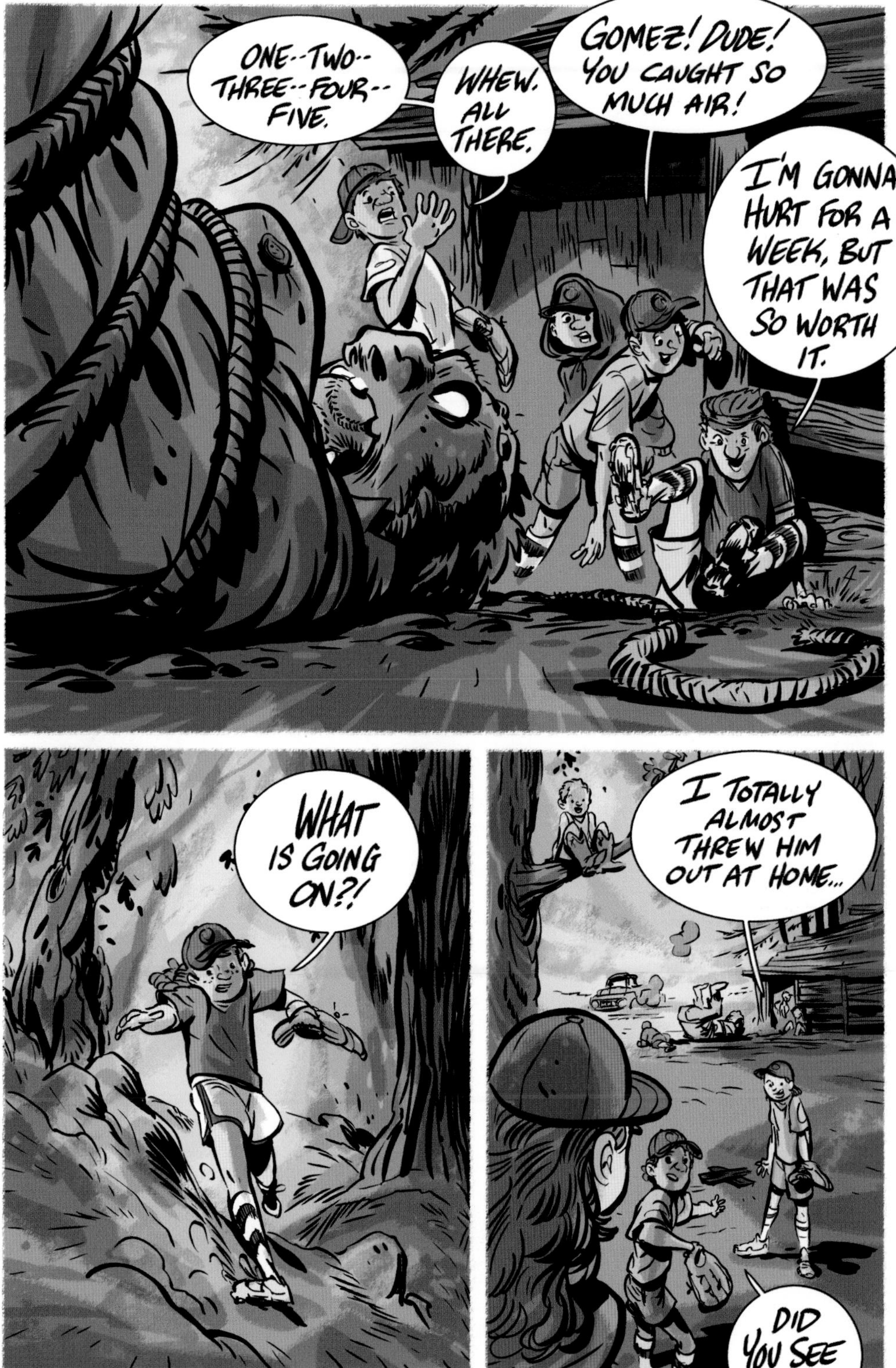
ONE--TWO--THREE--FOUR--FIVE.
WHEW. ALL THERE.
GOMEZ! DUDE! YOU CAUGHT SO MUCH AIR!
I'M GONNA HURT FOR A WEEK, BUT THAT WAS SO WORTH IT.
WHAT IS GOING ON?!
I TOTALLY ALMOST THREW HIM OUT AT HOME...
DID YOU SEE THAT?

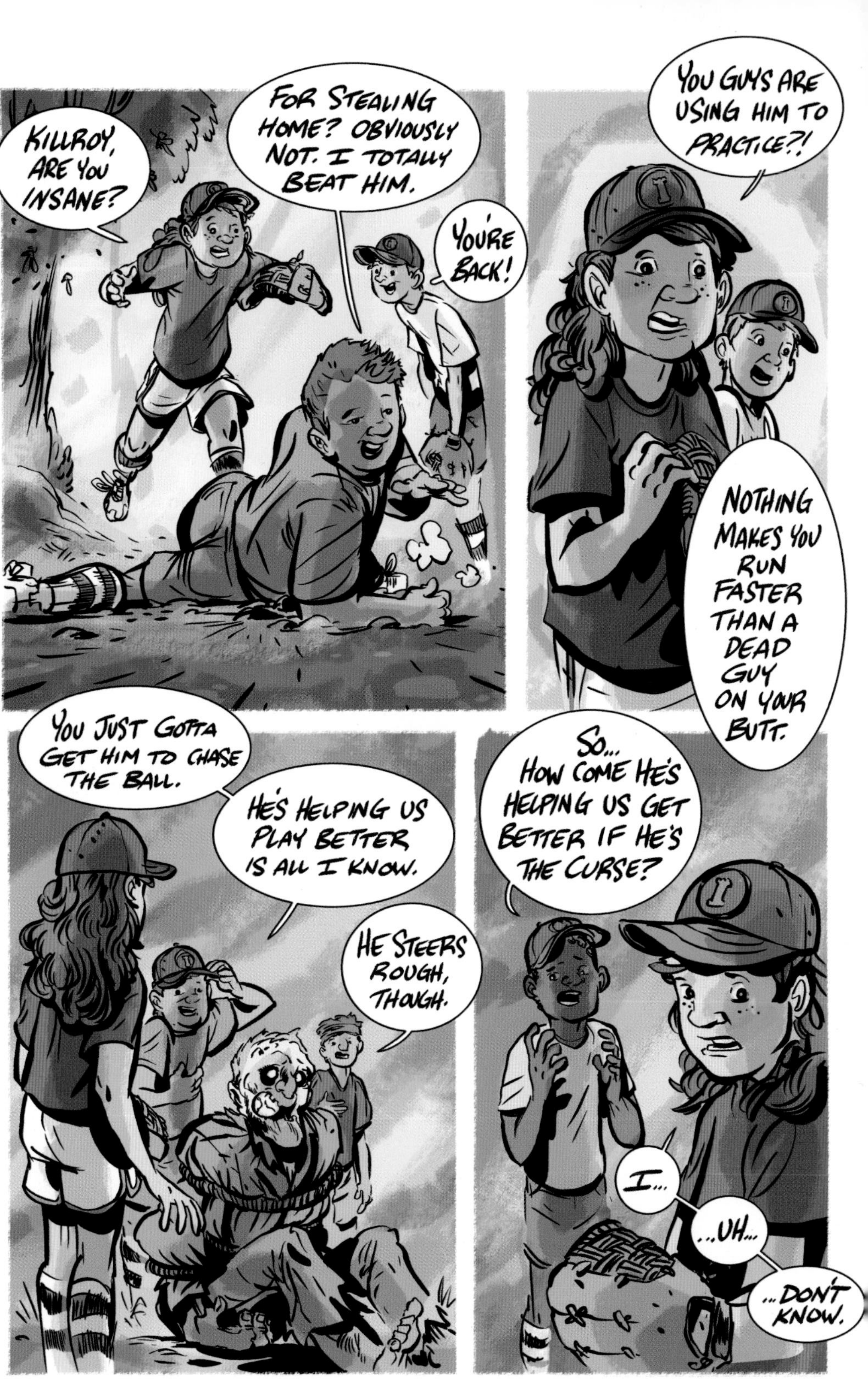
KILLROY, ARE YOU INSANE?
FOR STEALING HOME? OBVIOUSLY NOT. I TOTALLY BEAT HIM.
YOU'RE BACK!
YOU GUYS ARE USING HIM TO PRACTICE?!
NOTHING MAKES YOU RUN FASTER THAN A DEAD GUY ON YOUR BUTT.
YOU JUST GOTTA GET HIM TO CHASE THE BALL.
HE'S HELPING US PLAY BETTER IS ALL I KNOW.
HE STEERS ROUGH, THOUGH.
SO... HOW COME HE'S HELPING US GET BETTER IF HE'S THE CURSE?
I...
...UH...
...DON'T KNOW.

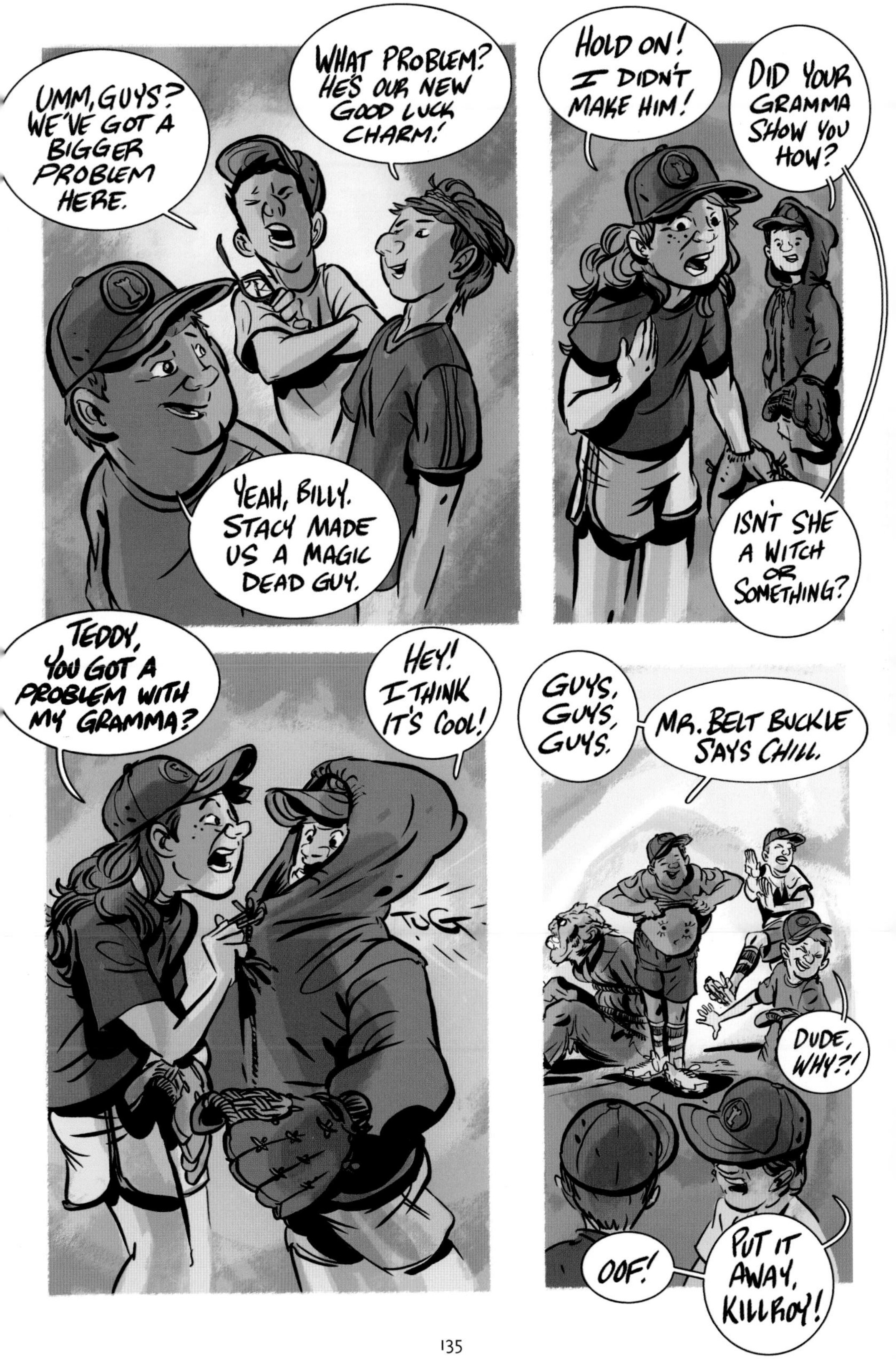
UMM, GUYS? WE'VE GOT A BIGGER PROBLEM HERE.
WHAT PROBLEM? HE'S OUR NEW GOOD LUCK CHARM!
YEAH, BILLY. STACY MADE US A MAGIC DEAD GUY.
HOLD ON! I DIDN'T MAKE HIM!
DID YOUR GRAMMA SHOW YOU HOW?
ISN'T SHE A WITCH OR SOMETHING?
TEDDY, YOU GOT A PROBLEM WITH MY GRAMMA?
HEY! I THINK IT'S COOL!
TUG
GUYS, GUYS, GUYS.
MR. BELT BUCKLE SAYS CHILL.
DUDE, WHY?!
OOF!
PUT IT AWAY, KILLROY!

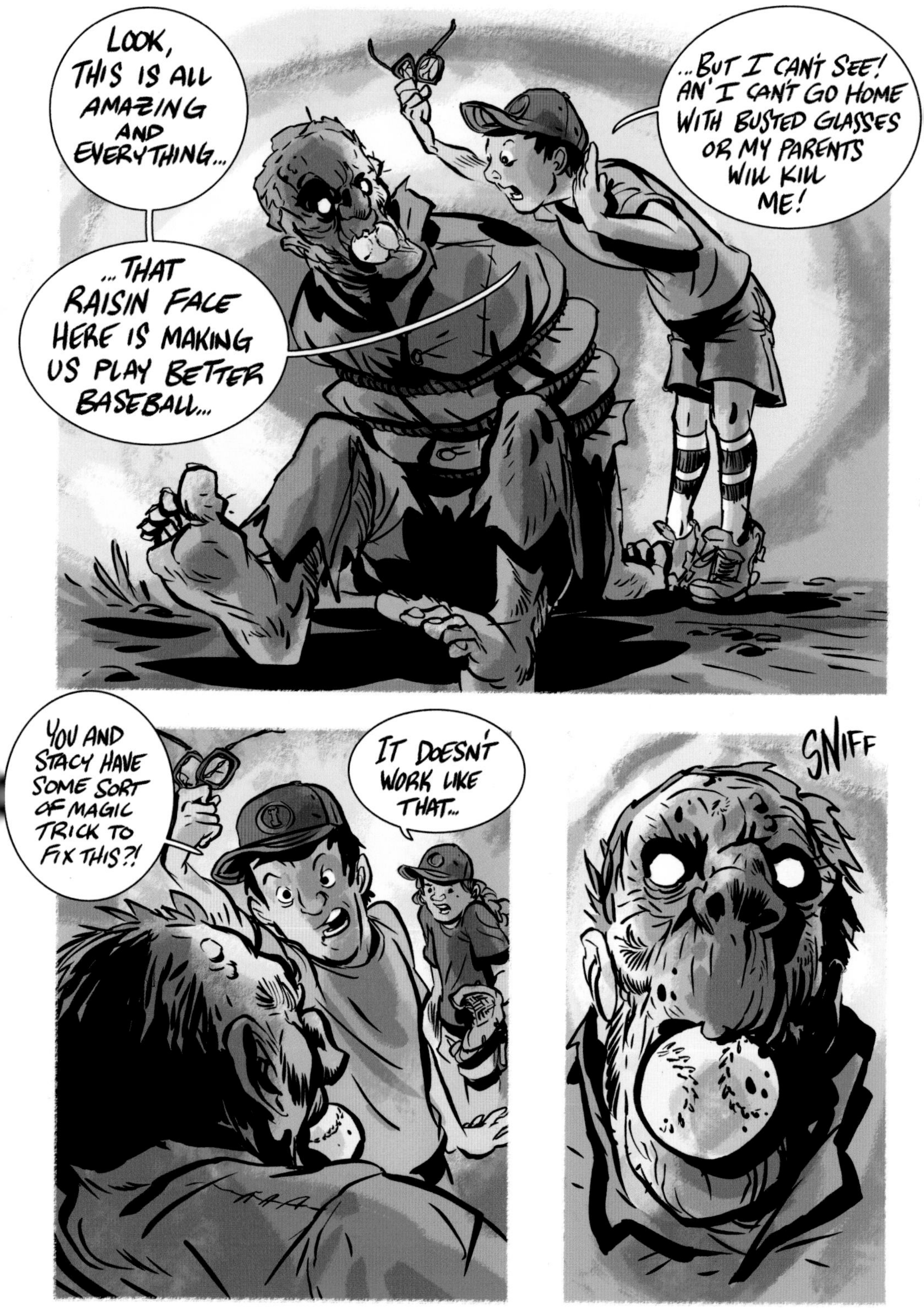
LOOK, THIS IS ALL AMAZING AND EVERYTHING...
...THAT RAISIN FACE HERE IS MAKING US PLAY BETTER BASEBALL...
...BUT I CAN'T SEE! AN' I CAN'T GO HOME WITH BUSTED GLASSES OR MY PARENTS WILL KILL ME!
YOU AND STACY HAVE SOME SORT OF MAGIC TRICK TO FIX THIS?!
IT DOESN'T WORK LIKE THAT...
SNIFF

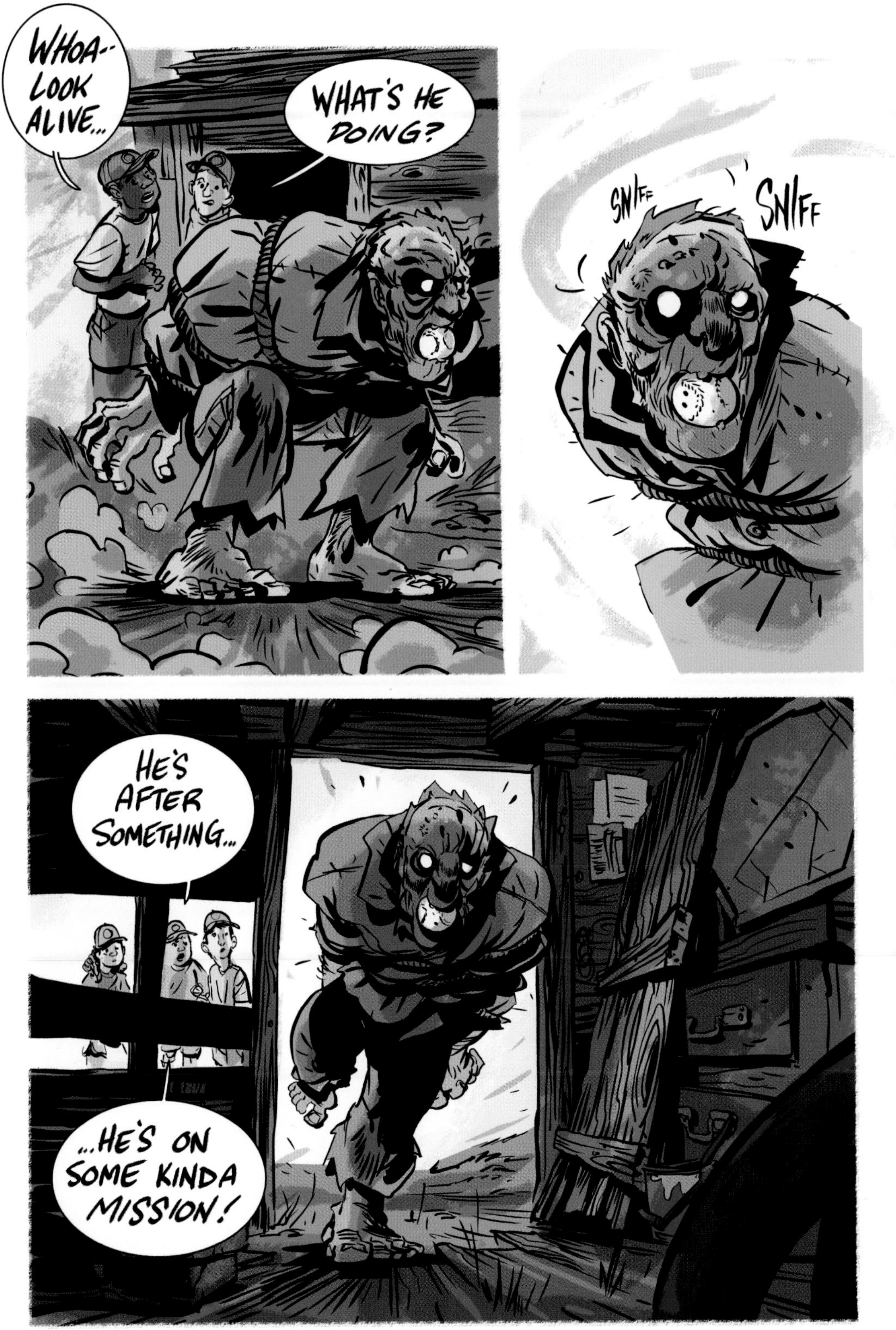
WHOA-- LOOK ALIVE...
WHAT'S HE DOING?
SNIFF
SNIFF
HE'S AFTER SOMETHING...
...HE'S ON SOME KINDA MISSION!

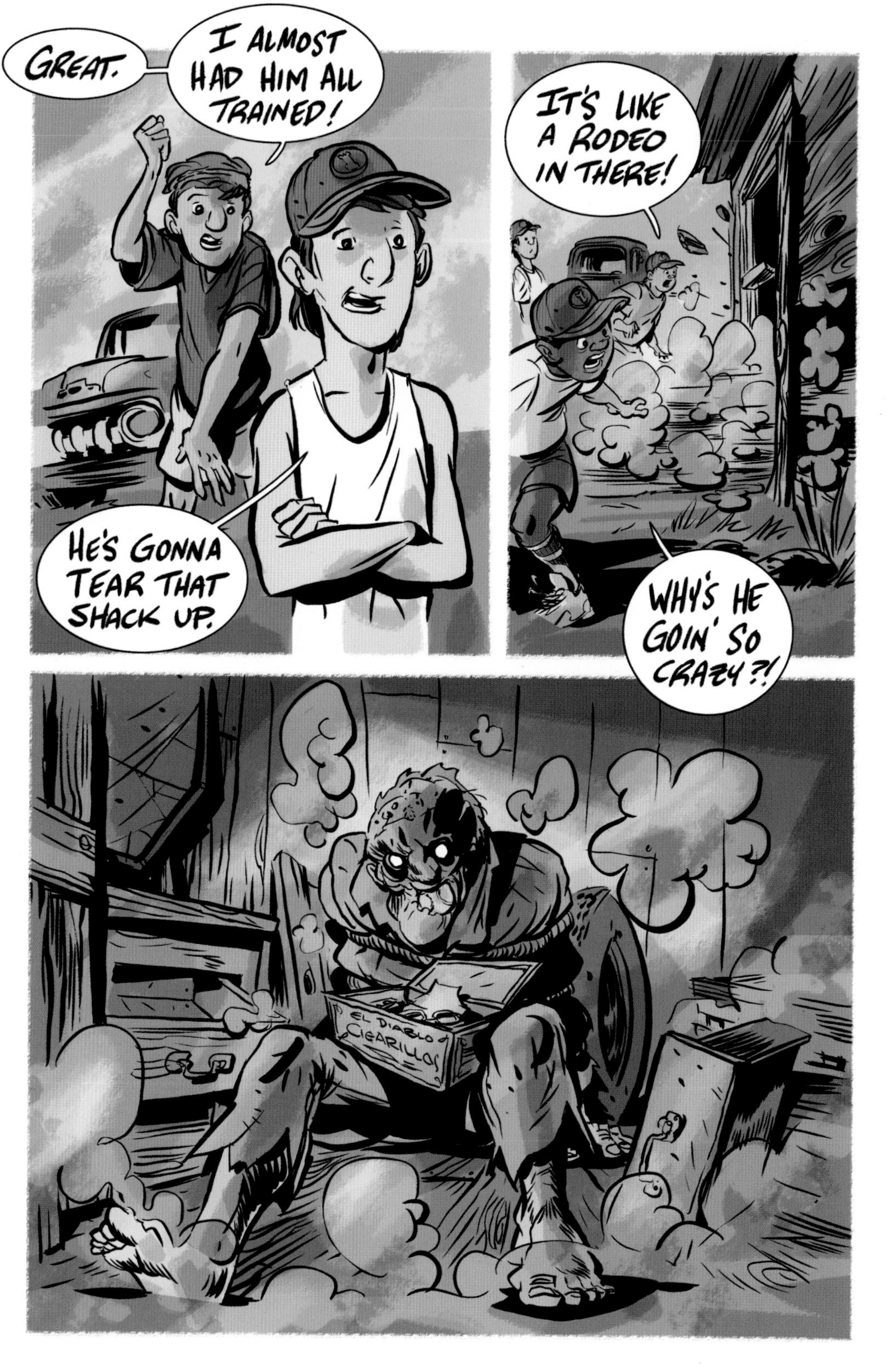
GREAT.
I ALMOST HAD HIM ALL TRAINED!
HE'S GONNA TEAR THAT SHACK UP.
IT'S LIKE A RODEO IN THERE!
WHY'S HE GOIN' SO CRAZY?!
EL DIABLO CIGARILLOS

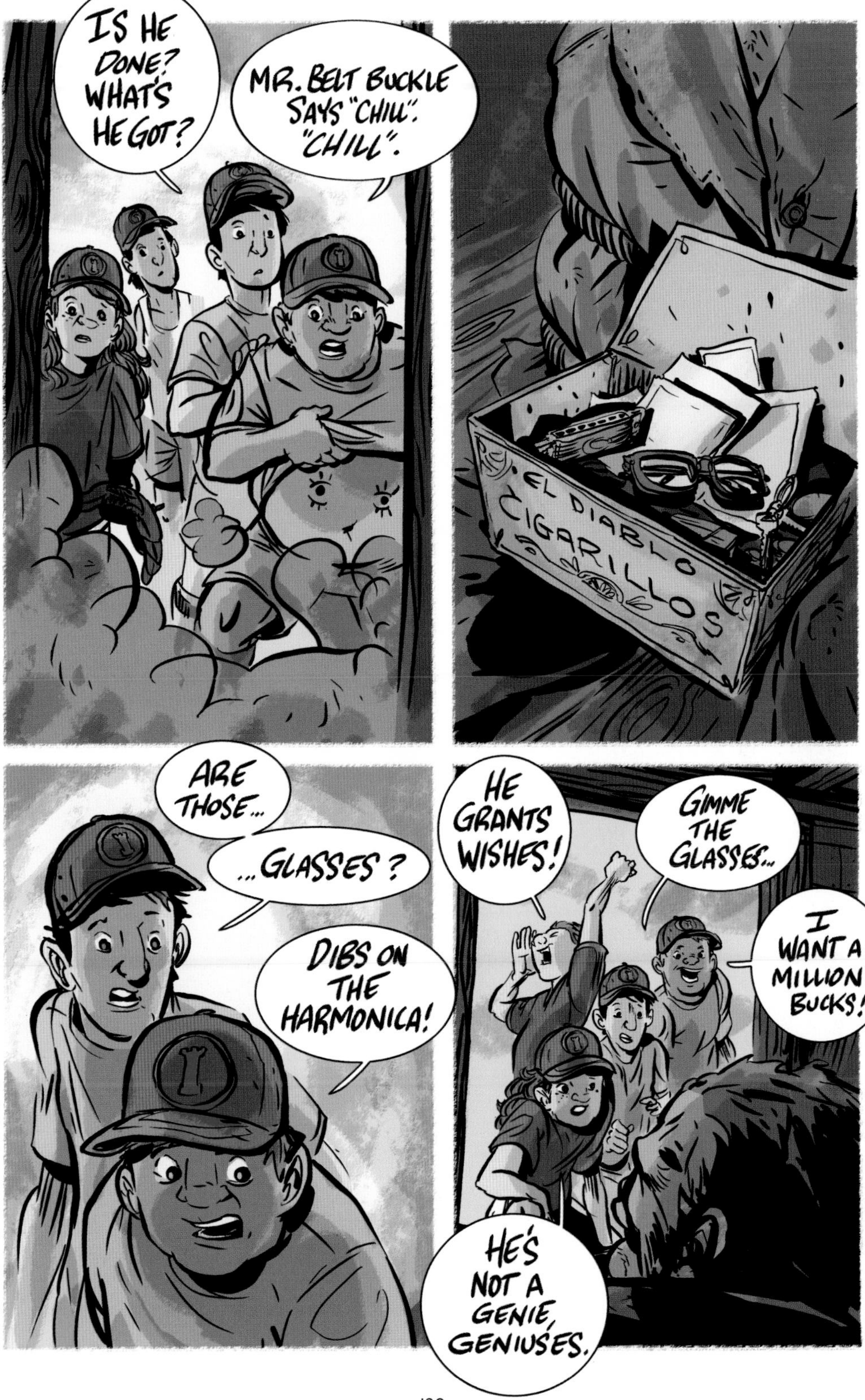
IS HE DONE? WHAT'S HE GOT?
MR. BELT BUCKLE SAYS "CHILL". "CHILL".
EL DIABLO CIGARILLOS
ARE THOSE...
...GLASSES?
DIBS ON THE HARMONICA!
HE GRANTS WISHES!
GIMME THE GLASSES...
I WANT A MILLION BUCKS!
HE'S NOT A GENIE, GENIUSES.

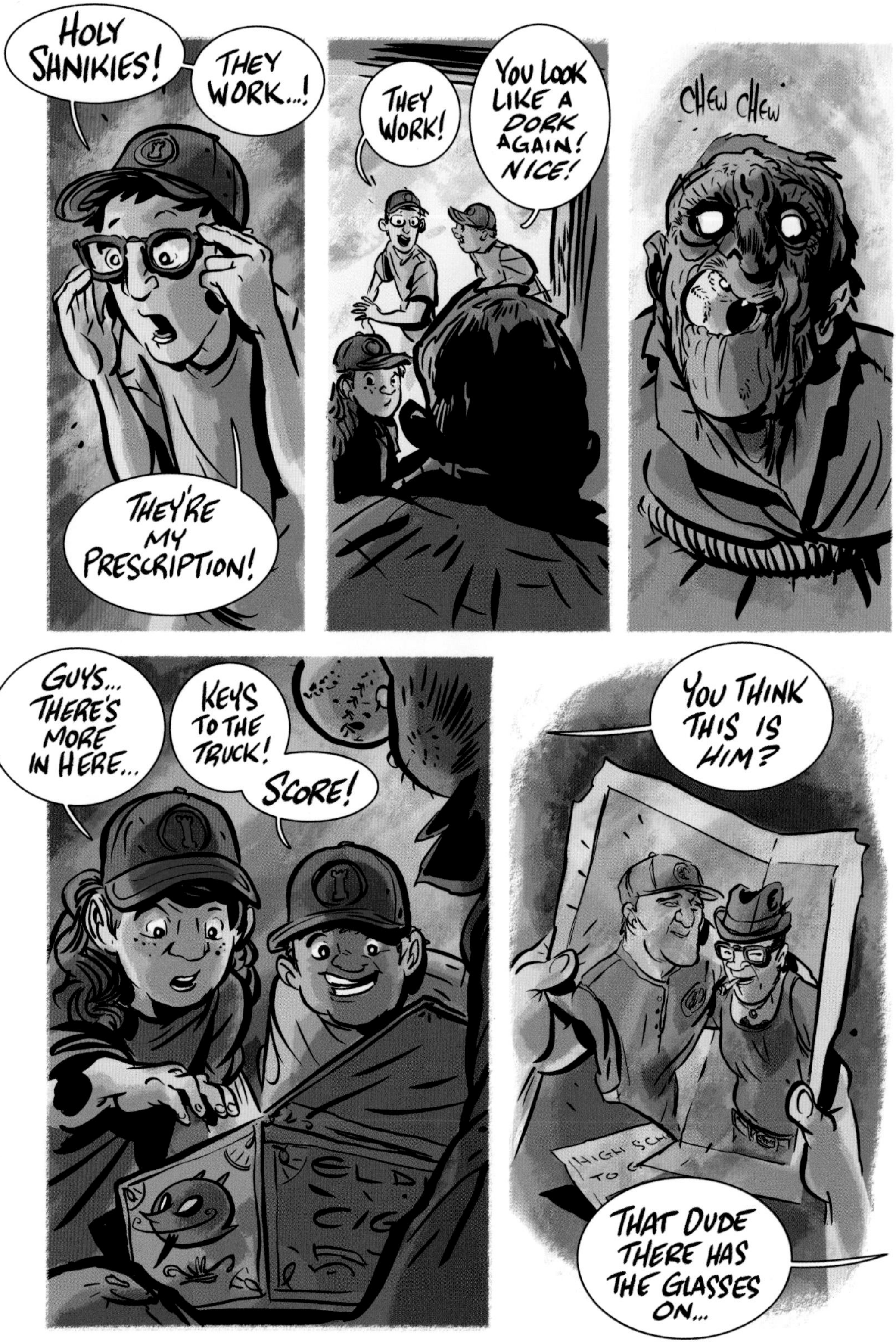
HOLY SHNIKIES!
THEY WORK...!
THEY'RE MY PRESCRIPTION!
THEY WORK!
YOU LOOK LIKE A DORK AGAIN! NICE!
CHEW CHEW
GUYS... THERE'S MORE IN HERE...
KEYS TO THE TRUCK!
SCORE!
YOU THINK THIS IS HIM?
THAT DUDE THERE HAS THE GLASSES ON...

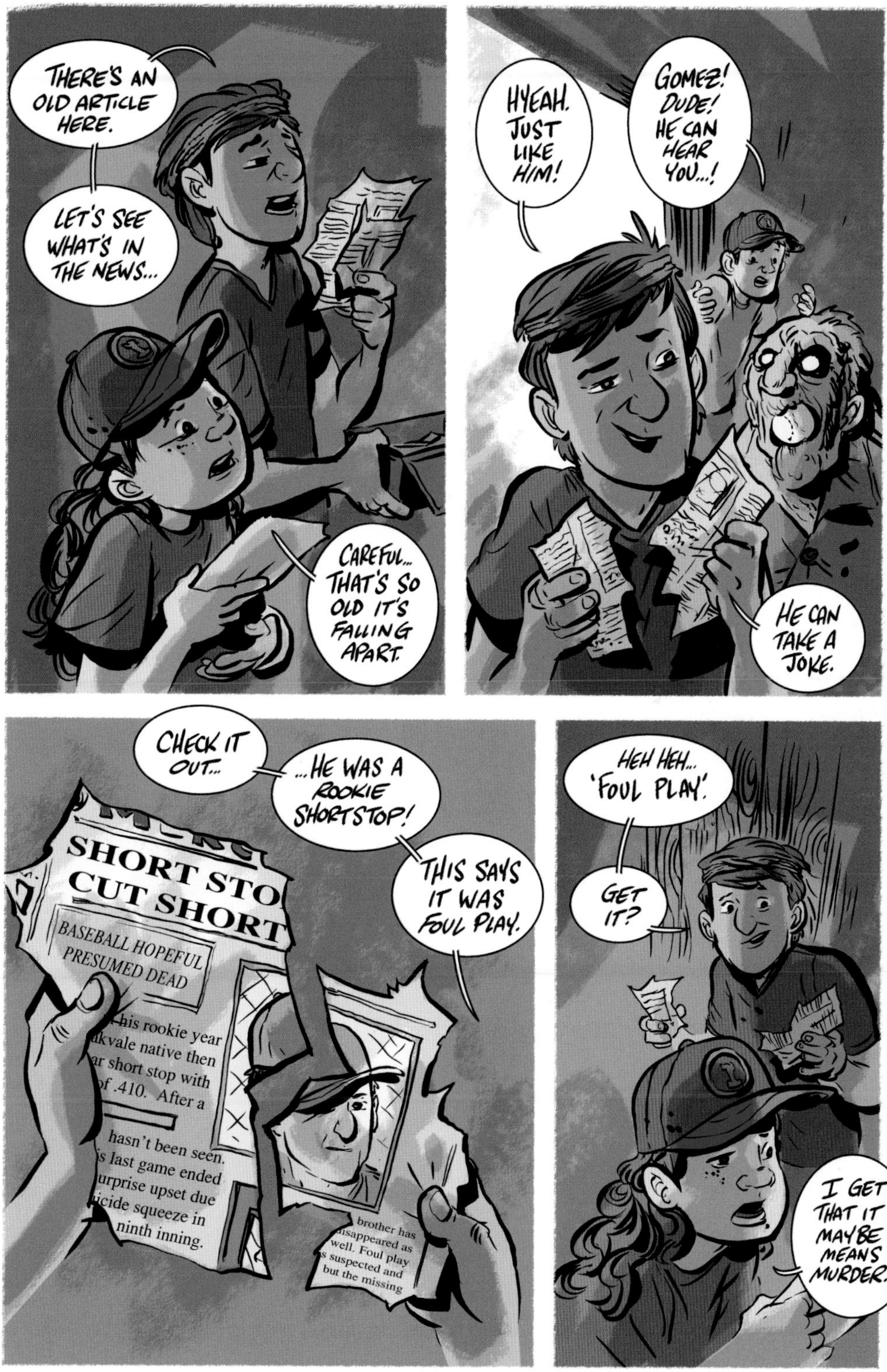
THERE'S AN OLD ARTICLE HERE.
LET'S SEE WHAT'S IN THE NEWS...
CAREFUL... THAT'S SO OLD IT'S FALLING APART.
GOMEZ! DUDE! HE CAN HEAR YOU...!
HYEAH. JUST LIKE HIM!
HE CAN TAKE A JOKE.
CHECK IT OUT...
...HE WAS A ROOKIE SHORTSTOP!
THIS SAYS IT WAS FOUL PLAY.
SHORT STO
CUT SHORT
BASEBALL HOPEFUL PRESUMED DEAD
his rookie year
akvale native then
ar short stop with
of .410. After a
hasn't been seen.
is last game ended
urprise upset due
icide squeeze in
ninth inning.
brother has
disappeared as
well. Foul play
s suspected and
but the missing
HEH HEH... 'FOUL PLAY'.
GET IT?
I GET THAT IT MAYBE MEANS MURDER.

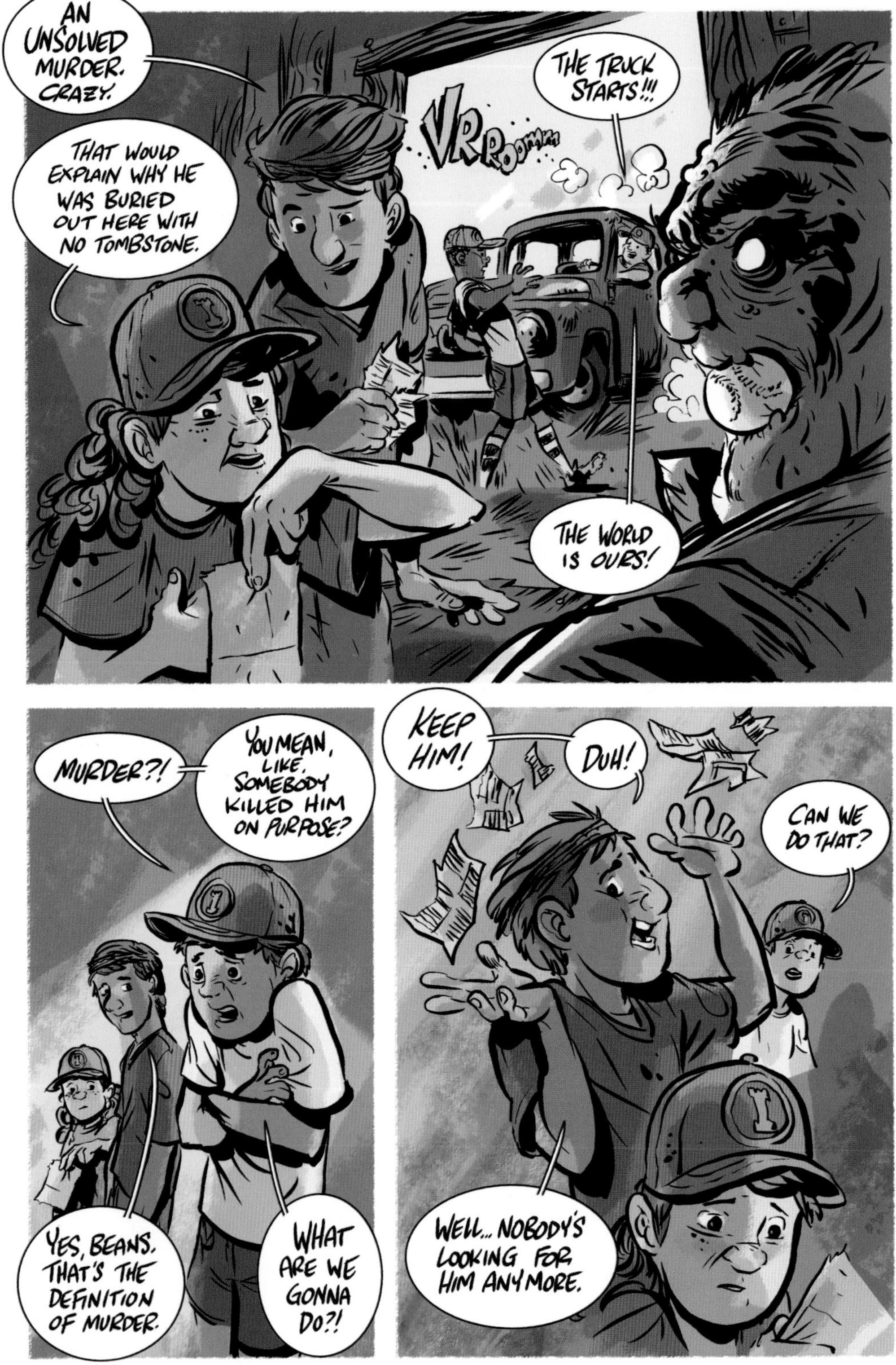
AN UNSOLVED MURDER. CRAZY.
THAT WOULD EXPLAIN WHY HE WAS BURIED OUT HERE WITH NO TOMBSTONE.
VRROOO
THE TRUCK STARTS!!!
THE WORLD IS OURS!
MURDER?!
YOU MEAN, LIKE, SOMEBODY KILLED HIM ON PURPOSE?
YES, BEANS. THAT'S THE DEFINITION OF MURDER.
WHAT ARE WE GONNA DO?!
KEEP HIM!
DUH!
CAN WE DO THAT?
WELL... NOBODY'S LOOKING FOR HIM ANYMORE.

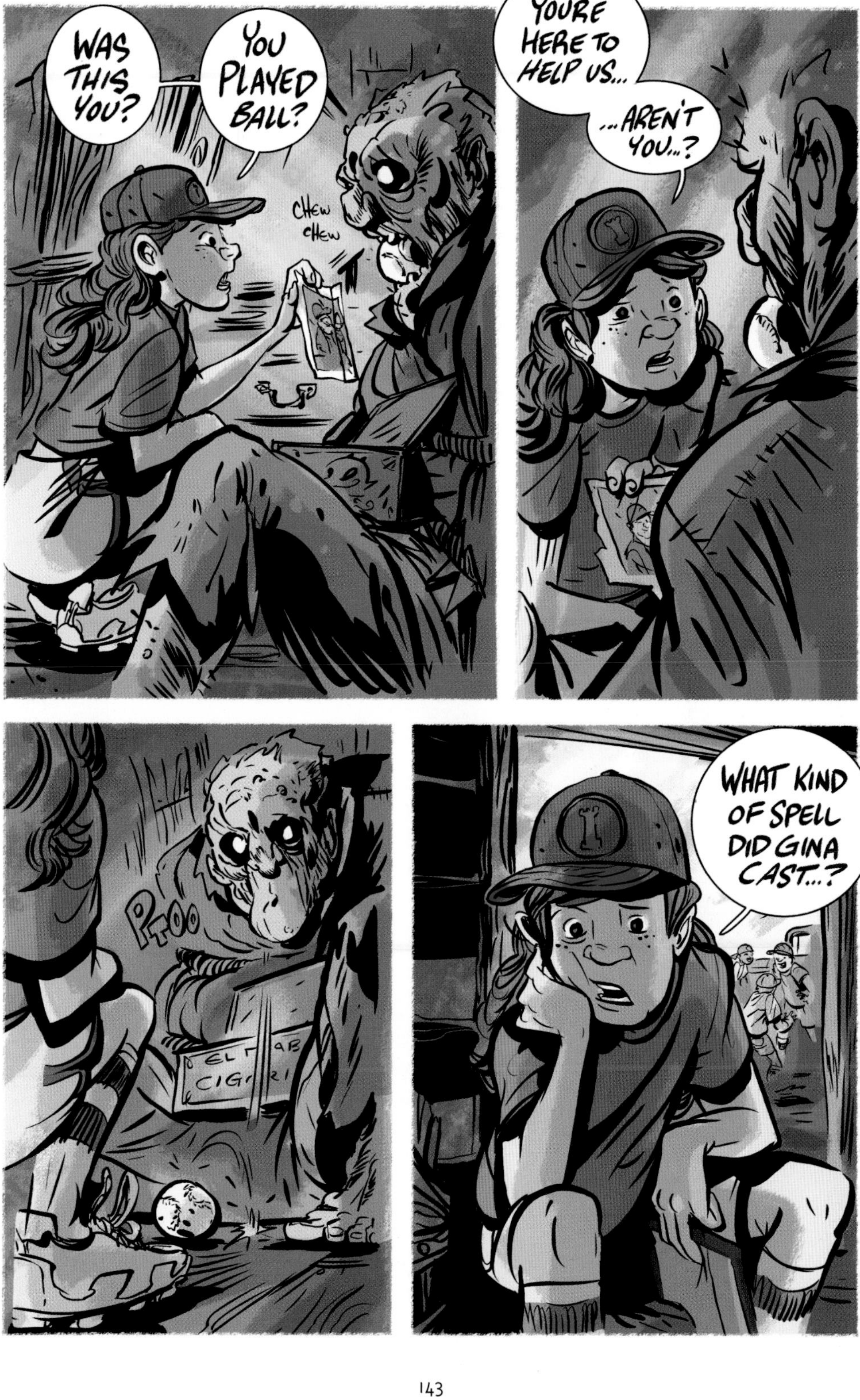
WAS THIS YOU?
YOU PLAYED BALL?
CHEW CHEW
YOU'RE HERE TO HELP US...
...AREN'T YOU...?
PTOO
WHAT KIND OF SPELL DID GINA CAST...?

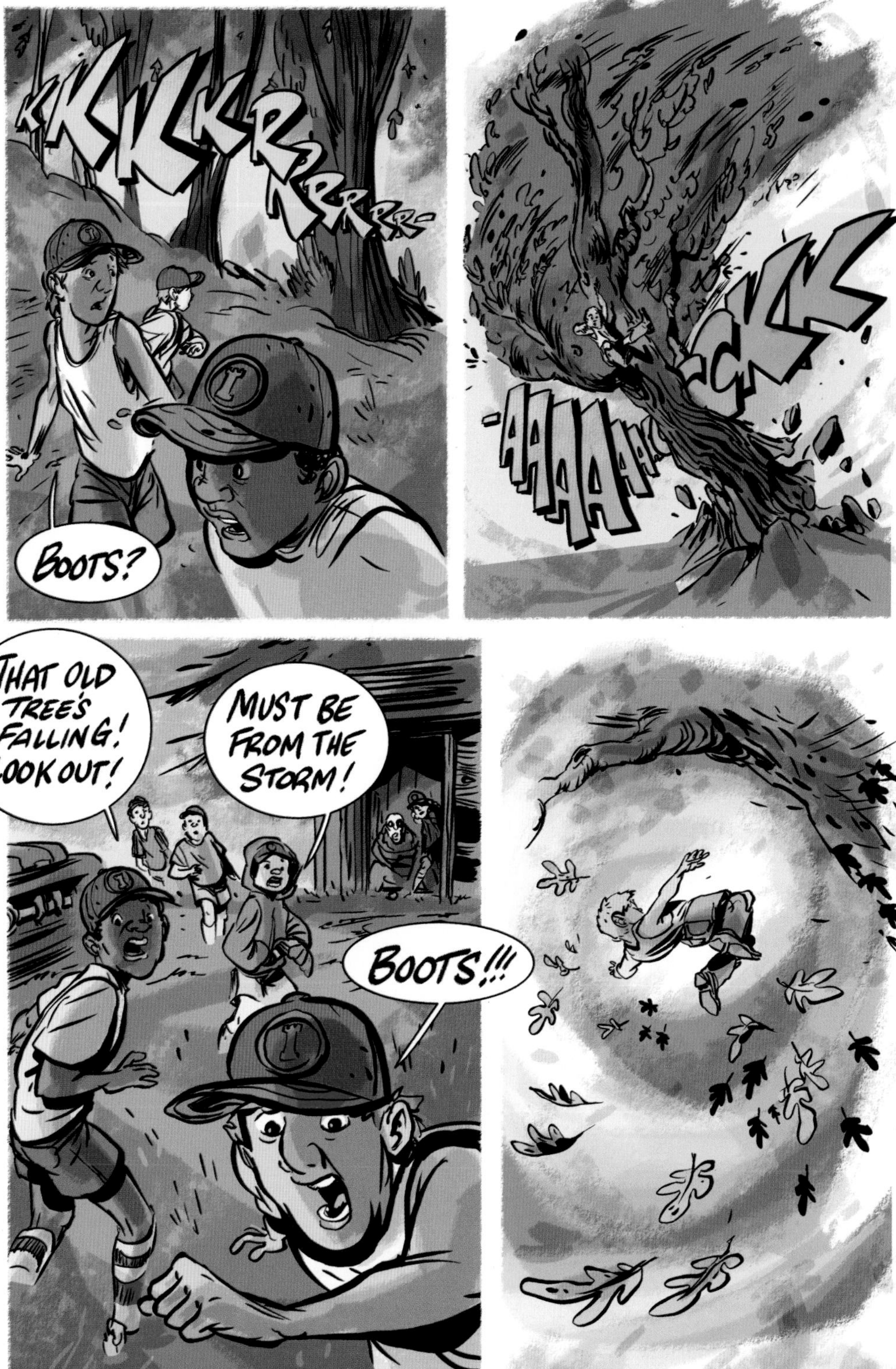
BOOTS?
THAT OLD TREE'S FALLING! LOOK OUT!
MUST BE FROM THE STORM!
BOOTS!!!

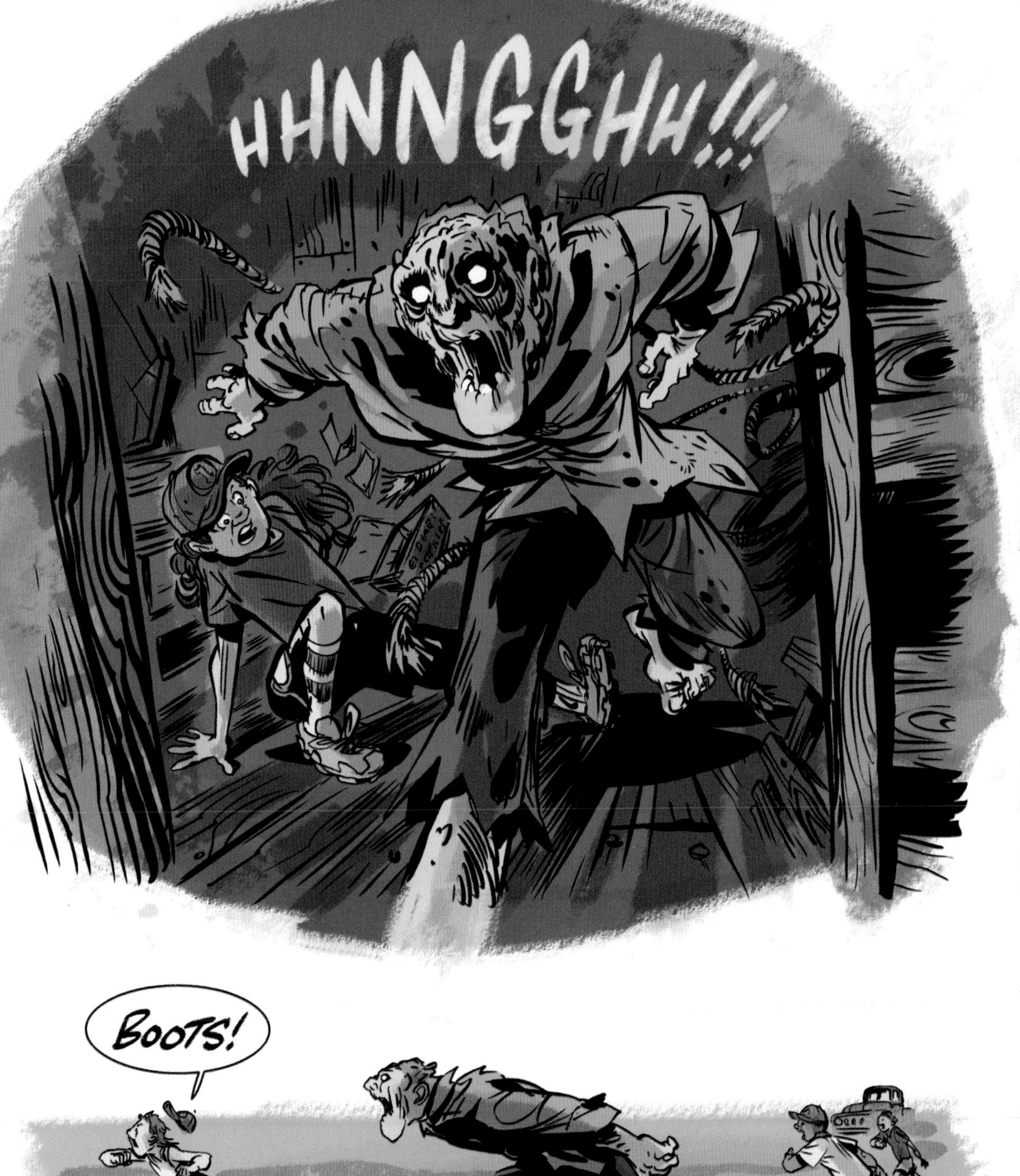
HHNNGGHH!!!

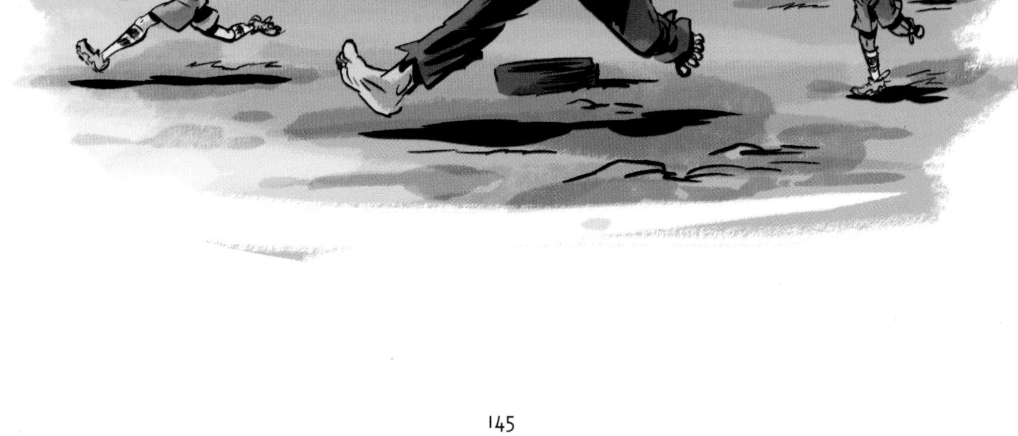
BOOTS!

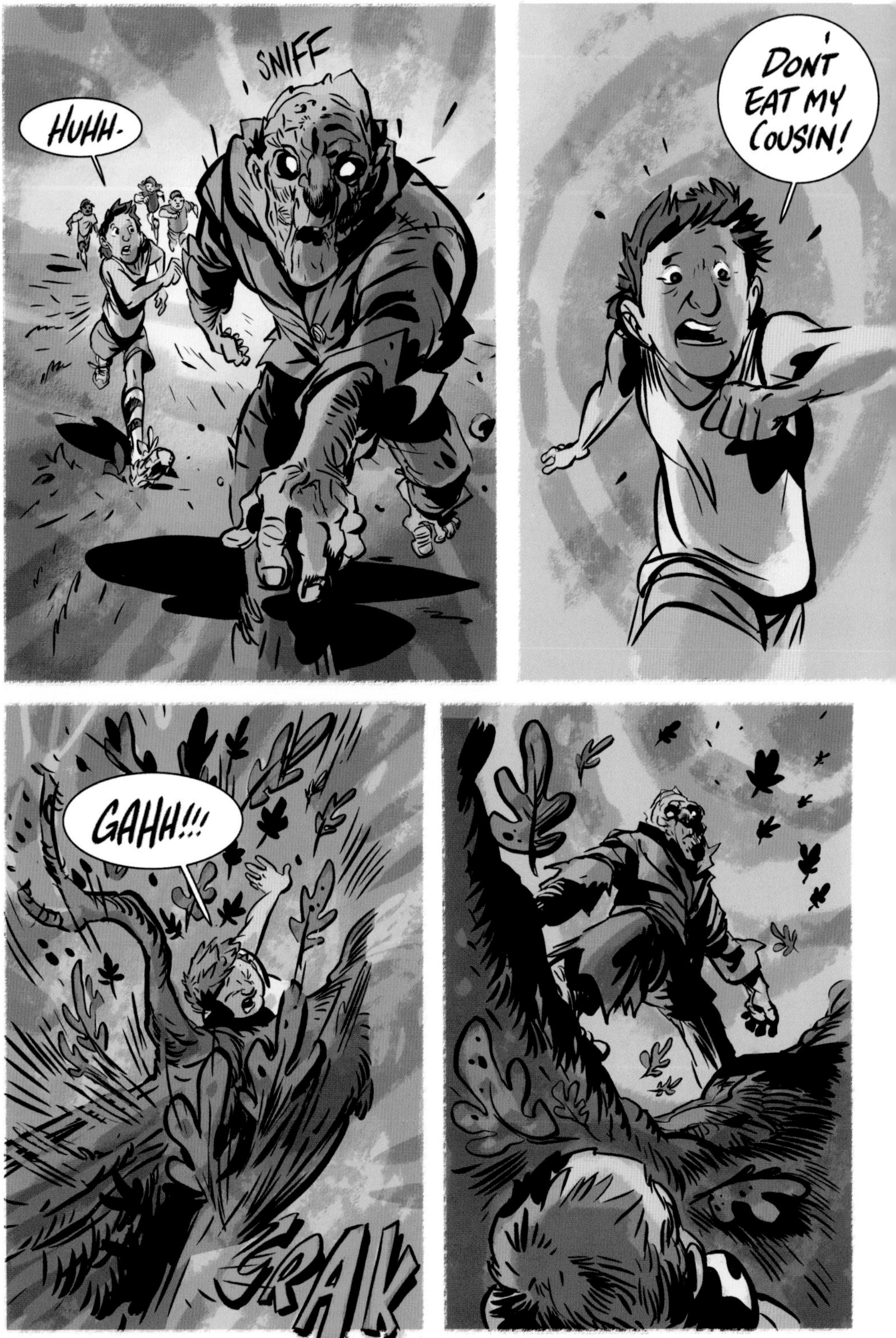
SNIFF
HUHH-
DON'T EAT MY COUSIN!
GAHH!!!
GRAK

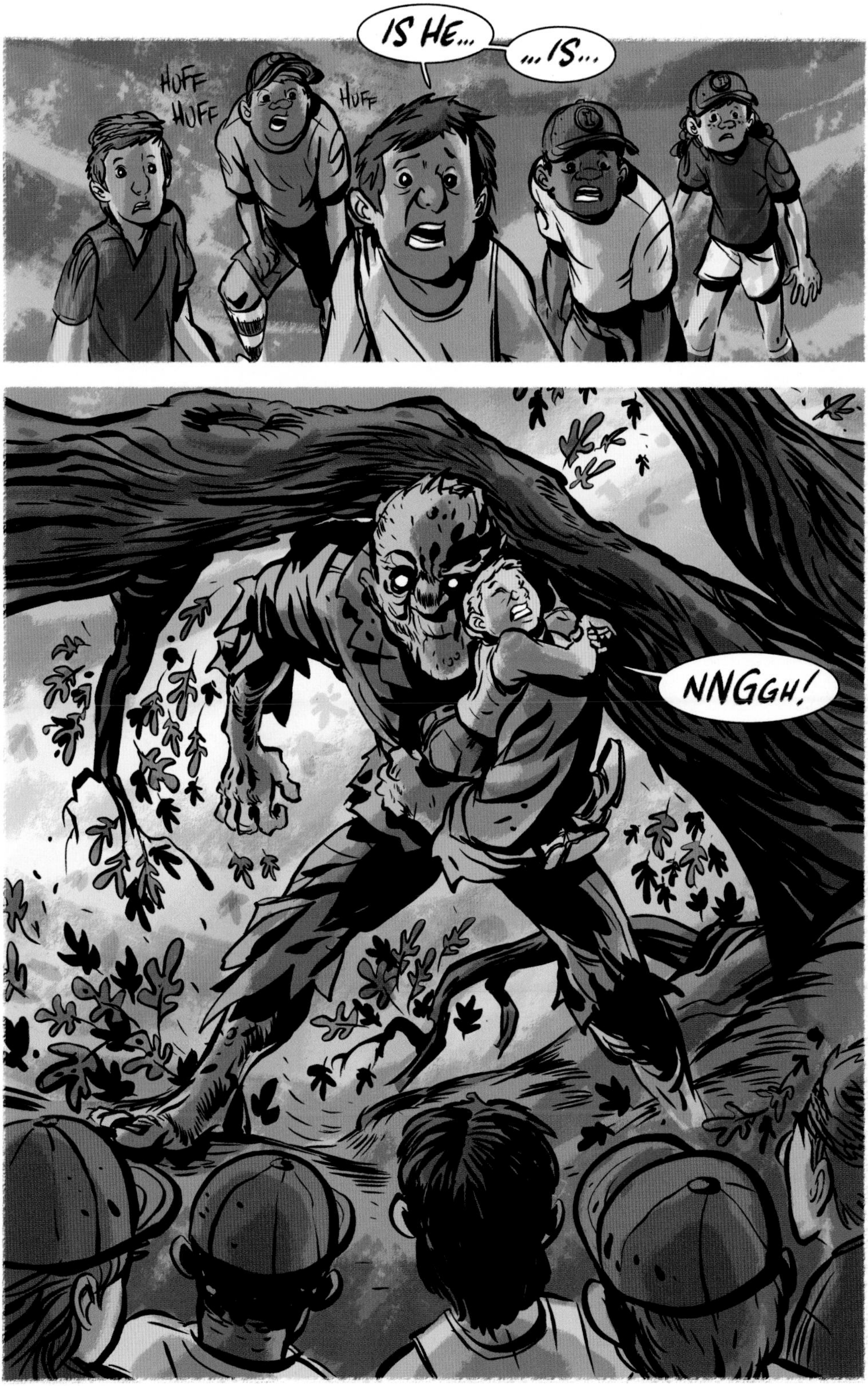
IS HE...
...IS...
HUFF
HUFF
HUFF
NNGGH!

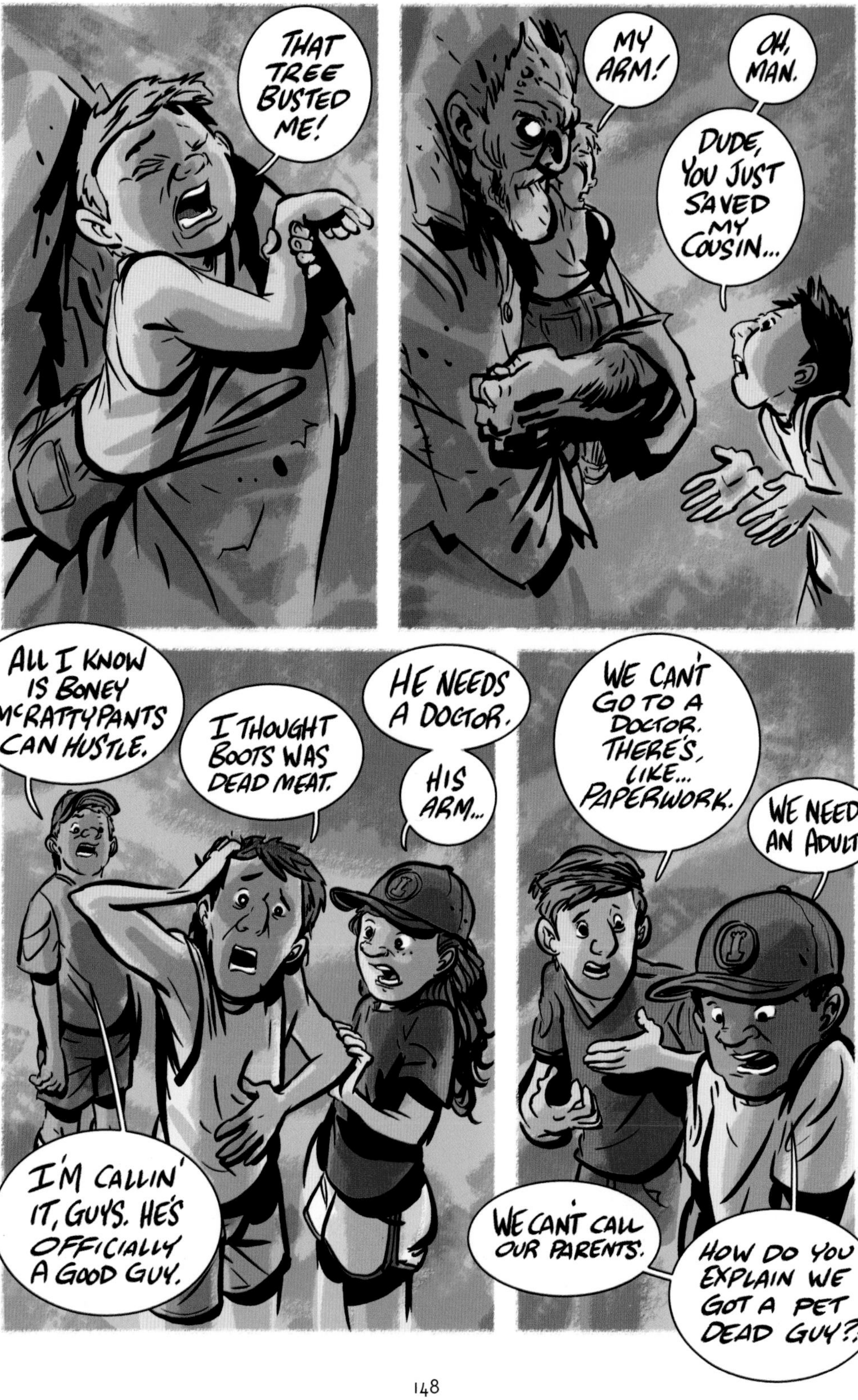
THAT TREE BUSTED ME!
MY ARM!
OH, MAN.
DUDE, YOU JUST SAVED MY COUSIN...
ALL I KNOW IS BONEY McRATTYPANTS CAN HUSTLE.
I THOUGHT BOOTS WAS DEAD MEAT.
HE NEEDS A DOCTOR.
HIS ARM...
I'M CALLIN' IT, GUYS. HE'S OFFICIALLY A GOOD GUY.
WE CAN'T GO TO A DOCTOR. THERE'S, LIKE... PAPERWORK.
WE NEED AN ADULT.
WE CAN'T CALL OUR PARENTS.
HOW DO YOU EXPLAIN WE GOT A PET DEAD GUY?!

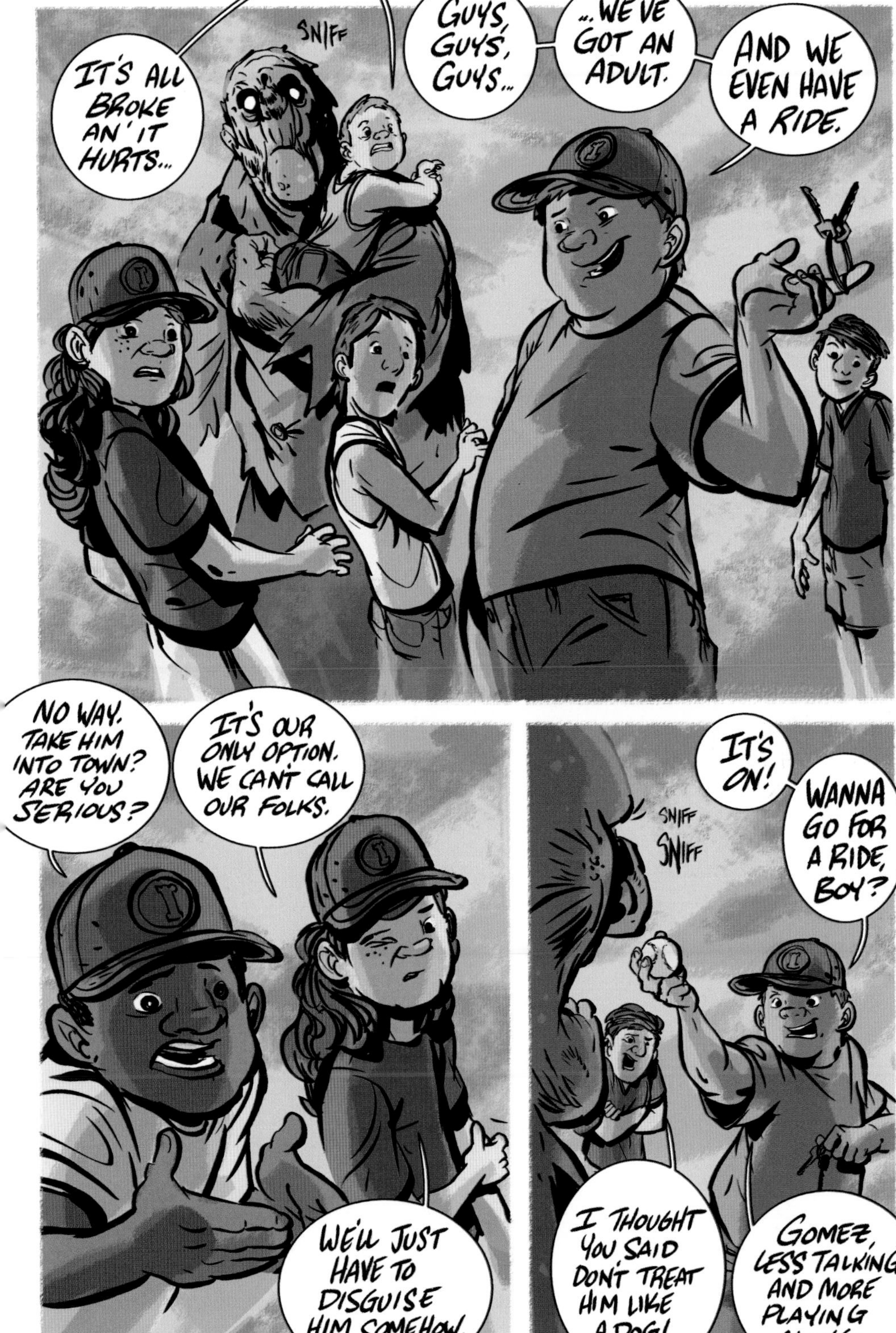
SNIFF
IT'S ALL BROKE AN' IT HURTS...
GUYS, GUYS, GUYS...
...WE'VE GOT AN ADULT.
AND WE EVEN HAVE A RIDE.
NO WAY. TAKE HIM INTO TOWN? ARE YOU SERIOUS?
IT'S OUR ONLY OPTION. WE CAN'T CALL OUR FOLKS.
WE'LL JUST HAVE TO DISGUISE HIM SOMEHOW.
SNIFF SNIFF
IT'S ON!
WANNA GO FOR A RIDE, BOY?
I THOUGHT YOU SAID DON'T TREAT HIM LIKE A DOG!
GOMEZ, LESS TALKING AND MORE PLAYING ALONG...

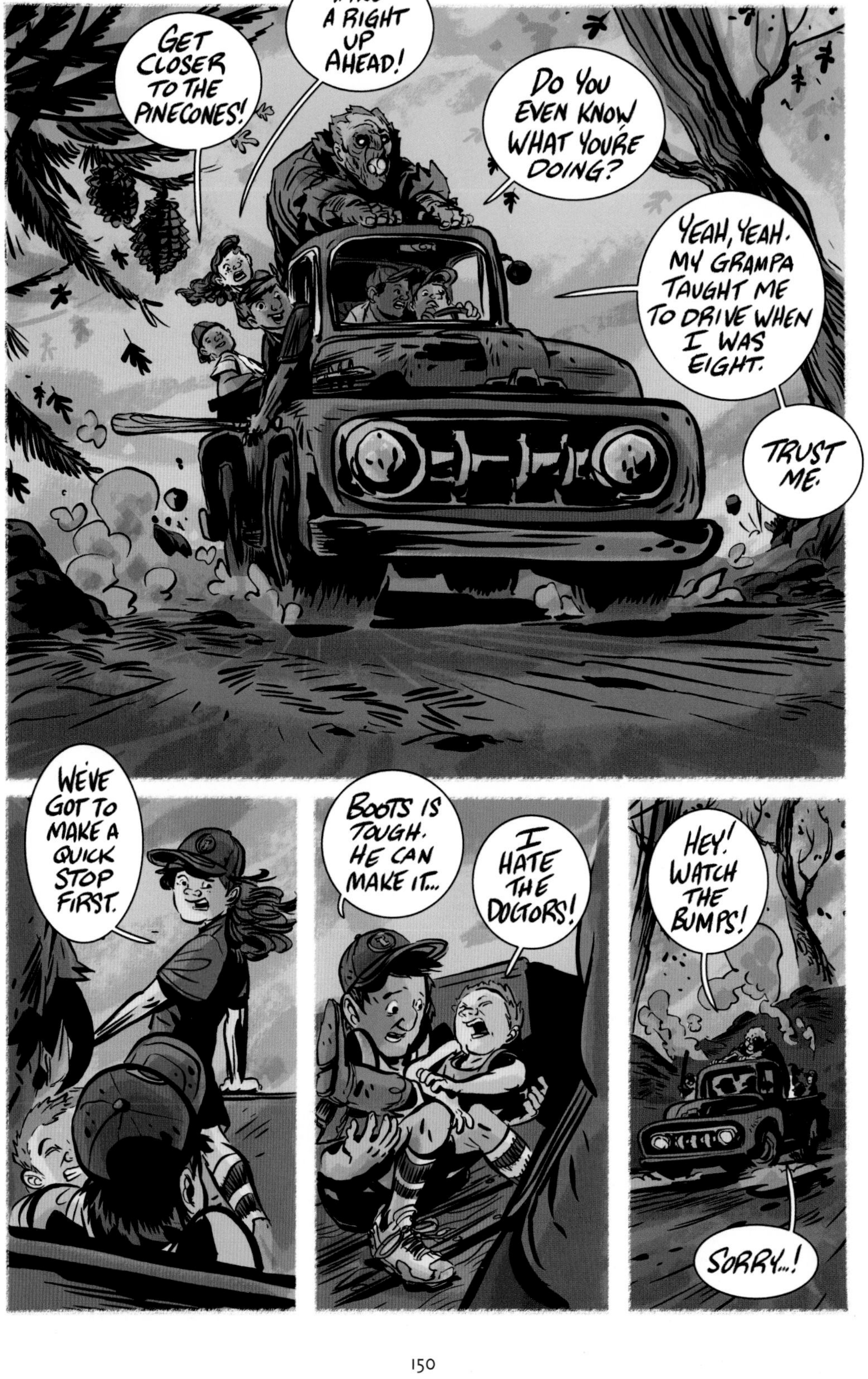
GET CLOSER TO THE PINECONES!
TAKE A RIGHT UP AHEAD!
DO YOU EVEN KNOW WHAT YOU'RE DOING?
YEAH, YEAH. MY GRAMPA TAUGHT ME TO DRIVE WHEN I WAS EIGHT.
TRUST ME.
WE'VE GOT TO MAKE A QUICK STOP FIRST.
BOOTS IS TOUGH. HE CAN MAKE IT...
I HATE THE DOCTORS!
HEY! WATCH THE BUMPS!
SORRY...!

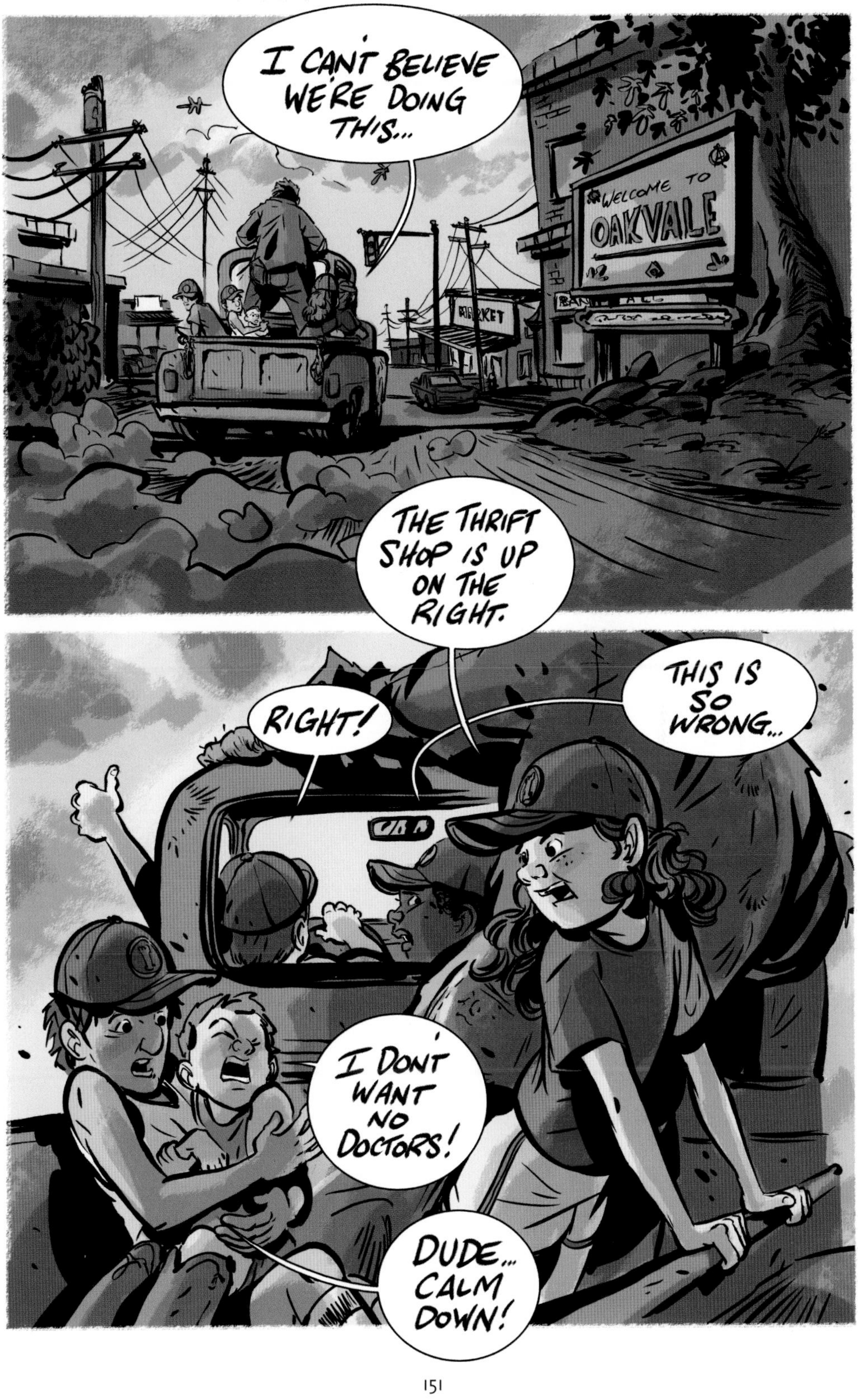
I CAN'T BELIEVE WE'RE DOING THIS...
WELCOME TO
OAKVALE
THE THRIFT SHOP IS UP ON THE RIGHT.
RIGHT!
THIS IS SO WRONG...
I DON'T WANT NO DOCTORS!
DUDE... CALM DOWN!

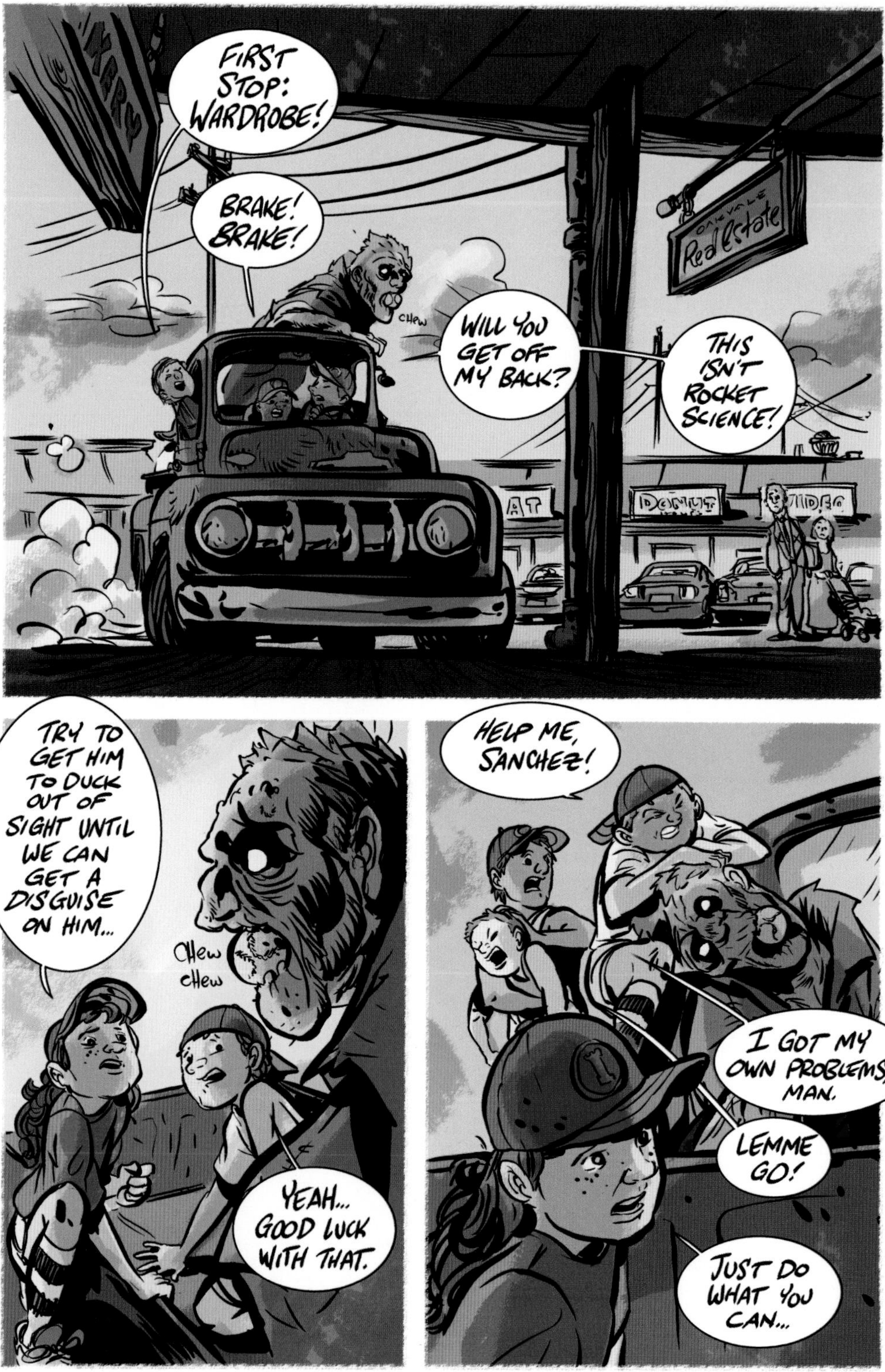
FIRST STOP: WARDROBE!
BRAKE! BRAKE!
CHEW
WILL YOU GET OFF MY BACK?
THIS ISN'T ROCKET SCIENCE!
OAKVALE Real Estate
DONUT
VIDEO
TRY TO GET HIM TO DUCK OUT OF SIGHT UNTIL WE CAN GET A DISGUISE ON HIM...
CHEW CHEW
YEAH... GOOD LUCK WITH THAT.
HELP ME, SANCHEZ!
I GOT MY OWN PROBLEMS, MAN.
LEMME GO!
JUST DO WHAT YOU CAN...

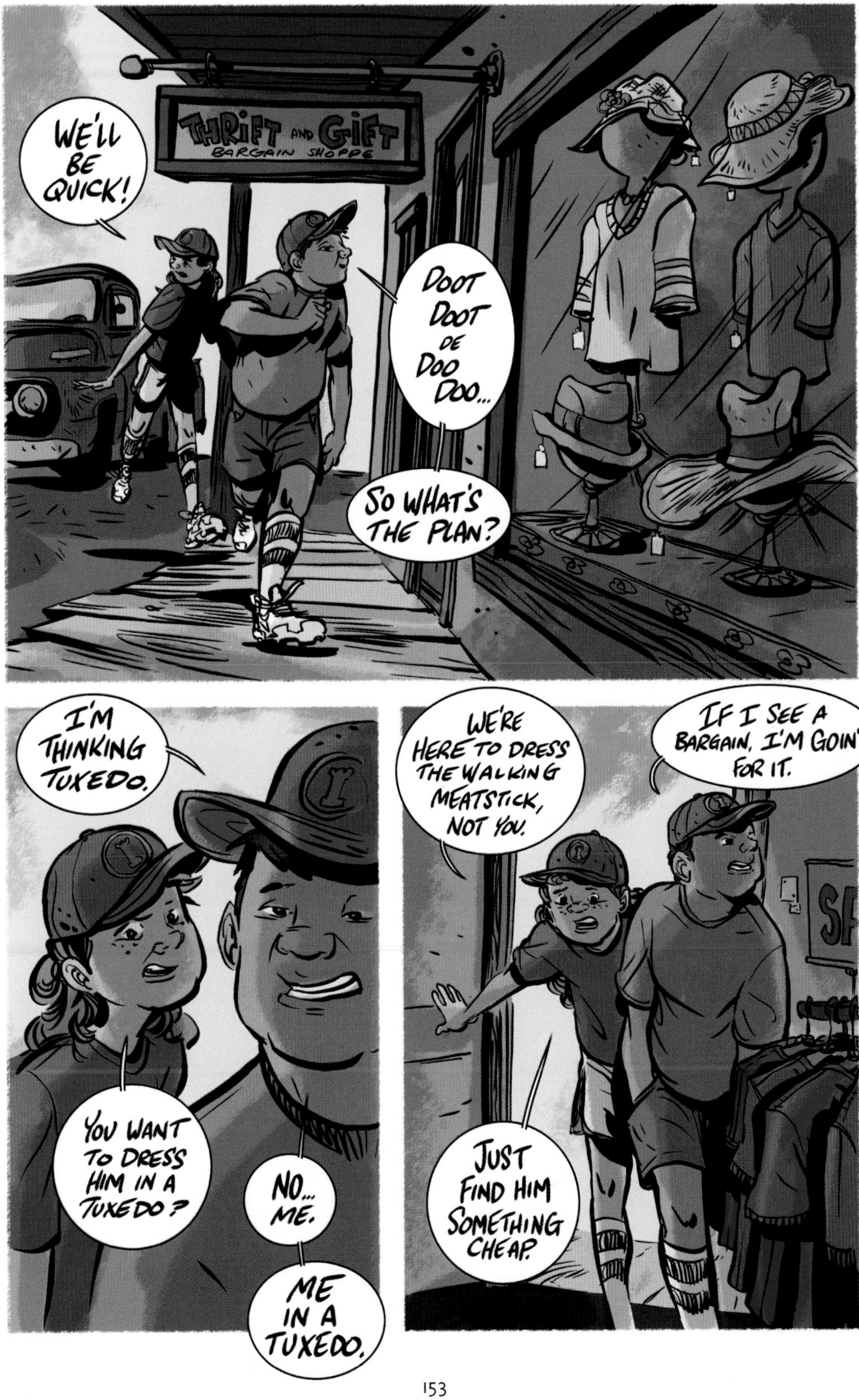
THRIFT AND GIFT
BARGAIN SHOPPE
WE'LL BE QUICK!
DOOT DOOT DE DOO DOO...
SO WHAT'S THE PLAN?
I'M THINKING TUXEDO.
YOU WANT TO DRESS HIM IN A TUXEDO?
NO... ME.
ME IN A TUXEDO.
WE'RE HERE TO DRESS THE WALKING MEATSTICK, NOT YOU.
IF I SEE A BARGAIN, I'M GOIN' FOR IT.
JUST FIND HIM SOMETHING CHEAP.

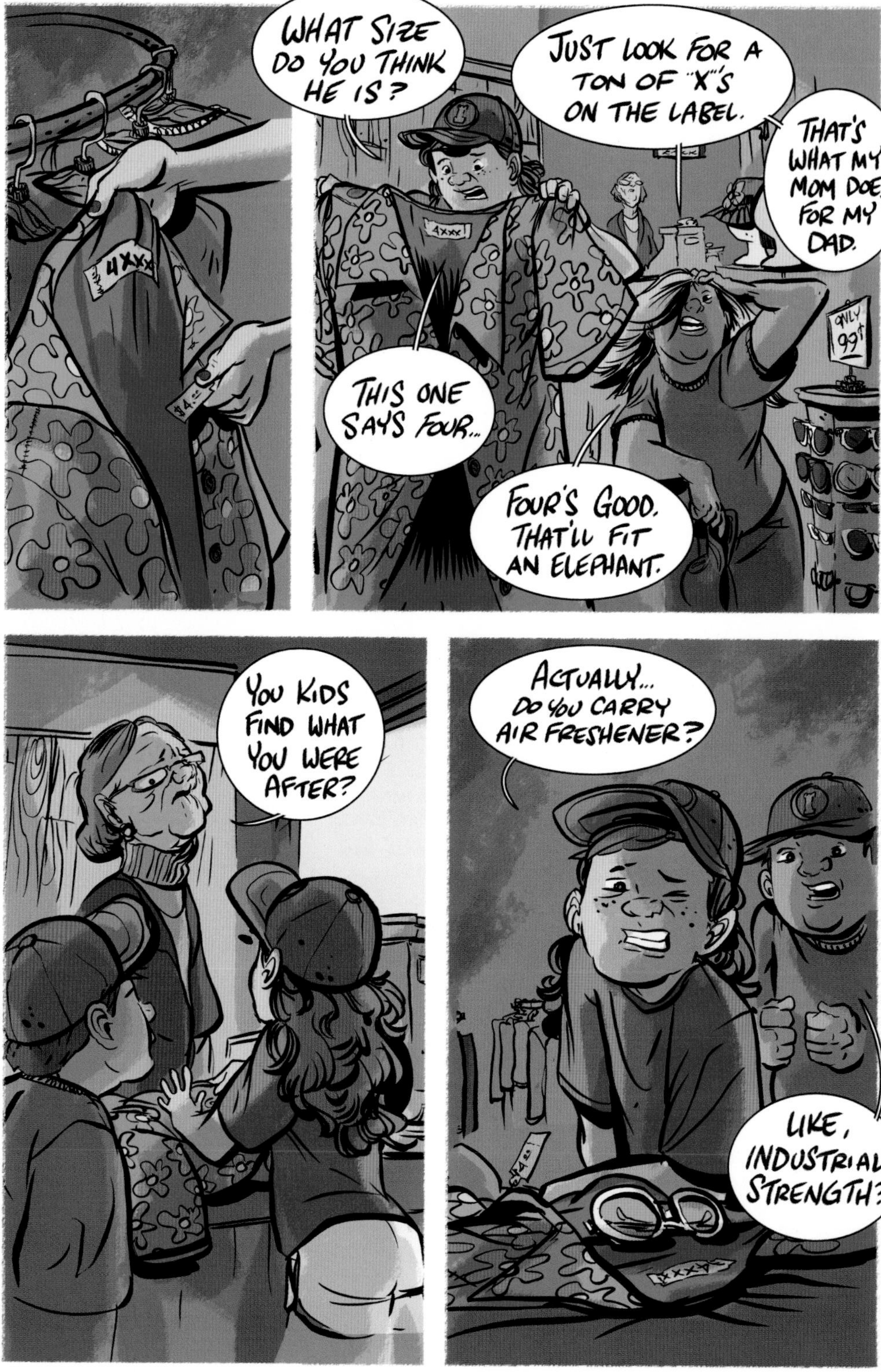
WHAT SIZE DO YOU THINK HE IS?
JUST LOOK FOR A TON OF "X"'S ON THE LABEL.
THAT'S WHAT MY MOM DOES FOR MY DAD.
THIS ONE SAYS FOUR...
FOUR'S GOOD. THAT'LL FIT AN ELEPHANT.
ONLY 99¢
YOU KIDS FIND WHAT YOU WERE AFTER?
ACTUALLY... DO YOU CARRY AIR FRESHENER?
LIKE, INDUSTRIAL STRENGTH?

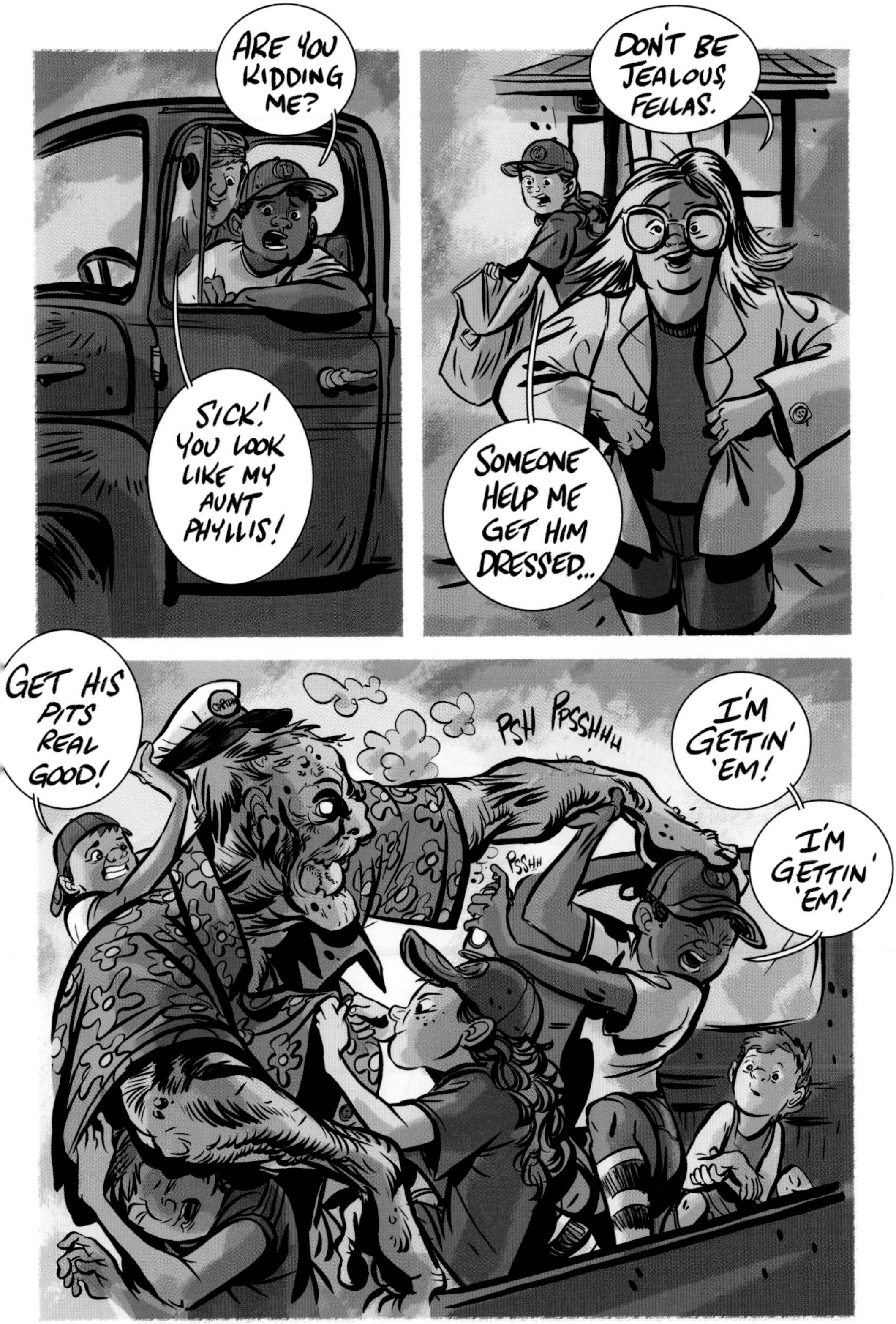
ARE YOU KIDDING ME?
SICK! YOU LOOK LIKE MY AUNT PHYLLIS!
DON'T BE JEALOUS, FELLAS.
SOMEONE HELP ME GET HIM DRESSED...
GET HIS PITS REAL GOOD!
PSH PPSSHHH
PSSHH
I'M GETTIN' 'EM!
I'M GETTIN' 'EM!

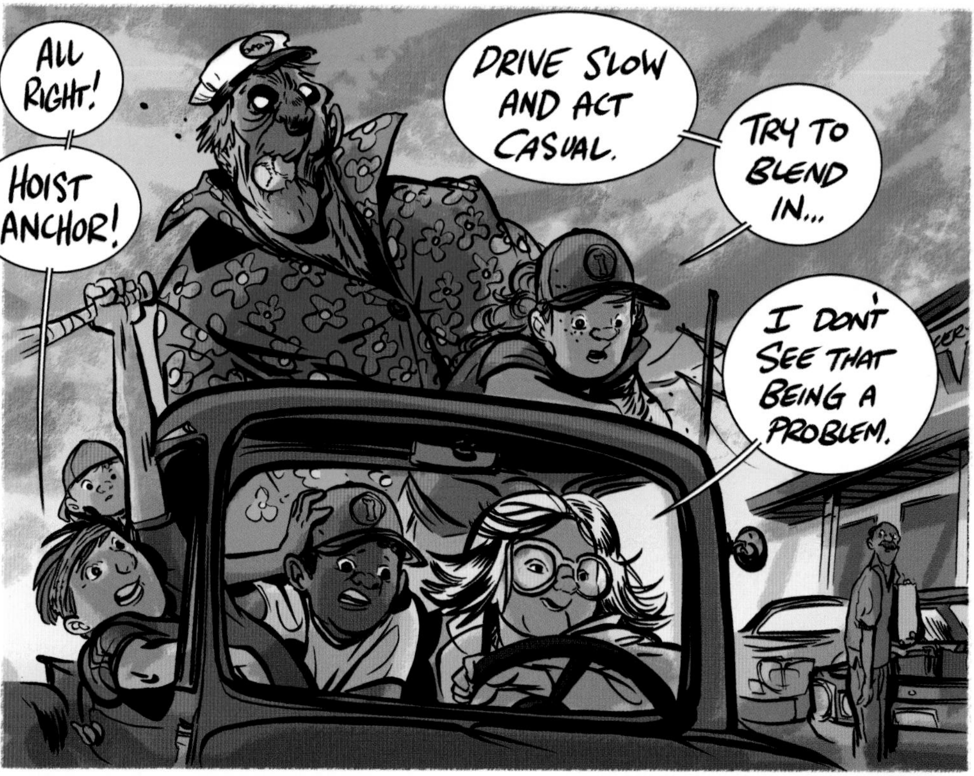
ALL RIGHT!
HOIST ANCHOR!
DRIVE SLOW AND ACT CASUAL.
TRY TO BLEND IN...
I DON'T SEE THAT BEING A PROBLEM.

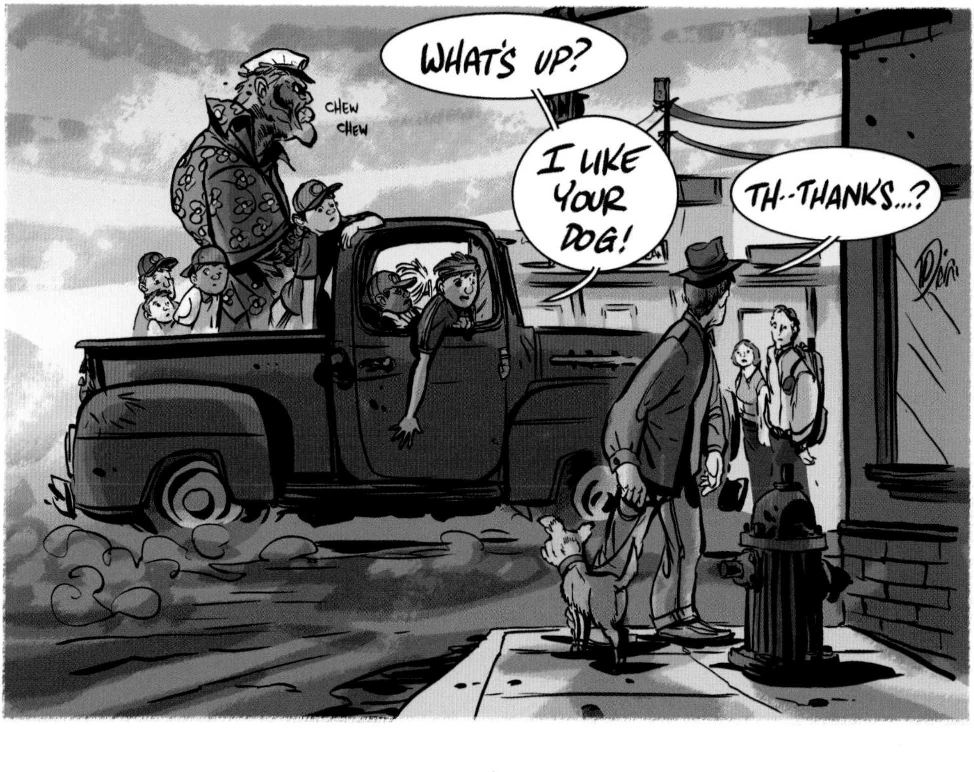
CHEW CHEW
WHAT'S UP?
I LIKE YOUR DOG!
TH-THANKS...?

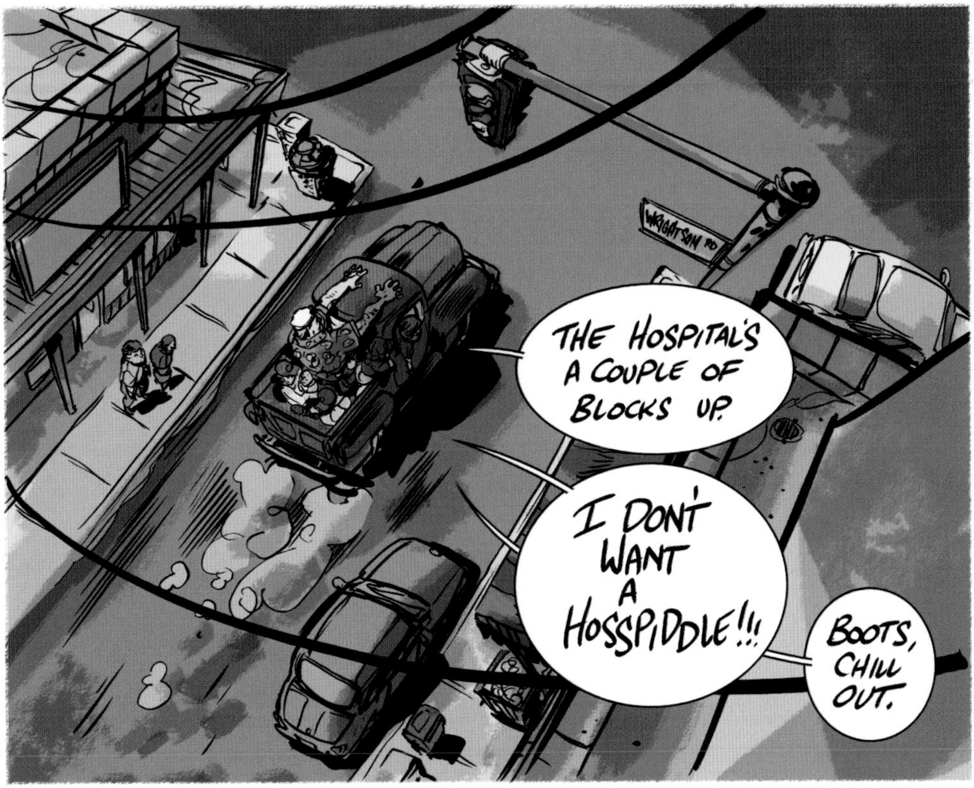
WRIGHTSON RD
THE HOSPITAL'S A COUPLE OF BLOCKS UP.
I DON'T WANT A HOSSPIDDLE!!!
BOOTS, CHILL OUT.

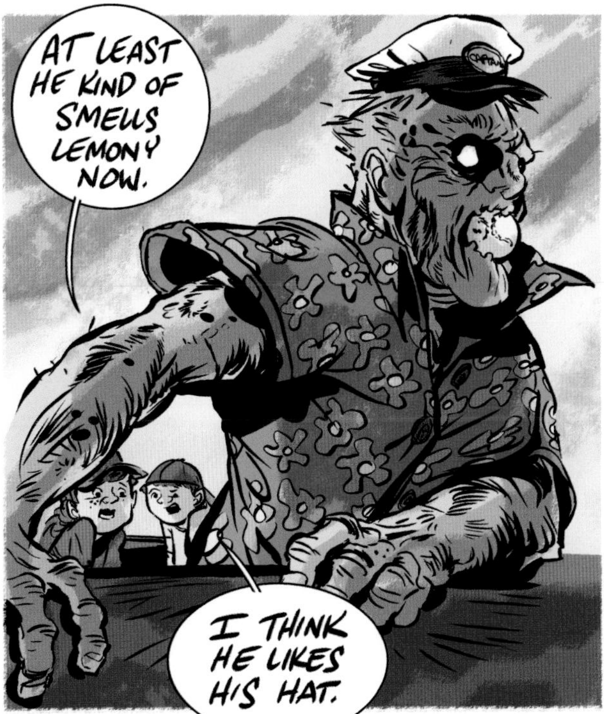
AT LEAST HE KIND OF SMELLS LEMONY NOW.
CAPTAIN
I THINK HE LIKES HIS HAT.

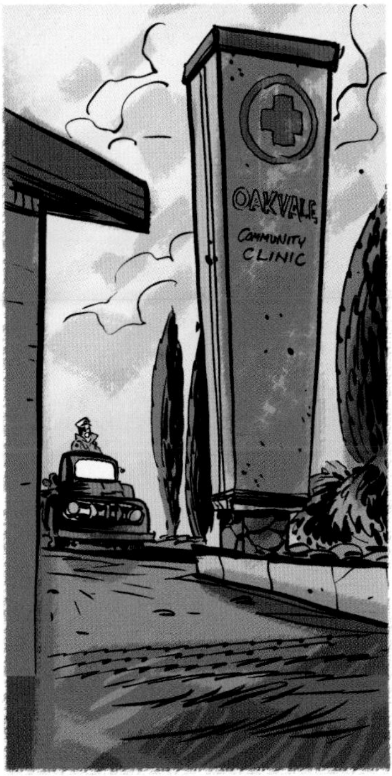
OAKVALE COMMUNITY CLINIC

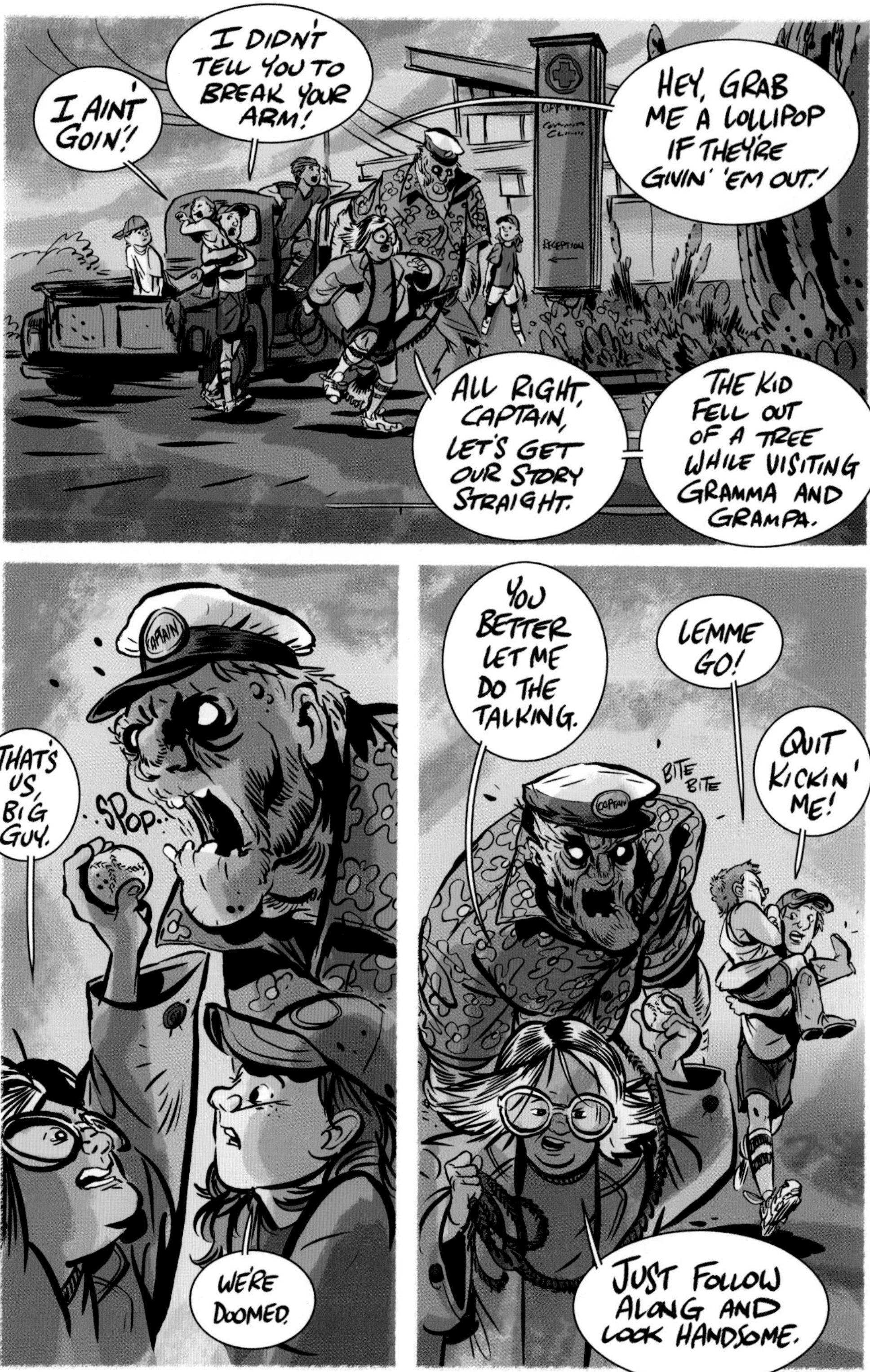
I AIN'T GOIN'!
I DIDN'T TELL YOU TO BREAK YOUR ARM!
HEY, GRAB ME A LOLLIPOP IF THEY'RE GIVIN' 'EM OUT!
RECEPTION
ALL RIGHT, CAPTAIN, LET'S GET OUR STORY STRAIGHT.
THE KID FELL OUT OF A TREE WHILE VISITING GRAMMA AND GRAMPA.
CAPTAIN
SPOP
THAT'S US, BIG GUY.
WE'RE DOOMED.
YOU BETTER LET ME DO THE TALKING.
LEMME GO!
BITE BITE
QUIT KICKIN' ME!
JUST FOLLOW ALONG AND LOOK HANDSOME.

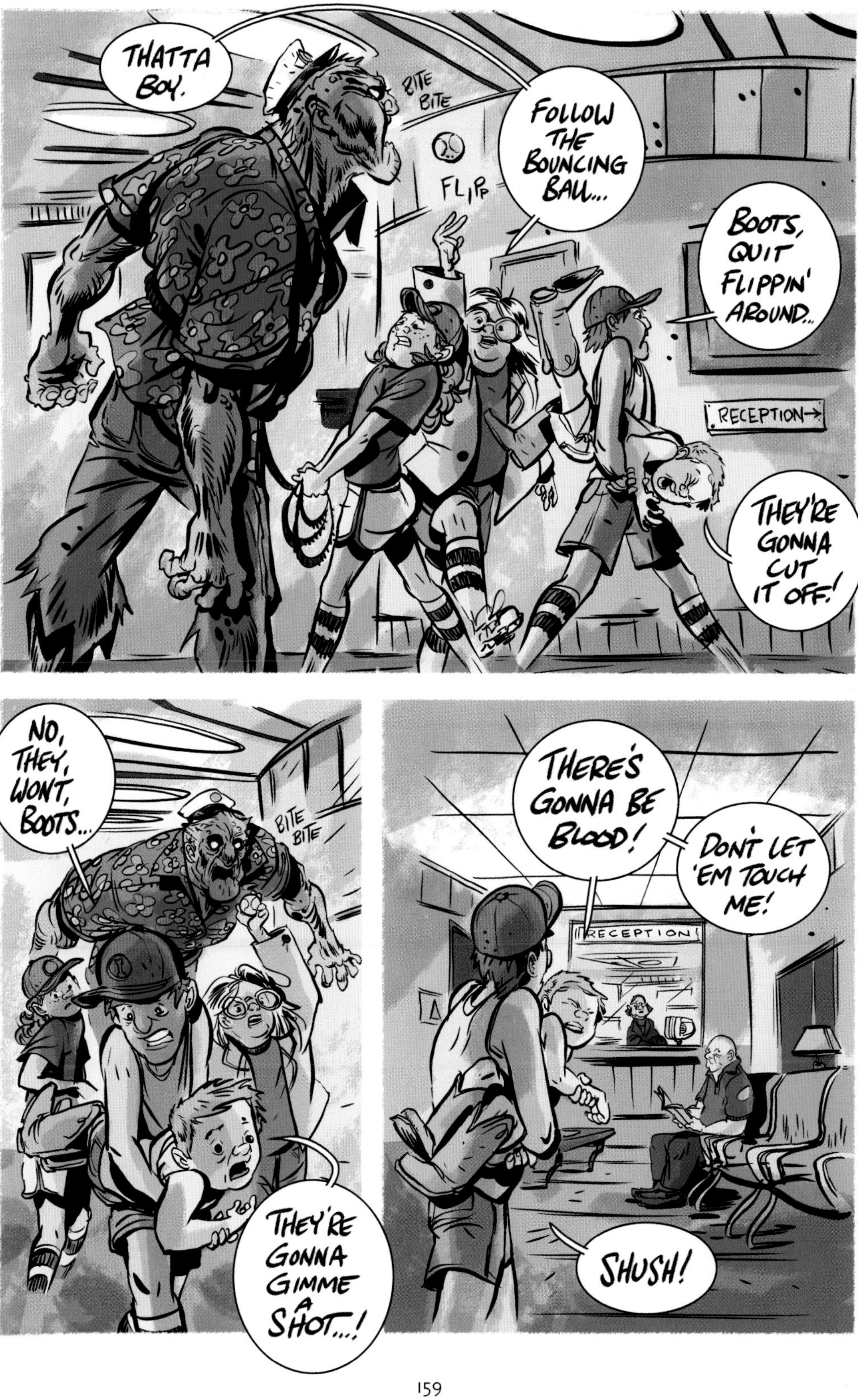
THATTA BOY.
BITE BITE
FOLLOW THE BOUNCING BALL...
FLIPP
BOOTS, QUIT FLIPPIN' AROUND...
RECEPTION→
THEY'RE GONNA CUT IT OFF!
NO, THEY WON'T, BOOTS...
BITE BITE
THEY'RE GONNA GIMME A SHOT...!
THERE'S GONNA BE BLOOD!
DON'T LET 'EM TOUCH ME!
RECEPTION
SHUSH!

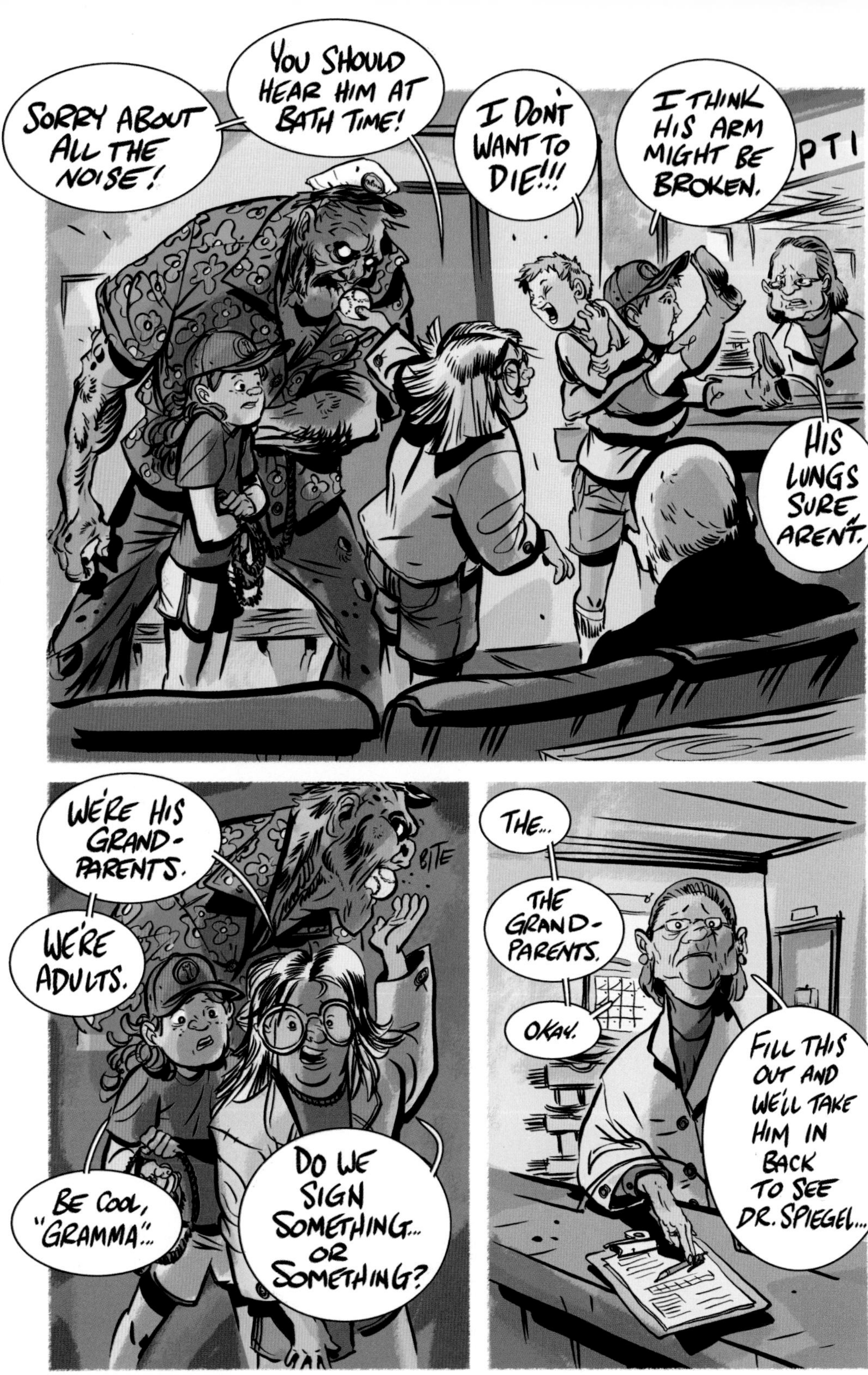
SORRY ABOUT ALL THE NOISE!
YOU SHOULD HEAR HIM AT BATH TIME!
I DON'T WANT TO DIE!!!
I THINK HIS ARM MIGHT BE BROKEN.
PTI
HIS LUNGS SURE AREN'T.
WE'RE HIS GRAND-PARENTS.
WE'RE ADULTS.
BITE
BE COOL, "GRAMMA"...
DO WE SIGN SOMETHING... OR SOMETHING?
THE...
THE GRAND-PARENTS.
OKAY.
FILL THIS OUT AND WE'LL TAKE HIM IN BACK TO SEE DR. SPIEGEL...

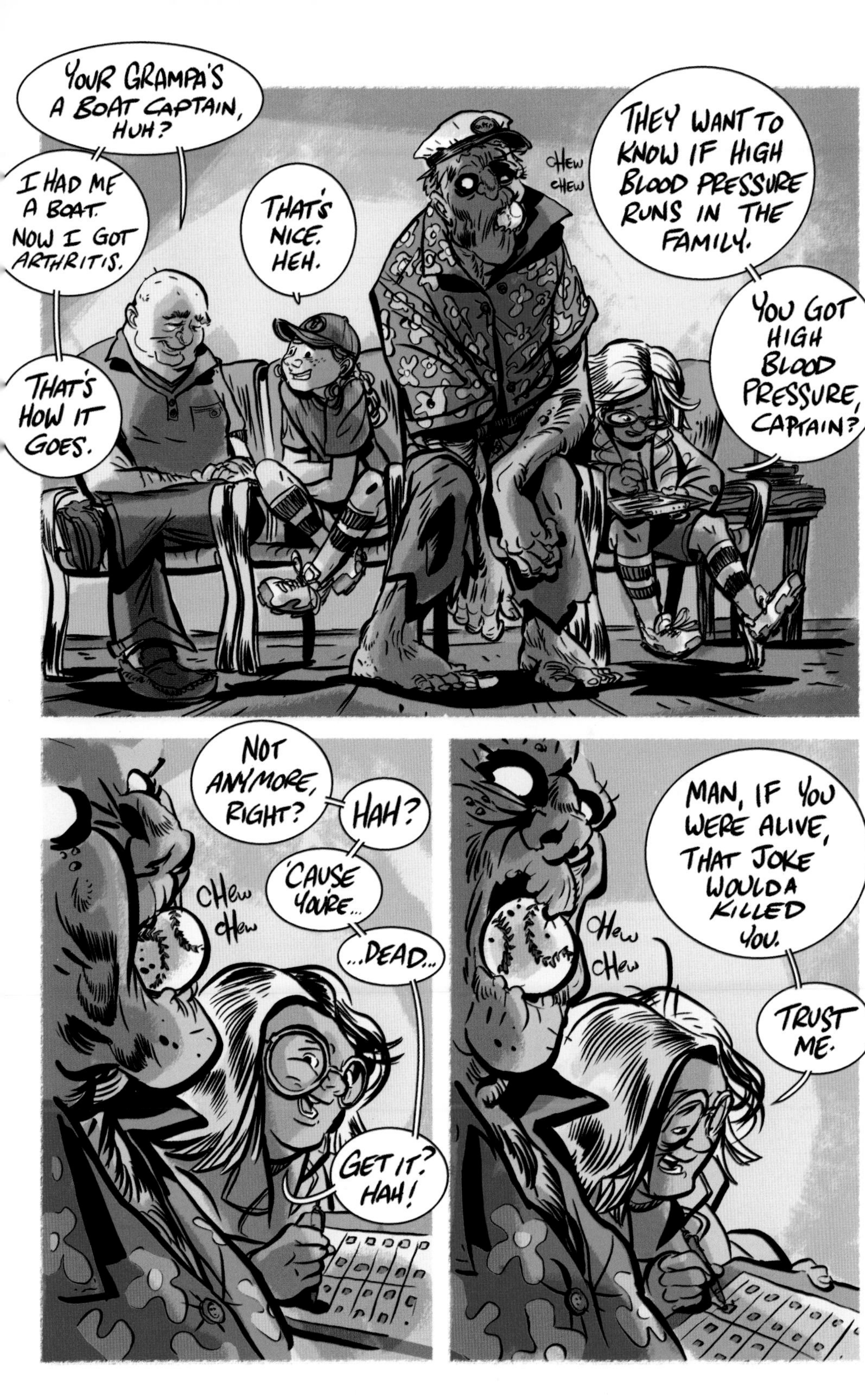
YOUR GRAMPA'S A BOAT CAPTAIN, HUH?
I HAD ME A BOAT. NOW I GOT ARTHRITIS.
THAT'S HOW IT GOES.
THAT'S NICE. HEH.
CHEW CHEW
THEY WANT TO KNOW IF HIGH BLOOD PRESSURE RUNS IN THE FAMILY.
YOU GOT HIGH BLOOD PRESSURE, CAPTAIN?
NOT ANYMORE, RIGHT?
HAH?
'CAUSE YOU'RE...
...DEAD...
GET IT? HAH!
CHEW CHEW
MAN, IF YOU WERE ALIVE, THAT JOKE WOULDA KILLED YOU.
TRUST ME.
CHEW CHEW

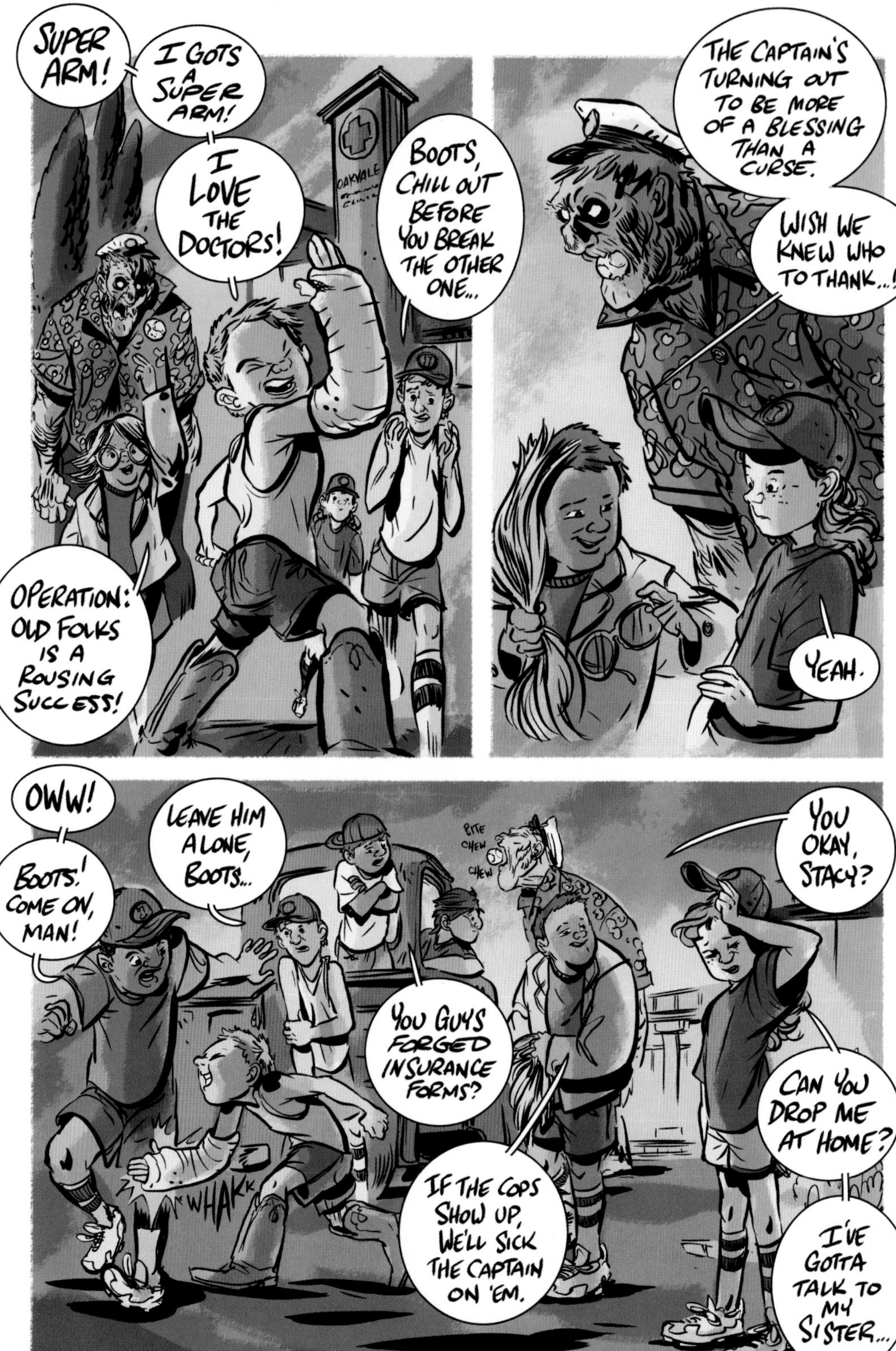
SUPER ARM!
I GOTS A SUPER ARM!
I LOVE THE DOCTORS!
OAKVALE CLINIC
BOOTS, CHILL OUT BEFORE YOU BREAK THE OTHER ONE...
OPERATION: OLD FOLKS IS A ROUSING SUCCESS!
THE CAPTAIN'S TURNING OUT TO BE MORE OF A BLESSING THAN A CURSE.
WISH WE KNEW WHO TO THANK...!
YEAH.
OWW!
BOOTS! COME ON, MAN!
LEAVE HIM ALONE, BOOTS...
BITE
CHEW
CHEW
YOU OKAY, STACY?
YOU GUYS FORGED INSURANCE FORMS?
WHAKK
IF THE COPS SHOW UP, WE'LL SICK THE CAPTAIN ON 'EM.
CAN YOU DROP ME AT HOME?
I'VE GOTTA TALK TO MY SISTER...

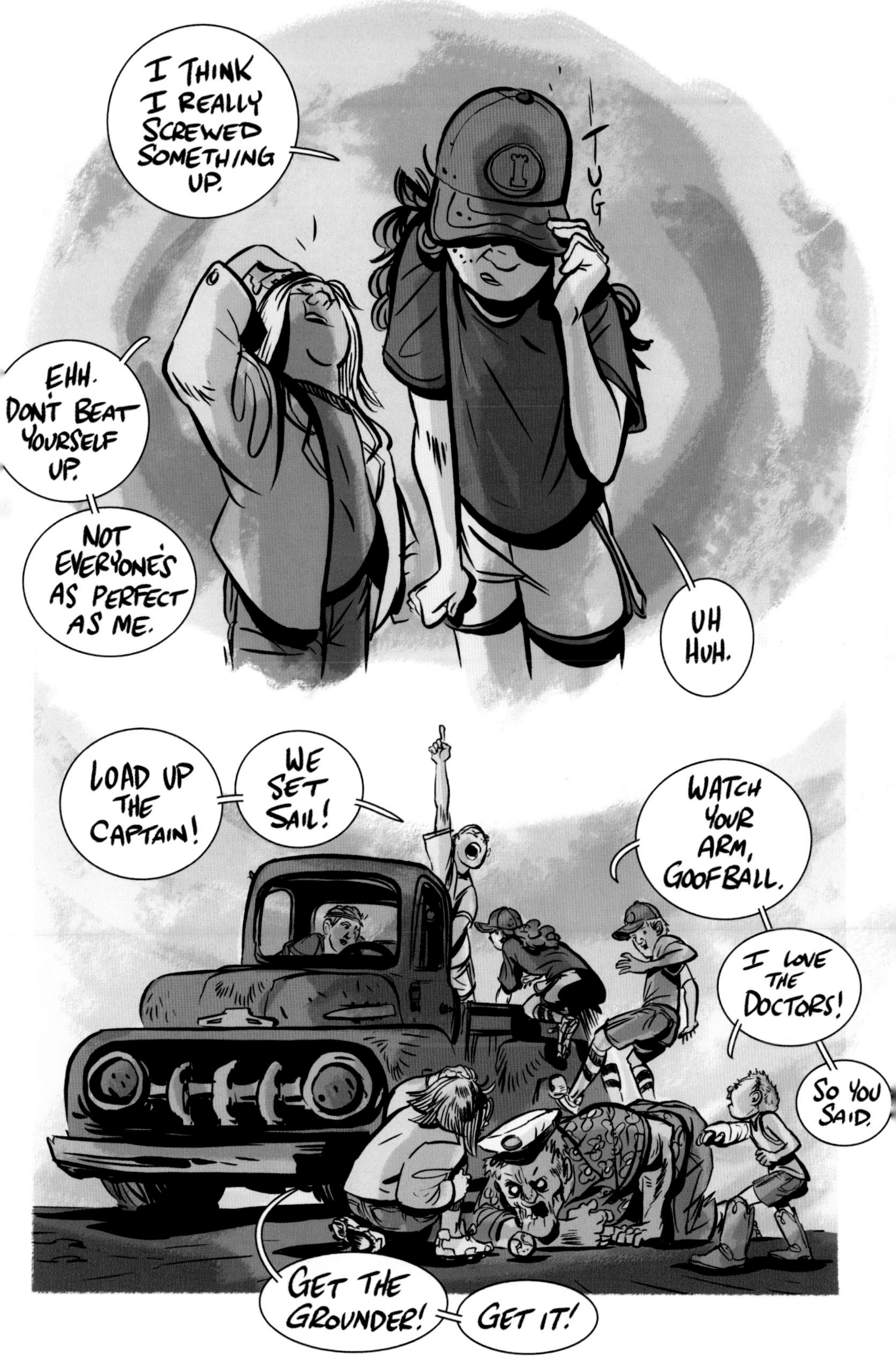
I THINK I REALLY SCREWED SOMETHING UP.
TUG
EHH. DON'T BEAT YOURSELF UP.
NOT EVERYONE'S AS PERFECT AS ME.
UH HUH.
LOAD UP THE CAPTAIN!
WE SET SAIL!
WATCH YOUR ARM, GOOFBALL.
I LOVE THE DOCTORS!
SO YOU SAID.
GET THE GROUNDER!
GET IT!

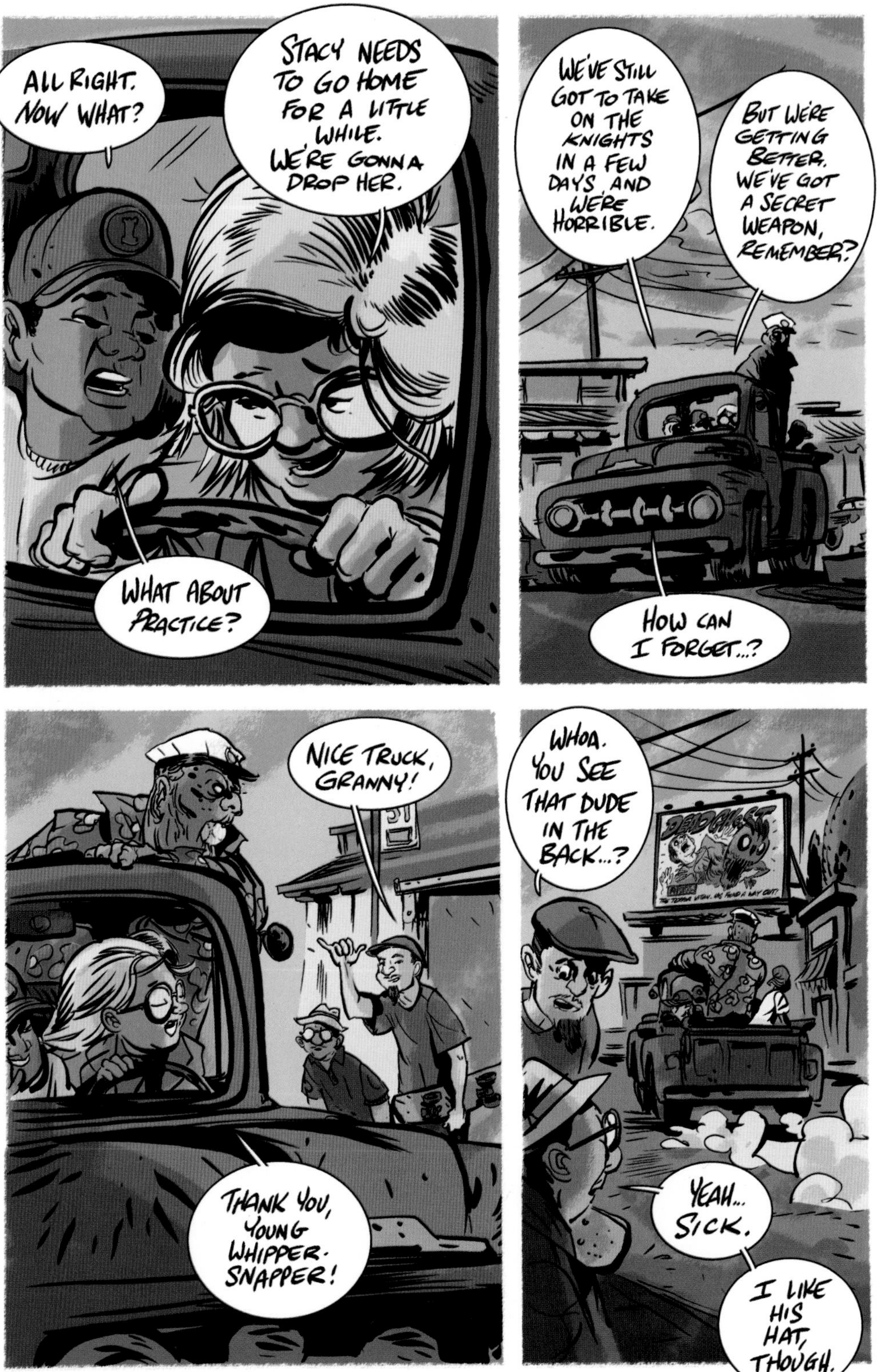
ALL RIGHT. NOW WHAT?
STACY NEEDS TO GO HOME FOR A LITTLE WHILE. WE'RE GONNA DROP HER.
WHAT ABOUT PRACTICE?
WE'VE STILL GOT TO TAKE ON THE KNIGHTS IN A FEW DAYS AND WE'RE HORRIBLE.
BUT WE'RE GETTING BETTER. WE'VE GOT A SECRET WEAPON, REMEMBER?
HOW CAN I FORGET...?
NICE TRUCK, GRANNY!
THANK YOU, YOUNG WHIPPER-SNAPPER!
WHOA. YOU SEE THAT DUDE IN THE BACK...?
YEAH... SICK.
I LIKE HIS HAT, THOUGH.

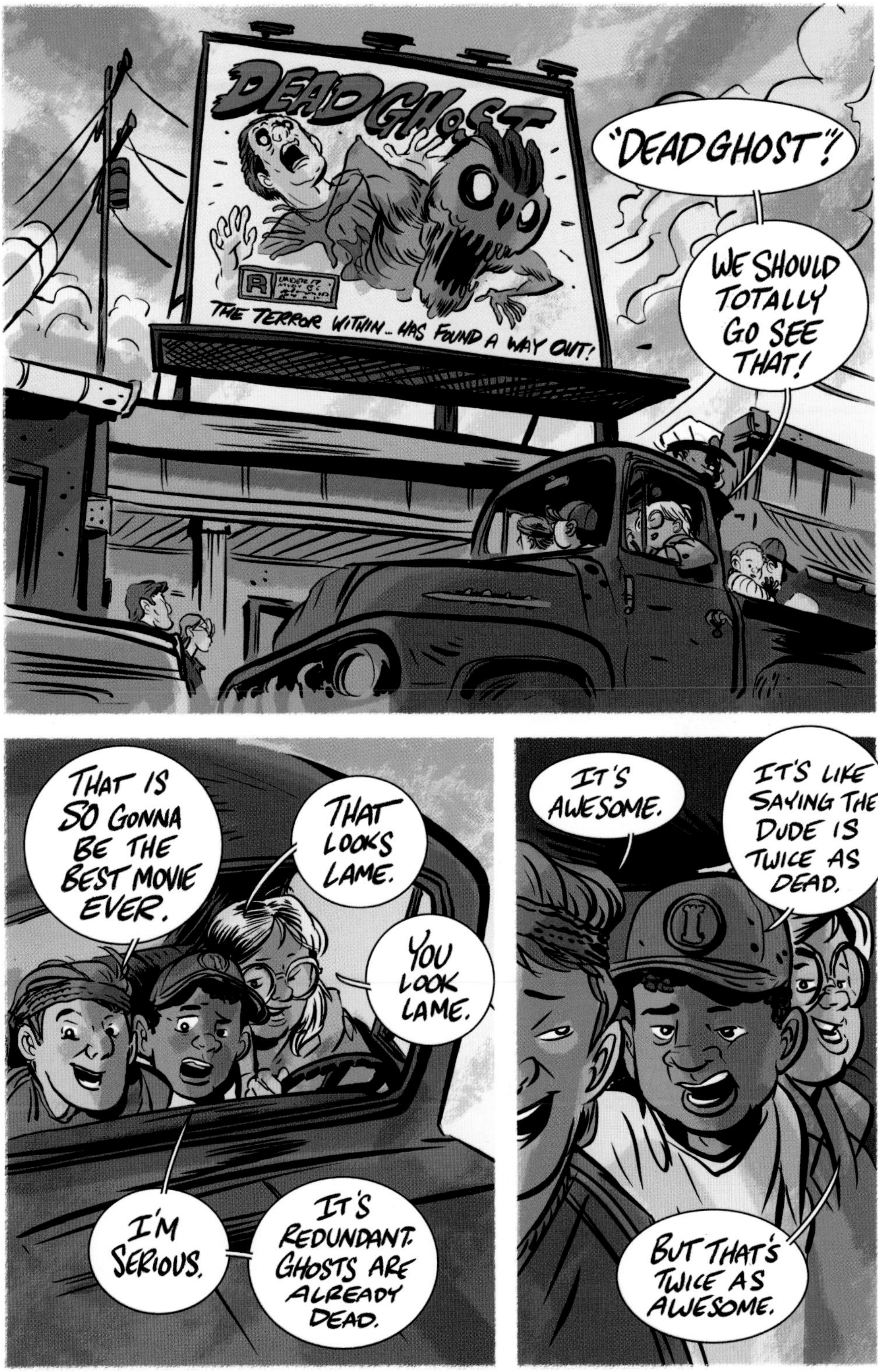
DEADGHOST
THE TERROR WITHIN... HAS FOUND A WAY OUT!
"DEADGHOST"!
WE SHOULD TOTALLY GO SEE THAT!
THAT IS SO GONNA BE THE BEST MOVIE EVER.
THAT LOOKS LAME.
YOU LOOK LAME.
I'M SERIOUS.
IT'S REDUNDANT. GHOSTS ARE ALREADY DEAD.
IT'S AWESOME.
IT'S LIKE SAYING THE DUDE IS TWICE AS DEAD.
BUT THAT'S TWICE AS AWESOME.

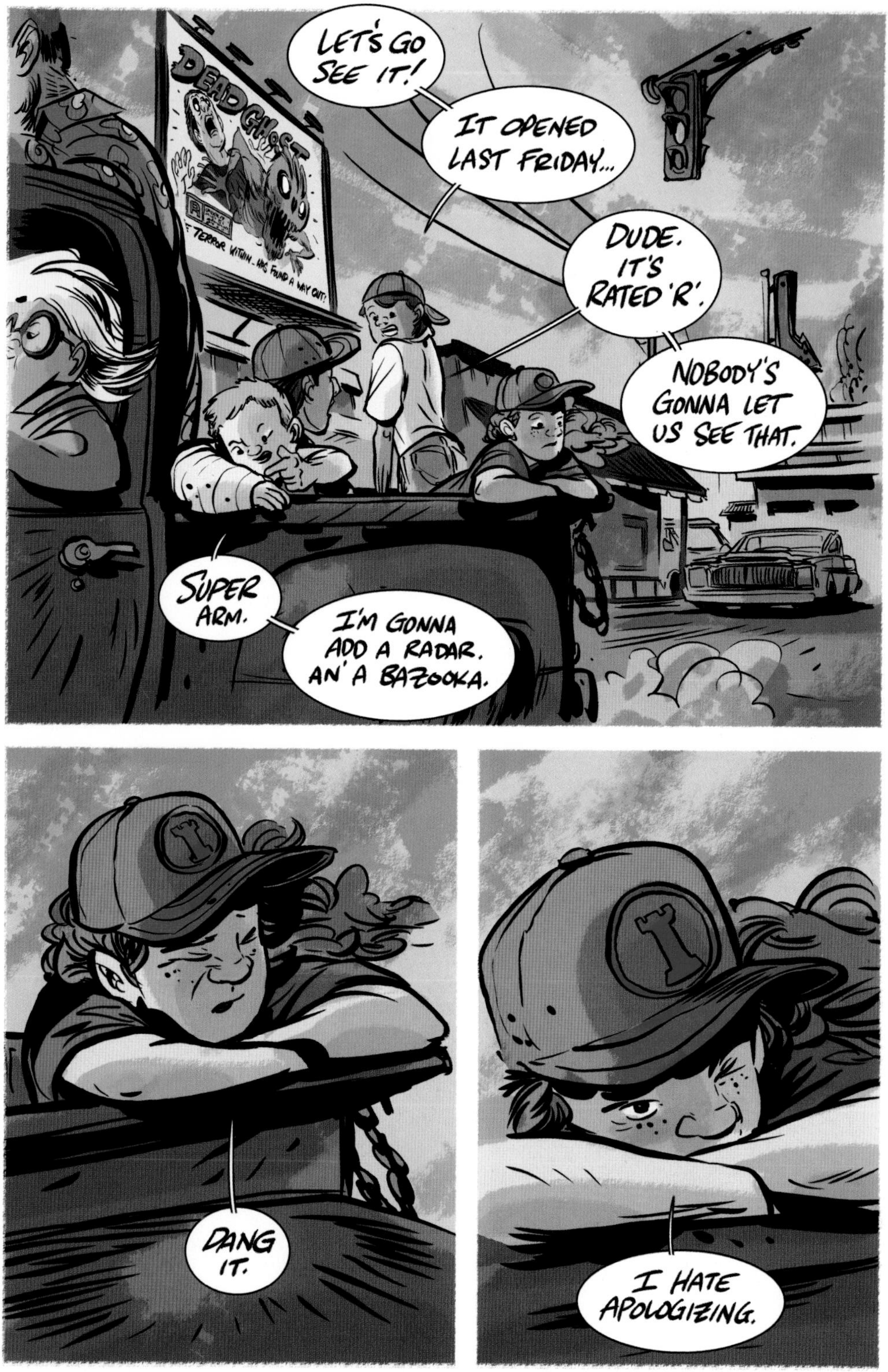
DEADGHOST
TERROR WITHIN... HAS FOUND A WAY OUT!
LET'S GO SEE IT!
IT OPENED LAST FRIDAY...
DUDE. IT'S RATED 'R'.
NOBODY'S GONNA LET US SEE THAT.
SUPER ARM.
I'M GONNA ADD A RADAR. AN' A BAZOOKA.
DANG IT.
I HATE APOLOGIZING.

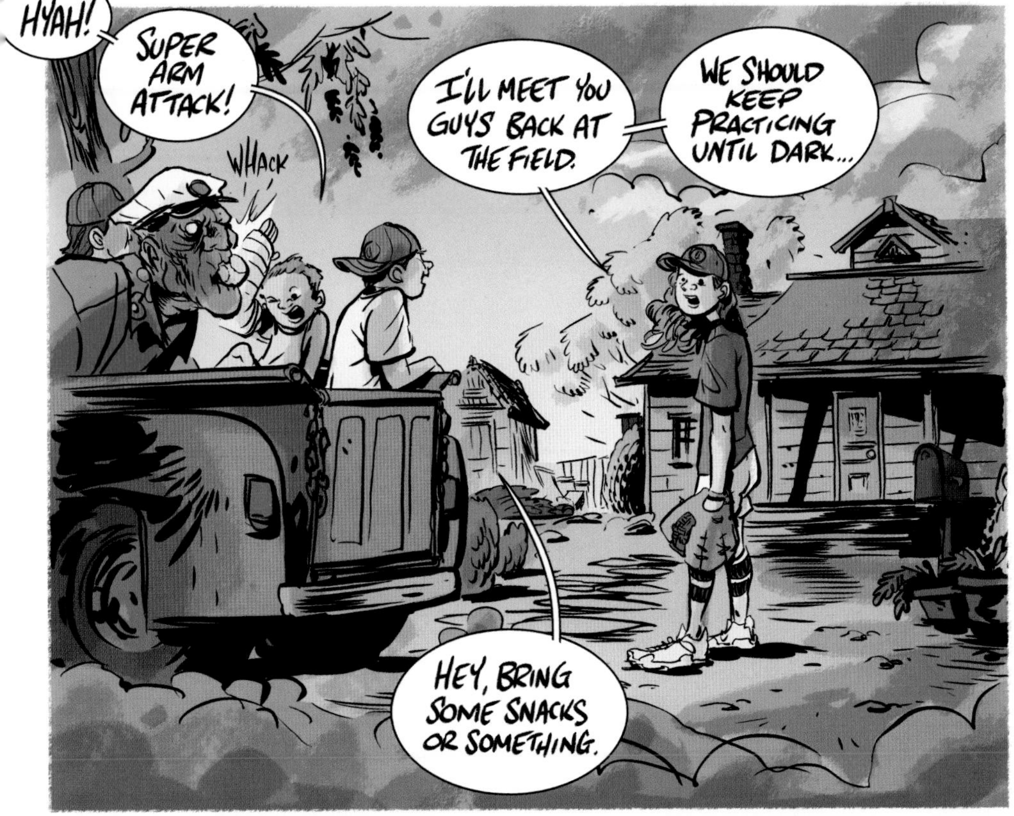
HYAH!
SUPER ARM ATTACK!
WHACK
I'LL MEET YOU GUYS BACK AT THE FIELD.
WE SHOULD KEEP PRACTICING UNTIL DARK...
HEY, BRING SOME SNACKS OR SOMETHING.

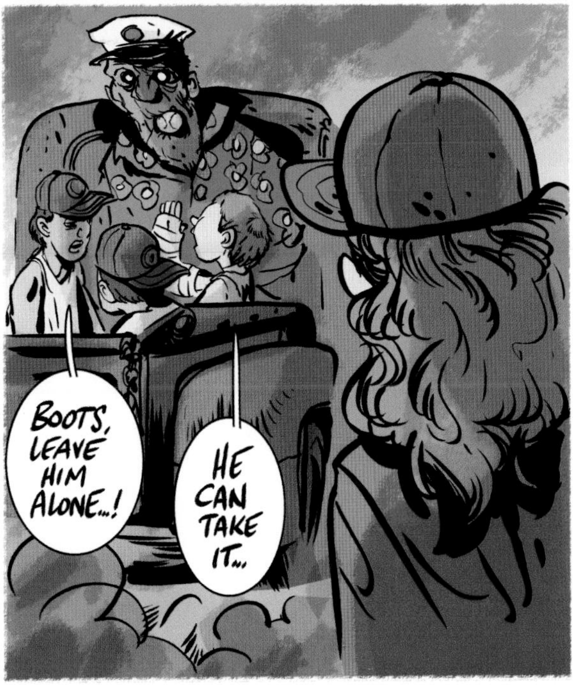
BOOTS, LEAVE HIM ALONE...!
HE CAN TAKE IT...

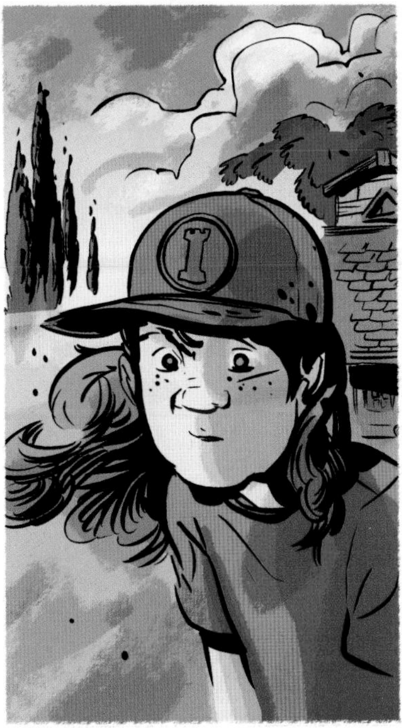

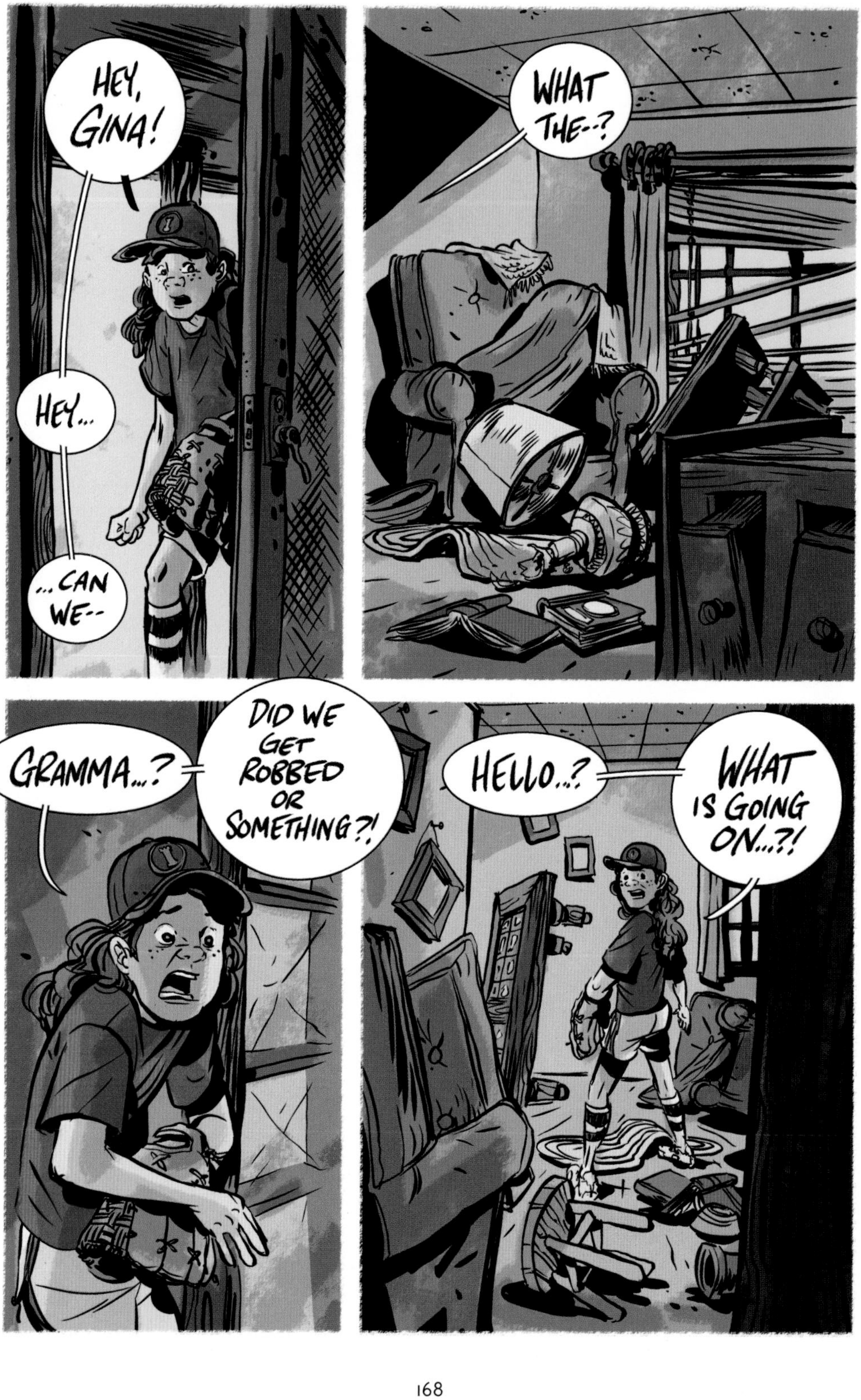
HEY, GINA!
HEY...
...CAN WE--
WHAT THE--?
GRAMMA...?
DID WE GET ROBBED OR SOMETHING?!
HELLO..?
WHAT IS GOING ON..?!

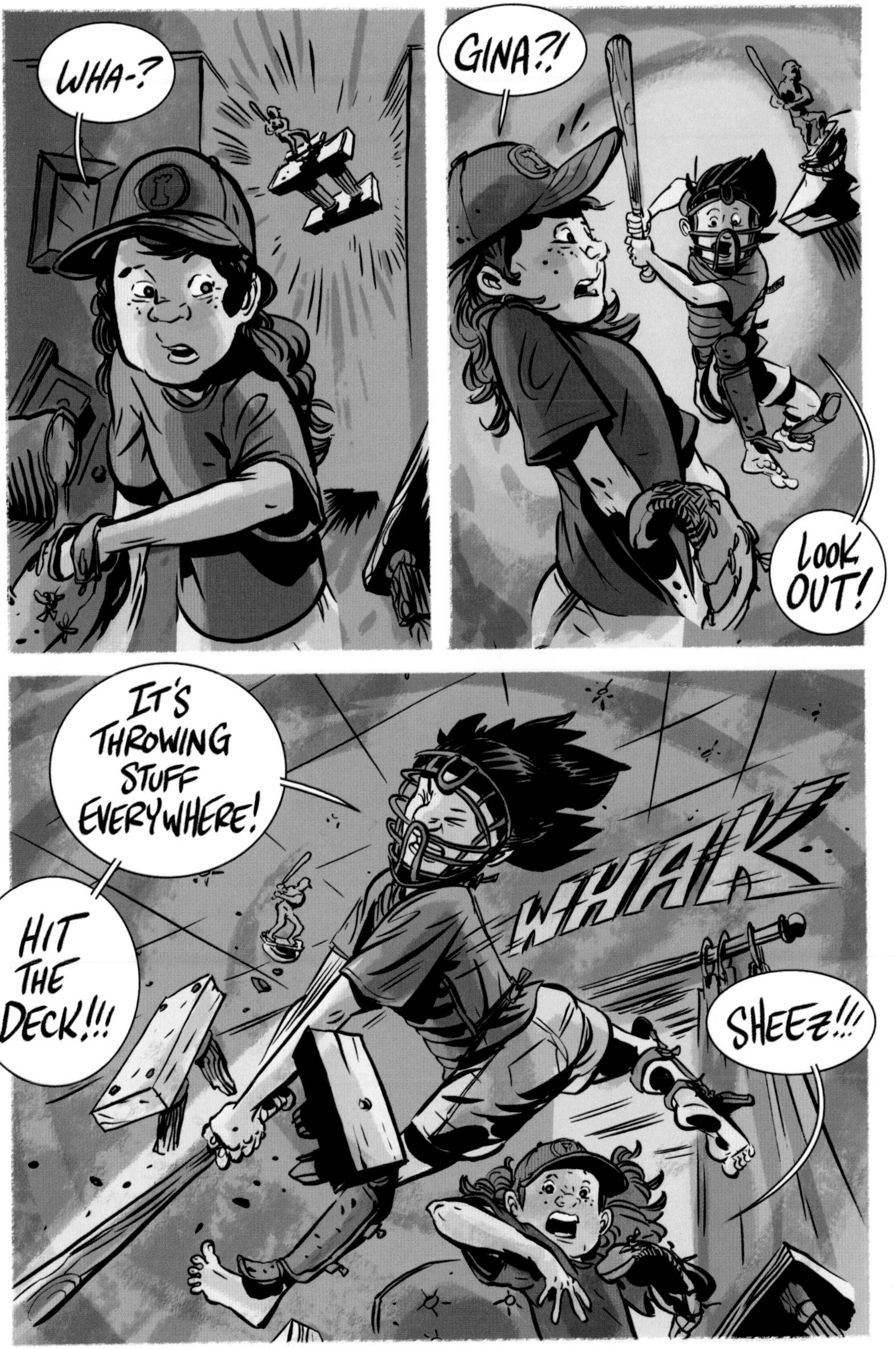
WHA-?
GINA?!
LOOK OUT!
IT'S THROWING STUFF EVERYWHERE!
HIT THE DECK!!!
WHAK
SHEEZ!!!

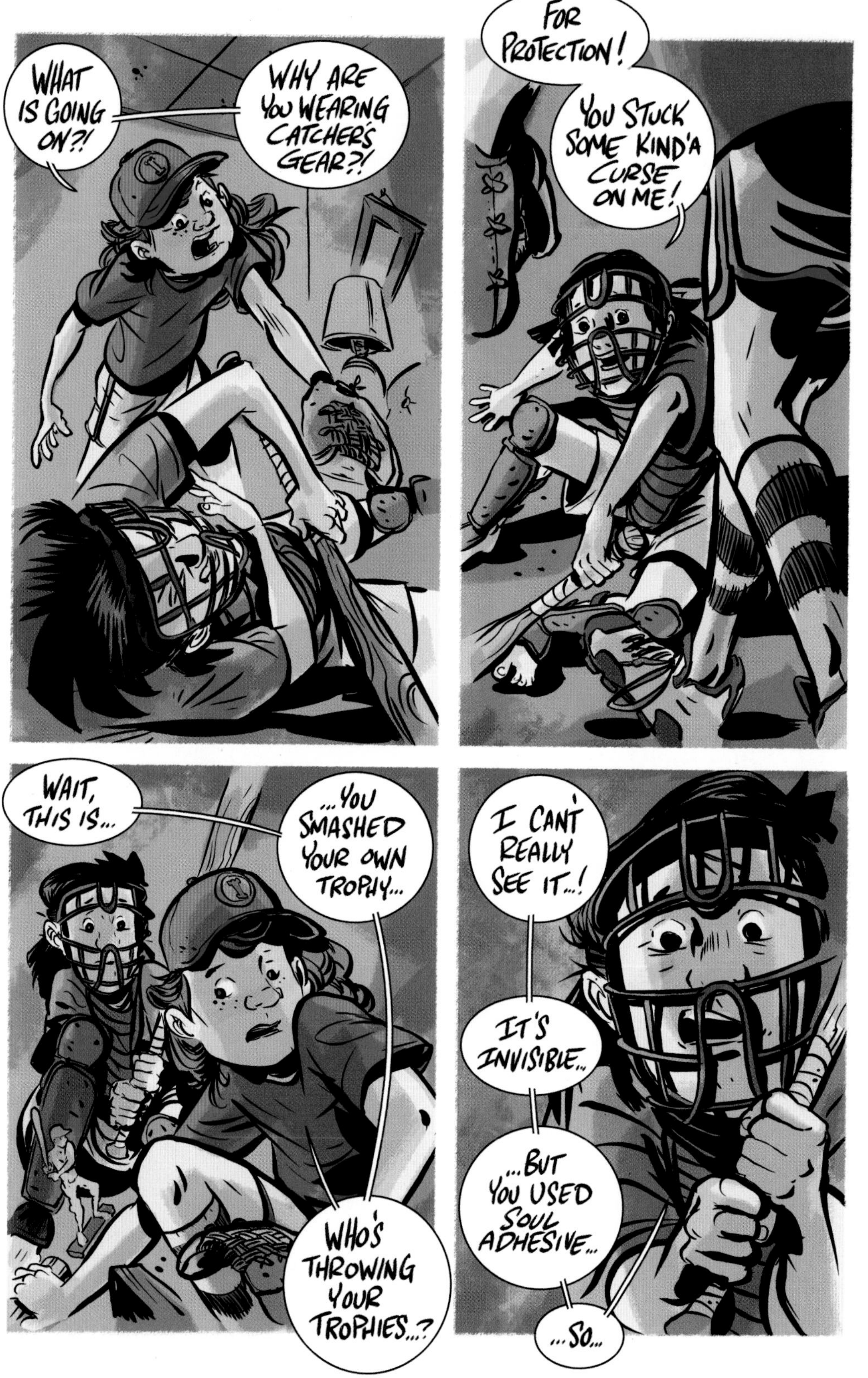
WHAT IS GOING ON?!
WHY ARE YOU WEARING CATCHER'S GEAR?!
FOR PROTECTION!
YOU STUCK SOME KIND'A CURSE ON ME!
WAIT, THIS IS...
...YOU SMASHED YOUR OWN TROPHY...
WHO'S THROWING YOUR TROPHIES...?
I CAN'T REALLY SEE IT...!
IT'S INVISIBLE...
...BUT YOU USED SOUL ADHESIVE...
...SO...

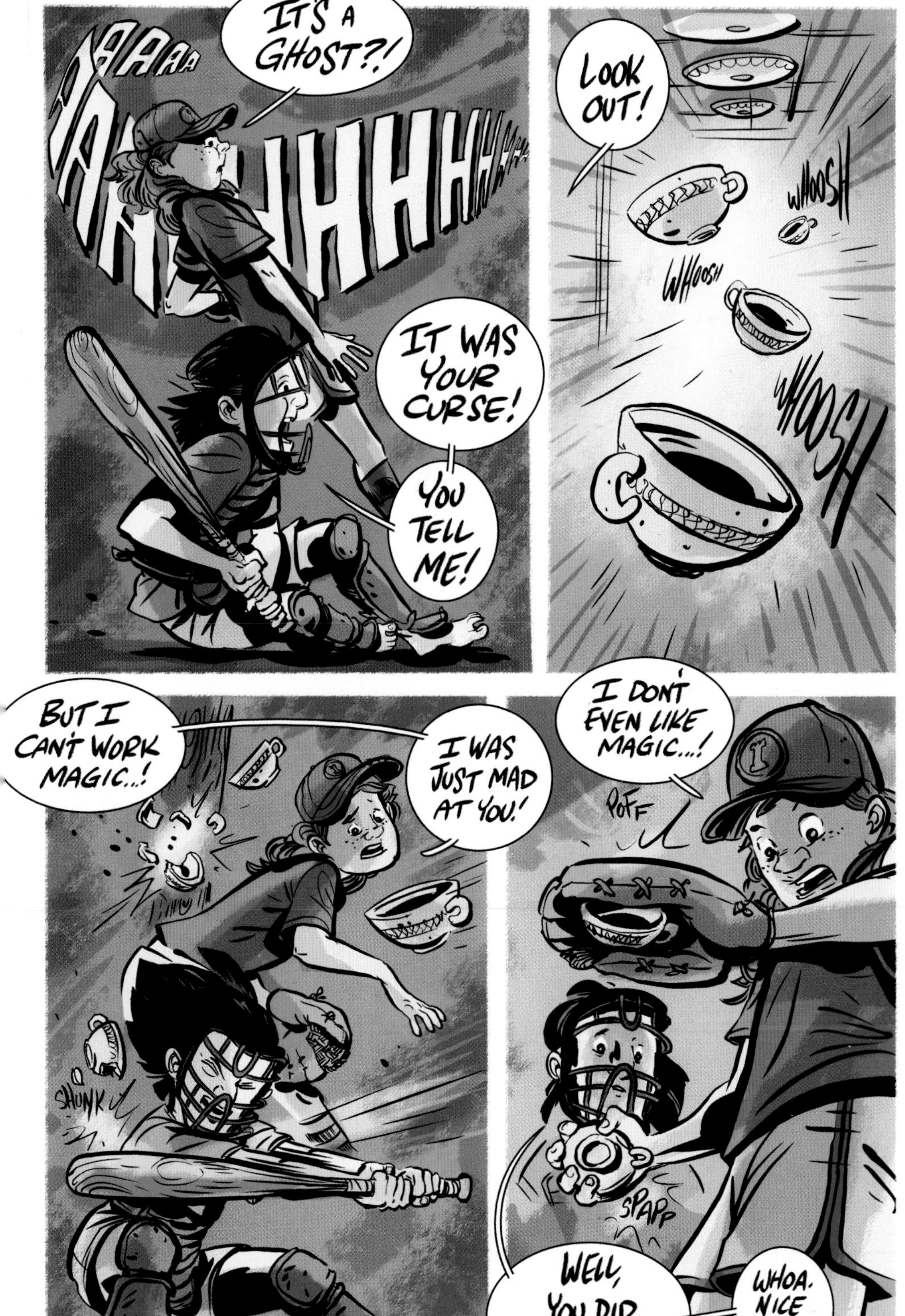
AAAAAAAHHHHHHH
IT'S A GHOST?!
IT WAS YOUR CURSE!
YOU TELL ME!
LOOK OUT!
WHOOSH
WHOOSH
WHOOSH
BUT I CAN'T WORK MAGIC...!
I WAS JUST MAD AT YOU!
SHUNK
I DON'T EVEN LIKE MAGIC...!
POFF
SPAPP
WELL, YOU DID SOMETHING!
WHOA. NICE CATCH.

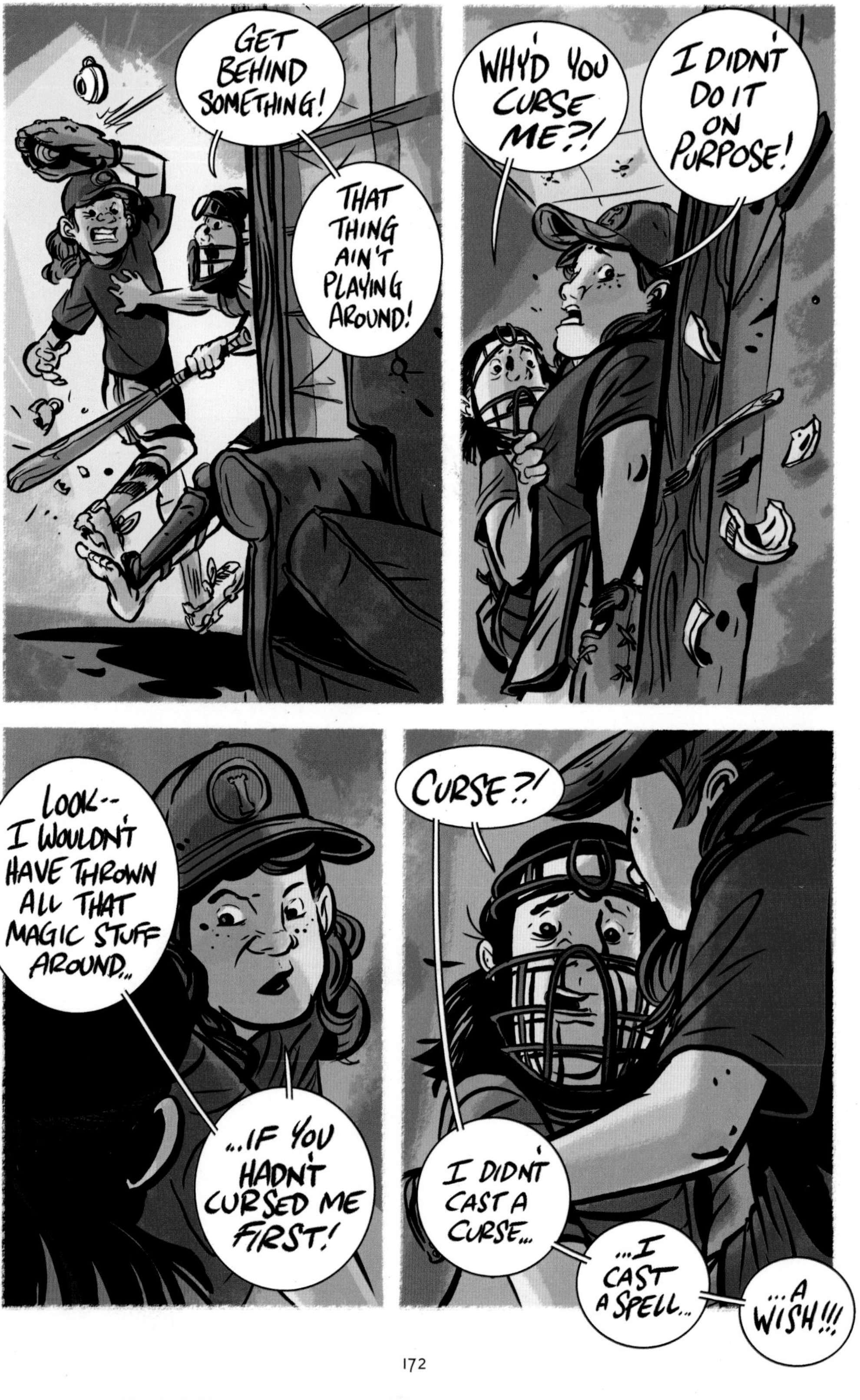
GET BEHIND SOMETHING!
THAT THING AIN'T PLAYING AROUND!
WHY'D YOU CURSE ME?!
I DIDN'T DO IT ON PURPOSE!
LOOK-- I WOULDN'T HAVE THROWN ALL THAT MAGIC STUFF AROUND...
...IF YOU HADN'T CURSED ME FIRST!
CURSE?!
I DIDN'T CAST A CURSE...
...I CAST A SPELL...
...A WISH!!!

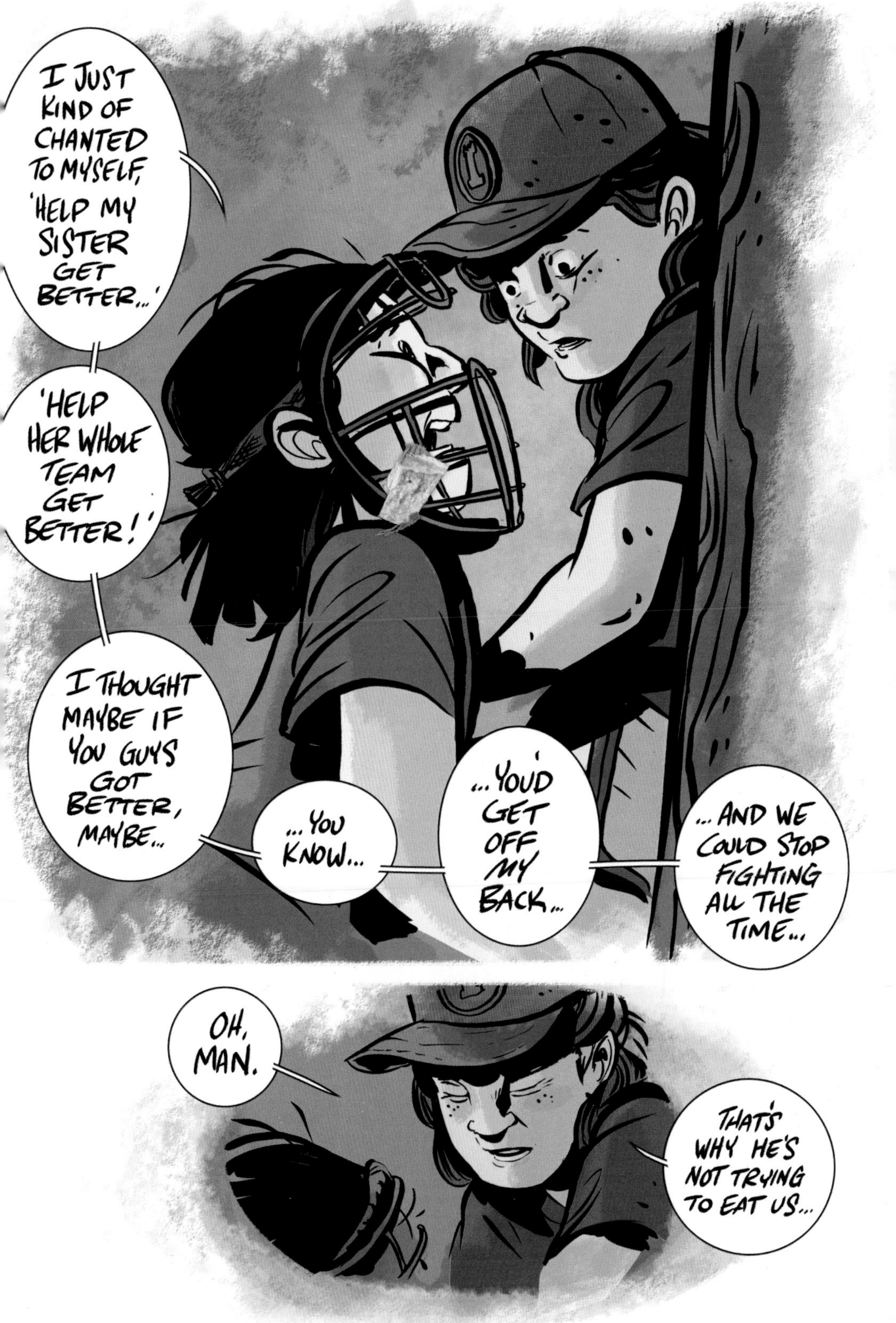
I JUST KIND OF CHANTED TO MYSELF, 'HELP MY SISTER GET BETTER...'
'HELP HER WHOLE TEAM GET BETTER!'
I THOUGHT MAYBE IF YOU GUYS GOT BETTER, MAYBE...
...YOU KNOW...
...YOU'D GET OFF MY BACK...
...AND WE COULD STOP FIGHTING ALL THE TIME...
OH, MAN.
THAT'S WHY HE'S NOT TRYING TO EAT US...

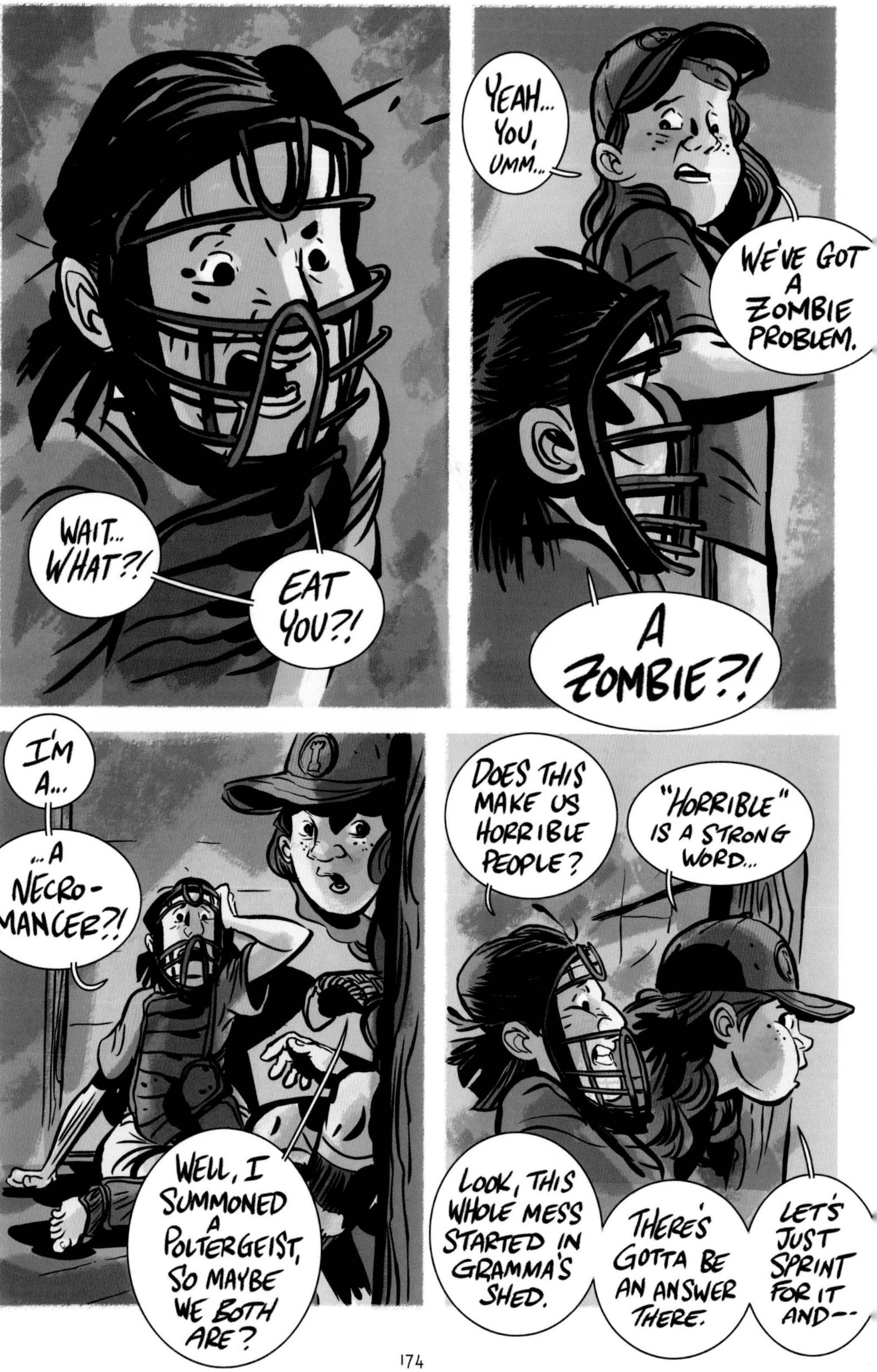
WAIT... WHAT?!
EAT YOU?!
YEAH... YOU, UMM...
WE'VE GOT A ZOMBIE PROBLEM.
A ZOMBIE?!
I'M A...
...A NECRO-MANCER?!
WELL, I SUMMONED A POLTERGEIST, SO MAYBE WE BOTH ARE?
DOES THIS MAKE US HORRIBLE PEOPLE?
"HORRIBLE" IS A STRONG WORD...
LOOK, THIS WHOLE MESS STARTED IN GRAMMA'S SHED.
THERE'S GOTTA BE AN ANSWER THERE.
LET'S JUST SPRINT FOR IT AND--

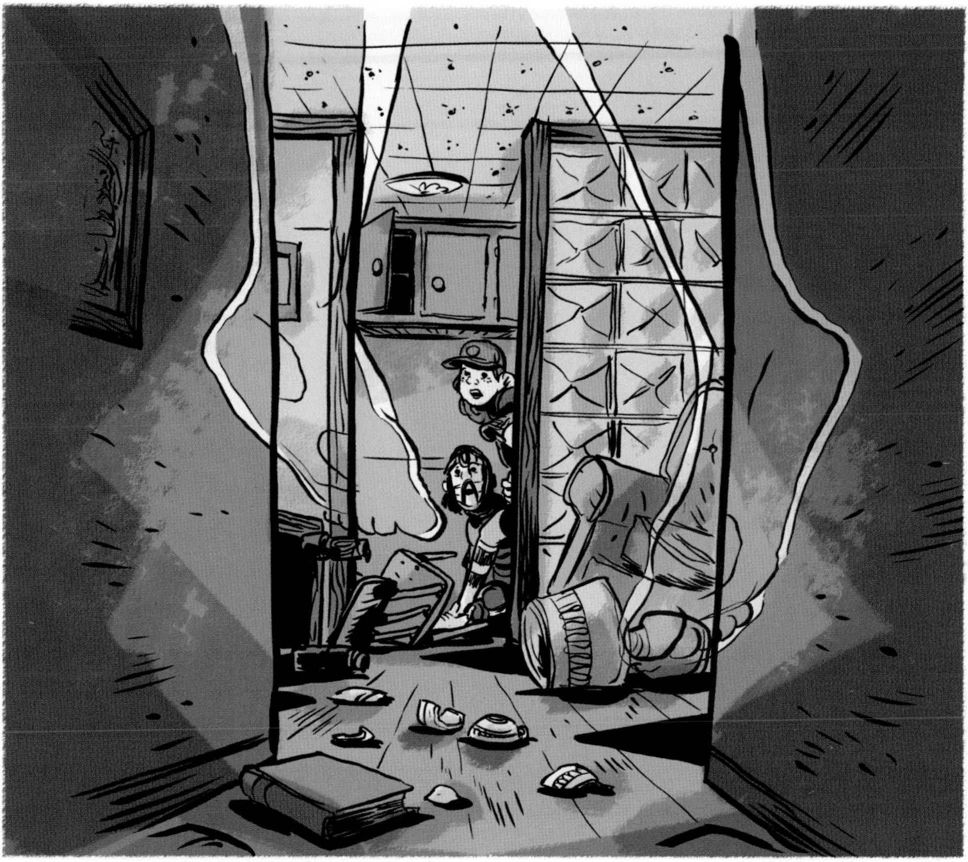

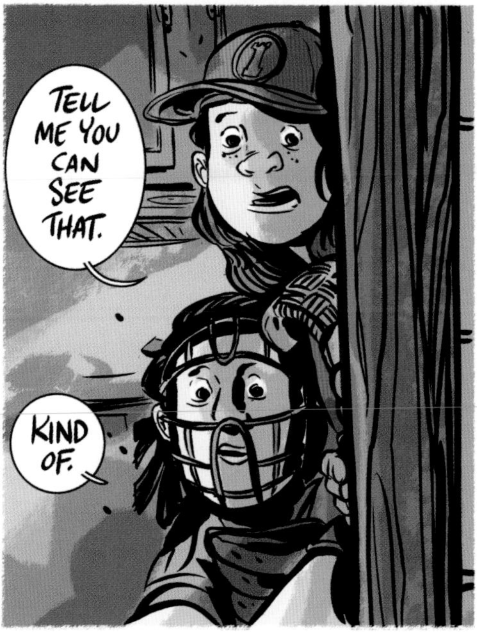
TELL ME YOU CAN SEE THAT.
KIND OF.

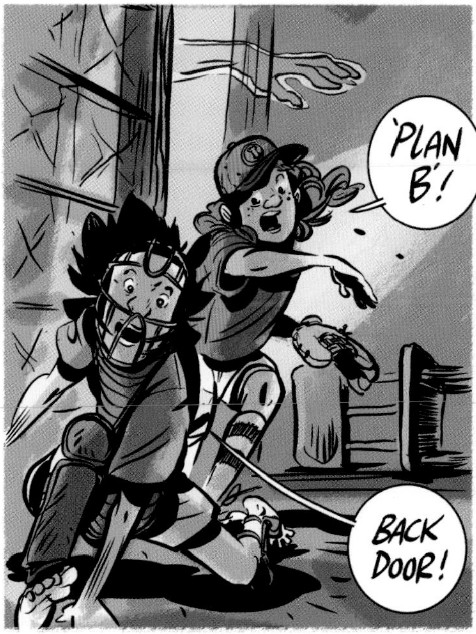
'PLAN B'!
BACK DOOR!

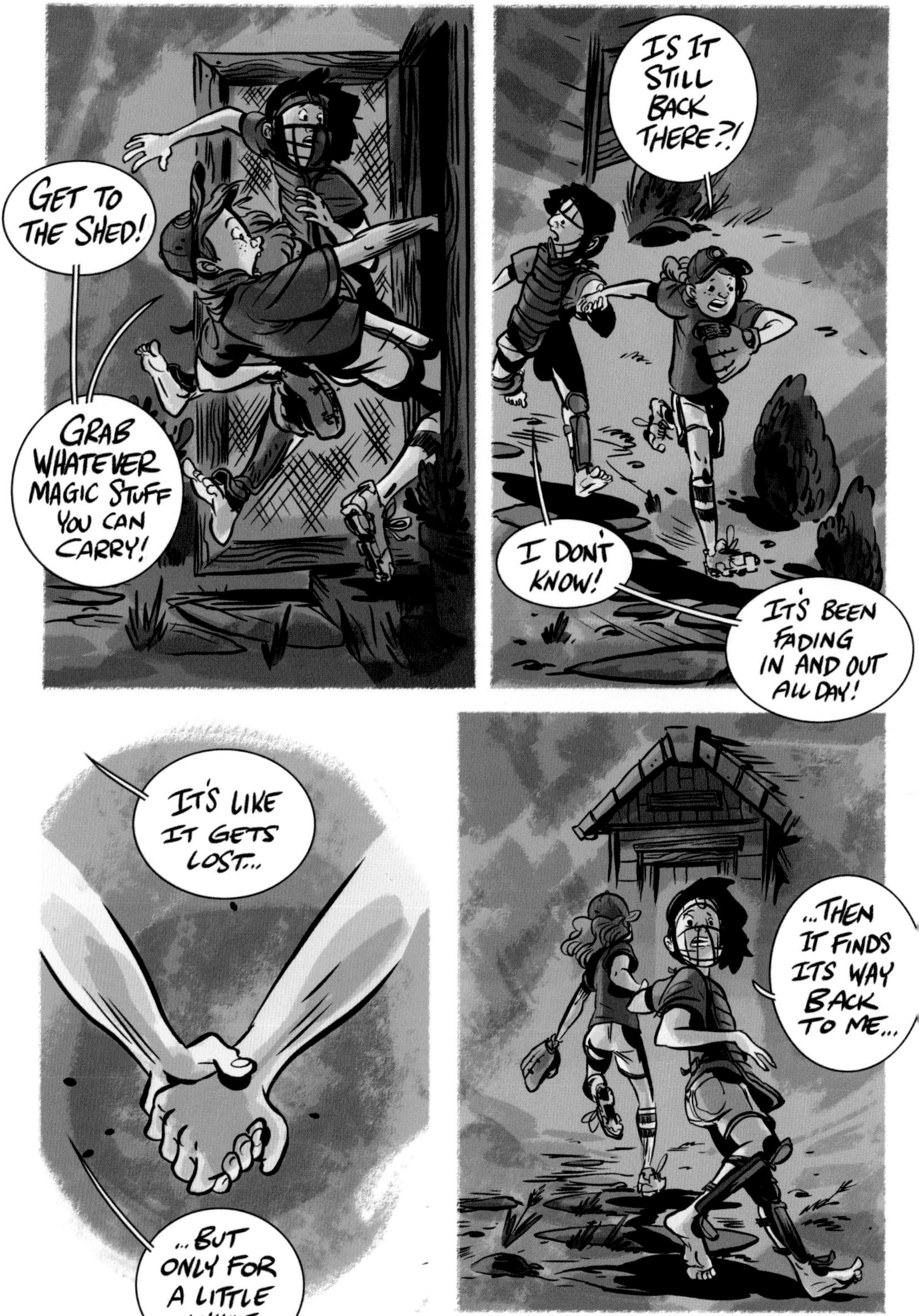
GET TO THE SHED!
GRAB WHATEVER MAGIC STUFF YOU CAN CARRY!
IS IT STILL BACK THERE?!
I DON'T KNOW!
IT'S BEEN FADING IN AND OUT ALL DAY!
IT'S LIKE IT GETS LOST...
...BUT ONLY FOR A LITTLE WHILE...
...THEN IT FINDS ITS WAY BACK TO ME...

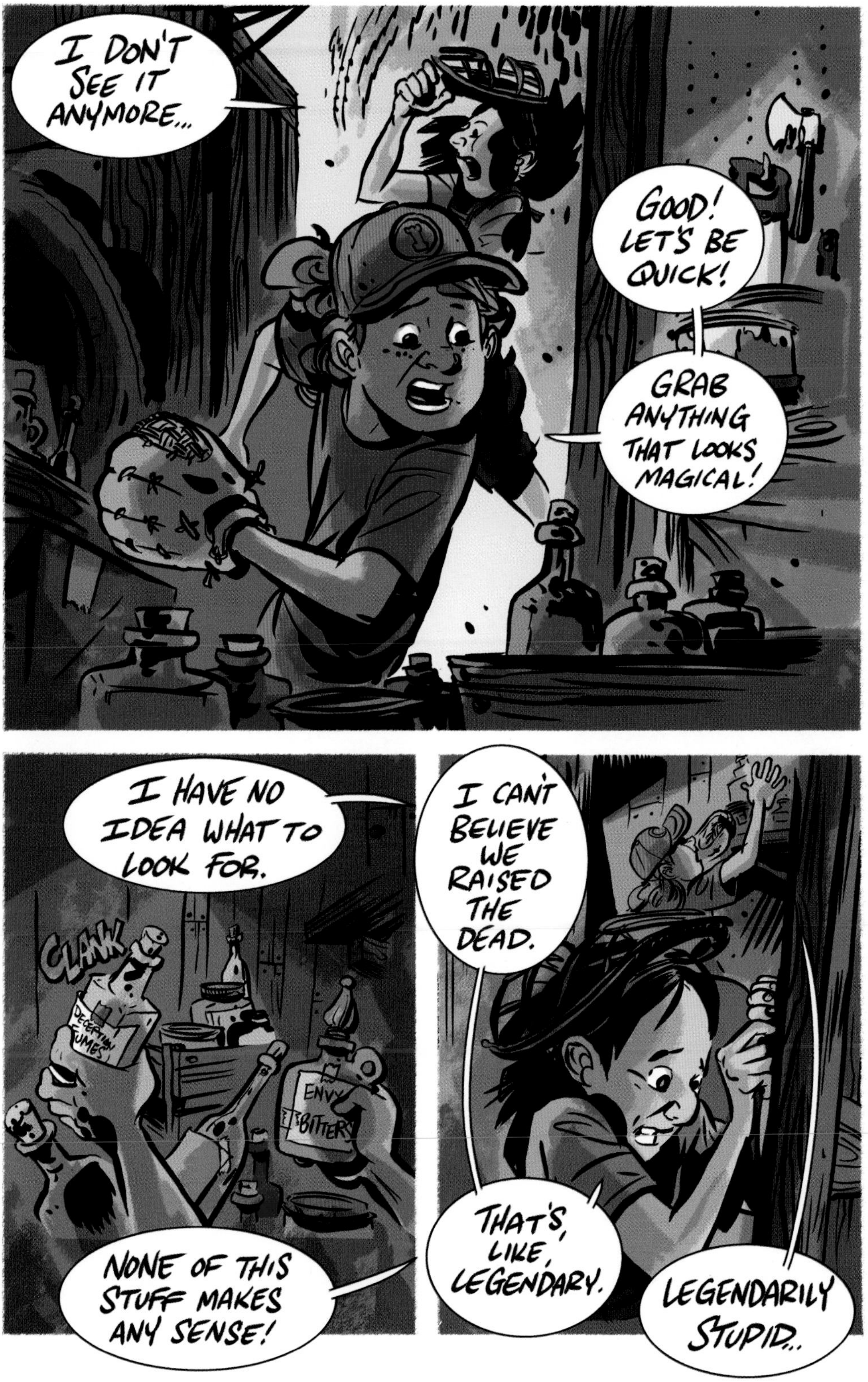
I DON'T SEE IT ANYMORE...
GOOD! LET'S BE QUICK!
GRAB ANYTHING THAT LOOKS MAGICAL!
I HAVE NO IDEA WHAT TO LOOK FOR.
CLANK
ENVY BITTERS
NONE OF THIS STUFF MAKES ANY SENSE!
I CAN'T BELIEVE WE RAISED THE DEAD.
THAT'S, LIKE, LEGENDARY.
LEGENDARILY STUPID...

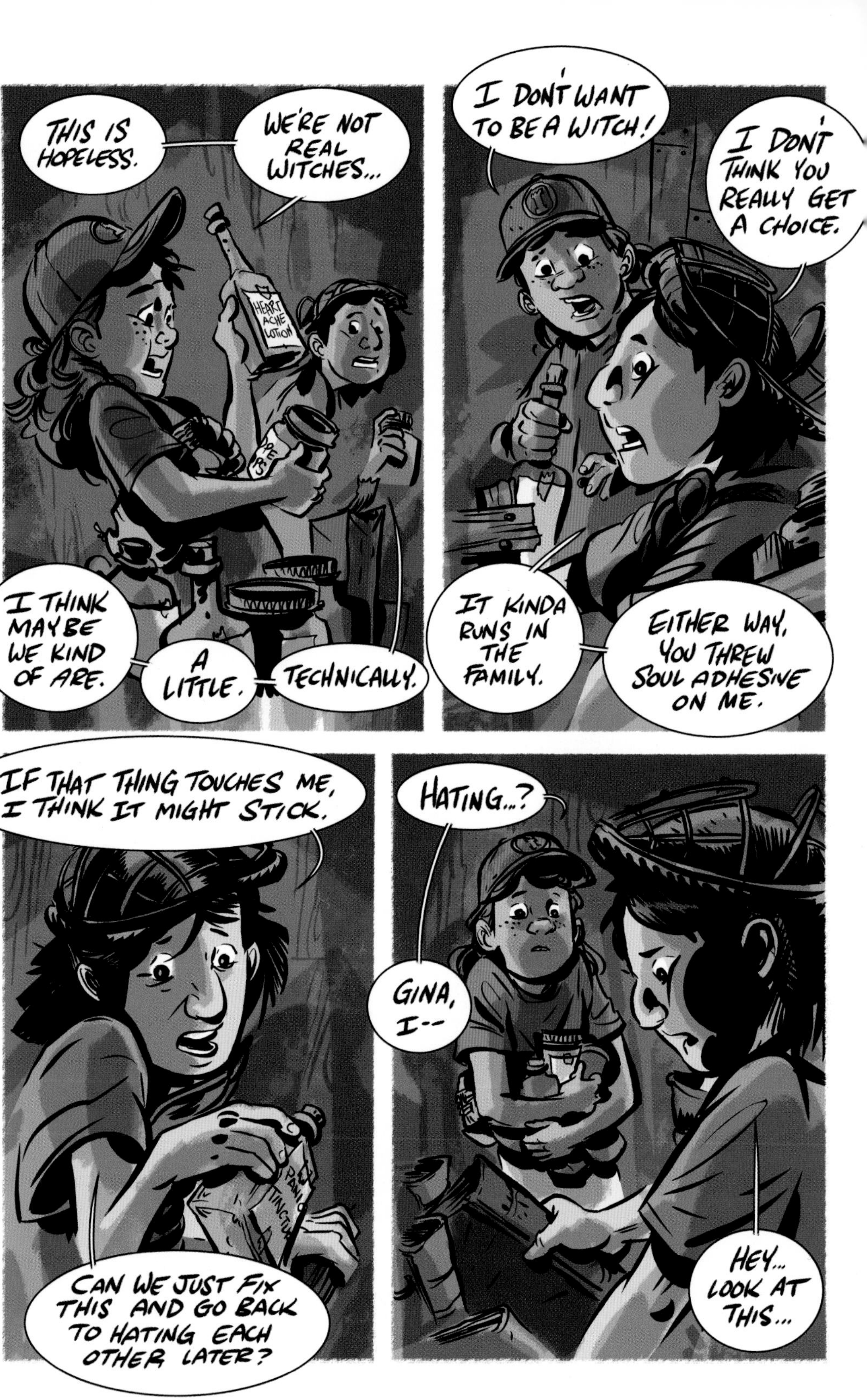
THIS IS HOPELESS.
WE'RE NOT REAL WITCHES...
HEART ACHE LOTION
I THINK MAYBE WE KIND OF ARE.
A LITTLE.
TECHNICALLY.
I DON'T WANT TO BE A WITCH!
I DON'T THINK YOU REALLY GET A CHOICE.
IT KINDA RUNS IN THE FAMILY.
EITHER WAY, YOU THREW SOUL ADHESIVE ON ME.
IF THAT THING TOUCHES ME, I THINK IT MIGHT STICK.
CAN WE JUST FIX THIS AND GO BACK TO HATING EACH OTHER LATER?
HATING...?
GINA, I--
HEY... LOOK AT THIS...

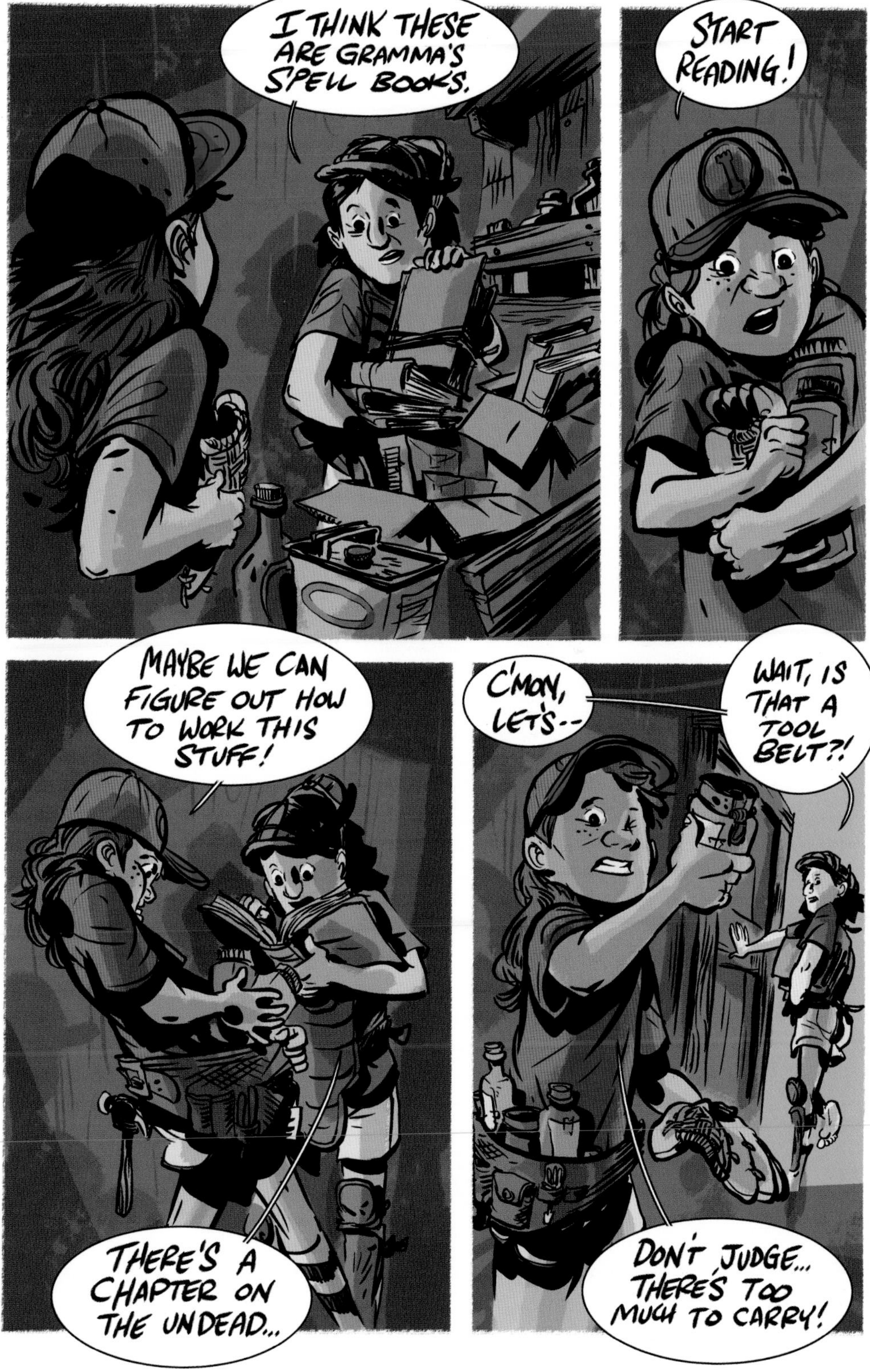
I THINK THESE ARE GRAMMA'S SPELL BOOKS.
START READING!
MAYBE WE CAN FIGURE OUT HOW TO WORK THIS STUFF!
THERE'S A CHAPTER ON THE UNDEAD...
C'MON, LET'S--
WAIT, IS THAT A TOOL BELT?!
DON'T JUDGE... THERE'S TOO MUCH TO CARRY!

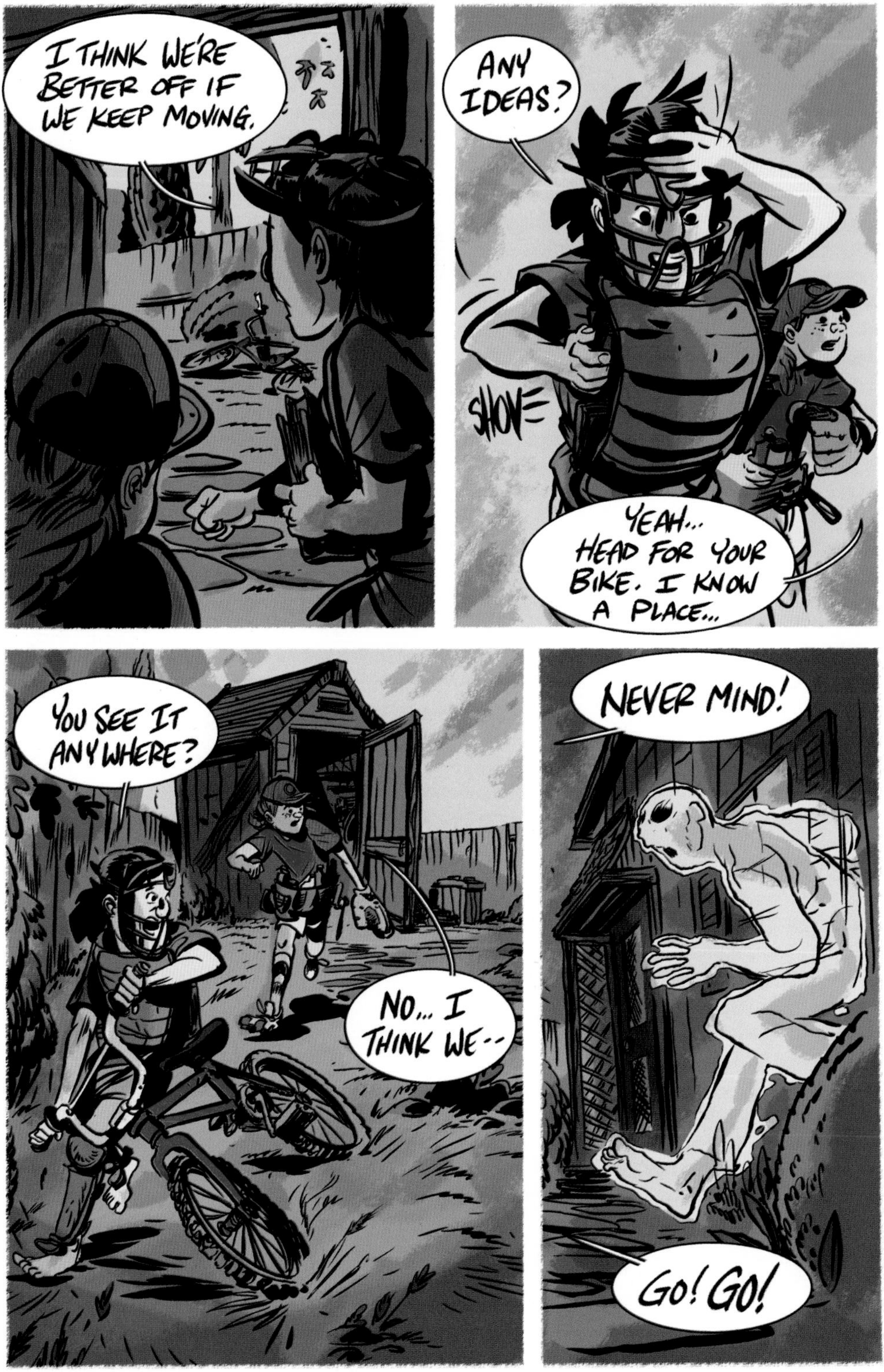
I THINK WE'RE BETTER OFF IF WE KEEP MOVING.
ANY IDEAS?
SHOVE
YEAH... HEAD FOR YOUR BIKE. I KNOW A PLACE...
YOU SEE IT ANYWHERE?
NO... I THINK WE--
NEVER MIND!
GO! GO!

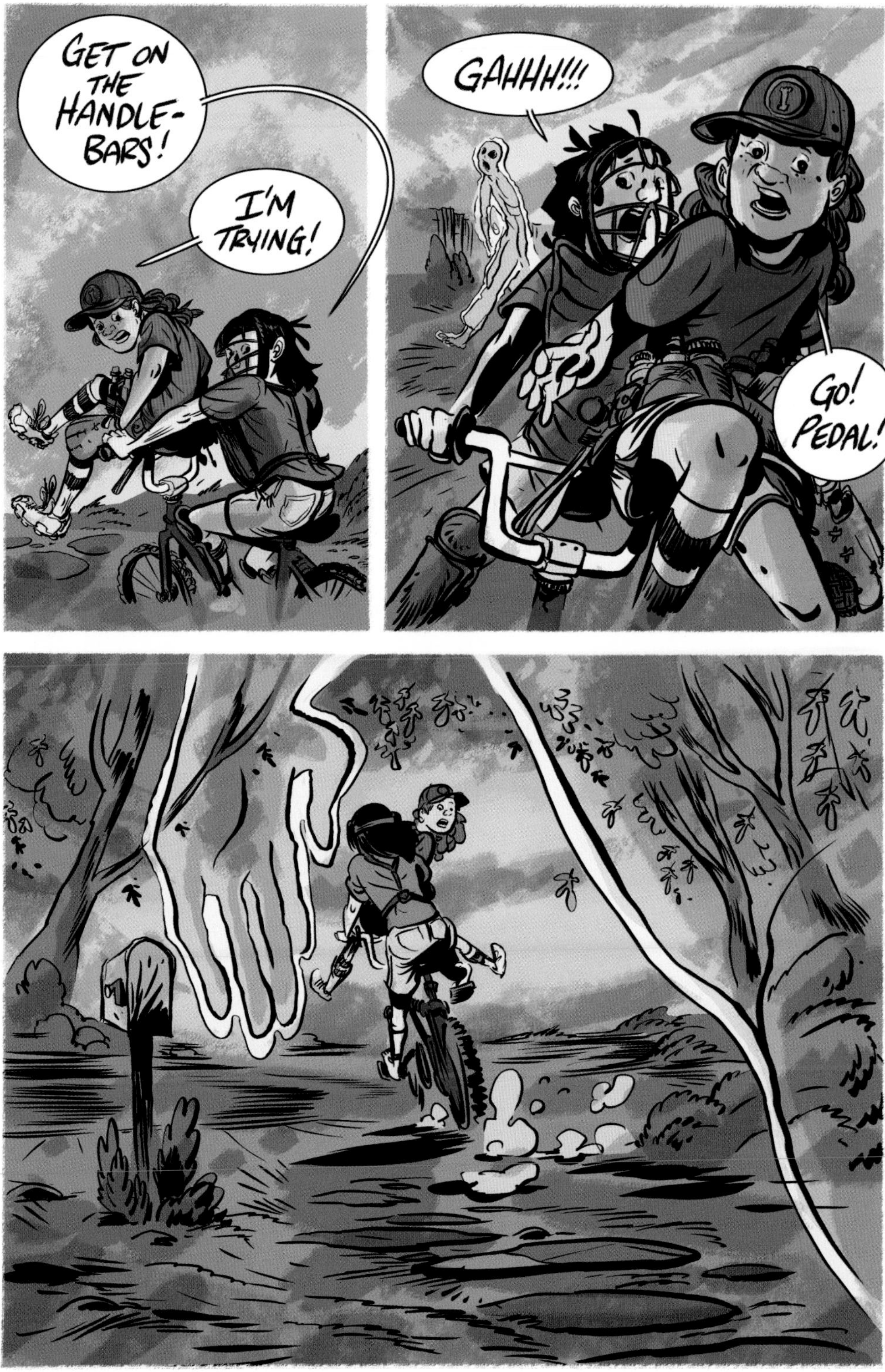
GET ON THE HANDLE-BARS!
I'M TRYING!
GAHHH!!!
GO! PEDAL!

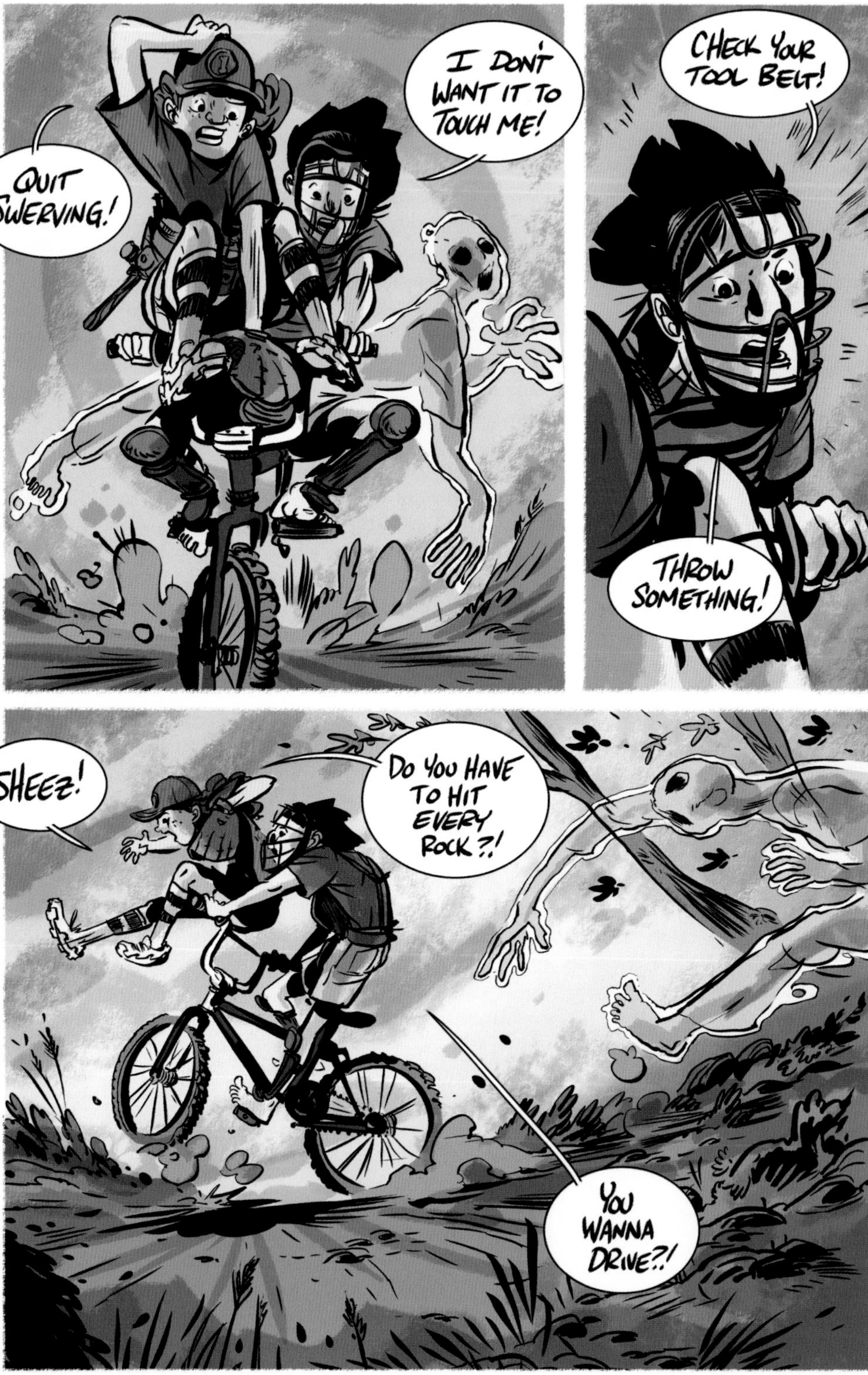
QUIT SWERVING!
I DON'T WANT IT TO TOUCH ME!
CHECK YOUR TOOL BELT!
THROW SOMETHING!
SHEEZ!
DO YOU HAVE TO HIT EVERY ROCK?!
YOU WANNA DRIVE?!

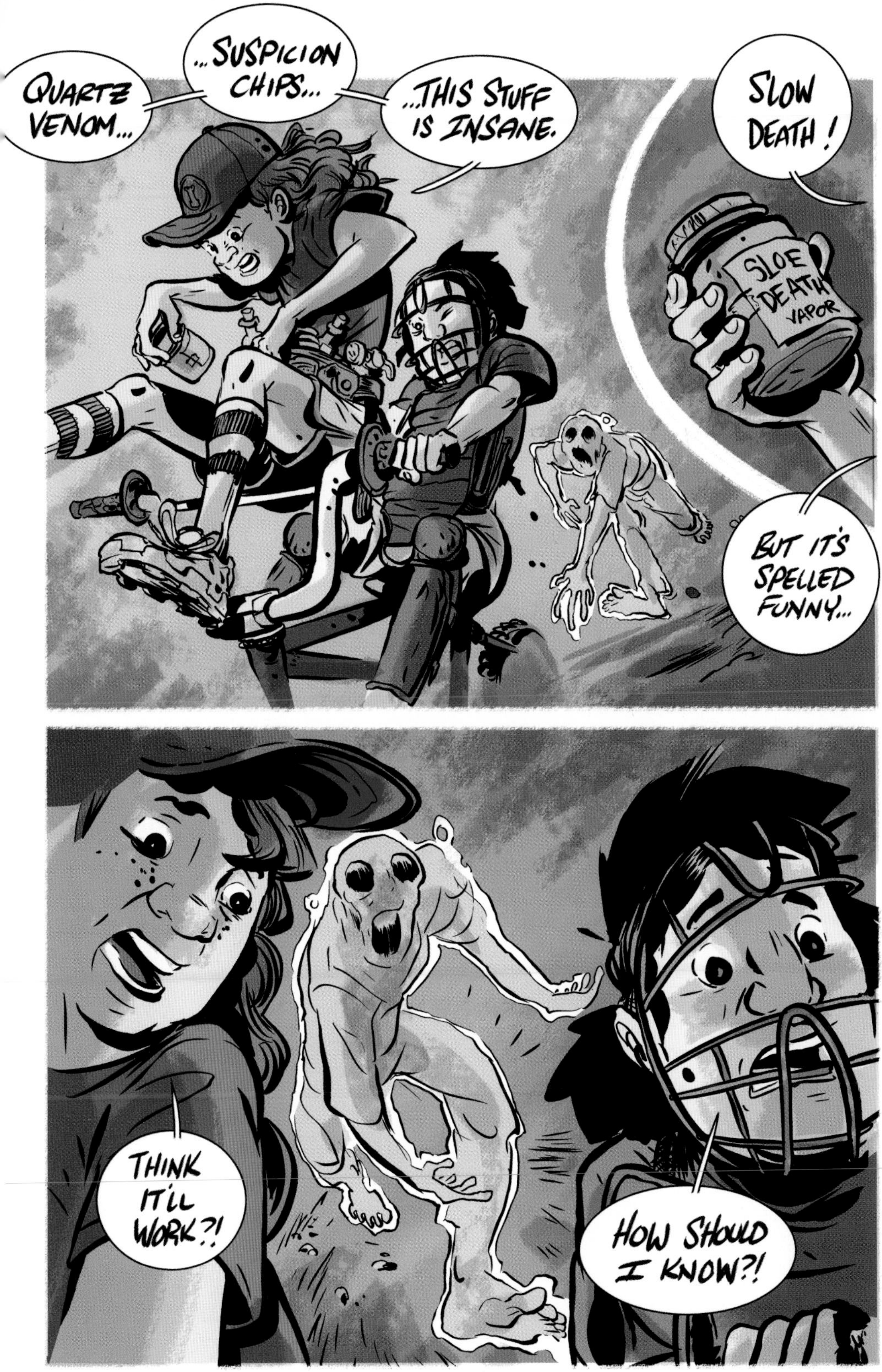
QUARTZ VENOM...
...SUSPICION CHIPS...
...THIS STUFF IS INSANE.
SLOW DEATH!
SLOE DEATH VAPOR
BUT IT'S SPELLED FUNNY...
THINK IT'LL WORK?!
HOW SHOULD I KNOW?!

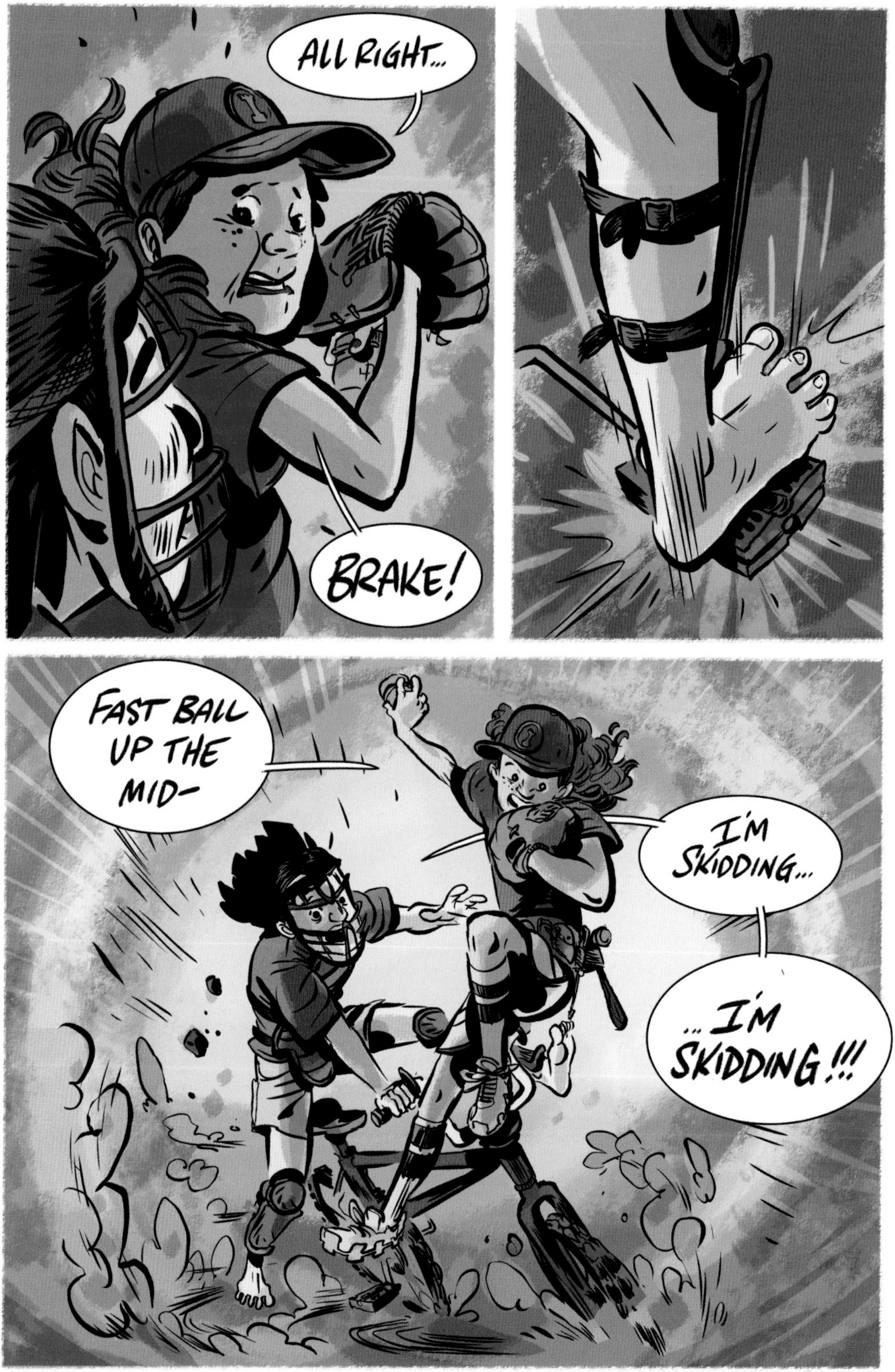
ALL RIGHT...
BRAKE!
FAST BALL UP THE MID-
I'M SKIDDING...
...I'M SKIDDING!!!

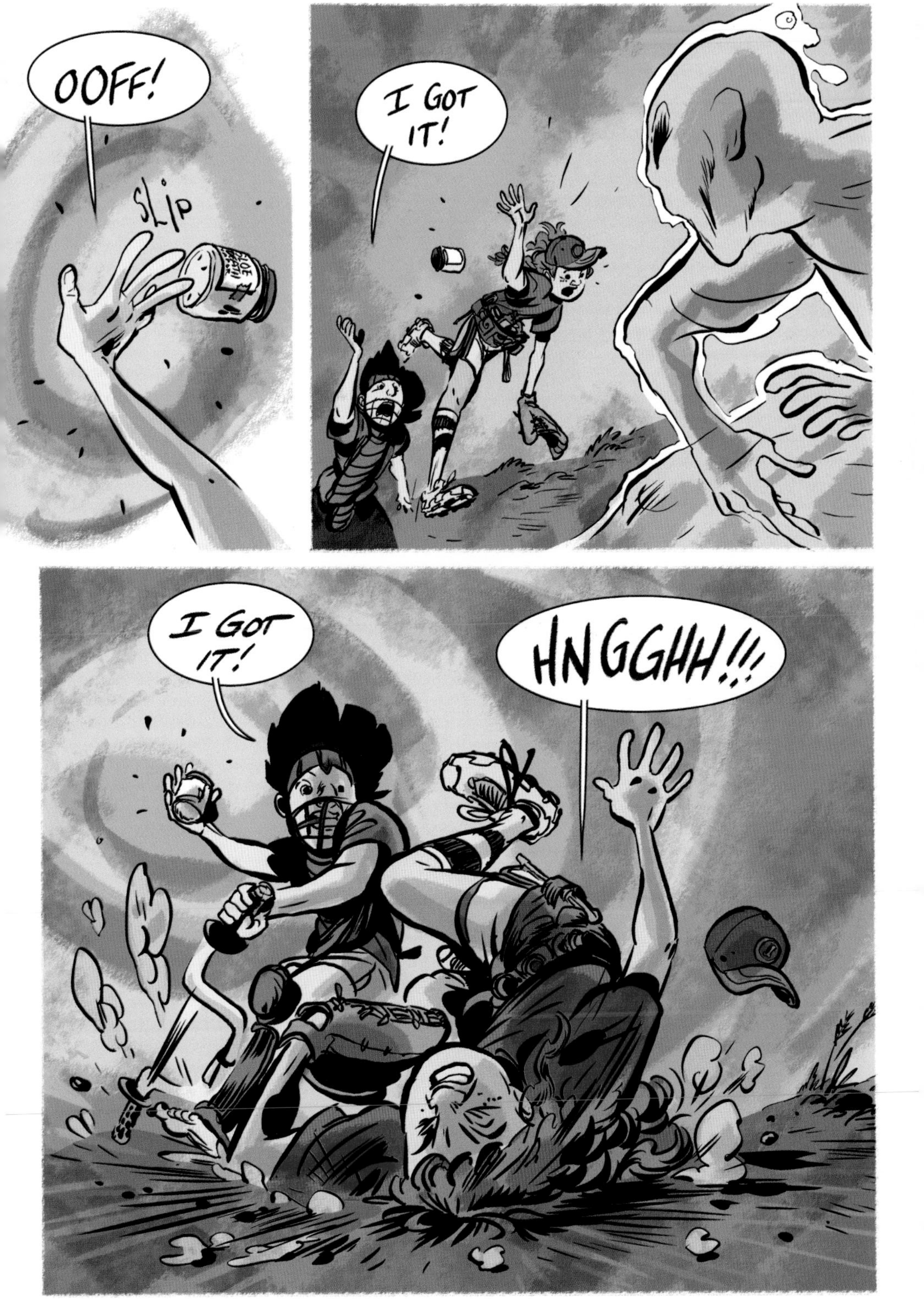
OOFF!
SLIP
I GOT IT!
I GOT IT!
HNGGHH!!!

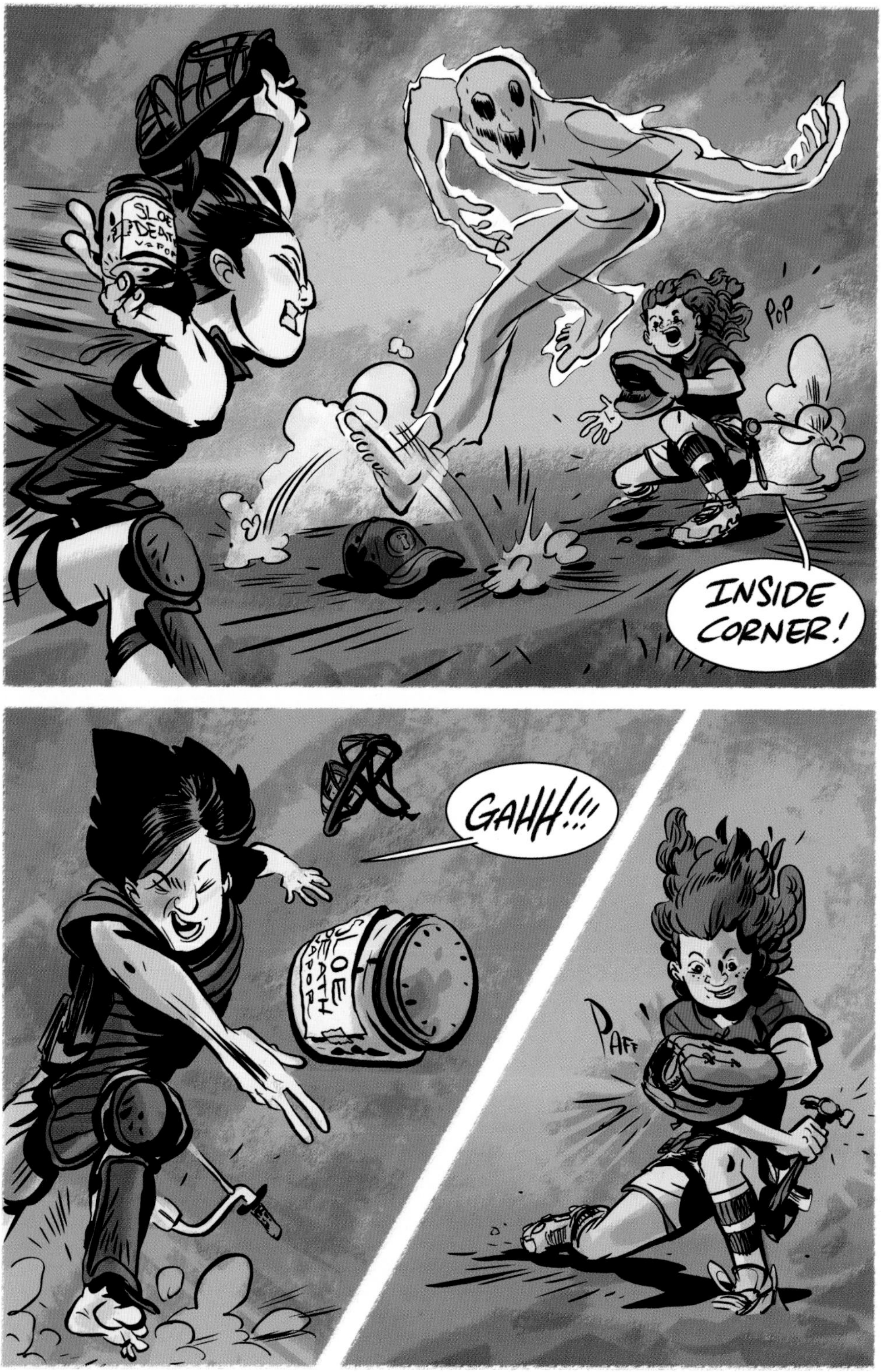
SLOE DEATH VAPOR
POP
INSIDE CORNER!
GAHH!!!
SLOE DEATH VAPOR
PAFF

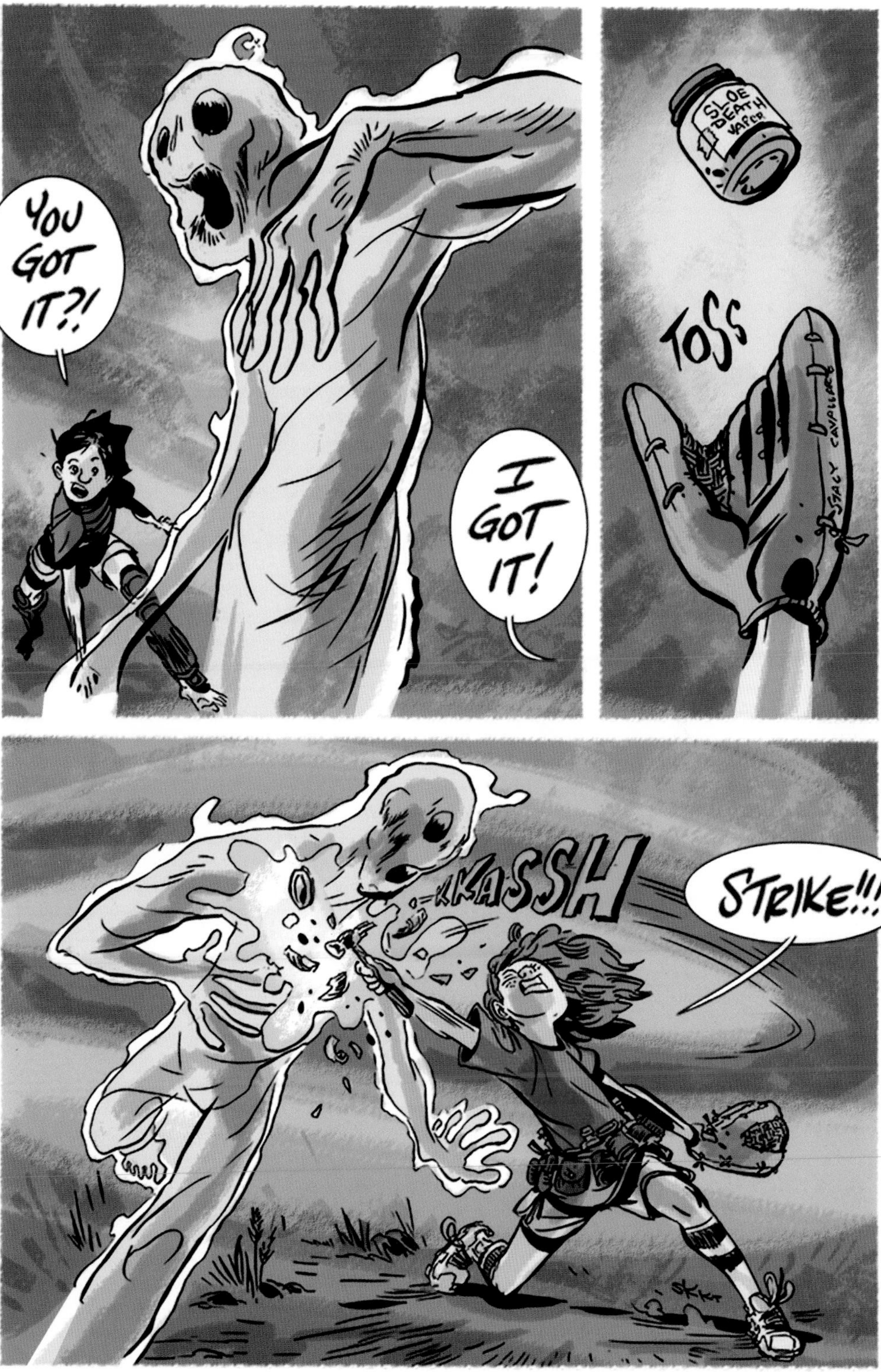
YOU GOT IT?!
I GOT IT!
SLOE DEATH VAPOR
TOSS
KKASSH
STRIKE!!!

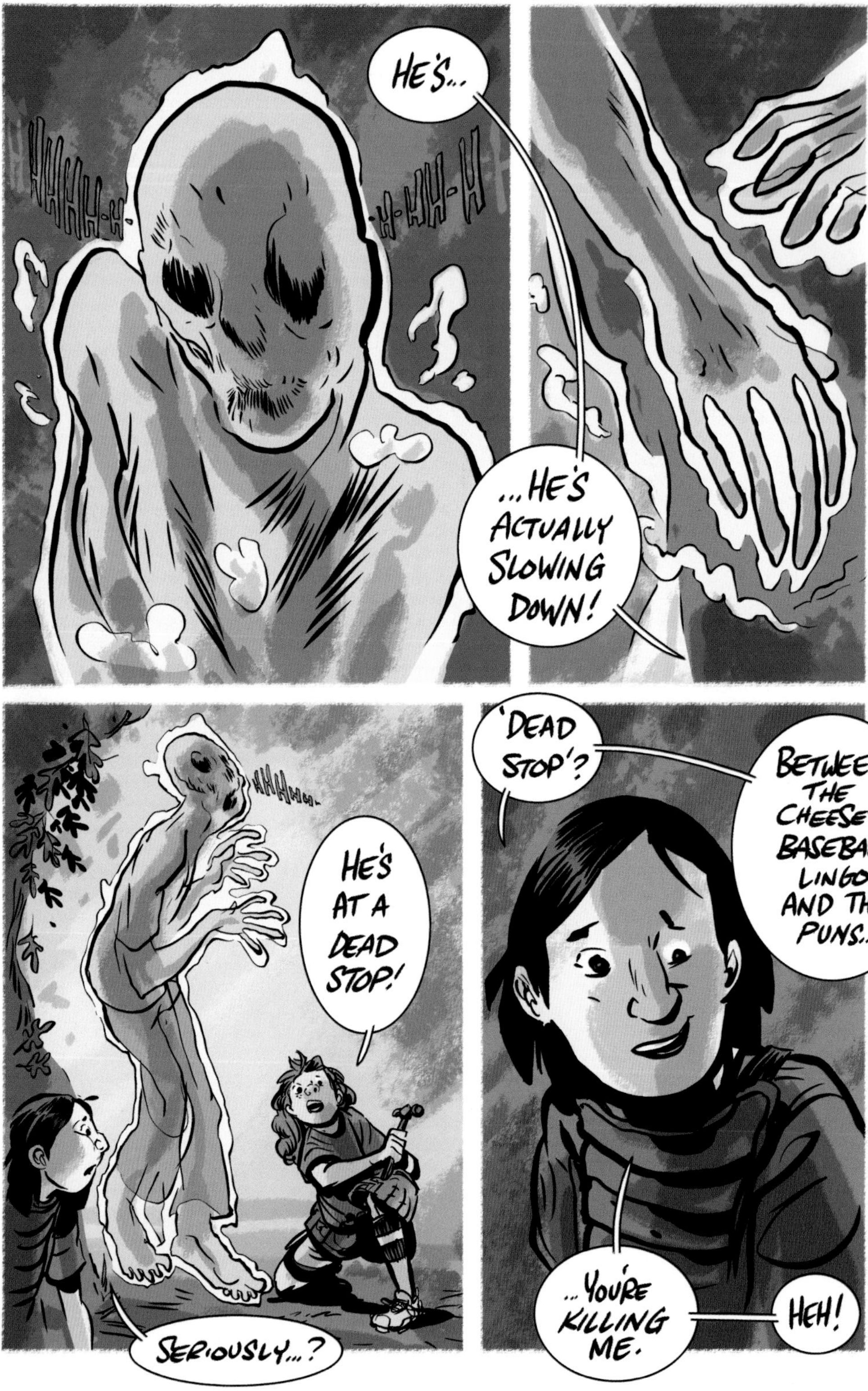
HHHHH-H-
-H-HH-H
HE'S...
...HE'S ACTUALLY SLOWING DOWN!
HHHHH...
HE'S AT A DEAD STOP!
SERIOUSLY...?
'DEAD STOP'?
BETWEEN THE CHEESEY BASEBALL LINGO AND THE PUNS...
...YOU'RE KILLING ME.
HEH!

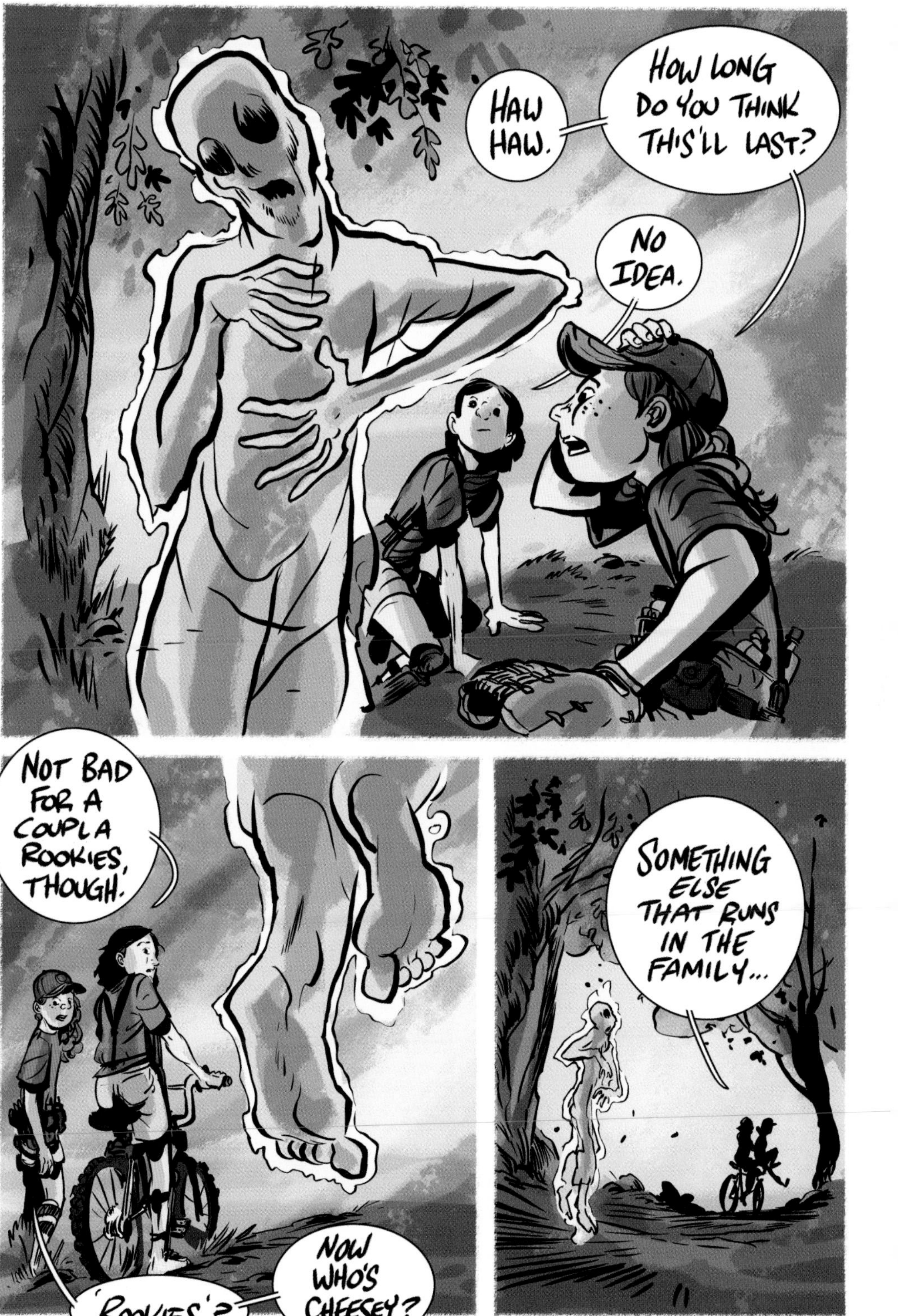
HAW HAW.
HOW LONG DO YOU THINK THIS'LL LAST?
NO IDEA.
NOT BAD FOR A COUPLA ROOKIES, THOUGH.
'ROOKIES'?
NOW WHO'S CHEESEY?
SOMETHING ELSE THAT RUNS IN THE FAMILY...

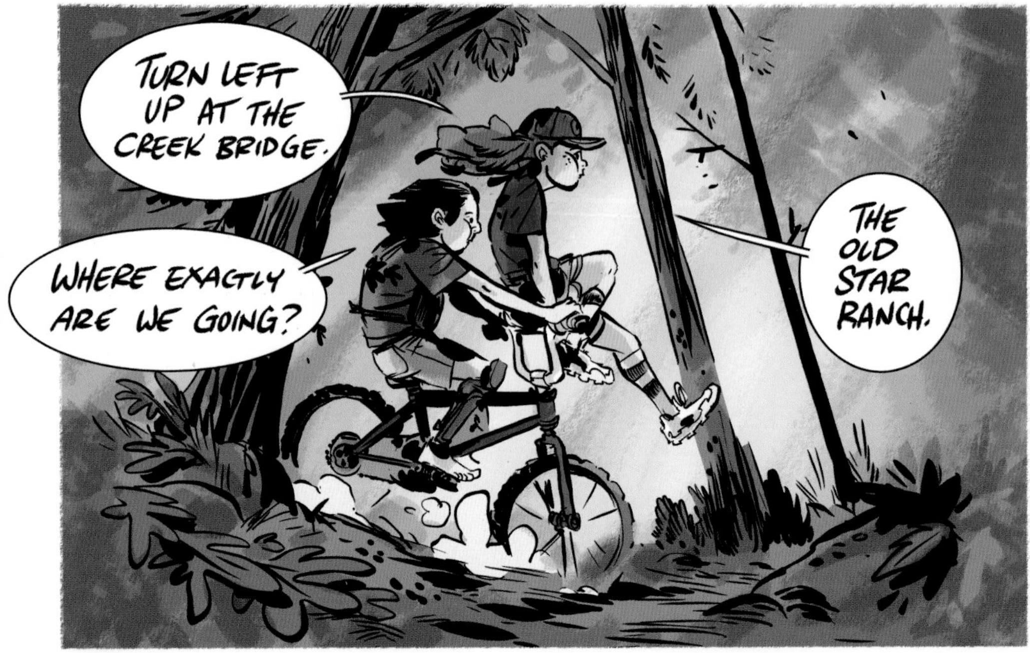
TURN LEFT UP AT THE CREEK BRIDGE.
WHERE EXACTLY ARE WE GOING?
THE OLD STAR RANCH.

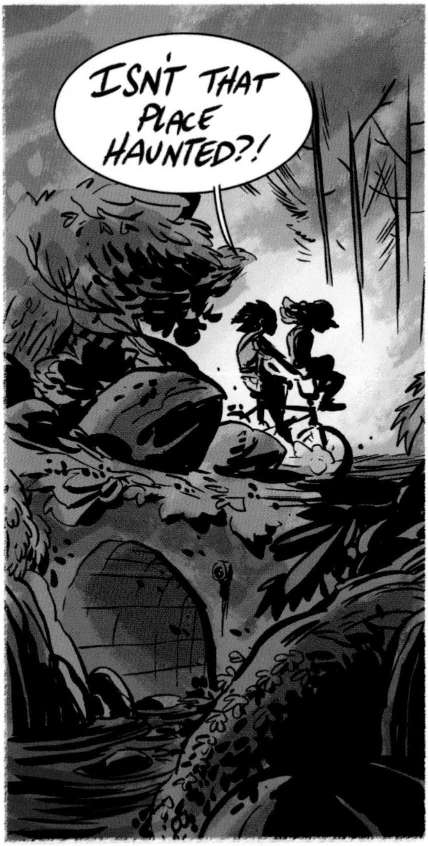
ISN'T THAT PLACE HAUNTED?!

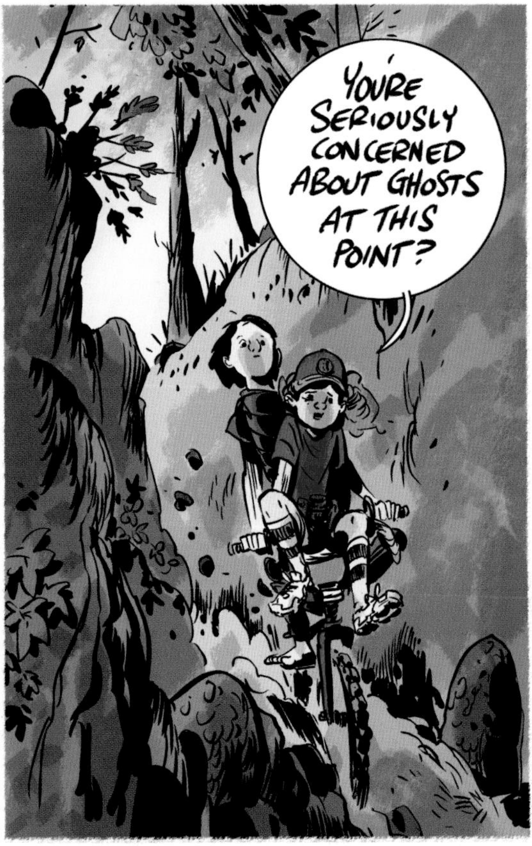
YOU'RE SERIOUSLY CONCERNED ABOUT GHOSTS AT THIS POINT?

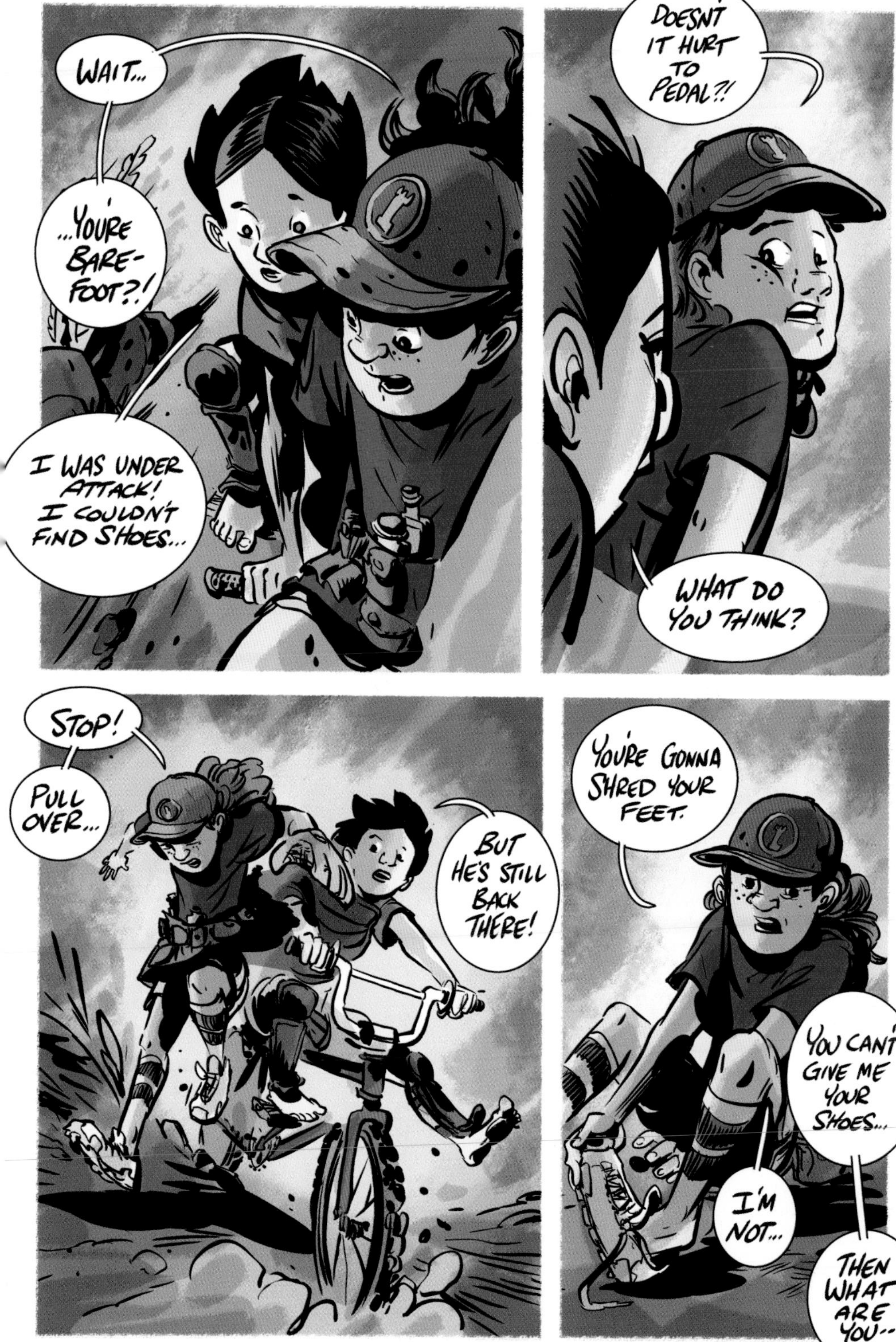
WAIT...
...YOU'RE BARE-FOOT?!
I WAS UNDER ATTACK! I COULDN'T FIND SHOES...
DOESN'T IT HURT TO PEDAL?!
WHAT DO YOU THINK?
STOP!
PULL OVER...
BUT HE'S STILL BACK THERE!
YOU'RE GONNA SHRED YOUR FEET.
YOU CAN'T GIVE ME YOUR SHOES...
I'M NOT...
THEN WHAT ARE YOU--

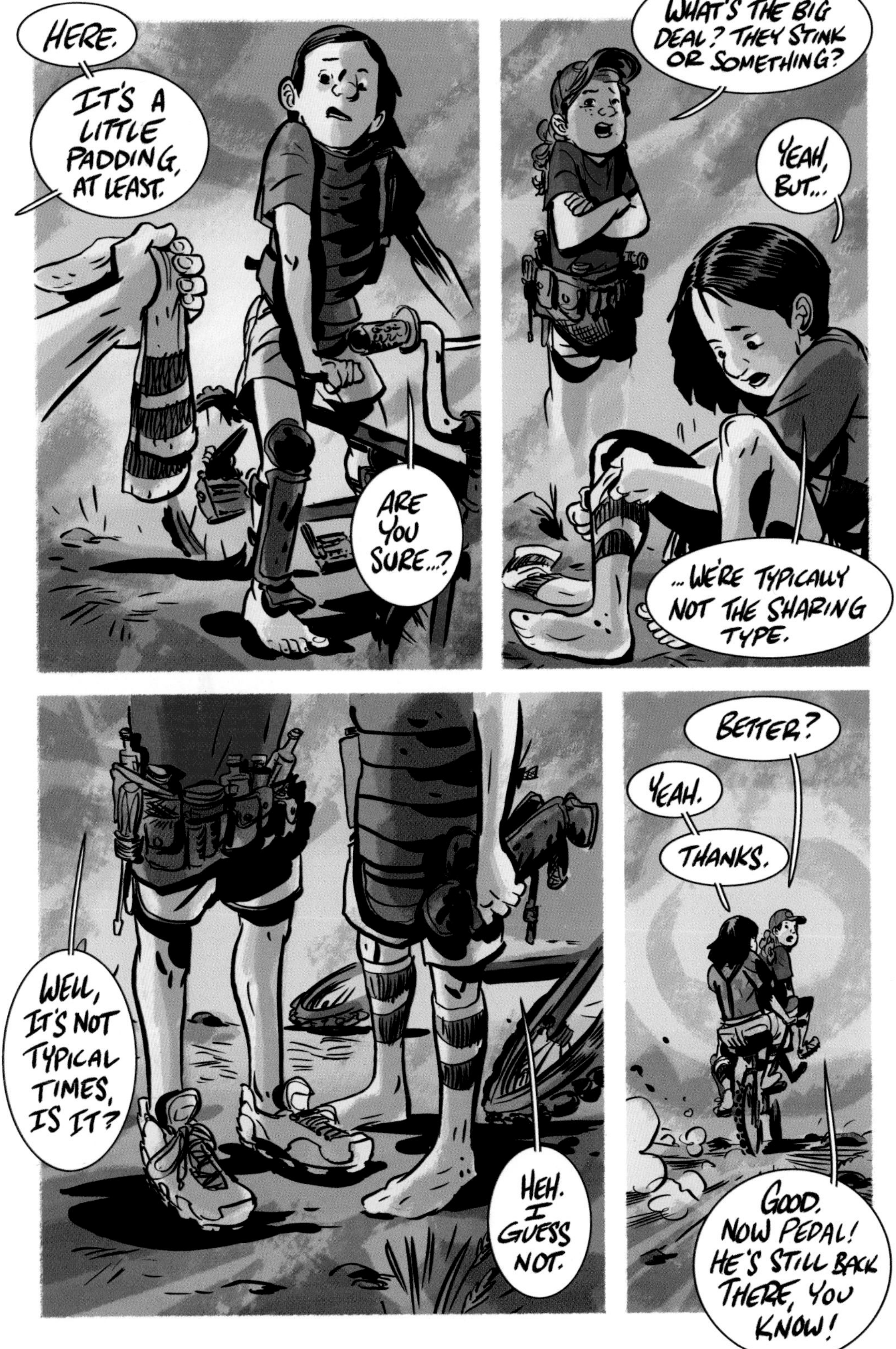
HERE.
IT'S A LITTLE PADDING, AT LEAST.
ARE YOU SURE...?
WHAT'S THE BIG DEAL? THEY STINK OR SOMETHING?
YEAH, BUT...
...WE'RE TYPICALLY NOT THE SHARING TYPE.
WELL, IT'S NOT TYPICAL TIMES, IS IT?
HEH. I GUESS NOT.
BETTER?
YEAH.
THANKS.
GOOD. NOW PEDAL! HE'S STILL BACK THERE, YOU KNOW!

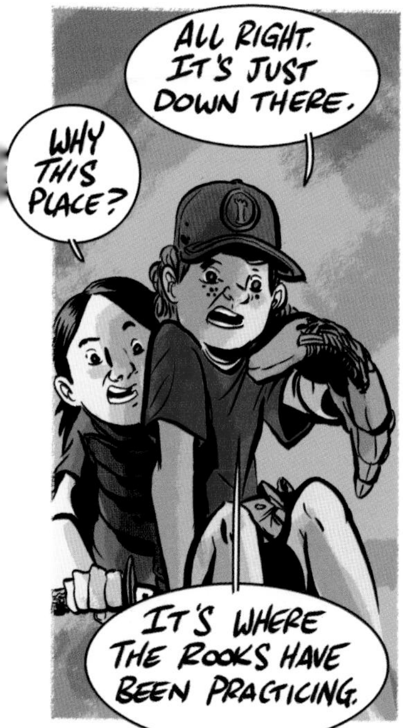
WHY THIS PLACE?
ALL RIGHT. IT'S JUST DOWN THERE.
IT'S WHERE THE ROOKS HAVE BEEN PRACTICING.

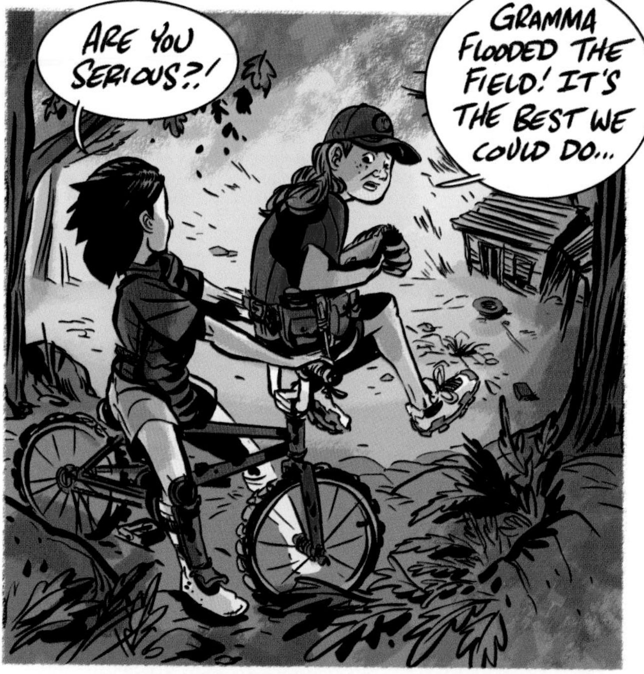
ARE YOU SERIOUS?!
GRAMMA FLOODED THE FIELD! IT'S THE BEST WE COULD DO...

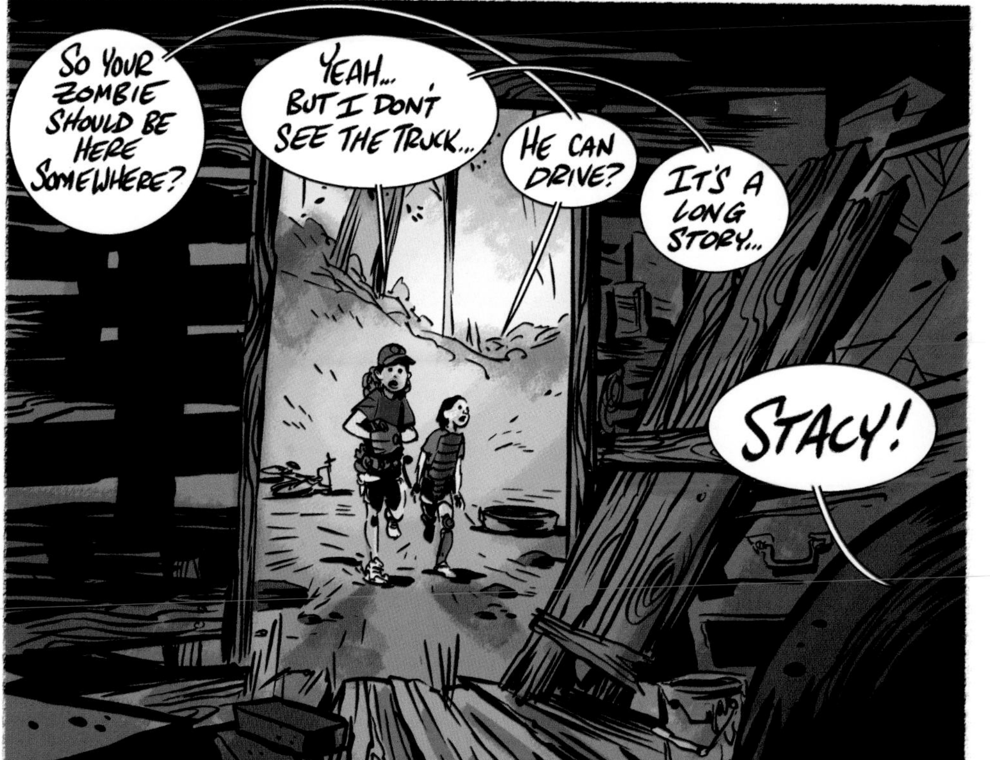
SO YOUR ZOMBIE SHOULD BE HERE SOMEWHERE?
YEAH... BUT I DON'T SEE THE TRUCK...
HE CAN DRIVE?
IT'S A LONG STORY...
STACY!

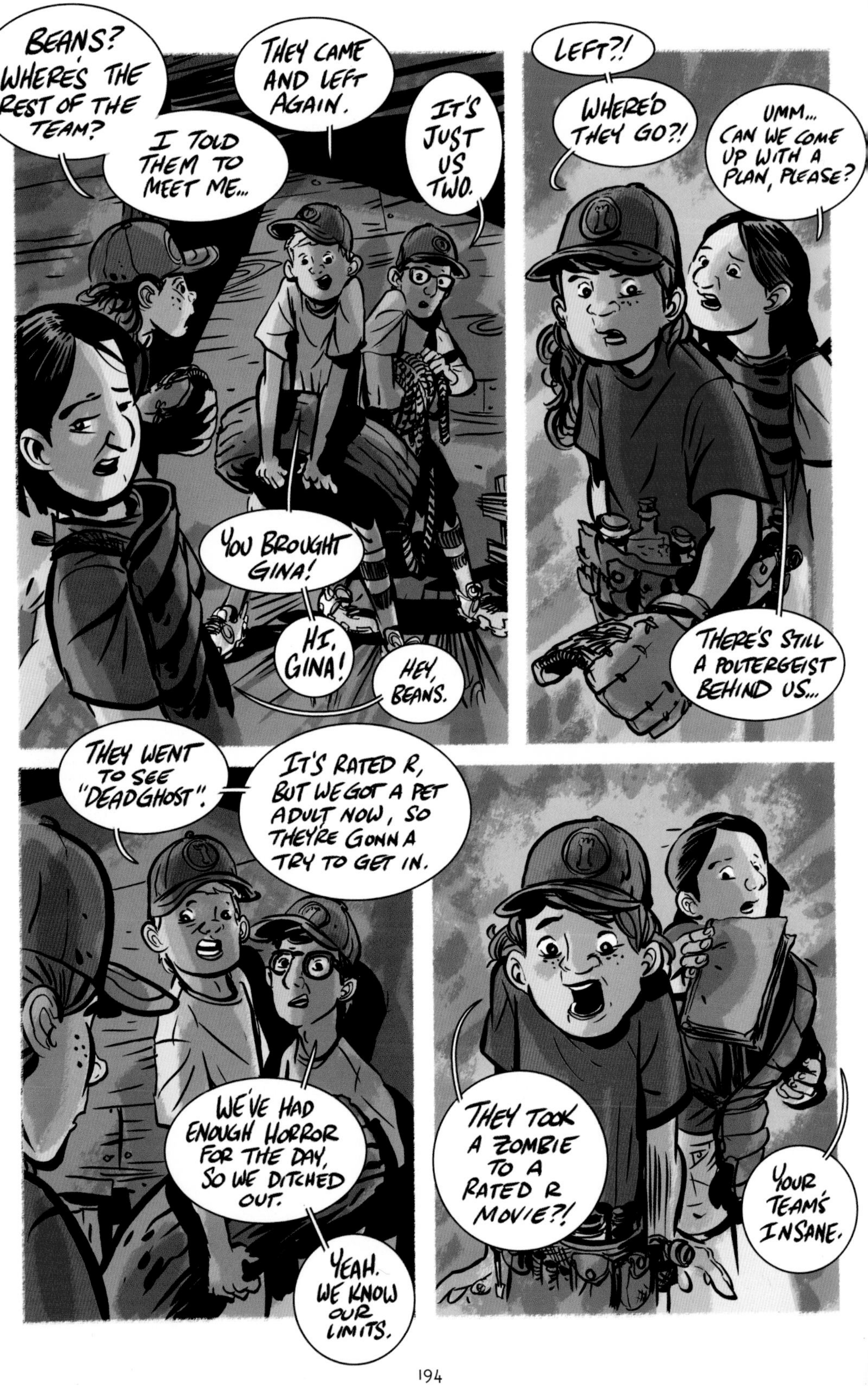

BEANS? WHERE'S THE REST OF THE TEAM?
I TOLD THEM TO MEET ME...
THEY CAME AND LEFT AGAIN.
IT'S JUST US TWO.
YOU BROUGHT GINA!
HI, GINA!
HEY, BEANS.
LEFT?!
WHERE'D THEY GO?!
UMM... CAN WE COME UP WITH A PLAN, PLEASE?
THERE'S STILL A POLTERGEIST BEHIND US...
THEY WENT TO SEE "DEADGHOST".
IT'S RATED R, BUT WE GOT A PET ADULT NOW, SO THEY'RE GONNA TRY TO GET IN.
WE'VE HAD ENOUGH HORROR FOR THE DAY, SO WE DITCHED OUT.
YEAH. WE KNOW OUR LIMITS.
THEY TOOK A ZOMBIE TO A RATED R MOVIE?!
YOUR TEAM'S INSANE.

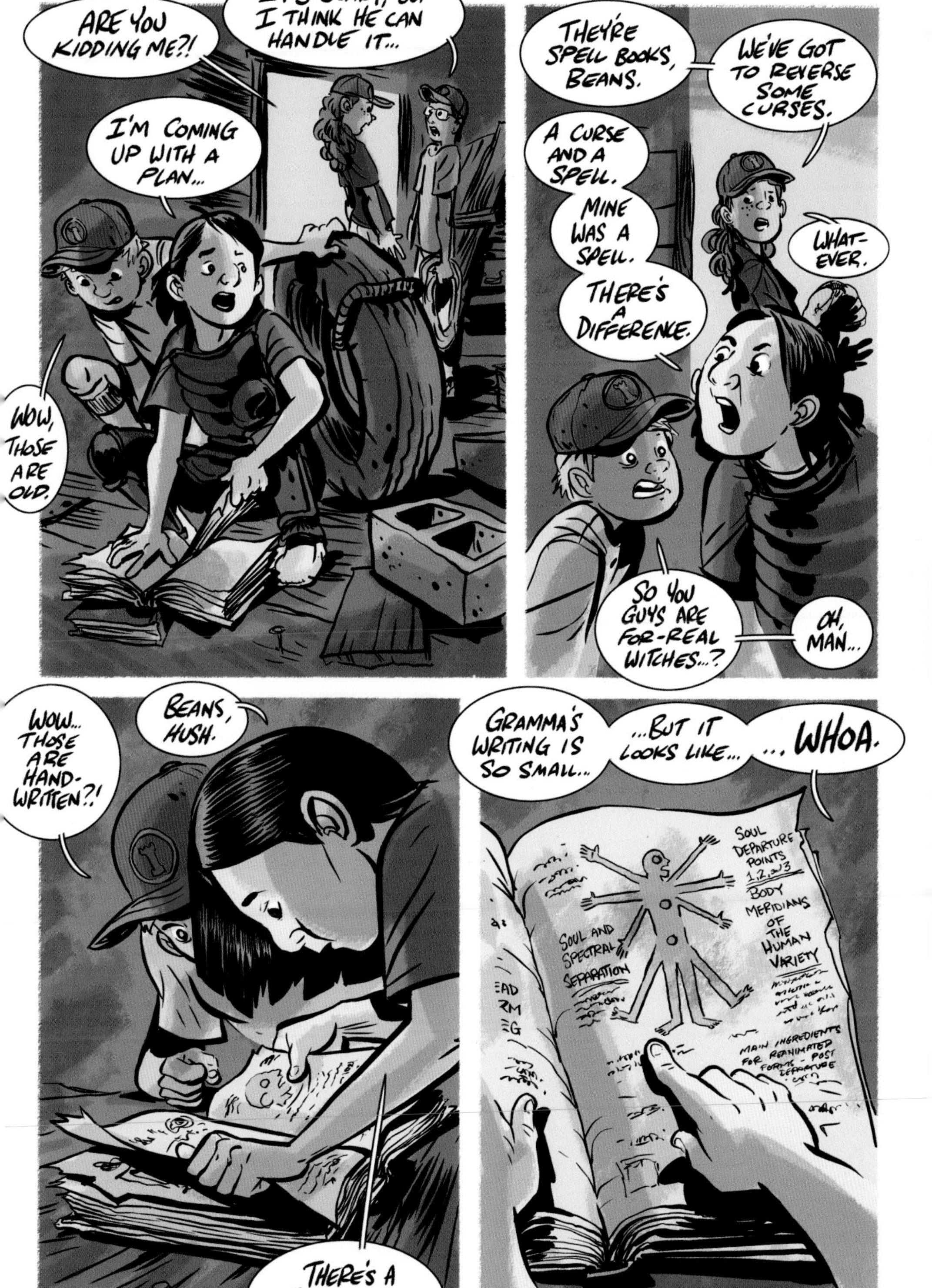
ARE YOU KIDDING ME?!
IT'S SCARY, BUT I THINK HE CAN HANDLE IT...
I'M COMING UP WITH A PLAN...
WOW, THOSE ARE OLD.
THEY'RE SPELL BOOKS, BEANS.
WE'VE GOT TO REVERSE SOME CURSES.
A CURSE AND A SPELL.
MINE WAS A SPELL.
THERE'S A DIFFERENCE.
WHAT-EVER.
SO YOU GUYS ARE FOR-REAL WITCHES...?
OH, MAN...
WOW... THOSE ARE HAND-WRITTEN?!
BEANS, HUSH.
THERE'S A SPECIFIC PAGE ON THE UNDEAD!
GRAMMA'S WRITING IS SO SMALL...
...BUT IT LOOKS LIKE...
...WHOA.
SOUL DEPARTURE POINTS 1, 2, & 3
BODY MERIDIANS OF THE HUMAN VARIETY
SOUL AND SPECTRAL SEPARATION
MAIN INGREDIENTS FOR REANIMATED FORMS - POST DEPARTURE

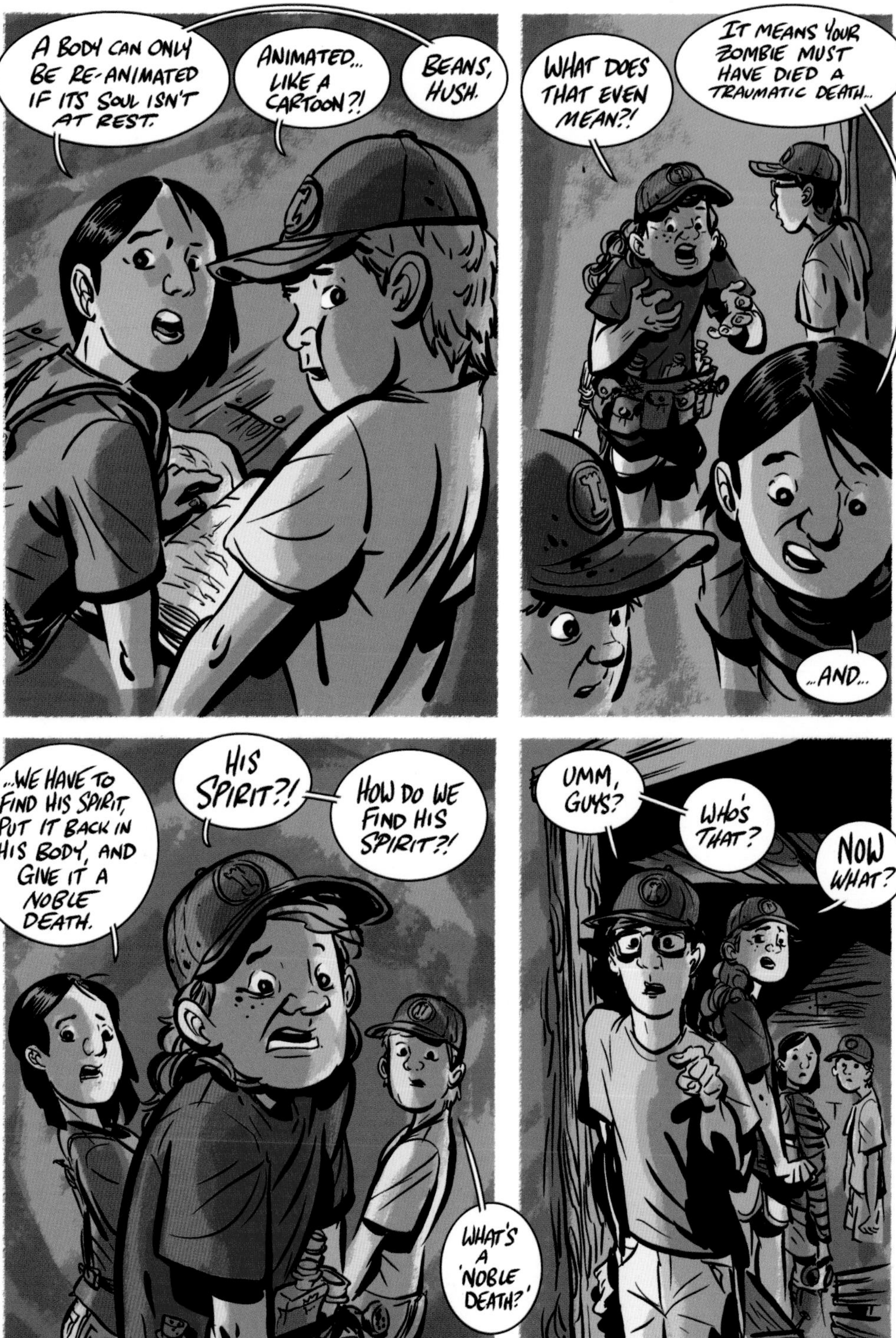
A BODY CAN ONLY BE RE-ANIMATED IF ITS SOUL ISN'T AT REST.
ANIMATED... LIKE A CARTOON?!
BEANS, HUSH.
WHAT DOES THAT EVEN MEAN?!
IT MEANS YOUR ZOMBIE MUST HAVE DIED A TRAUMATIC DEATH...
...AND...
...WE HAVE TO FIND HIS SPIRIT, PUT IT BACK IN HIS BODY, AND GIVE IT A NOBLE DEATH.
HIS SPIRIT?!
HOW DO WE FIND HIS SPIRIT?!
WHAT'S A 'NOBLE DEATH?'
UMM, GUYS?
WHO'S THAT?
NOW WHAT?

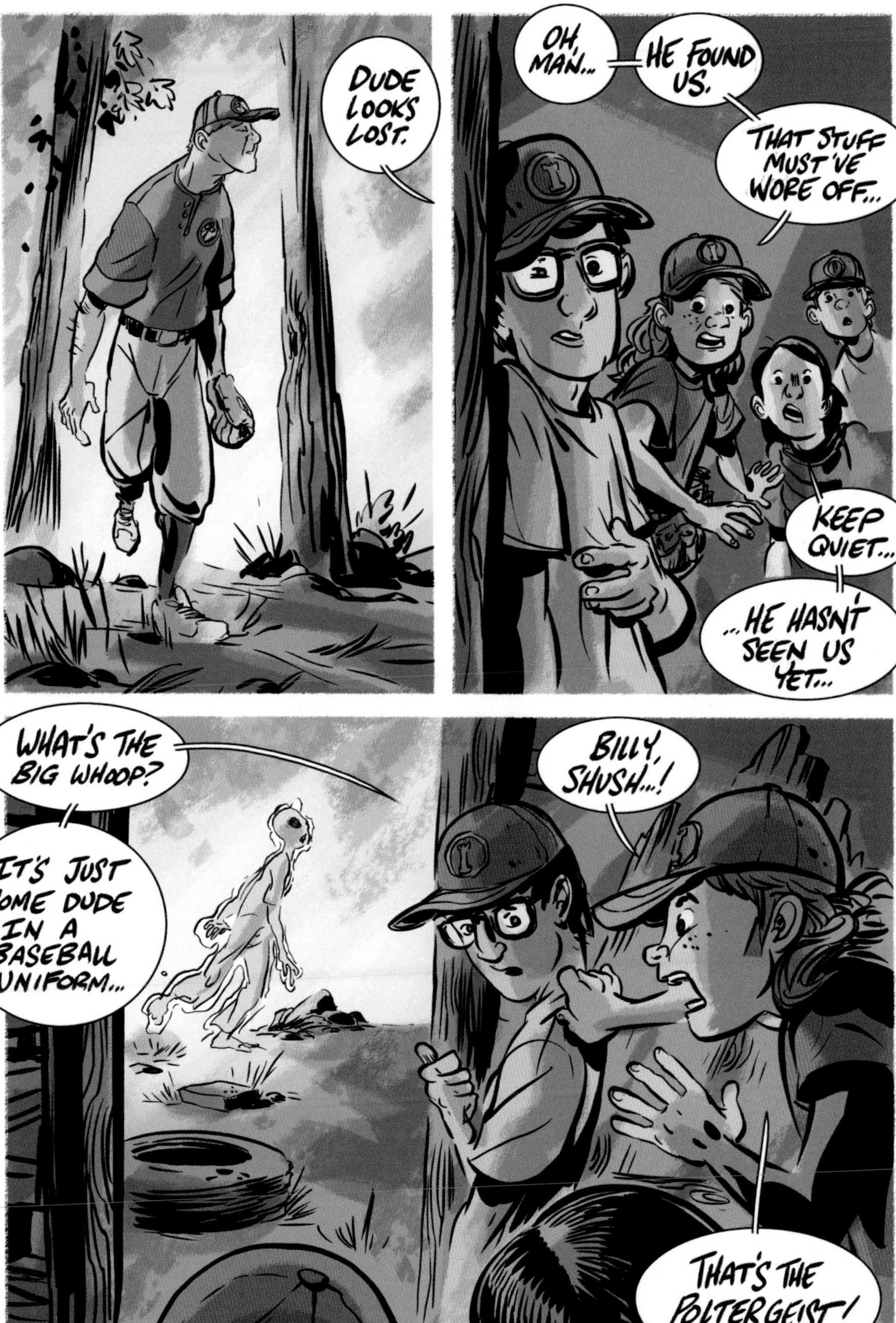

DUDE LOOKS LOST.
OH, MAN...
HE FOUND US.
THAT STUFF MUST'VE WORE OFF...
KEEP QUIET...
...HE HASN'T SEEN US YET...
WHAT'S THE BIG WHOOP?
IT'S JUST SOME DUDE IN A BASEBALL UNIFORM...
BILLY, SHUSH...!
THAT'S THE POLTERGEIST!

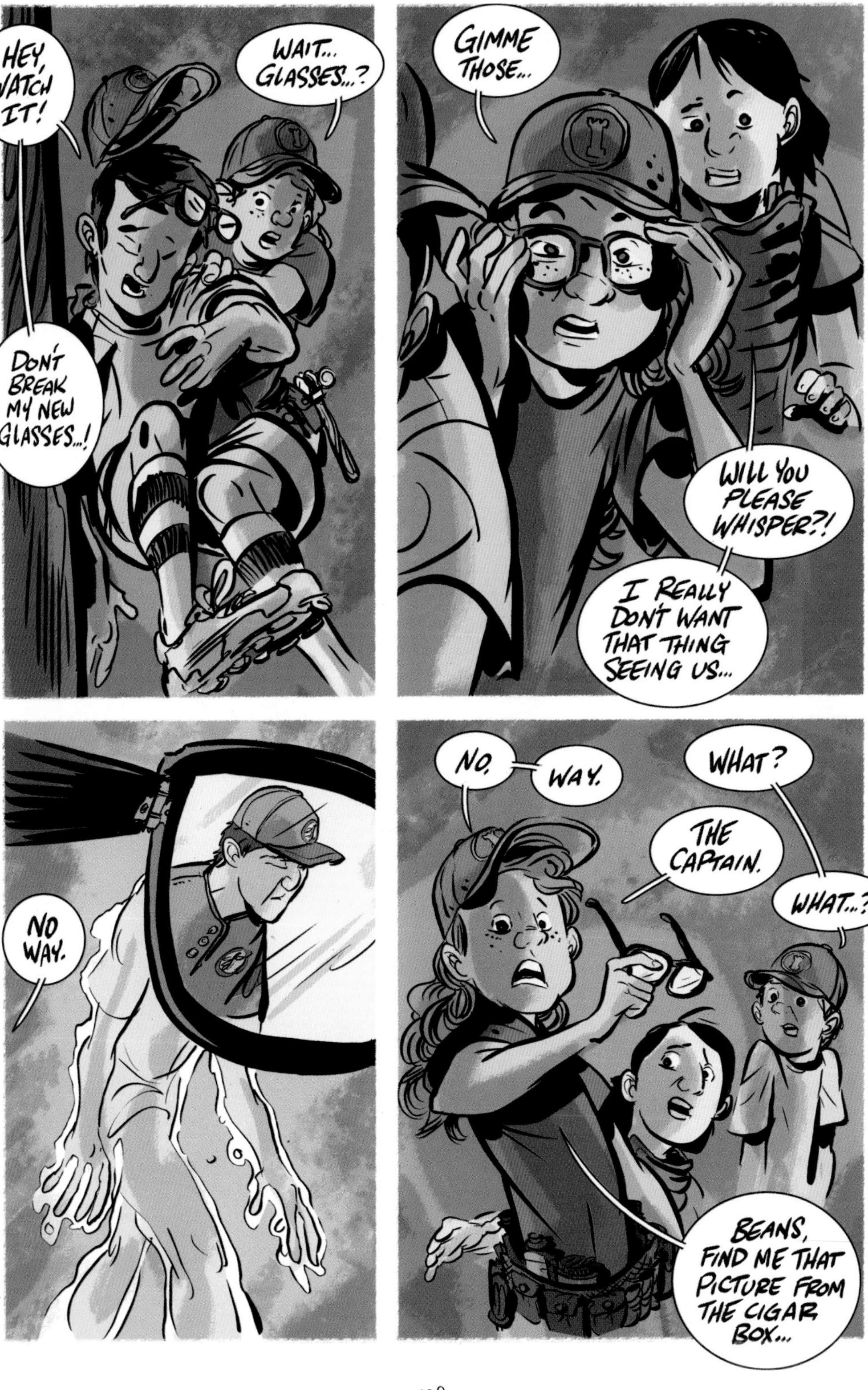
HEY, WATCH IT!
WAIT... GLASSES...?
DON'T BREAK MY NEW GLASSES...!
GIMME THOSE...
WILL YOU PLEASE WHISPER?!
I REALLY DON'T WANT THAT THING SEEING US...
NO WAY.
NO.
WAY.
WHAT?
THE CAPTAIN.
WHAT...?
BEANS, FIND ME THAT PICTURE FROM THE CIGAR BOX...

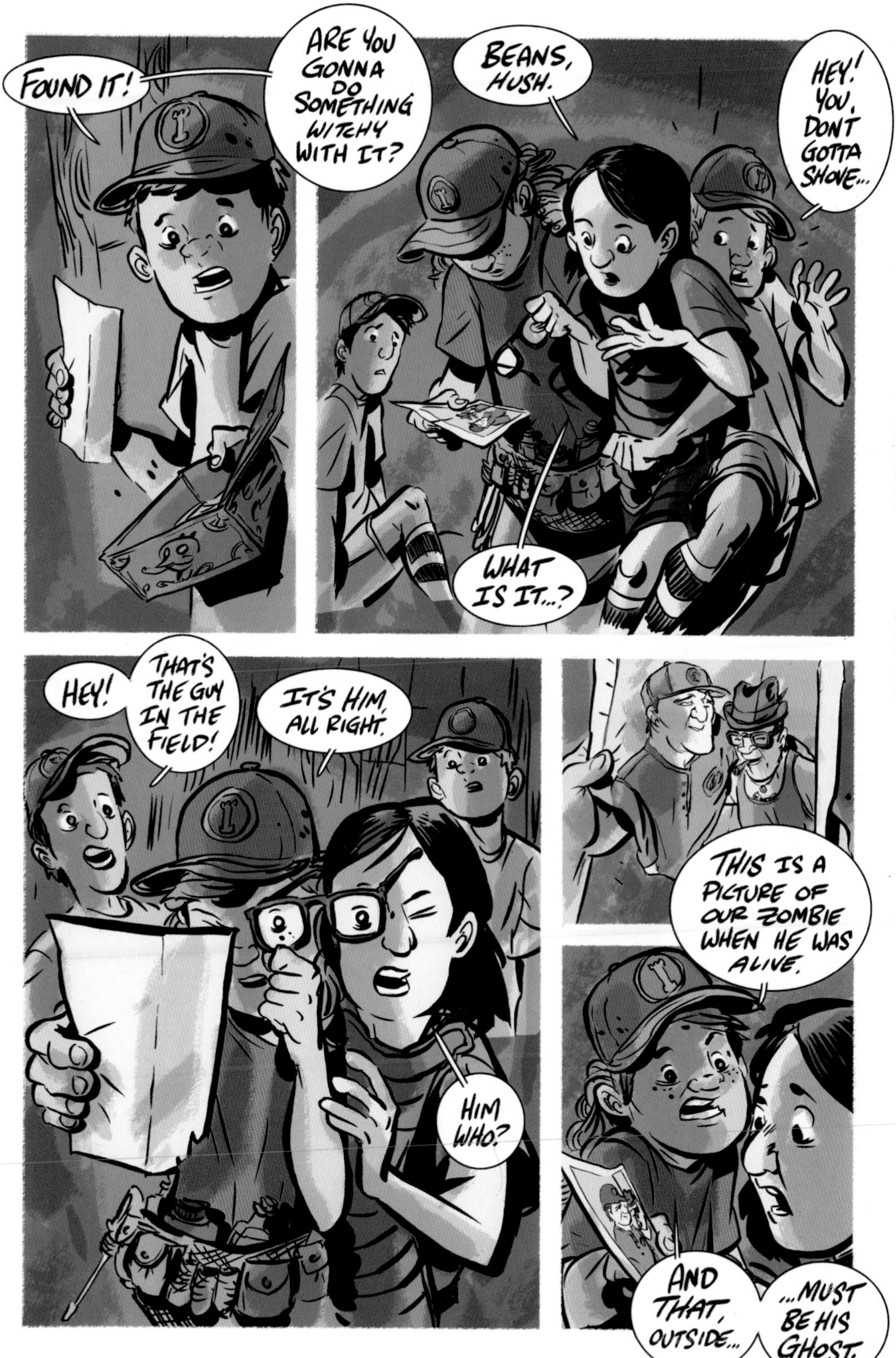
FOUND IT!
ARE YOU GONNA DO SOMETHING WITCHY WITH IT?
BEANS, HUSH.
HEY! YOU, DON'T GOTTA SHOVE...
WHAT IS IT...?
HEY!
THAT'S THE GUY IN THE FIELD!
IT'S HIM, ALL RIGHT.
HIM WHO?
THIS IS A PICTURE OF OUR ZOMBIE WHEN HE WAS ALIVE.
AND THAT, OUTSIDE...
...MUST BE HIS GHOST.

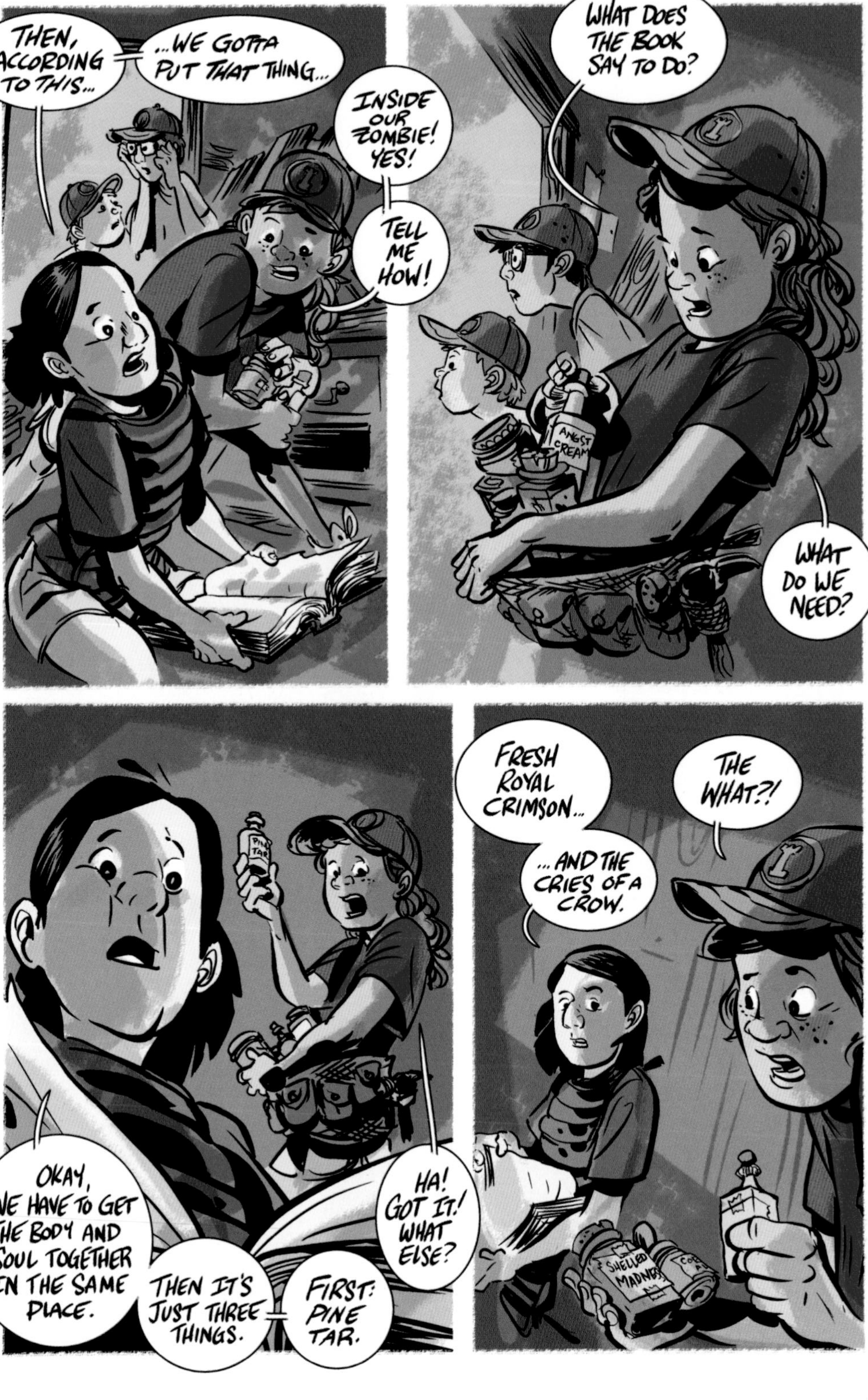
THEN, ACCORDING TO THIS...
...WE GOTTA PUT THAT THING...
INSIDE OUR ZOMBIE! YES!
TELL ME HOW!
WHAT DOES THE BOOK SAY TO DO?
ANGST CREAM
WHAT DO WE NEED?
OKAY, WE HAVE TO GET THE BODY AND SOUL TOGETHER IN THE SAME PLACE.
THEN IT'S JUST THREE THINGS.
FIRST: PINE TAR.
HA! GOT IT! WHAT ELSE?
FRESH ROYAL CRIMSON...
...AND THE CRIES OF A CROW.
THE WHAT?!

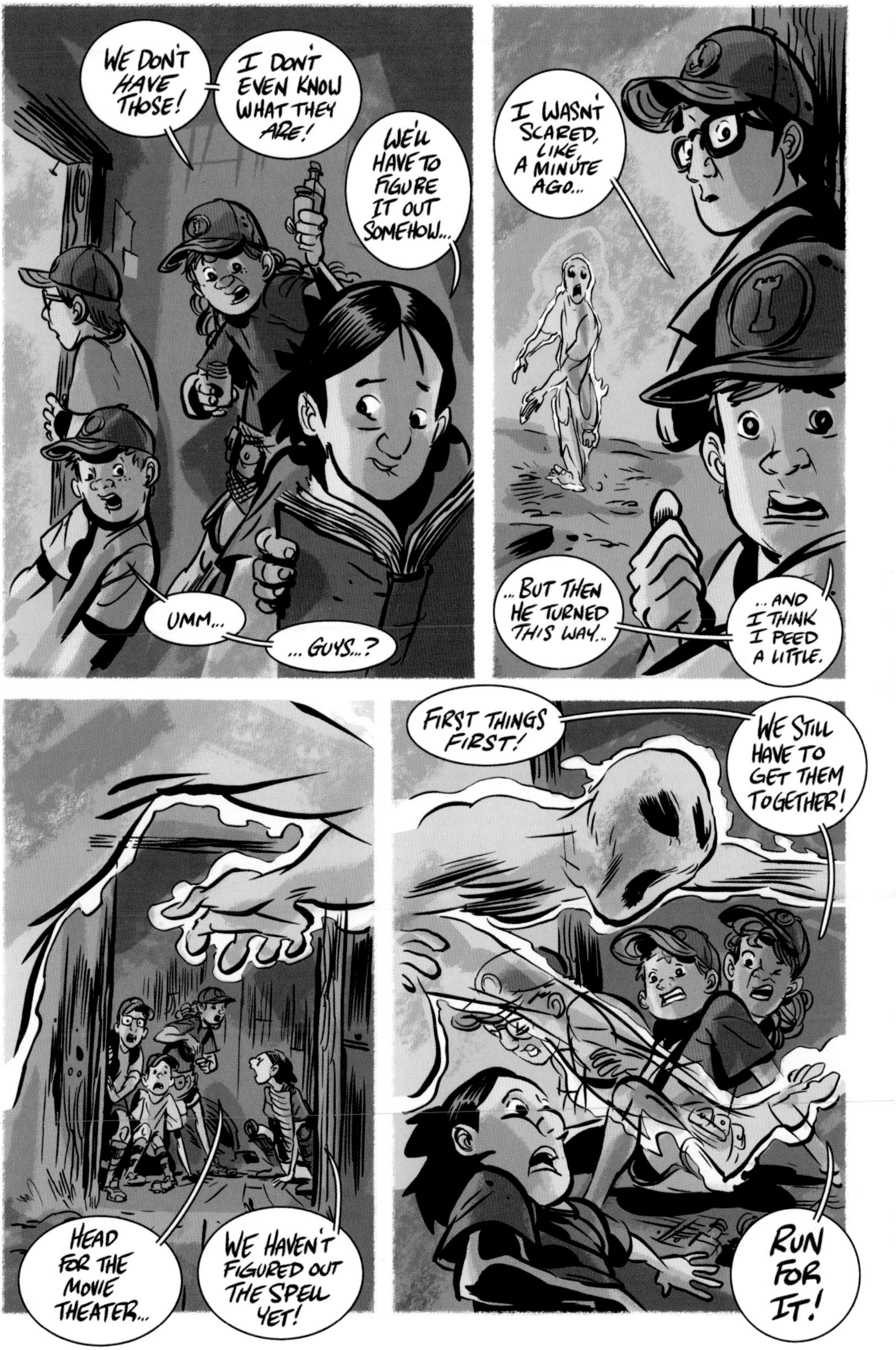
WE DON'T HAVE THOSE!
I DON'T EVEN KNOW WHAT THEY ARE!
WE'LL HAVE TO FIGURE IT OUT SOMEHOW...
UMM...
...GUYS...?
I WASN'T SCARED, LIKE, A MINUTE AGO...
...BUT THEN HE TURNED THIS WAY...
...AND I THINK I PEED A LITTLE.
HEAD FOR THE MOVIE THEATER...
WE HAVEN'T FIGURED OUT THE SPELL YET!
FIRST THINGS FIRST!
WE STILL HAVE TO GET THEM TOGETHER!
RUN FOR IT!

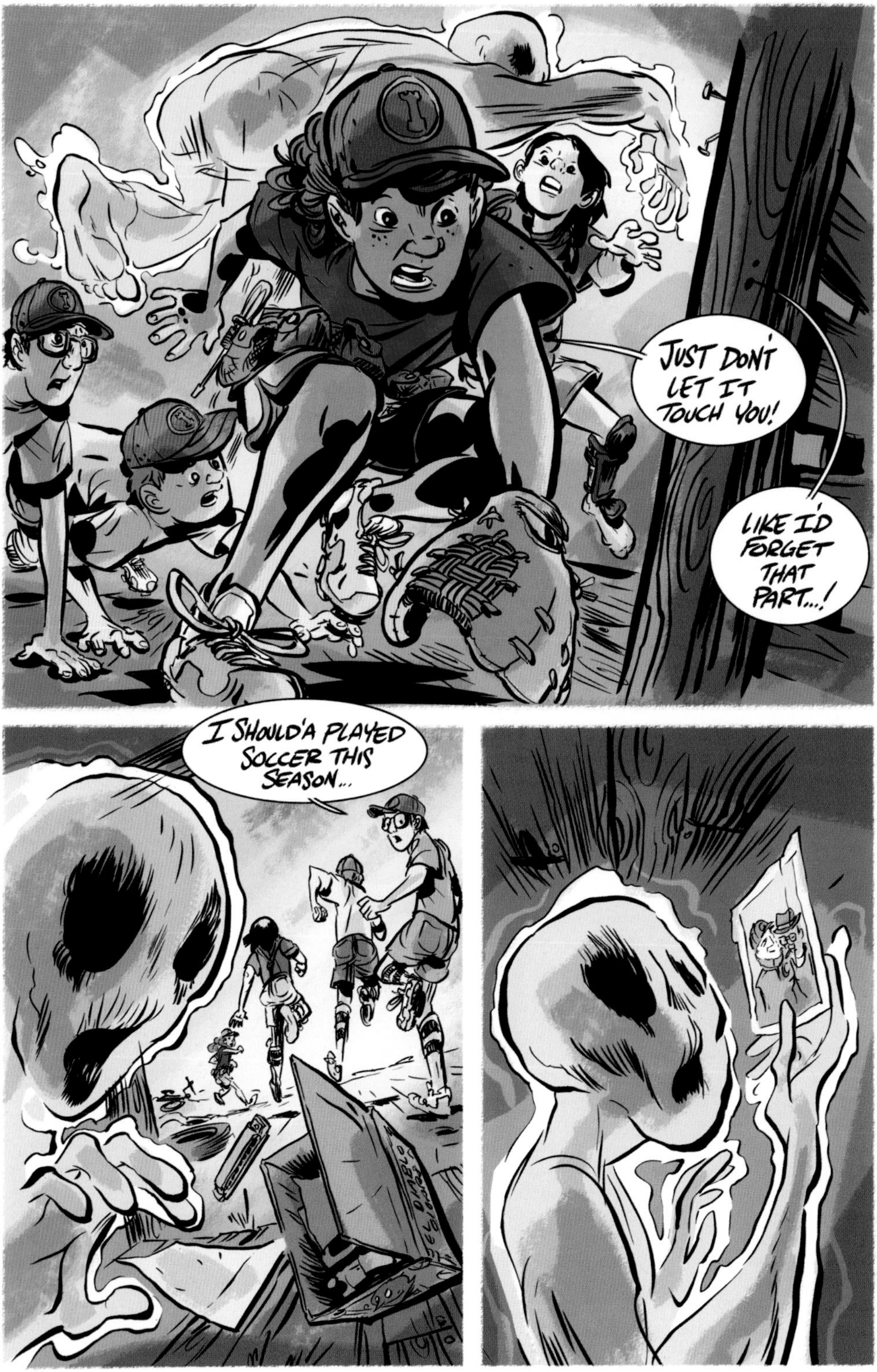
JUST DON'T LET IT TOUCH YOU!
LIKE I'D FORGET THAT PART...!
I SHOULD'A PLAYED SOCCER THIS SEASON...

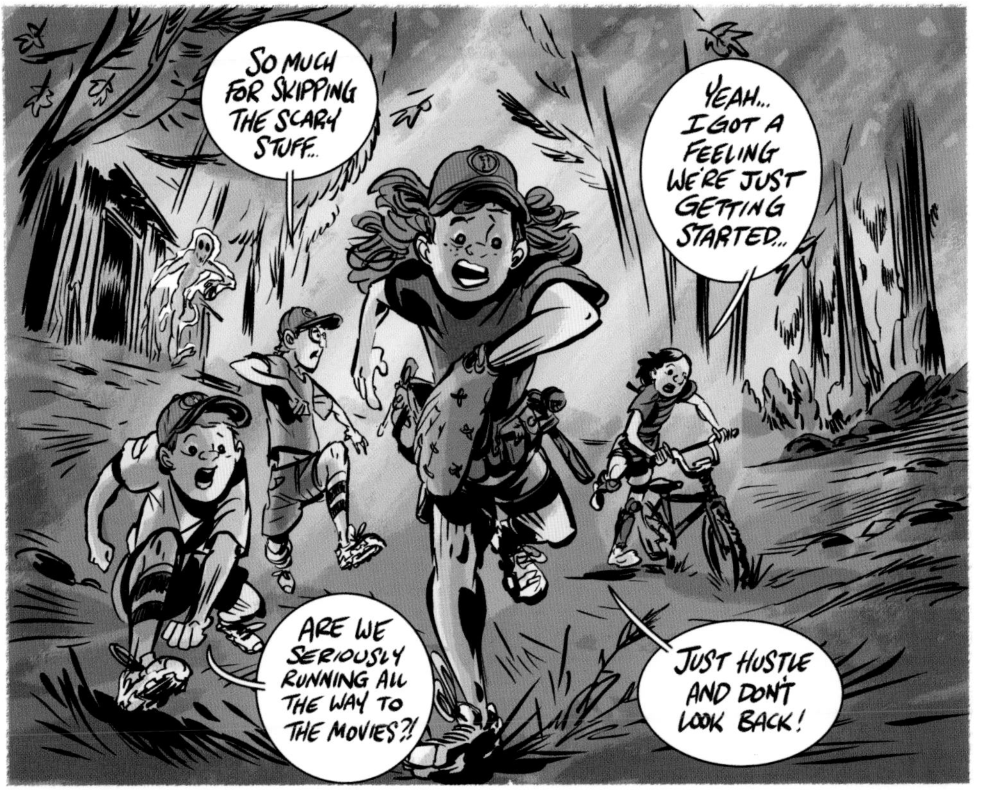
SO MUCH FOR SKIPPING THE SCARY STUFF...
YEAH... I GOT A FEELING WE'RE JUST GETTING STARTED...
ARE WE SERIOUSLY RUNNING ALL THE WAY TO THE MOVIES?!
JUST HUSTLE AND DON'T LOOK BACK!

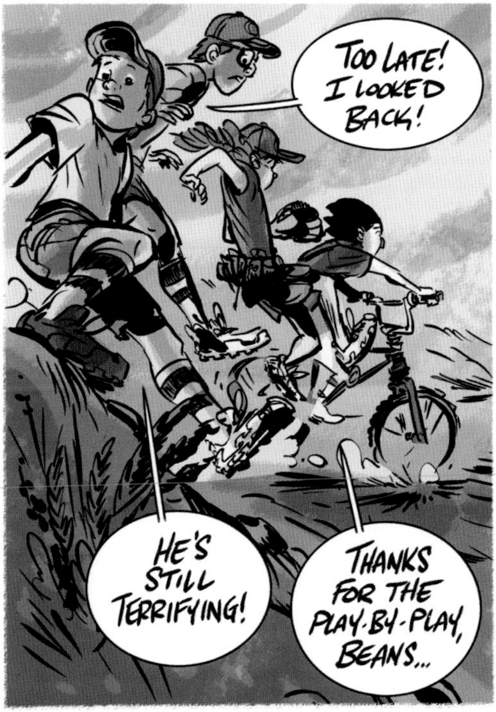
TOO LATE! I LOOKED BACK!
HE'S STILL TERRIFYING!
THANKS FOR THE PLAY-BY-PLAY, BEANS...

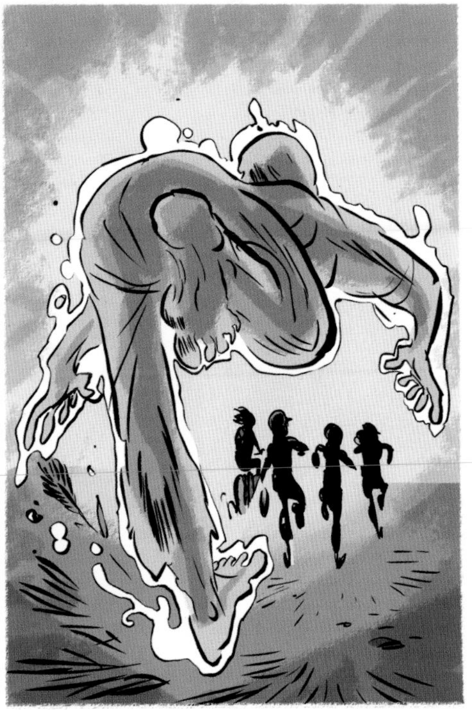

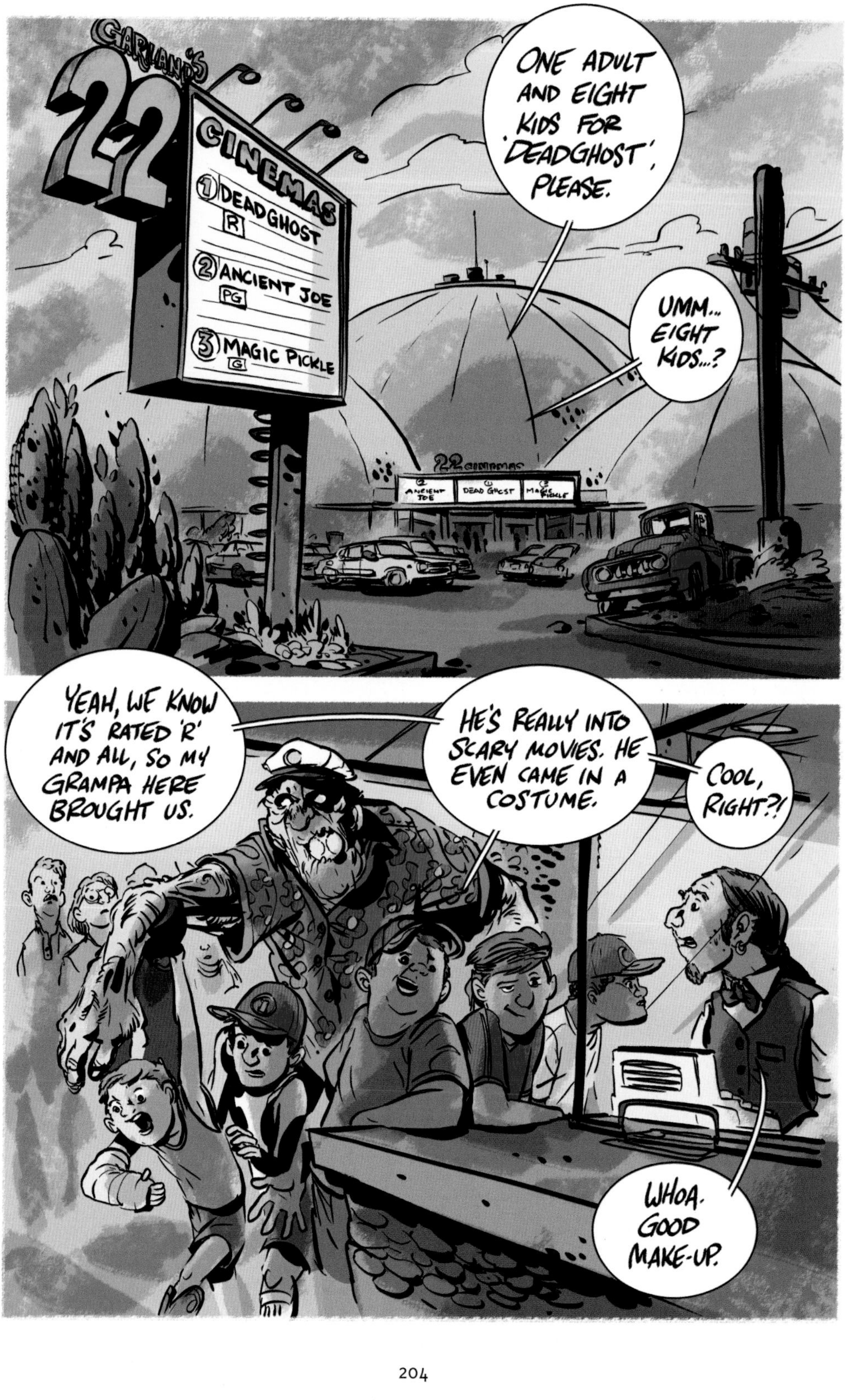
GARLAND'S 22 CINEMAS
1 DEADGHOST R
2 ANCIENT JOE PG
3 MAGIC PICKLE G
ONE ADULT AND EIGHT KIDS FOR 'DEADGHOST', PLEASE.
UMM... EIGHT KIDS...?
22 CINEMAS
YEAH, WE KNOW IT'S RATED 'R' AND ALL, SO MY GRAMPA HERE BROUGHT US.
HE'S REALLY INTO SCARY MOVIES. HE EVEN CAME IN A COSTUME.
COOL, RIGHT?!
WHOA. GOOD MAKE-UP.

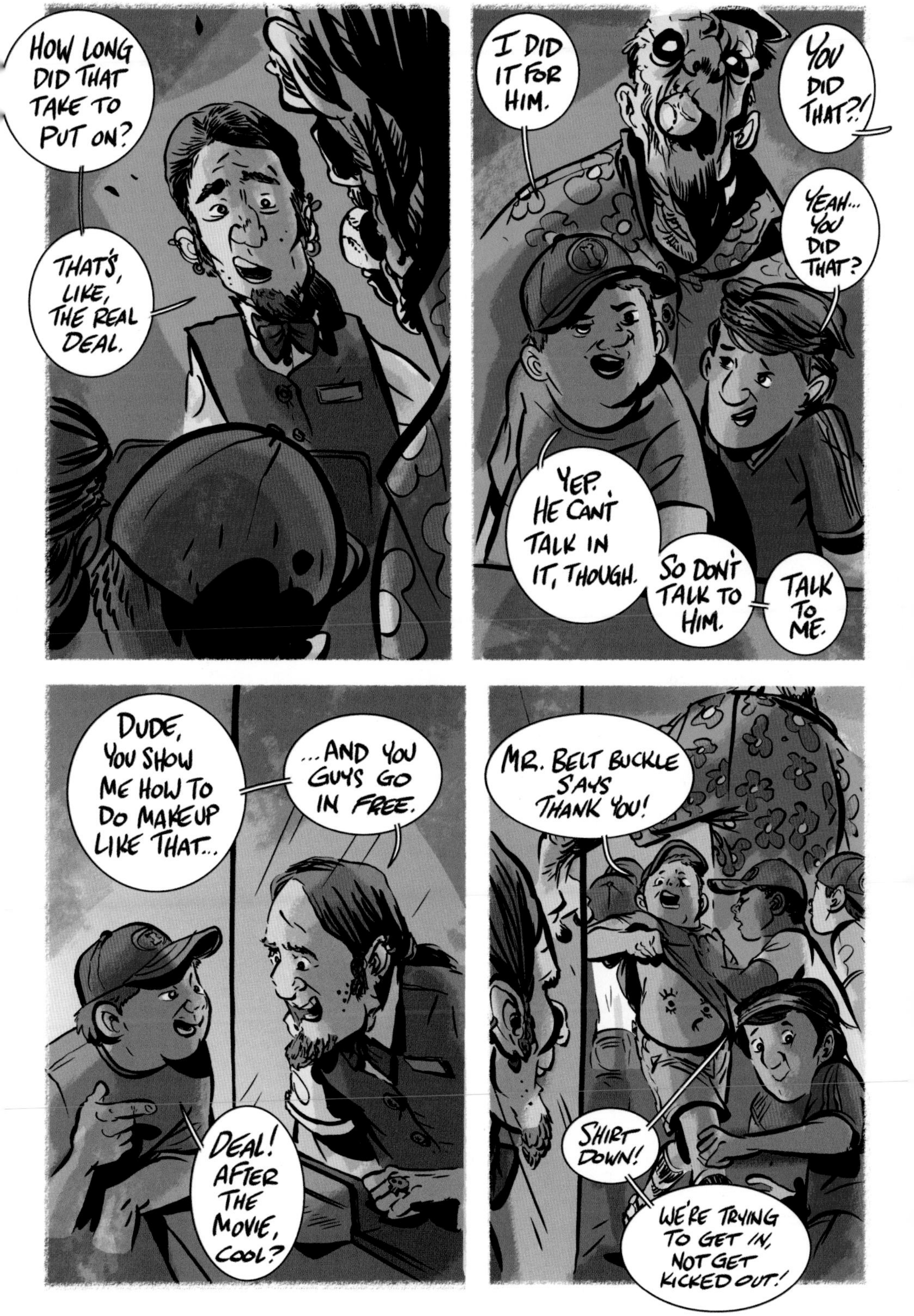
HOW LONG DID THAT TAKE TO PUT ON?
THAT'S, LIKE, THE REAL DEAL.
I DID IT FOR HIM.
YOU DID THAT?!
YEAH... YOU DID THAT?
YEP. HE CAN'T TALK IN IT, THOUGH.
SO DON'T TALK TO HIM.
TALK TO ME.
DUDE, YOU SHOW ME HOW TO DO MAKEUP LIKE THAT...
...AND YOU GUYS GO IN FREE.
DEAL! AFTER THE MOVIE, COOL?
MR. BELT BUCKLE SAYS THANK YOU!
SHIRT DOWN!
WE'RE TRYING TO GET IN, NOT GET KICKED OUT!

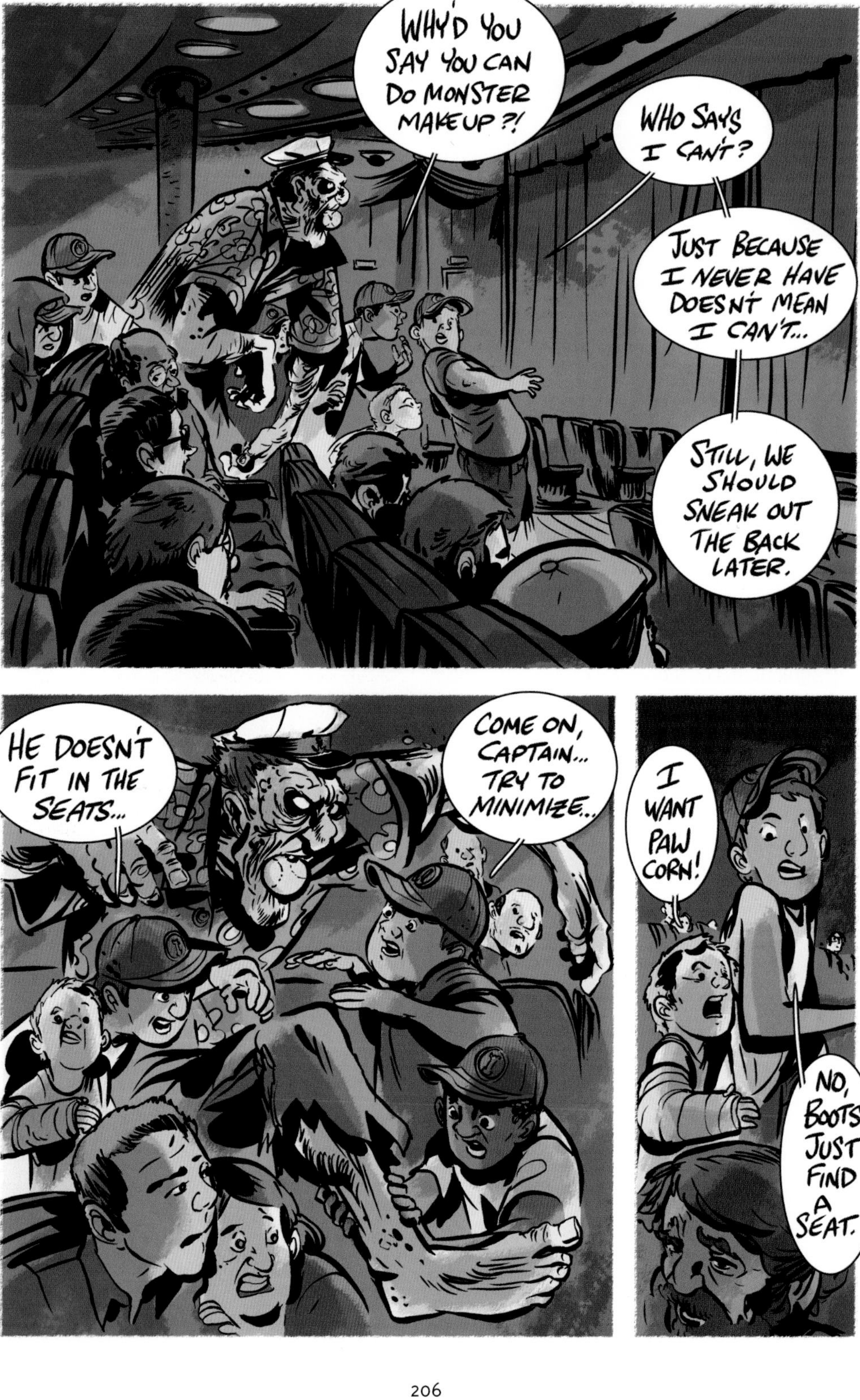
WHY'D YOU SAY YOU CAN DO MONSTER MAKEUP?!
WHO SAYS I CAN'T?
JUST BECAUSE I NEVER HAVE DOESN'T MEAN I CAN'T...
STILL, WE SHOULD SNEAK OUT THE BACK LATER.
HE DOESN'T FIT IN THE SEATS...
COME ON, CAPTAIN... TRY TO MINIMIZE...
I WANT PAW CORN!
NO, BOOTS. JUST FIND A SEAT.

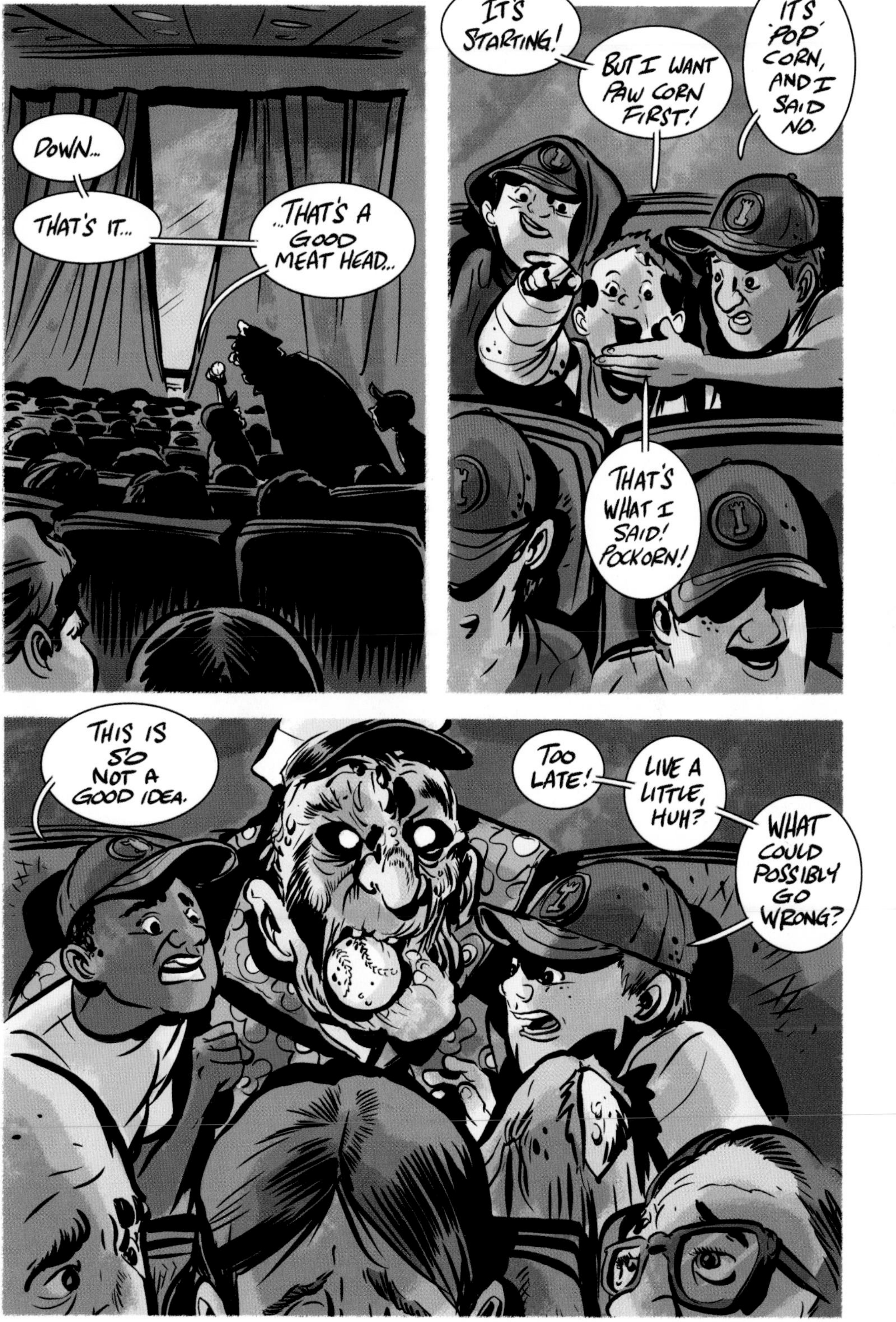
DOWN...
THAT'S IT...
...THAT'S A GOOD MEAT HEAD...
IT'S STARTING!
BUT I WANT PAW CORN FIRST!
IT'S 'POP' CORN, AND I SAID NO.
THAT'S WHAT I SAID! POCKORN!
THIS IS SO NOT A GOOD IDEA.
TOO LATE!
LIVE A LITTLE, HUH?
WHAT COULD POSSIBLY GO WRONG?

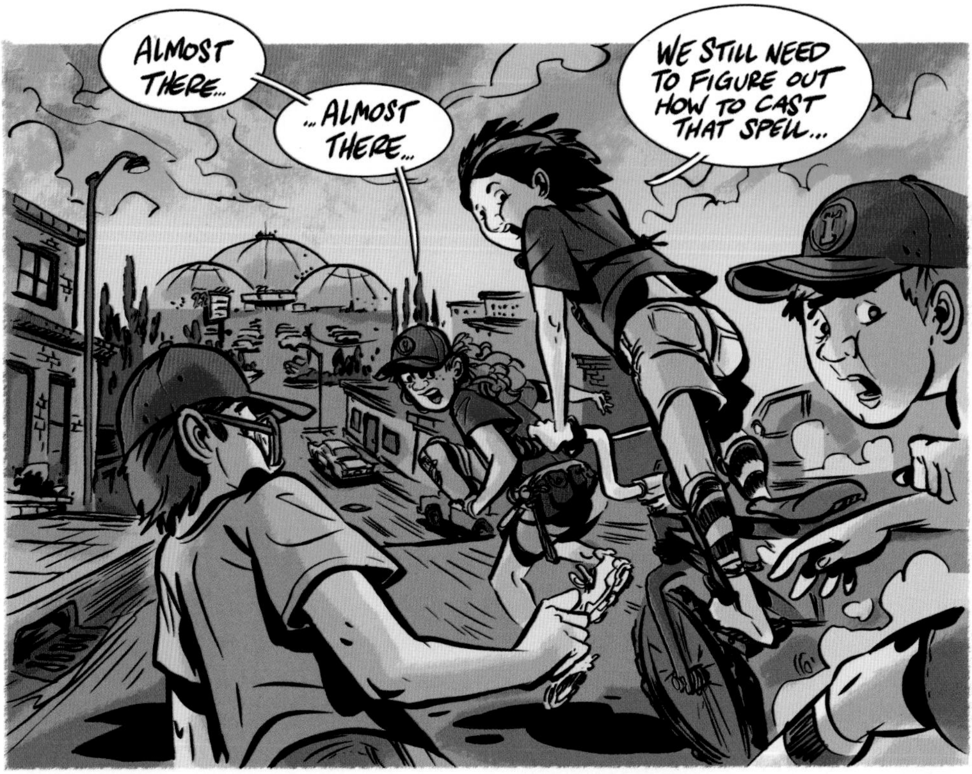
ALMOST THERE...
...ALMOST THERE...
WE STILL NEED TO FIGURE OUT HOW TO CAST THAT SPELL...

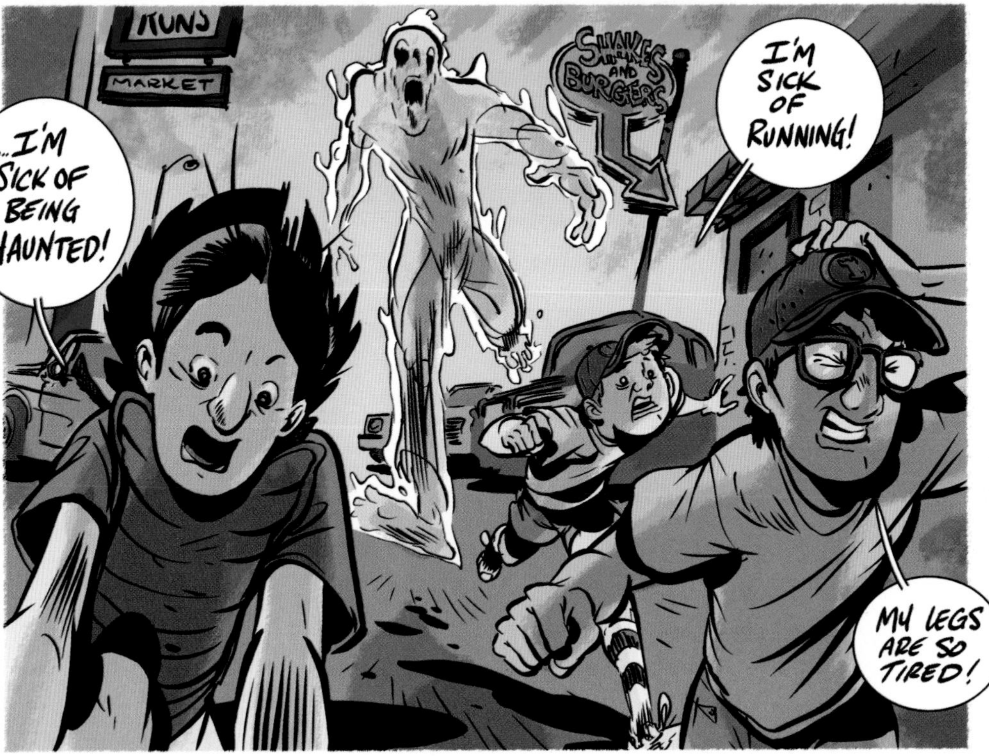
MARKET
...I'M SICK OF BEING HAUNTED!
I'M SICK OF RUNNING!
MY LEGS ARE SO TIRED!

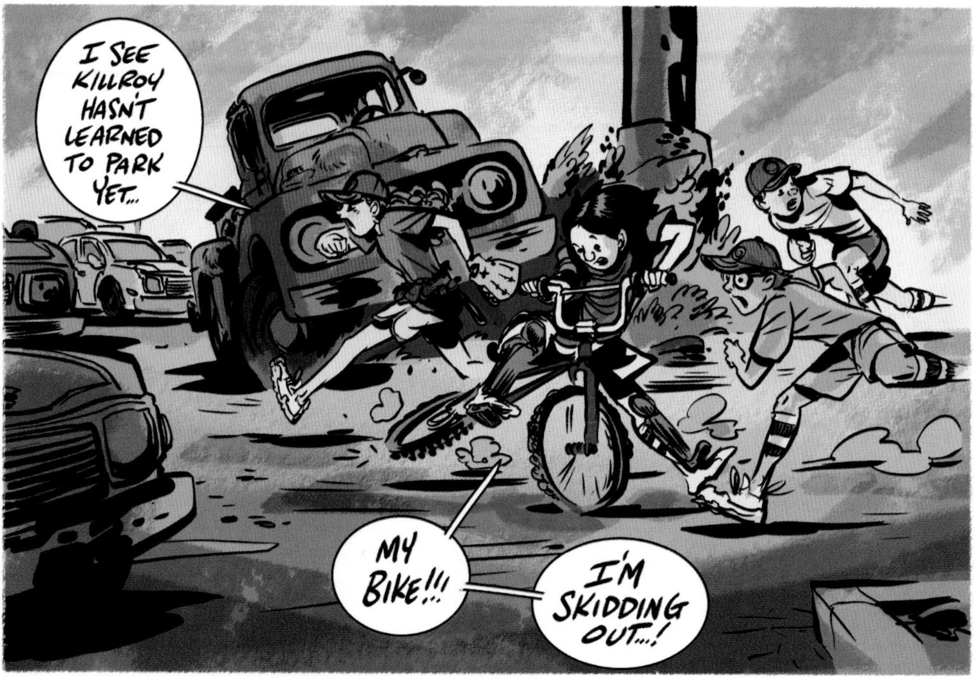
I SEE KILLROY HASN'T LEARNED TO PARK YET...
MY BIKE!!!
I'M SKIDDING OUT...!

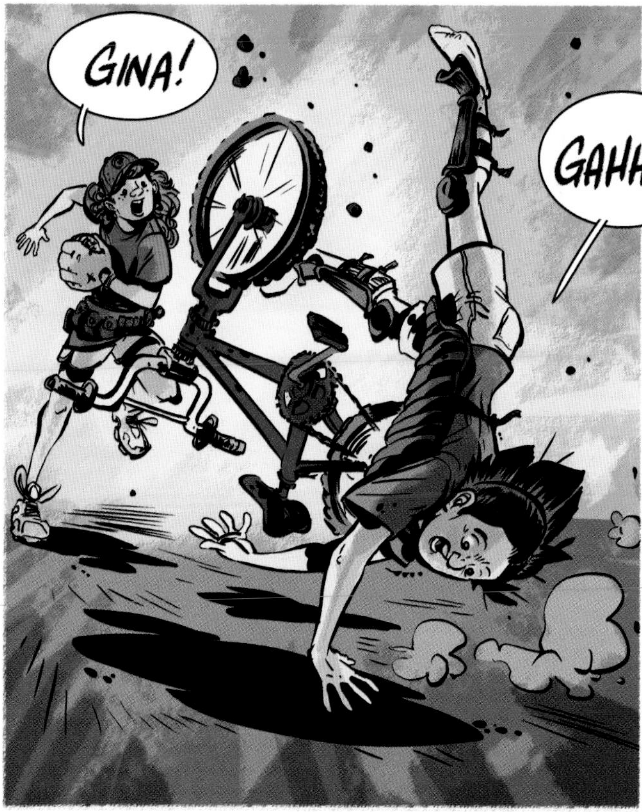
GINA!
GAHH!!!

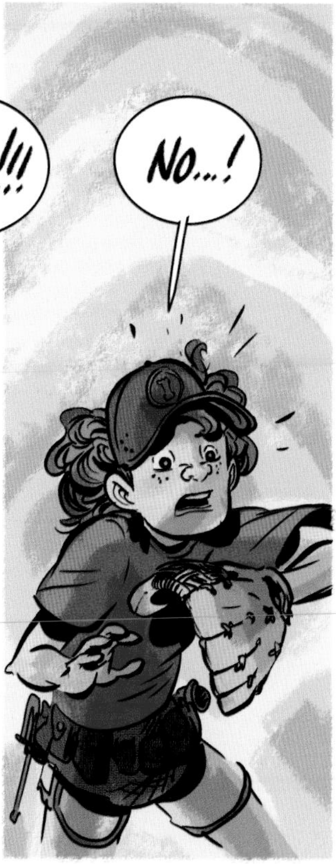
NO...!

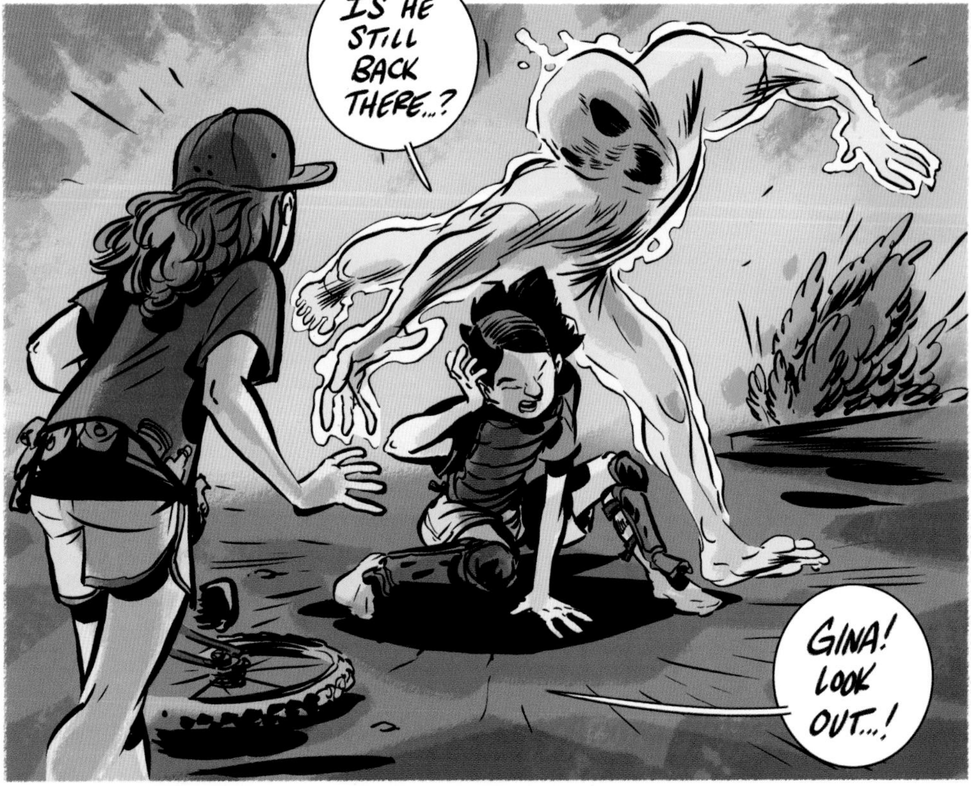
IS HE STILL BACK THERE...?
GINA! LOOK OUT...!

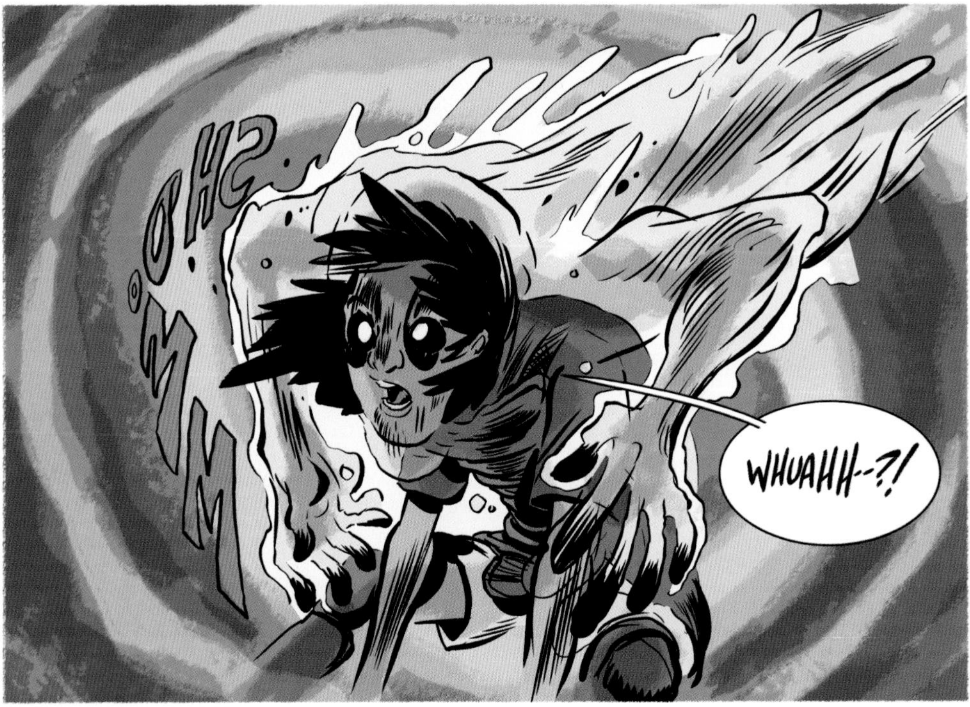
SHOOMM
WHUAHH--?!

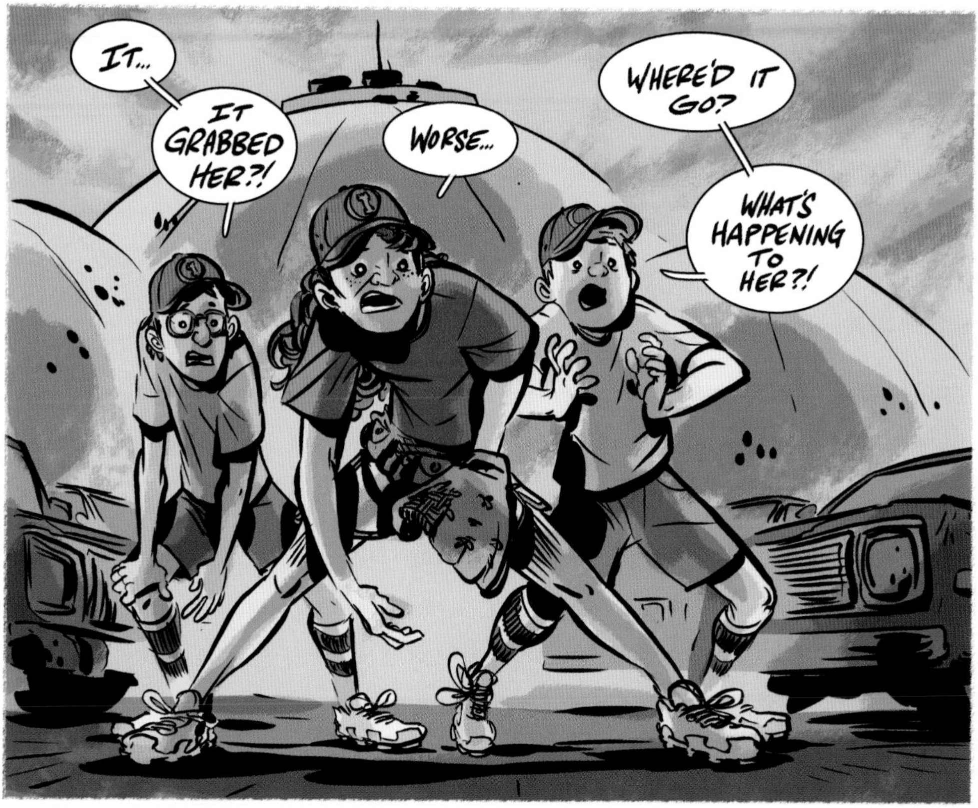
IT...
IT GRABBED HER?!
WORSE...
WHERE'D IT GO?
WHAT'S HAPPENING TO HER?!

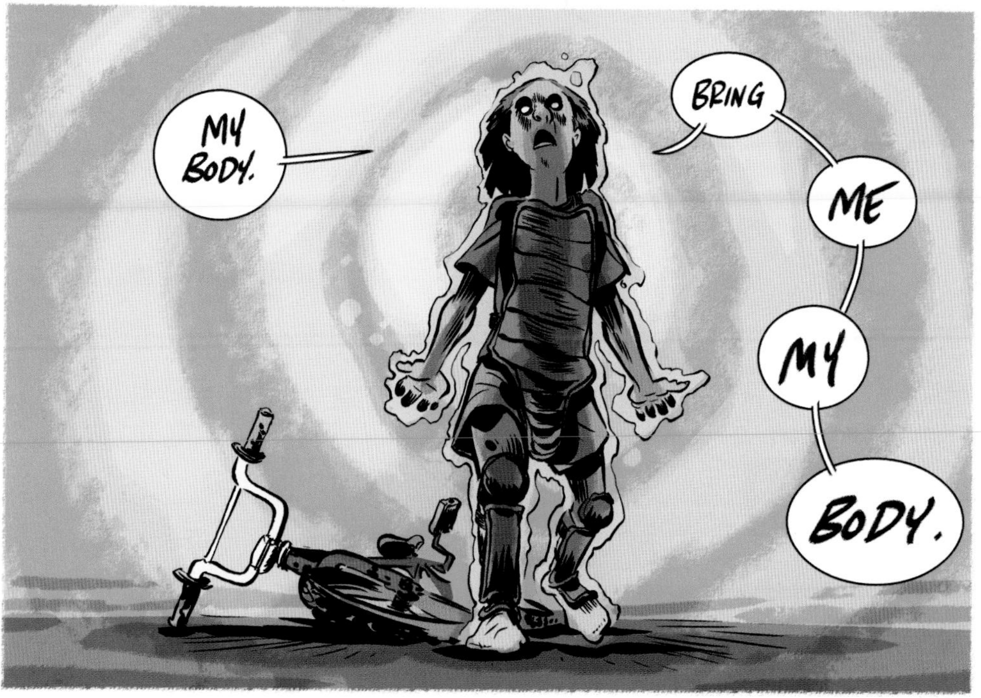
MY BODY.
BRING
ME
MY
BODY.

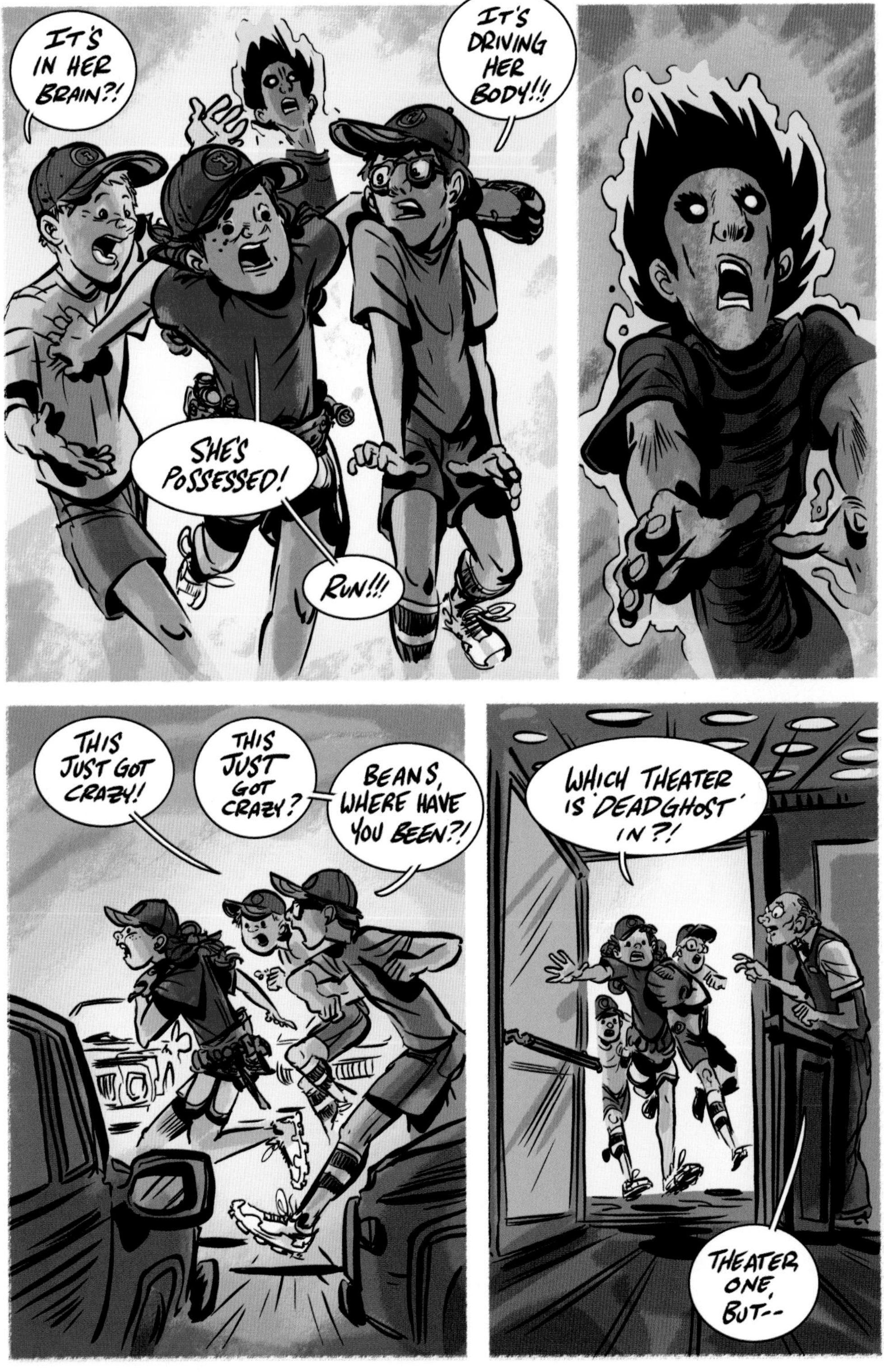
IT'S IN HER BRAIN?!
IT'S DRIVING HER BODY!!!
SHE'S POSSESSED!
RUN!!!
THIS JUST GOT CRAZY!
THIS JUST GOT CRAZY?
BEANS, WHERE HAVE YOU BEEN?!
WHICH THEATER IS 'DEADGHOST' IN?!
THEATER ONE, BUT--

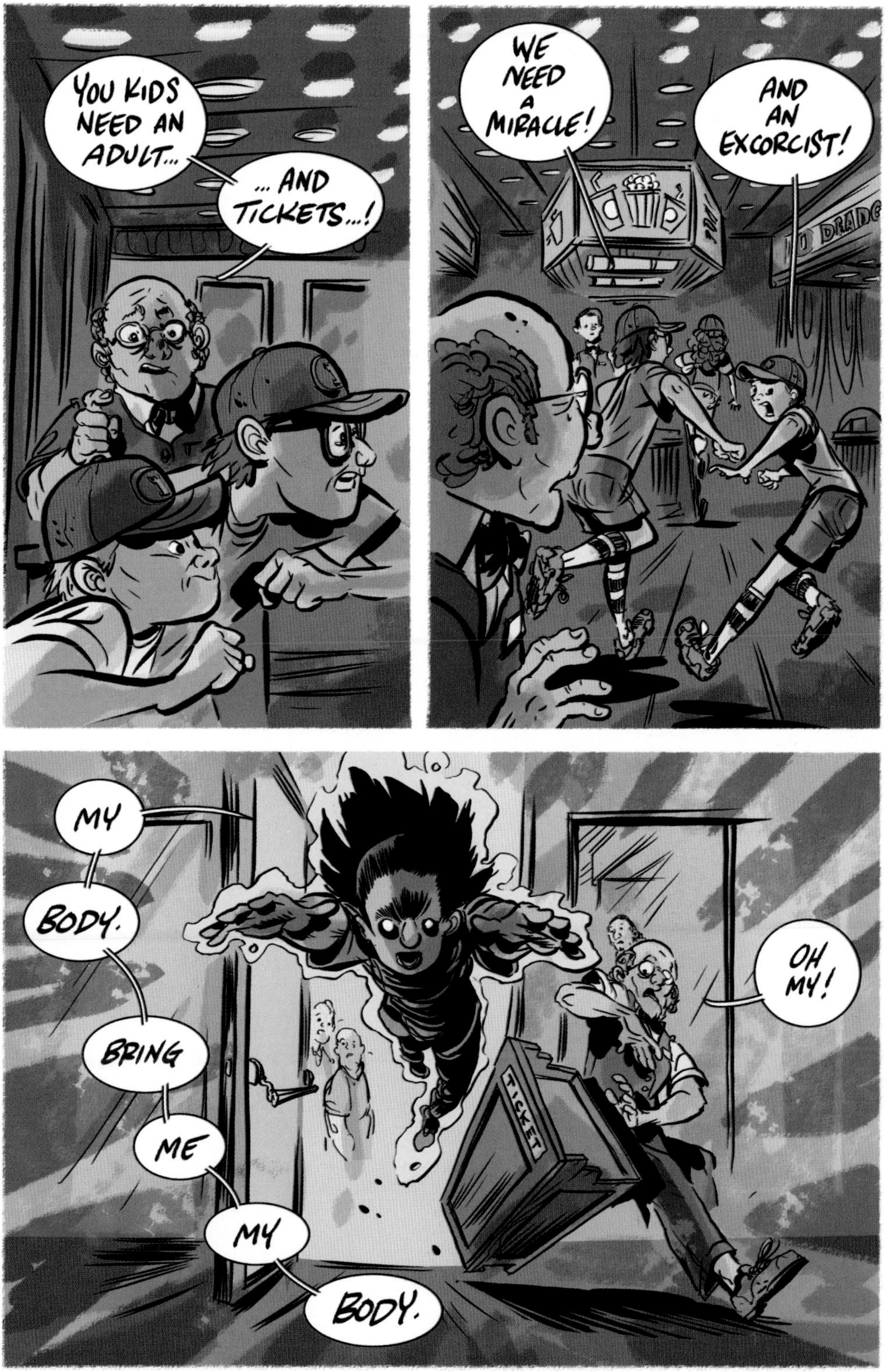
YOU KIDS NEED AN ADULT...
...AND TICKETS...!
WE NEED A MIRACLE!
AND AN EXCORCIST!
MY
BODY.
BRING
ME
MY
BODY.
OH MY!
TICKET

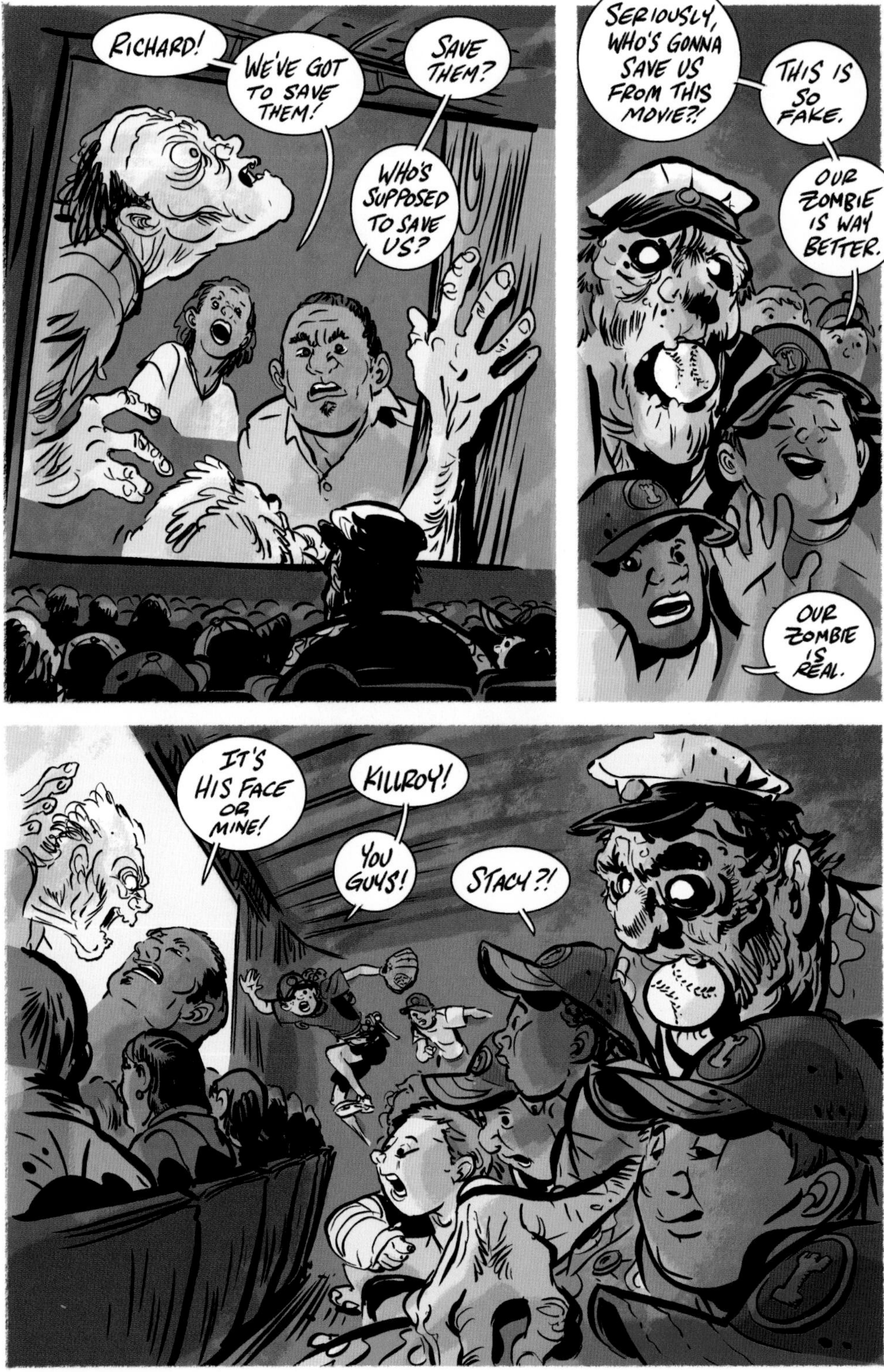
RICHARD!
WE'VE GOT TO SAVE THEM!
SAVE THEM?
WHO'S SUPPOSED TO SAVE US?
SERIOUSLY, WHO'S GONNA SAVE US FROM THIS MOVIE?!
THIS IS SO FAKE.
OUR ZOMBIE IS WAY BETTER.
OUR ZOMBIE IS REAL.
IT'S HIS FACE OR MINE!
KILLROY!
YOU GUYS!
STACY?!

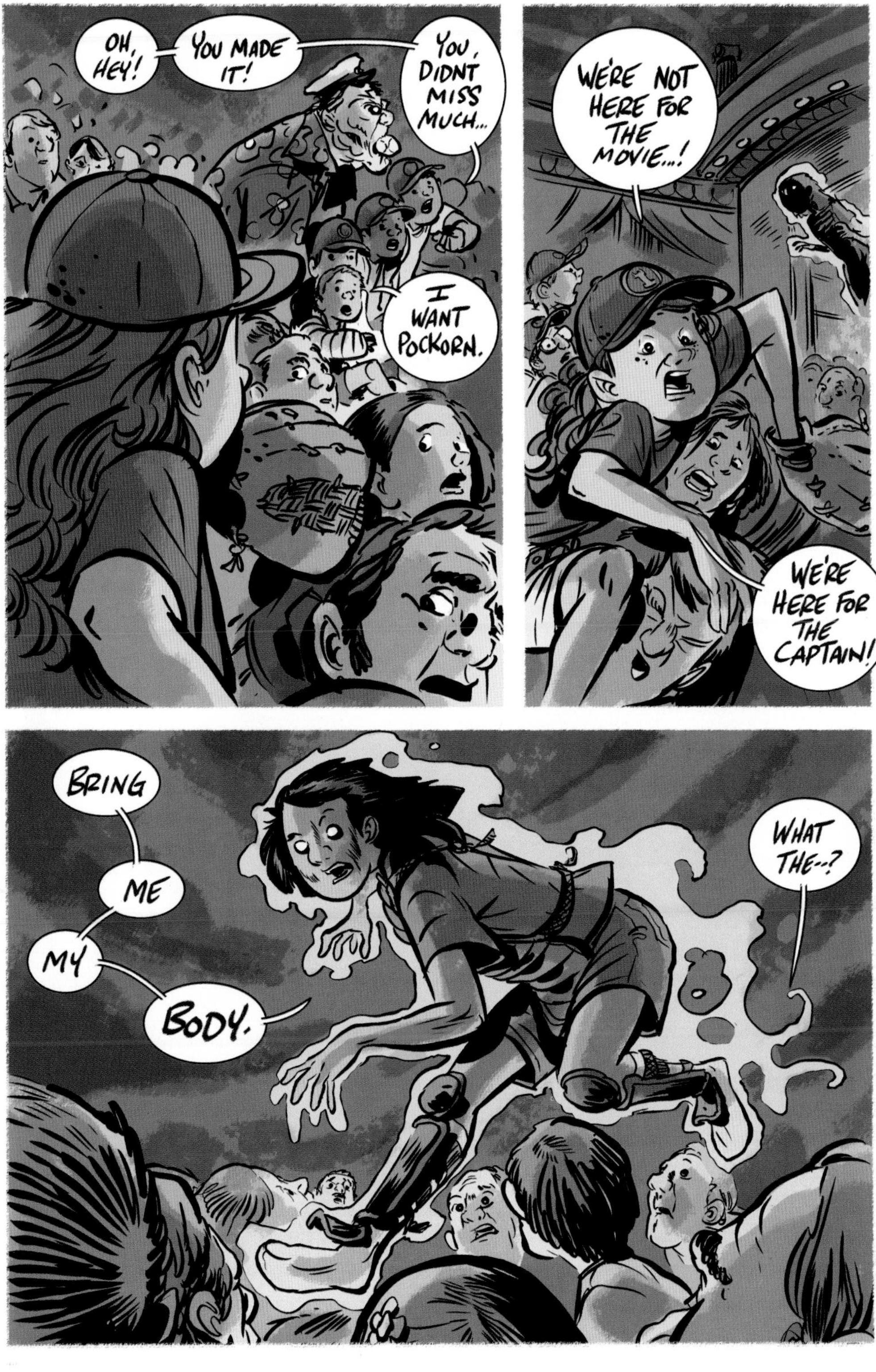
OH, HEY!
YOU MADE IT!
YOU DIDNT MISS MUCH...
I WANT POCKORN.
WE'RE NOT HERE FOR THE MOVIE...!
WE'RE HERE FOR THE CAPTAIN!
BRING
ME
MY
BODY.
WHAT THE--?

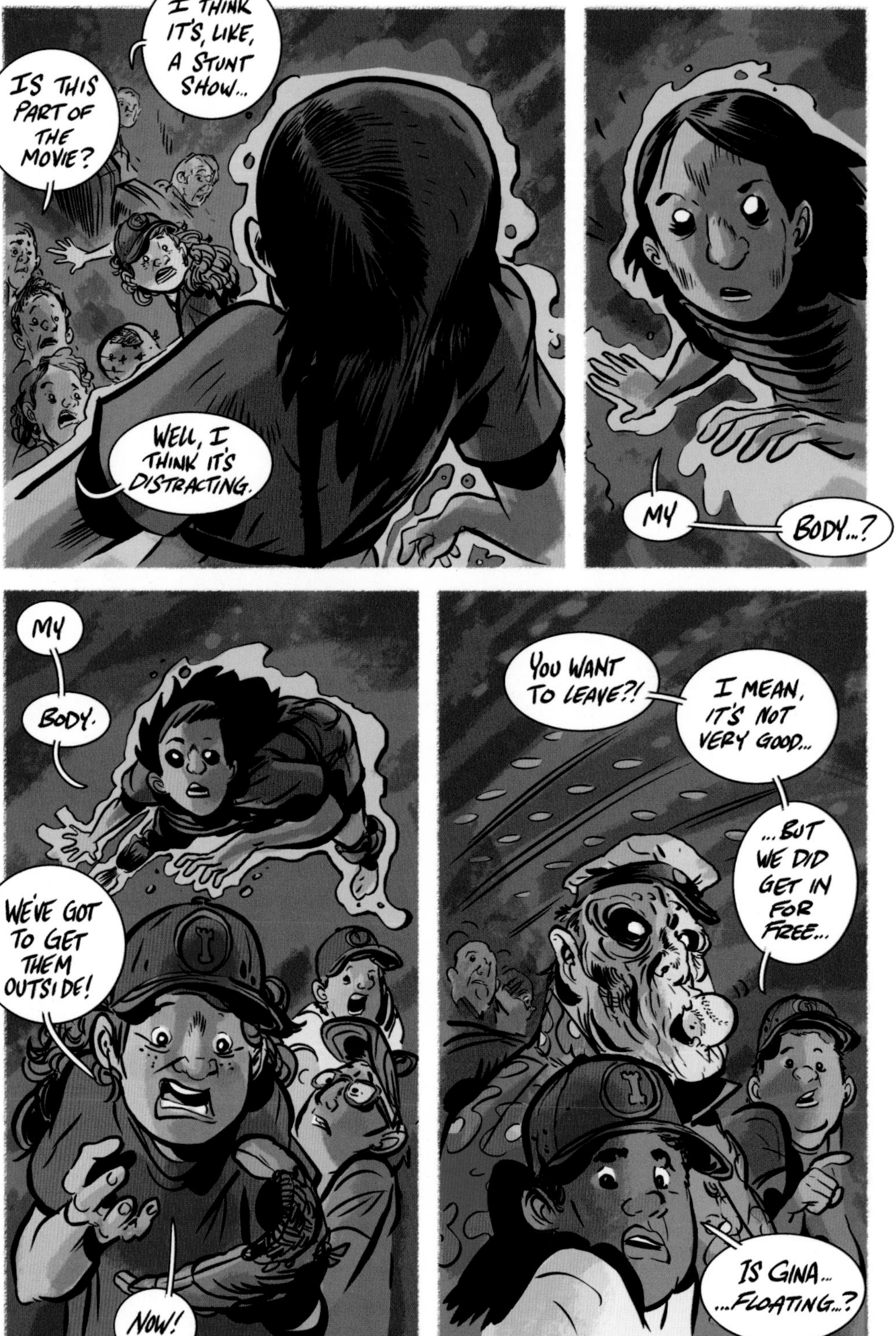
IS THIS PART OF THE MOVIE?
I THINK IT'S, LIKE, A STUNT SHOW...
WELL, I THINK IT'S DISTRACTING.
MY
BODY...?
MY
BODY.
WE'VE GOT TO GET THEM OUTSIDE!
NOW!
YOU WANT TO LEAVE?!
I MEAN, IT'S NOT VERY GOOD...
...BUT WE DID GET IN FOR FREE...
IS GINA...
...FLOATING...?

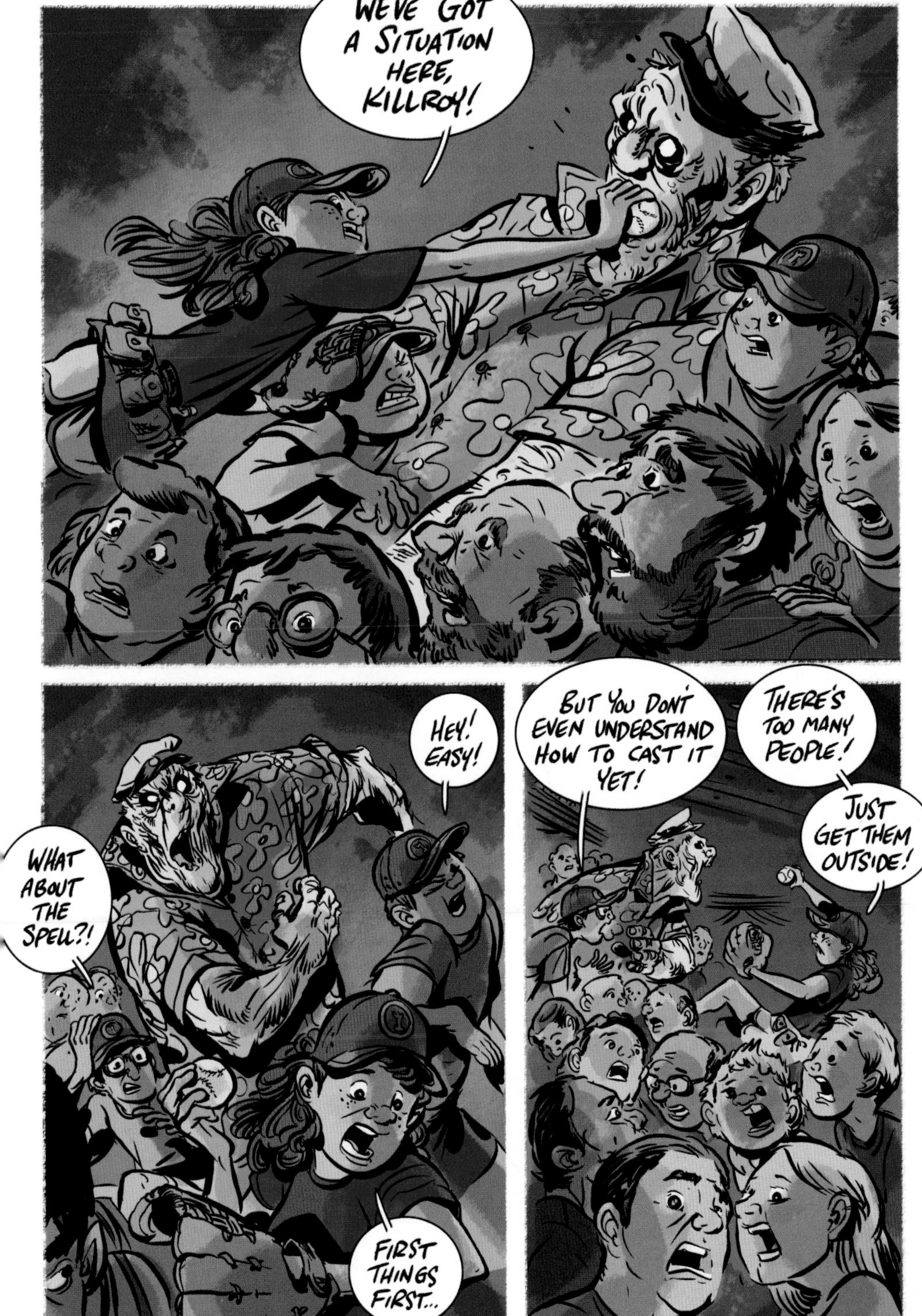
WE'VE GOT A SITUATION HERE, KILLROY!
HEY! EASY!
WHAT ABOUT THE SPELL?!
FIRST THINGS FIRST...
BUT YOU DON'T EVEN UNDERSTAND HOW TO CAST IT YET!
THERE'S TOO MANY PEOPLE!
JUST GET THEM OUTSIDE!

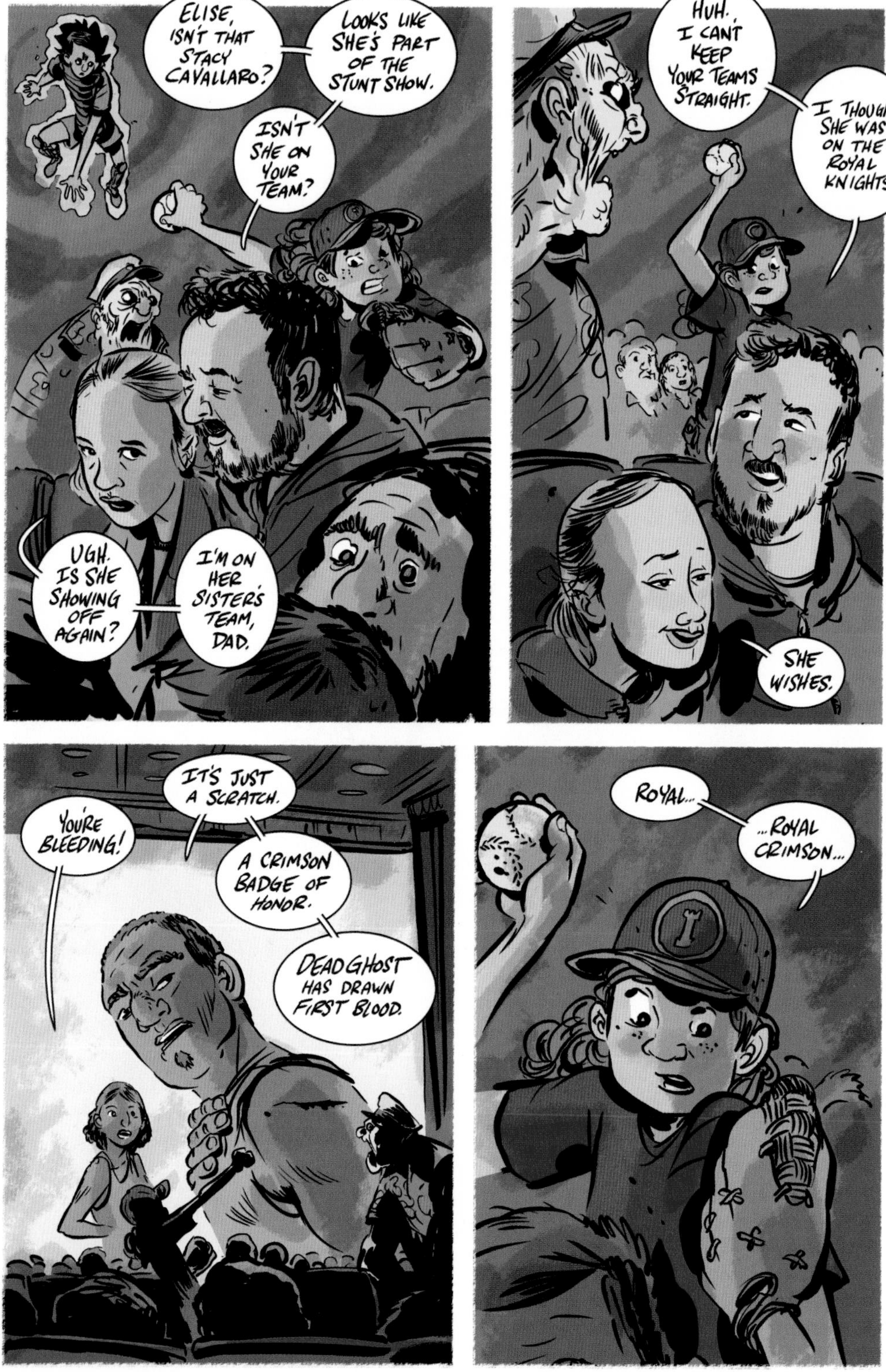
ELISE, ISN'T THAT STACY CAVALLARO?
LOOKS LIKE SHE'S PART OF THE STUNT SHOW.
ISN'T SHE ON YOUR TEAM?
UGH. IS SHE SHOWING OFF AGAIN?
I'M ON HER SISTER'S TEAM, DAD.
HUH. I CAN'T KEEP YOUR TEAMS STRAIGHT.
I THOUGHT SHE WAS ON THE ROYAL KNIGHTS.
SHE WISHES.
YOU'RE BLEEDING!
IT'S JUST A SCRATCH.
A CRIMSON BADGE OF HONOR.
DEADGHOST HAS DRAWN FIRST BLOOD.
ROYAL...
...ROYAL CRIMSON...

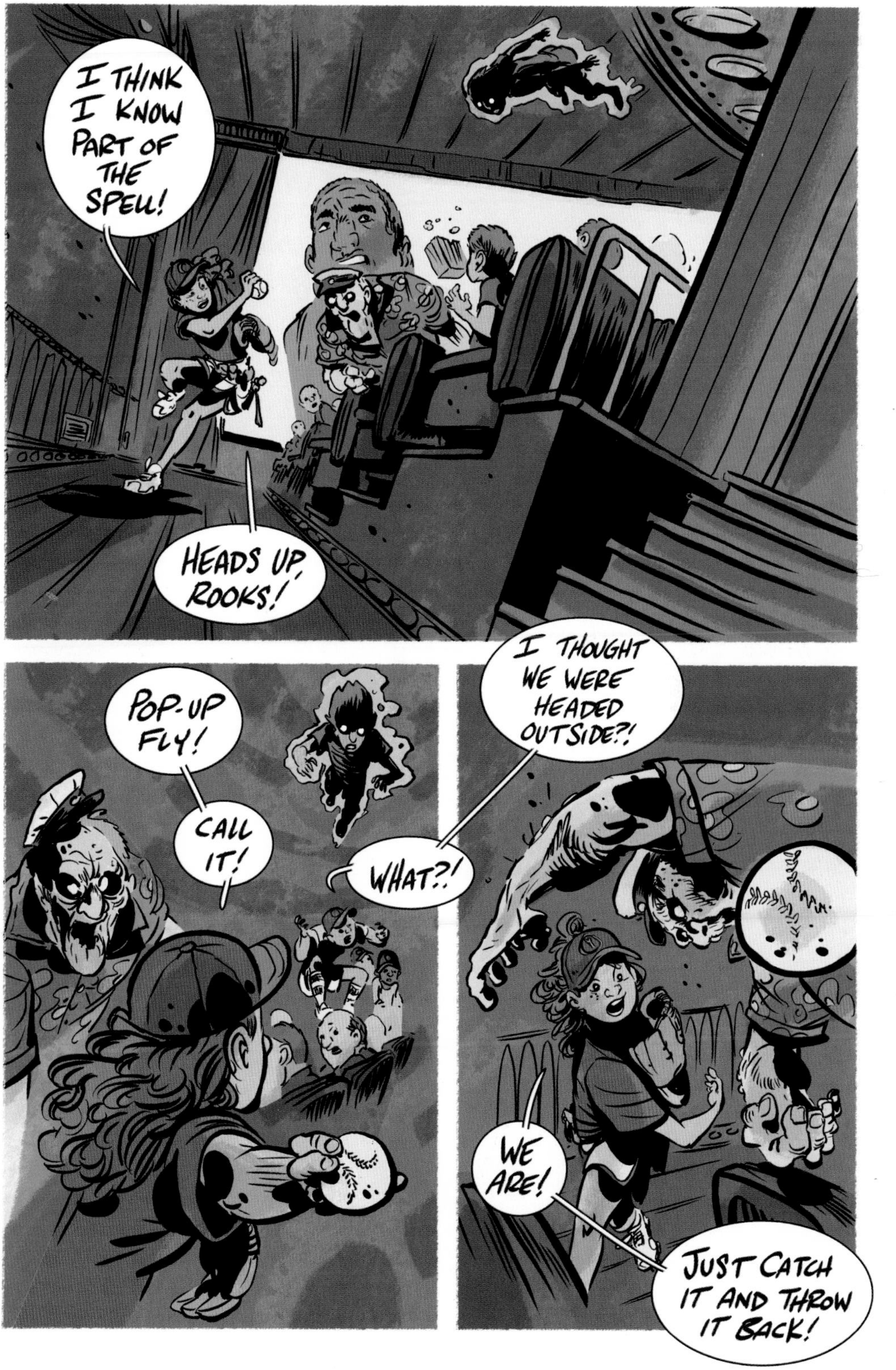
I THINK I KNOW PART OF THE SPELL!
HEADS UP, ROOKS!
POP-UP FLY!
CALL IT!
WHAT?!
I THOUGHT WE WERE HEADED OUTSIDE?!
WE ARE!
JUST CATCH IT AND THROW IT BACK!

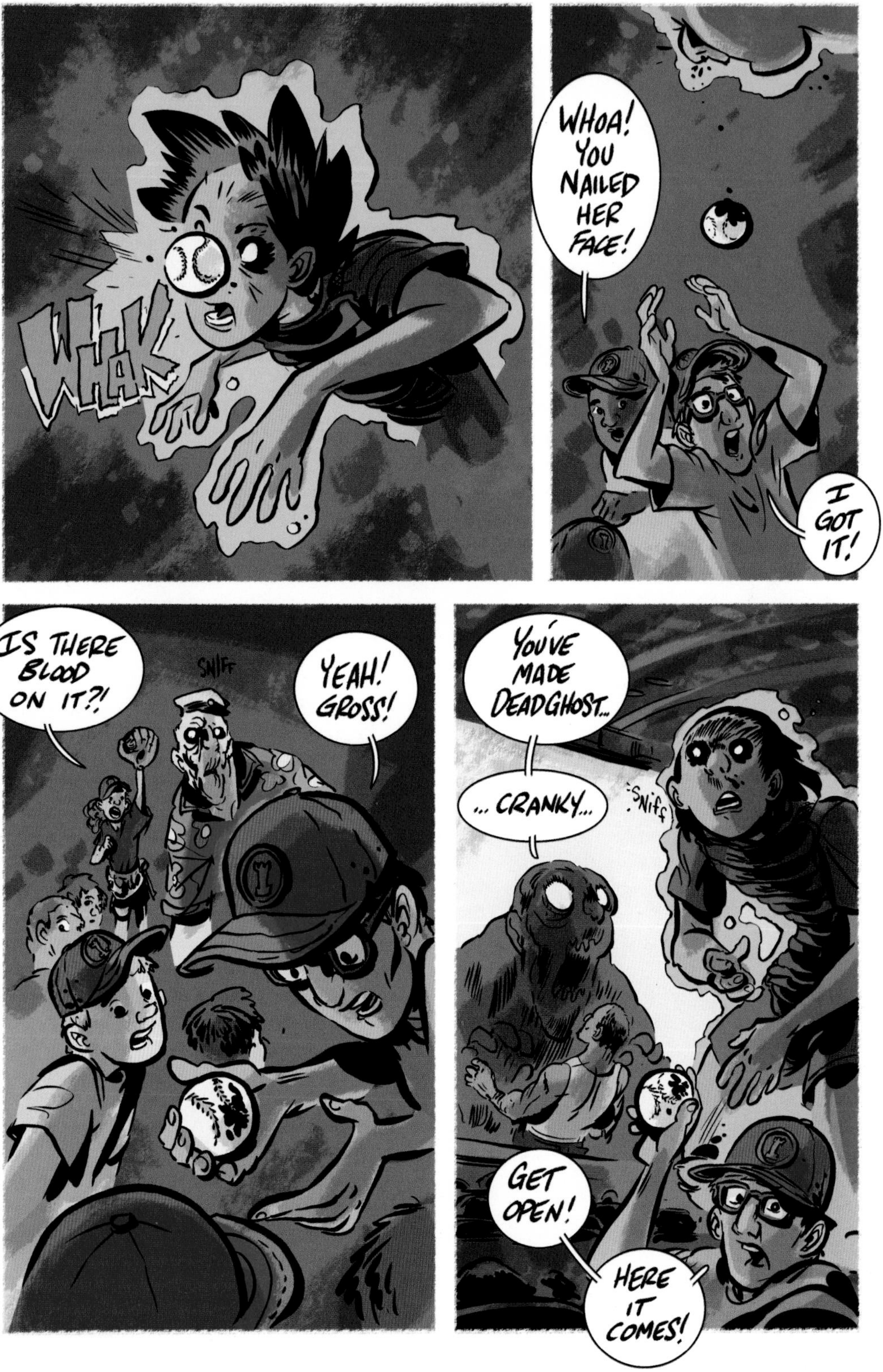
WHAK
WHOA! YOU NAILED HER FACE!
I GOT IT!
IS THERE BLOOD ON IT?!
SNIFF
YEAH! GROSS!
YOU'VE MADE DEADGHOST...
... CRANKY...
SNIFF
GET OPEN!
HERE IT COMES!

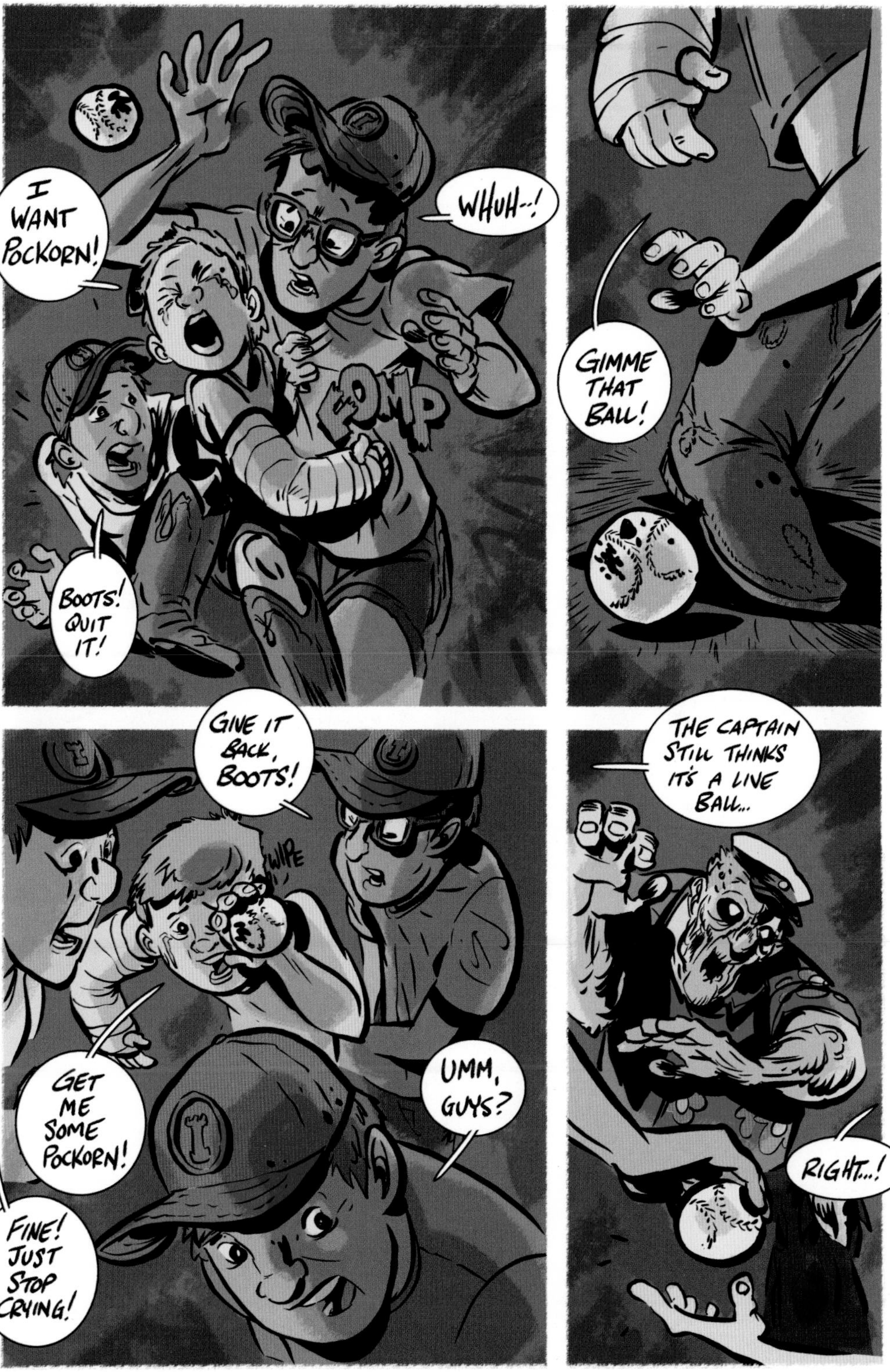
I WANT POCKORN!
WHUH--!
FOMP
BOOTS! QUIT IT!
GIMME THAT BALL!
GIVE IT BACK, BOOTS!
WIPE
GET ME SOME POCKORN!
FINE! JUST STOP CRYING!
UMM, GUYS?
THE CAPTAIN STILL THINKS IT'S A LIVE BALL...
RIGHT...!

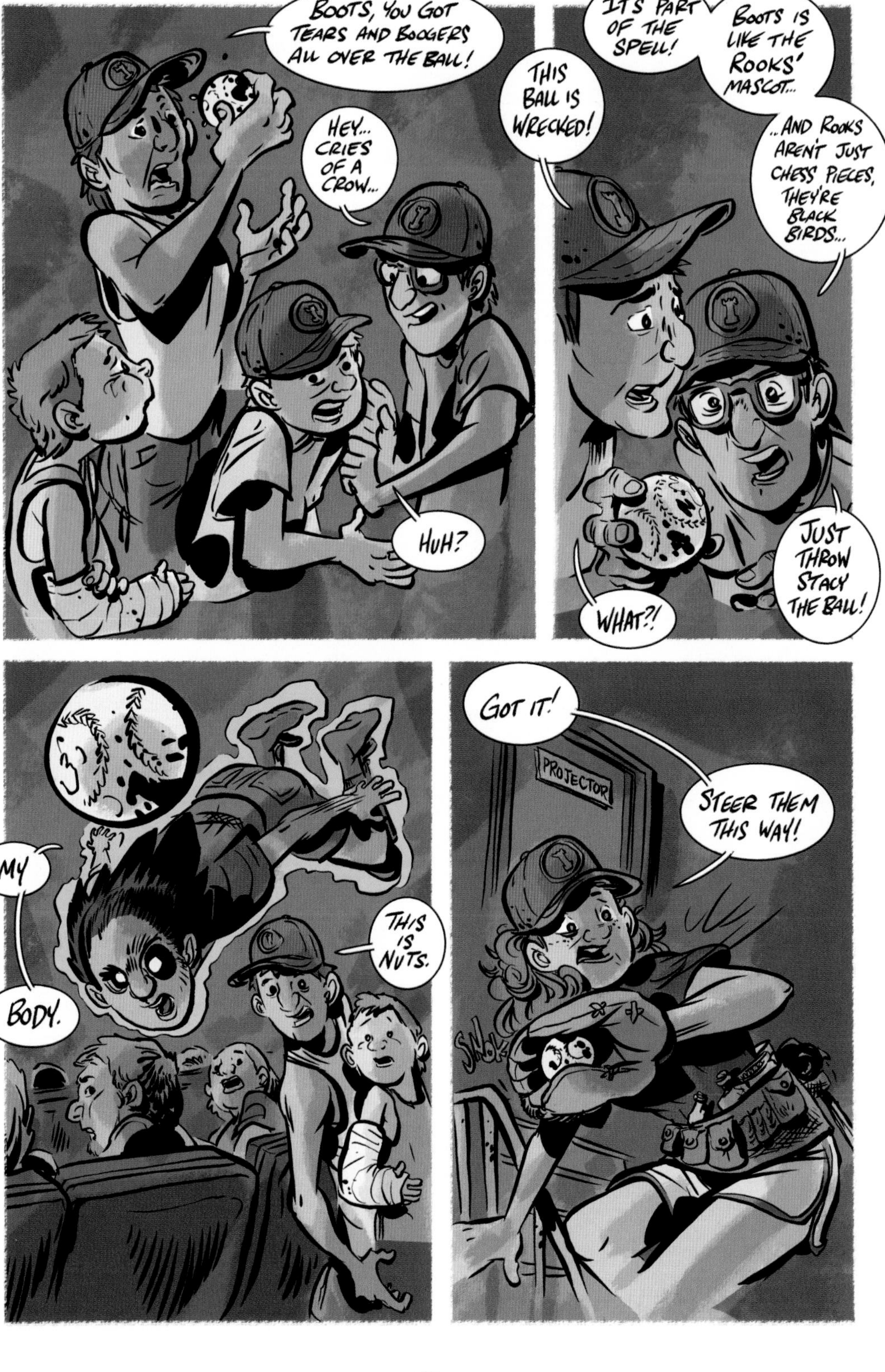
BOOTS, YOU GOT TEARS AND BOOGERS ALL OVER THE BALL!
HEY... CRIES OF A CROW...
HUH?
THIS BALL IS WRECKED!
IT'S PART OF THE SPELL!
BOOTS IS LIKE THE ROOKS' MASCOT...
...AND ROOKS AREN'T JUST CHESS PIECES, THEY'RE BLACK BIRDS...
WHAT?!
JUST THROW STACY THE BALL!
MY
BODY.
THIS IS NUTS.
GOT IT!
PROJECTOR
STEER THEM THIS WAY!
SNOK

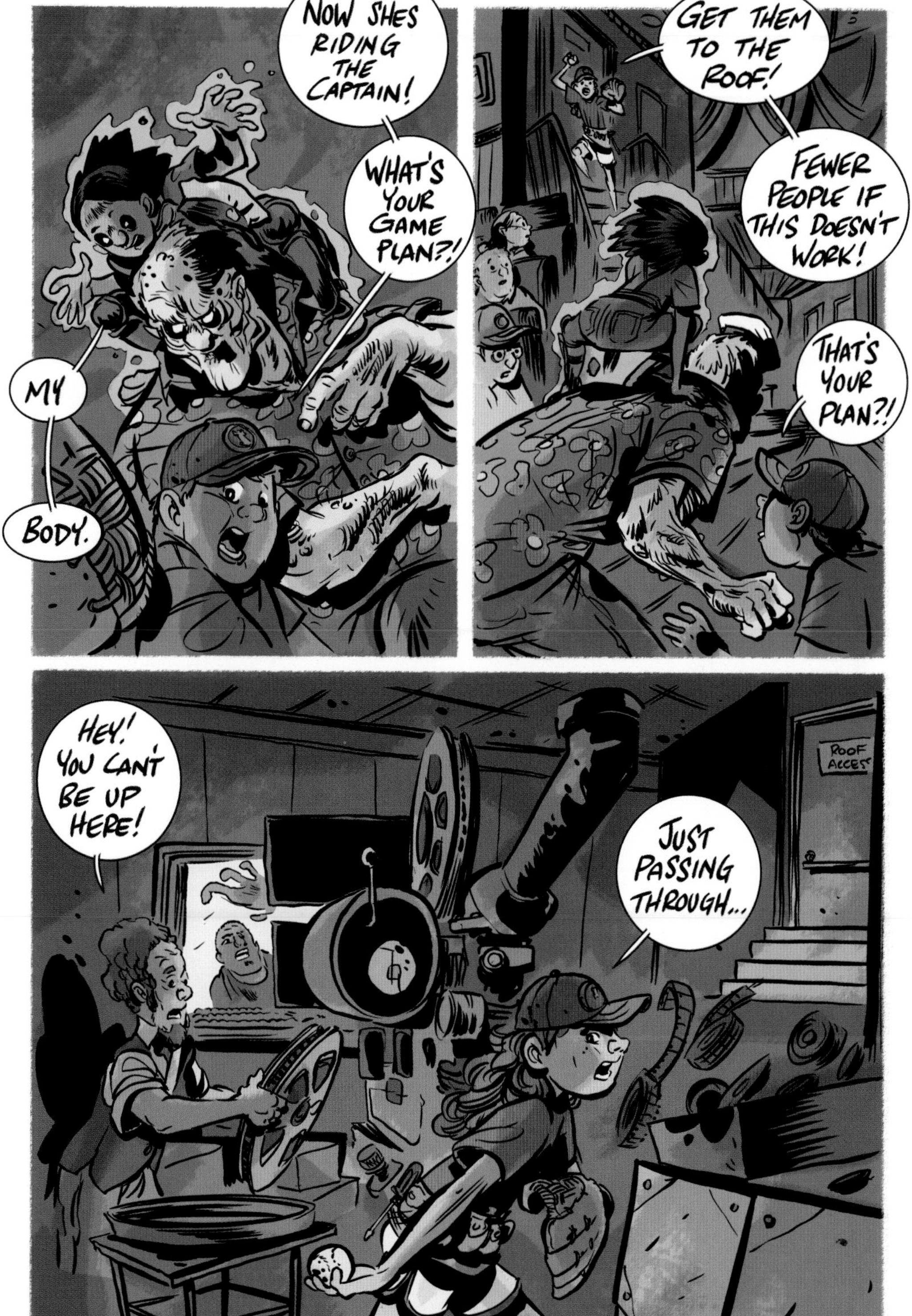
NOW SHE'S RIDING THE CAPTAIN!
WHAT'S YOUR GAME PLAN?!
MY
BODY.
GET THEM TO THE ROOF!
FEWER PEOPLE IF THIS DOESN'T WORK!
THAT'S YOUR PLAN?!
HEY! YOU CAN'T BE UP HERE!
ROOF ACCESS
JUST PASSING THROUGH...

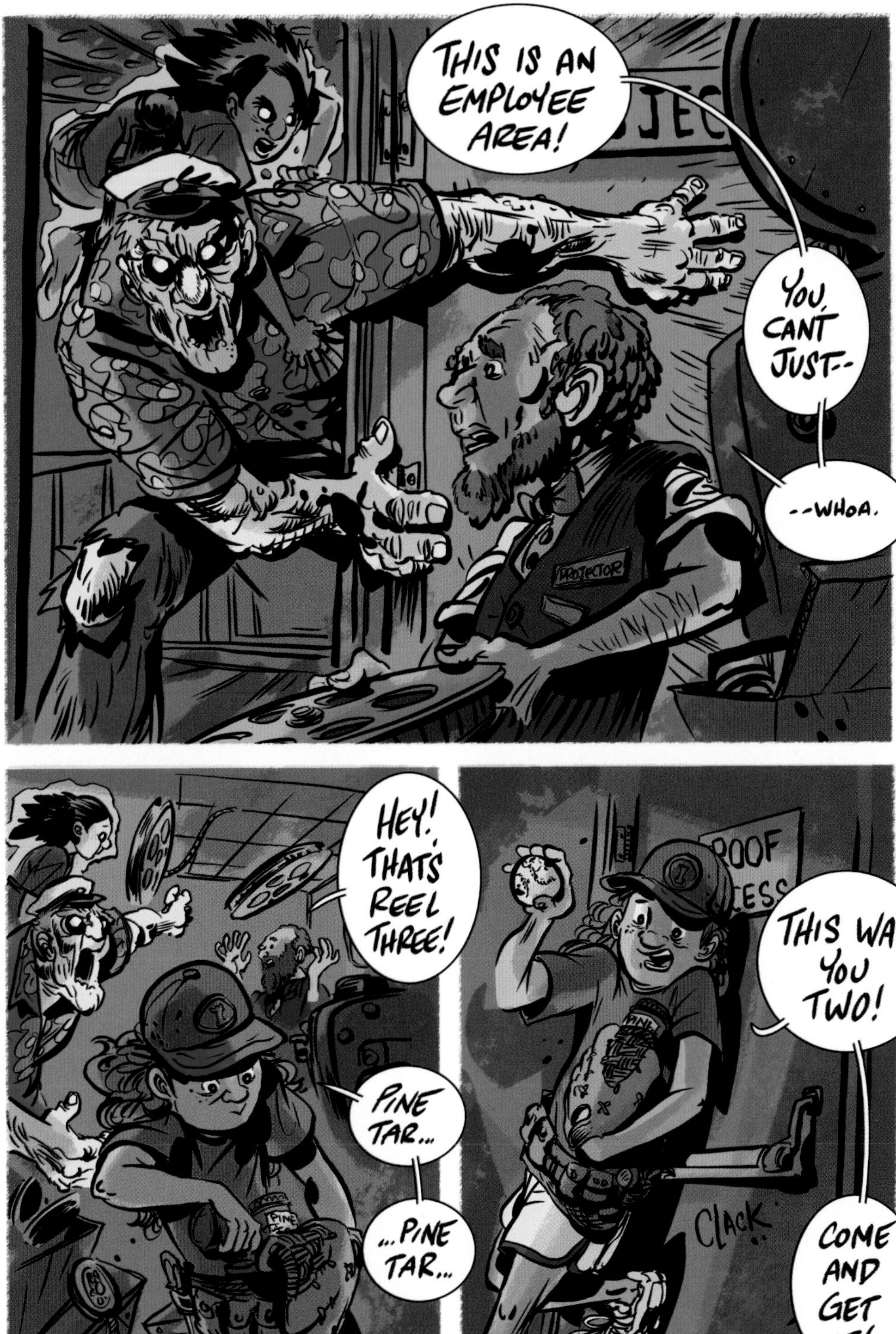
THIS IS AN EMPLOYEE AREA!
YOU CAN'T JUST--
--WHOA.
PROJECTOR
HEY! THAT'S REEL THREE!
PINE TAR...
...PINE TAR...
THIS WAY, YOU TWO!
CLACK
COME AND GET IT!

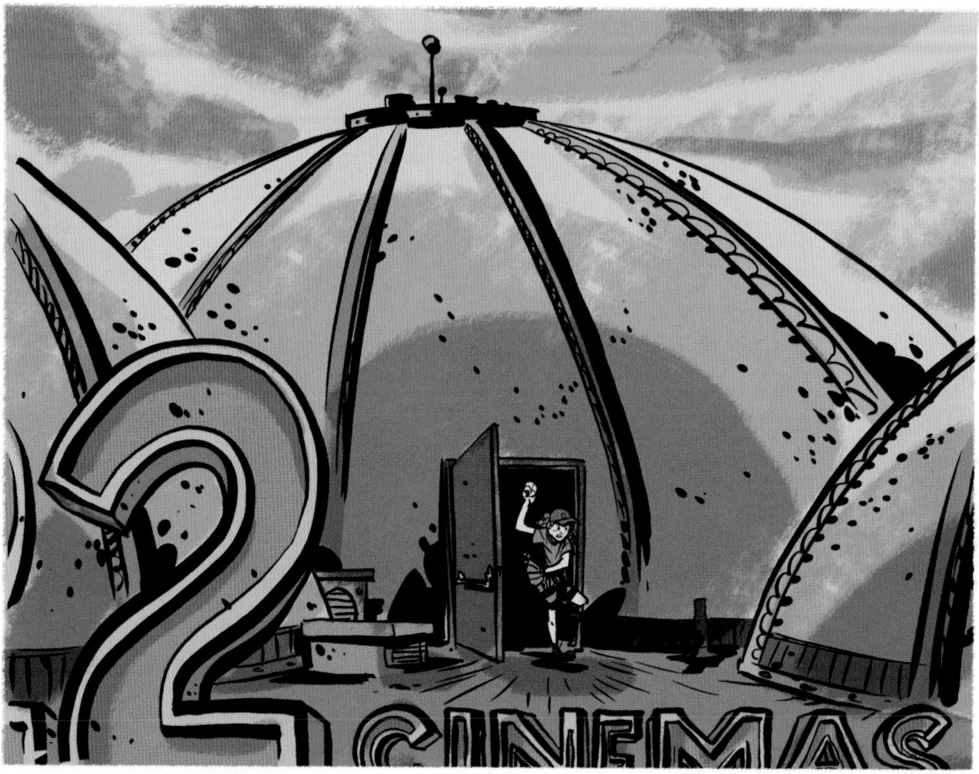

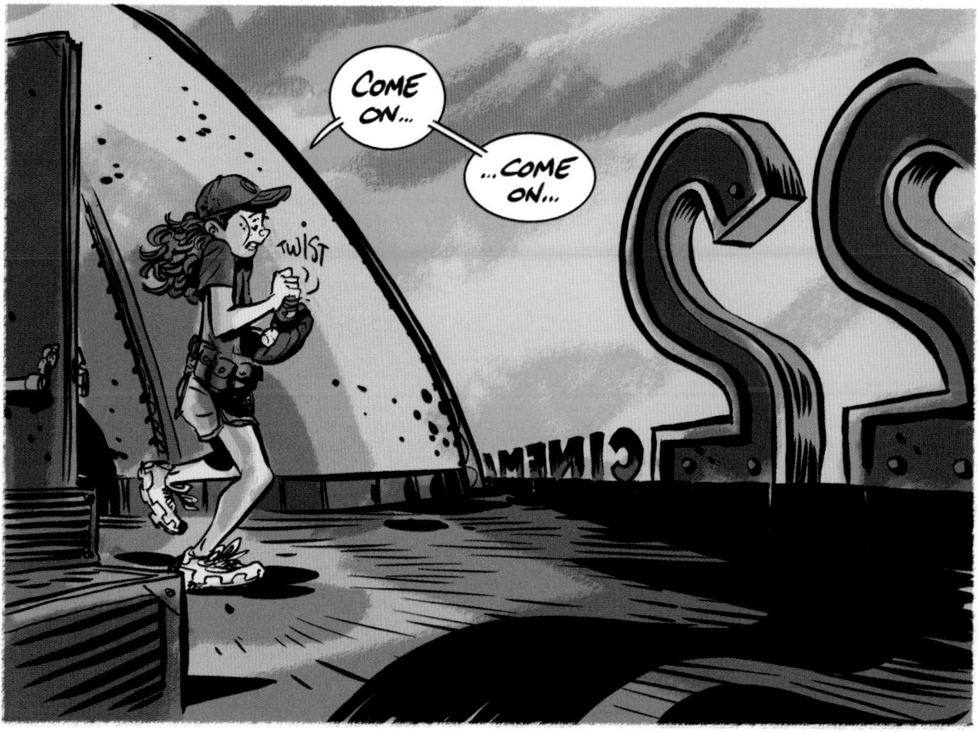
COME ON...
...COME ON...
TWIST

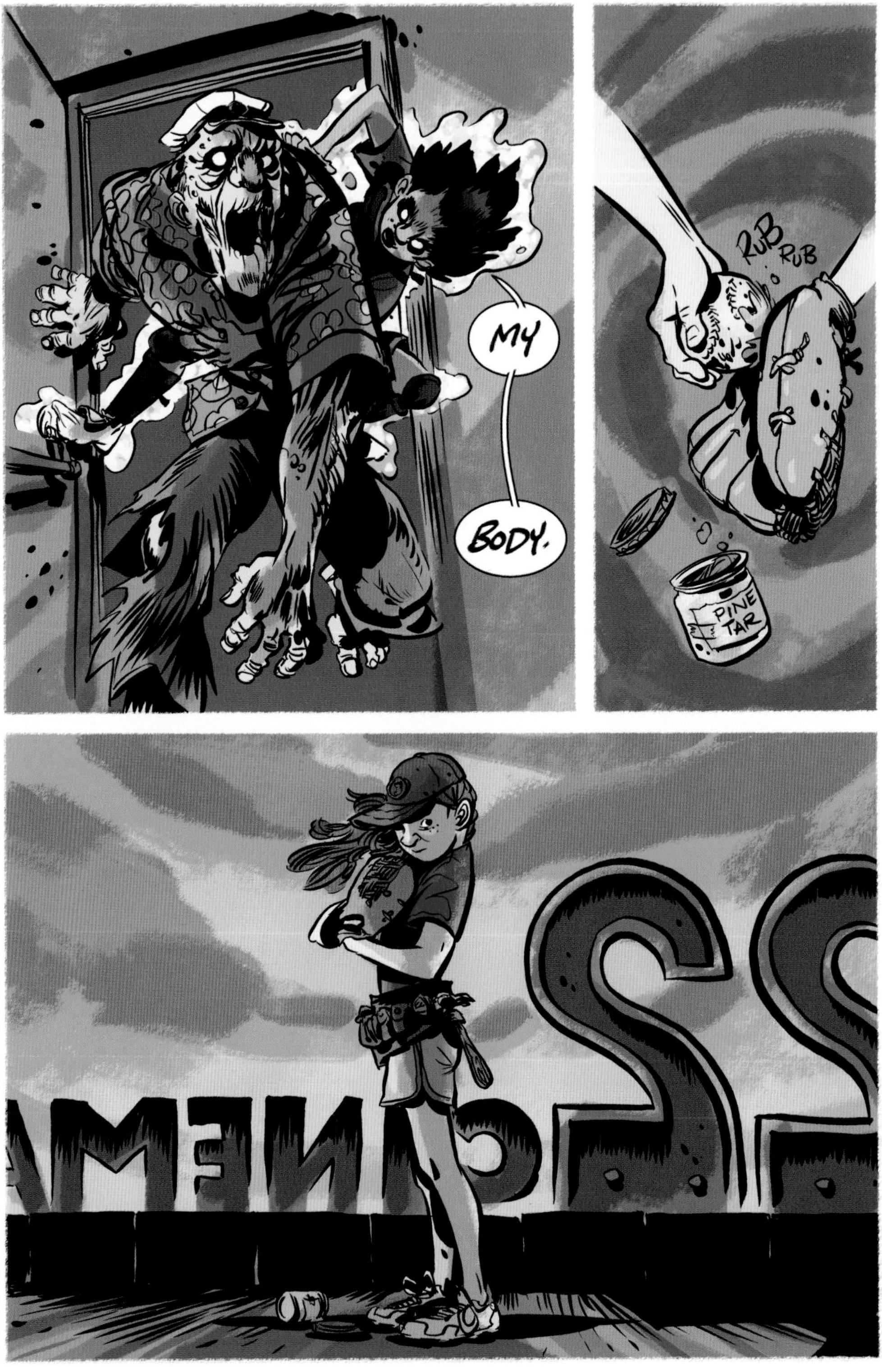
MY
BODY.
RUB RUB
PINE TAR

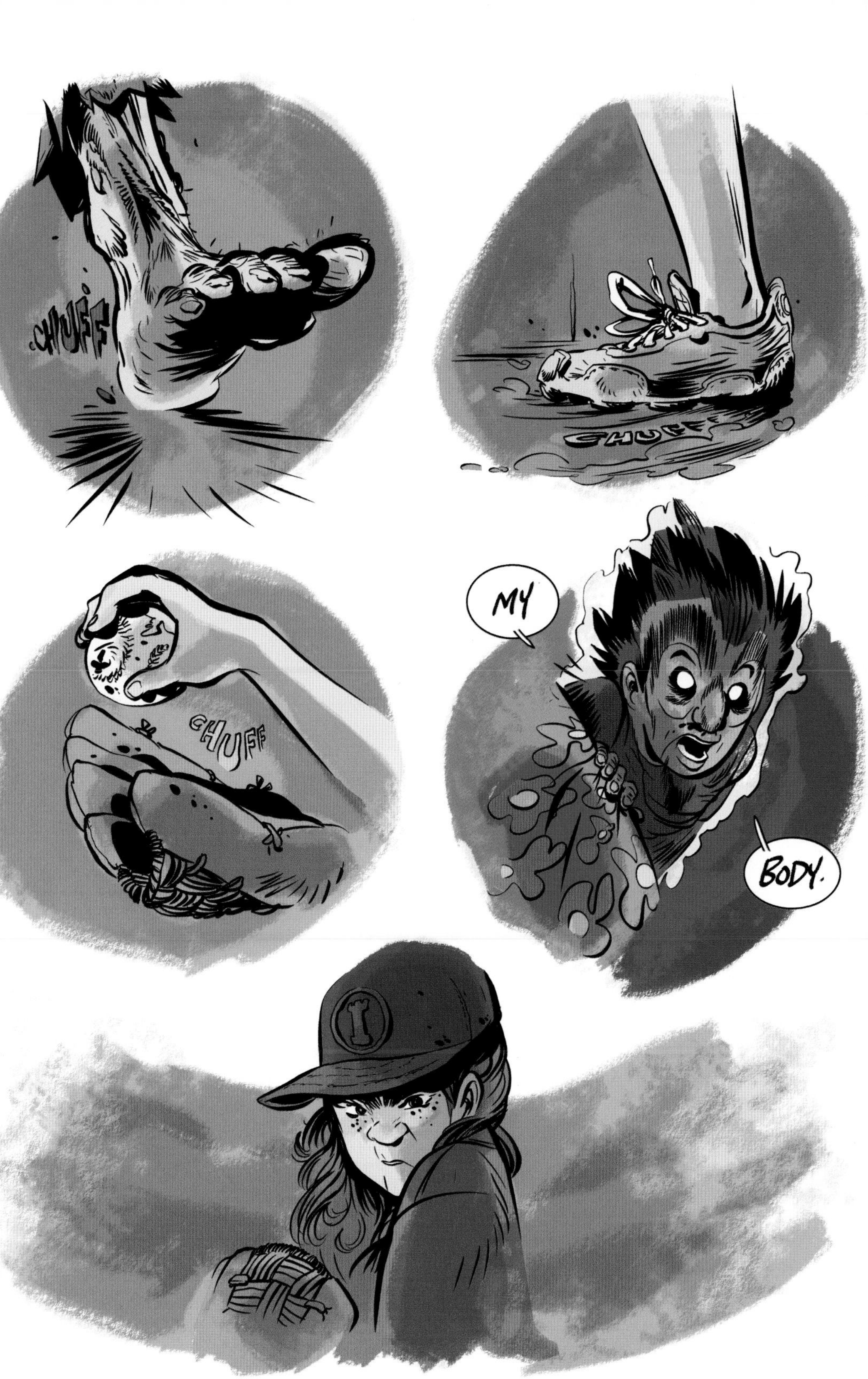
CHUFF
CHUFF
CHUFF
MY
BODY.

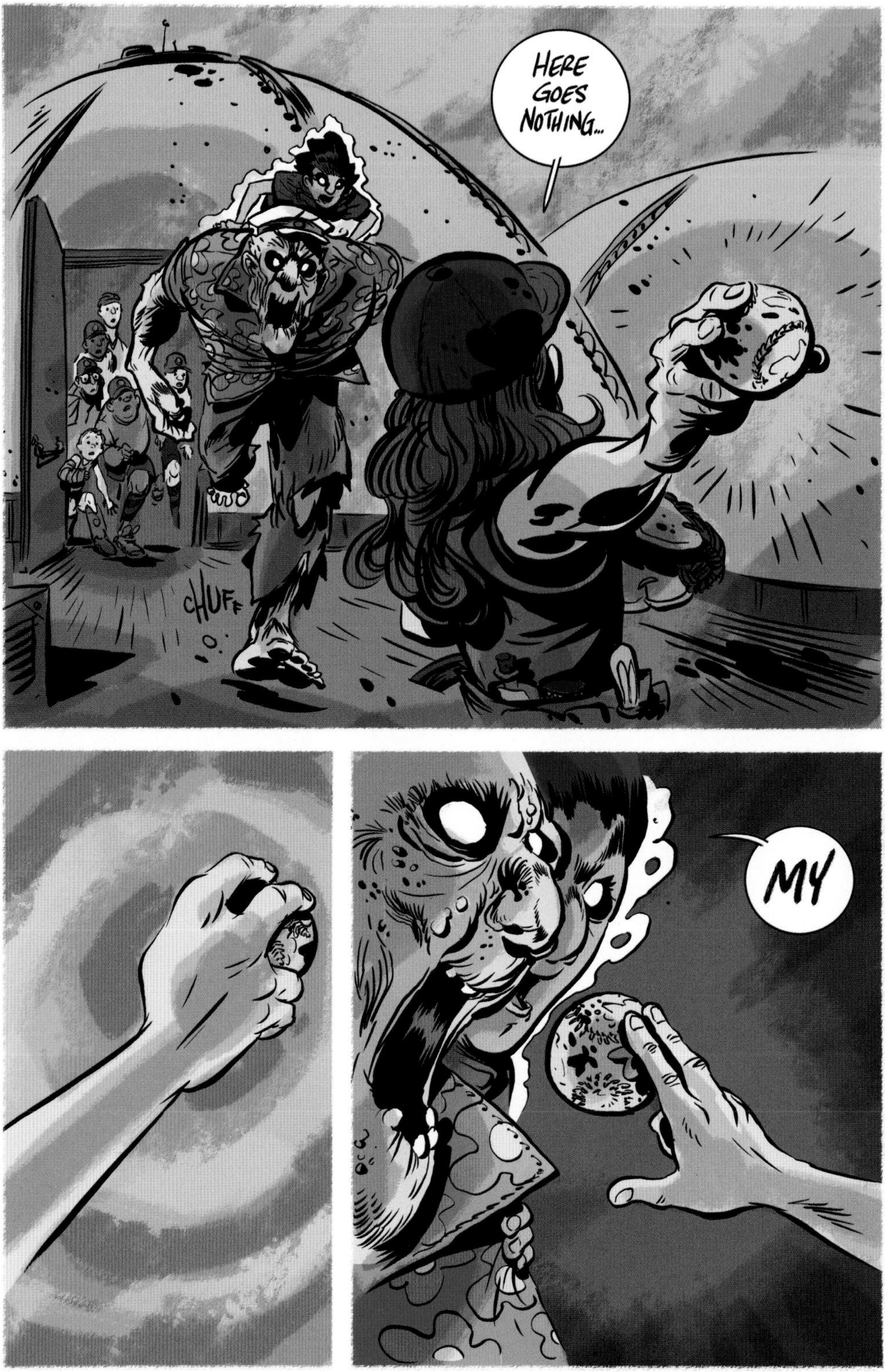
HERE GOES NOTHING...
CHUFF
MY

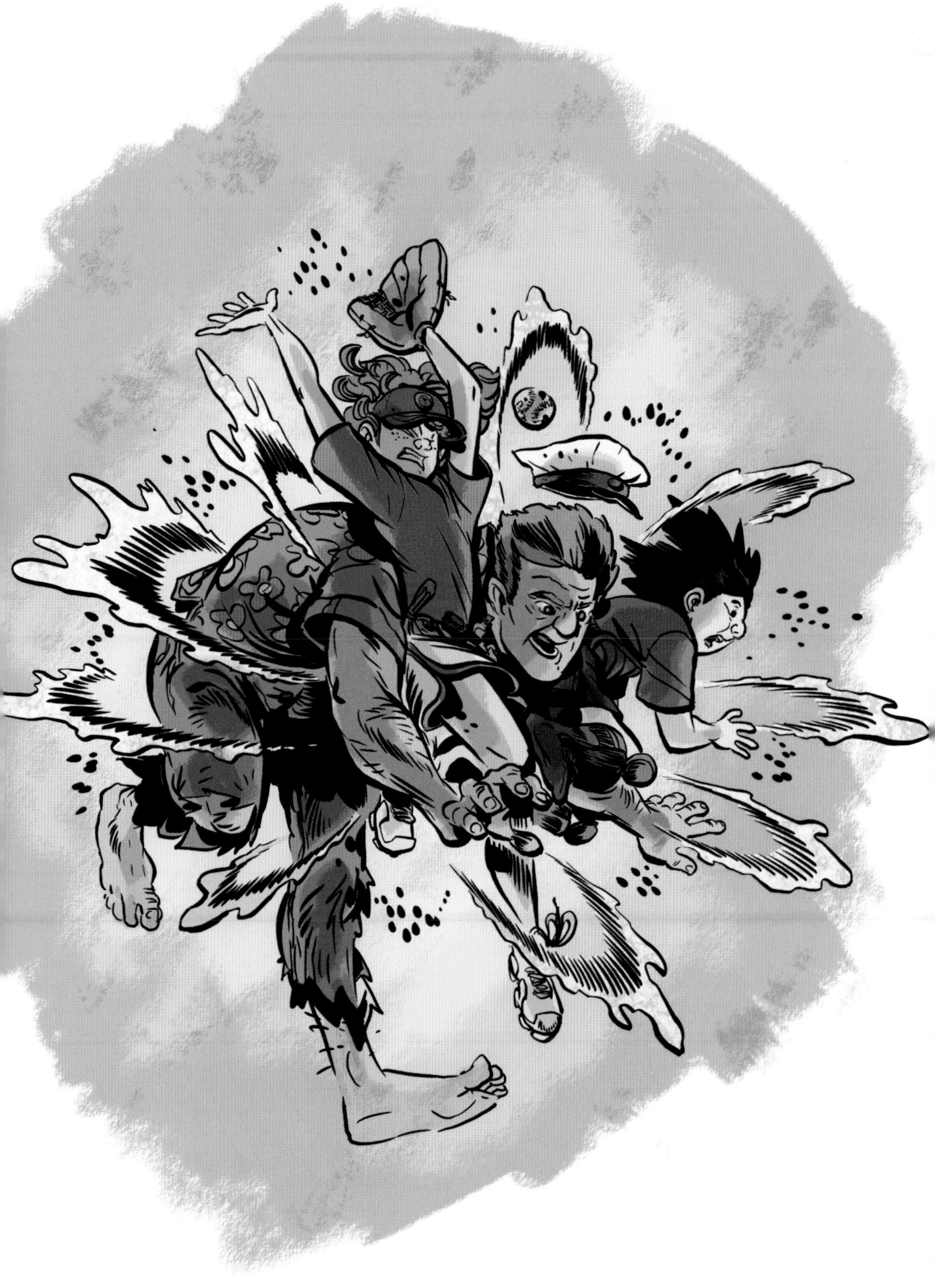

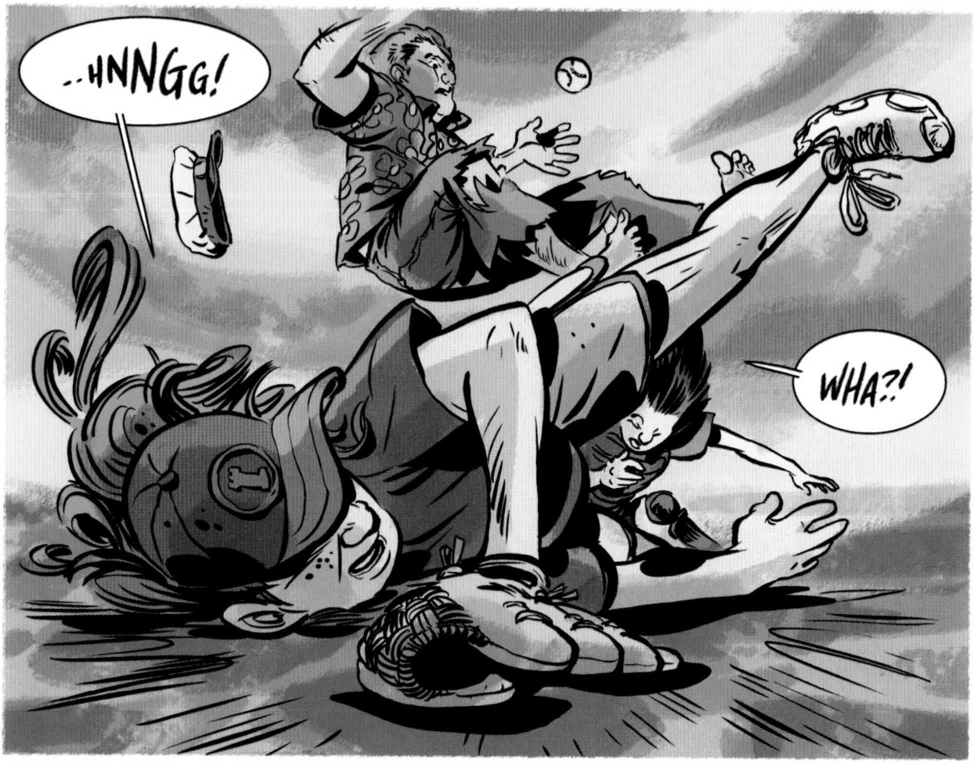
--HNNGG!
WHA?!

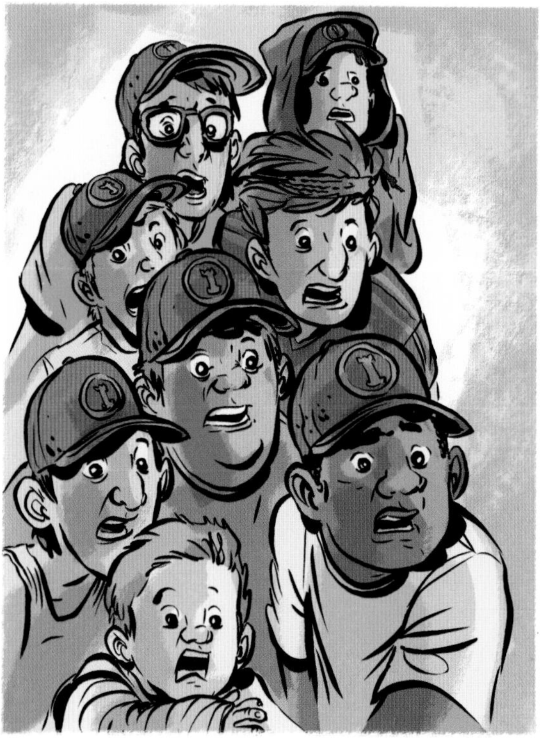

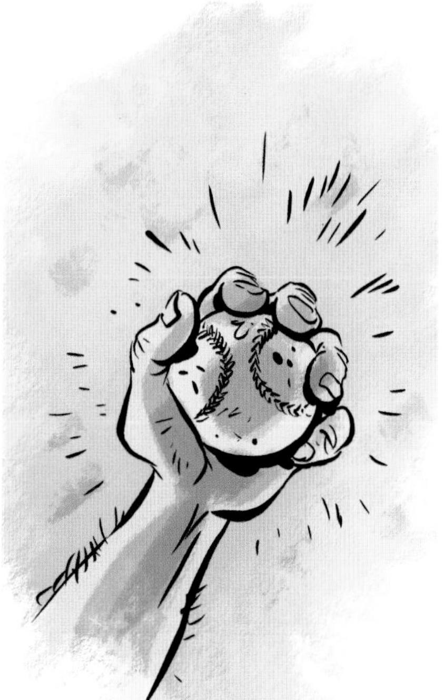

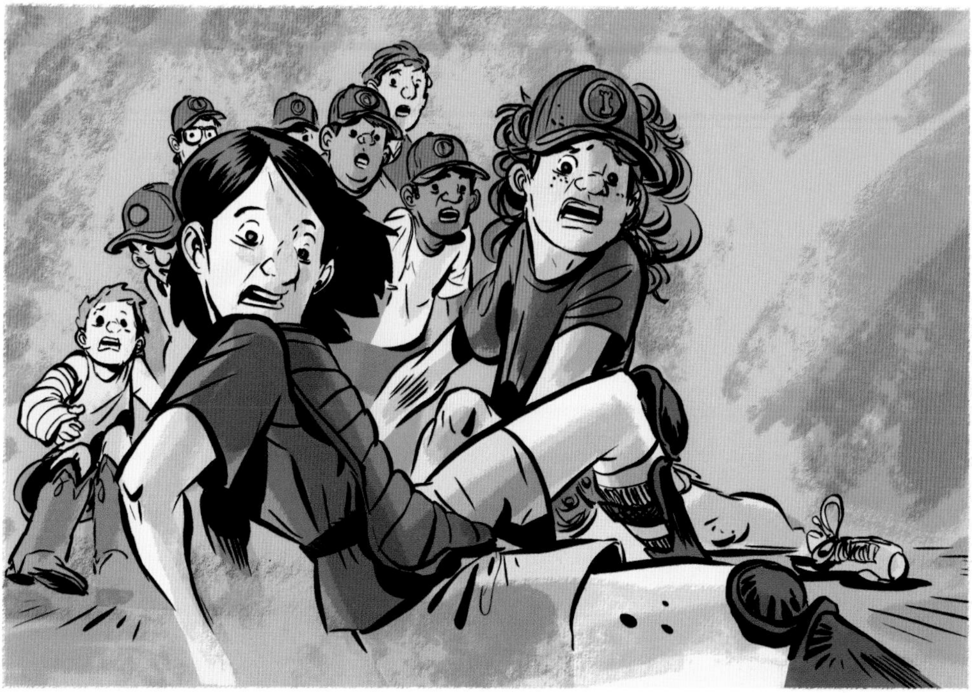

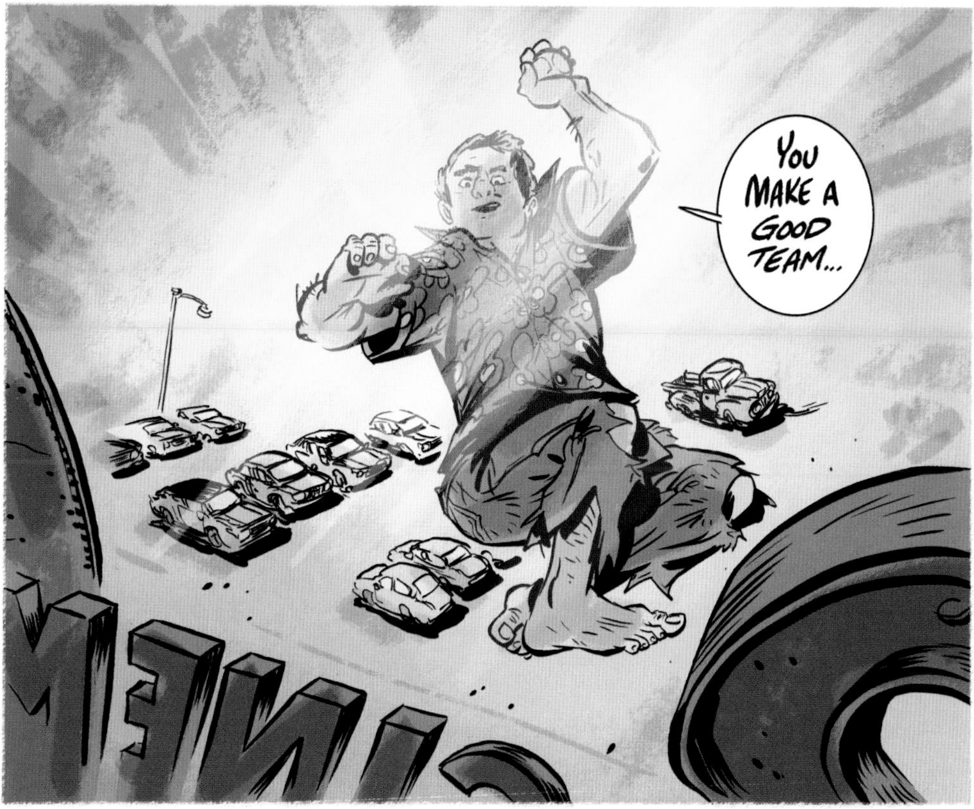
YOU MAKE A GOOD TEAM...

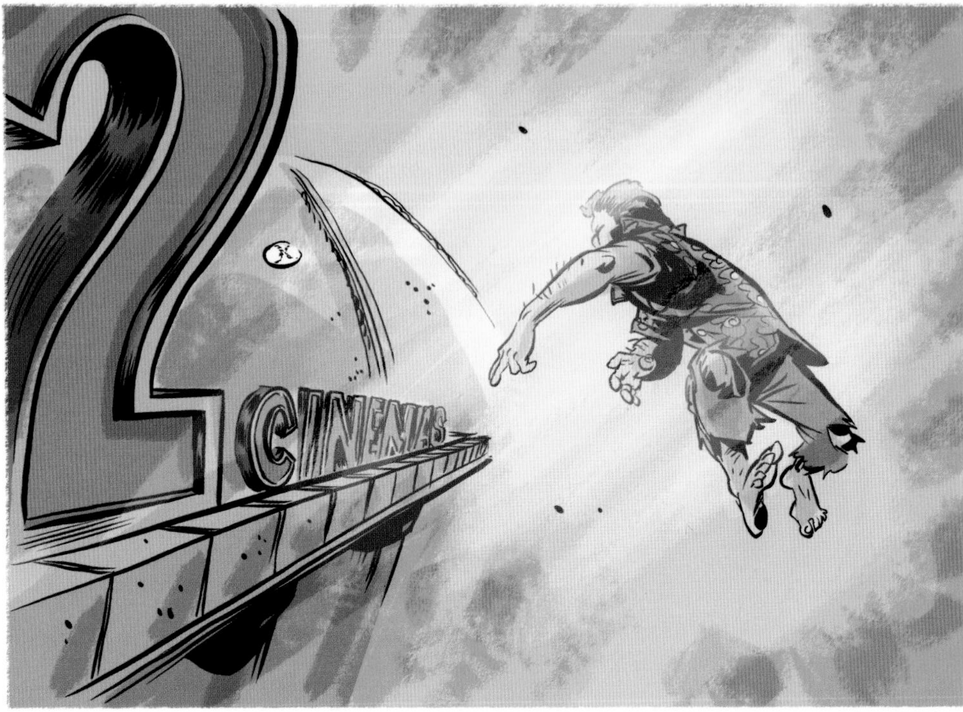
2 CINEMAS

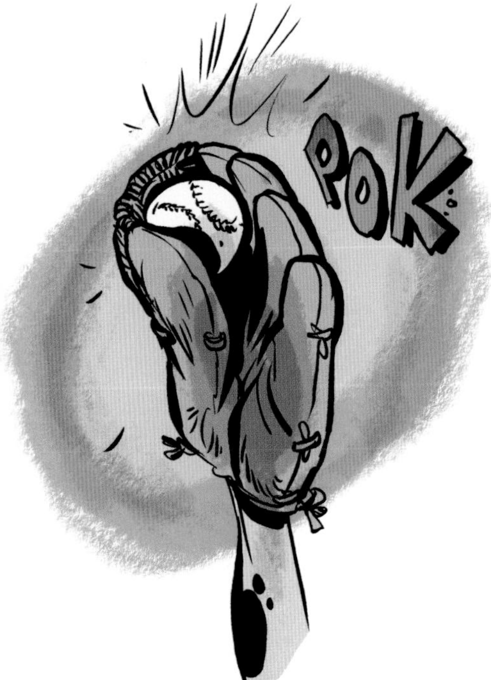
POK

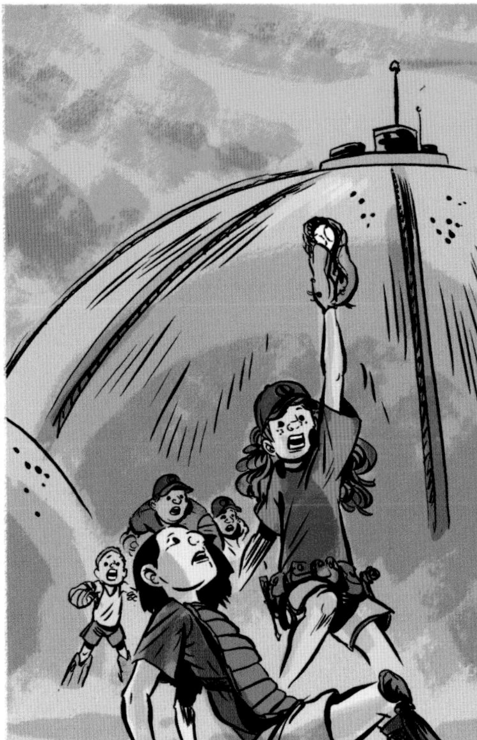

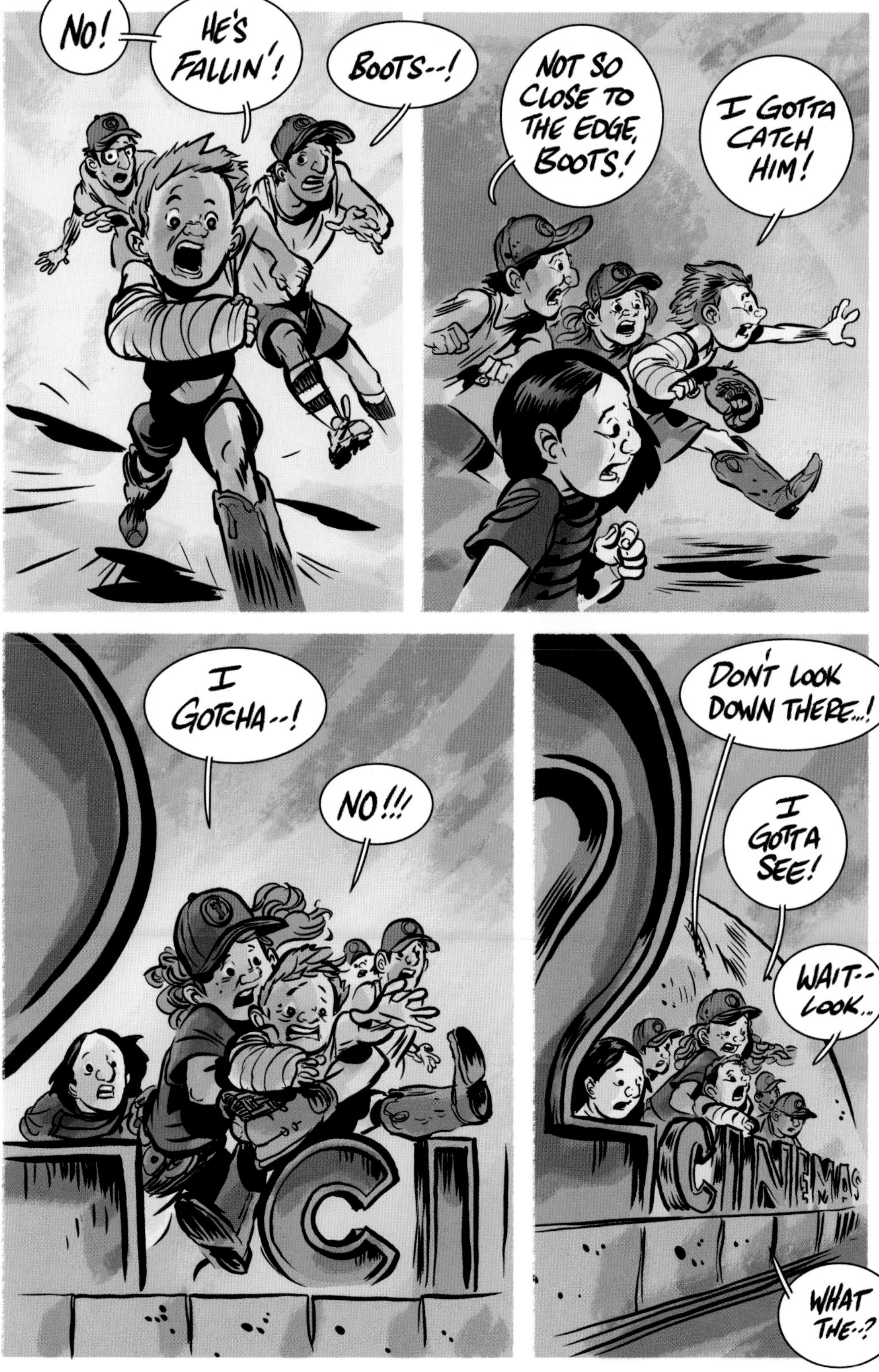
NO!
HE'S FALLIN'!
BOOTS--!
NOT SO CLOSE TO THE EDGE, BOOTS!
I GOTTA CATCH HIM!
I GOTCHA--!
NO!!!
DON'T LOOK DOWN THERE...!
I GOTTA SEE!
WAIT-- LOOK...
WHAT THE--?
CINEMAS

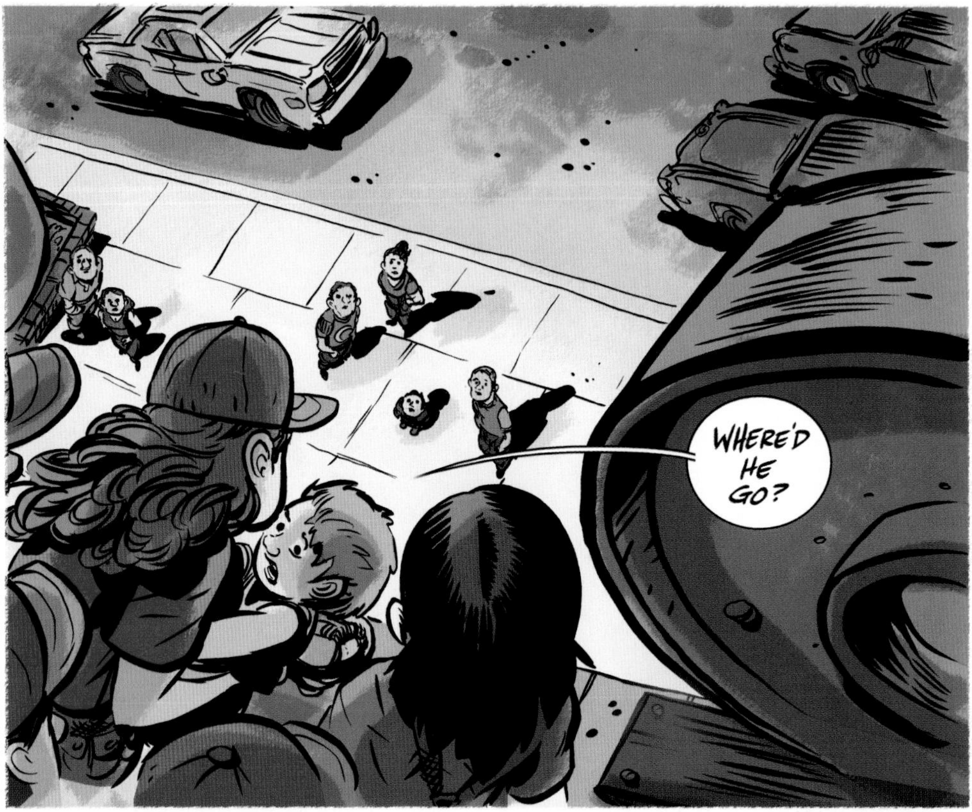
WHERE'D HE GO?

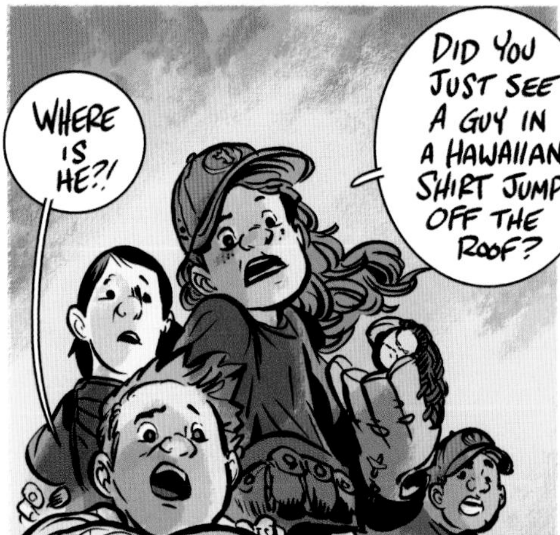
WHERE IS HE?!
DID YOU JUST SEE A GUY IN A HAWAIIAN SHIRT JUMP OFF THE ROOF?
CINEMAS

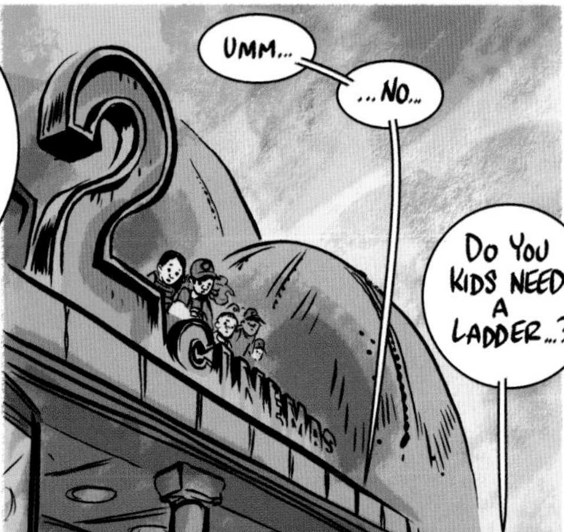
UMM...
...NO...
DO YOU KIDS NEED A LADDER...?
CINEMAS

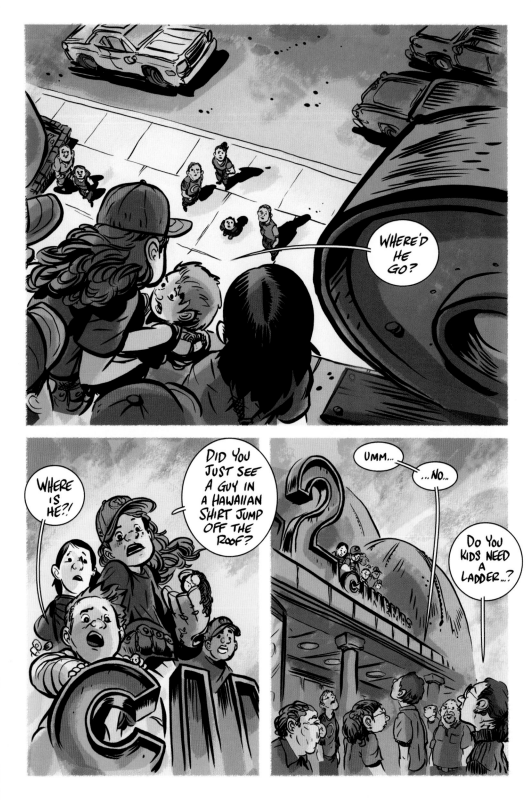

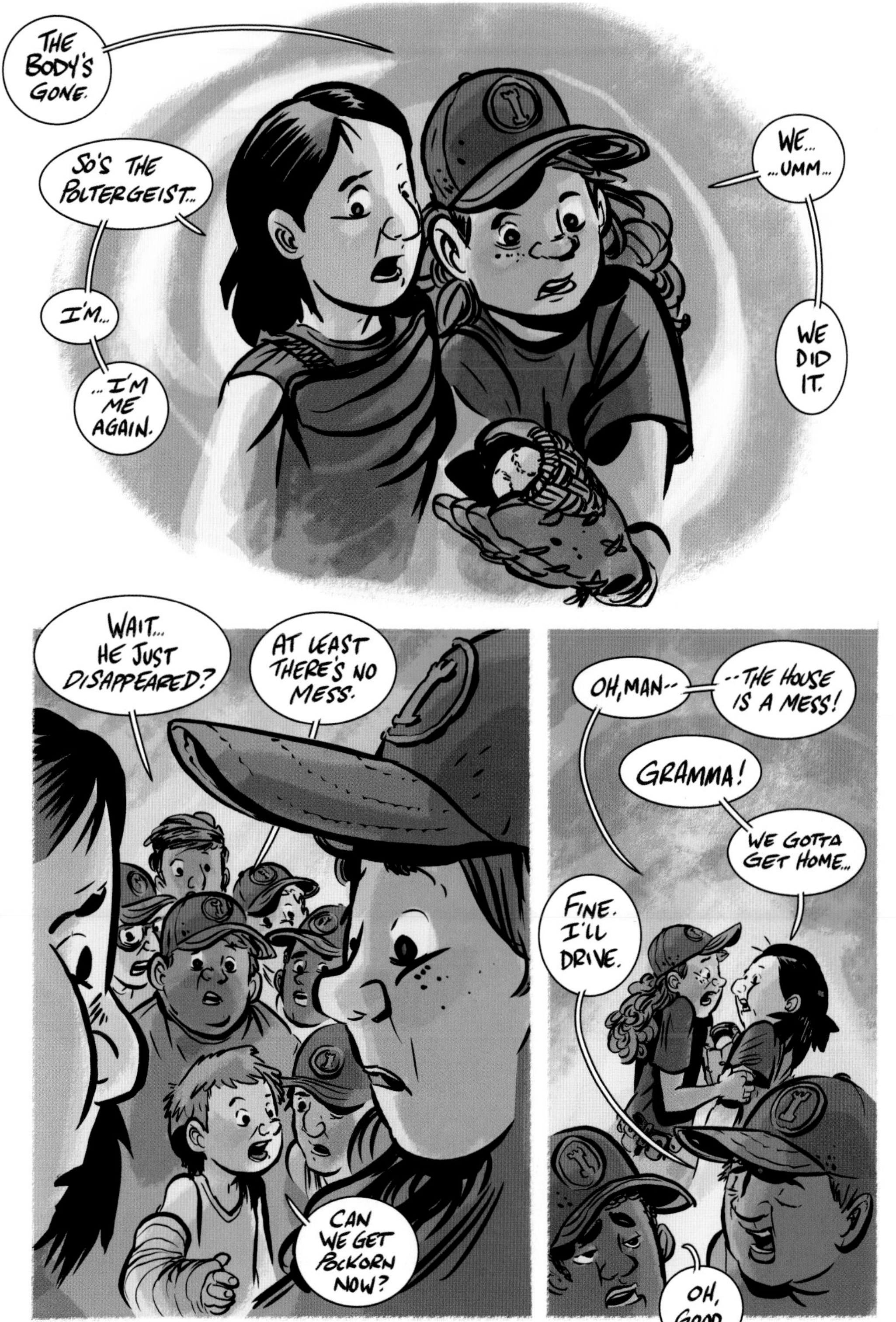
THE BODY'S GONE.
SO'S THE POLTERGEIST...
I'M...
...I'M ME AGAIN.
WE... ...UMM...
WE DID IT.
WAIT... HE JUST DISAPPEARED?
AT LEAST THERE'S NO MESS.
CAN WE GET POCKORN NOW?
OH, MAN--
--THE HOUSE IS A MESS!
GRAMMA!
WE GOTTA GET HOME...
FINE. I'LL DRIVE.
OH, GOOD...

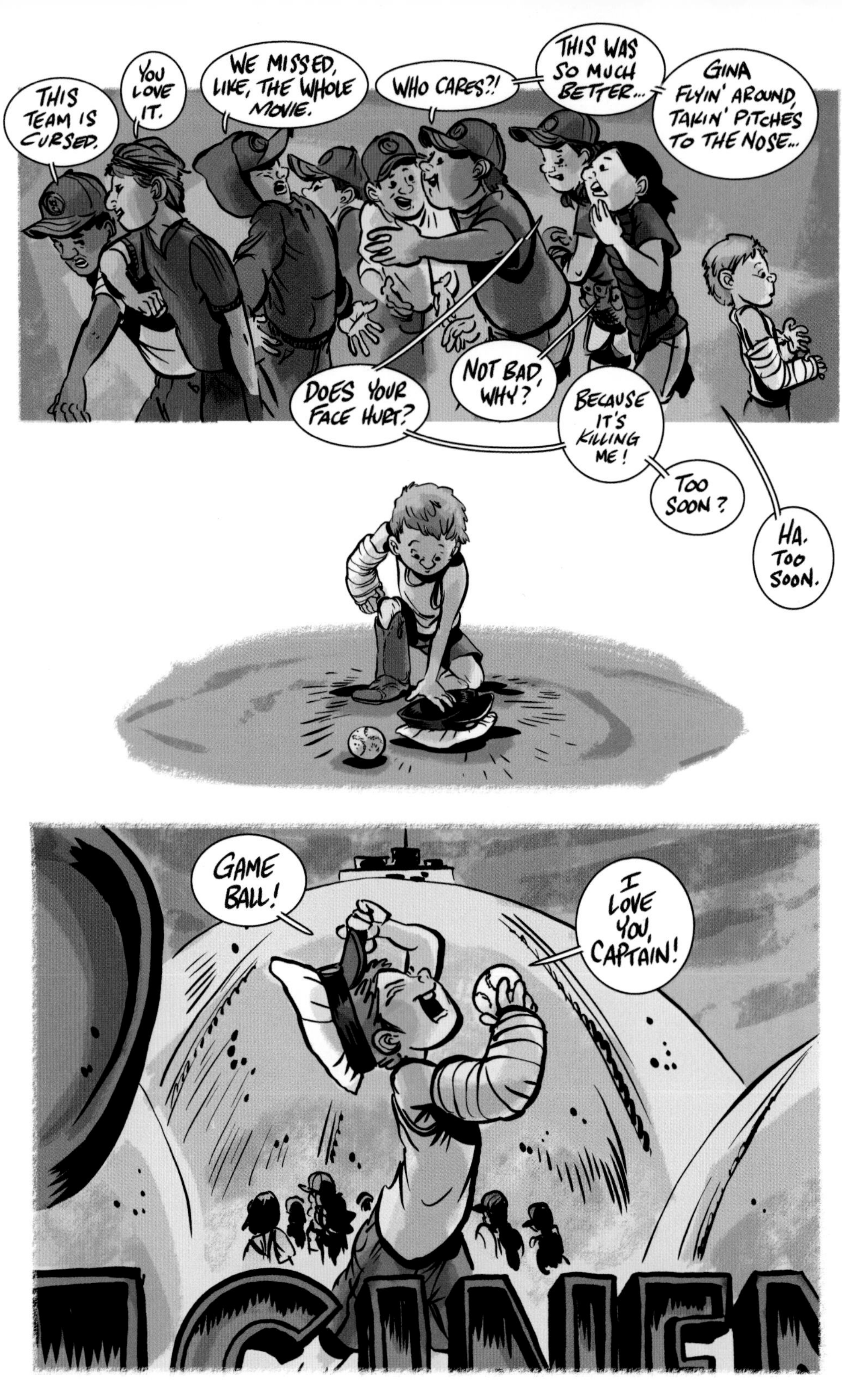
THIS TEAM IS CURSED.
YOU LOVE IT.
WE MISSED, LIKE, THE WHOLE MOVIE.
WHO CARES?!
THIS WAS SO MUCH BETTER...
GINA FLYIN' AROUND, TAKIN' PITCHES TO THE NOSE...
DOES YOUR FACE HURT?
NOT BAD, WHY?
BECAUSE IT'S KILLING ME!
TOO SOON?
HA. TOO SOON.
GAME BALL!
I LOVE YOU, CAPTAIN!

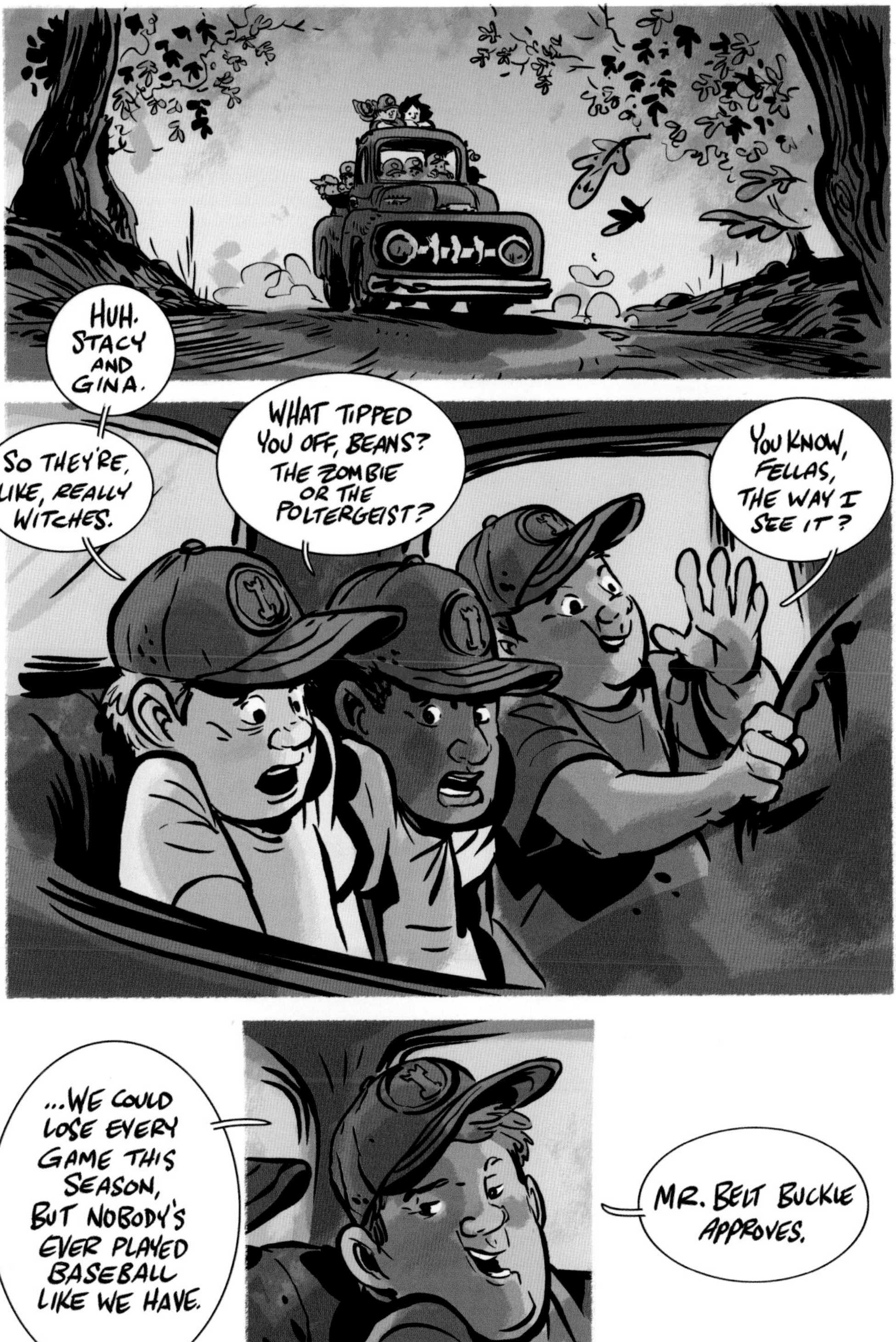
HUH. STACY AND GINA.
SO THEY'RE, LIKE, REALLY WITCHES.
WHAT TIPPED YOU OFF, BEANS? THE ZOMBIE OR THE POLTERGEIST?
YOU KNOW, FELLAS, THE WAY I SEE IT?
...WE COULD LOSE EVERY GAME THIS SEASON, BUT NOBODY'S EVER PLAYED BASEBALL LIKE WE HAVE.
MR. BELT BUCKLE APPROVES.

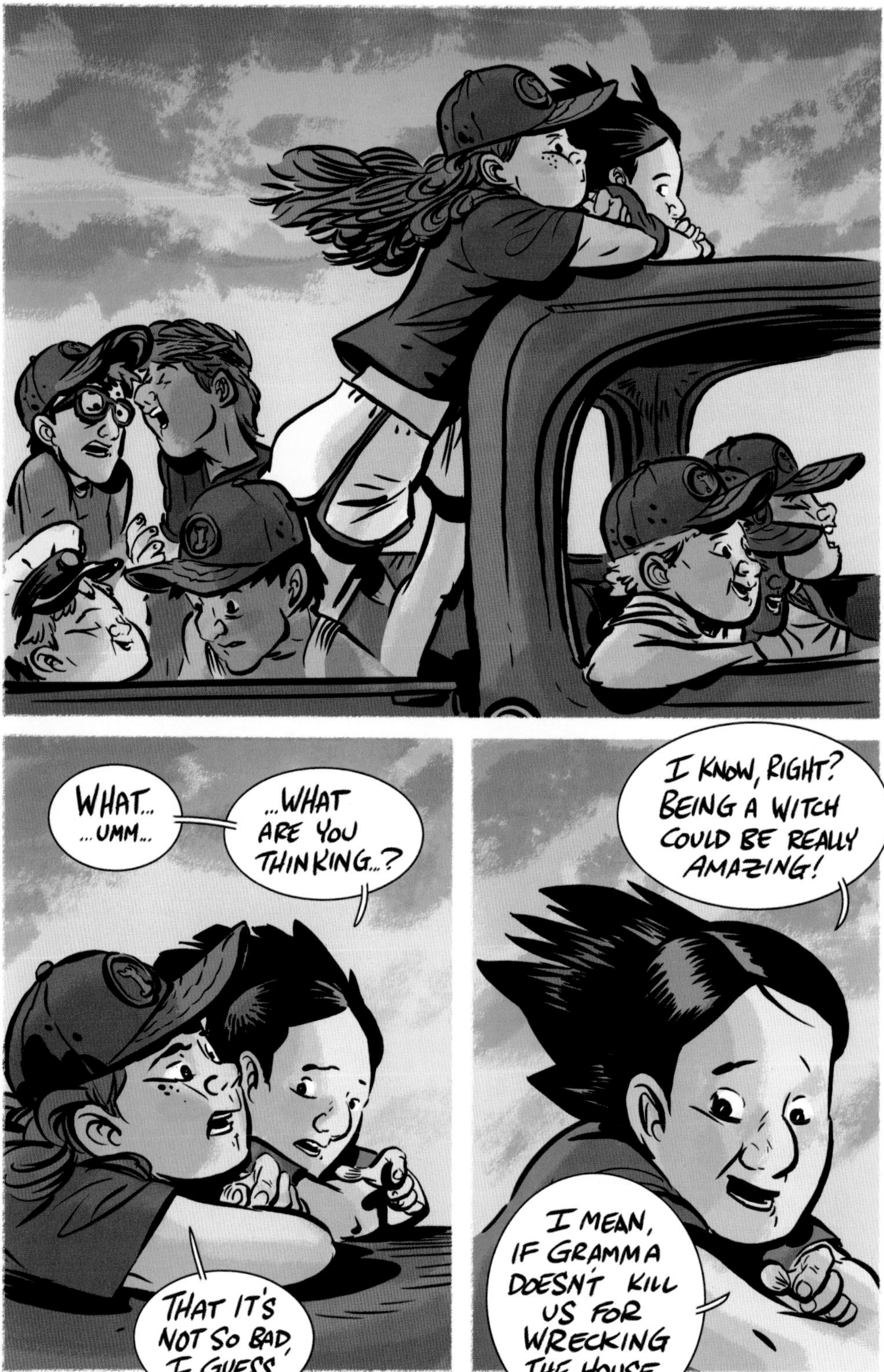
WHAT... ...UMM...
...WHAT ARE YOU THINKING...?
THAT IT'S NOT SO BAD, I GUESS.
I KNOW, RIGHT? BEING A WITCH COULD BE REALLY AMAZING!
I MEAN, IF GRAMMA DOESN'T KILL US FOR WRECKING THE HOUSE...

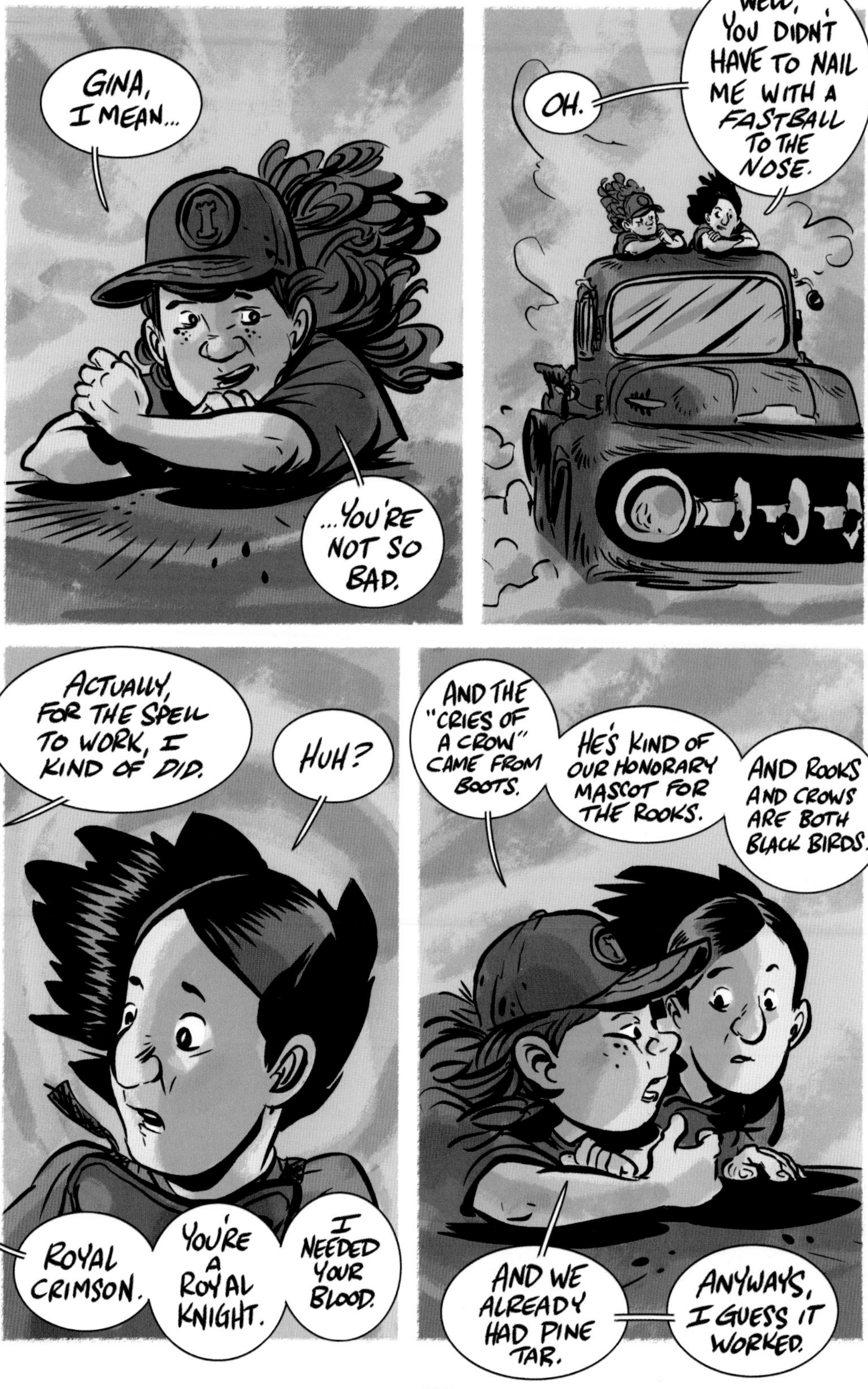
GINA, I MEAN...
...YOU'RE NOT SO BAD.
OH.
WELL, YOU DIDN'T HAVE TO NAIL ME WITH A FASTBALL TO THE NOSE.
ACTUALLY, FOR THE SPELL TO WORK, I KIND OF DID.
HUH?
ROYAL CRIMSON.
YOU'RE A ROYAL KNIGHT.
I NEEDED YOUR BLOOD.
AND THE "CRIES OF A CROW" CAME FROM BOOTS.
HE'S KIND OF OUR HONORARY MASCOT FOR THE ROOKS.
AND ROOKS AND CROWS ARE BOTH BLACK BIRDS.
AND WE ALREADY HAD PINE TAR.
ANYWAYS, I GUESS IT WORKED.

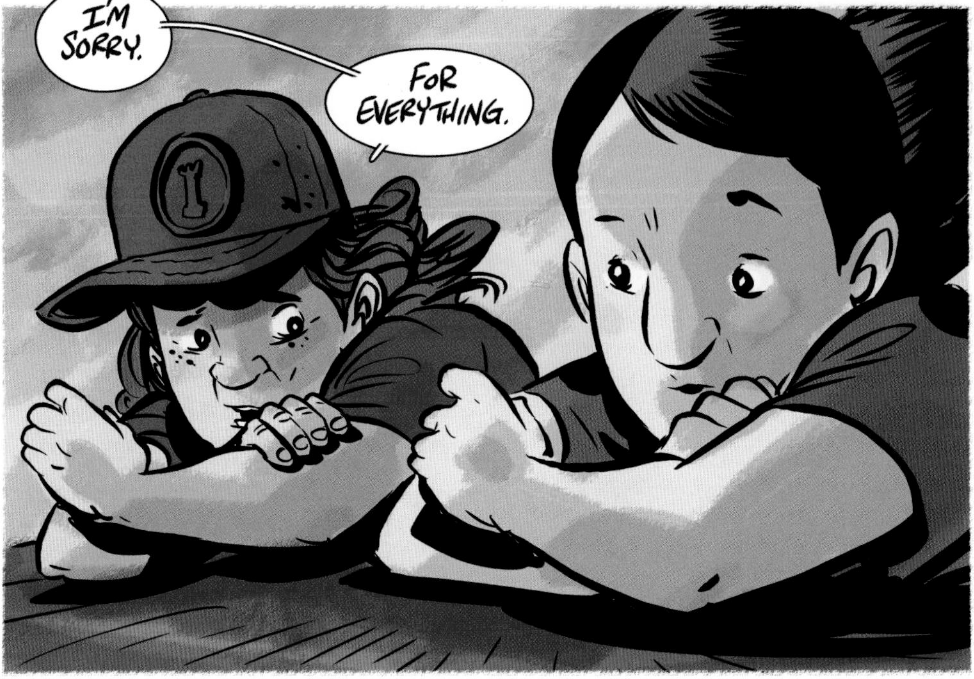
I'M SORRY.
FOR EVERYTHING.

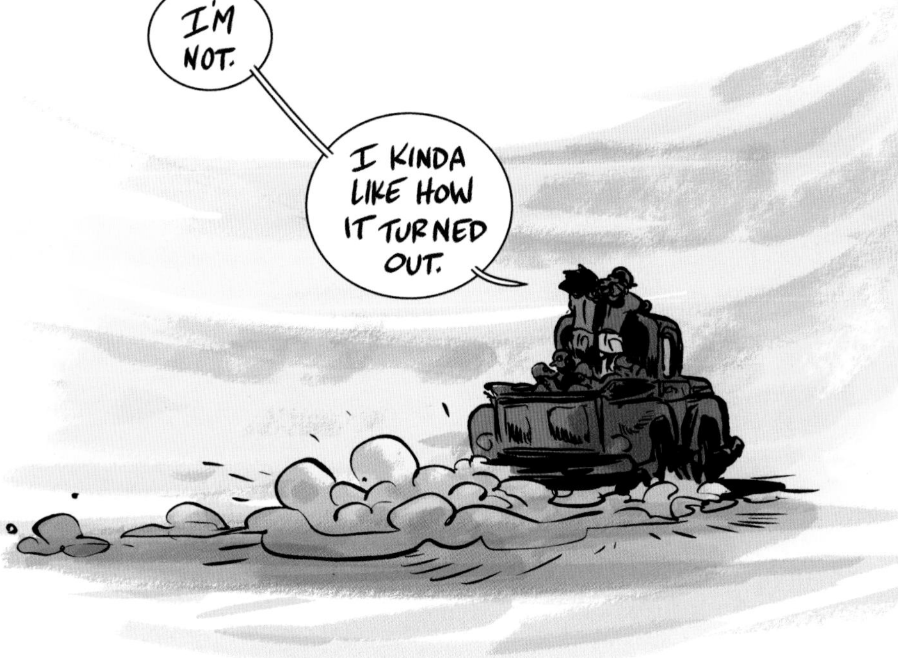
I'M NOT.
I KINDA LIKE HOW IT TURNED OUT.

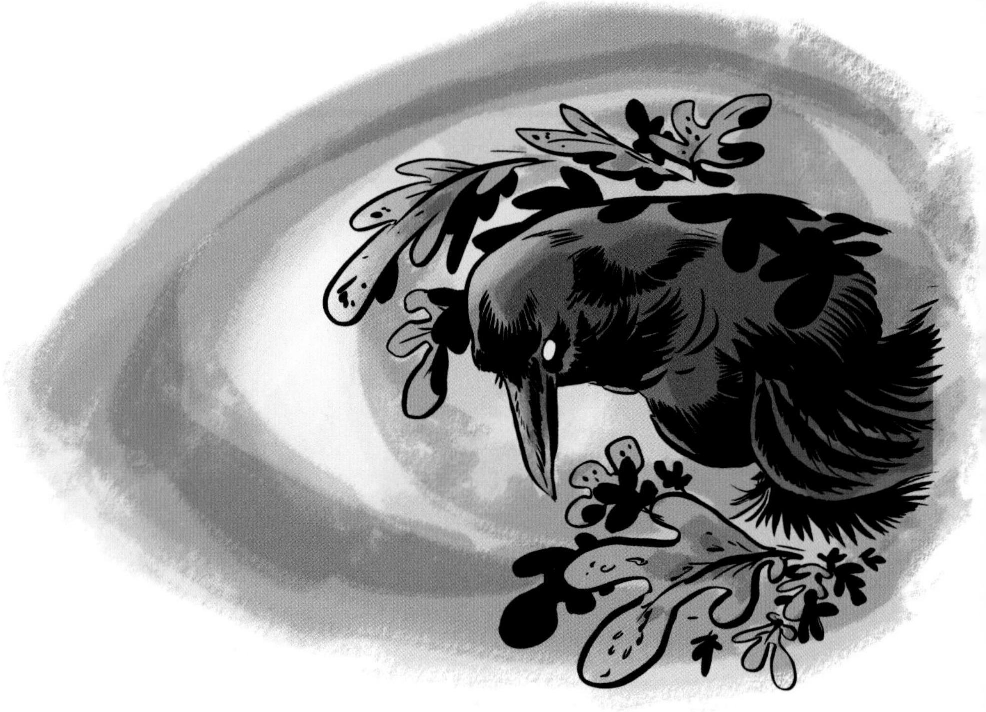

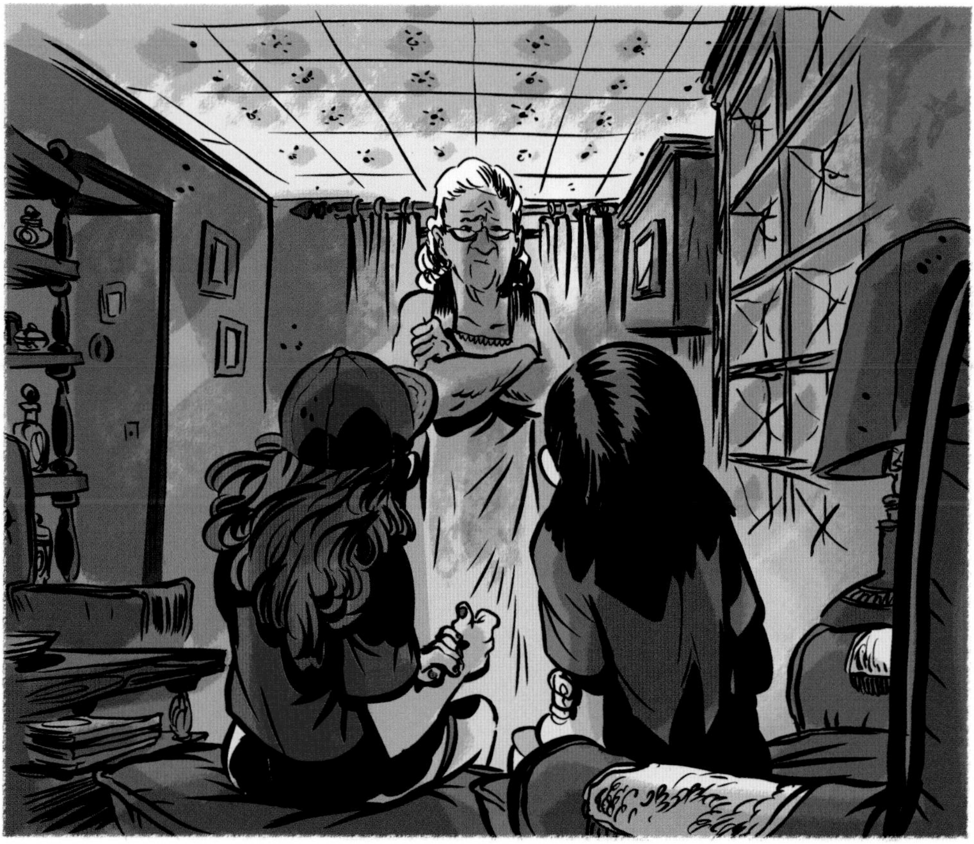

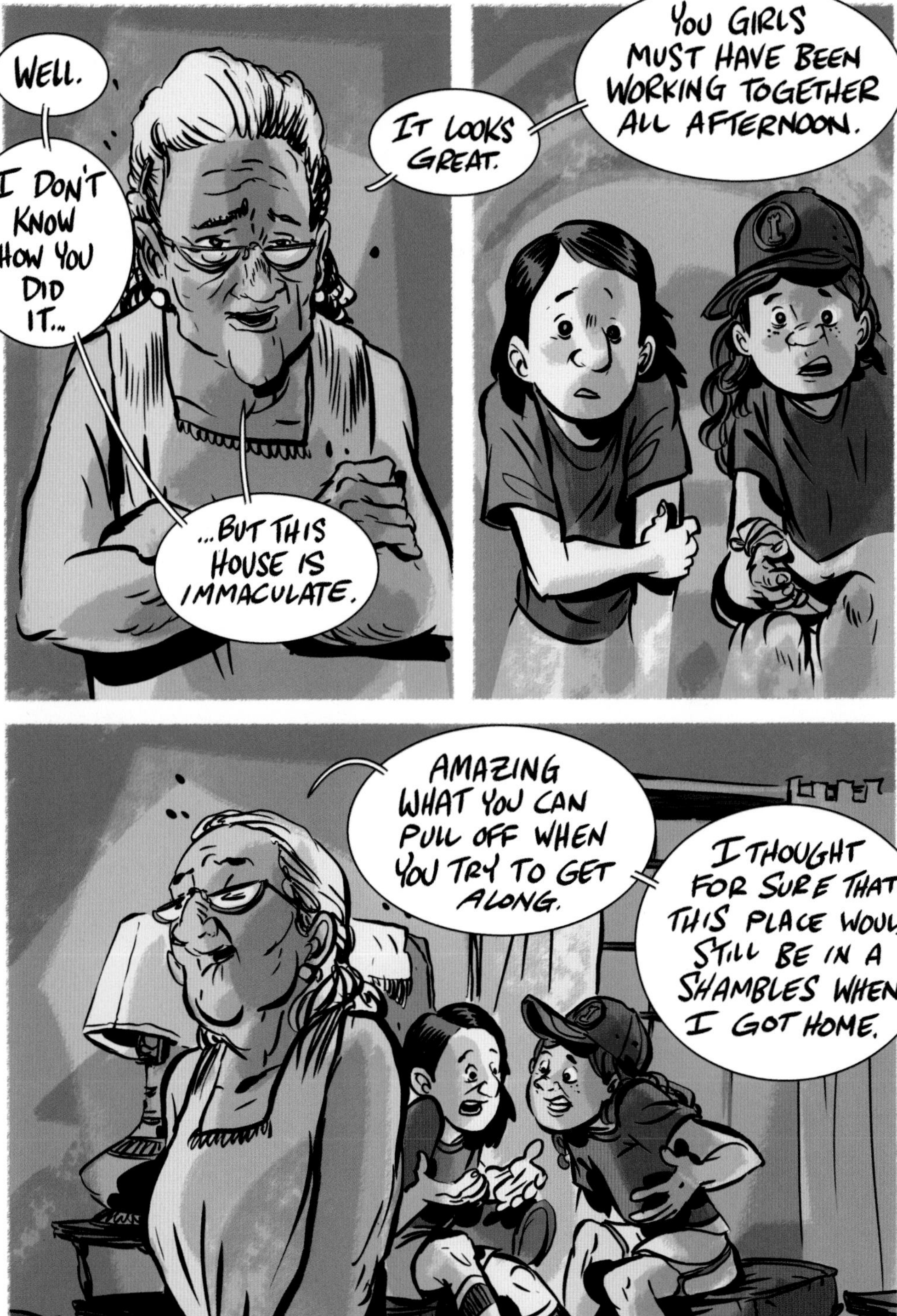
WELL.
I DON'T KNOW HOW YOU DID IT...
...BUT THIS HOUSE IS IMMACULATE.
IT LOOKS GREAT.
YOU GIRLS MUST HAVE BEEN WORKING TOGETHER ALL AFTERNOON.
AMAZING WHAT YOU CAN PULL OFF WHEN YOU TRY TO GET ALONG.
I THOUGHT FOR SURE THAT THIS PLACE WOULD STILL BE IN A SHAMBLES WHEN I GOT HOME.

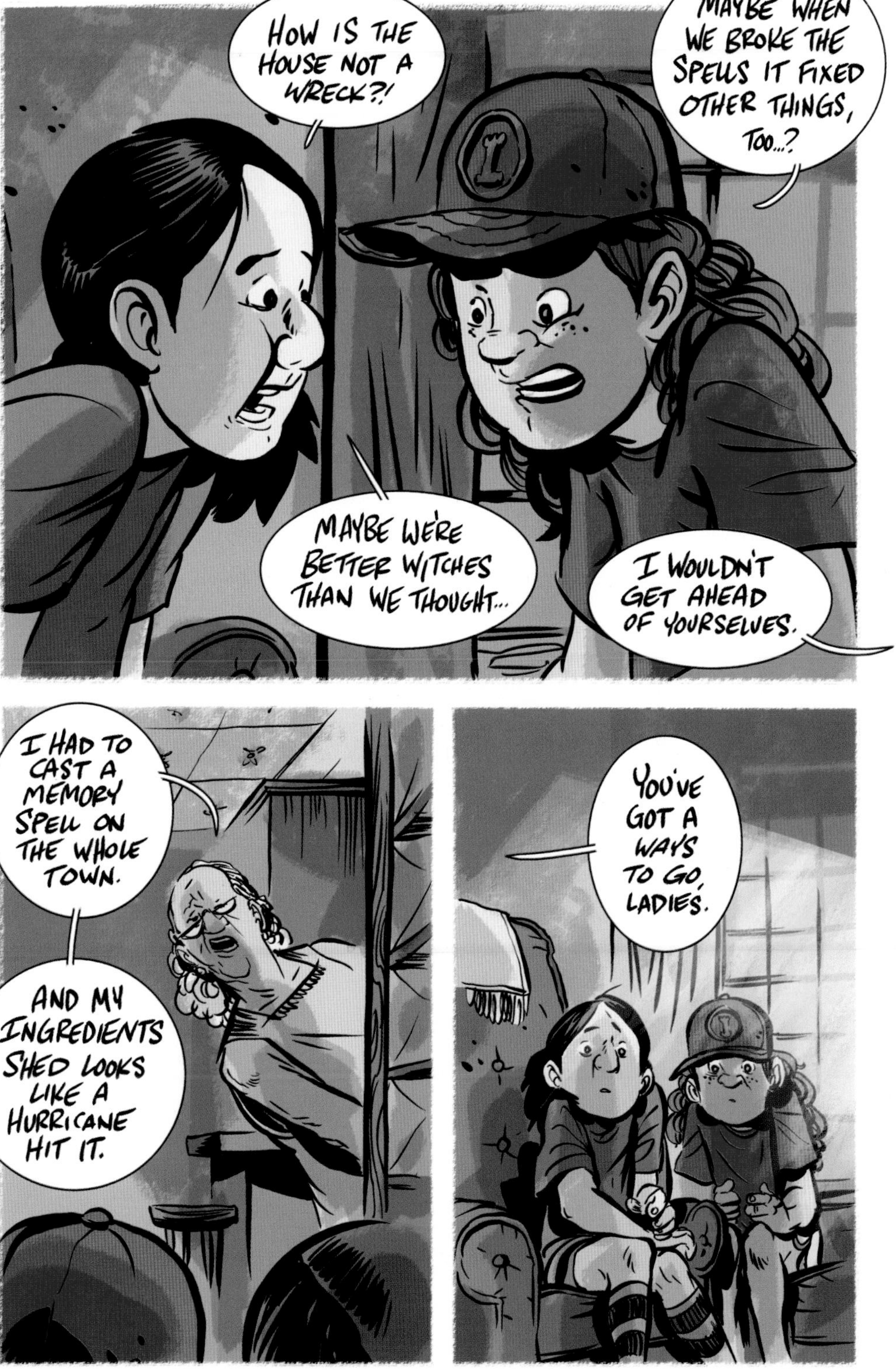
HOW IS THE HOUSE NOT A WRECK?!
MAYBE WHEN WE BROKE THE SPELLS IT FIXED OTHER THINGS, TOO...?
MAYBE WE'RE BETTER WITCHES THAN WE THOUGHT...
I WOULDN'T GET AHEAD OF YOURSELVES.
I HAD TO CAST A MEMORY SPELL ON THE WHOLE TOWN.
AND MY INGREDIENTS SHED LOOKS LIKE A HURRICANE HIT IT.
YOU'VE GOT A WAYS TO GO, LADIES.

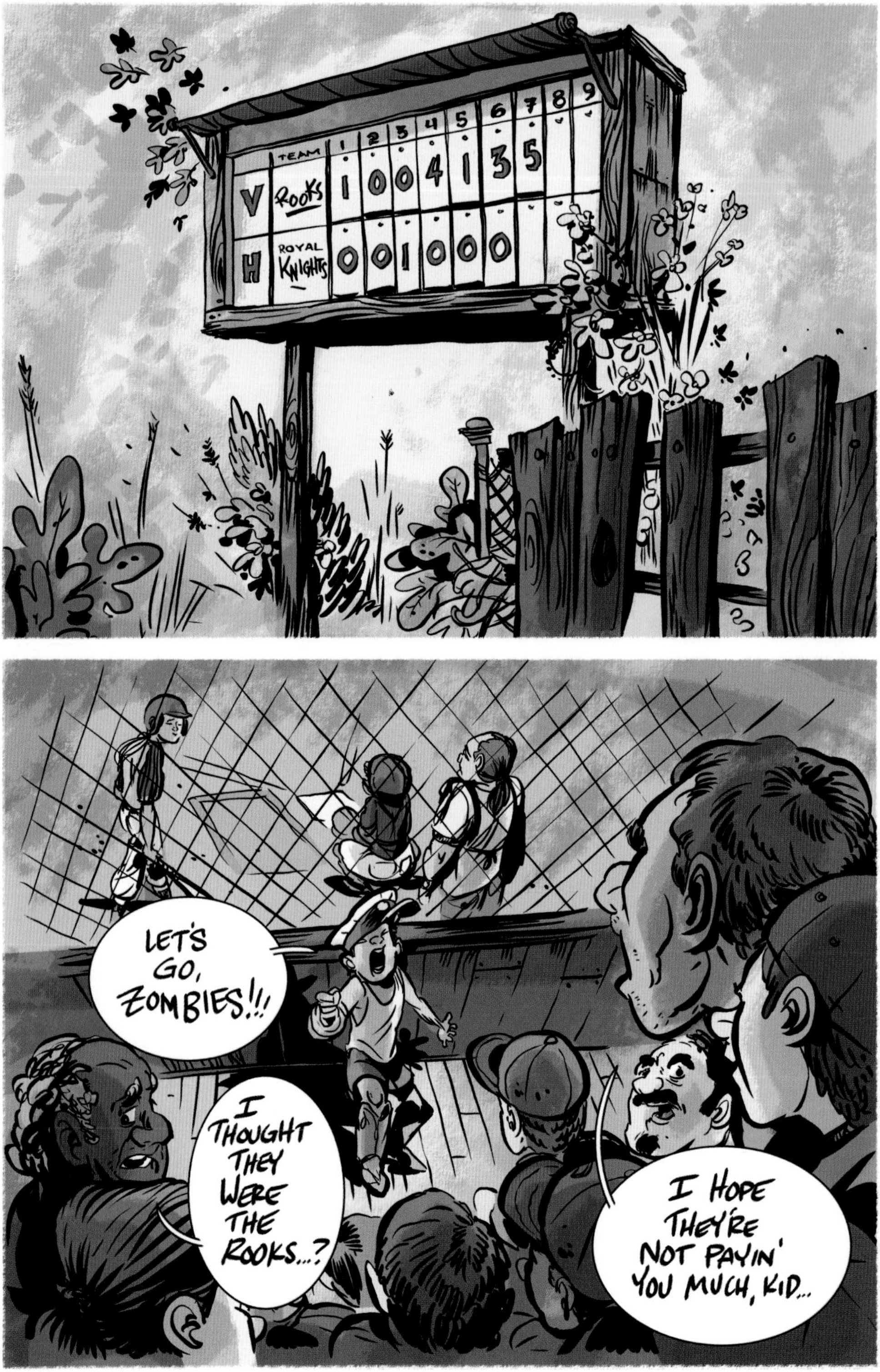
TEAM 1 2 3 4 5 6 7 8 9
V ROOKS 1 0 0 4 1 3 5
H ROYAL KNIGHTS 0 0 1 0 0 0
LET'S GO, ZOMBIES!!!
I THOUGHT THEY WERE THE ROOKS...?
I HOPE THEY'RE NOT PAYIN' YOU MUCH, KID...

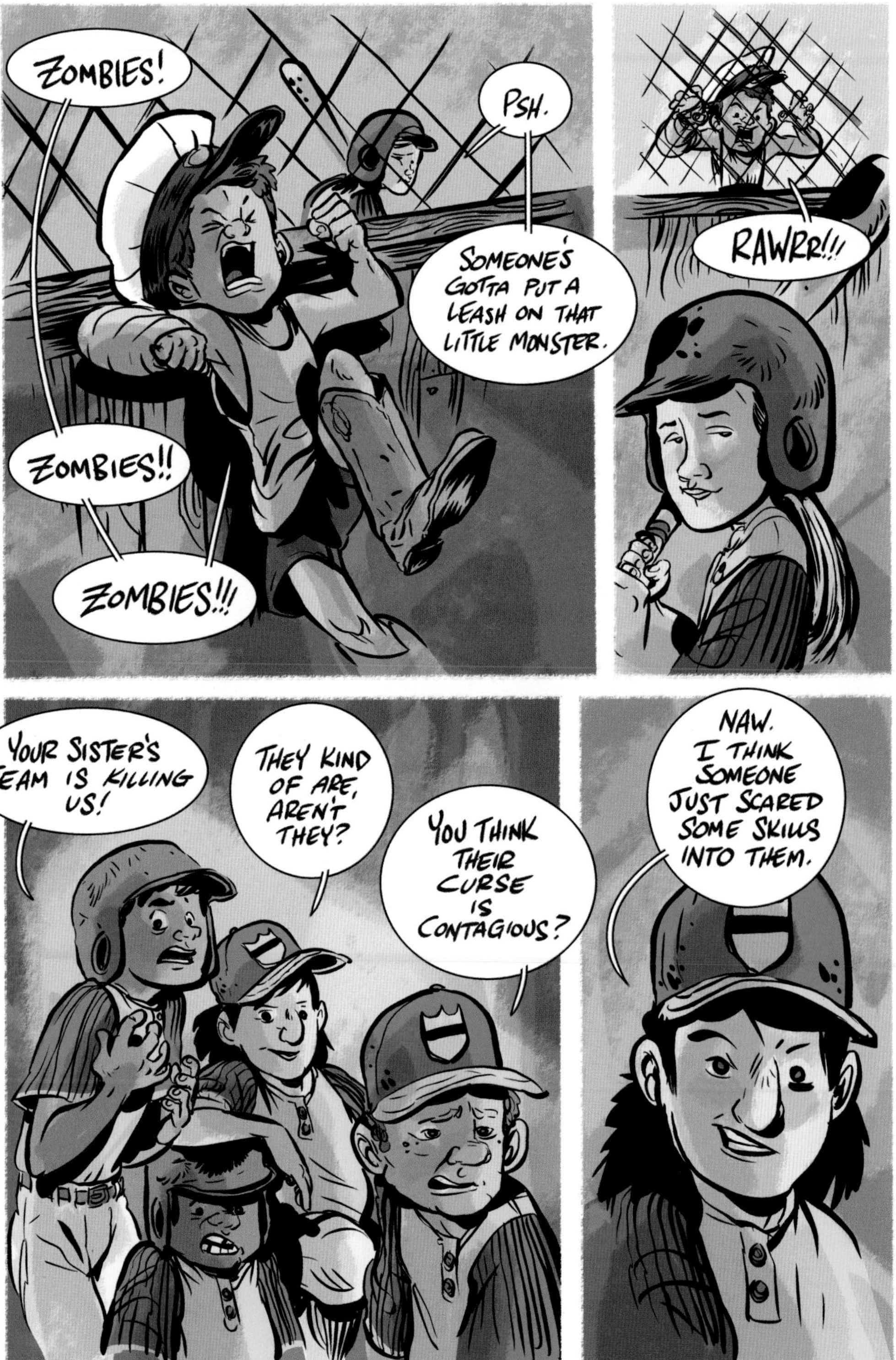
ZOMBIES!
PSH.
SOMEONE'S GOTTA PUT A LEASH ON THAT LITTLE MONSTER.
ZOMBIES!!
ZOMBIES!!!
RAWRR!!!
YOUR SISTER'S TEAM IS KILLING US!
THEY KIND OF ARE, AREN'T THEY?
YOU THINK THEIR CURSE IS CONTAGIOUS?
NAW. I THINK SOMEONE JUST SCARED SOME SKILLS INTO THEM.

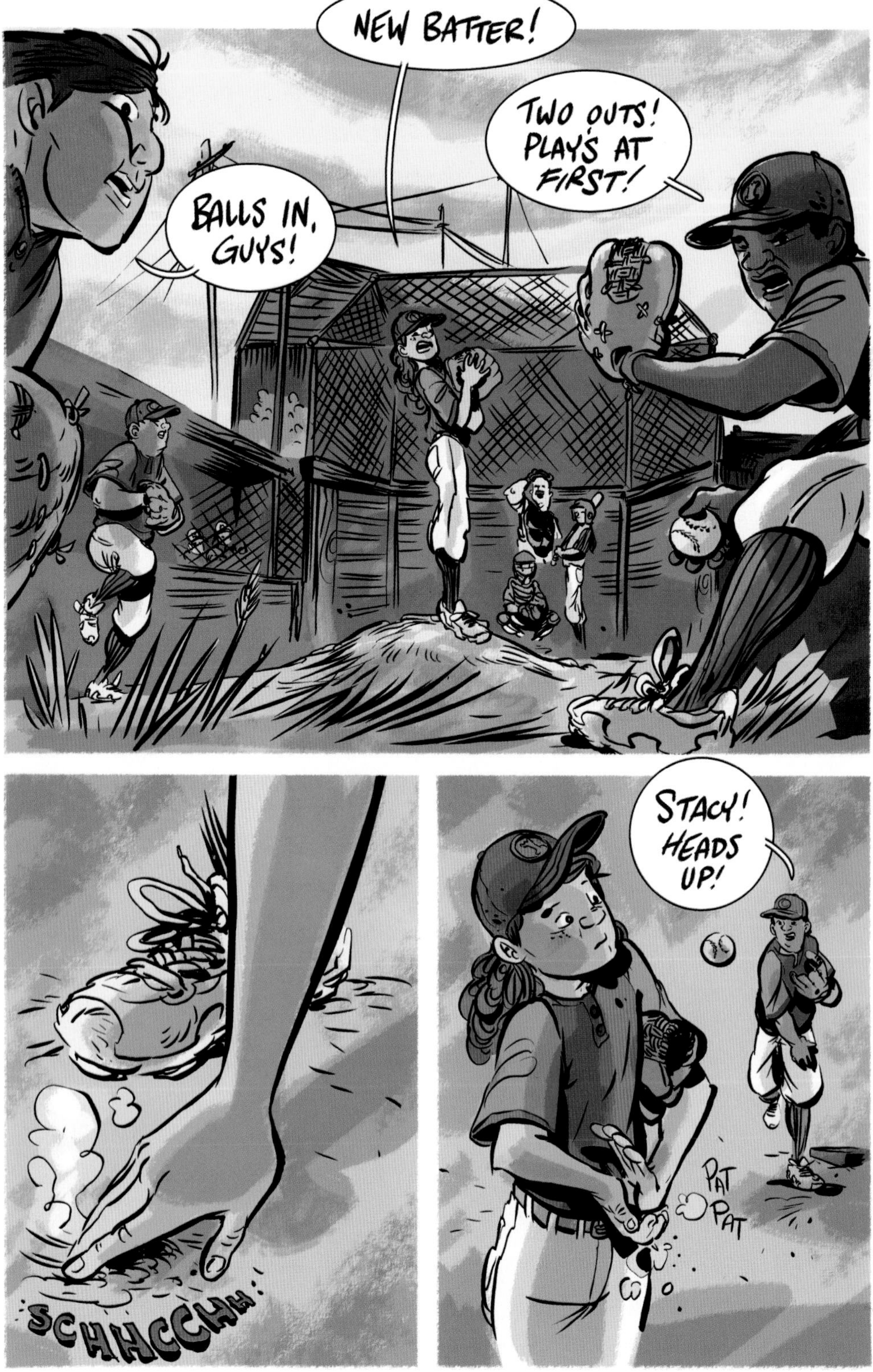
NEW BATTER!
TWO OUTS! PLAY'S AT FIRST!
BALLS IN, GUYS!
SCHHCCHH
STACY! HEADS UP!
PAT PAT

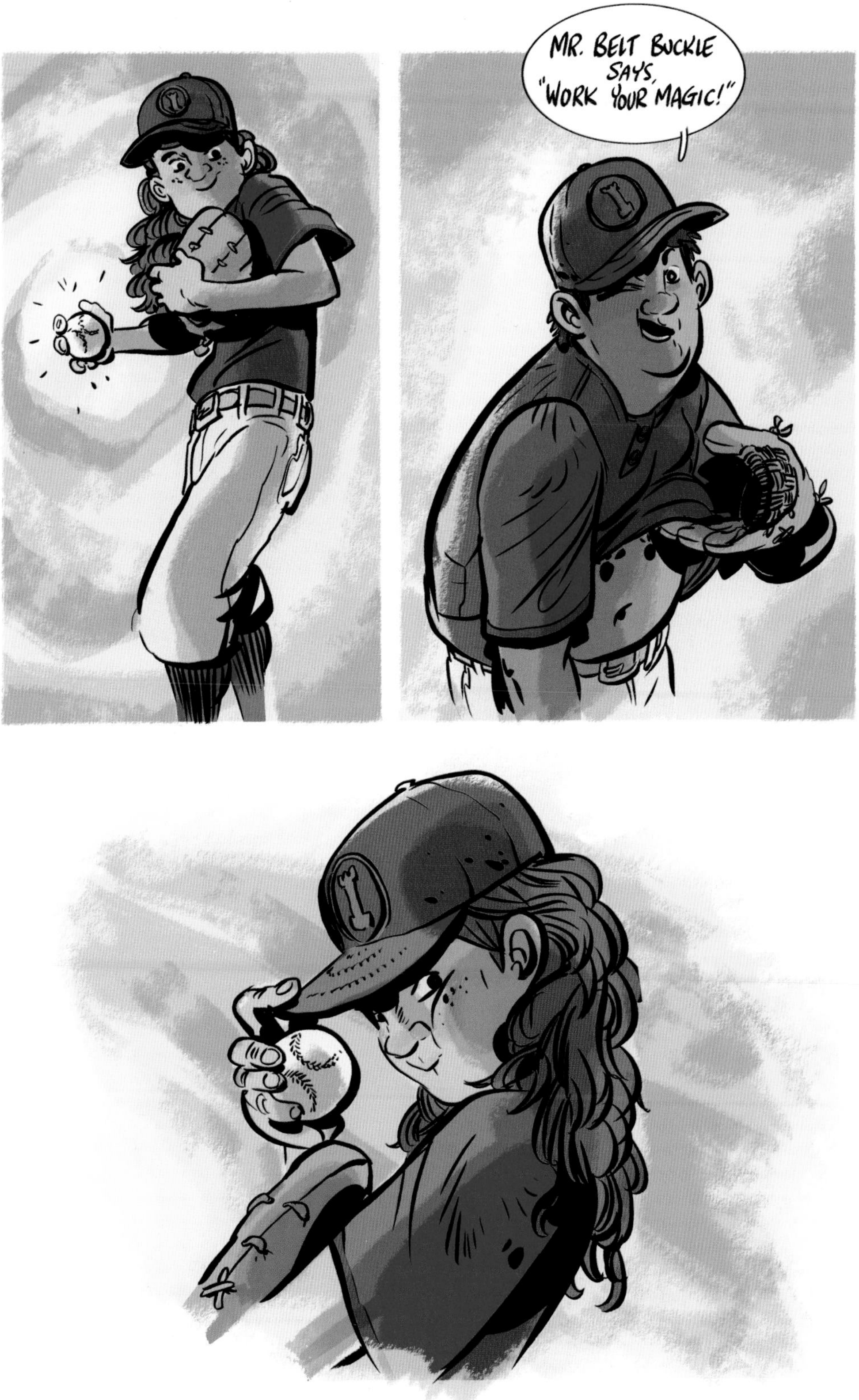
MR. BELT BUCKLE SAYS, "WORK YOUR MAGIC!"

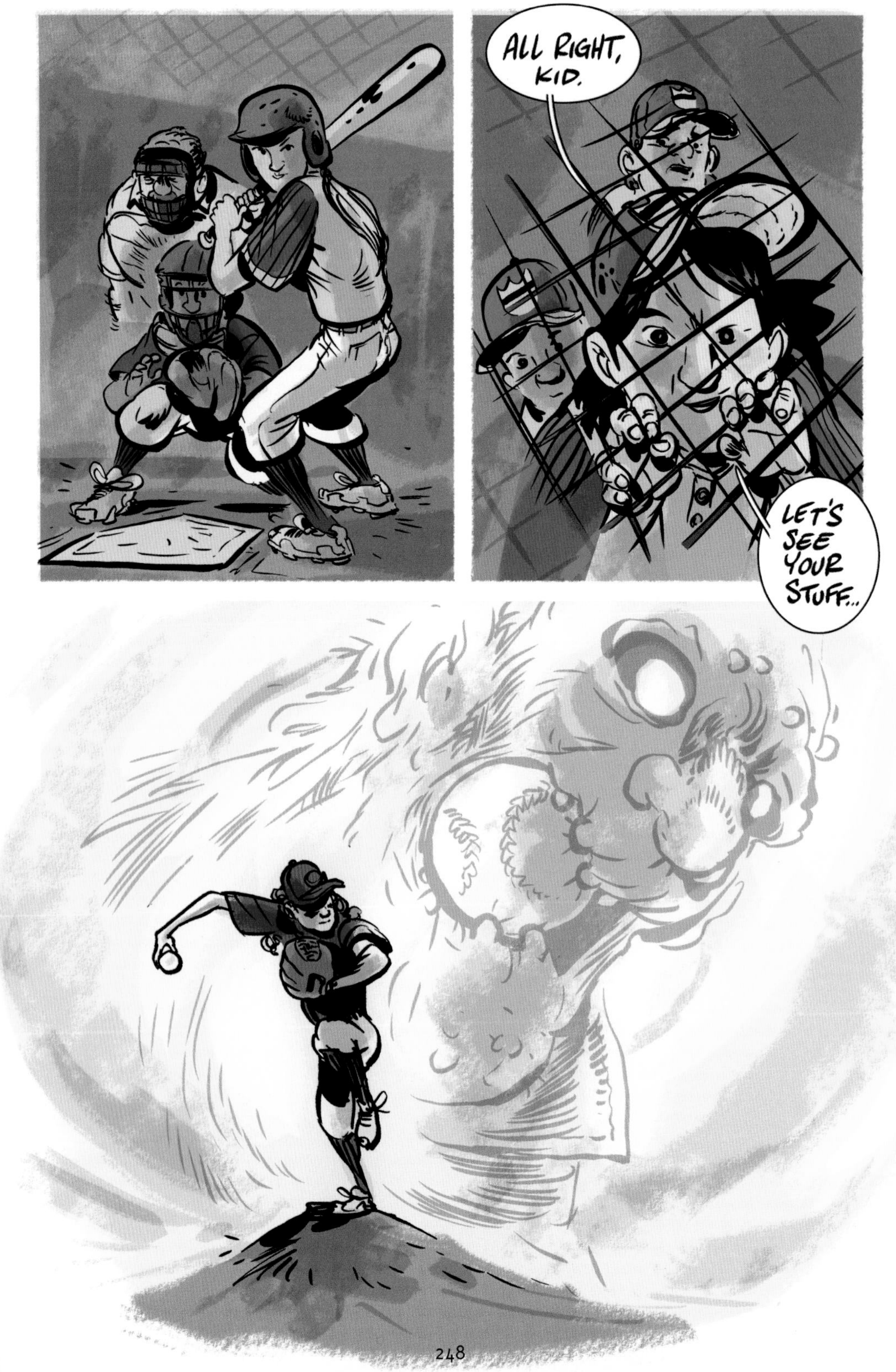
ALL RIGHT, KID.
LET'S SEE YOUR STUFF...

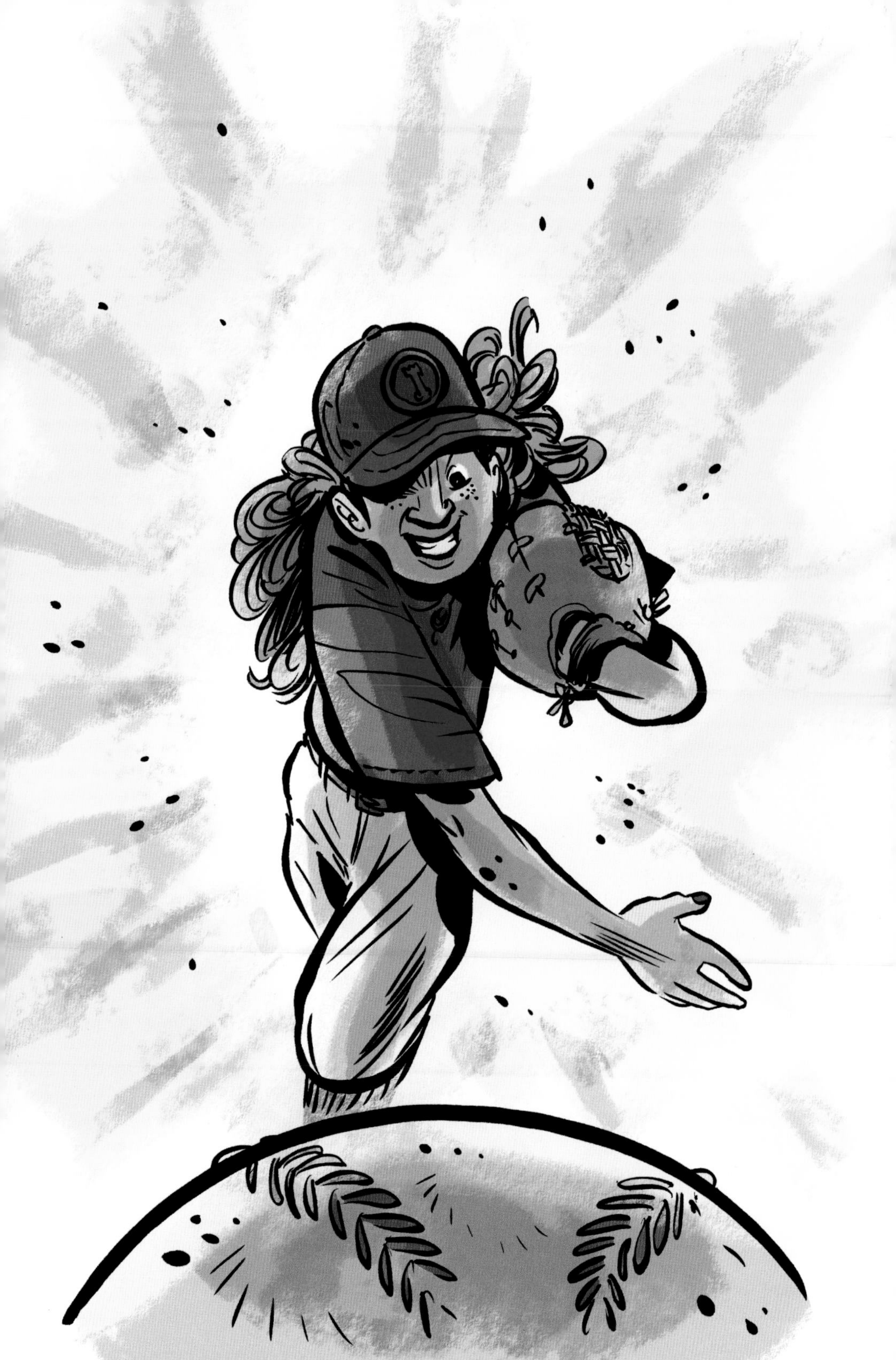

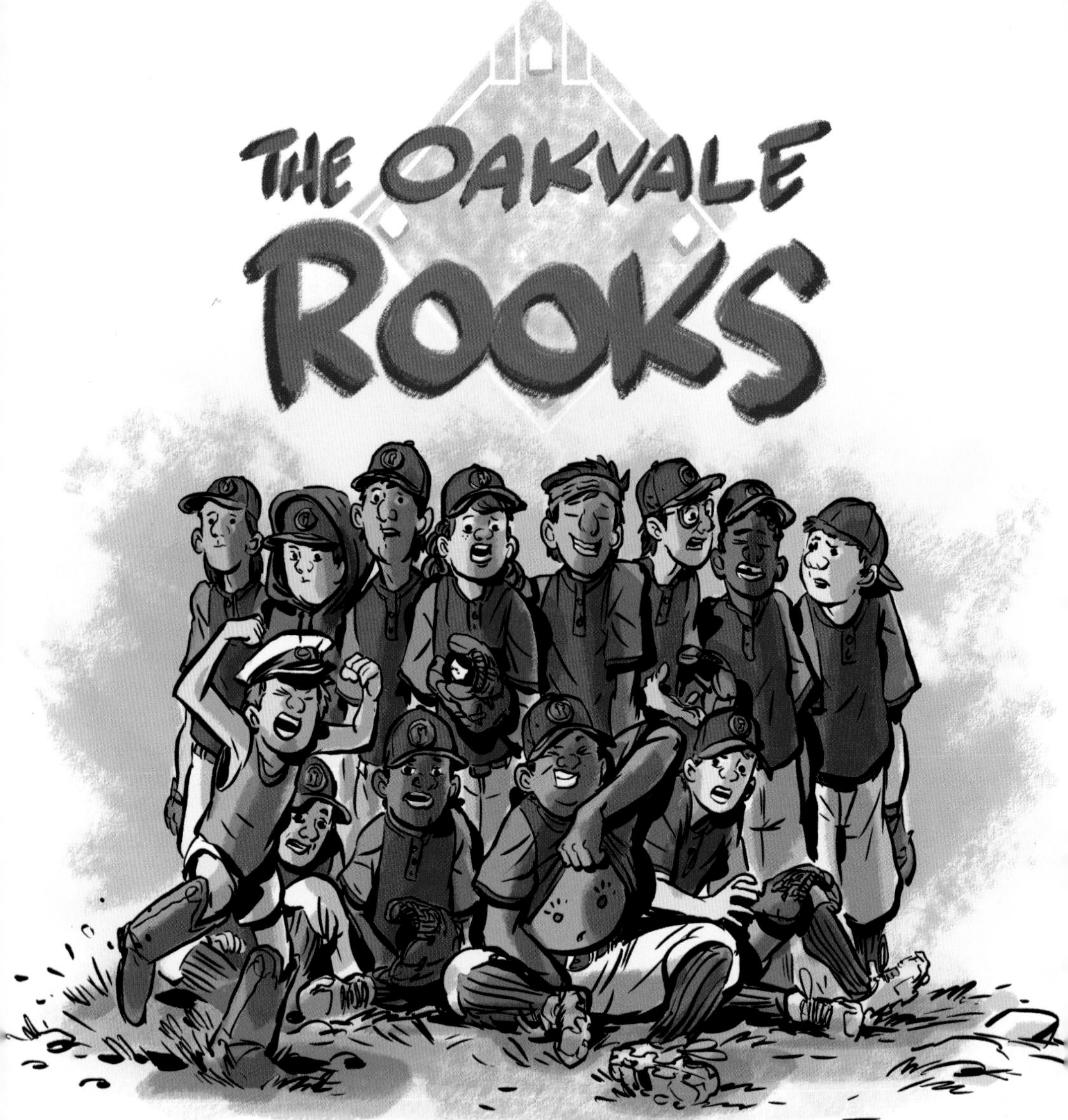
THE OAKVALE
ROOKS

BACK ROW: JOAQUIN MARTINEZ, TEDDY GRASSO, TYLER SANCHEZ, STACY CAVALLARO, CASEY GOMEZ, BILLY TAKEUCHI, SOLOMON HAMPTON, MARKO LARSONOVAN

FRONT ROW: LEVI ISACCS, CHRIS GORDO, LOUIE "KILLROY" NUNES, PETEY "BEANS" DWYER

PHOTO BOMBER: HENRY "BOOTS" SANCHEZ

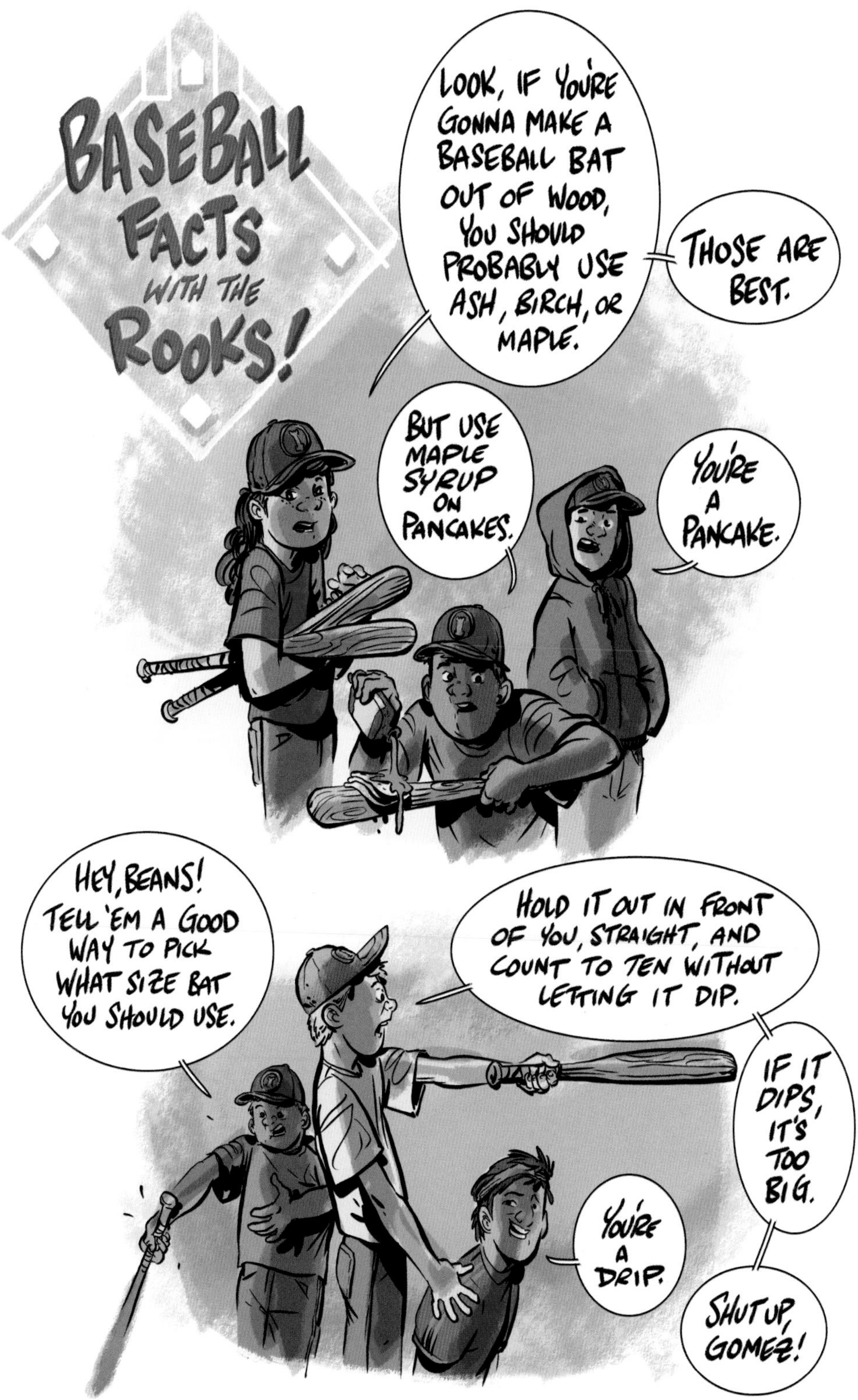
BASEBALL FACTS WITH THE ROOKS!
LOOK, IF YOU'RE GONNA MAKE A BASEBALL BAT OUT OF WOOD, YOU SHOULD PROBABLY USE ASH, BIRCH, OR MAPLE.
THOSE ARE BEST.
BUT USE MAPLE SYRUP ON PANCAKES.
YOU'RE A PANCAKE.
HEY, BEANS! TELL 'EM A GOOD WAY TO PICK WHAT SIZE BAT YOU SHOULD USE.
HOLD IT OUT IN FRONT OF YOU, STRAIGHT, AND COUNT TO TEN WITHOUT LETTING IT DIP.
IF IT DIPS, IT'S TOO BIG.
YOU'RE A DRIP.
SHUT UP, GOMEZ!

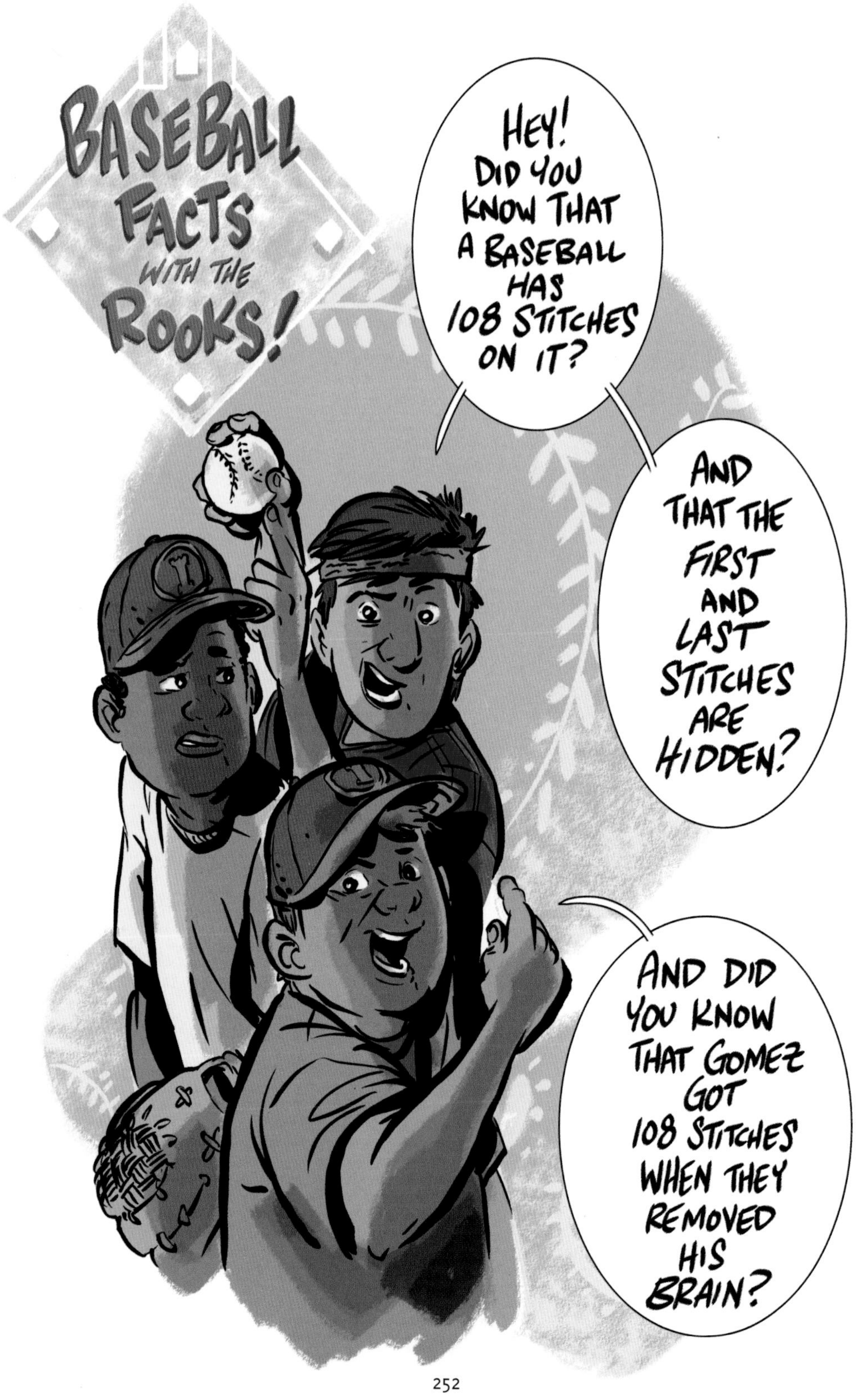
BASEBALL FACTS WITH THE ROOKS!
HEY! DID YOU KNOW THAT A BASEBALL HAS 108 STITCHES ON IT?
AND THAT THE FIRST AND LAST STITCHES ARE HIDDEN?
AND DID YOU KNOW THAT GOMEZ GOT 108 STITCHES WHEN THEY REMOVED HIS BRAIN?

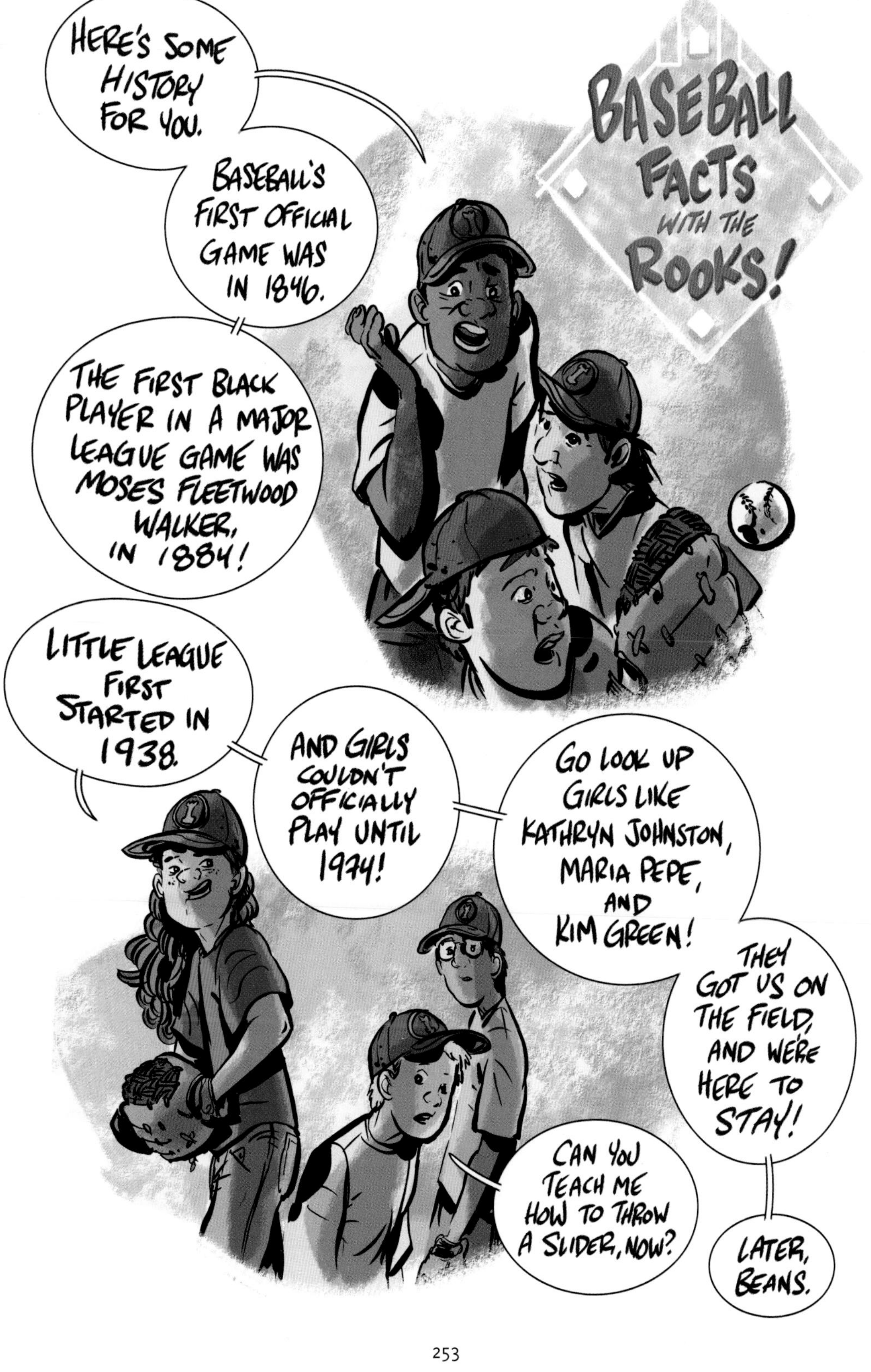
HERE'S SOME HISTORY FOR YOU.
BASEBALL FACTS WITH THE ROOKS!
BASEBALL'S FIRST OFFICIAL GAME WAS IN 1846.
THE FIRST BLACK PLAYER IN A MAJOR LEAGUE GAME WAS MOSES FLEETWOOD WALKER, IN 1884!
LITTLE LEAGUE FIRST STARTED IN 1938.
AND GIRLS COULDN'T OFFICIALLY PLAY UNTIL 1974!
GO LOOK UP GIRLS LIKE KATHRYN JOHNSTON, MARIA PEPE, AND KIM GREEN!
THEY GOT US ON THE FIELD, AND WE'RE HERE TO STAY!
CAN YOU TEACH ME HOW TO THROW A SLIDER, NOW?
LATER, BEANS.

SCOTT MORSE is the award-winning author of many graphic novels for children and adults, including the *Magic Pickle* graphic novel and the Magic Pickle series for Scholastic/Graphix. In film and animation, he's worked with Cartoon Network, Nickelodeon, Disney, and Pixar. He's built old cars with his Dad (including the 1951 Ford truck featured in DUGOUT!) and has coached ten Little League teams. He lives with his family in Northern California and rarely draws faces on his belly.

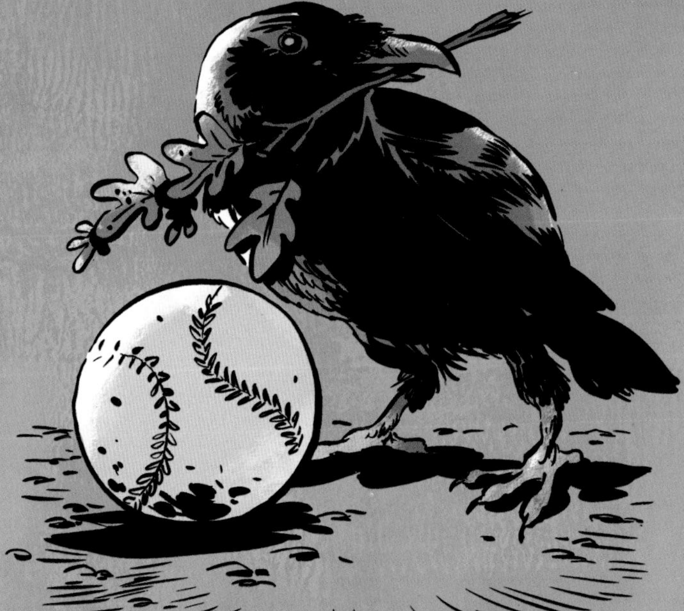